THE KING OF VINLAND'S SAGA

THE KING OF VINLAND'S SAGA

Stuart W. Mirsky

0190-MIRS

Library of Congress Number: 98-88295
ISBN#:   Hardcover   0-7388-0151-8
                    Softcover   0-7388-0152-6

This is a work of fiction. Names, characters, places and incidents either are the
product of the author's imagination or are used fictitiously, and any resemblance
to any actual persons, living or dead, or events, is entirely coincidental.

This book was printed in the United States of America.

To order additional copies of this book, contact:
Xlibris Corporation   1-888-7-XLIBRIS
PO Box 2199   1-609-278-0075
Princeton, NJ 08543-2199   www.Xlibris.com
USA   Orders@Xlibris.com

CONTENTS

Part 3
BLOOD TIES

FOR BRENDA, HEATHER, ELISSA
...AND HAREK BECAUSE IT TOOK SO LONG.

PROLOGUE

When Leif Eiriksson went to Norway, before he had done anything else of note, he stayed for a summer on an island in the Hebrides where his ship had been blown by a severe storm. There he met and fell in love with a certain young woman of noble birth, Thorgunna by name, who was said by some to be a daughter of the king of Russia. Now after that eastern prince, who had been something of a viking in the lands about the Baltic in his youth, had returned to his own country, this Thorgunna was brought west to live with her kinsmen in the Hebrides. There she grew into a tall, black-haired woman, dark-browed and altogether gloomy in appearance. Yet most folk agreed she was handsome to look upon and not the sort to go unnoticed for long.

Leif found no cause to disagree with this judgement for he thought her fine company and somewhat far-sighted to boot since she seemed to know a great many things which others did not. Thus he spent a pleasing summer with her, with both of them finding a great deal to say to one another, even after most other people had gone off to their beds.

Still, when the winds freshened, Leif made his ship ready to sail. Thorgunna saw this and asked what he was planning to do.

"I mean to travel to Norway," he answered her, "to win the king's favor."

She asked if he were willing to take her along, but Leif replied that he doubted her kinsmen would approve of that, for his own blood was not so noble as hers was and he had little in the way of worldly wealth to offer her. Thorgunna said she was not overly concerned with what her family thought since she believed Leif would prove a great man and succeed at whatever he put his hand to. Nevertheless, Leif said he thought it unwise to abduct such a well-born woman in a foreign land "since there are so few of us."

"I am not sure you will prefer the alternative," Thorgunna replied.

"I shall take that risk," said Leif.

"Then," said Thorgunna, "I must tell you that I am with child and you are the cause of it. If it is a boy, as I think likely, I intend to send him to you when he is grown; nor do I think you will find having a son by me any more pleasant than our parting now warrants."

Leif said Thorgunna must do as she thought best and gave her a gold ring, a woolen mantle and a belt of walrus ivory by way of making amends. Still these did not make this parting of theirs any easier.

Afterwards, Leif went on to Norway just as he had planned, where he won the friendship of King Olaf Tryggvesson and became a Christian at the king's urging. Still later he won fame and no little wealth when he discovered new lands to the west across the Greenland Sea. The best of these countries he named Vinland, for the wild grapes he found growing there, and he built a number of houses there for himself and his crew, exploring the countryside and stocking his ship from that land's natural abundance. Then he returned to his father's holdings in Greenland, carrying back with him timber, grapes and self-sown wheat, all of which were to be found in the new country, though they were unknown in Greenland.

Not long after this Leif's father, Eirik the Red, fell ill and died and so Leif settled down on his father's Greenland estate at Brattahlid and took over affairs there, for Eirik had been chieftain over all the Greenland folk and Leif took this chieftaincy after him. Leif's younger brothers also died about this time, Thorvald out in Vinland, where he had gone in search of that country's wealth, and Thorstein by disease in Greenland so that Leif alone came to inherit all the property and goods which had formerly belonged to his kinsmen.

Now it happened, some years afterwards, that a boy, about 16 years of age, came out to Greenland. Giving his name as Thorgils, he said he was Leif's son and presented the three gifts which Leif had left with Thorgunna by way of proof.

When he saw these, the Greenland chief acknowledged the boy at once and took him into his house. But Leif had a wife, by this time, and other sons at Brattahlid and these did not warmly receive their new kinsman who had something of his mother's dark nature about him and Leif soon regretted his generosity toward Thorgunna's son. Still, since the boy was of his blood, he would not send him away and so he purchased a small piece of land at the edge of his holdings and built a house and barn for him there, stocking it with a few cattle and goats. These he gave to the boy, Thorgils, saying "Here is your share of my goods, since your mother has sent you here to claim them of me. You can do what you like with them, either live here or sell them up for what they're worth and take your profits with you back to the Hebrides."

Thorgils said he would just as soon make his home there, since he had no desire to return to his mother's kin, and this he did for many years, though he never got on any better with his father's household than he had at the first. Mostly he kept to himself and worked the land, though he was often seen wandering off alone so that none in the district would have sight of him from one winter to the next. As he grew older he went out on his own in this manner for longer and longer periods and this did not improve his standing any with his neighbors, since he generally left his land and houses untended and his animals dying.

This was the state of things right up until Leif Eiriksson himself died, after which things became much worse than before. Thorgils' three half-brothers, the sons of Leif Eiriksson, took over Brattahlid upon Leif's death and seized all the wealth which Leif had accumulated in his years as chieftain there. But they offered Thorgils no part in the division of this property. Since he had neither friends nor kinsmen of his own to come to his support, Thorgunna's son was unable to press any sort of claim in the matter and the end of it was that he got no share in his father's goods. Nor did Thorgils' family ties with the Leifssons serve him any better in other matters. Once, when a certain woman of middle-age was widowed, Thorgils went to the eldest of his half-brothers, Thorkel, and asked him to speak to the woman's kinsmen on his behalf, since he wanted to make a proposal of marriage to her. But Thorkel Leifsson said he was unwilling to play any part in the affair and the end of it was that the woman married another.

Thereafter, Thorgils took more and more to wandering off by himself so that his farm fell into disrepair for extended periods and he was rarely seen there. He went out onto the ice behind the Greenland settlement or by boat along the fjords to the westernmost farms or beyond these, where few Greenlanders had gone before, and lived off the land there, hunting and fishing. His kinsmen and neighbors were not sorry to see him go either and, when he had been away for several years, the Leifssons announced one day that he had most likely died in their opinion and so they took over that farm which had been his.

Now the tale tells how, after a time and to everyone's great surprise, Thorgils returned to the settled parts of Greenland one day and that he had with him a small child who, he told people, was his own son. Folk were much amazed at this, since he had never taken a wife, to anyone's knowledge, nor even lived among men for many years. Yet the presence of the boy was undeniable. Thorgils said the babe was his by a woman he had befriended in the frigid northern wastes — a woman of unusual stock and unlike any people had ever seen before. She was quite remarkable in appearance and spoke a strange tongue which no ordinary person could hope to understand, Thorgils said, explaining that he had taken her for his wife despite these drawbacks and lived for a time with her until she had died. Then he had brought the babe back with him, for he said the wastelands were no place to raise a young child.

Now few folk believed the tale as Thorgils told it, for he was no better liked now than before, and it was well-known that none but a few outlaws and renegades made their homes in the northern wastes. Accordingly, many held the child to be the offspring of some settler's daughter in the western settlement who, because she wished to avoid marriage with the luckless Thorgils, had given him the babe when it was born. Still others said the child must be the issue of some witch or troll-woman who had ensorcelled Thorgils out on the wastes. Yet, everyone agreed that the child was most unusual to look upon, for he was large and swarthy in appearance and his face was as flat as a slab of ice.

Thorgils named this babe Sigtrygg, for he said that was as good a name as any for so uncommon a child, and he took him with him back to his farm. But now he saw that the Leifssons had entirely taken over this property and had placed tenants in his house. Therefore he went to see his brothers about the matter.

Thorkel, the eldest, said: "It was not our doing brother that you abandoned the farm which our father gave you. But land is scarce in Greenland, as you well know, and it's better to make use of it than leave it empty. So now we have placed tenants in the house, who are maintaining it and the barn in good repair. And they are tending the land and keeping herds of livestock on it, which is more than you did when these things were in your keeping."

"Even so," said Thorgils, "since I have returned with my son, I will need a place to stay, and where is better than my own farm?"

The three brothers consulted with one another, having little desire to see Thorgils as their neighbor again, though they did not think they could keep him away if he were intent on returning to his own land. After a time, Thorkel spoke again.

"Kinsman," said he, "while you must agree that we have done right by your property up till now, you must also see that it would be an ill thing to turn these tenants out, who are living there and seeing so ably to the upkeep of your holdings. Then that household would be without a livelihood while your farm would surely lie abandoned once more, when next you took it in mind to travel out onto the ice. Therefore let us make an agreement. If you will allow us to keep these people on your land, we will see to your business affairs here and collect the farm rental on your behalf, save for a small portion which we will keep as our fee. In this way, your holdings will be attended to while you, yourself, will be free to come and go as you like with whatever proceeds in your purse a well-run farm may yield you."

Thorgils thought the matter over and said it seemed a good arrangement to him, for he had little liking for farming as was by now quite clear. Therefore he said he would consent to his brothers' proposal so long as they agreed, in their turn, to take on the fosterage of Sigtrygg, his son, until such time as the child was old enough to go out on his own or until Thorgils, himself, should claim the babe again. Although they did not wish it, the brothers consented, seeing no other way to get their will in the matter. Thus, it came about that Sigtrygg Thorgilsson was turned over to his uncles, dwelling in each of their houses by turns, while his father took up residence in the wilderness once more, returning only at intervals to collect the monies owed him.

But Sigtrygg Thorgilsson did not fare any better with the Leifssons than his father had before him, for he was, first of all, the son of a man for whom they had little feeling of kinship and, second, of uncertain and suspect parentage himself. His looks alone set him apart from his other kinsmen and constantly recalled to their minds that his mother was unknown to them, either a settler's wayward daughter or a troll capable of luring and bewitching a man upon the ice. As a consequence, they reared him apart from their own children and shunted him from household to household, when the seasons permitted it. This made the boy more sullen than most and folk said he favored his father in this regard.

Now as for Thorgils, this man came less and less often to see his son until, at length, he left off coming altogether and it was commonly thought that this time he had indeed died out on the ice. Sigtrygg had little to say about this, one way or the other when he heard the news, though he was often seen afterwards, wandering the shores of the fjord, his eyes toward the distant sea.

Now, when he had grown into a large and strapping youth, his uncles came to him one day, while he was tending a herd of cattle at the water's edge, and asked him what he meant to do since he was now old enough to go out on his own.

Sigtrygg said he hadn't given much thought to that but was content to see to their cows, if they were willing to keep him on. Then Thorkel said: "Kinsman, Greenland is a poor country and we have too many mouths to feed already. We brothers think it best if you seek your fortune abroad. There is a ship in the fjord which will leave for Iceland within the day and we have bought you passage on it, if you are willing to go."

Sigtrygg replied that he was willing to leave if that was what they wanted but that, like his father before him, he had no desire to leave Greenland entirely and certainly no reason to go to Iceland, where he had neither kinsmen nor connections. "Rather", said he, "would I prefer to seek my father, or search out my mother's kin, if there are any remaining, in the northern wastes."

His uncles advised against this but Sigtrygg was determined and the end of it was that he took his belongings and departed Brattahlid in a small boat and went out into the wastes. Then, for several years, Sigtrygg lived as his father had done before him, hunting and fishing to supply his wants and visiting the far-flung farms of Greenland, carrying news from household to household and selling the furs and skins and walrus tusks he took for his upkeep, when this seemed needful. Word of Sigtrygg's doings came back to the Leifssons and they only shook their heads when they heard, for they thought him no better than his father had been in matters concerning a man's livelihood.

Still, Sigtrygg prospered among the Greenland settlers, for all the oddness of his appearance, and men came in time to think highly of him and to praise him.

PART 1
INHERITANCE

CHAPTER I

KINSMEN

The people at Brattahlid first learned of the return of their kinsman, Sigtrygg Thorgilsson, when news of this was brought to them by several farmhands from down the fjord. These told how a small sail had been sighted at the place where the fjord emptied into the sea in the early morning hours, when people were first getting about to see to their beasts and other chores, and there was a great deal of excitement throughout the settlement when people heard of this. Visitors were not a commonplace in that part of the world, and the first thought which anyone had was that a ship had come to them from overseas.

But it was soon clear from what these men had to say that the sail they had seen was much too small for that and that no more than one man had been sighted aboard the vessel which carried her. The people who first saw the vessel while standing on shore had seen this man take down both mast and sail and then watched as he began to row his small boat into the fjord. Then they had sent the others inland, along the fjord, to tell the news. Still, the excitement which word of the traveller brought with it to Brattahlid was great enough, for news was scarce in that country and people were always glad to welcome strangers.

All along the fjord folk came out to wave at the rowing man or just to watch him as he pushed his small vessel along with strong, steady strokes, passing deeper up the fjord with each bend of his back. The stranger in the boat stopped only briefly at a small farm which lay just past Eirik's Island, opposite the open sea, and then he pushed onward, despite the friendly calls to stop awhile which reached him from those who watched from the shore.

In those days Brattahlid was the largest of all the farmsteads in Greenland, and this for good reason, since the people who lived there marked their descent from Eirik the Red who first found and settled that country. These people had the best land in that part of the world, for their farm was set well back from the open sea, in the place where the fjord in which they had settled turned north-ward into the land, so that it was well-protected from the harsh winter storms which commonly blew in off the ocean there. All the houses and outbuildings of Brattahlid were built high above Eirikssfjord, as this neck of the sea was called, on sloping land which dipped sharply down to the blue waters below and which was covered, in summer, with a rich shieling of green grass almost to the very edge of the icy waters which jutted landward there, but which was entirely buried under snow and ice at other times.

There were several large halls amidst the other buildings, well spread out along the green sward of sloping land that overlooked the narrow blue strip of the sea, and, above these, the white caps of the inland ice stood silent watch, barring passage to the interior of the country. The biggest of the halls at Brattahlid was set in the very midst of the other buildings, for this was that hall which Eirik the Red had raised for himself, built entirely of stone and turf, with low walls, set deep in the ground and bearing a steeply pitched roof. In the short Greenland summer this roof bristled with fresh grass, no less than the ground out of which it seemed to rise, and the farm beasts found ready grazing there — as they did on all the buildings on that farmstead. But at other times of the year these buildings were a place of refuge to all the inhabitants from the bitter cold, for even in those days summers were shorter there than elsewhere in the world and the winters much harsher.

When the people at Brattahlid learned that the rowing man had come round the bend in the fjord, they came out of their houses and down to the water's edge to see for themselves and then it was not long before they had a clear view of who it was who

sat athwart the oars. Then the men on shore stood back and separated themselves from the women and children there and, after a
time, went back up the steeply sloped ground to see to other tasks,
for Brattahlid was a working farm and there were always things
which needed doing when the weather was clear. But the women
and youngsters remained by the edge of the fjord, watching the
slow but deliberate progress of the little vessel.

After awhile the man in the rowing boat beached it and then
he leaped from its belly to lug it up behind him onto the stony
ground. It was not easy work, for the vessel was loaded with bulky
goods which seemed to chiefly consist of the dried skins and furs
of wild beasts and several bound packs of glistening white bone
which, on closer inspection, could be seen to be the tusks of the
great walrus which made its home in those Greenland waters. Only
the few farm women who met the newcomer on the shore lent him
a hand so that he must do the bulk of the unloading himself. Still,
he did it briskly and afterwards the women and children who had
come down to greet him seemed to have a great deal to say to him
and the man gave a fine fur pelt to each of them from among those
goods which he had taken out of his boat.

Sigtrygg Thorgilsson was a good-sized man, well formed and
strongly built, but somewhat dark in appearance and wild-look-
ing in his dress, for he was garbed almost entirely in skins like
those he carried with him in the boat. The youngsters of Brattahlid
found this most appealing of all and they plucked at his garments
even as he piled each of them with what goods he thought they
could carry and urged them up the hill toward the waiting houses.
Then he took hold of the largest share, himself, and slung these
over his back, making his way up the sloping ground in the midst
of that company.

The younger men who were about the farm looked up from
their chores as he passed them and some few gave a nod of recogni-
tion but the older ones seemed entirely oblivious to this man's
passing and went on with whatever tasks they had set themselves.
Sigtrygg returned the greetings he got, however paltry these seemed,

and went on up the steeply sloped ground until he came to a halt before the entrance to the main hall. There he set down his burden and looked about him, although he said nothing.

One of the women now came up from behind him and abruptly pushed her way past into the house and, after a time, a serving woman appeared in the doorway where the first woman had disappeared. This woman said Sigtrygg was to come in with his goods if that was what he wanted.

"I don't think I came all this way to make my sleeping place in the doorway," he answered her, and now he lifted his burden again and took it indoors with him. He found a place for his goods up against one of the interior walls and then he went to the cooking fire which burned steadily in the long pit at one end of the hall. He made a place for himself there and, after a time, this same serving woman, making a great deal of commotion, brought him a small plate of braised meat and a bowl of curds and he ate these without speaking. When he had finished he asked where everyone had gone and the woman answered that they were all about their business, as all good farm folk should be, "for a farm doesn't run itself, and certainly not such a big one as this is."

Sigtrygg said he didn't doubt it but that he thought the arrival of guests would have been an occasion of greater note than this visit of his now seemed to be.

"You shouldn't treat yourself with such importance," the serving woman replied sharply, "for many people have come out here to visit the Leifssons from other parts of the world, and most have carried a great deal more weight in their names and reputations than a man like you can hope to do."

"Nevertheless," answered Sigtrygg, "I now want to know whether or not I am to find a welcome here, for I am not without goods and, it seems to me, this place has been as much a home to me as to any of you others who make your sleeping places under the shelter of Brattahlid's roof."

When he said this, Sigtrygg could see the faces of some of the youngsters peering at him from just outside the doorway and he laughed as he picked up a small stone and threw it toward them. The children scattered at this. Then he turned with great seriousness again and asked where his three uncles, the sons of Leif Eiriksson, could be found.

"Where they are always to be found at this time of the day," answered the woman.

"And where might that be?" Sigtrygg asked her.

"With the livestock," she said. "Or up on the ridge above the houses, seeing to the fencing. Or perhaps you can find them caulking the boats or mending netting. There's always more to do on a farm like this than men to do it. And you don't make matters any easier by sitting around here plying me with questions. Or didn't you see them when you came up here from the fjord?"

"Gunnar and Eirik I saw, well enough," answered Sigtrygg slowly, "although it's not certain they saw me. Or, if they did, they made no great show of it, for none but the little ones and my aunts thought to accompany me up from the boat. And no one seems to have thought well enough of the matter to have followed me in here in any case."

"Then it's not to be helped," said the woman. "But no one has turned you out either and that's nothing to be sneered at."

Sigtrygg replied that this was so but now he added that he wanted to know whether or not he could expect guest-rights over winter, "for, if not, I shall need to look elsewhere since I have already come far down the coast."

The serving woman said he was to wait where he was and he agreed to this, after which she put away the things she had been carrying and went out.

When she returned, Sigtrygg asked how things had gone and the woman replied: "Well enough for you, since I found Thorkel, your father's brother, and he says you are to stay, if you want to; but the terms are to be no different than before, for you are to winter in each of your kinsman's households by turns, if you are willing to share in the work which is to be done there." Sigtrygg said this was acceptable to him and that was how they left it.

Now Gunnar Leifsson, the second of the three brothers, had a daughter called Thjodhild, named for her great-grandmother, the wife of Eirik the Red. This girl was renowned in Greenland for her hair which was red-gold in color and which many thought no less remarkable than Eirik's own had been since it shone, they said, as brightly as the sun on a high summer's eve. This Thjodhild, though hardly more than a child at this time, took an instant liking to her kinsman Sigtrygg for she had not laid eyes on him in several years. Thus, when the time came for him to take up residence in her father's household in accordance with the terms of his welcome at Brattahlid, she contrived to place herself in his company. On those nights when Sigtrygg sat at table with the other members of the household, Thjodhild would sit as near to him as possible and, when he told the tales of his travels, she was always the first to seek him out and the last to desert him when the fire in the pit burned down. She refilled his cup too, when he emptied it, and brought him the choicest meats; and, when he helped her brothers with their driftwood gathering or in tending the cattle, she was generally to be found by his side, as well.

Her brothers, thinking this unseemly, went to Gunnar at last and told him how things stood. But Gunnar replied that he was reluctant to send Sigtrygg away for, he said, the presence of a stranger in the household was likely to make the dreary evenings pass more agreeably. Still, he called his half-brother's son to him one evening, after everyone else had gone to bed, and advised him concerning Thjodhild, saying, "though she is but a child, it is now evident she has already begun to think like a woman, so it were better to give her a wide berth, kinsman. Besides, you are no fit match for her, as you already know."

Sigtrygg said he had no such intentions toward Thjodhild but had merely been observing the courtesies of kinship, and so the matter passed.

Still it came about one day, when Sigtrygg was feeding Gunnar's cattle in the barn, that Thjodhild came up suddenly beside him and placed a hand on his arm. Sigtrygg at once drew back, saying, "Cousin, have a care, since even the white bear which dwells on the ice knows better than to come upon a man in such wise, lest he get his death wound thereby."

But Thjodhild said: "Are you so mighty a hunter then, Sigtrygg, that even the white bears fear you?"

"And why not," said he, "since I have killed my share of them?"

"Yet I think you a gentler man than your tales would tell," she replied.

Sigtrygg said he didn't understand what she meant, but was reluctant to leave her, all the same, so that these two stood awhile amidst the hay and the lowing beasts. After a time, Sigtrygg said he must see to the cattle as he had promised Gunnar. He took up an armful of hay and went among the cows but Thjodhild called him back, saying he must not be too hasty to depart, since she thought highly of his company. Sigtrygg answered that this was not uncommon, for folk in Greenland were often starved for news and other diversions in the winter months, whereupon he walked toward Thjodhild with the hay in his arms.

"Am I bear, then, or cow in your eyes now hunter?" laughed Thjodhild.

And Sigtrygg answered: "Neither, but only the fairest maid which my eyes have ever seen."

Thjodhild said she was satisfied with this response and asked him if he now meant to seek other prey than the bear and walrus and northern seal which he was accustomed to pursue. But Sigtrygg answered that he saw little luck in the game she was proposing, for he was a landless man with none of the world's wealth to his name, nor was he held in high esteem by her kinsmen.

"Yet," said she, "you have your father's farm and the rent which is due you from it, since your father has not collected on it these many years. This holding is now divided between my father and his brothers, though by rights it is yours as Thorgils' heir."

Sigtrygg said: "Still, I am no farmer, nor have I any wish to clash with my father's brothers over the matter."

"Then," said Thjodhild, "you shall never achieve what your heart desires, for you are a better tale-teller than a hunter, since it seems graver to you to face three kinsmen than to chase white bear."

After this, few words passed between them and each spent their time in other company, insofar as this were possible in the close quarters of a Greenland farm.

Sigtrygg now kept to his part of the bargain and lent his hand in the winter's work, getting the goodwill of Gunnar and his sons, thereby, while Thjodhild devoted herself to other pursuits. After a time, Sigtrygg moved on to his third uncle's household in accordance with the agreement which had been made. Yet, when the winter was over, Sigtrygg recalled Thjodhild's words and so he went up to his father's holding to see how it fared.

He found the farm there prosperous, with numerous goats and cattle on the land and the out-buildings well kept up, and now he could see no reason why he should not have a share in the proceeds of this holding as Thjodhild had urged. Accordingly, Sigtrygg went to each of his father's brothers, in turn, and told them what was on his mind and that he now intended to collect the rental fees which they had formerly promised to pay to his father, both that which they owed him from prior years and that which would be owed henceforth.

This news caused the Leifssons to become greatly agitated so that the three brothers called Sigtrygg aside one day, shortly after this, in order to urge him to see the matter from their viewpoint. They said that since his father had not claimed his due in many years, they had quite naturally put the proceeds to other uses and could not pay what he demanded. But Sigtrygg replied that he would willingly take payment in whatever form seemed mutually agreeable to them and over a number of years, if that were more convenient, but that he meant to have his due, nonetheless. "Barring that," said he, "I will take back the farm entirely and bring an action against you to regain my rights."

The Leifssons were not prepared for this and sought to reason with Sigtrygg, reminding him that they were his closest kin. Nor, said they, was he likely to have much success with a lawsuit against them in any case since he had neither supporters nor the means to obtain these in order to press such an action. On the other hand, they reminded him that they were well-known in Greenland and were accounted among its leading men so that they would have little trouble in finding backers for their claim.

But Sigtrygg answered saying, "Surely my blood is as good as yours. Nor is my claim a weak one."

Now the brothers thought there was some truth to this and were reluctant to see the matter come to court. Yet, since Greenland was a poor country for good farm land, and they less prosperous than seemed desirable, despite their standing among the Greenland settlers, they did not want to part with Thorgils' farm.

So now Thorkel, the eldest, said to Sigtrygg, "Kinsman, it were a hard matter to quarrel now, since we have been as foster-fathers to you, for our brother's sake. But matters are such that we cannot settle the debt as you would have it, since land is scarce and each of us must provide for the support of his family on the portion of the land which our father, Leif, left to us. Where Leif kept one household we now keep three, while, if you are minded to take up farming on Thorgils' farm, as you have said, perhaps there will be four before too long."

"That may well be," said Sigtrygg, "but what do you propose, instead?"

"Only this," said Thorkel, "that there is another holding which Leif Eiriksson owned, which was richer, by far, than anything in Greenland, but which none of us has yet laid claim to. We intend to give you all the rights to this property, if you will give up your claims here in Greenland in its place. And, in addition, we will provide you with the means to take possession of it."

Sigtrygg said he would not oppose such an arrangement, if the worth of the holding was as good as what he stood to lose in

Greenland, but first they must tell him where this other property was to be found.

"That's easy," said Thorkel, "for it is in Vinland."

Sigtrygg said: "Here is a strange matter, for you wish to give me a land which none of you has ever seen and which lies in a distant country, unpeopled by any save the savage Skraelings who drove our kinsmen out in earlier times. How am I to come to such a land or establish myself, thereafter, seeing as I am without goods or followers to achieve this?"

"Kinsman," said Thorkel, "as to your passage, we brothers will gladly purchase a suitable ship and stock it with provisions for your journey. But the ship's crew you must find for yourself from among the landless men of Greenland of whom there are, in these days, no small number. Such men will readily join themselves to your venture, when they learn that the houses which Leif Eiriksson formerly built in Vinland are now come into your possession, together with all the lands adjacent to them. In this way you may get sufficient followers to take possession of the land, if you desire it, while we shall have paid our debt to you."

"Yet, how is it payment," asked Sigtrygg, "to give me what you, yourselves, have never owned? For Leif Eiriksson abandoned those houses, after he built them, as is well known, nor are they in your possession now."

"Not so," answered the brothers, "for the truth is our father never sold or otherwise disposed of these houses, but only lent them, first of all to Thorvald, his brother, and later to Thorfinn the Icelander and lastly to Freydis, our father's sister, who made such bloody use of them that folk gave off seeking that distant place, thereafter. For Freydis committed murders there and the houses got somewhat of a bad name, so that no one ever had the heart to try that land again. Or so people say. But whatever has been said, the truth of the matter is somewhat different, for we tell you that folk gave up the settlement in Vinland for no other reason than that the country lay too far away, while they had good land closer to home. But you need have no such concern, kinsman, for if you

take Leif's houses from us you must give up Thorgils' farm. Therefore, you will have no reason to forsake Vinland for other holdings,
as those have done who went out there before you."

Sigtrygg now said he would have to think about this proposal
and the Leifssons answered that this was only right. "But," said
they, "while we have no desire to force these terms on you, we may
not pay our debt in any other way. Should you try to bring suit
against us over this matter, it will be solely on your own luck you
must depend, while we will trust to our influence and standing in
the district. Then it may be less likely that you will get satisfaction
from us than if you had accepted our offer now, for Vinland is a
whole country, freely given, whereas Thorgils' farm is a small holding. And one for which you will have to fight, if you would have
it."

The end of it was that Sigtrygg consented to the terms which
the Leifssons offered him, for he thought it better to gain something for certain, at whatever distance, than to risk all on an uncertain toss. Therefore witnesses were called and Sigtrygg renounced
all claim to his father's farm, in favor of his uncles, and they did as
much for him regarding Vinland. And in addition they swore to
provide him with a ship and provisions as already described.

Afterwards the kinsmen parted amicably enough and Sigtrygg
went out among the farms of Greenland to seek a crew, for he said
"even the best ship is useless to its owner without good men to
man it," and he spent the rest of that summer in search of these.

CHAPTER II

ON HERJOLFSNESS

Now word quickly spread that the Leifssons meant to finance a new expedition to Vinland and there was no dearth of people who had something to say about the matter. Most thought it a foolhardy venture, for many had died in search of this land or in the settling of it, since Leif's time, and there were not so many good ships among the Greenlanders, or good men, that these could be readily spared. Thjodhild, herself, when she heard of this, said very little, either one way or the other, save that she thought it very like Thorgils' son, to follow in his father's footsteps and go off in search of foreign lands, with neither wealth nor good luck to commend him, although his prospects had been so much better closer to home. Afterwards she shut herself in her bed and would not speak with anyone in the household. This state of affairs lasted for three days, and then she emerged as though nothing had happened and with nothing further to say on the subject.

That summer, the Leifssons bought a small ship from a farmer who lived at the mouth of Eiriksfjord, and refitted it and stocked provisions for it, both dried meats and barley cakes, and made it over to Sigtrygg, saying, "Here is the steed which will carry you to your inheritance." But Sigtrygg had as yet found himself no crew, for very few men cared to leave the good grass lands of Greenland's sheltered coasts to venture out into the uncharted sea in those days, and this was certainly a great change from Eirik the Red's time.

When he saw that he could not raise the crew he needed in

Eiriksfjord to man his ship, Sigtrygg told his uncles that he would not be able to sail as quickly as had been agreed and now he asked leave of them to lay up his ship at Brattahlid over winter.

"I don't know if we have the facilities for that," replied Thorkel, "though you may find some other farmer in the district with a boat house, if you can pay him for its use. As for us Leifssons, it seems to me we have already done more than enough since we have kept exactly to the terms of our agreement."

Sigtrygg now thought that there was little to be gained by talking the matter over any further with his uncles, so he took his leave of them and went down to the water's edge to see that vessel for himself on which his hopes now rode. The ship sat on the stony beach below the Leifssons' home field at Brattahlid and was neither large nor well-appointed, being a simple twenty-oared boat of rough hewn planking with a short oak mast, lying nearby, which must be mounted in the ship's center to carry her sail. She had been covered, inside and out, with pitch and tallow and numerous of her upper boards were split or broken.

Sigtrygg strode round this boat till it was clear to him she was sea-worthy, at the least, though one man alone could never hope to sail her. Then, when he thought he had taken her full measure, he found a long pole and placed it under the stern and began to drive this pole deep into the ground. At length the ship began to tremble and then to rise up off the beach, where the length of the pole was exerted against it, and Sigtrygg pressed his back further into it, till the bow of the ship began to nose down to the fjord.

Now, while he was about this, he heard a voice behind him and he straightened up at once to see who was there. Thjodhild stood above him on an outcropping of rock, loosely wrapped in a fur cloak, her sun-red hair whipped out above her head by the wind.

"Do you think to sail alone, then, to your holdings, kinsman?" she now asked him, "or have you a crew for this poor boat hidden in the fjord?"

"Neither," said he, "but it does no one much good to leave the vessel on this beach, so close to the shore, where any sudden storm can wash over and carry her out to sea unmanned. Then your father and his brothers shall have kept their word, concerning me, whereas I will be without means of claiming my inheritance."

"It were better for you to claim it here in Greenland than to risk all, in this boat, on the open sea," said Thjodhild, "for, in that case, they shall have your farm and be well-rid of their half-brother's son, to boot."

"That may be, but I don't think there's much likelihood I shall be a farmer if I stay here now," Sigtrygg replied, "since my uncles have kept their side of our agreement and placed this ship in my hands."

"Yet you have no experience with such sailing vessels," said Thjodhild, "and riding the seas is not so light a matter as the coastal rowing you are accustomed to."

"It seems to me that one boat is very like another," he answered, "and the sea is the sea, either here or out beyond the sight of land. But if I cannot find the crew I need, then one man can cross the ocean as well as twenty."

Thjodhild said she thought this very foolish of him and that it only proved how little he knew of real sea travel which all men understood to be a perilous affair. Still, if he was set on taking his ship into such dangerous circumstances, she said she would not stand in his way, but "you might do better for a crew if you looked where men know a thing or two about such matters," she added.

"What do you suggest?" he asked.

"Only that you hunt for your rowers where such ships as these are most likely to be found, and that would be Herjolfsness where those who come out from Iceland and Norway first strike land in our country; for, where ships find a ready welcome, you are most likely to find the men who sail them."

Sigtrygg said he thought this good advice, though he doubted he could raise a crew among such experienced seafarers, for who, he asked, would abandon one of those large and well-kept vessels, which make the crossing to Greenland, in favor of his own less certain enterprise?

"Then that is as it should be," said Thjodhild. "Yet if you are as intent on this business as you have let on, I doubt this will be an obstacle for you. In my opinion, you should now seek out one of those landless men who makes his living by trade with the foreign ships, when you come to Herjolfsness. Then, it may happen, he will lead you to a man or two who can serve your purpose."

"The old saying is true enough," replied Sigtrygg, "that wisdom comes from unlikely quarters, for you are the last person I would have expected to further my plans for crossing the sea."

"You need not find it so surprising, kinsman," she said, "since I don't think you will be much good to anyone if you are thwarted in this matter. And now I want to offer to look after this ship of yours, till you come back to us in the summer. If you have found a crew for it, that will be soon enough to sail it on the open seas and, if not, perhaps you will have some other use in mind for it."

"I don't see how you can do more for this ship than I can do myself," he answered.

"It's easy enough to see," said Thjodhild, "for I have brothers and other able-bodied men to call on in this place, who will gladly do as I ask, but there is no one here who would do as much for you. But, if you will not place your trust in my word now, I don't see how you can hope to move this ship to a safer berth before winter. And then you may find it somewhat harder to row your way to Vinland."

Sigtrygg said he thought Thjodhild's plan was not without merit and after they had discussed the matter a little further, he agreed to leave the ship in her keeping. So now they parted and Thjodhild said he was to keep to his purpose, if he meant to find a crew, "but if you cannot, I will speak with our kinsmen for you, and see what else can be done."

Not long afterwards Sigtrygg left Brattahlid and, though it was already late in the season, he followed Thjodhild's advice, traveling by boat along the fjords and down the coast, where the drift ice was already beginning to float in from the sea, till he came in sight of the headland called Herjolfsness. There were, by this time, no ships to be seen on the beach there, for all those with plans to sail had long since departed, before the ice and winter storms should make the seaways impassable, and those who meant to stay the winter had by now found shelter, both for crew and ship. The booths of the men who traded with the foreign ships had also largely been struck, so that there was now little, if any, activity to be seen. Still, when he got to the headland, Sigtrygg pulled his boat up out of the sea and made his way among the booths that were still standing, asking everyone he met if any ship's crews were still nearby.

There was a man then on the beach at this time, called Vragi Skeggjasson, who was living in the Ketilsfjord district. This man had come out to Greenland only a few years before and seemed to be well on in years, grey-haired and somewhat stooped in stature. He had neither land nor household of his own in the country, but made his living entirely on the Herjolfsness beach, where he traded with the farmers and those merchants who came out in their ships during the summer months. He was, said some, the son of a certain Killer-Skeggi, a man of Norwegian extraction who had gone out to the Faroes in the time of King Eirik Bloody-Axe and who later became a retainer of the Orkney earls.

In his younger days, this Vragi Skeggjasson had, it was said, been something of a harsh fighting man and a sea rover himself, who had fought in many hard battles along the Irish coast. He had lost an eye in one of these, though this had been so long before that no one had any recollection of the battle in which this had occurred. Vragi, himself, told people that he could not recall where he had left the eye, though he thought it most likely to have fallen out somewhere between Ireland and the Orkneys.

At the time when Sigtrygg was there seeking a crew on Herjolfsness this man was still about on the beach, for he was late in pulling down his belongings and shutting up his booth. When he heard Sigtrygg wandering here and there among the half-empty structures, asking if there were still seamen to be found, he came outside to see what all the commotion was about and asked Sigtrygg his business.

"I have a ship to man and a profitable voyage in mind," Sigtrygg replied, "and, according to some, there is no better place than here to find the right sort of people for such an enterprise."

"Now that depends," replied the old man, "since there are men who know ships and men who know the sea, but these are not always one and the same. And it will do you little good if you find the one sort but not the other, even among the ships' crews housed here over winter, especially if you have something out of the ordinary in mind."

"You seem to know a little bit about my plans," said Sigtrygg when he heard the tone of the old man's reply.

"Don't be too surprised at that," replied the other, "for Greenland is a small country and few have not heard of the Leifssons and their kin, especially one as remarkable as Sigtrygg Thorgilsson, and that ship he means to sail in search of his grandfather's land claim in the west. But, in my opinion, there are not many left in this country who are up to such a task."

Sigtrygg said he thought it strange the old man should know so much about him while he, himself, remained nameless and the old man laughed and told Sigtrygg that his name was Vragi, "though some have called me One-Eye, for obvious reasons. And you are free to do so, if you like."

Sigtrygg said it was all the same to him, whatever name a man chose for himself, "but I mean to sail abroad, just the same, whatever others have to say in the matter," and now he asked if the old man could direct him to anyone who might be willing to ship out with him.

Vragi One-Eye replied that there were at least two ship's crews in harbor for the winter but that both had already found lodgings and were now well inland with local farmers. "You won't find anyone fit for sailing out on the ness this late in the year," he added.

"Then what are you doing here still counting up your goods, if the trading's all dried up?" asked Sigtrygg.

The old man laughed again, even louder this time than before, and said he was slower than most, since his profits had been better, and now he had to pay the price for his good judgement in his dealings with the foreign ships, for he had more than he could easily carry away with him from the beach. "But if you will give me a hand in this, perhaps I can offer you some good advice, at the least."

Seeing nothing else to be done, Sigtrygg agreed to help him and now these two went inside the booth. There were all manner of cloths and tools and foodstuffs within, which Vragi One-Eye had gathered in his trading with the foreign ships; far more, it seemed to Sigtrygg, than one man, alone, could make use of. In one corner there was also a dented and somewhat rusted shield and an old sword which lay up against it. These were weapons such as a viking might once have carried but, because of their poor condition, they did not look like the kind of goods a clever man would trade for. There was also a wooden keg of fine ale, which the old man now bent over. After a moment, he poured out a large cup for his guest, placing it in Sigtrygg's hands. "You won't find anything better than this for drinking in all of Greenland," he said.

"I don't know about that," Sigtrygg replied, "but it seems to me I have found an open-handed host, at the least, who has some skill in trading, though a flawed eye for good weapons."

The old man, seeing Sigtrygg's gaze upon the sword and shield, shrugged and agreed they were not worth very much. But, he said, he kept them for sentimental reasons, "since they once belonged to a red-handed sea raider who made a name for himself along the Irish coast. And, if they're not much to look at these days, it only shows how much use their master had once put them to."

"And who might this famous viking have been?" asked Sigtrygg.

"People called him Vragi Skeggjasson, before he lost an eye," the old man said.

Sigtrygg laughed and asked how a man like that, if he had been such a well-known viking, should come to be living on the coast of Greenland and how he managed to support himself in the winter months.

"Such a man has no need to live like other people," replied Vragi, "for my trading is generally so successful that I get everything I need in the summer from those ships which come here to Herjolfsness. These goods," the old man added, "more than support me when things turn bitterly cold, for every farmer has food and drink to trade for what I gather. And besides, I have an interest in a ship or two, which is even now overseas, in Iceland and Norway."

"That seems a poor risk, to me, to count for one's livelihood on the ships which fare abroad," said Sigtrygg.

"It's not so different from a hunter's life," the old man replied, "who trades his skins and carcasses for a winter's shelter. But I keep to myself and have little need of anyone else's hospitality. And as to how I came to Greenland, well an old man gets little good from a viking's ways and must find his home where he can, once he has outlived the time for sword and shield play."

Sigtrygg said he was not surprised that a man who had spent so much of his life as a viking should need to make his home in Greenland, "since a man of war makes many enemies." And now he asked the old man whether he had any advice for him concerning the ship's crew he was seeking.

"Not much," admitted Vragi, "for your enterprise is too bold for most people these days and I know the crews remaining here over winter. There is not a man among them I would want on a vessel in which I had a share, if it were bound for the lands you have your eye on. And, by the looks of you, you are not much of a sea captain, either."

Sigtrygg said he thought he would prove as good a seaman as Vragi had been a viking, when the thing were put to the test, and after this they had very little to say to one another, though Sigtrygg remained to help the old man tie up his goods and cart them inland behind a small horse which Vragi kept for this purpose. When they had finished this work and gone a ways off the beach with the old man's goods, Sigtrygg suddenly stopped and turned to Vragi, asking if he knew of anyone in the district with whom he might find lodging for the winter.

"I don't have much to say about that, either," the old man replied, "since I'm not in the habit of bothering people for my upkeep. Nor can I offer you accommodations with me, since I live simply enough. By the time winter is over I shall have barely what I need for myself."

"In that case," said Sigtrygg, "I think we may as well part company here, since I have got little enough for my troubles so far."

Sigtrygg turned back toward the ness whereupon Vragi stuck out a staff he was carrying and blocked his way. "Since you are so intent upon this business of yours," he said, "I don't think it's right for you to go off empty-handed. So now I want you to pick out anything from among my goods which you want and take it for yourself. That is small enough repayment for the help you've given me and a gesture of friendship which I would like to make to you."

Sigtrygg said he wouldn't deny the old man this favor and he went over to the wagon behind the trader's horse, reaching deep into the bundled goods. When his hand came out again, he held the dented sword in it.

"Although it is in such poor condition," said Sigtrygg, "I don't think there is anything else in your store of goods I would rather have than this, if it's all the same to you."

The old man squinted his one good eye at the battered sword and leaned on his staff. "It doesn't pay to argue the value of things with the young," he said. "If that's all you want, I won't stop you. However I don't think it makes sense to separate two companions of such long standing," and, so saying, he went to the wagon and pulled out the shield which went with the sword and handed it to Sigtrygg, as well. "These two have not been parted in many years and I don't think much good can come of sending them on their separate ways now."

Sigtrygg thanked the old man for these gifts and turned to leave once more, but now Vragi took hold of his arm and pulled him back toward the wagon.

"It doesn't look to me as though you will feel you've gained much from our meeting, if all you go away with now are these old weapons," he said and Sigtrygg agreed that this was probably so.

"In that case," said Vragi, "perhaps there's one more thing I can provide you with before we part company."

"And what's that?" asked Sigtrygg.

"The advice which you were seeking," replied the old man, "for, unless I miss my guess, it was for that reason only that you stayed behind to help me with my goods. Now if I were a young fellow, like you, seeking a winter's accommodations, I think I would find no better path than over that nearby ridge and up along the fjord. And then I would go as far as my legs would take me till I came to a certain farm, set well back from the sea and nestled under the rocky promontory which juts out there from the inland ice. A farmer lives there who goes by the name of Torfi Gudvesson and who is, among all the people of this district, the most suitable for a man like yourself to be begging hospitality from. Then, if you've any luck with him, come see me when summer returns and we'll see whether your luck's as good at raising a crew."

Sigtrygg thanked the old man again and promised to do just as he advised, "for," he said, "it's always best, in strange waters, to sail in the wake of one who knows the port." And now he turned inland and went off over the ridge in the direction in which the old man had pointed.

CHAPTER III

THE FARMER'S SON

Placing the sword and shield in a bundle on his back, with his other goods, Sigtrygg went overland, at first, until he came to the coast and there the sea narrowed, as it poured into Ketilsfjord, between the steep sides of the land. He went back along the coast there, up the fjord, till he came at last to a small farm nestled far back from the water, much where Vragi Skeggjasson had said it would be. The stone walls, which ringed the farmhouse and the outbuildings, were broken in several places and only a few scruffy looking goats were grazing nearby. Nor was there much activity, other than this, to be seen in the home field.

When Sigtrygg came within hailing distance of the house, he called aloud to see if anyone was about. At first there was no response but, after a time, two boys came out and these looked to Sigtrygg rather on the thin side and somewhat unsure of themselves when they saw him. They were soon followed by a woman who proved to be somewhat bolder, for she greeted him warmly and asked his news and how far he was traveling.

"No farther than here," Sigtrygg replied, "if you are in need of a helping hand over winter, for it seems to me there is a great deal of work to be done in this place but not many men about to do it."

"That would be up to my husband," said the farm wife quickly, "since he has the final say in everything concerning our upkeep. But I don't think he would object if we showed you a little hospitality till he returned." Then she invited Sigtrygg into the house and offered him goat cheese, which he ate readily, and goat's milk to drink.

Now he spent a good deal of time with the housewife, telling her something of his travels and how he was planning a lengthy sea voyage the following summer. The farmer's wife said it had been a long time since they had played host to such a traveler as he was and Sigtrygg brought out the goods he was carrying and showed the woman two seal skins he had taken the previous winter, which were without blemish or other imperfection. He said she was to take these for herself.

"Such gifts deserve a fair return," said the housewife somewhat dejectedly, "but we are not so well off as other farmers in this district and have nothing comparable to give you."

"There's no need for that," Sigtrygg replied, "since I have never tasted such fine cheese in all my life."

The farm wife laughed. "The old saying is certainly true," she said, "that the hungry belly is easiest to fill."

Sigtrygg answered that it was likely to be much harder to fill over winter, if he did not soon find a place to stay, since he could not go back to Eiriksfjord now. The farmer's wife promised to speak to her husband about the matter, when he returned, and there they let the matter rest.

Not long afterwards, a large heavy-set fellow came into the house and he said he was Torfi Gudvesson, that same man of whom Vragi One-Eye had spoken. But it was soon quite clear that he was less than pleased to see a stranger at his table. "We don't have a great deal of food to spare, and even less when the winter shuts us in," he said to Sigtrygg, "so we are not in the habit of putting up travelers."

"It seems to me folk are a lot less hospitable in this part of the country than in the districts I am accustomed to," Sigtrygg replied when he heard the farmer's words, "and that is a very strange thing, seeing as this is the region where foreigners find the most welcome, when first they come out to our country."

"Have it your own way," answered the farmer, "but in my

opinion you would be better off seeking accommodations with people who have more than we do."

"Still I think you could use the extra hands," said Sigtrygg, looking across the room at the two frail boys.

"It's true enough that there's plenty of work for everyone here," said the farmer, "but provisions are not equally abundant; and you don't bring much of that with you either, from what I can see."

Sigtrygg said he would not deny this but that he thought there was something else on the farmer's mind which was making him so reluctant to accept a guest, "although this was not what I looked for when Vragi One-Eye sent me this way to find a winter's lodging."

The farmer now asked if it were true that he was a friend of Vragi Skeggjasson and Sigtrygg said that it was, bringing out the old viking's sword and shield by way of proof.

Now the farmer's wife said: "You're not showing much respect for an old friend, husband, if you turn this man away, since he came to our door expecting better. And, besides, he looks like a man who knows his way about a farm such as ours."

The farmer said he thought it highly unusual that his wife should be supporting the stranger so readily, but he could not deny the strength of her case if it were indeed true that Sigtrygg had been sent to them by the old sea trader out on the ness, for Vragi was well-known to him and not one whose wishes he would lightly disregard. "You don't know as much as you should about this fellow to be taking his side like this, wife," said Torfi Gudvesson. "Nevertheless, I wont stand in your way, if you are intent on taking him in. I only wish to stipulate one thing and that is that, in addition to help on the farm over winter, our guest must agree to grant me one request, whenever I ask it of him, without my saying anything more about it now than this."

"These are strange terms," said Sigtrygg, "if I am not to know in advance what request you have in mind."

"Nevertheless, they are my conditions," answered the farmer, "though, I assure you, they will not seem so hard for you to agree to, when the time comes."

"In that case," said Sigtrygg, "I wont hold back, so long as your request is an honorable one" and he told the farmer he would consent to his terms. Thereupon, they shook hands and Sigtrygg took up residence in the farmer's house.

Some time afterward, when they were sitting at table for the evening meal, the farmer's wife brought out a watery gruel with thin strips of meat in it, which Sigtrygg did not appear to find altogether to his liking. Torfi Gudvesson noticed that his guest seemed perturbed and asked him if he thought he could find better up at Eiriksfjord. Sigtrygg said he thought that he could, but added that food was only worth the strength it put in a man's back, "and by the looks of you, this food's as good as any I've tasted elsewhere in Greenland."

The farmer thought this very funny and now his manner became somewhat less harsh toward Sigtrygg and the two men appeared to get on better than before. They were soon spending a great deal of time together, talking about the doings in the Ketilsfjord district and elsewhere.

Torfi told Sigtrygg that the most important farmer in the district was a certain Grimkel Vesteinsson who had the largest and best land holdings in Ketilsfjord and was the person with the most authority, as well. "Whenever anyone has anything of importance to decide," said the farmer, "it is to Grimkel they take the matter; and they always abide by his decisions."

"He's not much of a chieftain, in my opinion," replied Sigtrygg, "if he doesn't do any better by his followers than he has with you, seeing as your household is so stretched for provisions over winter, when others in the district must have so much more."

"I don't count myself one of Grimkel's men," said Torfi and then he seemed to lose interest in the discussion. But Sigtrygg pressed the matter, telling Torfi he would like to go over to this Grimkel's hall and meet such an important man.

"I don't see how that can do either of us much good," replied the farmer. "Besides, it's not altogether clear what you have in mind."

"Just this," said Sigtrygg. "My father may not have been the most highly regarded of Leif Eiriksson's sons, but my blood is certainly as good as any in Greenland. Perhaps this will convince your neighbor to play the chieftain's part with a more open hand."

"I don't think it will have the effect you desire," said the farmer, "for this Grimkel is already well-acquainted with your kinsmen, since they have made common cause in matters of mutual concern, before this." And now the farmer got up from his place without saying anything more on the subject.

Not long afterwards, Sigtrygg noticed that the farmer kept a number of fine looking weapons on the wall and that these did not have the look of a poor man's possessions. They included several spears and shields, two swords, and a very old looking, long-handled axe with a two-edged blade at one end of the shaft. Each of the blades had a rather peculiar shape, being somewhat asymmetrical and wider at the top than at the bottom. Nor were they perfectly matched on either side as was the custom for such weapons.

Sigtrygg said he thought it unusual for a man to be keeping weapons like these, "especially when he seems to be so short of other things."

The farmer replied that they were family heirlooms, which he was unwilling to part with, and that the axe was especially valued by him for it had belonged to his father, Gudve Arnliotsson, and to Gudve's father, Arnliot the Strong, before that. "Both were exceedingly accomplished men in their day," said the farmer, "and well-known vikings."

Sigtrygg said: "Still, I have never seen a weapon quite like that axe. In my opinion, it would fetch a good price if you chose to sell it; and that would go a long way toward feeding this family of yours."

"Are you offering to buy it from me, then?" asked the farmer.

"Not at all," replied Sigtrygg, "for I don't have much use for such a large weapon. But I am certain there are many who would desire it, and not least of all those men who come hence to us from over the sea."

"That may be," replied the farmer, "but this weapon has one serious flaw, for its virtues are double edged, no less than its blade is, and most men, to my way of thinking, will feel they are better off without it once they have heard the matter out."

Sigtrygg said the farmer should explain himself.

The farmer said that the axe was called "hand-biter," and that for no small reason, "since whoever wields it in battle is assured of victory; but it will cause his death in the end. And that's how it was with my own kinsmen for each came to an untimely end, though the weapon brought them victory in every fight."

"Some people," said Sigtrygg, "would think that a price worth paying."

But the farmer answered that those were a young man's words, "for this axe has an uncanny way of bringing about events to cause harm to its owner, and that due to the harsh manner in which it was acquired by my kinsman, Arnliot the Strong. For he took it by force from a certain Lappish man, having come on him unawares, and the man placed this curse upon it before he died, that whoever owned it after him must meet a similar fate."

"Is there nothing, then, which will avert the weapon's doom?" Sigtrygg asked.

"Just one thing," replied the farmer, "and that is for its owner to willingly give it to another, before the doom ring has closed. But that is not easily done, for few men can carry such a weapon or wield it in war-play, so few will take it when it is offered. Nor will that man who has once claimed it, and carried it into battle, gladly give it up again, after he has seen the workings of its two-sided blade in the spear-storm."

Sigtrygg said he thought it a great shame that such a handsome weapon should be left to hang untouched on a farmhouse wall for so many years, "because of old tales and superstitions."

But he let the matter lie, for it was plain to him the farmer took
the matter much more seriously than he did, himself.

Soon enough the winter came on and it grew much colder
than anyone then living in Greenland could remember. The farmer
now saw that he had very little reason to regret giving hospitality
to Sigtrygg because his guest took on all the heaviest work, himself, and tended the farmer's animals, even when the cold was most
bitter and no one else in the household was willing to venture
away from the fire pit in the main hall. In those days it was said
that there was no one alive in Greenland who could endure the
cold better than Sigtrygg Thorgilsson, and most folk thought this
was due to the fact that he had been born out on the ice.

Now, one night, not long after Sigtrygg had taken up with
these people, while they were yet at table, there was a loud commotion outside. Sigtrygg thought it very unusual for people to be
about, because of the cold, and he rose from his place to see who or
what might be causing the disturbance. But the farmer rose more
quickly and, before Sigtrygg could reach the door, the farmer had
gone outside. The farmer's wife now told Sigtrygg that he must sit
down, since there was nothing to be concerned about, and she
brought him a large drinking cup filled to the brim with that
same ale which Vragi had offered him out on the ness the previous
summer. Sigtrygg said he thought it strange she had not served
this before, since the farmer and his wife were always complaining
about how little they had, "while this is just the thing to take the
edge off a cold night."

"The wise sailor does not eat and drink the best he has, the
first day at sea," answered the housewife. Sigtrygg agreed that this
was probably so and asked her if this meant that landfall was now
not far off.

"It is certainly much closer than before," agreed the woman.

Just then the doors of the farmhouse were thrown wide and in
strode a number of harsh looking fellows with Sigtrygg's host in

tow. They clustered about the farther end of the table, nearest the doorway, and spoke in low tones to the farmer and his wife.

At the head of this group was a large and long-legged fellow, who stood so much taller than the others he seemed to have to stoop to hear the muffled words the newcomers were speaking among themselves. After a moment, this man noticed Sigtrygg, in the smoky light of the hall, and he now detached himself from his companions and walked up the length of the table to where Sigtrygg sat, the cup of ale which the farmer's wife had given him still in his hand. The tall man walked round Sigtrygg and grinned at him through half-closed eyes, his mouth stretched taut as a ship's rope.

"You didn't tell me you had guests, this winter," said the man to the farmer and his wife, "particularly of such an unusual sort as this fellow."

The farmer's wife made no response but brought the big man a cup of ale, as large as the one Sigtrygg held, and he drained it in a single swallow and then he turned away, as quickly as he had come, and returned to his companions who were clustered near the door. Now the farmer came over to Sigtrygg and asked him if he would mind sharing the table with these newcomers for, said he, they were men of the district who had travelled far over the ice and were just now arrived from up the fjord. Sigtrygg replied that his host should do as he thought best "for it's your house and no one has any more say here than you do. But," he added, "they don't have the look of good drinking companions, to my way of thinking."

Places were now set at the farther end of the table and, in no time at all, the five strangers, for Sigtrygg could now see they were no more than this number, were seated and scooping the housewife's thin gruel into their mouths. For a time there were no sounds in the farmer's hall, save those noises which hungry men make at the food bowl, while the farmer's wife and children made a great fuss over the newcomers. As for the farmer, he now sat himself down beside Sigtrygg and made show of engaging his guest in conversation, as though nothing out of the ordinary had occurred. Sigtrygg thought this even more unusual than what had gone before but, since the farmer made no attempt to explain himself, Sigtrygg did not press the matter.

Then suddenly, and without warning, the strangers arose and left the farmer's house with the same rush and whispering as before, nor did they pause to thank the farmer and his wife nor to exchange any departing pleasantries with anyone at all in the household. After they were gone, Sigtrygg remarked that this was very strange behavior indeed and that it did not speak well for the manners of the people in the district.

But Torfi Gudvesson replied that it was all the same to him how people received his hospitality, so long as they took it when it was needed, and there they let the matter lie.

Now there is not much more to tell, until the winter had passed and the ice began to break up out on the fjord. Then, one morning, the farmer asked Sigtrygg to get up and follow him outside. He led the way to a stone building which stood at some distance from the main farm, behind a low hill. It was built into the side of the hill and had lain abandoned all winter, since the farmer had said it was too far from the rest of his holdings to maintain any animals in it, nor did he have so many beasts as to require the extra shelter. Farmer Torfi now asked Sigtrygg to help him clean out the structure and so they went inside.

Sigtrygg could see that the place had a lived-in look, since there was fresh ash strewn about the earthen floor, as though a fire had been lit not long before, and there were particles of food and other debris. He said that he thought they had had unlooked for guests, over winter, and he asked his host what this could mean.

"Not as much as it appears to," replied the farmer, "since we didn't lack for food or warmth all winter, no matter who made use of this building. But I want to put it to better use now."

Then he and Sigtrygg cleared out the inside and began to rebuild the stone enclosure which surrounded it. This was heavy work and they were at it for a very long time, neither speaking overmuch to the other, until they had finished. Then Torfi said:

"It's not often that a poor man, like myself, gets his help from the hands of a man of Leif Eirikson's kin, whatever else folk may say of your parentage."

Sigtrygg straightened and wiped the sweat from his eyes. "There's not much to be said, at any event," he replied, "since up at Eiriksfjord we are not accustomed to judging the value of a man's work by the blood that flows in his veins."

"Nevertheless," said Torfi, "I count it a great honor that a man of your standing has helped to rebuild this wall, since in my opinion it will be the better for your efforts."

Sigtrygg now said he thought the farmer should say clearly what he had on his mind "for a man like you does not often turn to flattery to get his way in things."

"Nor would I do so now," agreed the farmer, "but it is in my mind to raise the matter of your board with us, since I doubt you will be staying much longer, now that the weather's changed."

Sigtrygg said that this was probably so, "but it seems to me I have more than repaid you for your hospitality — and given a lot more than you'd have expected from lesser men."

The farmer said he would not deny this, but that there was still the matter of Sigtrygg's promise to grant whatever was asked of him.

"Most people would think I'd already paid more than enough for the right to tend your farm over winter," Sigtrygg replied.

Now Torfi fell silent and Sigtrygg told him that those pleas were best made which were spoken plainly. But the farmer answered that it was little use pressing a matter with people who did not remember what they had said the previous winter and he got up from where he was sitting and went back to the house without any more words. After a time, Sigtrygg followed him, and now there arose a certain coolness between them.

Soon after, Sigtrygg prepared to take his leave of the farmer and his family, since he said he had a great deal to do if he were going to find a crew to man his ship. The farmer's wife was just as friendly toward him as before, and she brought him whatever food-stuffs she could spare from her larder and wrapped these carefully and placed them in his pack. The two boys, for their part, had grown somewhat fond of their guest over the winter as well, and they now helped Sigtrygg to put his things in order for the journey back to Eiriksfjord. But while he was gathering his goods, Sigtrygg saw that the sword and shield which he had gotten from Vragi Skeggjasson were no longer among them.

When it was clear to him that neither the farmer's wife nor her two sons knew anything about the missing items, he went out to the barn where Torfi Gudvesson was seeing to his goats.

"I suppose you have it in mind to take your leave now," said the farmer without looking up from his work.

Sigtrygg said that was exactly what he was planning to do but that he had lost certain of his goods which he intended to find before moving on. "You wouldn't know where I can find these, farmer Torfi?" he asked.

"I would, if they are an old sword and shield," replied the farmer.

Sigtrygg said those were exactly the items he was seeking and now he asked the farmer how he had come by them.

"That's easy," said Torfi, "for I am no stranger to swordplay and have wielded many a good weapon in my younger days. It was in my mind to sample those battle tools you carry around, like wadmal, on your back."

Sigtrygg said it was not anyone's concern how he carried his weapons, but that he now intended to do whatever was required to ensure they were returned.

"I won't prevent you from doing that," said the farmer, "but first I wish to know why you find it so difficult to keep your share of our bargain."

"You haven't told me what you want, yet," said Sigtrygg, "so how can I say if it will be hard, or not?"

"Yet, you are somewhat less eager in this matter, than you

were last winter, when you were so anxious to find a household to take you in."

"It would have been easier," Sigtrygg agreed, "had things stayed as they were when we first met, but now it seems you have kept a great deal to yourself. Until you are more open concerning certain matters, it is unlikely we will find much to agree on."

"In that case," said the farmer, "you may as well ask me whatever is on your mind, for I don't think our parting will satisfy either of us, if you continue to harbor doubts about my goodwill."

Sigtrygg now said he thought this was fair enough, but that "nothing will settle things between us unless you tell me who those ill-mannered men were, who paid us a visit one night, last winter, and who spent the season in your goat shed on the other side of the hill."

The farmer said he was not surprised that Sigtrygg had noticed these men but that there was not a great deal to tell, "for they are men from the district, as I told you at the time, nor have I kept anything from you concerning that."

"Yet, I think you were somewhat close-mouthed about them, all the same, for otherwise they'd have been guests in your house, as I was."

"This only shows the difference between your luck and theirs," answered the farmer, "since their stay was so much less comfortable than your own."

"In that case, I don't suppose you will find it hard to tell me who that big, unlucky-looking fellow was at their head, for this, it seems to me, will surely have a bearing on the matter."

"That's no harder to say than the rest," answered Torfi, "for these are all local men, as I have said before. But as to their leader, there are not many people in these parts who do not know Arnliot Keelfoot who is thought, by some, to be the most promising man in the district. Nor is that to be wondered at, for he is also my son."

Sigtrygg now asked how it was that a man's son came to be living in an outbuilding, over winter, while a stranger shared the warmth and provender of the household with the man and his wife?

"This is not hard to tell, either," said the farmer, "for Arnliot, who some call Keelfoot for the size of his feet, though in truth they are not so much larger than any other part of him, is a man of no small prowess, as anyone with eyes can readily see. But he is also somewhat overeager, as young men sometimes will be, and this has occasionally thrust him into difficult situations."

"What manner of trouble, then," asked Sigtrygg, "will drive a man from his father's house in such a fashion as this?"

"Arnliot is my oldest son," said the farmer, "and there's no use denying his accomplishments. He is among the fastest and most daring men in all Greenland, but somewhat puffed up about it, to the bargain. There are few who can leap the spaces between the ice floes, as he can — a risky business, at best — and he has often enough raced others across the fjord in this fashion. But such races do not always end as well as they begin, and so it was in my son's case. Many a man has lost his footing on the sea ice and drowned in the freezing fjord waters beneath. No doubt you will recall the outcome of some of these games from your days at Eiriksfjord?"

"We were not so frivolous as that," said Sigtrygg, "though I have, myself, walked the ice for other purposes."

"No matter," said the farmer. "It's a pastime of the young here. But Arnliot is better than most and, for this reason, he engaged in a race with a certain Jarlabanki who, while not so young as Arnliot, was a man of no small repute, nonetheless."

"A man who thought he knew the ice floes as well as any?"

"Even so," said Torfi, "but also a man who was the younger brother of that same Grimkel Vesteinsson of whom we spoke last winter. The outcome, as you have guessed, was less than satisfactory, for Jarlabanki lost both footing and life in the freezing waters of Ketilsfjord, and my son won his wager."

"It seems to me," said Sigtrygg, "that things could be a lot worse than you have described them, for death is the risk a man takes in such contests, while your son is alive and well, despite his companion's mishap."

"But that is the point," replied Torfi, "for there were those on shore who supported either man and these did not see eye to eye concerning events out on the ice. Some said Jarlabanki was pushed into the sea while others thought Arnliot did less than he could have, to pull him out again. For my part, I think the man was too old to pit himself against a youngster and was overmatched. But, no matter, for Grimkel, his brother, demanded self-judgement in the case and, since he is so important in this part of the country, I was unable to obtain better terms. It is for this reason you see my household in the state it is, for Grimkel took most of what we had and would have taken our land, as well, but for Vragi Skeggjasson who paid the remainder of the fine which Grimkel levied against me."

"This is certainly a sorry tale," said Sigtrygg, "and now I understand why that old man sent me to your household, since he thought he had some claim on you, as perhaps he does. But I don't see why this son of yours should now be hiding under hills, if the fine's been paid."

"Because," said the farmer, "Grimkel is no easy man to run afoul of, and he took it badly that our land was saved and that we continue to live in peace in this district. He has sworn to get vengeance on Arnliot, despite the settlement. And, truth be told, I am unable to prevent him, since there is no one stronger than he is in Ketilsfjord."

Sigtrygg now said that he understood why his host had been so secretive all winter, if he was looking to shield his son, but that he didn't think Arnliot was the kind of man to stay hidden for long, by the looks of him.

"That's true enough," replied the farmer, "and that's just the reason I agreed to take you in when you came to us at the beginning of the winter."

"I can't offer you much support, in this matter," Sigtrygg said, "for, though I am kin to the Leifssons up in Eiriksfjord, I am not in the highest standing with them, as you well know. Nevertheless, I will speak with them on your behalf. Perhaps they will give you some help or find someone to exchange farms with you from another district."

"That is not the kind of help I had in mind," said Torfi.

"What then?"

"When you came to us you promised to honor any request I made of you, at the end of your stay with us, and now I want you to make good on that pledge."

"Since you have been so honest with me," said Sigtrygg, "despite the pain it has caused you, I don't see how I can be any less forthright with you. Ask what you will."

"That is no less than I would have expected of you," said the farmer, and now he arose and went to a corner of the barn and drew out from behind the hay a cloth-wrapped package. He placed it before Sigtrygg and carefully unwound the cloth. When the grey material came away, Sigtrygg's sword and shield lay unclad on the hay. Both were well-burnished and the sword shone with a gleam which betrayed newly sharpened edges.

"I don't think these weapons would have done you much good in the condition they were in, when you first brought them here," said Torfi. "Still, it has been a long time since I hammered and ground a blade as fine as this one is."

Sigtrygg lifted the sword and weighed it carefully in his hands. He said he thought it felt entirely different from before and the farmer replied that it was often the case that a newly tooled weapon seemed different, even to familiar hands.

"Now I want you to promise to put these to good use, when you have gone out to Vinland," said the farmer. "But, as for your oath to grant me whatever I ask of you, I want to know if you are now prepared to fulfill it?"

"And why not," said Sigtrygg, "since you have treated me more nobly than I have so far treated you?" He could not take his eyes from the gleam on the sword's freshly sharpened edge, which seemed to quiver in the pale white sunlight streaming in from the half-opened barn door.

"In that case," said Torfi Gudvesson, "I want you to accept my son and his companions aboard your ship, for I don't think there's anywhere safer than Vinland for these five, while Grimkel Vesteinsson remains the chieftain in this district."

Sigtrygg said he thought it strange the farmer would make such a big thing of this request, knowing that this was the very purpose for which he had come out to Ketilsfjord, "especially since I have so far found it difficult to turn away even the least likely of prospects."

"I feared this Grimkel's enmity would sway you in the matter," said Torfi, "since he carries some weight with your kinsmen."

"I don't see how pleasing my kinsmen in this will get me any closer to Vinland," Sigtrygg replied, "nor failing to satisfy them, lessen my standing much in their eyes."

"Then," said the farmer, "I will bring you to where they are in hiding for, if truth be told, I thought it best they were well away from here, before winter was past. Yet, now I think it will be hard enough to keep them hid, or from crossing paths with Grimkel, once the ice is gone in the fjords and people are again moving about."

Shortly afterwards, farmer Torfi brought Sigtrygg to a place in the hills, behind his steading, just under the lip of the ice which lay up over Ketilsfjord. There was a small, steep cleft there in the high ground, overgrown with moss and newly sprouting grass. Torfi and Sigtrygg climbed down into this ravine. When they had got to the bottom, Sigtrygg saw a small booth of turf, covered over with moss and brush and inside this five men were sitting.

"What brings you out so early in the year, father?" asked their leader, who now got up from his place and greeted his guests. "It is certainly too soon for you to be thinking we are short of food."

"I am more concerned that you are suffering for want of companionship," answered Torfi, "and I would rather spend my time visiting you, than have you salve your loneliness by paying your respects to any of our neighbors."

"That may yet come," said Arnliot, "since there are some who are eager enough for my company, and the guest quarters here are rather tight. But I see you have brought your own house guest along this time." He now turned to Sigtrygg and said: "How did you find my father's quarters over winter, then, fellow? Were they warm enough and to your liking?"

Sigtrygg said he had no doubt they were a great deal more comfortable than Arnliot's own winter lodgings had been.

"In that case, you won't mind if I do not invite you to stay with us here," answered Arnliot, "for our accommodations are skimpier than most, these days."

"That is exactly why I have brought this man with me," Torfi now interjected, "for until a short time ago, he had not much more to his name than you men have here. But he is now become a man of substance, for he is kin to the Leifssons and has taken over Leif Eiriksson's land claim in the west."

Arnliot said: "Then it's true, as I thought, that you are that fellow whom the Leifssons swindled out of his farm, up in Eiriksfjord."

"Call it what you will," said Sigtrygg, "but my uncles and I have come to a satisfactory arrangement in the matter. And now I am intending to raise a crew to sail with me to the west. I could certainly use men like yourselves, if you're willing to throw in with me."

Torfi now told Arnliot and his friends what he had in mind and how Sigtrygg had a fully provisioned ship waiting up in Eiriksfjord which he meant to put to sea in, that very summer.

"I don't think farmer Grimkel will take it kindly if we go overseas so suddenly," replied Arnliot, "without first paying our proper respects to him."

"There's no need to do that," said Torfi, "for no man has any claim against any of you, as things now stand. But if you have your way in this matter, it may soon happen there will be no way to untie that knot you are now so intent on binding."

"Even so," said Arnliot, "it is not my way to scoot out of the way of every hungry little fox, who happens across my path, like some fearful hare. It is only out of respect for you, father, that I have kept out of sight this long, but now I think this time of sneaking about has run its course."

Sigtrygg said that Arnliot would do better to heed his father's words "for there's plenty of time to put matters right, so why not do it when you are better placed than you are now? As everyone knows," he continued, "this Vinland, where we are headed, is an unusually rich and well-stocked country. A man can make his mark there and, when he comes home, most people will know he has done something."

"Have you sailed out there, then," asked Arnliot, "that you can speak so assuredly of what lies to the west?"

Sigtrygg now admitted that he had never seen the western lands nor even sailed on any kind of ship out of Greenland waters.

"I don't see how you can offer much to men like us, then," said Arnliot, "for I have, myself, been out to Iceland on one of Vragi Skeggjasson's ships, while still only a boy, and all of us here have sailed the Greenland waters in the ships men use to hunt the walrus and whale."

"It's all the same to me what sailing you've done" answered Sigtrygg, "and, indeed, I hold it better that you have some knowledge of ships than otherwise. But if you want a share in the ship I mean to sail, you must sail it with me, since the ship and the country we're bound for both are mine."

Now Torfi added that they were unlikely to find a better skipper than Sigtrygg anywhere in Greenland, for all his inexperience on the open seas, for he had in him the blood of Leif Eiriksson and, besides, Vragi Skeggjasson had already given him his backing. Arnliot asked what kind of backing the trader had committed to and Torfi told him about the sword and shield and how Vragi had sent Sigtrygg to him for lodging.

"It does not sound like he is placing much confidence in this man's enterprise in that case, father," answered Arnliot, once he had heard the farmer out, "since everyone knows that old sea trader is more accustomed to backing up a voyage with money and goods, than a few gifts and some free advice."

"Still, kinsman," said Torfi, "a man does not often get a chance to do something like this in his lifetime, and even more so in Greenland, in our day. Grimkel Vesteinsson, on the other hand, will be here a good many years yet, and you'll find plenty of time to deal with him then."

"I'd rather have the matter out now and go off to Vinland in my own time."

"In that case," answered Sigtrygg, "you will need to find another ship than mine, for I am not proposing to hold my plans hostage to your pride. If you entangle yourself with this Ketilsfjord farmer, I will not wait around until matters are cleared up and you are free to sail. But join me in this venture now and there is nothing to keep you from coming back, when things are quieter, and doing what's needful. Besides, it's well-known that a man who flees with the dogs nipping at his heels often finds it hardest to come back in through the front door."

The end of it was that Torfi Gudvesson had his way in the matter and his son, Arnliot, along with his four companions agreed to sail on Sigtrygg's ship, though this Arnliot was somewhat ill-humored about it since it was plain he thought himself the better man, where Sigtrygg was concerned. Sigtrygg now advised them to sit quietly, where they were, for the time being, and to come up to Eiriksfjord before midsummer, for he thought to have his full crew by then. But he said they were to keep a low profile and make their way north over land, staying well behind the main farms, for he said the best journey was often the one which attracted the least attention and that this was especially so in this case.

CHAPTER IV

A KING'S MAN

When they returned to Torfi's steading, Sigtrygg asked the farmer how he planned to manage if his oldest son now went overseas, seeing as he was so short of help. Torfi replied that he had two other sons who, while not yet grown, were unlikely to remain undersized forever.

"Do you think either of them will show the same promise as that fellow we have just been visiting?" asked Sigtrygg.

"That's certainly hard to predict," agreed the farmer, "but it is not unknown for one family to produce more than one outstanding man."

"In that case," said Sigtrygg, "I shall know where to look for my crewmen in the future. But, for now, I want to see who else I can find in this district, either farmers' sons or hired hands who are willing to throw their lot in with mine, since it's no use sailing where I mean to go, if we start out too late in the season. And I am still short a few fellows."

"I don't think you will find your men here in Ketilsfjord," said Torfi, "for none will join you in these parts without the agreement of Grimkel Vesteinsson."

"Then he is the first one I must seek out," replied Sigtrygg.

Torfi Gudvesson said it wouldn't be much to his liking if Sigtrygg were to pay a visit to Grimkel but Sigtrygg replied that he planned to do it, just the same. Sigtrygg now left Torfi's steading and went on his way, up the length of the fjord. At every farm he told his purpose and inquired whether there were any men willing to sail out with him to the western lands. But, just as Torfi had foretold, there was very little interest in this enterprise, though it appeared to Sigtrygg that this was as much due to the quality of the people in the district as to any concern for their chieftain's wishes.

Nevertheless, by the time Sigtrygg had come to Grimkel's steading, word had already reached those who lived there as to his purpose. The people on the farm made him a good welcome and were greatly interested in his plans and, afterwards, they brought him into the main house where he found Grimkel sitting on a high seat, which had been built at the farthest end of the hall. When the farmer saw him, he gave him a fair greeting and asked his news.

Sigtrygg now told him who he was and "that I am come out of Eiriksfjord in search of a crew to sail to Vinland this summer, since my kinsmen have made over to me those houses which Leif Eiriksson built there while he was yet a young man."

Grimkel said he was not surprised that Sigtrygg had brought this matter to him, for it was well-known that he and the Leifssons thought highly of one another. He said he was now prepared to treat Sigtrygg with the same regard as he would any of his kin, "though you are clearly from the less well-established side of that family."

Sigtrygg answered that he was gratified by such kind words but that if Grimkel really wanted to be of help, he must support him in his search for a crew, "since," he said, "ships do not sail of themselves."

Grimkel now had his men clear a place for Sigtrygg at the board, by his right hand and, when they had eaten and drunk somewhat, he asked his guest what backing he had so far secured.

"I don't have much need of that," said Sigtrygg, "since my kinsmen have undertaken to fully stock the ship, though I would certainly consider your friendship when I return with my cargo, for no one has any more claim on the goods I shall carry than I have, myself." So saying, he brought out a bundle of walrus ivory which he had with him and laid these on the table before Grimkel. The farmer's eyes opened at this sight, for these items were highly regarded by the traders who came out to Greenland from other countries and were known to fetch a very good price.

"I want you to have these, friend Grimkel," said Sigtrygg, "in exchange for your support and agreement not to hinder my search for men in this part of the country."

"What kind of support do you have in mind?" asked the farmer.

"Only that you say a few kind words to the people in this district, who count you their chieftain, concerning my undertaking and agree to let those under your sway, who choose to, join themselves to me, without holding anything against them because of it. And, lastly, I want you to promise safe passage for any of my crew through your territory, should this be needed, since it may happen that one or another of them will find himself in your hands. For my part, I will certainly not let anyone have the choice of any goods I bring back to Greenland before you, yourself, have had the opportunity to look them over and select what you need."

Grimkel thought this a very interesting proposition, for it was well-known that Vinland was a country where many things could be found, which could not be had in Greenland, and it did not seem he was being asked to take much risk for the chance to buy these goods before anyone else could see them. Still, he wanted to know what say the Leifssons had in all this, since he knew they were powerful men and might not find such a turn of events to their liking.

"Not much," Sigtrygg replied, "since we have made a fair exchange — my father's farm for the fully stocked ship and the houses in Vinland."

The chief of the Ketilsfjord men now picked up the walrus tusks and turned them over in his hands. "I don't see why we should not pledge our friendship on these terms, just as you are asking," he said and he had his serving women pour out drinks for them and named witnesses to the terms of their agreement.

"Now I want to offer you my hospitality for as long as you

wish to stay in our district," said Grimkel, after they had drained their cups, "unless you have already made other arrangements with one of my neighbors, in which case I will invite him and all his household, too, to the drinking under my roof."

"There won't be any necessity for that," Sigtrygg replied, "since I will not be spending much more time in these parts than I have already. The sailing season's short enough for what I have in mind. But if you wish to reward those neighbors of yours who took me in over winter, I would not find that amiss."

Grimkel said he would be more than happy to do as Sigtrygg wanted, though he had not been told, till then, that Sigtrygg had wintered in Ketilsfjord, "for had I known of this, I'd have insisted that you had stayed here with me."

"Then we have both spent a somewhat drearier winter than we might have had cause to expect," answered Sigtrygg. "Yet, I was directed elsewhere and, if the truth is to be told, I did not find the company as uncongenial as some others might have."

Grimkel now said he wished to know the name of the farmer who had sheltered Sigtrygg over the winter and Sigtrygg replied that that was easy enough to say for, "he is well-known to you, unless I miss my guess, a man with whom you have recently had dealings — Torfi Gudvesson."

Now Grimkel dropped the bundle of tusks which he had been handling hard on the table before him and asked Sigtrygg what this meant, since it could not have been a mystery that there were difficulties between him and the farmer whom Sigtrygg had just named.

"And yet I had been told," said Sigtrygg, "that you have made a settlement over these matters with this man; and not one which you are likely to have found unsatisfying, since you set the terms yourself."

Grimkel replied that this was quite beside the point and that he did not take it kindly when those with whom he was associated had dealings with people he disapproved of.

"It's all the same to me how you see things," said Sigtrygg, who now reminded him of the oath of friendship they had just sworn and of Grimkel's agreement not to hinder his efforts to raise a crew in his district. "Still, I don't see how my choice of shelter over the winter should have any bearing on what is now between us. And, if you are a man who is true to his word, you will now send for my host and treat him with the same deference you promised before I gave you his name."

"It won't do you any good to insist on that," answered the Ketilsfjord chief, "but I won't allow this to come between us, so long as you now let the matter drop." But his face seemed a good deal paler than it had been before.

Then Sigtrygg replied that he did not much care how Grimkel chose his friends, for his interests were over the western sea and not in Greenland. But, he added, there were some things a man had best let lie, and one such was a settlement which had been duly paid and sworn to.

Thereafter, Sigtrygg took his leave and it must now be told how, for all his words and efforts, he could not find even one other man, in all that district, to join him on his ship. But, afterwards, Grimkel Vesteinsson had a great deal to say about how things had turned out and people thought he took it very badly that Sigtrygg had first extracted the oath of friendship from him, before telling him of his relationship with the farmer, Torfi Gudvesson.

Now there is not much to tell until Sigtrygg returned to Herjolfsness to seek out that same sea trader who had directed him to lodgings earlier. He found him already in his booth and trading briskly with other men who had come out early onto the ness.

When he entered the booth, the old man asked him for his news and Sigtrygg said there was not much to tell, except that he had gained a few crewmen and tried his hand at peacemaking among the Ketilsfjord farmers. He now told everything that had happened over the winter and the old man said this was no less than he had expected, "since it's unlikely such headstrong people would ever allow themselves to be guided by others, and this is especially the case with Grimkel Vesteinsson."

Sigtrygg agreed, saying: "It doesn't seem as though my efforts to raise a crew have borne much fruit either, since the Ketilsfjordmen do not seem a very adventurous lot. And now I want to ask you where else I should be looking, or for whatever other advice you can provide me, since I don't think there's much to be gained if I let another season go by without sailing."

The old man laughed and said he had the best advice of all to give, "since I have, myself, found you five men, while you were mucking about inland among those Ketilsfjord fellows. And while these are not the very best, they are sailors, nonetheless, from the ships' crews which lodged here over winter, and perhaps they are the best you are likely to find in these times. So now you have ten men and not just five, which is half the number you are seeking."

Sigtrygg said he thought this welcome news, but that in his view, Vragi had miscounted, "for I, myself, am one more and that brings us more than halfway home. And now I want to ask if you are willing to share the command of my ship with me, for I have by now heard much of your exploits on the seas."

Vragi said: "It's clear enough you don't see the grey head and old bones which stand here before you, or do you think I gave up the viking life out of love for dickering with these farmers over money? It is not likely I shall ride the seas again, before this body lies moldering beneath Greenland's rocky shores."

"And yet the tale holds you won an earldom out in Ireland and were a most feared viking and a ship's captain."

"These are old tales," said Vragi One-Eye, "now best forgotten — by you as well as others."

"Nevertheless," said Sigtrygg, "I have heard it said you can see a change coming in the weather before the sea birds can and that you feel the sea swells on dry land better than most sailors aboard ship. That, I hear, is why you are so shrewd a trader, since you put your backing only in those vessels which have the best chance of profit. And I would count it lucky, indeed, if I had your backing for my venture."

"If backing's all you need," said the old man, "I'll buy a share in this ship of yours for, against my better judgement, I think I smell a seafaring man in you. At the least, you're more determined than most."

"I don't want money from you, old man," answered Sigtrygg, "but many people would deem my ship well-manned, if you were aboard her."

Vragi now shut his one good eye and said: "I've only half the tools a good sailor needs to mark his course and that which is left is not so good as it once was. Besides, I cannot pull at the oars like you younger men."

"Then I will pull for both of us, if you will guide the ship; for, though I took it badly when you judged me a poor seafaring prospect, I know only too well the truth of your words and misdoubt my own luck to bring the vessel safe to port in untried waters."

"No man ever improved his luck by speaking ill of it before he tried it out," warned Vragi, "and you're not likely to make things any better by doing so now."

"In that case, I will certainly need a man of your background to weight the scales more firmly in my favor; and, besides, how many more voyages can an old fellow like yourself expect? So, if you join us now, we are twelve, and not eleven; and that is a lucky number, and one man less which we must scour the countryside for."

The old man turned his face away and walked out of the booth and now Sigtrygg followed him and found him standing on a rise, a few feet away, looking out toward the dark grey waters. "The western sea is treacherous and few enough men from this country, or any other, have sailed her," Vragi said, "and the route out to Vinland was never a well-traveled one. Besides, it is already nearly too late in the year to undertake this sort of journey, for there are a great many shoals and hidden rocks along some of those shores.

And not every ship which has ever gone out there has found her way home again."

"Then that is even more reason I need a man like yourself who has been to foreign waters and knows somewhat of the sea's ways," said Sigtrygg. "Now tell me if you are willing to take my offer. Or why have you grown so silent? What are you thinking?"

"That now there are twelve of us," answered Vragi, "though I don't think I will be making many more voyages, after this one."

Sigtrygg said he thought this the best of news and now he asked the old man how he thought they should proceed.

"We have a ship to launch," said Vragi, "and that is no small task. In my opinion we must now raise whatever crew we can; but not worry overmuch about their number, so we get enough to pull the oars on both her sides."

Sigtrygg said he would abide by whatever decisions Vragi saw fit to make in these matters, for he welcomed the old viking as his partner in their western venture. But Vragi answered that a partner was often a good thing to have in battle, "though, in matters of business, a man is certainly better off alone."

Then they conferred for awhile as to the courses of action which were open to them and, on the following day, Vragi took Sigtrygg to meet the men he had enlisted for their voyage. These seemed to Sigtrygg to be a sorry lot. Two, who were from Iceland, showed only scant interest in their destination, since they were in outlawry at home and could not hope to go back to their country until their term abroad had expired. Therefore, they were only concerned to secure a berth for themselves on a ship which was not yet returning to Iceland, since the ship they had come on would certainly put into Iceland on its return voyage and, they said, they did not find it congenial to remain longer in Greenland.

The other three were also unimpressive fellows, out of the Faeroe Islands and the Orkneys, who had run afoul of their fellow crewmen and were no longer welcome aboard the ships they had come out to Greenland on.

"These are certainly not the men I would have chosen myself,"

Sigtrygg told Vragi, after he had taken him aside, "for they seem to be little more than troublemakers in their own countries with very little, besides, to commend them."

"Still they are seamen," answered Vragi, "and you have not got an overabundance of these. In my opinion, you ought to be glad for the men you find, at this point, or do you think I have lost my touch at manning ships? You are certainly singing a different song now than you sang yesterday."

Sigtrygg agreed that this was so and asked the old man's pardon for forgetting, even for the moment, the terms of their partnership. He now said he would not raise any further questions regarding the crew, "but at least I want to know from you how soon you think we will be ready to sail?"

"That depends," replied Vragi, "on how soon you think you will be ready to reclaim your ship."

Now as these two stood thus on the beach at Herjolfsness discussing these matters, the wind suddenly changed direction and began to blow up from the south. Then Vragi got very quiet, listening to the sea birds and looking more carefully down the coast. He walked toward a large, flat rock and began to climb onto it. Sigtrygg asked him what he was looking at so intently.

"Maybe nothing," replied the old sea rover, "but, unless I have lost the sight in my remaining eye, I think we shall have visitors before very long."

Sigtrygg said that he could not see very much in the direction in which Vragi was staring, but Vragi said that only showed how different their talents were, since he, himself, doubted he would be much good tracking bear out on the ice. After awhile Sigtrygg said he thought he could see a dark spot moving up along the coast, and asked the sea trader if that was what he saw, too.

"I think we shall need to get a closer look before we know if we have sighted the same thing," said Vragi. But, before he could come down off the rock where he was standing, to get closer to the sea's edge, there was a great commotion on the beach below them, as men came out of their booths and ran down to the shore line. In very short order a sail was clearly distinguishable, poking above the surf, and soon they could see a dark, broad-bellied ship beneath the straining sail, leaning toward them out of the sea.

"It seems," said Vragi, "we have not come out onto the ness a moment too soon to catch the first ship of the season," and he told Sigtrygg to follow him down to the water's edge and this he did.

The ship soon came up into full view and it was not long before the men on board her pulled down their sail and threw the anchor over the side. It was a large, sea-going vessel and she now stood close to the land, just out beyond the breaking surf, and a number of the crew began to row into the shore on the ship's boat. They soon landed and were very quickly the center of everyone's attention, for the Greenlanders were eager, as always, for news from abroad. But Vragi noticed that those still out on the ship made no effort to ready it for beaching and he told Sigtrygg that, in his opinion, the trading did not look entirely promising.

"Most people would be glad enough to hear what is happening in other lands," Sigtrygg replied, "without worrying about the opportunities for profit."

"Still, after a lengthy winter," said Vragi, "many a farmer will have need of the wares such a ship brings. It won't do anyone much good if these sailors content themselves with chatter."

They now made their way into the press of people and it was then that Sigtrygg saw a man among the newcomers, standing near the center of the crowd, who was not entirely unknown to him. This man saw Sigtrygg, too, and these two now exchanged warm greetings, one with the other. The man was very well-dressed, wearing a short coat of eastern brocade and linen breeches. He had a fine long knife, whose handle was a handsomely carved wooden dragon, strapped to his side. He was neither taller nor shorter than the other people in the crowd and he had thick chestnut-colored hair, close cropped about the head and face. He was very straight-limbed, if somewhat small boned, and the features of his face were straight and fine. Beside him stood a grizzled-looking fellow, grey-haired and bearded, with a face not altogether unlike the rough seas on which these two had but lately been sailing.

Sigtrygg said to the man with the chestnut-colored hair: "I did not look to meet you here, kinsman, when last we parted and I went out onto the ice."

"Nor I to find you among the trading men on Herjolfsness," the man replied.

Sigtrygg now told Vragi that this man was Girstein Eiriksson, whose father was the youngest of the three Leifssons and who had been, of all his kinsmen, the closest to him when he was a boy at Brattahlid. Vragi agreed that he had heard a great deal about this Girstein, who was accounted, of all the Leifssons' kin, to be the most promising, and he now asked Girstein how he came to be on this ship and where it had sailed from.

"It's easy enough to tell how he came to the ship," said Sigtrygg, "since he took passage abroad, some years earlier, on that ship which was to take me out of Greenland. But I had other business in mind then, while this cousin of mine was glad enough to take my berth."

Girstein, who was only a little older than Sigtrygg, said that this was so and that he had been readier to travel to foreign parts than Sigtrygg was at the time, and now he asked them for their news.

"There's certainly a great deal to tell, kinsman," agreed Sigtrygg, "but first we would learn something of this ship of yours."

Girstein replied that their ship was a Norwegian vessel, out of Trondheim, and that the man beside him was its skipper, Osvif Thorleiksson by name. This man, said Girstein, was a retainer of King Harald Sigurdsson who was newly come to kingship in Norway. "King Harald is somewhat of a harsh fellow, but a bold and fierce warrior, who has traveled widely and fought in many lands," said Girstein. "And most people think him a clever man."

"Cleverness in kings is not always to be sought for," Vragi said, "but do you count yourself one of this king's men?"

Girstein said he had not been so fortunate, but that he would certainly try his luck with the king, if they were to meet again.

"But for now I mean to see Eiriksfjord and my kinsmen and the lands up at Brattahlid."

"Then you must stay with us for a little, first," urged Sigtrygg, "for this man, Vragi, is my partner and he would take it amiss if I failed to extend the proper courtesies to such important visitors to our country as you men are."

Now, on hearing this, the Norwegian king's retainer said he thought this nobly done but that he did not have any desire to berth his ship until he came to Brattahlid "for we have other matters to attend to and Girstein has promised us lodging and good trading in Eiriksfjord."

Sigtrygg replied: "You'll certainly find plenty of that among my kinsmen, but we think you should put ashore here and sample our hospitality first, for we are no less able to pay you for your wares than they are up at Eiriksfjord. And you are not wanting for cargo, as we can see from the size of your ship and how low she is riding in the water."

Osvif now asked Girstein what manner of man this kinsman of his was and Girstein answered he was the best sort, for he was descended from no less a personage than Leif Eiriksson and from that Hebridean woman, Thorgunna, whom many held to have been a daughter of King Valdemar of Russia. And now he explained how Sigtrygg's father had come out to Greenland to claim his rights, years after Leif Eiriksson had visited the Hebrides.

"In that case, these are fortuitous circumstances, indeed," said Osvif, "for this kinsman of yours is related by marriage to our King Harald, since Harald has Queen Elisif to wife, who is, herself, the granddaughter of that same Russian king."

"Then," said Sigtrygg, "it would certainly be an ill thing if you were to have come this far, yet spurn the hospitality offered by a member of your king's own family. I cannot think King Harald would take such news without any reaction at all."

Osvif now agreed that this was probably the case and so he gave orders for his men to go back to the ship and bring some of their goods ashore. This was soon accomplished and then the trading went briskly enough, though the men at Herjolfsness had much less to offer than could be got at Eiriksfjord. Still, Girstein thought it great sport that Sigtrygg had persuaded the Norwegian to unload some of his wares, much against his will, and Girstein and Sigtrygg now went apart from the others, for Girstein was anxious to learn what had passed in Greenland during the years he had been away.

Sigtrygg now told him how he had made his way up onto the ice, after they had last parted company, and traveled into the waste lands, north of the most far-flung farms in Greenland, where he had become somewhat of a hunter, as his father had been before him. And then he told of the arrangement his uncles had made with him, to give him the land in Vinland for his father's Greenland farm, and how he had come to Herjolfsness and gained the backing of the trader, Vragi Skeggjasson, in order to raise his crew. But he said nothing to Girstein about Thjodhild, or how it had been her words which had spurred him to claim his due.

Girstein now looked very thoughtful and Sigtrygg asked him what was on his mind.

"Not much," said Girstein, "except that I think it will be a very good joke on our Norwegian friend, when he learns that our grandfather's houses are in your hands."

"How so?" asked Sigtrygg.

"Because his business with my father and his brothers is as much for this as for the Greenland trade which he can get at Eiriksfjord. In truth, he had it in mind to buy this holding of our kinsmen or, failing that, at least to secure their use for a short while, that he might bring back to King Harald the riches which abound in that land."

Sigtrygg said: "I don't think there will be much luck for him in this now, unless he deals with me."

"Then you will sell him your holdings, kinsman, if he asks this of you?"

"Certainly not," replied Sigtrygg, "though I am not above giving him trading rights."

"I would do no less, myself," Girstein agreed. "And now I want to invite you and your companions to come on board ship with us, for we will soon put out for Eiriksfjord where, if I take your words aright, you have your ship berthed and from where you plan to set sail for the west."

Sigtrygg said he would need to talk this over with Vragi, since he counted him a partner in the Vinland venture, and Girstein agreed that this was only right. "But I don't think you should take overlong in making this decision, for my Norwegian shipmates are eager to see Brattahlid."

"A quick arrival won't do them much good, if their purpose is as you have described it," said Sigtrygg.

Girstein said that this was probably true but that any man with a ship could sail out to the west, "for Vinland is said to be a very large country, if it is also hard to come to. Still, in my opinion, it would be best if you kept your own counsel with these Norwegians and told them as little as possible, until we are come in to Eiriksfjord."

Sigtrygg agreed that this was good advice and now he went aside to speak with Vragi. He told the sea trader all that Girstein had said and asked him if he thought they would gain more by joining forces with these newcomers, who clearly had the ship and crew for the kind of voyage they were planning, or if they should stick by their original intention and gather their own crew, "for now it seems to me that providence has sent us the men we need to reach the Vinland sea."

Vragi replied: "I know something of this Norwegian king and I do not think he is a partner worth having; he is a hard and ruthless fellow and not entirely to be trusted. As for this Osvif, can a king's man be so very different from his king?"

"Still," said Sigtrygg, "it won't do to let them go up to Eiriksfjord alone, since my kinsmen may misgive the oaths they have sworn to me, when they hear this Norwegian sea captain's errand."

"That is certainly true," said Vragi, "and the advice of your kinsman, Girstein, is no less sound. Therefore, I propose that you accept his offer and go back with them to Brattahlid and speak up for your claim in the presence of your kinsmen, when the matter is raised, for they would not dare deny their oaths in that case. And then you must make the best terms you can with these foreigners. As for me, I will come up with what crewmen I can find, as we have heretofore agreed, before midsummer, and then we shall see if we can raise Vinland before the ice shuts us in for another year."

Sigtrygg said that, as always, Vragi could be relied upon to give the best advice. And that was how they left it.

CHAPTER V

A GUEST-ALE AT BRATTAHLID

Now it must be told that Sigtrygg took ship with the Norwegians and they soon sailed up the coast to Eiriksfjord. But, when they were come into the mouth of the inlet, Osvif, the ship's skipper, came up to Sigtrygg, where he stood on the ship's prow, and asked him how he liked the journey thus far and if he now desired to relay any sort of message to his kinsman, King Harald, when the time came for them to return to Norway, "or would you rather carry your own words to the king?"

"I have no intention of doing either," answered Sigtrygg, "since there is more than enough to keep a man busy in this part of the world. As for messages, I don't see much reason to worry about that now."

"Still," said the Norwegian, "it can do you no harm to seek the king out yourself, for Harald has a long reach and most people find it better to make him their friend than otherwise."

"I will take my chances on that score," said Sigtrygg. And now there did not seem much left to be said between them so that the skipper returned to the business of guiding his ship up the fjord while Sigtrygg remained upon the prow to watch the farm houses and the cattle, which were grazing all along the water's edge, glide by. Their coming now occasioned great excitement, as the arrival of a foreign ship always did among the Greenland folk, and many people who were out in the fields came down to the sea to mark their arrival or to launch their own small boats and follow the ship on its course to Brattahlid, which lay well up the fjord.

Girstein had been watching Sigtrygg on the prow and now he came up to join him. He said: "In all my travels in other countries, kinsman, I had forgotten how fair the home fields of Greenland are, when first you sight them from the ice-covered seas. And now I know why our ancestor, Eirik the Red, brought people out to settle here for there are no finer grasslands in all the northern nations."

"Yet," replied Sigtrygg, "there are certainly better lands, if a man can reach them."

Girstein turned from the green shoreline and looked carefully at his kinsman's dark features, as though seeing these for the first time. It seemed to him that, while they both watched the same place along the fjord's coastline, they were looking at altogether different countries.

"That may well be," he agreed.

After a time, the ship came up under the halls and out buildings of Brattahlid, which stood well up the slope from the rock strewn beach, and cast anchor there. The people who lived there saw the ship's arrival and hastened down to the shore to await the crew's landing. Foremost among these was Thorkel Leifsson and his two sons, Thord and Thorstein, and after them came the women and servants of the household and the younger children. Nor were Thorkel's brothers far behind, for each of them had a portion of the holdings at Brattahlid and the surrounding farms, though the main part was in Thorkel's keeping.

But when they saw the first of the ship's crew row ashore and realized that Girstein Eiriksson was among these, there was a great deal more excitement than before, for Girstein had been considered a highly accomplished man, even before he had gone out to Iceland, and his kinsmen certainly thought no less of him on his return than when he had departed the country.

Thorkel Leifsson was the first of the brothers to see Girstein, amidst the Norwegians, and he pushed all the others aside saying: "Welcome, kinsman, since you bring such a rich trading ship in your wake, as was only to be looked for from you."

Girstein replied: "The ship's not mine, kinsman, though I'd hoped to do somewhat better during my time in foreign lands. Still, this vessel's skipper is a retainer of the king of Norway and that, in most people's opinion, is no small thing. And now I want you to offer these men every consideration, for they have passed up trading elsewhere in the country to give the folk of Eiriksfjord first claim on their goods."

Thorkel thought this well-done and promised to do just as Girstein had asked. When Gunnar and Eirik joined them, Thorkel told his brothers they must each take a third of the crew and house them in their homes over winter. "As for me," said Thorkel, "I will offer hospitality to the ship's captain and any of the crew he wishes to have accompany him."

The Norwegian skipper now thanked the brothers for their hospitality and the talk quickly turned to the disposition of the ship's goods. Thorkel offered Osvif the storerooms at Brattahlid for any of the goods he was in no hurry to sell, but everything else he said they should arrange to offer to the farmers of Eiriksfjord as soon as possible. Osvif said he would do just as the Leifssons advised him and he now had his cargo brought ashore. This consisted mostly of grain and ale and such metal weapons and tools as could not readily be obtained in Greenland, along with fine cloths and other decorative items. From these last, he took several bronze brooches and made gifts of them to the Leifssons and he gave sections of his best cloths to the women of their three households.

Now among these women stood Thjodhild who, when she had received her share of the cloth, remarked that she thought it strange the Leifssons should see fit to greet one kinsman, who had come to them in this ship's crew, but to ignore another, though he was certainly no less worthy or accomplished.

"Whom do you have in mind, daughter?" asked Gunnar.

"That's easy enough to say," replied Thjodhild, "for, unless my eyes have been blinded by the glare from the ice, that is Sigtrygg Thorgilsson still aboard this Norwegian's ship, and he is helping the other crewmen to unload the ship's wares and make her fast in the fjord."

Girstein now said that her eyes had always been sharper than other people's and that it was, indeed, Sigtrygg whom she could see on board the ship; and he described how they had come upon Sigtrygg at Herjolfsness and invited him to sail up with them to Eiriksfjord. "And now, it seems to me, he is proving a steadier crewman than most, and a man who knows his way about a ship as well as any."

"We'll see what kind of a sailor he makes, soon enough," said Thorkel, "if he's ready to take the gift we Leifssons have given him. But, if not, we are out very little, while we have gained old Thorgils' farm."

Now, when Girstein heard this, he took his uncle aside and asked if it were true, as he had heard "that you have sold our family's rights in Vinland for one poor farm?"

"There's no use denying it," answered Thorkel, "but I don't think our kinsman will find it very much easier to come to his holdings this summer than he did the summer before, since there are not many people in Greenland who are eager to risk their lives in such a venture."

"Yet, there may be enough," said Girstein, "since not every man is as unwilling to sail new seas as you Greenlanders are. As for me, I think we kinsmen will certainly have cause to regret this business, for much has been given up here, in exchange for very little."

But Thorkel said: "He has still to come to that country in the small ship we have given him. And this will be no easy thing, or do you think he will raid this Norwegian for men, though these are surely bone-tired after a hard sail across the sea from Norway?"

Girstein said he thought Sigtrygg would do whatever he had to, to claim what he considered his, and that this was only to be expected. "But no one would have expected the sons of Leif Eiriksson to part with that holding their father had insisted on retaining all his life."

Thorkel said there was no use complaining about it now and what's done is done, "but I advise you, kinsman, to enjoy the hospitality we offer to you and your friends in the meantime, since the end proves all, as the saw has it."

The Leifssons now declared that they would lay a feast in one week's time for all the leading men in the district, to honor the Norwegians and the return, with them, of Girstein Eiriksson. Thorkel, himself, directed his servants to take word of this to all the farms in Eiriksfjord, as well as to those in nearby Isafjord and Einarsfjord, for these waterways, between them, held all the largest and most prosperous farms in Greenland in those days.

Now as soon as the ship's crew had all come on shore, the Leifssons took a hand in dividing them into three parties, according to the number who should receive hospitality in each household, and Thorkel gave instructions as to the disposition of Osvif's cargo. But, when they had counted out the guests, it was soon clear that the Leifssons had made no provision for Sigtrygg, who stood apart from all the others by the water's edge. Seeing this, Thjodhild went down to the lapping surf and gave Sigtrygg a good greeting.

"It seems you have not fared as poorly as some would have hoped, cousin," she said, "since there are many good sailors in this crew who in my opinion would gladly test their mettle on the sea, if the journey's prospects were to their liking. But that may not be entirely to the liking of some others here at Brattahlid."

Sigtrygg replied that it was all the same to him what his kinsmen at Brattahlid thought, adding that he was more concerned with the condition of his ship. And he now asked Thjodhild where it was to be found.

"There's no need to rush that," Thjodhild said, "for I would like to know, before anything else, whether you are willing to reconsider this venture of yours to distant lands, since it is not unlikely my father and his brothers will alter their agreement with you, if you urge it; and then it may seem somewhat easier for you to settle here in Greenland than it seemed to you before."

"There's no use hoping for that," answered Sigtrygg, "for my mind is made up. Besides, I don't see how a farmer's life here in Eiriksfjord is likely to be any more promising than seeking Leif Eiriksson's lands across the sea. But, as for a crew, these Norwegians are not the men I have in mind, though they are certainly as capable as any."

"Then how do you mean to reach Vinland, if not with these men?" asked Thjodhild.

Sigtrygg replied that he preferred to speak first with his uncles about his plans, before discussing them with others, though he agreed that Thjodhild had as strong a claim on him as anyone in Brattahlid; and now he gathered up his things, adding that he hoped he would still find something of a welcome in his kinsmen's holdings, although they were so preoccupied with their foreign guests.

Thjodhild said: "I don't think you will find a worse welcome here now, than before."

"In that case," said he, "a speedy sailing makes good guesting."

When the time came for the feast, which Thorkel Leifsson had proclaimed in honor of Girstein and his Norwegian shipmates, people came from the entire district and from further still to see the foreigners, since word of their arrival had spread throughout Greenland and most people thought it an event worth noting. For three days new boats rowed in, some from Hrafnsfjord and Siglufjord, smaller and more distant districts than those three fjords which were most directly under the Leifssons' sway as were named before. But Thorkel was unwilling to turn anyone away for, he said, there was no use skimping when such important people were involved and he offered hospitality to anyone who sought it.

This made Brattahlid rather more crowded than folk there were accustomed to, but Thorkel told Osvif this would be better for the trading he desired; and now these two agreed that Osvif would contribute to the upkeep of the guests, too, since he was likely to derive the most profit from such a large influx of people.

Accordingly, the Leifssons set out the benches down the length of the main hall and spread their tables with all manner of game and fish and beef which was then to be had in that country. But Osvif made over to them as much ale as they thought necessary for so large an assemblage since ale was not easily come by in Greenland where no grain could be grown.

Then the farmers and the Norwegian sailors sat for three nights exchanging news and other pleasantries over the free-flowing ale and meats, which the Leifssons provided, and everyone thought this the best guesting which had been seen in Greenland in many years. The Leifssons got much praise for their efforts and most people thought Thorkel especially had greatly enhanced his honor by this show.

Now, after the third night of feasting and carousing, when most people were ready to take their leave, it was told to Thorkel that two more boats had rowed in over night and that in the larger of these were twelve men, from the district around Herjolfsness, and that their leader was a round faced fellow of no small girth who was exceedingly well-dressed. This fellow, it was said, bore himself very straight, for all his size, and made much of his pre-rogatives over other men, even as he was seeing to the beaching of his vessel, for he did not assist his followers in any way as they were about this work. Around his neck he wore a wide silver ring and his garments were fur trimmed. In his right hand he held a dark wooden staff topped with carved walrus ivory.

"That would be Grimkel Vesteinsson," said Thorkel, when he had heard all this, "who, among all the farmers who make their homes in Ketilsfjord, is accounted the chief. Nor is he any less a friend to our kin for that, though he is somewhat of a popinjay, as some would have it. He is certainly a welcome visitor to this house. Let him come in."

"And yet, there is another boat, smaller than the first, which also came ashore only this morning," said that same servant who brought the news of Grimkel's arrival. "This one carries eight men and their leader is not known to any of us, for he is somewhat advanced in age and stooped over and has but one eye."

Thorkel now asked if anyone in the hall knew who this might be. Girstein was then standing by his uncle's bench and he looked down the length of the hall till his eyes found Sigtrygg, who sat over against a corner, showing little enough interest in the proceedings. "That would be Vragi Skeggjason," Girstein said at last, "who is a trader out on Herjolfsness and a friend to our kinsman, Sigtrygg Thorgilsson."

"Is this true?" Thorkel now asked Sigtrygg.

"There's no reason to deny it," Sigtrygg answered him, looking up from his bench.

"In that case," said Eirik Leifsson to his brother Thorkel, "let him come in, as well. Though the feasting's mostly done, there's no reason to be niggardly with what's left. It will be a long time in Greenland before people see another feast like the one we have thrown here, brother."

Girstein said that his father had spoken well and now he himself told the servant to invite both boatloads of men up to the house. But Thorkel added that he thought it rather strange that these men had come up from as far away as Herjolfsness, "since the eating and drinking's no less good in that part of the country than here, or so I've been told."

Nevertheless, the new men were soon brought into the hall and people made room for them on the benches. Girstein now directed the servants and women of the house to bring out whatever food was left, of that which had not yet been served, and ale cups were quickly passed to the newcomers. Vragi One-Eye gave Sigtrygg only the slightest nod of his head upon entering, and did not dally at the board, for he and his following were famished with hard rowing and they soon fell on the food before them.

But Grimkel made a great show of his entrance and strode up to Thorkel Leifsson and his brothers and gave them an elaborate greeting, nor would he take a seat till those nearest the Leifssons moved down somewhat along the benches.

Thorkel now asked Grimkel and his Ketilsfjordmen what brought them up to Eiriksfjord, since the trading season must now be in full swing on Herjolfsness, where they held sway.

"Only this," answered Grimkel, "that by the good offices of your kinsman Girstein Eiriksson, the best trading this year has surely come to Eiriksfjord and we thought to partake, somewhat, of this Norwegian's wares. And yet I understand he gave the men on Herjolfsness a tasting of his goods when he held over briefly in our part of the country, though he did not seek hospitality from me."

Thorkel asked if this were true, adding: "I thought first trading was only to be done here at Brattahlid?"

"We were persuaded by your kinsman Sigtrygg," replied the Norwegian skipper, "to share our goods with the merchants on the ness, though we did not stay with them long enough to garner much profit."

Thorkel asked Girstein if this were so and he answered that it was.

"But that is the very cause of my own concern," Grimkel now added, "since everyone knows I am the chief of all the farmers in that district and all such trading is to be conducted according to the terms I set. Yet now you kinsmen have usurped my place and stolen the best trading in the country to boot. And this before I'd even come out to the ness to set up my booth. Still, everyone knows that the Leifssons are the most pre-eminent family in Greenland and I, for one, am not minded to dispute their rank with them. Only give me the chance to do my trading up here, with every other common farmer, and I will not hold this matter against anyone, let alone your nephew, Sigtrygg Thorgilsson, with whom I have made separate arrangements concerning trading rights, in any case."

"I know nothing of these matters which you are speaking about," Thorkel answered, "nor of the doings of our kinsman, nor of any arrangements he has taken it upon himself to make with others. Nor will I be bound by these."

Grimkel now looked to Sigtrygg but, seeing no support from that quarter, he seemed to become quite uncomfortable. "Yet, we have exchanged oaths before proper witnesses, concerning the Vinland trade, and it would not be well-done to cast these aside," he urged.

"Even so," replied Thorkel, "no one has consulted with me on the matter."

Now Grimkel seemed much put out and again he looked to where Sigtrygg sat, as though for some word of agreement, but Sigtrygg did not speak up. With great annoyance, Grimkel now lifted the staff he had been carrying about with him, with such show, and brought it down hard on the table, cracking its finely carved head of walrus ivory. "Now are fair words dashed, no less than this carved stick," he said in anger, "for I thought to be dealing with honorable men; or did I grant you, Sigtrygg Thorgilsson, free passage and my support in Ketilsfjord for empty promises?"

"Not empty to be sure," said Sigtrygg softly, at last, "for we have yet to complete the terms of that agreement which I have made with my uncles, though we are soon enough about this, now that my support has arrived. But as to my promises, be assured, chieftain, they are as good as your own."

"What promises, friend Grimkel, have been made you?" Thorkel asked, for he was now anxious to know the reason for the Ketilsfjord chief's words.

"Only this," replied the big man, "that first trading rights out of Vinland are to be mine, once your kinsman has come into his own in that country. And this was to be without need of consent from you Leifssons since you have given up all claim on the lands to the west, as your kinsman tells it. In exchange, I gave him board and my support in his efforts to raise a crew from among the people who owe me their allegiance. And now I want to know if the terms of this bargain are to be kept?"

Osvif, the Norwegian, leaned over and asked whether it was true that the Leifssons had indeed withdrawn their claims on their father's landfall in the unknown countries beyond the Greenland sea, "since many a brave man has contemplated raising those shores for the wealth to be gained there, nor would I fail to count myself among these."

"What is true," answered Thorkel, "is that we have exchanged a small land holding in this country for a distant holding over the sea, but our kinsman must go out there to claim it, which he has so far failed to do; nor is that land so small that only one man may build his home there."

Sigtrygg now rose from his seat and glowered at his uncle with such a gaze that Thorkel Leifsson must shrink back in his seat, his eyes upon the roughhewn boards of the table top. "These are not the terms we swore, kinsman, when I gave over my father's farm to you for all time," Sigtrygg said evenly, "for then you held that all rights to the lands around your father's houses, in the country he named Vinland, had been granted to me and no other, and that you would henceforth forsake all claims concerning these lands. Therefore trading rights and all land takings in that place are mine to dispense; in exchange you have enriched your holdings here in Greenland. Thus, it is in my power to treat with the men of Ketilsfjord or whomsoever else I see fit to make terms with."

Gunnar now came to the aid of his brother, saying: "Yet, you must first come to those houses you are claiming, kinsman, and this you have so far been unable to do. Nor do I think you will find this any easier to do now than before, unless you make terms with men who are in a position to sail out to those lands." And now he he cast a look at the Norwegians, and added "but such men owe more to us than they do to you."

"Nor is it altogether clear," said Thorkel, "that a pledge of houses is a pledge of country and this may well require a judgement of those best versed in the law. But if you are willing, kinsman, we will gladly amend the terms of our bargain now, that these things will be settled to everyone's satisfaction."

Now all this while Vragi Skeggjasson had kept his silence at the table. But when he saw how things went, he put down the joint of meat he had been troubling over and said: "There's no need for that now, since oaths have already been sworn and witnessed to. And as for your kinsman's ability to lay claim to his holdings, you see before you the men of his crew who now want but the ship, which you have already pledged, to take them over the sea."

Gunnar said: "Who are you that you have inserted yourself into this matter which ought to be between kinsmen only and not strangers?"

"No one but a simple trader, lately come out to Greenland, who makes his living by dickering with the farmers and sailors who exchange their goods when the seas are calm enough to let the one pass over, to the betterment of the other. But if my name is not already known to you, I am called Vragi One-Eye, though some have named me other things."

Thorkel said: "Still, my brother speaks truly for this is no concern of yours since it is a dispute between kinsmen and a matter entirely within our power to resolve."

"Yet every man has an interest in matters pertaining to his partner's well-being and the legitimacy of his claim," answered Vragi gently. "And your kinsman has pledged me half interest in his ship. Therefore my claim in this affair is no less strong than your own."

Now when he heard this, Thorkel leaned over to Girstein and the Norwegian, both, and asked them what they knew of this Vragi who, while unimpressive in appearance, spoke, said Thorkel, with a certainty which belied that. Girstein said he knew no more about the fellow than what had already been said.

Grimkel now leaned over to where Thorkel conferred with his kinsman and volunteered as to how this fellow, while obviously unknown in their part of the country, was at least well-known to the men of Ketilsfjord. Though not residing long in their district, said Grimkel, word had it he was a very successful trader with a keen eye for a good ship and an understanding of the sea. But, the Ketilsfjord chief added, he was not above meddling in other people's business and had made some enemies, thereby.

"If he has not been long in Greenland," asked Thorkel, "then from where has he come and to what purpose?"

"Rumor has it," whispered Grimkel, "that he was something of a fighting man in his youth and, for that, has never been able to take up the farming life; and so he lives a solitary existence, eking out a livelihood from trade alone."

"And keeps no animals?" asked Gunnar.

"No."

"Nor hunts his food, as our kinsman does?" said Thorkel.

"He is certainly too old for that," answered Grimkel.

Now Osvif the Norwegian said: "It is a rare man who can live such a life out here in this country, for your winters are harsher than in most other lands. I doubt there are many others who could subsist as you say this fellow does on trade alone. Yet, he is not as unknown to me as to you Greenlanders."

Thorkel said if he knew who the fellow was he should now speak up, "for he has interposed himself in matters which are of great concern to us, and we must know how to deal with him."

Osvif turned to the old man and caught the gleam of his one good eye. "Forgive my inquisitive nature, friend," he said, "but, are you that Vragi Skeggjasson who fought under the banner of King Sigtrygg Silky Beard of Dublin, when he made his stand at Clontarf; and later with Earl Rognvald Brusason who challenged his uncle, Thorfinn Sigurdsson, Earl of Orkney and Caithness, in the sea fight which those two fought off Roberry?"

"These are certainly places I have been," the old man said and cast Osvif a friendly grin. Then he spoke these verses:

> Ill-starred the struggle
> where kinsmen contend,
> companions and brothers
> in the midst of the spear-storm.
>
> Hard lessons learned there
> harder the lives lost,

when gold-byrnied Brusason
met Thorfinn, his uncle
that shaggy-browed scatterer
of warrior's treasure.

Two wolves lapping war's rain,
where wolf-riding women
called ravens to shield rims,
there blood ties were broken.

Everyone thought the verses well-formed and now it seemed to them that this trader was no common sort but a man of some accomplishment since he had something of the poet's skill with words. Osvif the Norwegian said: "Then you were with Rognvald when he tried to burn Thorfinn in his hall? And fled, no doubt, when Thorfinn paid his nephew back the compliment and basted him to a well-cooked turn in his own bed?"

"All of these things are true enough," answered Vragi. "And now I am come to Greenland to live out my days far from the old feuds in more peaceful fashion."

"Then no wonder you are here," said the Norwegian, "since Earl Thorfinn has a long memory and little pleasure in granting peace to those he counts as enemies. But I do not see how you will get peace here if you involve yourself in others' affairs now. If living below the horizon is your purpose, far from the eyes of those harsh sea birds which trouble the waters in the home countries, you gain little by raising your mast out here, for word of your presence must surely find its way back to your enemies in Orkney."

Vragi laughed and said he didn't think Earl Thorfinn had much reason to pursue an old man to such distant parts as Greenland, "even if he knew I were here for I've heard he has problems much closer to home since there's little enough love to be spared between the earl and your king."

"That is true enough," Osvif agreed. "But now I want to know what part you mean to play in this Vinland affair, since these kinsmen have certainly taken it on themselves to complicate matters for those others of us who have an interest in that country."

"I mean to keep my word to that man who made me a partner in his venture," replied Vragi, "for I can do no less than that. Nor do I think him any less a man than his namesake was, under whose banner so many bold men fought and died out in Ireland these many years past. And while some people say that Sigtrygg Silky Beard fled before his enemies, when King Brian of the Irish led them out against him, I think they would be hard-pressed to find the cause to make this other Sigtrygg take flight."

"Yet," said Osvif, "there is that in our two histories which argues that we join our forces here and try to bring a settlement about between these people, for in that fashion we may both gain some good of them."

"I think a settlement has already been made," said Vragi, "or what is that oath which exchanged one man's holdings for another's and left both sides so well content, but a short time ago?"

"There's no use talking any further about a settlement," Thorkel now broke in, for he had grown tired of the bantering between these two foreigners, "unless you have the means to come by this land claim; and by the looks of you, and the men you have with you, there are not nearly enough to sail even the small ship we have purchased for this venture, and that will be the end of the matter. Nor are we of a mind to turn over this ship, which we found hard enough to come by, for so foolish a venture, unless she be manned by the full complement of men required to sail her."

"This is ill-spoke," said Sigtrygg who had been listening in silence all this while, "since an oath is an oath, as all men know, nor was the giving of this ship contingent on how many men should man it."

"Even so," replied Thorkel, "there's no sense throwing good after bad, and if you cannot safely sail this ship of ours, we should lose both ship and kinsman in this foolish venture. No, I have decided this arrangement of ours is flawed and must be put to rest and a new bargain struck in its place."

Now Sigtrygg said it was clear to him how things stood, since he lacked the backing to enforce the terms of that oath they had all sworn. But Vragi told him to hold his peace and let the matter rest for the while.

"There's no use hoping for that," replied Sigtrygg in hot anger, "since these kinsmen of mine have certainly forgotten the meaning of the words they spoke when it seemed so important to them to get my father's farm of me, back when the value of its rental outweighed all else in their minds."

Thorkel said: "If you would have the rental kinsman, then that is certainly a way this matter may be righted."

"I will have nothing but what already is my due," said Sigtrygg, "but if you brothers cannot abide this, then we shall see who among us is the stronger." And, when he had spoken these last words, the son of Thorgils Leifsson stood up in his place and left the hall, nor did he look back or speak any further to those who stayed behind and not even to those men who were pledged to his own enterprise.

Now after he had gone out in this manner Vragi turned to the Leifssons and asked them how many men they required "to sail this ship of yours," for he thought to make an end of the matter with fair words.

"She is twenty-oared," replied Gunnar Leifsson, "and so should carry no fewer than that number."

"What if eighteen?" asked Vragi.

"The very least," Gunnar said. "But you are only eight men, by the looks of you, well short of the needed number."

"We are nine with your kinsman," said Vragi, "and five more on the way."

"Then that is fourteen," answered Thorkel, "and still well short of the needed number so have done with this quibbling, for we have all grown tired of it."

But Vragi said since they were in need of only four more men that it was not unlikely they might find those they needed at Brattahlid. And now he asked Osvif if he had any likely fellows he would be willing to spare for this venture so that the kinsmen could keep to the terms of that bargain which they had honorably struck.

Grimkel, the Ketilsfjord chieftain, now added that he thought this a fair way to settle all differences for, of a truth, he was already reckoning up the gain he would come by should Sigtrygg be in a position to keep his word on the matter of first trading rights.

But the Norwegian skipper said to Vragi that he did not see how he could offer much help in the matter, since he needed all his crew to man his own ship. And besides, he added, "no man of them is fit now for this kind of voyage since they'll need to winter over in Greenland to gain their strength back." When he said this last, he cast his eyes over at Thorkel Leifsson.

Vragi marked the looks between them then and saw how it was, that guest would not gainsay host. So now he arose from his place, as Sigtrygg had done before him, and got his men up behind him.

"There's no use trying to make an end to hard feelings when even the peacemakers carry spears in their hands," he said, turning a sharp look on the Norwegian. "In my opinion, the best hope for settling things now lies in a night's sleep, after which some people may see things differently than they do at this moment. Therefore," he continued, turning to Thorkel Leifsson, "I now ask that you direct us to those sleeping places we can expect from you for the night, since we have had hard rowing to come up to this part of the country."

"There's not much room for that," replied Thorkel quickly, "for all the guests we have been entertaining these past three days."

But when he said this he thought he saw a hard look pass over the old viking's face and those others who were present said they thought it unseemly to begrudge accommodations to men who had been guests at their table however unwelcome they may now have become. So Thorkel said he thought he could offer them quarters "for a night or two, at the least, after which you and your men are to be on your way."

Vragi said that that would be sufficient for them. So now Thorkel called a servant to him, who had been standing at the farthest end of the hall, and told the fellow to take Vragi and his companions down to the cowshed, nearest the fjord, and prepare sleeping quarters for them there, "though," he added, "it is not my desire that these men be allowed to inconvenience the cows in any way."

CHAPTER VI

BENEATH THE ICE

Now, when Sigtrygg had fled out of the big hall at Brattahlid in hot anger, he took himself into the field above the farm's houses and strode briskly up the land's slope till he could see all the farm buildings and fenced-in pastures below him, and the fjord beyond these, in one sweep. Then he thought the people and buildings of Brattahlid seemed small and without great import, against the great sheathe of white ice which towered above all that country from the interior; and the long neck of Eirikssfjord was no more than a dark blue trickle of the great ocean which lay out past Greenland. At such times, when such anger came upon him, these were the thoughts which alone brought him comfort and now he turned them around in his heart, finding in them the same solace which the wastelands and the ice brought him, when he was wont to hunt in those places alone.

Yet, as he paced thus on the ridge overlooking the fjord, he heard footsteps on the loose rock below and, seeking their source, he saw that Thjodhild was pressing close behind him. Holding her long skirt out above the sliding earth, she arduously made her way up the sloping face of the land till, stumbling, she caught the ground with both her hands and would have slipped still further had not he lurched downward toward her and seized her by her shoulders, fetching her up to him so that these two now stood face to face in the fading light of the evening sun.

"My thanks, kinsman," said she, brushing off hands and skirt and tugging at her sleeves. "I'd have fallen, of a certainty, into the privy below, had you not reached your hands out thus."

For a moment the anger left him and Sigtrygg laughed at the thought of the steep descent and untimely landing place she described and then, of a sudden, he grew serious again, saying "why follow me now, since matters have gone just as you have urged from the start; and you should be well-satisfied with the doings of your father and his brothers?"

"Yet," said she, "things are not altogether bleak, for you can now lay claim again to your father's holdings; and I think our uncle will not be altogether indisposed to grant you this."

"My claim is for a ship, which I left in his hands, at your urging, and now it is her return alone that I seek."

"Then have you not heard the words spoke in the hall, that she is undermanned and cannot sail as you would have it?"

"She shall sail, if I sail her," said Sigtrygg, "only I get back what is mine."

Thjodhild stood silent awhile, for it seemed to her he was a more stubborn man than most. "Will you take her out against all good advice to perish on the open sea, though there are better prospects for you here? If such sailing were the easy thing you purpose, then would not many others have done it before you? But even this Norwegian seafarer shies from such an enterprise, until his men are well-rested, and his is a bigger and a better ship than yours."

"Even so," said Sigtrygg, "I will have my due and that more speedily than some would expect."

"You won't get very far contending with our kinsmen at Brattahlid, for these are no dumb beasts to be sought for and slain on the ice, but men; and more numerous than those that old man has brought up to you from Herjolfsness."

"Yet it were your words sent me there," he said "and there I found the men I need. Or do you think I adventured all this past winter, among the poor farmers at Ketilsfjord, for no purpose?"

"For good purpose, but bad end," Thjodhild replied. "And

now I want to urge you to give way in this and accept our kinsmen's offer, for there is good farming in this country and a man may make much of the land he gets here."

Sigtrygg now saw there was something in Thjodhild's eyes which urged him more strongly than her words, for she looked hard on him and her hands sought his.

"Would you have me forsake the land which Leif Eiriksson found and which has come to me now as my inheritance, though I am surely no less a man than he was and better suited than all his kin to do what he did?"

Thjodhild said Leif Eiriksson was her grandfather, too, and that there were many in Eiriksfjord could claim a share in his blood "and many a good man in this place, besides. Or do you think you are the only one to do big things?"

Now Sigtrygg broke free of her grasp and turned to look at the great ice which overtopped the whole fjord and, indeed, all that country. "No man of them knows the wastes as I do or has traveled as fearlessly in those places. And if I am not the sailor some are, there are others in my company can serve that purpose."

"Old men make poor traveling companions," said she.

"Yet they may offer in wisdom what they lack in vitality. Besides, there are younger in my company, and these not without some sailing skills. The ship can be sailed without full complement and still be brought safe to port. Oaths have been sworn and I'll not waver from my purpose though kinsmen and oathtakers fail me."

"I see you are yet the same man as before," said Thjodhild, "and have grown little in judgement by your time in the south."

"Judgement is that a man do what is meant for him," said Sigtrygg. "And this, since it first was offered, I have known was mine to do."

"Then I'll not stop you," she said.

"And you could not."

"Only come back with me now," she begged him, "and we'll

set things right with Thorkel; for my father can move him, as few others can. Nor is my father hard stone to me."

"There's no use pressing this any further with those men, for Thorkel has other dealings in mind, or did you miss the interest of that Norwegian in the Vinland holdings?"

"Yet the world is large," said she, "and many ships can sail on the sea, nor will one man's claim hinder another's. There's room enough for all."

"That may be," Sigtrygg answered her, "but Leif's claim was in a good place and it may happen that none were better in all that country, for he explored widely there and never found a place more to his liking. Let our Norwegian friend make other landfalls, if he will. But Leif's houses are mine, freely given, and I'll not hand them back. Now, tell me, lady, where lies that ship I put in your keeping when last we bandied words on the fjord's edge?"

"This," said Thjodhild, "is not now in my hands to give, for Thorkel Leifsson and his sons took charge of it, after you were gone and keep it now well-locked in one of the farms they hold up the fjord, though I know not in which place, exactly, it has been laid up."

"Then you have kept ill to your part of our bargain when I put my goods into your hands. How shall I get my rights now?"

"Let me speak with our uncle, kinsman," said she, "and then we will see if this wrong can be undone."

Sigtrygg told her she should do as she thought best and now he said: "It is my desire that you return to your kinsmen below and leave me to my own ways in this place."

"I will stay with you, kinsman," said she, "and then we two can go down together to the farmstead in the morning, for this is a cold place and not fit for sleeping alone on such a height."

"I have slept in worse places," he said. "But this is no fit resting place for you. Besides, it cannot speed my case if it is discovered we have shared even these bare rocks. Go down to your father's house and seek the farm's comfort and I will find you in the morning. Then, we may yet make a good end of this night's work."

"You are a strange man, Sigtrygg," said she, "and not easy to understand. Yet I would rather abide by your words than trouble you further, seeing it is I have brought you to this impasse. Still, it were best if you came down with me now and sought your shelter in our kinsmen's houses, like other men, for there is no telling what dark things prowl these high places when the night lays on us."

He laughed. "There's naught but what men tell one another over the house fire, to while away the dark hours," he said. "In truth, the open sky's a better roof than thatch, to my mind, and less to be feared, but for the winter's cold and the skulking of other men. Go home, kinswoman, and we'll settle things in the morning."

Then she left him, but without gladness, and worked her way back down the path on which she had come. And Sigtrygg, when he had satisfied himself that she had got safely down again, found shelter under a broken overhang of rock and lay down within it, though he did not find sleep for a long while, seeing as the shadows of the great ice at the fjord's end played over him and looked, ever and again, like the prow and keel of a great ship, slipping and jumping over the broken surface of the sea.

Now all that night he slept fitfully and it seemed to him that many loud noises came down from the ice, as though the great ice sheet, itself, cracked and groaned and shifted under its own weight. And these sounds continued without cease, becoming harsher and louder than before, so that they troubled his sleep and he awoke several times in the night, until he thought he must give up sleeping altogether to listen to that cracking din, which now seemed to lay over the entire fjord. But, as he bent his ear to the rising sounds, he thought the rumbling ice changed slowly until it sounded more to him like the noises of men than shifting ice sheets and, as he lay there, he thought he could make out words and then voices, though he could not say whose voices they were. Yet, he thought he knew the voices and the men who made them.

After awhile, he slept again, his back against the rock ledge which he had chosen for his shelter. But, because of the hardness of the rock and its roughened surface, he soon found he could sleep there no better than before. And now the noises returned, but this time they were distinctly the voices of men, so that Sigtrygg thought he must raise himself up and see who it was that came his way. Yet, the voices remained garbled, though he thought they were much closer than they were before, and he could not make out what they were saying.

With great effort, Sigtrygg lifted his face above the rock ledge and struggled to open his eyes, seeking the cause of this night's disturbance. Above him and toward the great mass of white ice which lay inland, above the fjord's head, he thought he could see the shapes of men, larger than any he had ever seen before, but still much further off than it had seemed from the nearness of their voices. And now it appeared that their leader was looking Sigtrygg's way, that he could see him, though in truth there was a huge gulf which lay between them. This giant seemed to know Sigtrygg and Sigtrygg, himself, thought that this was not unusual since he thought he knew the giant, too, though he still had no clear view of him.

Then the giant began to lope along the edge of the ice and the others followed him and Sigtrygg watched them go, for they made their way, not to the side of the fjord on which Sigtrygg lay, but to the opposite shore and there they stood, facing Sigtrygg in complete silence, only staring at him, their faces vaguely familiar to his eyes, though he could not recall them by name. Now they seemed to be much like other men, having lost that great size they had appeared to have before, and Sigtrygg thought this a trick of the ice which sometimes fooled even the most experienced hunter's eye. But the men on the far side of the fjord continued to stand there, as though they had no other work to attend to and seemed to see Sigtrygg as well as he saw them, though it was an even greater distance between them now than before.

Sigtrygg thought that there were five of these men and that

they were waiting for him for some purpose, but he could not understand why they stood by so silently, as though they thought he already knew what it was they were seeking. And then he saw their leader, a head and more above the others, grinning as his shadow seemed to roll out from the place where he stood and slide across the fjord till it touched the houses of Brattahlid; he thought he saw the main hall of the farm burst into flames, then, as the shadow touched it, and he heard voices coming from the farm houses, screaming as though in pain, and he sat suddenly upright, trying to discern if these were men's voices he was hearing or the voices of the women.

Vragi and those who were with him were awakened in the early morning hours, not by the cows with whom they were sharing accommodations but by the heavy sound of a man's feet moving among them. They reached for their weapons but a sharp, whispering voice warned them to be still.

"Who's there, troubling an old man's sleep like this?" asked Vragi at length.

Sigtrygg said it was no one else but him and that now they were to get up, at once, since there was work to be done.

"What do you have in mind?" Vragi said, and he saw that Sigtrygg had his sword belted to his side and his shield on his arm.

"I want you to take these men of yours and row across the fjord and see what's on the other side, for I have a feeling you won't be disappointed."

Vragi agreed but said he thought it a good idea to leave two of their men with Sigtrygg on this side of the fjord, "since your kinsmen are not likely to be in any better mood now than they were when we last saw them."

"Do as you think best," said Sigtrygg, "only hurry back to me with whatever you find waiting on the other side."

Vragi now left the two Icelanders with Sigtrygg and got the rest of his men into their boat. These, together with the Icelanders, had numbered seven men in all, since he had recruited two others after he and Sigtrygg had last parted company on Herjolfsness. Thus, he took five with him to row across the fjord and left the Icelanders, who were called Asmund and Thorolf, in Sigtrygg's company.

When Vragi and his crew had pushed the boat into the water and begun to pull at the oars, Sigtrygg told the Icelanders they were to follow him up to the main hall. Thorolf and Asmund said they were more than willing to do this sort of work and they each grabbed their weapons.

"I don't want you men to say anything more than I'm willing to say myself," Sigtrygg now warned them. "In fact, I think it would be best if you kept to yourselves in this affair and left the talking entirely to me."

The two exchanged glances but agreed that they would not do anything more than Sigtrygg asked of them, "for", they said, "it's clear enough that no one has anything more to say in this matter than you."

They now followed Sigtrygg up to the main house and by this time in the morning a number of folk were already about. The young men of the household were sitting on the porch, which was rather a wide affair and deep enough to accommodate a large group of people. Girstein Eiriksson was there with the Thorkelssons, both Thord and Thorstein, and the Gunnarssons, Thjodhild's brothers. Lambi Gunnarsson was the eldest; he was a big man with broad shoulders and dark hair, but folk knew him mostly for the sternness of his eyes, which were what most people remarked on, before anything else, when they met him for the first time. He took things very seriously and was not much given to joking or lightheartedness, though he and Sigtrygg had known each other since they were both small boys and had always gotten on well together. Lambi's younger brothers, Helgi and Thorvald, sat on either side of him. Helgi was only a year older than Thjodhild, but Thorvald was still barely more than a boy and had not yet attained his full height. Both were fairer than Lambi but neither could match him for size or strength. Also with them were a number of the guests who had been staying on at the house and several of the Norwegians from Osvif's ship.

When they saw Sigtrygg coming up from the fjord, Lambi asked him whether he had now decided to accept the hospitality of Brattahlid, afterall, seeing as he had behaved so churlishly the night before.

"I have no apologies to make for that," Sigtrygg replied. "I have merely come to have a word with my uncles and get back what is mine."

"In that case, you are certainly welcome here, kinsman," said Girstein, and he made a place for Sigtrygg beside himself, on the porch.

"I wouldn't speak too hastily," said Thord Thorkelsson, "for it is not yet clear to me if our cousin has accepted matters as they now stand. Or does he think to sway us with this armed company?"

There was general laughter at Thord's words and everyone on the porch thought it a very funny joke, except for Lambi and Girstein. Girstein said he thought such words as Thord's were unlikely to advance matters, as things now stood, and that, if a settlement was now needed between the kinsmen, the best thing was that they talk the thing out when people were no longer brooding over their ale. But Lambi asked if it were true that Sigtrygg was still unwilling to accept the Leifssons decision in the matter?

"That is certainly true," answered Sigtrygg, "since oaths were sworn and I have fulfilled my part in the matter exactly as my kinsmen required."

"This may be so," said Thord, "but matters have changed since you went off a year ago to raise a crew, nor have you been altogether successful at that, as these sorry fellows you are dragging along behind you must readily show. No one promised you a ship to wreck in vain wanderings out on the sea, whatever the oaths, so it now seems to me that this is a matter which you must submit to arbitration. If you won't take judgement from your own kin, then it is better to try it out at the assembly, according to the laws of the country."

"I don't see how I am any more likely to get my rights in a court proceeding now than before," Sigtrygg replied.

"Even so," said Thord, "you haven't much choice, since it's unlikely you are prepared to swim all the way to Vinland."

That company again thought Thord's words very clever and there was just as much laughter as before.

"You wouldn't be speaking this way if you and I were alone out on the ice," said Sigtrygg.

"Perhaps not," Thord agreed, "but then it's not very likely I will ever find myself in such a position, since I am not as fond of wandering about as you are."

Girstein now rose from his place and went to the edge of the porch, placing himself between Thord and Thorstein, where they were standing, on the one hand, and Sigtrygg and his companions, on the other. "It's not often that things can be satisfactorily settled when such hard words precede action," he said. "Now it is my advice that we kinsmen put this matter aside, till the assembly can be called, and then let things be sorted out by those who are most knowledgeable concerning such affairs. In the meantime, I think our kinsman must be somewhat hungry, after the hard night he has spent on the hillside, and there's plenty of food left in the kitchen for any who wish to claim it. That's certainly an easier claiming than these Vinland houses which our grandfather built."

At this Asmund and Thorolf, who were still standing somewhat uneasily behind Sigtrygg, brightened considerably, since it seemed to them a long time since they'd eaten; and this was not made any easier by the nature of the accommodations in which they had taken their night's rest. "I certainly wouldn't object to a little morning meat," said Thorolf under his breath and Asmund said he agreed.

"It seems your retinue is somewhat under-provisioned," said Thord. "In my opinion, you are better off seeing to their groaning bellies, than worrying about how you will get these two unlikely fellows across the sea. Take what you have, when you can't have what you are seeking, is always the best advice."

Sigtrygg replied that he planned to feed them well enough, both in Greenland and Vinland, when they came to that country, but in the meantime his business was with the Leifssons, not their wet-eared offspring, and he told Thord to stop bandying words about and blocking his way "but go into the house and bring out your father, for these are man's matters."

Lambi got up from the bench he had been sitting on, and his two brothers with him, and Thord and Thorstein also stepped forward from their places. "There's no use throwing such words about here, kinsman Sigtrygg," said Lambi, "for these are things which only the wisest among us can right. Until then, you'd do best to remember how many there are of us, and how many of you, and who has possession of the holdings here at Brattahlid."

"Brattahlid is not my concern," answered Sigtrygg, "only what is here which is mine; and that is a ship which I left in good faith when last I passed this way, at the urging of your own sister. Until that is returned to me, I count my business with the Leifssons unfinished."

"It won't do you any good bringing our sister into this," Lambi said, "for what she did was much against our will and the advice we gave her. But, if she saw to your ship for you, it was only because she too grasped the folly of your plans to ride over the seas, though you've never sailed a vessel out of these coastal waters before, and hunt for distant lands. Or do you think you can sail in the wake of those who preceded you and who were certainly much more accomplished men than you are?"

"I intend to do whatever is necessary," answered Sigtrygg, "nor do I count myself, in any way, a lesser man than those who have sailed before me. As for you Gunnarssons and you Thorkelssons, and Girstein Eiriksson, too, you will all see that you will not get much of a bargain in your dealings with me, if you mean to block my way now."

"I don't think you are in any position to make such threats, as things now stand," warned Lambi. "If I were you, I'd skulk off, while I were still able, with my two outlawed friends, and find a place to winter, out on the ice, for I don't think you are likely to get much more of a welcome in these parts, than you have now found."

At these words, Thorolf and Asmund began to fidget even more, for it certainly seemed to them that the odds were very much in the Leifssons' favor. It began to look to the two Icelanders as though they had lined up on the wrong side of things; that now they would not only be denied passage to the western lands, however far off these lay, but also that they were likely to find it hard going even to get shelter for themselves in Greenland over the winter, when matters were the least promising for homeless men such as they now were. Asmund now whispered to Sigtrygg that, in his opinion, it would be best if he were willing to back off and make a settlement with his kinsmen, since there were clearly too many of them for him to make a fight of it.

The men on the porch heard this and it proved no less an occasion for laughter than Thord's words had before. Lambi now said this only showed how good a judge he was of men, since this was just what he had expected when he first saw Sigtrygg coming up the hillside with these fellows in tow. "And now I want to advise you to cut these two loose, as soon as you have left us, for I don't think they will do you much good in the waste lands," he said.

Sigtrygg turned to Asmund and Thorolf and told them to hold their tongues, "since it was not for your deep thinking or fine speeches that I brought you along." Then he told his kinsmen they must now bring out the Leifssons, if they wanted him to leave, for otherwise they were not likely to be rid of him, however hard they tried to make things.

"If that's all it will take," answered Thord, "I will certainly be happy to oblige you, for my father will count it well worth his effort if, by speaking with you now, he can put an end to this incessant haggling." He then sent Thorstein, his brother, into the house and, in a very short time, the Leifssons appeared, with Thorkel in the lead. The Norwegian merchant, Osvif Thorleiksson and Grimkel Vesteinsson, the Ketilsfjord chieftain, came out right behind them.

"So this is how you repay me for raising you up like one of my own," said Thorkel at once when he saw Sigtrygg standing below him, "by picking fights with your kinsmen and making threats against my household? It's not often a man gets such a poor return for his generosity and good will. Now I'm told you are ready to make a settlement with us over this little dispute of ours, and I'm willing enough to do that, so long as you are reasonable and do not ask too much of me."

"I only want what is already mine," Sigtrygg replied, "and as to a settlement, these are your words, not my own."

Thorkel said: "I don't have a great deal of time to toss words about with you like this. If you've something on your mind, I would advise you to say it now, if you want my reply. But if not, then it's plain little has changed; and then you are not likely to get any more from this meeting of ours than you have got from me so far."

"I've come for that ship which I left in the safekeeping of my kinsmen," Sigtrygg said. "After that I will be no more a burden on you or your household, than those who lay no claim of kinship upon you at all. But, until this is resolved, it is unlikely you will find any respite from me, so long as I am alive."

Thorkel said he thought this one of the most amusing threats any man had ever made to him, "for you are no more a problem for us Leifssons than a flea on a horse's backside. And now I want to advise you that you are not doing your case very much good by comporting yourself in this fashion and resorting to threats in front of all these men, for I will certainly call upon them as witnesses when the assembly is convened. And then we will see which of us will have his way in this matter."

Sigtrygg replied that Thorkel could certainly have it his own way now, as he did most of the time, but that others might not always feel constrained to play the game by his rules.

"If you mean to draw your weapon," counseled Thorkel, "you have, in my opinion, chosen a poor place and a poorer time, for never have you been so outnumbered as you are right now, and anyone seeing such an act would certainly agree that we Leifssons had a great deal of provocation, if we thought it necessary to respond."

"I am not such a fool," said Sigtrygg, "as to think the advantages are all with me, should we come to blows in this place, for you have certainly marked the difference in strengths between our two sides. But I have brought these arms with me for another purpose and that is to offer you Leifssons a chance to make an end of the issue according to the laws of the country. And if we settle up in this way, I will be well-content, however things fall out."

"What do you have in mind, then?" asked Thorkel.

"Only this. That I will fight a duel with any man of your choosing, over this question, according to the ancient laws which our fathers brought with them out of Iceland, and out of Norway before that. Then, let all men who are here now hold this in witness: if I fail, I shall give up my claim to the ship and Leif's houses, and to my father's farm here in Greenland, too. But, if successful, I shall have the ship, and all the provisions you have already pledged me and your goodwill, besides, to go out to Vinland and lay claim to the land which Leif Eiriksson held."

Thorkel said: "And why should I agree to this, since I already have the ship in my hands and the farm, too, and it is in my power to dispose of both? Nor do I think it is in the interests of our kin that duels be fought between men of the same blood, while I am chieftain in this family and over all the district. Or do you think it is your place to force me to a decision, which overturns that judgement I have already given?"

"It is my right, as these men here know, and no one will take it harder than you when this is laid before the assembly," said Sigtrygg.

"Is it a right in this country, then?" asked Osvif the Norwegian who had, up to that moment, stood silently behind the Leifssons.

Thorkel said some held it such, but that no duels had been fought, in this fashion, since Eirik the Red's time and that most people thought this law a relic from earlier days, more fit for honoring in memory than in practice.

"Still it is the law," said Sigtrygg, "and no man may say otherwise. And I claim my rights according to its terms now."

"Do you think you can take with sword play what you cannot secure by more peaceful means?" asked Osvif.

"When all doors are shut, to a man," said Sigtrygg, "even the barred window looks promising."

"This is certainly nonsense and a waste of all our times," said Thorkel, "since I have no more intention of agreeing to this duel than of handing a boat over to you, to lose for us on the open sea. And surely you are no swordsman, though you carry that old weapon about, as though you had fought with it in some far off battle. What does a hunter and a killer of dumb beasts know of sword play and man-fighting?"

Osvif now added that he thought this was true enough and advised Sigtrygg to accept a settlement with his kinsmen. "Besides," said he, "that country you are seeking is, as I hear it, big enough for more than one man's claim, and it may yet fall out that you will find your way there, if not in your own ship, then in some other's."

Girstein said the Norwegian's words were well-spoken and he urged Sigtrygg to accept the advice given, promising that he, himself, would do whatever he could to get a fair settlement for Sigtrygg, in accordance with the true worth of Thorgils' farm.

"Still, my sword and shield are before you," answered Sigtrygg when he had heard these men out, "just as the old laws require it. And I will not take my leave, till I have got an answer."

"My answer has already been given you," said Thorkel.

Now, while they were about this, the men on the porch could see that a boat had come across from the other side of the fjord and a group of men had disembarked and were now coming up the hillside to the main hall. These numbered eleven in all and appeared to be well-armed; at their head was a big man, towering above the others, and he carried a large round shield slung across his back and a sword strapped at his waist. Over his shoulder he bore a long-handled, two-sided war axe which he held lightly against his body as he strode briskly toward them. Beside him walked Vragi One-Eye, whom they knew for Sigtrygg's supporter from the night before.

Seeing where their eyes went, Sigtrygg said: "Now we are somewhat more evenly matched, since my crew is come."

Thord replied that the odds were still not in Sigtrygg's favor since "you are now only fourteen, by my count, while there are a great deal more men here at Brattahlid than that."

"That may be," answered Sigtrygg, "but how many of these are your men? I do not think this Norwegian will willingly spare his crew for fighting in a matter which is not his concern, while these guests of yours have certainly not come here for manslaughter."

Thorkel said: "Is it your intention, then, kinsman to press this matter with blood?"

"Only one man's blood need be shed or, at the worst, two, if the fighting proves hard enough," Sigtrygg replied, "for I will stand by my summons to settle this matter, according to the old laws, by single combat, if I can get no good in any other way."

Now Vragi came up to Sigtrygg and asked how matters stood and Sigtrygg told him everything and that he had determined to settle things by dueling, if his kinsmen were unwilling to resolve the issue in a more peaceful way. The big man who was with the newcomers also came up beside them then and it was soon seen that this was none other than Arnliot Torfisson, from the Ketilsfjord district, whom men called Keelfoot for his great size. When this man heard Sigtrygg's words, he lowered his long, two-handed axe to the ground and rested his big hands atop its blade, grinning, much as he had the night before in Sigtrygg's dream.

"Things have certainly taken a different turn now, as it seems to me," said Osvif Thorleiksson when he had looked for a time at the newcomers and especially at the big man who now stood by Sigtrygg's side. "Still, I would urge you kinsmen to avoid any blood-letting, if this is still possible. In my opinion, you are now much more evenly matched, though there is little good can come of the kind of settlement which you, Sigtrygg, are proposing. If it were up to me, I would man this ship of yours jointly, for neither of the two sides has enough men for a full ship's complement. Yet to-gether you are certainly more than enough. And as for you, Sigtrygg, I think you will find it hard enough to come to your holdings, let alone settle down there, if you persist in this folly for there are so few of you."

Sigtrygg replied that he did not see much to be gained by making common cause with his kinsmen in this affair and Thorkel said the same, adding that he had not expected such repayment as Osvif had now given him, for the guesting he had already pro-vided to both ship and crew. "Had I known you would take the side of my enemies, I would certainly have urged you to find your lodgings in some other fjord," he said.

It was now quite clear to everyone that neither side was pre-pared to budge in this matter. But Grimkel Vesteinsson seemed more enraged than anyone else, since he saw that Arnliot Torfisson was among Sigtrygg's following and he thought this the height of arrogance as he had counted himself Sigtrygg's backer, however quietly, before this. But now he said that he thought the Leifssons ought to settle things to their own benefit, whatever it took, and he promised them the support of his own men.

"If manslaughter is being urged," said Osvif, "then it were better between two men than all of us here. And, as this fellow Sigtrygg is kin to my own king by marriage, however distantly, I will see that neutral ground is provided and that all the terms of the duel are kept."

Vragi said: "That is well-done. And I will stand as his second, if he will have it so. Who will fight for you Leifssons?"

"There's no need to ask that," said Lambi Gunnarsson, "for no one here is better suited to this than me."

But Thord said: "I think our kinsman Girstein has as good a claim. And he, alone of us, has been abroad and seen how these things are done in other countries. Besides, I hear he's somewhat of a handy man with the sword."

"That's true enough," answered Girstein, "but I think Lambi, or you Thord, have each a better right to this than I, for you men seem to find it hardest to accept the terms of Sigtrygg's oath with our fathers."

"Enough," said Thorkel. "If it will take a duel to settle this, I am not opposed and will do whatever is required to make the matter right. But I will choose our champion and the place where this fight is to be held. And now I select Lambi, for he is most eager to settle things, as it seems to me, and, perhaps, has more reason than you others. Besides, he is certainly the strongest of you kinsmen and the keenest of you men in a fight."

Sigtrygg said this was acceptable to him and now Thorkel told Girstein he was to be Lambi's second. Girstein replied that he was willing, if that was Thorkel's wish and everyone now agreed on how the fight should be fought. Each man was to have a sword; and the seconds were to hold the shields, after the manner of the ancient duels which they used to hold in Iceland and in Norway. And the first man who was cut must pay fine to the other and own himself beaten, or else be killed in single combat, if he would not yield. But the winner should have his rights, as the law required.

CHAPTER VII

AN UNLOOKED FOR GIFT

It was now agreed that Lambi and Sigtrygg were to fight it out on the following day, on an island near the mouth of Eiriksfjord, and those members of both parties who would attend were now named. Then Thorkel told Sigtrygg he could have the cow shed for himself and his men this one night more, but afterwards, however things fell out, he would find no further welcome at Brattahlid. Sigtrygg said it was all the same to him and accepted the offer.

"Now," said Arnliot, when they had settled in among the cow stalls, "one thing or the other will certainly happen: either that big farmer will crack your skull, friend Sigtrygg, and we shall find our accommodations a good deal worse than they are now, or you will find your luck and cut the legs out from under him. And then we will be in for some hard sailing."

"I did not think the prospect of a little rough work at the oars would scare you so easily," said Sigtrygg.

"It's not the rowing I'm worried about," Arnliot replied, "but how you will be able to stand up under the blows of Lambi Gunnarsson, for he strikes me as a man who has hefted a sword or two before, and to no small purpose. As for you, I know how you came by your weapon and how you have used it since."

"There's no need to worry about that," said Sigtrygg, "for I have done my share of killing, if only with a hunter's weapons, and I know my kinsman, both how he moves and how he thinks."

"Still," said Arnliot, "it is in my mind to offer to stand up in your place and kill that fellow, for otherwise I don't know if any of us shall see the other side of the western sea."

"I will do my own fighting," said Sigtrygg, "where my kinsmen are concerned."

"Yet," said Vragi, "it may not be unwise to accept Arnliot Keelfoot's offer, since it is never easy killing a kinsman, if it should come to that, and this may stay your hand when the blow is most needed. Besides, you will have less to amend if another strikes the death blow."

"It's no use arguing about it," said Sigtrygg, "for my mind is made up and no one shall fight this duel but me. As to the outcome, if things go as planned, we shall soon be at sea. But, if not, then I want you to look after these men and see they get lodging over winter and do not lack for anything, till summer comes and they can be on their way again. As to this Keelfoot fellow, you must see he gets a final settlement with Grimkel Vesteinsson, for I owe this much, at least, to his father."

Vragi agreed and told him he was not to worry about any of it, though Arnliot said he thought this all very funny, since a man who expected to defeat his enemy did not make plans for his own death. "And that is even more of a reason why I should fight this duel instead of you."

Sigtrygg said everything would happen as it was fated and now he looked hard at the large axe which Arnliot had brought with him up from the fjord and which he now cradled beneath him, as he lay across the cold earth, as though it were his most valued possession. The big Ketilsfjordman saw where Sigtrygg's eyes went and asked him if he thought he had some special interest in the axe, to which Sigtrygg replied that he had none, "except that it seems to me that I have seen that weapon of yours before, and then the farmer who owned it did not seem overly eager to part with it. And he thought he had good reason."

Arnliot said: "It's not surprising that a man will share with his kinsmen what he will not willingly give to strangers."

Sigtrygg agreed that this was probably so and turned his attention elsewhere. Now he asked Vragi to see to it that Thjodhild should have his goods, if things went against him, and especially the sword and shield, which he counted among the best of his possessions.

"They could find no better home," said Vragi.

"Then there's nothing more to be done till tomorrow," Sigtrygg said, "so I advise you men to take your ease here, for the time being, and stay out of the way of my kinsmen, since we must be well-rested when the new day comes, however things fall out."

Now the day passed without incident for Sigtrygg's men stayed close by the cow shed, as he had instructed them, and no one came down from the farm houses, until evening, and then a servant came in and brought with her a basket of dried meats and some whey. She said these were sent by Thjodhild, who thought they might be hungry, since they had made no effort to come up to the hall to eat with the others in the household.

Arnliot grabbed the serving girl's arm and said it was not only dried meats they were in need of, but she only laughed, saying Thjodhild had forbidden them anything else and especially ale, since she thought they should have a clear head on the following day.

"A man can't clear his head, if he hasn't fogged it first," said Arnliot.

"Are they drinking up at the house?" asked Vragi.

"They certainly are," said the girl.

"And who's drinking the most?" he asked.

"That would be Thord Thorkelsson," she said, "though the Gunnarssons are certainly no slouches, either. Thjodhild has ordered that all the ale vats be brought out and opened, and no one thinks he is any less entitled to his share than anyone else. Only Girstein Eiriksson shows no interest in the ale, for he seems to have his thoughts on other things."

"That is just what I would have expected from Girstein," said Sigtrygg, "for, of all my kinsmen, he is certainly the cleverest."

"He's not so clever," said Thorolf the Icelander, "if they are finishing all the ale tonight and he is passing up his share."

"What are they saying while they are drinking?" asked Vragi.

"That tomorrow will see an end to all this fuss about Leif Eiriksson's houses," said the serving girl. "And then they will see if the Norwegians have any ideas about how the houses are to be disposed of. They think Lambi will make quick enough work of Sigtrygg, for Lambi is very strong in the arms and shoulders and can strike a cow's head off its neck with a single sword stroke."

"It's just as I told you," said Arnliot. "It will take a man of equal or greater power to fell that tree. But there's no use talking to people when they're not disposed to listen."

Sigtrygg asked the serving girl if Thjodhild thought the same as everyone else.

"It's not easy to tell," said the girl, "for she's not saying a great deal about it, either one way or the other. But she's certainly very open-handed with the food and drink. A person would think it was her own household, the way she is encouraging them all to fill their bellies."

Vragi thanked the girl and said she must now be on her way, before she was missed, but he told her to keep her ears open and let them know if anything out of the ordinary was said. She promised to do just that and asked if she was to come back to them again, if she heard anything.

"Only if it is very important," said Vragi, "or if your mistress sends you."

They slept well that night, and Sigtrygg slept the soundest, though some of the men thought it particularly galling that the fare had been so poor, when there was so much better to be had only a short distance away, and complained about this. Vragi told them that it didn't pay to grumble about what other people had, since they would soon be eating a whole lot worse, once they were at sea, "and there are other hardships, which a sea-going man must face, besides skimpy rations," he added.

"In any case," said Arnliot, "it would make things a whole lot easier if we knew for sure that we would win the ship tomorrow; and I, for one, would certainly prefer to arrange it so." But Sigtrygg appeared to have already fallen asleep so no one paid any more attention to Arnliot's words.

Late in the night, when the sounds had all died down from the main farmhouse, they heard a scratching outside the shed door. Vragi was the first to waken and he took his staff and poked at the door, pushing it open slightly. When he heard the scratching again, he asked who was out there. The serving girl said it was only her. Vragi told her to come inside, but to do so as quietly as she could.

By this time a number of the others had also awakened, including Sigtrygg and Arnliot, and Arnliot asked her what news she was bringing with her this time, "or have you finally put some ale aside for these thirsty fellows who must take their entertainment with the cows?"

The girl said she was to tell them that Thjodhild was outside and that she wanted to speak with Sigtrygg.

"Tell her to come in here," Sigtrygg said quickly, "for I have no secrets from these men."

The girl went out and when she came back Thjodhild was close behind her.

"You are certainly in a sorry way now, kinsman," said Thjodhild, when she saw where Sigtrygg was lying, stretched out upon the earth not far from a mound of cow dung.

"I've slept in poorer places," he answered her. "And in better."

"Is this better, then, or worse than the bed you chose for yourself last night?"

"It's warmer here," Sigtrygg replied, "although the smell is stronger."

Vragi asked if everyone was now asleep up at the main house and Thjodhild said that that was certainly the case. "Only one or two of us are still about," she added, "and that for our own reasons."

Sigtrygg said: "I thank you for the food, kinswoman, since

these men were growing restive on their empty bellies."

"There was no use having them cut your throat, in anger," Thjodhild replied, "before Lambi has had his chance to take your head tomorrow."

Arnliot thought this highly amusing. "It seems there are not a great many people who have their wagers on you," he told Sigtrygg.

"It's all the same to me where people put their money," Sigtrygg said, "for things will happen as they will; but I, for one, do not intend to give up my ship."

Thjodhild said: "Most people will say that it is my fault the ship is now withheld from you, though I doubt you could have done any better with it, had you followed other counsel. Still, I would rather fix things now, than leave matters to chance tomorrow."

"Are you afraid for your brother's life, then?" asked Sigtrygg.

"Only say I think it better if my kinsmen do not shed one another's blood," Thjodhild answered, "though you are certainly anxious enough to cut through this matter with your sword."

"If you have a better proposal," said Sigtrygg, "I am not unwilling to hear it."

"Then get up and come with me tonight," she said quickly, "away from this place, before the Leifssons and their households are risen in the morning, since there's still time to undo the knot you've tied here."

"I don't think there's any use in our running away now," Sigtrygg replied, "for some words cannot be unsaid, nor other things undone. Besides, I mean to have the ship, either one way or the other. If my uncles will not produce it, I will take it with their blood."

"I thought you would say as much," Thjodhild said, "and that's why I did not come empty-handed. I have your ship for you, if you will take it tonight and leave before the duel is to be fought."

"Where is the ship?" asked Sigtrygg.

"You must first give me your oath you will not fight tomorrow but will take the ship and go."

"Shall I flee like a thief with my own vessel?" asked Sigtrygg.

"If you are eager enough to have it," answered Thjodhild. "And that is a better chance of recovering the ship, than if you fight my brother."

Arnliot leaned forward and whispered loudly that this was coward's work, to steal a man's property in the night without striking a blow, and flee before the duel was fought.

"That may be," said Thjodhild, "but if Sigtrygg is lost tomorrow, what prospects do any of you have? Or will you lay all upon the faltering of my brother's sword arm?"

Vragi said: "There's no use fighting a duel over a thing which is already in our hands. In my opinion we can't ask for any better turn of events than this, that the object of the fight is won before the first blow is struck."

"I'd like it a whole lot better," said Arnliot, "if I could first cut that big goat down."

Thjodhild asked: "Will you come with me then, kinsman, and let me undo the wrong I've done you?"

"And why not," said he, "since you have asked it."

He now told his followers to get up and they did so, as quietly as they could, and gathered up their belongings and crept, one by one, outside. Since it was already high summer, the night sky was not dark and so they must move low along the fence of the home field, that no one coming out of the main house to relieve himself in the night should lay eyes on them and raise the alarm. Sigtrygg asked Thjodhild how far they had to go and how she had found out where the ship was being kept.

"That's not hard to tell," she said, "for men speak most freely when they are full of ale. The ship is in a barn, not far down the fjord, and it will be hard work to get it out and onto the water, and then you will still have to sail her past Brattahlid. And that will be the hardest part of this."

"Is she sea-worthy?" asked Vragi. "For she has lain up all winter with none to look after her."

"The Leifssons have not let her dry out or go to rot," answered

Thjodhild, "for Thord and Thorstein, especially, have taken a fancy to her; and my own brothers, it seems, have also had a hand in this. I think they mean to sail her, themselves, when they deem the time right."

"Then they will certainly take this loss very hard," said Arnliot.

They went in a single line as low to the ground along the shore as they could, till they had left the buildings of Brattahlid behind them, and then they broke into a run, still clutching their goods and weapons close to their bodies. Thjodhild led the way and she went as swiftly as any of the men, lifting her long skirt off the ground so she would not trip over it. But the serving girl could not keep up, so Arnliot scooped her up in his arms, as though she were just another sack of goods, his pace never faltering.

When they came to some distant outbuildings, Thjodhild told them to stop and now they must approach more cautiously. "There it is," she told them, "but let me go first."

Sigtrygg said she should do as she thought best and he told his men to lie down on the ground. Arnliot replied that he was only too glad to follow these orders and he fell on the little serving maid, causing her to let out a sharp squeal.

"If you don't act with more care, we may all be undone," said Sigtrygg.

Vragi took a knife from his person and handed it to Arnliot. "Now you must do one thing or the other," he said. "Either silence the girl or cut her throat with this." Arnliot accepted the weapon and placed it across the girl's throat and told her to keep silent. Her eyes widened and he stretched his body over hers, covering her face with his own.

They now watched Thjodhild go up to the building and behind it. In a little while she appeared again and waved them to come up. Sigtrygg rose first and, after him, each of his men in turn, except for Arnliot who stayed behind, still tussling with the maid. When they had gone about half-way, Sigtrygg stopped suddenly and the men behind him halted, too.

"What's the matter?" Vragi asked him.

"It's a very strange thing," said Sigtrygg, "but I thought I saw a glint of metal just a moment ago, behind Thjodhild's skirt."

"Is there any reason to mistrust the woman?" asked Vragi.

"None that I know of," said Sigtrygg.

"Then go forward and pay it no mind."

Sigtrygg did just that and they came up to where Thjodhild stood. "Where is my ship?" Sigtrygg asked her.

"Inside," she said.

"Then you must lead the way."

They followed her into the barn and, when their eyes had adjusted to the dimmer light, they saw before them a single helmeted man, fully armed in war gear, leaning up against the side of the ship. He had a long oaken spear in his left hand and a drawn sword in his right; a large round war shield was propped against his legs. At once they began to look around for other men, but there was no one else to be seen. Sigtrygg asked the man who he was.

The man stuck his sword into the earthen floor and lifted up the visor of the helmet he was wearing. It was an elaborate headpiece, of southern make, and not the sort of armament which was commonly seen that far north. Underneath the raised visor, the close-cropped, chestnut colored beard of Girstein Eiriksson was plainly visible. "Welcome, kinsman, I thought you would never make up your mind to come," he said.

Sigtrygg now asked Thjodhild what this meant and she said that Girstein had been with her in this matter from the beginning, since he did not see much more sense in their two kinsmen fighting over a boat than she did. "And the truth is, it was his idea to take the ship, before anyone at Brattahlid could waken," she now added.

"But I did not know if you'd have the courage to forego a chance to split Lambi's gut with that new sword of yours," Girstein said.

Now, as they were speaking thus, Arnliot came rushing into the barn, the little servant girl in tow. When he saw Girstein, fully armed, he stopped in his place and let the girl go. "What have we here?" he asked. "Have the Leifssons finally found their guts and sent their champion out to stop us?"

"Here is one you'd certainly be better off without, kinsman," said Girstein, his eyes on the big yellow-haired man. "Why don't you let me relieve you of the problem?"

"There's no need for that," said Sigtrygg, "for I need every one of these men, as things now stand. And now I want to thank you for your help in this matter, since I have a feeling things will not go easy for you, once your part in this is known."

"Nothing ventured, nothing gained," answered Girstein, "though I still hold it a mistake that my father and his brothers sold you our grandfather's land claim for one poor farm here in Greenland."

"I would have fought it out and settled the matter, one way or the other," said Sigtrygg.

"No doubt," Girstein replied, "but I don't think such a settlement as that would have held for long."

"And why not," asked Sigtrygg, "since I have no close kinsman, hereabouts, to seek compensation for my death?"

"It was not compensation for you that concerned me," answered Girstein.

Thjodhild now said that it would not help any of them very much if they continued to stand about exchanging pleasantries, while the Leifssons and their guests were already dreaming their last at Brattahlid. "If you don't get a move on and roll this boat out of the barn and down to the water, you may as well invite them up here for the morning meal; and then you can all go down to the island and fight your duel together," she said.

Everyone agreed that Thjodhild's words made sense, so now they got the barn doors open and, placing rounded planking under the ship's hull and tying long leads of walrus hide rope to the fore and aft sections, they began to maneuver the vessel out into the open air. No one held back from this task and even Thjodhild and her serving girl did what they could. Vragi told them how they must guide the ship down the steepest parts of the slope, holding tight to the cables so the ship would not plunge unchecked into the hard sand and rocks below. And he went round the vessel, as they moved her, to see that the hull did not take any damage. When they had got her down by the water, he told them how she must be eased in and, when they were done, he stood back to see how she rode on the sea.

"She's not much of a ship," he said, "but she'll sail alright."

Then they brought the oars and whatever meager provisions they could find in the barn, which were not overmuch, and put these into the ship. The last things they fetched were the sail and mast and the ship's awnings, and then they loaded these, too. Now, when they had done these things they began to look about them and somebody said there was no tow-boat. At once Sigtrygg and some of the others hastened back to the barn, but in a little while they returned looking somewhat dejected, for they had been unable to find the tow-boat anywhere. Now they all began to mill about and some of them seemed unsure of what was to be done next for, they said, sailing out on such a perilous voyage as they were now proposing was not something to be done lightly, "or without the benefits of a boat to carry us to safety, should this ship of ours fail us."

Vragi asked if they thought they had any other choice, "for the new day is certainly upon us and the Leifssons are soon up and about. And I'm not certain how they will take it if they find us out here with this ship upon the fjord, and we men set to sail her, but hanging back for want of a tow-boat."

Sigtrygg said: "Some people would think it foolhardy to make such a dangerous crossing as we are now proposing, without any means of getting to safety, thereafter, should matters go against us."

Vragi replied that this was true, "but many would not hazard the trip at all. So now you are to decide if we want to greet the Leifssons and their following here upon the beach and show them how finely this ship of theirs sits upon the fjord waters, for it is certainly too late to undo all that we have now done, or if you prefer to take your chances out on the open sea."

Sigtrygg said he preferred the sea and now the others said the same.

"Good," said Vragi and he walked down to the fjord edge and looked over the ship, once more, carefully noting how she stood in the water. "Well, we are certainly not over-provisioned, for this voyage," he said at last.

Girstein said: "Time was short, and it did not seem the wisest course to raid the stores at Brattahlid."

"It will certainly do for the while," Sigtrygg said, "for I have travelled more lightly in my time."

Now Thjodhild said: "Kinsman, most people would think us quit, since I have restored what was taken from you. But, in my opinion, this just marks another debt, for I want you to promise, when you have tired of travelling about in foreign parts, to come back home to Brattahlid and settle here with us. And, that, I deem, should be sooner rather than later, if you would claim your due in this country."

"Lady," said Sigtrygg, "you have certainly kept your word in all that you have undertaken to do and your advice has always been of the best. Yet, what you propose is no easy thing and many obstacles lie between us, not least that you are my close kinswoman, which, some folk would think, renders us unfit. It is enough that you have stood by me in my need and given me the means to come to my inheritance. Now let us part on those terms."

"That was not the parting which I foresaw," said she.

Now Girstein saw how things were between them and that Thjodhild held tightly to Sigtrygg's hands and would not let them fall from her own. Accordingly, he went up to these two and stood nearby till Sigtrygg turned about to him.

"You are certainly in need of a few more men," Girstein said then, "and I am of a mind to give you at least one extra hand at the oars."

"Then that is why you came out here fully armed?" asked

Sigtrygg. "I thought you meant to hold the ship from us till our kinsmen came."

"I'd have done that, too, had I thought you meant us ill. But, in the end it seems to me a good thing we did not come to blows."

Thjodhild asked Girstein if he were serious about going out with Sigtrygg and his crew, despite Thorkel's feelings in the matter.

"Most assuredly," answered Girstein, "if our kinsman will have me, for there are not many good chances, in this part of the world, to win a name which others will remember."

Arnliot now went to the ship and climbed into her, his men with him, and the others, whom Vragi had brought, followed suit. When they were all on board, Arnliot called out to Sigtrygg and asked him if he meant to spend the rest of the day there on the beach with his kinsmen, "or are you waiting for those other fellows to come up from Brattahlid and skewer you like a stuck seal?"

Now the little serving girl went out up to her chest into the cold waters of the fjord and stood under the boat's prow. Arnliot made his way to her and reached down, grasping her by the wrists; then he pulled her up out of the water and held her above the ship's side, in the air, kissing her face.

"You take yours and I'll take this one," he said to Sigtrygg, "and we'll people the new country between us. But as for that peacock of a kinsman of yours, with his fine armor, I'd sooner throw him into the sea and let the whales have him." Then he dangled the serving girl at arms length from his chest and dropped her into the cold, grey waters with a loud splash.

"That one will certainly need killing, before your travels are done," Girstein said quietly. "If you bring me along, I'll do the deed myself when the time is right."

"He's under my care," said Sigtrygg, "for his father's sake. And that, I think, is reason enough to deny your request to sail with us, though there's no other man I'd rather have at my back in this venture than you, kinsman."

"Then sail with a good wind," said Girstein, "and may the ocean carry you, without turmoil, to your destination."

"And come back to us as soon as you are able," added Thjodhild, "that we may put things right here in the end."

When she had said these words, Thjodhild clasped Sigtrygg's arms and her eyes seemed to pierce his. "We will wait your return," she whispered. He raised her hands up to his chest at this, his own fists fiercely clutching hers.

Vragi now said they must soon be off, since the new day was already upon them and the people at Brattahlid were no doubt already up and about. "It will be hard enough sailing with this crew, tired and fractious as they are," he said, "so there's no need to make things worse now."

Sigtrygg replied that he would do as Vragi advised, and he now let go of Thjodhild's hands, and turned toward the ship. Then he followed the older man into the surf. Everyone watching that day was much amazed at the ease with which the old viking got himself up the boat's side, for they had no gangplank there and no proper mooring; yet Vragi got himself on board the little ship with the agility of a much younger man though he lost his staff there as he climbed over the ship's side. Sigtrygg waded into the surf to retrieve it, for the current had already begun to pull it out toward the open sea, but Vragi stopped him saying "there's no need for that, since we will be following that stick's course ourselves before too long. Besides, I have the feeling these fellows here would think it rather frivolous of me, to bring a walking stick on board a sailing ship."

When the last of them were aboard, they took their places along the two sides of the ship, each man finding an oar stem and pulling as hard as he might. But Vragi went to the ship's stern and took the helm in his two hands and now he steered the ship out toward the middle of the fjord as the others used the oars.

"They are certainly short of men," said Girstein as he watched the ship move slowly out from the shore, away from them, "though," he added, "one more had been no great help."

"Let them have a smooth and fast journey, in any event," Thjodhild replied, standing still and watchful beside him, "the quicker they may see the folly of this enterprise of theirs." But when she said these last words her voice caught, as a bird's foot is trapped by the hunter's snare and her words were lost, deep in her throat. Girstein marked this and marked, too, how her eyes glistened, like the great ice sheets which lie inland above the fjords of that country, when the sun is shining full on them, and then he took her by the shoulders and gently drew her back to Brattahlid.

CHAPTER VIII

FLIGHT FROM THE FJORD

Now there was no wind, to speak of, out on the fjord, when they had got the ship into deep water, save only a light breeze which blew in at them from the sea. Vragi said there was no use unfurling the sail, the way things were, and he told them to bend their backs into the oars instead, since only thus could they get past Brattahlid and out to the open sea. "But row as quietly as you can," he added. "There's no use waking the farmers who live in these parts."

For a time they pushed slowly through the grey water, till the houses of Brattahlid loomed up to starboard. Then they looked at the shore and thought they could see some movement around the houses; Sigtrygg said these would be the house servants, drawing water for the people still inside and seeing to the animals.

"In that case," said Vragi, "we won't gain much by trying to avoid discovery now," and he told the crew they were to pay no more attention to the sounds the oars made when they drove them into the icy fjord waters, but must now row for all they were worth.

About this time someone in the home field saw the slow moving ship and soon there was a great deal of movement around the houses with people running back and forth. Then a large body of men could be seen running out of the main hall and these made straight for the fjord, where a number of skiffs were beached, not far from where the big Norwegian merchant ship lay.

"It looks like your kinsmen are not taking this at all well," said Arnliot when they saw the movement on shore. "My advice is that we waste no more time with lengthy farewells if we hope to get this ship of ours out of the fjord."

Sigtrygg now said every man was to pull for two, "and then we'll see what kind of crew we have raised."

The people on shore were running along the water by this time, shouting at the men on the ship and waving their fists, hurling whatever was to hand, spears and rocks and farm axes, but these fell well short of Sigtrygg and his crew.

"There's not much to worry about," said Asmund, when he saw how the weapons were landing harmlessly in the grey waters, "if that's the best they can do. It's unlikely any of their threats can reach us out here."

But, as they were pulling past the farm's outer buildings, Sigtrygg saw that the Leifssons were launching three of the skiffs which had been laid up on the beach. "Rocks and spears are one thing," he said, "but those boats they are launching are certainly swift enough, and it will not take much for them to outrun us in them."

"I don't see how they can do us much harm," answered Asmund, "since their vessels are so much smaller than our own."

"That only shows how little you know, for a sailing man," said Vragi, who was still holding fast to the helm, though he kept his one good eye peeled shoreward, "for we are undermanned and cannot both row and fight. If they catch us, it will be hard going to keep them off, but if we pause to fight with them, we'll make no more progress to the sea, and then they'll be on us like hounds on a bear."

"I don't think they'll find the going any easier for that," said Arnliot.

Sigtrygg looked back at the three boats and said he thought he could now see who their pursuers were. "In the first skiff are a number of the Leifssons' hired men," he said, "the shepherd and the cowherd and several of the household servants. There are six in all and that is a bit of luck for us, since theirs is the first boat out and is rowing harder than the others. Behind them I see the

Thorkelssons and some of their companions. But they do not seem as keen to catch us as the first boat, for they know that the first to come up with us will find it the hardest going."

"Who is in the third boat?" asked Arnliot.

"That would be Grimkel Vesteinsson's skiff, but she is undermanned, with only ten men, though she can carry twelve. I see Thjodhild's brother, Lambi Gunnarsson, in the prow of her and the other Gunnarssons are helping the Ketilsfjordmen with the rowing. And they are rowing the hardest."

"Then it will go poorly with us, if all three of these boats catch us," said Vragi. "Do you see any others putting to sea?"

"Another boat, maybe two," answered Sigtrygg.

"What of the Norwegian?" asked Vragi.

"There are men around his ship, but I cannot see clearly what they are about."

Now the first skiff came on at a very quick pace, the men in her rowing hard and fast, as they bounded over the face of the sea. Behind that vessel it could be seen that the Ketilsfjordmen were coming up with the Thorkelssons. "If they keep up this pace," said Vragi, "there will be nothing for it, but we turn about and fight. And then it will be anybody's guess how things turn out."

Sigtrygg now said they were to pull in their oars at once. "Let the first skiff come up to us," he said, "before the others are within striking distance."

"What do you have in mind?" asked Vragi.

"I'd rather fight the one boat now, than three or more after they have run us to ground. Besides, these first fellows are not so formidable as those coming after."

Sigtrygg's crew now raised their oars, as he told them, and, in no time, the first skiff found itself plunging headlong into the ship's side, causing the larger vessel to shudder and roll to the left. But the skiff had the harder time of it, for the impact it made upon striking Sigtrygg's ship caused the smaller vessel to fly up onto its prow nearly hurling the men in her into the sea. Then the crew of Sigtrygg's ship took their oars and began to pound at the smaller boat. When those in the skiff realized their predicament, that they were alone against the larger ship without any support, they lost heart and rushed to the farthest end of their vessel, to avoid the hard blows of the ship's oars. But this only swamped their boat, causing her to capsize, and now the sea rushed in, tossing the men on board into the fjord.

"Now we must finish them off," said Arnliot, and he used his oar to smash the skull of the man swimming nearest the ship's side.

But Sigtrygg told them not to waste their time churning up the sea like that, "but pull in your oars and fish these fellows out."

Arnliot replied that, in his opinion, it would be better to put an end to those already in the water "so there will be fewer to contend against us later. But at the least, it is my advice we leave them where they have landed, and then they will slow their fellows when they come up to them, for it is unlikely the Leifssons' kin would willingly part with these servants of theirs."

But Sigtrygg said they must now do exactly as he said, whatever the consequences, "for this will show who has the authority on this ship." And so they pulled out four of the men, who were thrashing about under their oars, but lost the fifth, who by this time had gone under in the cold waters. Now, when they had got the four safely on board, Sigtrygg told his men that things had suddenly gotten a great deal harder for them since they could no longer hope to outrun their pursuers because of this delay. But, he told them they were not to row any less hard than before, "since the Gunnarssons and the Thorkelssons are nearly on us."

Those two boats were now prow to prow and within hailing distance of Sigtrygg's ship and, because they were lighter vessels and more fully manned, there was no way for Sigtrygg to increase the distance between them. Lambi, who was standing up in the prow of his boat, called to them to ship their oars and give over the chase for, he said, there was not much hope they would get off lightly once the Leifssons had laid hands on them, if they persisted in this theft. But Sigtrygg told his men they were to keep rowing and pay no attention to the threats of their pursuers.

Lambi said: "I did not look for this from you kinsman, to run like a coward from a fight of your own choosing. Or was it all a sham to steal that ship of ours?"

Sigtrygg replied that Lambi could think whatever he liked, but would get no more of an answer from him than that, "since it's hard enough work moving this ship with the few men I have. But you might do better in your boat if you pulled at an oar yourself, instead of depending on others."

Sigtrygg now went to the Leifssons' hired men, who had been pulled from the sea and who sat huddled and wet, wrapped in woolen blankets beneath the ship's mast. "It's not likely we'll be putting you ashore anytime soon in these parts," he told them, "so now you must choose how you want to leave this vessel. Either get up and pull at an oar, with the rest of us men, or go back into the sea; and then you can swim home to Brattahlid."

The hired men said they would rather help out on the ship, if they had the choice, than go back into the sea so Sigtrygg put each one at an oar and said they were to row as hard as they could. "Now we are eighteen," he shouted above the crash of the oars to Vragi, who still had his arms locked on the helm, "and that is the price my kinsmen set on this ship of ours, though I doubt they thought we would be paying it in this manner."

But Arnliot said: "Had I known you meant to bring slaves on board, I'd have taken the little maid along with us for I think she'd have been a better companion than any of these."

Now the Thorkelssons and the Gunnarssons were come up hard astern, against the ship; and, though Sigtrygg had got four more rowers than before, they could not pull away fast enough from the two skiffs. Not far behind these, Sigtrygg said he could make out two more boats coming from the shore and that it would not be long till these came up with them, too, if the first two boats succeeded in slowing them down. Vragi said this was most certainly the case and that "now we shall see if this crew of ours is as ready to fight for our ship as they are to sail her."

At this time, Lambi Gunnarsson was leaning across the gulf which lay between him and Sigtrygg's ship, trying to catch hold of the hull. When Vragi saw this, he brought the steering paddle hard to the left so that the ship's stern veered out and away, causing Lambi to lose his footing, and then he would have pitched headlong into the sea but for his brothers, who grabbed him by the waist and held him fast. Seeing how things were Lambi now seized a spear and, planting his feet firmly beneath him, threw it with all his strength at the fleeing ship. It landed hard, amidship, and Sigtrygg asked if anyone had been hurt.

"I have taken a scratch in my side," answered Thorolf the Icelander, "though I won't be tugging at this oar any the less for that."

Sigtrygg went to the man and saw the spear had stuck in his upper leg, the blood already soaking his leggings and forming a dark pool at his feet. "Do you think you can spare this splinter for a few moments, Icelander?" he asked.

Thorolf replied that he would be glad enough to lend it for awhile, if Sigtrygg could think of a better use for it than the one it was now serving. Sigtrygg took his knife and cut the flesh around the spear point, till he had got the head of the spear out of the fatty part of the leg, and then he pulled it free. Thorolf did not cease to pull at his oar during the entire proceeding.

Then Sigtrygg took the weapon in his hand, still wet with Thorolf's blood, and ran aft. He stood on the stern, till he had Lambi clearly in sight and then he hurled the spear down with such force it took Lambi full in the shoulder and pierced him there, toppling him into the sea.

When Lambi fell, the Ketilsfjord men pulled up on their oars and let their skiff spin away from the ship, for every man of them was keen to pull their companion out of the cold waters. But, when they had got their hands on Lambi, and were pulling him back onto the boat, it could be seen that he was already near death, for his eyes were shut fast and his face and limbs were blue as the sea itself, as much from the blood loss as from the icy fjord waters, while the thick wooden shaft of the spear stuck hard in the joint of his shoulder below his neck.

When Thord saw how things had gone with Lambi, he told his men to row less vigorously for he did not think they would be much of a match for the men on the ship if they overtook them alone. He now said he thought it wiser to let the other boats which the Leifssons had sent out come up to them, before they pressed their pursuit.

All of these things the Leifssons saw plainly from the shore and, when they saw Lambi fall, they thought it a very serious loss indeed. Thorkel said this was not what he had expected when he had sent those kinsmen of his out to fetch back his property, for he had now lost a skiff and six good men and finally a man of his own blood. Nor did he see any greater likelihood he would be getting the ship back, for all his losses, "since those who have got her are rowing even harder than before while my own boats are paddling about like lost seals."

Osvif Thorleiksson said that Sigtrygg and his crew were a lot more determined than anyone could have foreseen and he now urged Thorkel to give over the pursuit "for these men are certainly prepared to make a fight of it."

"It's no wonder things have taken such a turn as this," said Grimkel, who had seen what happened to Lambi on the Ketilsfjord skiff, "since they have some very bad fellows in that company."

Thorkel now asked Osvif whether he was prepared to repay him for the guesting he had been given at Brattahlid by putting out to sea with his crew "to run these killers down"?

"My ship's not yet ready for that kind of work since she's been laid up on the beach all this while, with no time to overhaul her," Osvif replied.

"Nevertheless, I think your ship and crew will make shorter work of these outlaws than we Leifssons now can," said Thorkel, "and, besides, I cannot afford to lose any more of my kinsmen."

"You are certainly prepared to part with at least one more," said Osvif, gesturing toward Sigtrygg's ship.

"That may be," answered Thorkel, "but nothing less is likely to bring this matter to an end and restore my property to me. Will you send out your ship?"

Osvif said that he didn't think he could do as Thorkel was asking just then, but advised the Leifssons to send men running down the coast, ahead of the fleeing ship, if they insisted on pursuing the matter; and to have the farmers who lived along the fjord put out, in their own boats, to block Sigtrygg's passage to the open sea. "In that way you will certainly hold your quarry in the trap and then you may wear him down till you can overcome him with the men from this district. But, in my opinion, you would be better off letting him sail out, as he desires, for I think there will be hard fighting and many more dead in the fjord before the chase is done."

Thorkel said this was just what he should have expected from a foreign born man, though he thought he had earned a better reply because of the hospitality he had already provided to Osvif and his crew.

"You certainly didn't scruple to ask us to pay our own way when you were laying out that feast for your neighbors," answered Osvif, "or was that ale I supplied you with less good than what you Greenlanders are used to?"

It was just about this time that Thorkel caught sight of Girstein Eiriksson walking toward him along the shore, fully armed and carrying his long spear. Thjodhild Gunnarsdottir was following close behind him.

"Welcome, kinsman," said Thorkel, "and just in time to persuade this Norwegian shipmate of yours to go after those thieves who are stealing our ship. You are certainly setting a warlike example for these king's courtiers."

"I don't know that I can be of any help, in this matter," Girstein replied, "for everyone knows it is the right of the ship's captain to dispose of his vessel however he likes. And sailing out now when she's been laid up may do more harm to the Norwegian's ship than good for us. Besides, our kinsman has only claimed his own, or do you deny you pledged him that ship he now sails on?"

"A fine thing," said Thorkel, "when a man's own blood will turn from him in his hour of need. And the bravest of those who answer his call must be struck down by those blackguards who are absconding with his property. I did not think to find you wanting, kinsman Girstein, when your own cousin has been speared through the heart, while seeking to defend Brattahlid."

Girstein now asked him whose blood had been shed and Thorkel told him how the first skiff had been overturned and her crew drowned, for Thorkel had not seen any of them pulled out of the sea from where he had been standing on the shore. "And Lambi Gunnarsson has been pierced like an ice bear, with a harpoon thrown from that fleeing ship," he added.

"Who did the killing," asked Girstein, "if, indeed, our kinsman is dead?"

"There's none other but Sigtrygg Thorgilsson can throw a spear like that," said Thorkel, "and now it is your duty, and the duty of every one of our kin, to avenge this blow."

Girstein said that things had certainly gotten out of hand, just as he had feared, and that this only proved the wisdom of letting the ship go peacefully, "although there's not much hope of that now."

He then turned to Osvif and asked him if he were willing to do as Thorkel had requested, "since there is blood spilt now and it is a question of manslaughter."

But Osvif gave the same answer as before, saying he didn't see much to be gained by interfering between the kinsmen, "though the Leifssons would have done better to take my advice in the first place and settle this matter by compromise."

Now Thorkel asked Girstein what he was prepared to do to get revenge for Lambi's killing and Girstein replied that he would do whatever honor required but that he still hoped they would find some more peaceful way to settle this. Then Thorkel told him he was to take the fastest men he could find at Brattahlid and run down the length of the fjord to alert the farmers who lived there to get out their boats and surround the fleeing ship "for," he said, "it is unlikely those thieves can row fast enough to get clear of the fjord before we can shut them in."

Girstein said he would do whatever was needful and he now turned to speak to Thjodhild. But she was already gone, for the boat on which Lambi Gunnarsson lay was rowing in fast toward shore and she had run into the surf to meet it.

Vragi, standing in his place at the ship's helm, asked Sigtrygg whether he could see the same thing that he was seeing.

"That depends," replied Sigtrygg, "if you are talking about those fellows who are trying to outrun us along the shore."

"They are exactly the ones I have in mind," Vragi replied. "What do you think they mean to do?"

"If I were them," said Sigtrygg, "I would try to bring out every boat along these shores and bottle us up in the fjord."

"I would do the same," answered Vragi.

He now began to sniff at the wind and he turned the ship in toward the shore.

"What do you think we ought to do now?" asked Sigtrygg. "It won't be much fun trying to hack our way through these Eiriksfjordmen, once they close off the way to the sea. But I don't see how we can hope to row out of this fjord any faster than we are now doing."

Vragi said they must put up their oars and unfurl the sail.

"There's not enough wind for that," said Sigtrygg, "unless I miss my guess; and, though I am not a sailor, as many have re-minded me before this, I at least know that you cannot hang your sail and row at the same time. In my opinion this will only slow us up and we don't have any time to waste."

"Nevertheless, we must now put up the sail," Vragi insisted, "and then we shall see how things turn out."

Sigtrygg told the crew they were to do as Vragi said and soon enough the ship lay drifting into the land as they pulled out the sail and hung her from the mast, watching it hang loosely above them. About this time Thord Thorkelsson saw that they had changed direction and were drifting toward the land and that two more skiffs were rowing hard out to meet them. Now he urged his own men to row more fiercely, for he said they would soon have enough support to give these interlopers something to worry about.

When the men on board the ship saw the skiffs closing in on them, they got themselves ready with whatever weapons they had brought along and went to the ship's sides. "If we can't outrow them," said Arnliot Keelfoot, "at least they'll know what kind of a fight men like us are prepared to put up. I don't think many of them will think they've seen harder sword play, when this thing's done."

The skiffs came round the ship, but they stayed at a respectful distance. The men in them began to throw their spears at Sigtrygg and his crew. "Put up your shields," said Sigtrygg, "and be ready if they come in to take the ship. Otherwise, let them be."

Arnliot said he would much rather fight back than let these fellows get off scot free, "for I didn't join this crew to be spitted by your kinsmen, while we are still out of sight of the open sea."

"Even so," said Sigtrygg, "I want you to throw nothing back at them whatever the provocation, but wait till they try to come in a little closer, if they are up to it."

When Thord saw that Sigtrygg was not fighting back, he asked if this meant that he was now prepared to row the ship ashore and submit the matter of Lambi's killing to his kinsmen's judgement?

"There's not much hope of that," Sigtrygg replied, "since I didn't fare particularly well, when I was last ashore with you Leifssons, and then it was just a question of a ship."

"In that case," said Thord, "we will have to take back what is ours by force of arms, and then things may go somewhat worse with you than they might have gone otherwise."

Sigtrygg told him they were welcome to try but that he didn't think they'd find it any easier going than Lambi Gunnarsson had found it before them. Now Thord seemed less eager to press the matter, when he heard this, and he began to look about him at the two other skiffs which sat on the sea nearby. The Ketilsfjordmen had already rowed back to the shore, with Lambi and his brothers on board their boat, and it did not seem to Thord that those men who were left with him in the three skiffs were half the fighting men that Lambi alone had been. But Sigtrygg and his following, he knew, had already shown themselves more than willing to shed blood over the matter.

Thord now told his men to row around the ship, to keep her from moving off, while they awaited reinforcements from on shore, for he was certain that Thorkel would soon send other boats to help them bring the ship in, especially when they saw how they now had the ship in their hands.

"This kinsman of yours is a timid sort," said Arnliot, when he saw how Thord was deploying his vessels. "I don't think it will take much to drive him off."

"Then we will use it to our advantage," answered Sigtrygg, "when the time is right. But I don't want you to begin to fight with them unless I say so, for those on shore will now think they have us when they see how we are sitting so still out here. In the meantime, my kinsman is certainly not likely to rush things."

"Yet," said Arnliot, "the longer we delay, the more time they'll have to put their boats out and then there'll be more of them than even we can hold off. And all the while, the farmers down the fjord will be launching their little boats to close us up in this place."

"Even so," answered Sigtrygg, "we can't outrow them, in any event. So we must trust to our luck, instead."

Now, when he said this last, the ship suddenly lurched to one side on a swell and Sigtrygg looked up at the sail. It was puffed out slightly; then another swell seemed to catch them, and the sail widened again.

"I think the wind has changed," said Vragi and he leant into the helm and began to guide the ship before the light wind which was now blowing down off the inland ice.

When Thord saw that they were beginning to sail, he called to his companions to row in on the ship's hull and force it closer to the shore. One of the skiffs made for the prow, but Sigtrygg told his men they were now to gather up the spears, which had been previously thrown against them, and give these back to the men in the skiff. This they did gladly and, when the men in the skiff saw how things were, they began to row as rapidly as they could out of range. Sigtrygg's crew thought this quite funny, except for the four servants of the Leifssons, who did not know what to do since they now found themselves on board a ship which was fighting against their own side.

"If you want to leave, I advise you to do so now," Sigtrygg told them, "for I don't think we will be putting into shore any sooner than before." He said they were free to go over the side and swim to the skiffs, if they were bold enough, but otherwise they had better be prepared to pull their weight, if they wanted to stay on board his ship. None of them made any effort to leave.

"In that case," said Sigtrygg, "you are now to go to your places, for we may need you at the oars before long."

Vragi now tacked leeward and the ship seemed to leap under them, for the wind was now beginning to grow much stronger and it soon filled the entire sail. Vragi took them close into the skiff in which Thord sat so that the men in it now had to row as hard as they could to get out from under the ship's hull or they had been cut in two by the larger vessel. In a moment Sigtrygg's ship had broken out of the circle, which the skiffs had made around her, and the men in the three boats began to row as fiercely as they could in the ship's wake. But now it was clear that the Eiriksfjordmen had waited too long, for the ship easily moved away from them, pushed by the wind.

Thord told the men on board his boat to put up their own mast and sail at once and then he called to the other two crews to do the same. But they replied that they had put out in such haste that they had failed to bring these along so that it was soon clear only Thord's vessel would be able to give chase. His men struggled to raise their mast and pull out the sail but this was slow work and, all the while, Sigtrygg's ship was moving steadily down the fjord. Thord said he thought they had been better off before Lambi was speared, since Grimkel Vesteinsson's skiff, on which Lambi had ridden, was a larger vessel and "would certainly not have been launched without her mast and sail."

Now, try as they might, they could not gain the speed from their sail which Sigtrygg's vessel could command, since his was a sea-going ship and her sail and rigging were well suited to make the most of the wind. Thord urged his crewmen to tighten their own rigging, but they could not close the widening gap which now appeared between them and the fleeing ship, and, soon enough, they could only make out the back of Vragi Skeggjasson's head where he sat in the stern of the ship, his arms wrapped tightly about the steering paddle as he guided the larger vessel before the wind.

"What do you see before us?" Vragi now shouted to Sigtrygg, on board the fleeing ship and Sigtrygg quickly ran up to the ship's prow. When he came back he said he could see a number of skiffs coming toward them from down the fjord, but no boats of any size.

Vragi asked if any of these were raising their sails.

"A few," answered Sigtrygg, "for, no doubt they have noticed the wind, as we have; but it won't do them much good, since this wind is at our backs and not at theirs. Still, it may make it more difficult for us to outrun them when they come up with us. Do you think we will be able to get through?"

"There's not much to be said for my seamanship," answered Vragi, laughing, "if I can't outsail this pitiful fleet. But what is the Norwegian doing?"

"Not much," said Sigtrygg, "for his ship is still on the beach and no one is making any effort to roll it down into the water."

"In that case," Vragi replied, "I don't think your kinsmen will find it as easy a matter as they thought, if they are still intent on cutting us off from the sea."

CHAPTER IX

WHAT HONOR DEMANDS

They now ran before a hard wind, blowing off the inland ice, the ship leaning sharply to port, and the people of Brattahlid fell away swiftly behind them. Those skiffs which Thord commanded were soon left vainly rowing in the ship's wake, as it swept down the center of the fjord and past where the sea's arm bent round the land, on the Brattahlid side. When they had run past that point, the Leifssons' farmhouses disappeared entirely from view, nor could any of the small vessels, which now could be seen coming at them from the shore, get close enough to hail them.

"It's unlikely they can shut us in now," shouted Vragi, "so long as the wind holds; and in my opinion this is no false breeze."

"Then we must not let up until we have made open sea," Sigtrygg replied.

"I won't argue with that," Vragi said, "but I think we must now give some thought to naming this ship of ours, before we have gone much further, for that is the custom in other countries. It would be the height of arrogance to expect a good voyage, if we do not look to our luck now."

Sigtrygg said that, in that case, he wanted to call the ship the Thjodhild. But Vragi advised against this, "for," said he, "I do not think that woman is destined to bring you much luck."

"I'd offer the name of the little serving maid," Arnliot said, "but I did not ask it of her."

"She is called Fridgerd," said Sigtrygg, "but that is no fit name for this ship, however small and bare she is, for she has already carried us out of harm's way and will now take us across the open sea, if this wind holds."

"Then we must name her for her attributes, however humble these appear, for it never pays to be overly proud. And that is especially so when you are sailing on the seas," said Vragi. "And now I propose we call her Gull, for she takes to the wind like one of those birds, and with any luck she will run thus all the way to Vinland."

"Have it your own way," Sigtrygg said, "though I'd have named her otherwise."

The little ship, newly named the Gull, now sped across the face of the fjord, without any slackening of her pace, for the wind was still at their backs and the sea was calm. They easily went past and around the small boats the farmers of Eiriksfjord sent out to nip at their heels and Sigtrygg ranged his crew along the ship's two sides to watch for any boats which might get too close, though there no longer seemed to be much likelihood of that.

Sigtrygg now went up to Thorolf the Icelander, who was sitting somewhat slumped over in his place, and asked him if things had gone well enough, to his way of thinking.

"I'd have been happier to avoid that pin-prick your kinsman gave me earlier," Thorolf replied, "but the wind came up just when it was needed, and that, I think, is a sign of your luck in this matter."

"Then why do you find it so difficult to leave your seat, Icelander?" Sigtrygg asked and Thorolf replied that he preferred to sit where the view was best, and now he let his chin slide onto his chest. Sigtrygg could see that the man was very pale, for the blood he had lost, and he gave orders to the others to lay Thorolf lengthwise in the middle of the ship. Asmund, who had accompanied Thorolf out of Iceland, now asked Sigtrygg if he thought his companion would live.

"That depends," Sigtrygg answered, "on how deep the spear point lodged and how much blood has been lost. But I will certainly do what I can in this matter."

He told the crewmen to bring strips of cloth and he took these and bound up the wound, which was a deep, sideways gash in the man's hip and thigh.

"I have certainly seen worse than this," he said, "but I have seen better, too."

Vragi now told the crew they must look to their posts and leave the healing arts to their ship's skipper, "for Sigtrygg knows, better than most, what harm a spear can do and how to stanch the blood flow, if that can be done."

Asmund said: "It would be an ill thing for this man to lose his life when there is but one year left to his outlawry, and we could as easily have stood in Greenland, however harsh the country."

Sigtrygg now put water on the man's lips and piled the remaining cloth under his head, saying there was not much else to be done, till they could bring the Gull to land. But Asmund stood over his friend, without speaking, until Sigtrygg sought to rise and then he held out his hand to him. Sigtrygg grasped it firmly and drew himself to his feet.

At that moment they heard a loud voice shouting at them and, when they looked up, they could see that it was Vragi. His voice had an urgent tone to it, too, and every man of them now looked out over the ship's bow, on the starboard side, in the direction in which he seemed to be pointing. Vragi said: "Hop to, lads, for there is a vessel not far up ahead which is coming out to greet us. And she is a sailing ship."

Sigtrygg asked him what he had seen and where and Vragi told him he had only to look for himself, "for the sail is there for all to see, heading out from the land."

Sigtrygg could now make out the ship, too. She was not much bigger than the Gull and leaning to starboard as she ran across the face of the wind, making right for them. Her crew was rowing vigorously to offset the Gull's advantage, with the wind at her stern. "I did not think they could put out a ship so large in this short a time," said Sigtrygg, "nor do I see how we can hope to outrun them, now."

"It would have taken a man of great speed and stamina to get this far ahead of us by land," Vragi said, "to give them the time to launch her. Yet, perhaps, they have not fitted her out as well as they might."

He now pulled hard on the helm and told the crew to get to their places by the oars, for they must do whatever they could to push the Gull ahead of the wind. Sigtrygg seated himself in Thorolf's place and took his oar, and every man of them did as much, for the new ship was closing rapidly with them since it was fully crewed and its men were fresh.

"I think we shall have some hard fighting, afterall," Arnliot said, "and I, for one, am not sorry for that. It was not manly to fly from these Eirikssfjord farmers without striking a few blows."

"There'll be plenty of opportunity for blows now," Sigtrygg agreed, "though I think it had been better to leave this place in quieter fashion."

The second ship was soon running alongside the Gull, to starboard, and within hailing distance. The men on board her began to shout, but Sigtrygg and his crew offered no response. Now a man in full war gear stood up on the other ship's deck, his helmet glinting brightly in the Greenland sun, and he asked where Sigtrygg might be found.

"I'm at the oars, like the rest of my crew," Sigtrygg shouted back, "but who is asking?"

The man answered that there was no one there with any more right to be asking than Girstein Eiriksson, and now he said Sigtrygg must drop sail and row back to Brattahlid, "for our kinsman's blood has been shed and compensation must be paid for it."

"There's no use hoping for that," Sigtrygg replied, "or do you think I took this ship out on the fjord for nothing more than a pleasure cruise in the warm morning sun?"

"It does not matter what purpose you had in mind, kinsman," Girstein said, "for Lambi has been speared like a walrus coming up out of the ice for air, and there must be a payment for that."

"In that case," answered Sigtrygg, "you would do well to look to that spear which struck him down, for I gave him back only what he first sought to give to me. And we have a man on board who is now near death because of that blow."

Girstein said that all of this must be sorted out with the Leifssons at Brattahlid and he told them to turn their vessel about, "for otherwise I am charged to take your ship and the men on board her."

"Then you will find it harder going than you had cause to think before, kinsman, for we are making for the open sea, whatever anyone else says."

Girstein now told his helmsman to steer into Sigtrygg's ship and snap her oars and the two ships slid toward each other, side against side. Vragi told the Gull's crew to ship their oars at once and he pulled hard on the rudder, driving the ship's stern against Girstein's vessel. At this, Girstein's crew let fly their spears and, with these, grappling hooks to catch the Gull's side. But Vragi caught the sea's swell with his turn and his ship rose up above the other and the hooks fell into the sea.

Girstein said: "We will ram and sink you kinsman, if you don't heave to, so we can board that ship of yours."

"Certainly one of us will sink the other," Sigtrygg agreed, "and then we will see who cares most to finish his journey."

Girstein told his crew to come about and drive their prow into Sigtrygg's vessel, but Vragi had held the ship too close to the other for that, giving them no maneuvering room. "Jump the distance between our two boats, if you've a mind to," Vragi shouted laughing at them, "for you'll never get any closer to us than this."

Girstein now said that if Sigtrygg had any hopes of getting a settlement with his kinsmen, he must give over his flight and the ship now, "for blood must first be assuaged, before other matters can be settled, whatever the causes of that mishap when you tried to sail past Brattahlid."

"This is certainly a different song than I heard from you when you helped me get hands on my ship," Sigtrygg replied. "Or do you now wish to undo that deed of yours which opened the Leifssons' boat house to me, where my property was hid?"

"The only way now, kinsman," said Girstein, "is to make good the slaying of Thjodhild's brother which, if I'd had my way, had been the deed left undone."

"And what does Thjodhild say to that?" asked Sigtrygg.

"She did not speak when they rowed Lambi in, but I saw her weeping in the surf," was Girstein's reply. "And that, too, is no light debt which now must be repaid."

"Was it for her brother then or me, that she shed those tears?" asked Sigtrygg.

"Both," said Girstein, "for you threw the weapon which took his life. Now give over that ship of yours and I will offer to stand by you and get the best settlement I can, though it's unlikely any of the men aboard your ship, even if dead, will be accounted the equal of Lambi Gunnarsson."

Vragi now asked Sigtrygg if he wanted to lower their sail, but Sigtrygg said they were to keep on, just as before, "and then we'll see if my kinsman's crew has the stuff which our boys have."

The two ships now ran before the wind, each trying to gain advantage over the other. Vragi told them to pull at the rigging and tighten up the sail, but Girstein's vessel held just as close to them as before, despite this, and then the Eiriksfjordmen began to move out ahead of them. Girstein shouted, "I don't see how you can hope to outsail me, kinsman, for I have spent these last years travelling about on ships, while you have been walking the ice," and he urged his helmsman to steer into Sigtrygg's ship in hopes of turning her into the wind.

Sigtrygg told his crew they must take out whatever weapons they had brought with them, "for now there will be fighting," and he ran to the ship's starboard side, his sword and shield raised.

"It would be better to cut the ropes which hold their sail," said Vragi, "but that is no light feat, and I've not seen it done on a moving ship since I was a young man."

"Where is the best place for that?" Sigtrygg asked.

Vragi replied that they must cut through the ropes which held the sail to the ship's frame "and that is near the sail's base, for there's no hope of cutting her higher than that."

Sigtrygg now asked for all the spears which they had on board and Asmund collected these, both those which they had carried onto the ship and those which others had thrown against them, and Sigtrygg laid them hastily out on the deck. Then he bent down and looked them over and selected the two which he thought best suited for his purpose. He chose a long spear with a very broad blade and a shorter one, which he held carefully in his hands, testing its weight and balance. He also took a small axe and thrust it into his belt, after which he gave his sword and shield to Asmund and told him to go stand at the ship's prow and "be prepared to make a fight of it." He then took a length of rope and wound it around his waist, and then he went up behind the Icelander, looping the other end of his rope around the peak of the Gull's prow.

"Let them run out ahead of us," Sigtrygg said, and his crew dropped their oars deep below the water line and held them there for a single stroke. At this, Girstein's ship suddenly lurched ahead of the Gull and Girstein, when he saw they had taken the lead, told his rowers they were now to turn across the Gull's path and drive the fleeing ship back into the wind.

With a great shout, the Eiriksfjordmen pulled up their oars on the port side, but stroked harder to starboard, and their helmsman cut the rudder so that the ship which Girstein sailed now slammed its side up against Sigtrygg's prow, rocking that vessel from stem to stern and sending a shiver through the beams which held her together. Asmund lost his footing where he stood but Sigtrygg, who was right behind him, pushed him forward, nearly into the Eiriksfjord ship. When the Eiriksfjordmen saw that Asmund was hanging over their vessel, with his sword raised, they rushed to attack him and now he had hard going against the swords and spears they were thrusting at him. Sigtrygg stood in close behind him but kept well out of the reach of the swordsmen on the other ship.

When he saw that the momentum of the two ships had brought them close enough, and all the Eiriksfjord crew, on that side of the ship, were trying to get at Asmund, Sigtrygg took the long spear he had chosen earlier and reached out from behind the Icelander and snagged the other ship's rigging with the broad side of the blade. Then he began to pull at it, cutting it through.

Girstein was standing forward of the mast and now, when he saw what Sigtrygg was trying to do, he ran into the melee, shouting at his men to seize the spear from Sigtrygg's hands, rather than continuing to exchange useless sword strokes with Asmund at the ship's prow. When they heard these words and saw Sigtrygg's blade doing its work, Girstein's crew left off worrying Asmund and began at once to strike, with all their weapons, at the shaft of Sigtrygg's long spear. Girstein, himself, now seized a blanket of wadmal and threw it over the spear point and then he threw a line of rope over that. All the men of his crew then flung themselves onto the long spear and began to contend with Sigtrygg for the weapon, so that Sigtrygg was no longer able to maintain his grip on it. With one final tug, they pulled it out of his hands and into their ship.

Then Sigtrygg pulled tight on the rope with which he had bound himself to his ship's prow and leaped onto the gunwale, the smaller spear in his right hand. Balancing himself precariously on that narrow ledge with the rope taut, he now stretched himself to his full height and raised the second spear over his head. Then he hurled it hard into the deck of the Eiriksfjord ship, over the heads of that ship's crew. There it struck, deep in the planking, with a loud thud and, there, too, the rope which bound the lower part of the sail to the ship's hull, on the starboard side, leapt apart, split by the spear's edge, leaving the sail flapping uselessly in the wind at its lower end. Then Sigtrygg ran swiftly up along the ship's rail, before anyone on the other ship could act, and struck with his axe at the nearer rope, severing that one, as well, so that the sail came completely away from the lower bonds which held it.

"Now row us backwards, as quickly as you can," Sigtrygg commanded and his crew reversed their oar strokes, pulling their vessel back and away from the other ship.

"That was well-done," cried Vragi, "for I have seen it cut with sword or axe, but never by spear throw. And that on the first cast."

Girstein, when he saw what had occurred, told his crew to row their ship about, after Sigtrygg, but Vragi now guided the Gull away from the struggling Eiriksfjord vessel, and the Eiriksfjorders must row hard behind, if they would overtake them.

"Let each man apply himself to his own oar now," Vragi said to the men on board Sigtrygg's ship, "and give this wind some help; then we'll see what our little bird can do," and he guided them out and away from the other vessel. The Gull now sailed on ahead, for Girstein's men must first tie down their loosened sail before they could hope to make the most of the wind again, which was now blowing steadily and strongly off the inland ice. And, though it did not take them overlong to repair their rigging, the Gull rushed on before them, seizing the lead and holding it thereafter.

Sigtrygg told his crew members they must now hold to their purpose and not let up on the oars, "for it is unlikely they will let me do to them again, what we have now accomplished, if once they catch up with us hereafter," he said, and everyone on board agreed that this was certainly the case.

Thus, it happened that Sigtrygg and his crew took their ship out of Eiriksfjord, though Girstein Eiriksson pursued them hotly, until they were well past Eirik's Isle, which lies at the mouth of the fjord, and were come into the open sea. Then Girstein let up the chase and hove to, for he said there was no use taking a shipload of farmers into unknown parts, adding that it was "not unlikely the harsh western sea will do our work for us, in any event."

PART 2

ACROSS THE WESTERN SEA

CHAPTER X

LANDFALL

Once he was certain no other ships would follow, Sigtrygg told Vragi that he wanted them to make for the north "since we are so short of provisions." Then they sailed slowly along the Greenland coast until they came to an area which was teeming with wild life, both birds and seals and reindeer, along the coast. Sigtrygg now told them they were to put in on the lee side of a nearby island and then he divided his men into three groups. He left Vragi and five others on board their ship, to see to her safekeeping, but split the remaining twelve of them into two parties. The first group he told to walk along the island's beach and gather what eggs and small game they could find and fill their water sacks. But Arnliot and Asmund and three others he said were to go off with him, to see if there was anything bigger worth taking.

Now about this time, the servants of the Leifssons, who had come along only through ill luck, got up their courage and asked Sigtrygg what he had in mind for them since they were certainly not willing participants in this enterprise of his. The man they appointed to speak for them was a certain Olvir, who was Thorkel Leifsson's chief steward and who had charge of all household matters at Brattahlid. He said: "We four now want to know when you are proposing to let us go back to our homes, for we are not the kind of men you will want along with you on this voyage. We are neither fighting men, nor hunters, nor are we experienced on ship board, though you have put us to work at the oars like common sailors. Besides, we think things will certainly go a whole lot harder for you, with the Leifssons, if you compound your crime against such important men by abducting us against our will."

Sigtrygg said: "It was not my wish that you row out to join my ship, as you have done, but things have certainly turned out better for you than you had a right to expect, since we pulled you out of the sea when we might as easily have done otherwise. And, if you wanted to go back to your homes, you had every opportunity to do so before this."

"Nevertheless," said Olvir, "now the chase is done, it seems to us you can return us to Eiriksfjord without taking much risk, and that is only the right thing to do."

"I don't see that I have any obligation to do that," answered Sigtrygg, "for, truth be told, I am not minded to take any further risks with my ship. And besides, I am still short a few crew members and you men can help me with that."

"We servants of the Leifssons," said Olvir, "are not eager to see these strange places, which lie over the western sea and which you are so intent on finding, for we have heard there is a great deal of danger in those lands and we are peaceful men. But if you take us back to our homes now, there is every chance that Thorkel Leifsson and his kin will look more kindly on you than you have otherwise given them reason to do. As for us, we will certainly speak up in your behalf."

Arnliot now said that he thought these men were obviously not fit to travel in their crew "for they are the most timid and cowardly sort of fellows I have ever met. My advice is that we leave them right here on this island, when we are through with this place, and let them find their own way back to Eiriksfjord, if they are up to it."

Many others in the crew now said the same thing, for they were not overjoyed to be sharing their ship and goods with members of the Leifssons' household.

Olvir said they would accept this arrangement, if they had to, so long as they had a chance of getting back to Brattahlid.

"You are certainly eager to return to serving your betters," said

Sigtrygg, "and maybe that is how it should be. But I think that leaving you out here, to fend for yourselves, is unlikely to hasten your return to Brattahlid. Unless some ship happens by, I think you will have very little chance of staying alive until you can find your way home again. And then it would seem to me that I had had a hand in your deaths. In my opinion, the best thing for you men is to stay on board ship with us and see what kind of sailors we can make of you."

Olvir said that was certainly the last thing any of them would wish, for they numbered a cowherd and a shepherd and a simple laborer in their midst, and none of these had any desire to try his luck on the seas. "We are neither overly clever nor overly bold, sir," said Olvir, "and we don't think you will find much cause to rejoice in our company, when things get rough."

Sigtrygg said they would have to let him be the judge of that and now he told Olvir he was to join himself to the hunting party, which Sigtrygg planned to lead, and the others were to divide up among the other two groups. Olvir went along with this very unwillingly, complaining all the way, as Sigtrygg took them to the other side of the island. But Arnliot thought it great sport and kept prodding the steward with the point of his spear.

Now they came to a beach which was dark with seals and Sigtrygg told them they were to advance as quietly as possible. They were to break into a run at the sleeping creatures only when he gave the word, he said, and then they were to spear as many of the biggest as they could find, "but leave the young ones and the females alone, for they will return to the sea and breed more of their kind for next year's hunting."

They crept up as close as they could get, until the wind shifted and brought their scent to the sleeping creatures, and then one large bull looked up, giving the alarm. Then the seals began to move like a slow, dark landslide across the face of the beach and Sigtrygg said they must run into the midst of the animals and kill what they could. Arnliot was the first into the herd and he began laying about with his spear until he was covered with the bellowing creatures' splattered blood. The other men also began striking here and there at the fleeing animals and soon they too were drenched in seal blood. Most of the beasts made it safely back into the sea, but the men got a good catch nonetheless and now Sigtrygg said they must skin and flay the meat and pack it with salt, for he thought this would carry them as far across the western sea as they had to go.

But when he looked for Olvir, he found him leaning on his spear at the edge of the beach, for he had been unable to bring himself to join in the hunt. "I'm not much good at such bloody work," he said, "for even at home I'm the last one to help out when the time comes for butchering the stock. Thorkel Leifsson often says it's a good thing I've a better head for managing the affairs of his house than most, or I'd be out in the cold when winter came, since I'm so little use to him in the cattle and sheep houses."

"You'll find," said Sigtrygg, "that, on a ship, the man who doesn't carry his weight often finds it hardest to fill his belly." And then he told Olvir to make himself useful by cutting the dead animals into strips, for salting.

When they were as fully provisioned as Sigtrygg thought necessary, he told Vragi that, in his opinion, there wasn't much reason for them to put off crossing the sea any longer, "if you know the way to Vinland."

"A great many people must think they know the way," Vragi answered, "for the passage was much talked about in your grandfather's time. But not many people have found their way there since. Yet, I have heard one thing and another about this journey, and made inquiries, so that I think I am as capable as any to guide us in the right direction."

Then Arnliot said: "The way is well-enough known, for there are three lands we must pass to come to our destination and each one is well described in the old tales. First we must cross to the country of flat stones, a barren and forbidding land, and from there we are to journey south to the country of forests and long

white beaches, or so I have heard. Then we have one more crossing, and that must bring us to Vinland. After that we must sail till
an island can be seen to our north and the landing place is then
not far, but can be seen from atop the island."

"This accords well enough with what I have heard," answered
Vragi, "though I doubt the voyage is as simple as this or it had
been sailed a great deal more often than it has."

"Nevertheless," said Sigtrygg, "I now think the best way to
test these directions is to try them out."

Since there was no one with any better proposal, they now
agreed to make preparations for their passage across the western
sea. Sigtrygg told each of the crew what his job on the sea voyage
was to be and, when he came to Arnliot, he said he should pull the
oar amidship, for there his strength would be put to the best use.
But the big Ketilsfjordman said he thought he would be most
useful at the helm, for he was larger and stronger than any other
man in the crew, should they encounter rough seas, "while Vragi
Skeggjasson is certainly too tired to handle such an important position, once we have set sail."

Sigtrygg said he thought Vragi was a better seaman than any
of the rest of them and that they would need his kind of experience, if they hit rough weather. But Vragi now said that Arnliot
had not been misguided in his advice, "for I am not as spry as I
used to be, and the helm is a post which should belong to younger
men. Besides, I have the feeling that farmer Torfi's son will prove
somewhat handy at this, or at whatever else he puts his mind to."

"In that case," said Sigtrygg, "I won't stand in his way, so long
as you agree to act as our pilot."

"Willingly," Vragi said.

They now put out from the island where they had sheltered
their ship, rowing away from the land until they had got a north-
easterly wind and then Vragi told them to put up their sail. Now
there is not much to speak of, for they got a calm sea and passed
over rather quickly and without incident until they raised land.
The first thing they saw was a high ice sheet in the distance and,

when they got close enough, they could see that the country which lay under it was all flat rocks and empty.

"This is just as the old tales describe it," said Sigtrygg, and he made them put into the land for fresh water.

Now while they were exploring this country, a strong wind came up and it blew a gale off the sea, driving their ship up against the rocks and this happened so suddenly that they had no chance to make any provision for it. Vragi said he hadn't noticed the signs of the storm coming, because he was unfamiliar with the seas in that part of the world. But now they had all they could do to get the ship away from the rocks and Sigtrygg said they had best put their backs into it, for there weren't any forests nearby for wood to mend their ship, if she were to take damage. Then, he said, they would be stranded in that useless country over winter, which would certainly be no less harsh than those winters which trouble the Greenland wastes.

They put ropes on the ship, fore and aft, and tried to hold her in the wind, but the sea surged up under the ship's hull and drove her onto the shore. Two of the Leifssons' servants took serious injuries at this time, but Olvir did everything he could to help Sigtrygg and the others. The end of it was that the ship was only lightly damaged, when the storm passed, and Sigtrygg said they must make quick work repairing her and be out of that country as soon as they were able, "for it is certainly getting late in the season to be cruising about on these seas."

Olvir took care of his two companions and, around this time, Thorolf the Icelander began to grow stronger and was soon up and about. Sigtrygg now told him to help Olvir with his work, and he and Asmund did everything they could for the Leifssons' servants. When the ship was ready, they got the injured men on board her and set sail due south, across the open sea.

They now sailed for a number of days and the sea was a lot rougher than before. Vragi made them take down the sail several times, out of fear the strong winds would damage it or blow them about too harshly on the ocean. Still, they made their way steadily south until they again sighted land, though this country did not appear to be much better than the first. It was also barren and empty and Sigtrygg said this was certainly not what they had expected after leaving the land of flat rocks, "for the tales say we are to look for forests and white beaches."

"Perhaps this is the first land we were to find," said Vragi, "and not the second; if so, we have only to hold our course and then we will come to the right landmarks."

Arnliot said that in his opinion this country was worth even less than the last one they had visited.

They now bore southeast along the coast and, after awhile, they thought the land began to look better than when they had first raised it, for they could see some poor looking trees, along the shoreline, and rivers emptying into the ocean.

"This certainly cannot be Vinland," said Arnliot, "for it is too harsh looking. Yet it begins to improve, the further down the coast we sail."

"Then we must go on," said Vragi.

They passed along that extensive coast, on their starboard side, and all the while they could see that the trees were growing thicker and taller, until they thought they had certainly made their second landfall. "This country is thickly wooded and overgrown," they said, "just as the old sailing directions foretold."

But Vragi said: "In my opinion, we have not yet found Markland, for this country is all one with our second landfall, which was a harsh and useless country. But Markland, they say, is a land entirely unto itself."

"Yet, the tales may be wrong," answered Sigtrygg, "or misremembered, for it has been quite a number of years since anyone has sailed out this way to tell about it."

"Still, we must look for another landfall, and then we will know what we have found."

Then they continued their journey, putting in here and there along the wild country which lay on their starboard side, to take on fresh water and see what manner of land they had come upon. They found no signs of human habitation, but plenty of beasts, and Sigtrygg said that he thought the hunting would be good if they wanted lay up there for awhile. But Vragi replied that he didn't think they had the time for that, since he thought the seas were already becoming pretty untrustworthy "and there's no telling how rough they're likely to become in this part of the world, once the winter is on us."

Now they had already been out for several weeks and were concerned that the weather had already begun to change for the worse, with all the rough seas they were beginning to see. Accordingly they held to their course, continuing to bear southwardly, until they came, one day, to a point where the land fell away from them to the west. But to the south and east, they could make out what looked to be another landfall entirely. Now Vragi said they had to decide whether they were to follow the same land they had been sailing along, on its westerly turn, or set out still following the same southerly course, to see what sort of land this new country might be.

Sigtrygg said: "If you are right, and this land we have been sailing by is one with our first landfall, then we have yet to find Markland, in which case that is as likely to lie directly south of us, as not."

"Then," said Vragi, "I think we should put the matter to the crew and see where most of them think we ought to be heading."

"There's no need for that," Sigtrygg answered him, "since you are along as our pilot and have so much more experience in these matters than the rest of us. In my opinion, we ought now to be sailing in the direction where you think Markland is most likely to be found."

"Then we sail south," said Vragi. And so they did.

They now sailed out from the land and into open waters until they came up with the second land. They made for it and at once began to sail down its coast, which lay on their port side. Now they could see that this land quickly became much more pleasant than the one they had just left. It was just as forested as the other, but it had the long white beaches which seemed to go on without ending which the old sailing directions had promised, and its trees seemed larger than those they had now left behind in the previous land.

"In my opinion," said Sigtrygg, "this is certainly more likely to be Markland than that other country." Everyone now agreed and Vragi said they must follow the white sandy beaches as far as these took them "and then we will see what lies before us."

Accordingly, they stayed on course, with Markland to port, for a good many days and everyone thought that this was the best country they had seen so far, though it did not look very hospitable for sheep and cattle, since, as Olvir said, "It is certainly too heavily forested for that."

"Yet, we will find plenty of wood for ship building, if that's what we need," said Vragi.

Arnliot answered that, "in any case, these trees will make a good cargo for us to take back, when we return to Greenland."

It now seemed to them that the long white beaches would never come to an end, but eventually this land, too, fell away from them, this time to the east. Vragi said: "Now we are faced with the same problem as before, whether to follow the land or strike out across the open sea, for there's no telling how dangerous the seas are likely to become this time of the year."

"I think we should settle it just as we did the last time," said Sigtrygg, "and leave the decision up to you."

"In that case, I think we must stay on our southerly course, because Vinland lies past Markland, as the story has it. Therefore, if this is Markland, we have yet another landfall to make."

They now put to sea once more and were out two days with no sign of land. Each man gazed anxiously at the horizon, for they had not been overly keen to leave the good Markland country behind them and venture out again into strange waters. While they were still searching thus for signs of a third landfall, Vragi suddenly announced that he thought things were about to get much worse for them, "for I don't like the way the wind is shifting."

"We had better turn back to Markland, in that case," said Arnliot, "for it's no use facing another storm out here, with no better prospects of finding shelter than we have now."

"We've come this far," Sigtrygg said, "so there's no reason to think about turning back."

"Nevertheless," said Arnliot, "we know there's land only two days' sail in the direction we have just come from, and that good enough for sheltering in a storm, with plenty of trees if we need to make repairs to the ship. But, we don't yet know what lies before us. If another storm catches us here, we may find it somewhat harder to come to Vinland than we had otherwise expected."

They went on like this for awhile, each pressing the merits of his case, but it was soon quite clear that Sigtrygg had no intention of giving in, whatever the risks to them on the open sea. Most of the crew thought Arnliot was making the most sense, but Sigtrygg said he thought they could not be far off from a third landfall, since they had been following the sailing directions so closely. Now Arnliot said that, since the crew was in agreement with him, the best thing to be done was turn their craft around and return to Markland, until the seas were calm again, and that he was in the best position to do this since he had the helm.

"I don't think that will do you as much good as you hope," Sigtrygg replied, "since few men can steer and defend themselves at the same time, even if they are as big as you are."

"Hard choices make for hard testing," said Arnliot, and now he prepared to turn the ship about.

At this point, Vragi stepped between these two and told them they would find it more profitable to pay closer attention to the sights and sounds on the ocean than to one another's harsh words, "for, unless I miss my guess, those are sea birds out ahead of us and, as everyone knows, you don't find them on the open sea but only when there is land nearby."

"Then we had better run for it," answered Sigtrygg, "for I have now been at sea long enough to smell a storm rising, as well as any old-timer, when the seas break up as they are now doing." And he left off bandying words with his helmsman.

They now tightened their rigging and put out the oars and made for where the birds could be seen circling in the sky. They came to land shortly thereafter, and none too soon, for the seas now turned stormy again and they had to run into the nearest harborage for shelter. This storm blew, on and off, for three days and they were unable to venture out of the haven which they had found until the third day. When they did come out, the coast where they had beached was covered with ocean debris and Sigtrygg asked Vragi if he thought this could be Vinland.

"It certainly could," Vragi agreed, "though it is rather bleak here and nothing like the stories we have heard about that country."

Sigtrygg now said they were to divide up and see what the land was like, and so they did. After they had spent three days more exploring the countryside, Vragi said to Sigtrygg that they now had another choice before them.

"If this is Vinland," he said, "then there is plenty of land here for the taking and good harborage; you may as well settle here as anywhere else. But, if not, then we have already wasted a great deal of our time in this place, since the seas seem to be getting rougher, the longer we wait. So we may as well sail as soon as possible and follow the lay of the land, southwards, to see where we come to."

Sigtrygg said he had no desire to make his claim anywhere else but where Leif Eiriksson had built his houses and now he asked Vragi if he thought he could find these.

"According to the old sailing directions," said Vragi, "we are to sail until we see an island to the north; and then we must make for it, since the place where Leif landed lay past a headland, to the west of that island."

"In that case," said Sigtrygg, "I don't see why we are spending any more time in this place than we already have, whatever country it is."

They now went back aboard ship and followed the coast as far as it would take them. The country looked rugged to them, but not inhospitable, however they made no further attempts to land until the shore line began to turn off to the west. Then Sigtrygg asked Vragi if he thought they ought to continue to follow that land or again put out to sea.

"This time I think we should stay close to the land for, if this is Vinland, who knows if there will be any land beyond this point? But, if not, at least we shall get a better sense of the country we have now found."

Accordingly, Sigtrygg told them to put into the land and they spent the night there and took on fresh water. Then, on the following day, they took to their ship again and sailed west, along the lie of the land. Now it happened that the coast they were following began to turn back to the north, after they had been at sea for a short while, and so they turned northwards too, steering close in to the shore line.

"It doesn't look like we will have gained much from travelling around this shore," said Sigtrygg, when they had gone a ways up the coast, "if it takes us back north, to where we have already been."

"In that case," said Vragi, "at least we shall know if we have found an island here or if this country is part of some other land."

While they were thus engaged, Olvir asked if anyone could see the same thing he was seeing.

"What's that?" Sigtrygg said.

"I'm not sure," he replied, "but it seems to me I can see birds flying to the north and west of us."

"What else can you see in that direction?" Sigtrygg asked.

"I thought I saw the top of a mountain."

Sigtrygg now climbed out on the ship's prow and remained there for short while. When he came down he went directly to where Olvir was standing and lifted him up off the deck. Then he threw him onto a pile of ropes and other gear which had been stored there.

"What have I done to you to warrant such harsh treatment?" Olvir asked. But he made no move to rise, for he was frightened by Sigtrygg's unusual behavior.

"Not a thing," Sigtrygg answered. "I merely wanted to see what kind of a man you were and whether or not you had become any stronger since you began sailing with us, for you have certainly become more useful, the longer you have been on board."

Vragi asked Sigtrygg what he had seen.

"Not as much as our friend Olvir," Sigtrygg admitted, "for there are no birds out there, unless this man's eyes are a good deal sharper than my own. But there is certainly land to the north of this coast, and it has the look of an island, just as the old tales have it."

CHAPTER XI

A NIGHT'S WATCH

Sigtrygg now told Arnliot to steer out from that shore, which they had been sailing under, and make for the open sea, to the north and west of their position, and Vragi had the crew adjust the sail's rigging to make the most of that wind which was then blowing behind them from the south and east. But, when they had gone about two thirds of the way toward the island, and everyone on board could now see clearly where it seemed to rise sharply out of the sea before them, the wind suddenly died down and left them drifting.

"There's no use waiting for this wind to come back," Sigtrygg told them, "if that is the island which marks the way to our intended landfall, for we are certainly capable of rowing a good deal farther than it now lies before us."

Vragi replied that it made no sense for them to expend themselves on such hard rowing and counseled that they now let the ship drift awhile, "until we get a proper wind." But Sigtrygg was impatient and said they were to put their backs into the oars "as though my kinsmen were yet rowing hotly in our wake." So they lowered the oars again into the sea and struck the swells with the oar blades with that same spirit they had shown before, when they departed Eiriksfjord.

Now they had hard rowing, for the island rose high above the ocean's surface and proved to be a great deal farther off than it had, at first, appeared. But Sigtrygg said they were not to let up in their efforts, whatever the distance between them and their destination, and every man of that crew pulled at his oar with the same vigor that Sigtrygg, himself, showed. When they had gotten closer to the land, they could make out the ocean birds which commonly circled about the skies of such places and they could see the forest greenery that swathed the steep island hillsides. Sigtrygg told Arnliot to steer for the sand on the beach, between two shoals which guarded the way, and the strong oar strokes of the crew soon brought their vessel hurtling up onto the soft, sandy shore. There the ship stuck fast in the wet sand and the men jumped from the vessel and fell to, beside her hull, on either side, in the loose ground which their feet found there. They were well-spent from their exertions and, save for Arnliot, who had passed his time at the helm, and Sigtrygg, himself, there was no man of them who now made any effort to rise from the place in which he had thrown himself down.

Vragi, too, lay quietly for a brief time and then he got to his feet and said: "That was poorly done, for a ship's skipper, since you asked so much from your crew that too little is left, should some unforeseen need now arise. Nor is it wise to strike an unknown beach in this fashion, when no man of us may know what lies beneath the surface of these shallow waters. Or was it for some other purpose you urged my involvement in this enterprise, than to guide you in the proper handling of your vessel?"

Sigtrygg laughed and said there was no use denying the purpose for which Vragi had been engaged, but that the sight of the island had gotten the better of him, after such a long voyage as they had just had. "Yet, I will certainly look to your counsel as regards this ship of ours, hereafter, if you are still willing to offer it."

Vragi replied that he had no intention of holding back, since they had come so far, but that he thought there would come a time when Sigtrygg's eagerness would lead him to disregard his advice again, "and that will cause you no little harm."

Sigtrygg now said he thought it advisable for them to go up to the highest point on the island and have a look around, noting that the old tales spoke of a landfall which could be seen from atop just such an island as the one they now found themselves on. "Besides," he added, "it's always best to get the lay of a strange country, in case there are enemies about."

Few in the crew showed much interest in this new enterprise, for they had not yet fully recovered themselves from the race to shore, which Sigtrygg had urged them to. Thus, he set off alone towards the tall grass which grew inland along the island's beaches. He had not gone far when he heard the steady stride of footsteps behind him and, turning, he saw that Arnliot Keelfoot meant to accompany him. Arnliot carried his long-handled war axe at his shoulder. When he came up to Sigtrygg, he grinned, after his fashion, and shifted the axe from one shoulder to another.

"I don't see how you can expect to give much of an account of yourself, if there are enemies about," he said, "when you go off into unfamiliar terrain without so much as a sword at your belt. I, at least, do not make it a point to leave my war tools on board ship, where they are likely to do me the least good."

"In my opinion," Sigtrygg replied, "that axe of yours is better suited for felling trees than hewing at enemies, which often require a subtler stroke. But it can't hurt to bring it along, since no one knows the size of the bushes we are likely to find blocking our path."

These two now made their way up the rugged slope and were soon in a wooded region of the island which was so overhung with trees that little of the sun's bright light shone through. Sigtrygg said that he thought Arnliot would find more than sufficient foes in this place, against which to wield his two-edged axe, and said he should now attack a number of the trees to see what kind of wood they were made of. Arnliot stepped into a small clearing, around which several trees were clustered, and he swung the axe in a great circle. With each stroke he cut into one of the trees which surrounded him, rarely striking the same tree twice in a row, until he stood alone in the clearing amidst the fallen carcasses of his green-shrouded foes. Sigtrygg counted seven felled trees and said he thought this exceedingly well-done, "since most men would have found one of these trees hard-going."

Arnliot replied that it was often the case that the measure of the tree was the measure of the man and Sigtrygg agreed that this might be so. "And now we have somewhat more cargo to carry aboard ship than we had before," he added, reminding his companion of their true purpose on the island.

They now pressed hard through the forest till they had made their way to the island's summit and there they cleared away the undergrowth which obscured their view. The clear sky above them, and the brightly shining sun, were soon made fully visible by the work of Arnliot's axe and Sigtrygg went out onto an overhang of rock at the clearing's edge to look about the place. He could now see that they had, indeed, come to a large island, for there appeared to be grey ocean in every direction. "In my opinion, we are now not far from our intended landfall," he said after a little while, "since there is that which appears to be a headland, lying to the west of this island, and that is where my ancestor, Leif Eiriksson, was said to have put in with his ship, if the old sailing directions are to be believed."

"In that case, there's no use trying to prove them by standing about and wrestling with this island's trees," Arnliot replied, "since we have already seen they are no match for a good Norseman's axe."

Sigtrygg agreed that this was probably so and, after he had gazed for a time at the somewhat shapeless and low-slung outline of the headland, he led the way back down the trail they had made.

When they came out onto the beach where the ship lay, they could see that the crew had begun to pull her up to higher ground at Vragi's urging. They had long ropes on her bow and stern and were towing and guiding the little vessel away from the lapping tide. Vragi stopped from his exertions at sight of them and asked what they thought they had found. Sigtrygg and Arnliot quickly described everything they had seen from the island's high point and added that they thought there was not much use in pulling the ship any further onto the shore, since they should be setting sail as quickly as possible, now that the object of their journey was within reach.

"It seems there are two here with rash counsel, where before only one of you thought enough of these matters to trouble an old man's sleep," Vragi replied. "Or do you think we should go rushing headlong into the seas around this island without taking proper precautions?"

Sigtrygg asked Vragi what precautions he had in mind and Vragi responded that, in his opinion, the day was already too far gone to be putting out to sea, even if only to make a nearby landfall, "for who knows what manner of surprises lie in wait for the unwary ship in these parts? Besides, the crew is still spent from our recent exertions to gain this island. To my way of thinking, the best thing now is for us to spend the night here and sail refreshed, when the sun finds us in the morning."

"In that case," replied Sigtrygg, "we shall lose a day in coming to Leif Eiriksson's land claim, and who knows what manner of landfall this island, itself, may turn out to be? Or if the seas will hold, to give us fair sailing in the morning?"

Vragi laughed loudly and said this only showed the wisdom of putting over for the night on the island they were now on, since the nearness of the headland seemed to have affected Sigtrygg's usual good judgement. "A night in this place," he added, "will certainly have a salutary affect on those of us in the crew who are willing to lay our heads on its rocks and dream the dreams it sends our way. As for the race to Leif Eiriksson's houses, that contest is already won, for it is unlikely anyone can make land there now before we do. But, if we try to seek that place out while the day is already waning, who knows how much we are likely to stumble about, once darkness has overtaken us, or if we shall even find our way to the proper landfall."

Sigtrygg said that Vragi's advice was, as usual, better than most but that he was concerned the weather might turn against them and strand them on the island. "Then there would be no telling how long we would be forced to lay up in this place," he added, "or how much farther to come to Vinland."

"There's no use worrying about that," Vragi said, "since bad weather doesn't last forever, even in this part of the world. But, as for Vinland, it cannot be far off, even if that headland of yours should prove to be some other place."

The end of it was that Sigtrygg agreed to follow Vragi's counsel and they now prepared to spend the night on the island. Sigtrygg gave orders to some of the crew to go inland and fetch the trees which Arnliot had felled and he took a number of others with him to see what manner of game was at hand. They soon found the island did not want for any of the necessities of life and that the birds were so thick, in certain parts, that they could get whatever they needed for their evening meal with very little exertion. When they had got a satisfactory catch, they came back to their encampment, at the highest point along the beach, where the tall grasses rose up out of the sand, and put up booths for the night. Then they ate their fill and lay down in the shelters they had raised and most slept soundly. But Vragi made them post a guard along the outer edge of their sleep-houses for, he said, there was no telling what kind of dangers they were likely to find in this unexplored country.

Sigtrygg took the watch throughout the first part of the night and would not accept any relief until Vragi, himself, came to him, some time after the stars had reached their full height in the black sky, and urged that another should now take his place. Sigtrygg replied that he didn't see much reason for that since the crew needed time to regain their strength while he was, himself, not weakened in the slightest by the day's exertions. Vragi said that Sigtrygg's stubbornness in this, as in other things, would only set a bad example for the crew, since every man must take his turn, both sleeping and keeping guard, "and no one is any good to his fellows in the morning, if he is still pining for the sleep he abandoned the night before."

"I am not unused to keeping my own watch," Sigtrygg replied, "nor is one night's sleep such a loss to me."

"Then you are certainly better off than an old man such as myself," answered Vragi, "who must find his sleep where he can. But now I want to urge you to think of these men whom you have in your care and on whom you are depending to bring you safely to your land claim. Few of them have the skills, which you may lay claim to, and that is no bad thing since men should admire their leader for those things they do not have themselves. But we may also have need of these talents you boast of, and which few others in this part of the world can equal, before too long. Yet, if you are unrested, you may find it harder to demonstrate them than otherwise."

"The bears up on the Greenland ice never found cause to complain about that," Sigtrygg answered him.

"Still, Greenland is, by now, a long way off," Vragi said. "Nor is it altogether certain what manner of welcome we shall find across that strait which divides us from the headland you sighted, once we have crossed over. But, you will certainly have a cooler and a clearer head, whatever awaits us, if you lay it down on some smooth rock now and let others keep the watch for you."

Sigtrygg looked out over the black line of the sea, which stretched beyond their sleeping-booths, and listened closely to the soft sweep of the surf along the island's coast and to the rustling of the tall grasses behind them. "I don't see how anyone can hope to find sleep on a night like this," he said, "when so much is at stake and the night sky is so clear."

"It will be clearer still in the morning, and then it will be good for sailing as well as for watching," Vragi replied. "And, as to the stakes of this game, they will be no less high after the sun has risen, than they seem to you now."

Sigtrygg agreed that this was probably so and now he got up from his place to seek his bed. Then Vragi sat for awhile, after

Sigtrygg had gone, and kept the watch himself, until it seemed to him that the morning's light was not far off. Thereupon, he arose and went to the place where Thorolf the Icelander was sleeping and pulled on his shoulder until the man lifted his head. He told Thorolf he was now to take his turn keeping a sharp eye on their encampment, but Thorolf protested that there wasn't much need for that, "since this place is quieter than a cow's shed, after the winter slaughter."

"Still, it will be good practice for you men, if we come to harsher countries," Vragi said. "You are to keep the watch till first light and then wake the rest of us, for it will be hard work taking down these booths and getting our ship out beyond the surf by the time the sun has risen. And I want to be sailing before the sun stands over the horizon by a distance exceeding the width of a man's hand."

After he had given these instructions, Vragi too, sought his sleeping place, leaving the well-being of the camp to the Icelander. Nor did anything occur that night to warrant the unusual precautions which the old viking had insisted on, and which most of the crew had found so out of keeping with what he had been in the habit of demanding of them, up till then. But no one thought it his place to dispute the matter and they slept soundly enough during the night so that none felt they had any cause for complaint once the morning sun was up.

On the following day they put out to sea with all the speed that Vragi had promised and they were soon sailing round the north of the island. When they passed its northernmost point, they could make out the headland which Sigtrygg and Arnliot had sighted and Vragi said they were to steer into that land. The wind was behind them, so they had no trouble crossing the sound which lay between the island and their destination, and they were soon sailing northward along the coast of the new country. Now they could see that this region was also well-wooded and they sailed up along the headland until they came to its end and there they turned westward, into an inlet which ran in from the sea. They found themselves in a body of water, with land on every side, and they spent a good part of the day cruising about that region. Toward midday Vragi said they were to head south, along the inside of the headland, and Sigtrygg asked him what he had in mind.

"Not much," Vragi replied, "except that I think it's time we gave some thought to this land claim of yours which, unless I miss my guess, is most likely to be found at the innermost part of this headland, where the best shelter will be when storms blow in off the sea."

Accordingly, they sailed down the inside coast of the headland. But now a strange thing happened. The tide ran out under their ship so swiftly that they struck a sand bar, before they realized how shallow the waters had become. Then they saw there was no choice but to walk the rest of the way to the land. They were greatly surprised by this turn of events and seemed at a loss for how to proceed. Most of them thought it would not be a good idea to abandon the ship where she had grounded, for there was no telling when the sea would come up again, and then it might come with enough force to sweep their little vessel entirely away. "We are certainly not skilled shipwrights, whatever other abilities we may have between us," Arnliot said. "And it is not clear we can build ourselves another ship with the seaworthiness that this little seabird of ours has shown."

"In that case," said Vragi, "one of two choices is now before us. Either we sit here until the sea rises again, and then who knows with what force it is likely to come, seeing how suddenly she fell under us, and this may do a great deal more damage than any of us is now prepared to accept. Or we must make for the land and drag this little vessel of ours in behind us. And, though this seems the harder choice, I think it the better one, since it is most likely to preserve our means of travel. But, if anyone doubts the circumstances in which we now find ourselves, this strange action of the sea should be seen as nothing out of the ordinary, for there are similar tides in other parts of the world which I have seen, though none so powerful as this outflow. And it is told of, besides, in the tales surrounding the Vinland ventures, so it is certainly another sign that we have made a true landfall."

They now agreed to follow Vragi's advice. They put ropes on the ship again and began to drag her through the soft sand of the seabed which lay under them. Olvir and his companions were the most unhappy about this turn of events and were heard to mutter that, in their opinion, this voyage got harder to bear, the longer they were about it.

"That may be," replied Sigtrygg, "but some might have thought it harder still to be left flailing about in the cold Eiriksfjord waters, when small boats were overturning faster than speared whales."

Dragging the ship to land now proved no light work, since the ground was so wet under them that it made for very slow going, but Vragi advised them not to let up "for the alternative may not be any better for us." Accordingly, they struggled throughout the remainder of the day to bring the ship in and were nearly to the shore by the time the tide began to roll back.

Then it swept the ship up, making the movement of that vessel somewhat easier than before and they made better progress, at first. But the strong rush of the sea was soon too much for them and it began to pull the ship back from their hands and out again toward the open ocean. Nor was it any less forceful on the men, themselves, for these soon found they had lost their footing in the deep waters which now engulfed them and many were pulled out, with the ship, only saving themselves by clinging to the ship's ropes.

"This has not turned out as well for us as I would have liked," Sigtrygg said, and now he asked Vragi what he thought they ought to do.

"There's only one thing to do," Vragi replied, "and that is to get back on board this ship of ours, if we can, and steer her into the shore."

The men now pulled themselves back aboard the Gull, one by

one, and, when they were mostly on board again, set about re-claiming control of their ship, which had now fallen entirely into the hands of the rough ocean current. It did not take them long to reassert their authority, with Vragi and Arnliot both at the helm and the others pulling hard at the oars, and they were able to bring the ship around and point her back toward the land.

"We'd have done better to follow the practices of your grand-father, Leif Eiriksson," Vragi said, "for he left his ship where she grounded and anchored her there, according to the tale, reclaim-ing her only after the tide had returned. That seemed to me overly risky before, but now events have shown the wisdom in it. Never-theless, this tidal ebbing is a good sign, since others have encoun-tered it before us."

It was not long after this that they beached the ship on the shore which Vragi directed them to. After they had rested from their struggle with the tide, they began to walk about, seeking some indication concerning that place where they had landed. Not far from the beach where they stood was an area covered over with tall grass and, beyond that, a wooded region, not unlike what they had found on the island, although the land here did not rise so sharply to those heights which the island attained. Sigtrygg told his men they were to divide up into three groups, one to be led by him, one by Arnliot and one by Vragi, and to spread out and investigate the countryside which now lay before them, to see what could be found.

The three parties went off in entirely different directions, past the high grass into the tree-covered regions. Towards evening all three came back and stood about on the beach, near where their ship lay, to see if anyone had had better luck than any of the others. Sigtrygg was the first to speak and he said there had not been much to find where he and his companions had traveled, but that the country had a good look to it and would certainly be worth exploring. Then Vragi said much the same, for he had not found any signs of prior habitation by Greenlanders either, "though," he added, "there is a lot more to this country than we have so far seen; if we don't find what we are searching for here, there are certainly many other landfalls nearby which seem to me worth making."

Now they turned to Arnliot and his following and asked them how their search had gone, or if they thought it made any sense, at all, to continue exploring this land where they now found themselves.

"I'm not so down in the mouth as you others," Arnliot replied, "for, while you were rooting about in those woods which lay up behind this little strip of sea coast, my men and I made better use of our time. And now we have found a place where any farsighted Greenlander would willingly lay down his claim; and there are houses there to prove it."

Sigtrygg said that Arnliot must lead the way at once, even though the better part of the day was now behind them and the night's darkness not far off. They followed him to a clearing beyond a thin line of trees. There they saw a number of houses, just where Arnliot had said they would be, laid out in a little meadow. These had walls of timber, but no roofs, and they looked as though they had lain empty for a great many years. They were all overgrown with grass and, inside their walls, there were benches and tables of roughhewn construction, all of which had fallen into disrepair.

"I don't see how you could have missed all this," Arnliot said after they had had a good look at the wooden structures, "since they were right out here in the open, for anyone with eyes to see."

"I'm not sure how easy these were to find," Sigtrygg replied, "for many have talked about Leif's houses, without coming much closer than that, but now it seems I am somewhat in your debt since we might have missed this place entirely, without your keen vigilance, and gone off to less likely spots than this has proved to be."

Sigtrygg now walked around the buildings and took their measure. Then he asked Vragi if he thought these could be the same houses which Leif Eiriksson had raised in the west.

"They certainly look like Greenlanders have built them," Vragi agreed, "since people in your part of the world don't have a great deal of experience with wood houses and these are rather roughly constructed. In my opinion, they are as likely to be Leif's houses as any others, for the signs we have seen all point to it; in which case," he continued, "most people would think I have done my part in this business, since it seems I have brought you safe to Vinland."

CHAPTER XII

DARK DEEDS AND DEAD MEN

On the very next day, Sigtrygg put the crew to work repairing the houses which they had found. They cut the lumber they needed from the nearby forest and roofed over the buildings with turf and timber. These houses were not overly large, but they proved more than sufficient for the small crew of the Gull and Sigtrygg took the largest of the structures for himself. He also made sure their ship was well-secured on high ground and covered over with a sturdy shed of newly cut timber to protect it from the elements. When they had finished these tasks, Sigtrygg told his men they must now find the proof they had made the landfall they were seeking, "for many countries may look the same and have houses of wood along the shore, but only one is likely to be the land which my grandfather found."

Accordingly, they again went out in small groups to explore the countryside, during the next few days, and it was not long before many of them returned with the news Sigtrygg was seeking. A number of the men brought wild grapes back with them to the encampment and showed these to Sigtrygg and Vragi. They said they had cut them from vines which were growing on the high ground, up above the coastal area where the houses were, and Sigtrygg said this was no less than he had expected. He now closely interrogated each of the men who had found grapes until he was satisfied that these were growing extensively throughout the area and then he said that this certainly proved their landfall beyond any doubt. And now he declared, in the presence of all those who

had accompanied him out to the west, that he was taking possession of that country, in accordance with his rights and the oaths
which his kinsmen had sworn to him, before he had left Greenland.
He promised those with him the choicest holdings in that land
and said they were now free to choose out what parts of it they
wanted for themselves.

Vragi said: "It is certainly your prerogative, to dispose of your
holdings as you will, but I think it wiser to hold off apportioning
this country, until we know more about it."

But Arnliot replied that they could already see there was plenty
of room for farming, if anyone was minded to try his hand at that
vocation, "for, by sailing in this region alone, we have sighted more
land for the taking than in all the fjords of Greenland."

"Even so," said Vragi, "there may still be a great deal more to
learn about this country. And now I want to know if any of you
men thinks he has seen anything else worth telling about in his
travels in search of the local produce?"

Now one of the Faroe Islanders stepped forward, Aki Erlendsson
by name, and he said that he thought he had seen another settlement, not unlike the one they were now occupying and not too far
inland from where they were encamped, along the edge of a small
lake. Vragi asked him why he had not mentioned this before and
Aki replied that he had been too busy looking for grapes though
he had, himself, not been fortunate enough to find any. Still, he
had wanted to bring back the sort of news which he thought Sigtrygg
was most anxious to receive.

"But what about these houses?" Vragi demanded. "Since you
passed so near them, you must have something more to tell us."

"Not particularly," was Aki's reply, "for I didn't see anything
growing in that area which had the right look to it."

Now there was much talk about the houses which Aki had
seen and what this might mean. After they had pressed Aki further, he told them he thought the houses were in as poor condition as the ones which had first been found by Arnliot and his
companions and that they were just as likely to have been aban-

doned. Vragi said that would certainly be the best circumstance, if it were true, "for it won't do having neighbors close by if we are already making land claims in this region."

Sigtrygg said he thought they now ought to go and have a look for themselves, but that it would be best if they took their weapons along. So now they got their arms, each man taking his shield and a sword, if he had one, or a spear or axe, otherwise, except for the four servants from Brattahlid, who had no weapons of their own.

These were each given a spear by Sigtrygg, who told them they were to keep a tight hold on these and not make any use of them unless they must, "for they are not your usual farming implements." Arnliot took his long-handled axe, and now they all went in the direction which Aki showed them.

When they had gone a little ways, they came out into another clearing and there they found the houses, just where Aki had told them they would be. These houses were fewer and somewhat smaller than the first group of buildings and seemed to be in worse condition. But they were no older than the other houses and looked as though they had been made by the same people.

"I'm not sure who is responsible for these buildings," Sigtrygg said, "but I have an unpleasant feeling about this place and I'm not sure we will be entirely happy with what we find here."

Now they went up to the structures for a closer look and, when they began to walk around in the high grass which grew all around these buildings, they heard sharp crunching under their feet and Sigtrygg said they had better see what the cause of these unusual sounds was. Then they searched around in the grass, until they found the source of the strange noises which, they could now see, were human bones which lay scattered all about the houses, half hidden where the tall grass was growing.

When they saw these they drew back at once, for it was plain the people, whose bones these were, had met with a violent end and had been left lying about, thereafter, without benefit of a Christian burial. Sigtrygg's crew thought this the worst possible turn of events for, from the look of the bones, the deaths of those who had lived in the houses had not been easy. Even Sigtrygg, who was bolder than most others and who had seen death more often than the rest, now turned aside at this sight for many of the bones appeared to have been chewed over and broken by marauding animals.

"What can this mean?" Arnliot asked, placing his axe head-down at his feet, though he did not seem any more comfortable among the dead than the others.

"Only one thing," Sigtrygg replied, "for I have the feeling we have found a grim reminder of past events here, unless I am very much mistaken, and there is little doubt that unworthy deeds have been done in this place."

Now all the crewmen began to mill about and none were too willing to go forward, seeing that the bones were underfoot wherever they stepped. But Vragi told them they must still enter the houses and have a look around nonetheless, "or else we will never be certain of what is to be found. And that will leave too much unknown for us to settle safely in this area. Though, unless I miss my guess, Sigtrygg already knows something of what took place here."

Sigtrygg replied that this was certainly true and now he told them that, in his opinion, this was the settlement of those two Icelanders, Helgi and Finnbogi, who had sailed out to Vinland with Leif Eiriksson's half-sister, Freydis, in Leif's time. These had gotten the use of Leif's houses from the Brattahlid chief, as a base for an expedition which they hoped would yield a very profitable shipload of goods to take back to Iceland. The brothers and Freydis had each contributed a ship and crew to the expedition. But things had not gone smoothly and the story had it that Freydis and her husband coveted the Icelanders' larger boat, since it could carry a great deal more cargo than their own smaller Greenland vessel.

Upon their arrival, Freydis had broken her agreement with the brothers, to share the houses which Leif had loaned to them, forc-ing the Icelanders to go elsewhere and build shelters for themselves. But later, when all the cargo had been gathered and the two crews were preparing to sail home, Freydis urged her husband and his men to surprise the Icelanders in their houses early one morning and kill them, so she could take their ship and cargo. Since none of her men would kill the women who were with the brothers, Freydis did this herself, according to the tale, to ensure that no witnesses survived to recount the events which she had instigated. Yet, the tale came out when one of her own crew let things slip, after they had returned to Greenland, and Leif was greatly disturbed about the whole affair. "Still," Sigtrygg added, "no compensation was ever paid for these killings, since none of the relatives of the murdered crew in Iceland ever pressed a claim. And now it seems no proper burial was provided for the corpses either."

Olvir said he had heard much the same tale at Brattahlid and did not think it unlikely that Sigtrygg had it right and that they had now stumbled on the site of Freydis' bloody deed.

Vragi said that he, too, knew of this matter although, until now, he had not been sure how much of it was true. "But now," he added, "I no longer see much reason to disbelieve any of it."

"In that case," Arnliot said, "we must decide what is to be done for, in truth, I don't see how we can carry on in this country with a place like this so near our backs."

Most of those present agreed with Arnliot, for they did not like the thought of so many, who had been so evilly slain, left without burial, to walk about in the night if they were so inclined.

"I don't put much stock in ghosts, myself," Sigtrygg now said, "but it is certainly my duty to see that these people get a burial, at the least, since it was my kinswoman who did the deed."

There was general agreement with this and Sigtrygg now asked who among them was willing to help him gather up and bury the bones. Not many wanted a hand in this task, however, until Vragi said that he, at least, would be more than willing to assist, since he thought the spirits of the dead would look more kindly on those who had collaborated in their burial, "should there still be some, among them, who are moved to walk about in the night."

Most of the others thought there was wisdom in this, for they could not see any other means of differentiating themselves from other men, in the ghosts' eyes, if these spirits should remain without peace, even after their burial. And laying them to rest in the earth at least offered some possibility of putting an end to the matter. Accordingly, there was now general consensus that they must all work together to bury the bones, since no man of them wanted to be thought backward in this affair. Vragi now said they must be careful to scour the entire area for every stray bone and that no piece of bone should be left unburied when they were done, if they were to get the full benefit of their efforts.

They spread out with great care and began to search through the tall grass all around the houses, and even within each structure, carrying back all the bones they could find and laying these carefully in a large pile in the middle of the meadow. Then they dug a number of graves nearby, as deeply as they could, and carefully laid each group of bones into the earth and covered these over with rocks and loose dirt. After this, they stamped down on the ground and packed the graves as tightly as possible so no one would be able to recognize the mounds they had made and inadvertently dig them up again.

When they were finished, Olvir looked up and said he thought they should not spend any more time in that place than they already had, "for there is only the ill-will of the dead here now," he said, "who may, perhaps, fail to distinguish between their benefactors and their killers, when things get dark."

Everyone thought this made sense, for no one wanted to be the last to leave the clearing; yet now, when they turned to go, there was a sudden rustling in the trees directly behind the houses. Each man froze in his place, so deeply had they been moved by the fate of the dead in that meadow, and they turned slowly toward the place where the sounds had come from.

Two dark, man-like forms seemed to be watching them from the shadows of the forest. The entire crew stood motionless, for, in their anxiety to bury the dead, they had lost track of everything else, and now it seemed to them that the very figures of the two aggrieved Icelanders, Helgi and Finnbogi, stood before them, glowering from the forest darkness.

One of the Brattahlid servants said: "Here are the two brothers come back to get their vengeance on Freydis' kin. Neither axe nor sword will bite on such as these, but only prayer can avail us now," and he fell to his knees and began to murmur vigorously to himself.

The Greenlanders stood stock still, watching the two weird apparitions which did not move in their turn, though these were hard enough to see, since they were well concealed by the shadows of the trees. For a long time nothing moved in that meadow, though Olvir's companions had all dropped down to their knees, by this time, and were praying in unison. Nor were the others in the crew any more eager to challenge these wraiths than the serving men from Brattahlid, since they thought this strange appearance must mean they had somehow failed in their efforts to bury the victims of Freydis' greed and, thereby, appease their wrath. Accordingly, a few of the crewmen now began to look furtively about them for any bones which might have been overlooked in the general burial or to see if, perhaps, one of the graves had not been satisfactorily closed.

But, after a few moments, Sigtrygg said to them in a quiet voice that they were to forget the search for bones and look to their weapons, instead, "for these are men, just as we are, and nothing extraordinary. Nor have they any advantage over us in numbers or strength. But, if we do not seize them, they may fetch their kinsmen, and that will be a cause of great concern to us, hereafter."

When they heard this, it was as though a shadow had passed from the Greenlanders' eyes, for they immediately lost their fear of the two apparitions and, as one man, they ran into the forest, where the dark figures had been, seeking to lay hands on these. But the two apparitions fled away as quickly as the Greenlanders began their pursuit, nor were those two any less fleet than the speediest of forest-dwelling creatures, for they dashed over the ground as lightly and as silently as the ghosts which the Greenlanders had first taken them for. It was hard running just to keep them in sight.

Now the men of Sigtrygg's crew spread out in a broad band as they plunged into the trees, where the fleeing figures had gone, making a great deal of noise as they broke through the branches and undergrowth which blocked their way. Arnliot at once took the lead, for his great strides enabled him to cover more ground than any of the others, while his companions from his Ketilsfjord days stayed close behind him.

Luck was with the men of Greenland that day, for one of the shadow men they were pursuing, and who had moved so swiftly as to make the Greenlanders doubt he was mortal afterall, suddenly caught his leg in a bramble and stumbled in his flight. This brought him to earth though nothing else, it had seemed, would be sufficient to accomplish this, despite all the Greenlanders' efforts. Then Arnliot and his fellows caught up with the fallen creature and fell on him, slaying him where he lay. The second figure, who had been somewhat ahead of his fallen comrade, now turned and, seeing the disaster which had befallen his fellow, broke off from his line of flight to seek shelter in a dense copse of trees which did not lay far from where he had been, just moments before. But Arnliot saw his change of direction and, without lingering over the fallen body of the first apparition, he immediately took off after the second.

Then the other crewmen plunged into the tight cluster of trees from every side and the fleeing figure suddenly burst from their midst with Arnliot right behind him. The big Ketilsfjord man now came up with the stranger, who was a great deal smaller than the Greenlanders were, and reached out his long arms to seize the fleeing figure. When he had finally got his hands on the fellow, Arnliot pulled him down and fell atop him, crushing him beneath his great weight. Then the Greenlander grasped a nearby rock with his right hand and raised it over his head to crush the fallen man's skull. No sound came from the stranger's mouth as he

saw the rock descending and this would have been his death blow
had not Sigtrygg suddenly come up to them and stayed Arnliot's
hand.

"There's no need for that," Sigtrygg told him, "for these two
have done us no harm, as yet."

But Arnliot replied that they had already killed the first one
and now they might as well do the same with this other, "so he
cannot bring any word of us to his fellows. For where two are
running," he added, "I do not doubt more will be found."

Sigtrygg said: "Enough evil has already been done, if the first
has been killed as you say, since it is unlikely we can kill them all.
In my opinion, they will know this country better than we do,
though now, it seems to me, we have made ourselves their enemies."

"Then that is all the more reason," continued Arnliot, "to slay
this one while we can, since we've already dug graves enough to
accommodate them both."

But Sigtrygg said he had something else in mind and now he
told Arnliot to allow the creature to rise, since he wanted to have a
better look at him. By this time the others of the crew had come
up with them and these now formed a circle around the captured
man. Thereupon Arnliot lifted himself up from his prisoner, though
he kept the man pinned to the earth with one of his large feet
which he pressed squarely into the man's chest. Now they saw that
they had taken a strange prey, indeed, for here was a young man
who seemed to them barely more than a boy, clad wholly in animal skins with nothing but pieces of stones in his belt, which,
upon closer inspection, appeared to be some sort of weapons. The
stranger was dark complexioned with thick black hair, which he
wore bound at the back of his neck, and he seemed entirely unable
to understand their speech. His face was long and, they thought,
rather ugly. He seemed in a great fright as he peered about at his
captors.

Sigtrygg said: "He must think we are as hideous as he appears
to us, for I don't imagine he has ever seen Greenlanders before."

Olvir now stepped forward and bent down to look at the stranger. When he straightened up again he seemed rather thoughtful. Sigtrygg asked him what he had on his mind.

"Not much," Olvir said, "except that I was curious as to what manner of man this is, for it seems to me I have heard tales at Brattahlid about an unpleasant and warlike race which dwells in this land. Some of them, I had even heard, were responsible for the death of Thorvald Eiriksson, Leif's brother. Yet this one does not look overly threatening to me."

"It's not easy to threaten others, when such a big foot as Keelfoot owns is pressing into your chest," Sigtrygg said.

"Still," said Olvir, "I don't see how this sort of man can pose much danger to us. In my opinion, he would be easy for even the least among us to overpower."

"Then you did not see how stealthily and swiftly these two came upon us in the clearing," Sigtrygg replied, "or what a hard chase they led us afterwards. A large number of such men would certainly be a serious matter, if they were to come upon us with evil intentions."

Vragi now said that Sigtrygg was showing just the sort of foresight they should expect from their leader, for it always paid to be on the alert for danger and no man, even one as unimpressive as this one lying under Arnliot's foot, should be underestimated. "And now," he added, "I think we have found one of those Skraelings which the tales tell of, who did so much harm to those expeditions which came out here before us."

"Yet," said Sigtrygg, "according to what I had heard, no evidence of these people has ever been found by Leif's houses, though they are said to dwell both east and west of here."

"In that case," Vragi answered, "you may consider him either easterner or westerner, but he is certainly here with us now. In my opinion, this will require careful thought, before we proceed any further."

Everyone now said this made sense and Arnliot added that it gave them even more reason to kill the prisoner than before, since the Skraelings were known to be dangerous foes. Sigtrygg asked Arnliot if this meant he was afraid of the captive he now had under his feet and Arnliot said that that was certainly not the case, "for I am not the sort of man who runs from his enemies, whatever their nature."

"In that case," Sigtrygg replied, "I don't think you will mind sharing your quarters with this little fellow we have found," and he told the others to bind the Skraeling with ropes and lead him along behind them, back to Leif's houses.

"What if there are others," Arnliot said, "and they have seen us and are even now running back to their kinsmen with word of what has happened here?"

"Then killing this one will certainly not make any difference in the outcome," Sigtrygg said. "But I have not seen any signs of this and most people would agree that my eyes are not the worse, for the time I have spent as a hunter in the waste lands." He now asked if any of the other members of the crew could see evidence that there were still more Skraelings lurking about. But none of them thought they could read the signs any better than Sigtrygg, himself, and so Sigtrygg told them to take their prisoner back to their encampment "but keep a tight hold on his ropes, since his escape would be more serious now, than before."

They first took the body of the other Skraeling and buried it in such a fashion as to make it difficult to find again, and then, looping a number of ropes tightly around the fellow they had left alive, they led him back to the clearing where they had first caught sight of him. There they took his stone implements from him and threw these away and then they tied another rope to his neck and led him, in their midst, back to Leif's houses.

When they came into the settlement, Sigtrygg had them drive a long stake into the ground and then he tied the other end of the rope, which bound their prisoner about the neck, to the stake and left him there for a time. After awhile, Sigtrygg returned and this time he was holding a long knife in his hand. The Skraeling watched him without attempting to move away and now Sigtrygg thought the creature seemed more curious than afraid, so he held out the knife for him to see. The small man's eyes widened and Sigtrygg said it seemed to him that the fellow had never seen iron before. He now placed the knife alongside the ropes which bound the Skraeling's hands and cut them with one stroke. At this, the little man leaped backward toward the stake which still held him prisoner.

"He is certainly somewhat bolder than before," Sigtrygg said, "though, in my opinion, this fellow knows very little about the things which we prize most."

The other crewmen now gathered closely around the captive and several of them began to push him about with their booted feet. Yet, he did not seem frightened, but appeared to be more interested in the garments and manners of the Greenlanders than in finding some way to flee from them.

"Here is a change," said Sigtrygg, "since he seems as eager to take our measure as we are to take his."

"Still, there's not a great deal to be said for these Skraelings, in my opinion," Arnliot replied, "since they are so ignorant and unimpressive to look at."

They could now see that the man's shoes were little more than thin wrappings of animal skin, sewn together with sinew, and that he wore a necklace of shells and feathers across his chest. Arnliot reached out suddenly and tore this from the Skraeling's neck, but the small man made no effort to resist him and even appeared not to notice his loss. Now Arnliot passed the necklace about to his companions and, when they had examined it at some length, he told them that this only proved his point about these people, since even their adornments were of no obvious value. Then he took the necklace and threw it into the nearby trees in disgust.

The Skraeling's eyes followed, though his face betrayed little concern. Yet, it was clear he could not keep from watching the large figure of Arnliot, as he moved about him, for that Greenlander must certainly have been the biggest and strangest looking man this creature of the western shores had ever seen.

Sigtrygg now said he thought it a good sign the Skraeling seemed to have lost some of his fear of them and that this would be a source of good luck for their enterprise.

"I don't see how this wretch's courage, if that is what you call it, can do us any good," answered Arnliot, "unless it is to tell us what manner of enemy these fellows will make. And I, for one, would rather have them fear us, than otherwise."

But Sigtrygg said he thought the young man's boldness deserved a name of them and, since no one else had offered to do it, he would take the task on himself. He now said he thought the Skraeling's long face reminded him of a bear's snout and so he proposed they call him Bjorn, "for he seems to have the courage of those beasts and does not smell so very different, if I am any judge."

There was much laughter about this but, since no one had any better proposal to make in the matter, Sigtrygg said the name should stand as he had given it. Then he walked over to the trees where Arnliot had thrown the stranger's necklace and picked this up, carrying it back to where the Skraeling stood, still surrounded by the Greenlanders. He placed it in the small man's hands and said he should put it on again. But the Skraeling did not make any attempt to do so, for it was clear he did not understand Sigtrygg's words.

"Do what you like with it, then, Bjorn," Sigtrygg said to him at last, "for this is yours, and no one has any better right to it than you do, yourself." Then he turned about and left the crew and their prisoner as though he had completely lost interest in the matter, going into that house which he had previously claimed for his own.

The others remained with the captive for a while longer, though they now seemed to feel somewhat differently toward the fellow than before. After a time, they brought him food and water from their stores, and the Skraeling took these readily enough for the hard chase had taken its toll of him.

Then there was much talk among the crew and they began to laugh and joke with their prisoner, as though he were an old ship-

mate and had shared their voyage across the western sea with them.
It seemed to them that the little man joined in the general merri-
ment, though he did not speak their language. Only Arnliot found
this new familiarity somewhat hard to take, but the others thought
it no great matter that their captive, whom they had been so intent on killing, but a short time before, should now seem so harmless to them and an object of such great interest. And so it fell out
that the Skraeling got his life from the Greenlanders, and a name
to boot, although it was a long time before he knew it.

The rest of that season passed without further incident, although Sigtrygg now placed a careful watch about their settlement lest more Skraelings should come upon them unawares. But
they saw no other signs of these people and were soon busy with
hunting and fishing, for Sigtrygg said they were to lay in a supply
of meat against the winter months. They also thickened and rein-
forced the walls of Leif's houses, filling in the cracks with turf or
ship's tar, since they had little idea how harsh the winter in that
part of the world might prove to be.

As for Bjorn the Skraeling, Sigtrygg now placed him in the
care of the crew, saying that no fewer than six men should have the
watch over their captive at any time and, if he were allowed to
walk about the settlement, one of these six must always have that
rope, which had been tied about the Skraeling's neck, in hand.
Sigtrygg made the crew take turns keeping a watch on their prisoner, in this fashion, and he told them they were to learn as much
of the man's tongue as they were capable of, while they were in his
company. Thus, Bjorn got some degree of freedom to move about
the settlement, since the Greenlanders did not prevent him from
going where he would, so long as one of them always had hold of
that rope which bound him.

Sigtrygg also encouraged the crew to take their meals with the
Skraeling, for he thought this most likely to lead to a quick familiarity with Bjorn's ways and he himself spent a good deal of his
own time with the captive, in order to teach him something of the

Norse language and to learn to speak a little in the Skraeling fashion. At times he even took the Skraeling out alone, without any of the crew, and then these two, who understood so little of one another's words, seemed to find other means of speaking, for both were keen of eye and ear and well-attuned to the movements of the beasts in the forest.

"This Skraeling of ours has something of a hunter's manner," Sigtrygg told Vragi one day, "since he moves about among the trees with such quiet and skill and seems to know the minds of the animals which dwell in these parts as well as they do themselves."

"In that case," Vragi replied, "you must be especially on your guard when you are alone with him, for he would be a hard one to catch again, if once he has broken from your grasp."

"There's no need to worry about that," Sigtrygg said, "for his rope is of the toughest walrus hide and no stone blades, such as he might fashion, are likely to do it harm. As for iron, such tools are forbidden him."

"Then see he doesn't spirit any away under your nose," Vragi said.

Sigtrygg agreed that this only made sense and now he took more care when he went with the Skraeling into the woods than he had before, but he did not desist from this practice. In many ways, he found their captive a more agreeable companion than any of his own men. The Skraeling seemed a man who could keep his silence in the forest and hear even the smallest and seemingly least significant sound, reading each murmur or rustle as though it were no more than letters in a book. Nor did he fail to see the changes in the pathways they trod, where the forest creatures had made their way and Sigtrygg said he thought this especially worthy of admiration for he was no poor hunter, himself, though his own trails had taken him to harsher regions, in the past, than the one they now found themselves in.

So little by little, Sigtrygg and Bjorn the Skraeling seemed to gain an understanding of one another and it soon fell out that the Skraeling could speak haltingly in the Greenlanders' tongue and that Sigtrygg, and a few of the others, could respond to him, somewhat, in the Skraeling manner. Bjorn told them, around this time, that his Skraeling name was W'tnalko and that the name of his companion, whom they had slain, was Aselekah. And so the Greenlanders called him by his own name afterwards, as much as by that name which Sigtrygg had given him.

Now, while Sigtrygg very quickly showed himself to be the best student of the Skraeling language among the Greenlanders, most of the crew thought it quite surprising that Olvir proved to be nearly as apt a pupil, though he spent much less time with their captive than most of the others. After Olvir, Thorolf and Asmund seemed to learn to speak the Skraeling tongue best, for they showed the most interest in doing as Sigtrygg wished. But Arnliot appeared to have the least desire of any of the crew to learn to speak like a Skraeling, saying he thought they would all be better off if they kept their own words out of the mouths of these wild people. As for Vragi, he was mostly silent on the matter and no one could tell how much of the Skraeling speech he had mastered, or if he had learned any at all, for he kept to himself a great deal more than before, and most of the crew thought this a very great change from the days when they had been sailing together, over untried waters, in search of new lands.

CHAPTER XIII

FELLOWSHIP

They spent that winter in Leif's houses, on the edge of the Vinland shore, nor did it seem to them that the season was overly harsh, since they were accustomed to much more severe weather than they now found in the new country. Although the leaves all fell off the trees, and everything took on a grey and brownish cast, there was very little snow, to speak of, and a man could walk about on the coldest days without fear of freezing. As for the grass, this did not die out but remained somewhat green, even during the worst part of the winter, and they thought this the best of luck since it meant that cattle and sheep would have very little trouble finding food there in the winter months.

Olvir, especially, commented on the usefulness of this land for grazing and now said he thought this meant they must think about returning to Greenland, as quickly as possible, "to fetch the proper sort of animals for a good farm or two, if we mean to establish ourselves here."

"You'd do better to start thinking about how you and the other Brattahlid men who are with you can be of more use to your shipmates while we are here," answered Sigtrygg when he heard this, "than about arranging your passage home. For, unlike the others in this crew, you men didn't bring much in the way of equipment along with you, when you came on board with us."

"That is hardly to be wondered at," said Olvir, "for we certainly didn't ask to travel out here on that ship of yours."

"And I suppose you didn't ask to be pulled out of the drink, either?" Sigtrygg replied. "Or not to be thrown overboard again, afterwards, once you had served your purpose? It seems to me," he went on, "that those of us on board the Gull did not ask to be pursued and speared by you Brattahlid men, so it is not entirely clear who owes more to whom in this matter. But, at the least, you fellows have gotten your lives from us, and that's nothing to be sneered at."

Olvir said that this was so but that he did not think Sigtrygg should be holding against them those actions which they had only performed out of a sense of duty, while servants at Brattahlid, "although by now we have certainly shared a few ship's meals together, and been through quite a bit with the rest of this crew."

Sigtrygg agreed that this was so but added that that only made it the more annoying, when they started talking about returning to Greenland, "for there's no use considering that question until I, myself, have decided on it," he said. "However, you Brattahlid men seem to me to be the least prepared, of all of us, should trouble arise, and I think it's time this matter were looked to."

"How is that to be done?" Olvir asked.

"Very simply," Sigtrygg replied. "Each of you has found a spear or axe, from among those weapons which our enemies threw at us in Eiriksfjord, or from the extra arms which we, ourselves, brought on board. But it's unlikely we shall be able to find you any armor or helmets in this part of the world, and we are certainly a long way those places where such goods may be procured. But at the least, it seems to me, you men should have shields, and there's plenty of material on hand for that."

"We are not accustomed to warfare," Olvir said, "nor is it altogether clear we will have need of such armaments, for this seems to be a peaceful country so far, except for the blood which we, ourselves, have already shed."

"Then that is even more reason to be prepared," said Sigtrygg, "or have you forgotten the stories of how Thorvald Eiriksson met his end? Or the troubles which beset Thorfinn Karlsefni's expedition? These Skraelings are not so harmless as their looks suggest and I, for one, have seen how softly they tread in the forest."

Olvir replied that Sigtrygg usually had things his own way, whatever anyone else in the crew had to say in the matter, and it was unlikely to be any different in this case, so he now agreed to do whatever Sigtrygg asked of him, "though we servants of the Leifssons have very little experience in fashioning arms."

"Then you will make good pupils," Sigtrygg replied, and he asked Vragi if he would be willing to teach the men from Brattahlid how to cut and shape wood for their shields.

"There are certainly enough trees around for that," Vragi agreed, "and I don't see how it can do these men much harm." So now he took them out with him into the nearby woods to find the right sort of trees for their work. In a very short time he found a stand of oak and then he set to work cutting the needed timber, with the Brattahlid men's help, and hauling it back to their settlement. There they trimmed the bark off the wood and, using their axes, cut it to the needed shapes. This caused a great clatter in the settlement and other members of the crew came out to assist them or just to watch the goings on, since there was not a great deal besides this, during the winter months, to occupy them. The Skraeling, W'tnalko, also found the work of interest and he watched with fascination as the Greenlanders used their iron tools to form the wood.

"Now we must leave it out to dry," Vragi told them, when they had finished preparing the pieces of oak, adding that "this country certainly has the best of everything which I have seen so far, for this is just the kind of wood to make strong shields, such as the men of old used to carry, before iron became so common in the world."

"I wish we had iron now," Olvir said, "for then, at least, we would be as well protected as you others, if trouble starts."

"In my opinion," Vragi replied, "there's just as much iron to be found in this part of the world as elsewhere. But that is a bigger matter than we can now attempt, for iron must be dug out of the ground and heated and forged, whereas these pieces of wood can be easily obtained and fashioned into the objects we need. Nor are they likely to be any less reliable, since they are cut from such stout trees."

He then showed them how to arrange the cut wood on flat ground, under the winter sun, making certain to bind the timber so that it would not shrink or warp as it dried. But he took a single length of wood, from among all those pieces, for himself, for he had earlier cut this from a young sapling; and now he shaped it into a thick shaft of unusual height and diameter, and, when he had done this, he began to walk away from the others with this pole in his hands.

When Olvir saw the shaft, which was a good deal longer than Vragi was tall, he asked what Vragi intended to do with such an unwieldy piece of wood.

Vragi answered that the shaft would serve very well to replace the one he had lost, when they were leaving Eiriksfjord, "for, it seems to me, I will have need of it, before our stay in this country is done. And maybe that is how it should be, since a thing which is found in a country is often best suited for use there."

Sigtrygg now asked the Brattahlid men each day how their weapons making with Vragi was progressing and, each day, Olvir told him that the wood had not yet sufficiently cured and that they thought they would need more time.

"Well then, when do you think it will be ready for fashioning into shields?" Sigtrygg inquired.

"Not until that old viking has satisfied himself that the tree's spirit has entirely gone from it. And then he has promised to show us how a man's soul can be put in its place."

"Our shipmate certainly has some very strange notions about wood working," Sigtrygg said. "Still, he has been right more often than not, and I, for one, am not willing to second guess him now."

One night, not long after this, when the moon shone full in

the clear black sky, Vragi came to where Olvir was sleeping and told him to rouse himself and his companions and come outside with him. It was quite cold and Olvir asked him what was wrong. "Nothing at all," was the reply, "but you men have got some work to do."

They followed him unhappily to the field where the pieces of oak had been lying and, because the moon was so bright, they could see every piece clearly, though the night shadows seemed to dance strangely across the bare wood. Vragi told them each to take certain pieces in their hands and now he went from man to man with his knife and cut a gash in each man's hands so that the blood flowed from these wounds over the piece of wood each was holding.

"I don't see what is to be gained from this," said Olvir, "since there's not much use in trying to fashion these into weapons when it's so dark, even if the moon is full, as it is now. Nor do I see any purpose to this bloodletting."

Vragi told him to keep silent and now he walked around the men in a wide circle, singing a strange song to himself in a voice so low none of them could make out the words he was mumbling. When he had circled them thus, several times, they began to become extremely uncomfortable and all but Olvir started to fidget. Vragi now bent down and took a handful of cold earth in his hands and walked to where the men stood huddled together. Without warning, he suddenly threw the dirt over the men and onto the pieces of wood they were holding. Then he went to each of the Brattahlid men, in turn, and cut runes in the wood which they held in their hands with the point of his knife. "Now rub the earth into the oak," he told them, "with the blood you have spilled here."

The men were too astonished to do anything but what Vragi instructed and so they did as they were told. When they were finished, Olvir said he thought this rather strange behavior for Christian men and asked Vragi to explain himself.

"The wood is ready to be worked," was all Vragi was willing to say at first. But, when he saw how concerned Olvir and the others were, he added: "Still, tomorrow will be soon enough for that. In the meantime I now advise you men to go back to your sleeping places and to do so as quietly as possible, so as not to wake the others. This kind of ceremony is most effective when others have no knowledge of it. But be sure to hold on to that piece of wood which you have washed tonight in your own blood, for it will be the heart of the shield each of you is to fashion when the sun has risen tomorrow morning."

Olvir said they were not accustomed to such pagan practices as this and that "some would think these forbidden rites, since the old gods have fallen into disrepute."

"I wouldn't worry overmuch about that," was Vragi's reply, "since this is a new country and it is not altogether clear which gods hold sway here. As for your prospects after tonight, they are, in my opinion, much better than they were before, since you will have the kind of armaments a man can rely on, if you follow my instructions in every detail from here on in. But, if not, no amount of blood or moonlight or earth will suffice to stiffen your backs."

The following morning Sigtrygg and the rest of the crew were awakened by a clatter of voices and axes, soon after the sun had risen, and they rushed outside to see what was causing such a commotion. They were astonished to see the Brattahlid men hard at work on their shields, as though they had been at it the entire night. Vragi was nowhere to be seen so Olvir was directing things. The large round shields already seemed to be taking shape. Sigtrygg asked Olvir if he thought they knew enough about their task to proceed without the old man's guidance and Olvir replied that they were certainly not unfamiliar with tools or carpentry, since they had been workers on a Greenland farm. "And as to the finer points of weapons making," he added, "we are more than capable of doing what is needed, from the advice which has already been provided to us."

Sigtrygg had to admit that the men seemed more involved in

their work than they had before and were going about things with a confidence and eagerness they had failed to show, up till then, even when they had been rowing for their lives in Eiriksfjord. Still, he thought it would have been better if Vragi were present and he now said as much.

"There's no use idling about, while we wait for one man," was Olvir's reply, "since there's so much around here that needs doing. Nor are we servants of the Leifssons likely to be backward in putting our time to good use."

Thereafter they continued, just as before, and they did not let up until the sun was near its highest point in the sky, and then they broke to eat, albeit reluctantly. By then, it seemed that the shields had been fully shaped and cut, and the men were quite pleased with themselves. About this time, Vragi Skeggjasson reappeared from the forest's edge, leaning on that tall staff of his, to which it could now be seen he had affixed a spear point from one of the weapons they had brought with them from Greenland.

No one said much about this weapon, for everyone knew that, like the Brattahlid men, Vragi had come out to Vinland with no arms of his own since Sigtrygg was carrying his sword and shield. But they all agreed the shaft certainly made an unusual spear, since it would be far too long for throwing.

Some of the crewmen now wanted to know if Vragi intended to construct a shield for himself, in the same fashion as the Brattahlid men had done, to carry alongside the spear. To this Vragi only laughed and said that a man of his years didn't have as much need for a shield as ordinary men, "since I have already lived so long that it's not likely a shield will make a great deal of difference, where my fate is concerned. But you others had better look to your own well-being. Besides, a spear like this will take both of a man's hands, if it's to be wielded properly."

Vragi now made his way into the camp, leaning on this spear, and came to the place where the Brattahlid men sat. He stopped to look at their handiwork, but did not seem overly interested. When he had finished his inspection, he went on his way again. It was quite clear he intended to say very little about the men's work, either one way or the other.

When Sigtrygg saw that Vragi was not going to comment, he went over to him and asked if he thought that everything was in order, "since these men have now taken it on themselves to finish that work which you have been guiding them in, until now, although you were nowhere about to see that things were done correctly."

Vragi asked Sigtrygg what he, himself, thought of the shields.

"They certainly look strong enough, and well-made to me," Sigtrygg replied, "but I have the feeling you will be the best judge of that."

"It's not certain which of us is likely to be the better judge, where this work is concerned," answered Vragi, "but some people would think that only the man who carries his own arms into battle will have anything of consequence to say on the matter."

Sigtrygg agreed that this was probably so, but now he asked what could possibly explain the change of heart which was so evident in these men, "since they have shown a spirit no one would have guessed at, before this, in finishing their work so quickly."

"It sometimes happens," Vragi replied, "that men become attached to the work they are engaged in, and feel as though it is no less a part of themselves than their own head or limbs. Then they are most anxious to finish things, and that with the greatest of care. Now, it seems, that these Brattahlid men have found cause to fashion arms for themselves which even the hardiest warriors, in days gone by, would have borne confidently against an enemy, and there's no use asking whether this is because of one thing or another. But these men have found their spirit, which before was sorely lacking, nor do I think you are likely to find them any less reliable, after this, than those others you have engaged to pull at your ship's oars."

Sigtrygg said that would remain to be seen, but that it was certainly true the other members of the crew seemed to find the activities of the Brattahlid men of great interest, for he could see how they clustered around them, admiring their oak shields.

Olvir and his companions were then putting the finishing touches on their handiwork, each man carving what he thought he would most like to carry before him into battle. The shepherd carved a large ram's head in the center of his shield since he thought such a creature most fitting for a warrior who had spent his life among sheep. The cowherd, on the other hand, thinking to do the shepherd one better, cut a scene of slaughter onto his own shield, showing how the men of Brattahlid were accustomed to butcher the weakest of their animals, before each winter, to conserve food for the rest of their herd and feed the farm's household over the coldest months. This, he thought, was certainly a scene to strike dread into any enemy he might encounter. The third man, who unlike his companions, had no set task at Brattahlid but did whatever work he was told to do, carved only a simple cross. But Olvir cut the figures of four men into his shield, and over them the image of the moon, and each of the men had his right hand extended with what seemed to be a gash in that hand, from which blood appeared to be falling.

Sigtrygg approached the men and examined each of their shields, in turn. When he came to Olvir's, he remarked on the strangeness of the images and the unusual markings to be seen on the shields. He asked Olvir what they meant.

"Not as much as they appear to," answered Olvir, "though men who have sworn an oath together will often find it easiest to stand side by side, should the need arise."

The other crewmen were so taken with the shields the Brattahlid men had made for themselves that many of them now said they wanted to do the same, despite the fact the new shields were larger and bulkier and certainly weighed more than those which they had carried with them from Greenland. Accordingly, they asked Vragi for his help. But he told them Olvir and his companions were now the best men to turn to for this, since they knew how the thing was to be done, and he said that Olvir should feel free to instruct his fellow crewmen in the intricacies of the craft, "though," he added in a hushed voice, "you are not to reveal anything about what has passed between us under the moon's light."

So it fell out that the crewmen busied themselves with the business of shield making and this kept them occupied for some time.

While they were thus engaged, Sigtrygg found time to wander about the camp or to speak with their Skraeling captive, which he did, with greater and greater skill so that it soon seemed to many of the crew that he spoke the Skraeling tongue with the same facility as W'tnalko, himself, did. Now not long after the crew had begun to make shields for themselves, Sigtrygg found himself sitting nearby those who were busily cutting and shaping the wood they had brought back from the forest, listening to the cracking and pounding they made. He thought these the best sounds to be heard in all that country and he leaned contentedly against the wall of one of the buildings and let the warmth of the winter sun fall onto his face.

He was soon lulled into a deep sleep by the sounds of the crew's hammering and the warmth of the sun and now he had a very strange dream, for he thought he stood on the edge of the shore, where they had first beached their ship in this new country, and that he could hear a distant pounding, though he could not say what the cause of this unusual noise might be. He looked all about him but he was entirely alone, with none of the crew to be seen, and he began to call to his men, but no one came in answer. He thought this the strangest thing of all, since he knew the men could not be far, as Leif's houses stood close by, where the men must be, and these within hailing distance. Yet, no one came in answer to his summons, though his shouts grew louder, each time, and his voice more commanding.

He walked along the shore and looked out onto the horizon, as though seeking some sign of a ship. But there was nothing to be seen and the noise grew louder in his ears, with each passing moment, and he thought he must find the men of his crew as quickly as possible, for fear of the sounds which seemed to grow so loud they now overwhelmed the entire countryside. All at once he began to run inland from the beach toward Leif's houses but, try as he might, the beach seemed to stretch on ahead of him and everything seemed just as far away as before, and he could not find its end. Yet he continued to run toward the settlement until it seemed to him he could run no more and now he fell to the ground and lay there as the noises became a great pounding above him.

When he looked up he saw that a dark swarm of black-winged birds hovered over him, pounding the sky with their wings.

Now the birds began to descend to earth, to the place where he lay, and they all circled over him and came down with their great wings flapping, and he saw that these were black ravens and that they croaked angrily among themselves as they came. Then he lifted his head and he could see, in every direction, these same birds arising out of the land and joining their fellows in the sky above where he lay, and all of these began to drop down onto his fallen body and cover him, burying their fierce beaks in his flesh. Then he struck out at these, his tormentors, to drive them away with his flailing arms and legs, but there were more of these birds than he could possibly have counted and they would not be chased off. Thereupon, he seized one of the creatures and twisted its neck till its face was turned toward him and now he could see that its face was the face of a man, and he thought that he knew it.

Then all the birds let out a cry of great anguish and they turned upon him with a fierceness they had not shown before, as though to tear his flesh from his bones. Sigtrygg sought to run these off with every bit of strength that remained in him but the ravens were more determined than he was, and they fought him with wings and sharp beaks, and he could now see no way to overcome the creatures. He thought they would devour him alive where he lay, though the dead raven, whose neck he had twisted, lay still in his hands. But now that raven in his hands became a man and no bird at all, and he found himself clutching the dead creature as though it were a dear brother and he felt hot tears fall from his eyes onto the fallen man's face. And when he looked down at this man and saw the face, still wet with his own tears, he could see that the face was the face of the Skraeling, Bjorn, whom he had made a captive in Leif's houses.

And now, all the other ravens, which swarmed over him, and those still circling in the sky or still rising up out of the land in every direction to fly in a great mass above him, also appeared to him to bear the faces of men and not of birds at all and, when he looked more closely, he could see that on every one of them was the self-same likeness which the first bird had worn and it, too, was the face of the Skraeling Bjorn, who called himself W'tnalko.

Sigtrygg woke abruptly from this strange dream and shook himself, as though to shed that sleep-inspired vision, and then he looked about him at the men still working nearby and at the sun which hung low, in the wintry sky. He got to his feet at once and walked uncertainly from that place where he had but lately slept, walking slowly among the houses, until he came to the place where the Skraeling sat, still tied by his rope to a large post in the ground, watching the men cut the shield wood with his dark, unmoving eyes. The Skraeling looked up at him then and the sight of his dark face struck Sigtrygg like an icy wind sweeping out of the northern wastes. He did not linger there but went quickly to find Vragi and when he saw him he took him aside and told him everything he had seen in his dream, asking if he thought it held any particular meaning.

"It is said," Vragi answered him, after some thought, "that every man is given three dreams in his lifetime which foretell his fate, though no single dream alone may suffice to tell the whole tale. But each will hold a portion of the truth. If this is one of those visions, I feel you must now pay it some heed."

"Then this will be the second of such dreams, which I have had, and not the first," said Sigtrygg, "for on the night you came to my uncles' holdings in Brattahlid, I dreamed similarly. And then I beheld our friend Arnliot Keelfoot, who appeared to me from the inland ice, casting a shadow across the fjord. This shadow seemed to grow larger and larger, the longer he stood there, until it engulfed all of my uncles' lands and buildings and caused a fire to ignite within their houses. And then it seemed to me that my kinsmen were trapped within these fires so that they were burnt alive."

"You should have told this to me sooner," said Vragi, "for the first dream will have a bearing on the second, and on how we conduct our affairs in this country, hereafter."

"Yet, do such visions speak truthfully?" Sigtrygg asked him, after awhile, "for I have certainly had rough sleeping before this, though there was little enough that came of it. In my opinion, a man should not put a great deal of faith in such things, since they may mislead and urge us down false roads."

"Then why did you ask me about it, if you thought it of such small note?"

"I was taken by the strangeness of the matter," Sigtrygg answered, "and, in truth, I thought it foretold my death."

"That it may certainly have done," said Vragi, "although there is yet a third dream to be read, and no telling when you will have the chance for that. But for now, I think we should give some thought to these two dreams which you have already had, for there will be some truth to be discerned in them."

"What do you think they mean, then?" asked Sigtrygg.

"That's hard to say," Vragi replied, "although I take it that farmer Torfi's son may yet cause you some harm, where your kinsmen are concerned. Still, we are here and not in Greenland, with the western sea between us, so there's no great likelihood of that, for the time being."

"And what of the second dream?" asked Sigtrygg.

"That is another matter," Vragi said, "for these birds you dreamed of are certainly much closer to hand and it won't do to take them lightly."

"Then what do you think we ought to do?"

Vragi was silent for awhile, looking up at the pale sky as though seeking the answer to Sigtrygg's question. At last he spoke and this time his voice was very low, for he seemed to be speaking more to himself than to his companion. "Some people would say that a dream like this is sent into the world to give a man a choice, and that rarely an easy one. In which case you are not likely to find safe harborage, now, however you tack your sails in the winds this dream-gale blows. Still, you must make for the land."

"It's all the same to me, how things turn out," Sigtrygg answered him, "for no man may live past his appointed time, and I don't think I'm likely to have any more luck in that than other people. But at the least I would know the courses before me, and in which direction you think I ought to be sailing."

"Then it's time you gave some thought to Arnliot Keelfoot's words when we found that Skraeling in the forest beside the Icelanders' houses," said Vragi, "for it seems to me our friend gave you certain advice then concerning this captive, which you thought very little of at the time; though perhaps you had been wiser to heed his words."

"And what words were these?" Sigtrygg asked him.

"That you cut the Skraeling's throat," said Vragi, "and bury him where we found him."

CHAPTER XIV

A WALK IN THE FOREST

Not long after this, Sigtrygg called his crew together and asked if anyone had any more to say about the Skraelings who lived in that part of the world than had been said before, "for I have the feeling that our success or failure in this enterprise will greatly depend on what we do now."

No one seemed to have much to add until Olvir stepped forward. He said he only knew what was told at night over the house fires in Brattahlid, concerning the journeys which the Eirikssons had made. "And now it must be recalled," said he, "that, while Leif Eiriksson never found any evidence of Skraelings in the part of Vinland he claimed for himself, his brother Thorvald was not so fortunate. It will be no surprise to any in our company to hear that Thorvald died from the arrow of one of these Skraelings, while he was exploring the country east of here. But some may not know that his men also found signs of these people to the west and south, along the coast. In which case, we must conclude that these people are to be found all around the place where Leif made his land claim and that we are unlikely to avoid them for very long now, if we remain in this place."

Arnliot remained silent and Sigtrygg asked him why he was so quiet, "since you are not the sort to let others have their say without making your own thoughts known."

"I have not been hesitant to offer my opinion about this to you in the past," said Arnliot, "and I don't think you will find me reticent now, though I doubt you will find my advice any more to your liking this time than before."

"I will be the judge of that," Sigtrygg answered him, "but I have the feeling you are still of the same mind concerning that Skraeling we have got in our keeping."

"I don't think there's any use keeping him alive," said Arnliot, "if that's what you mean. Once he breaks free, it will not be long before he brings his kinsmen down on our heads. And then we will find it hard going to keep a foothold in this country."

"Some people would think it will not be long, in any event, before we meet more of these Skraelings, if they are as numerous in this country as the tales suggest," Sigtrygg said. "Perhaps our manner of treating this one fellow will have a bearing on how we are received by his kin."

"I would certainly not want to pin my hopes on that," answered Arnliot, "for history has shown these to be a harsh and unfriendly people. Or have you forgotten the dealings which Thorfinn Karlsefni had with them?"

"He had trading with them, to be sure," said Sigtrygg.

"Still, blood was spilled; and the Icelander and his followers had to flee this country, with what they could carry, if they would save their lives," said Arnliot.

"I don't think it's entirely clear what caused the falling out between the two parties, since the tales are all garbled where this matter is concerned," Sigtrygg replied. "Or if those were even Skraelings of the same race as the ones we think must dwell near here. Some hold the Icelander made his landing at a place which is far removed from my grandfather's holdings; and that because he sought to make a permanent settlement, which he could not hope to do on Leif Eiriksson's land."

"Still," said Arnliot, "there's no telling if they are the same or different. And I, for one, am not anxious to test the matter out by letting this captive of ours run free to report our whereabouts to his fellows."

Sigtrygg now asked if anyone else thought he had something

to add. No one stepped forward so he turned to Vragi and asked what he advised.

"That is best left to you," the old viking told him, "since you are the one most concerned with this matter. But, if I were the one to decide, I would not find it difficult to follow the advice of those who counsel prudence."

Sigtrygg now said they were to bring the captive to him and Thorolf and Asmund went off to bring W'tnalko in, for they had kept him bound during their deliberations in one corner of one of the smaller houses which Leif had built. The Skraeling saw the faces of the Greenlanders when they brought him in and it was soon clear to him that matters had taken a rather serious turn. Where smiles and gruff good fellowship had been their manner of greeting him in the past, only somber looks met him now. Olvir, who had been somewhat more friendly to the Skraeling than the others, now only averted his eyes when the man looked in his direction.

"Now the matter will be put to the test," Sigtrygg said and he told Thorolf to place the rope which hung about the Skraeling's neck in his hands. Then he asked the Skraeling if he thought he would like to walk awhile in the forest, as was their custom.

W'tnalko said he would be glad to do this for, in truth, he found the Greenlanders' company somewhat wearying and he longed for the tree-covered pathways which lay so near, yet which were now beyond his reach because of the rope which Sigtrygg and his crew kept always about his neck. Sigtrygg replied that he also felt the need to leave the settlement and so he took hold of the walrus hide rope and led the Skraeling into the nearby trees while the others looked on.

He took no one else along with him and carried nothing else but the sword at his belt and a long knife, which he was accustomed to keep on his person since his hunting days in the northern waste lands. Then he disappeared with the Skraeling among the trees' shadows, for both men were swift and silent walkers. They walked on for awhile among the forest paths, until they had gone much further than Sigtrygg had ever ventured with his captive before and the branches of the trees became so thick and gnarled, overhead, that it seemed as though they were walking beneath the shadow of a giant fish net which had been cast over them by the white winter sun.

When they had gone so far that Sigtrygg began to notice they had come to unfamiliar ground, he stopped in his tracks and told W'tnalko to sit down beneath a large tree. Then he seated himself a short distance away on a rock, which thrust up out of the earth, and let the end of the rope, which bound the Skraeling, fall to the earth beside him. He also took out his sword and laid it across his knees. W'tnalko looked at the weapon and at the rope, which he could see had not been bound to anything nearby and which now lay unattended at Sigtrygg's feet. But he said nothing.

Sigtrygg now asked the Skraeling if he thought the hunting was likely to be good when the seasons changed, for they could already see some shoots coming up out of the ground and, here and there, new buds upon the trees.

The Skraeling replied that, in his opinion, the hunting was likely to be especially good, since all the signs pointed to it.

Sigtrygg said: "Then you certainly have a better nose for these things than I have, myself, Bjorn, for I am not as familiar with the animals' signs in this part of the world as you. Still, I doubt you would be much good in my country, out on the ice."

W'tnalko said he did not have much to say about that since he could not imagine a land which was, as Sigtrygg had so often described it, always covered by ice and snow and where a man was as likely to hunt his food out on the open sea as on dry land. Still, he said that, in his opinion, Sigtrygg's own skills as a hunter were certainly unlikely to be small.

"Is this a good area, then, for hunting," Sigtrygg asked him, "when the weather changes?"

W'tnalko replied that it certainly was.

"In that case," said Sigtrygg, "I now want to ask you whether or not you think it strange that we have not seen any of your kinsmen in this part of the world, since that day we found you with your companion wandering in the woods? Or were you two the only men left in all this wide country?"

W'tnalko replied that there were certainly other Skraelings like himself about.

"Then how is it that none have been seen since that day we found you?"

W'tnalko was silent for a time but it could be seen that Sigtrygg was intent on having an answer. So now the Skraeling cast his eyes about him and offered this answer, saying that not many of the Skraelings' settlements were likely to be found so near the sea, since most of those people preferred to live further inland, sheltered by the trees. Still, he added, there were Skraelings to be found all about in the woodlands, "if a man knows where to look for them."

"Yet we saw no sign of these as we sailed down the coasts of this country, and these were heavily wooded," Sigtrygg said.

W'tnalko replied that that wasn't surprising, "for we Skraelings do not readily show ourselves to strangers."

"Then how is it," asked Sigtrygg, "that you fell so easily into our hands, for most people would think it rather clumsily done, to be taken, as you were, standing about and gawking at others."

W'tnalko now told him that this was because he was not so different from others of his kind, for all the Skraelings were very much afraid of the place where Leif's houses stood, since they had never seen such structures before and had no idea of the kind of men who had built them. Or if these houses had even been built by men at all. Some held, he said, that the houses were the work of spirits who were not friendly to ordinary people, so most of the Skraelings were unwilling to venture too near to them, especially because of the strange looking, unburied corpses which had long lain beside the houses.

Still, W'tnalko said, he and his companion had been overcome by curiosity to see the strange houses and had made a special journey to them. Yet, they had been quite as surprised as the Greenlanders, themselves, at what was to be found there.

"Then you were travellers, just as we are," answered Sigtrygg after a time, "and that is not to be wondered at, for many people will think it worthwhile to seek their fortunes in other places. But what did you hope to see here?"

W'tnalko said it was considered an honorable thing, in his country, to go into places of great danger and return again unharmed. Besides, he added, "there is good hunting where other men fear to follow the game."

Sigtrygg laughed and said that this was certainly not surprising, "for the best lands are often those in which fear has kept others away. And now, it seems to me, you Skraelings are not so different from my own Greenland crew, since you both took the dried bones of these poor Icelanders for something more than what they were."

W'tnalko said nothing to this and Sigtrygg told him that he now wished to know more about the Skraelings who made their home in that part of the world, how many they numbered, what kinds of dwellings they built for themselves and where they were to be found. "And I am especially keen to learn what manner of men they are," he added, "since I find myself living so close by to them."

W'tnalko now grew more quiet than before and Sigtrygg asked if this meant he was unable to speak knowledgeably about these matters.

"I can certainly tell you what you want to know," the Skraeling replied, "but I am not sure who has the most to gain from it."

Sigtrygg said it was not clear that anyone would receive any more benefit than anyone else, by the conversation they were now having, "although some people would think it in their interest to speak freely, in the company of stronger men than themselves."

W'tnalko said he did not see much reason to be concerned about that.

Sigtrygg laughed again for he thought the Skraeling manly, despite his unimpressive appearance. "Then, at the least, you must acquaint me with the manner in which you Skraelings travel about, since that may help to avoid more bloodshed such as another chance meeting, like the last one, with men of your kind, is likely to bring."

W'tnalko replied that he thought it highly unlikely other Skraelings would soon come out in search of him, "for they will think me slain by the spirits who dwell in this place, and it will be some time before any are bold enough to come see the truth for themselves." In which case, he added, it was highly unlikely that he would be the one to greet them and tell what had occurred.

"Then that is even more reason to speak up now," Sigtrygg urged him, "for you have little enough to lose, in any event, and not much likelihood of parting company with us on your own terms, as things now stand."

But W'tnalko replied that he had no intention of being the cause of harm to his kinsmen, whatever else might happen to him, and now he sat in his place, still as stone.

They sat thus for some time, neither man breaking the silence. Then, after awhile, Sigtrygg took the sword which lay upon his knees and, stretching his arm away from the outcropping of rock on which he sat, placed the weapon, point downward, into the ground before him. Then he kicked the end of the Skraeling's neck rope away from him with his foot.

"There's no use arguing with stubborn people," he said, at length, "nor in slaughtering a man as though he were a beast in some farmer's barn. In my opinion, there are now only two choices before us and neither one is likely to be easy for a man such as yourself to make. For you must either take your chances among these trees, and hope you are quicker than I am, or else we are to become friends. In which case, it won't do to hold anything back concerning the nature of this country and the people who are to be found in it."

W'tnalko saw that Sigtrygg meant to bring matters to a head and that his chances were now not much better than a beast whose trail had been freshly struck and so he said he would accept the offer of friendship, "if you will tell me first what you want to know."

"Firstly," said Sigtrygg, "how many Skraelings, like yourself, are to be found in this part of the world and where do they make their homes?"

W'tnalko said he had no answer to that, "for I have no knowledge of such things. Only that there are a great many, some of whom live nearby, while others are much farther away. Nor are all of us Skraelings alike, for some are more numerous than others; and some more warlike."

"Then how do they go about?" asked Sigtrygg. "In large groups or alone? And what manner of transport do they rely on?"

"That depends," replied the Skraeling, "for some band together while others do not." As to travel, he added that this was accomplished by each man on his own feet. "But, if we must cross any kind of waterway, we do so in small boats, for we have no vessels such as you Greenlanders have, and have never seen their like before."

"And what of the houses?" Sigtrygg pressed him. "Certainly you have nothing after the fashion of those which we are accustomed to build, or you would not have found ours so unusual."

W'tnalko agreed that this was true, "for," he said, "we do not build in the same manner as you. But there are people who live far to the south and west of here who build even larger houses than you Greenlanders. They make these of earth, which they pile higher than the tallest trees in the forest; and they make their homes inside of them. But I have not seen this with my own eyes."

Sigtrygg now asked him how near the closest Skraelings were and whether it was difficult to come to their part of the country, or for those Skraelings to come there to them. W'tnalko replied that he did not know what was to be found in every direction but that he thought the nearest Skraelings were no further than a fortnight's journey by foot through the forest "though a man must know the path, or he may never find his way home again."

"And do all the Skraelings go about as you do, with weapons of stone and entirely clad in animal skins?"

W'tnalko answered that they did, as far as he knew, and that none of them had ever seen weapons or garments like those which belonged to the Greenlanders.

"Then that is no less than I had thought," Sigtrygg replied, "for had there been Skraelings who possessed such things, you would not have acted as you did when first we found you. And now you will be thinking how unlikely it is that you will ever see your kinsmen again, since you have fallen in with us."

W'tnalko said it was all the same to him, whatever happened, for he had known beforehand of the dangers in coming to this place, if not of the nature of those men who had built their dwellings here, adding that he was now prepared for whatever might befall.

"In that case," said Sigtrygg, "you may not find my plans entirely to your liking, for it was in my mind to offer you life, rather than a hero's death, if you are willing to do one more service for me."

Most people will choose life, when it is offered, and this Skraeling was no different than others in this regard so now he asked Sigtrygg what he had in mind.

"Only this," Sigtrygg replied. "I want you to guide me and my companions through the forest, to that place where your kinsmen make their home, for it is in my mind to pay a visit to them before they decide to visit me. And then we will see what manner of welcome I am likely to find in this country and whether there is any chance our two peoples can live peaceably as neighbors, with so little distance between us."

When he heard this, W'tnalko replied that he was prepared to do a great many things to save his life, if that was what was required of him, but that he was unwilling to do this last thing which Sigtrygg now asked of him, "for I am not sure my kinsmen will thank me for it."

Sigtrygg took up his sword again and the end of that rope which hung from the Skraeling's neck. "Nevertheless," he said in a faraway voice, "that is what you are now to do."

CHAPTER XV

INTO THE WEST

When he returned to the settlement, Sigtrygg had the Skraeling in tow and he gave him at once into Thorolf's keeping, telling him to keep an especially sharp eye on the prisoner, "since it will be much more serious for us now, if this fellow should run off, than before." But aside from these instructions, he had very little to say to Thorolf, or to any of the others. Arnliot remarked that he thought it surprising Sigtrygg had returned with the Skraeling at all.

Several days now passed and Thorolf kept the Skraeling hobbled and bound at the wrists, for it seemed to him that Sigtrygg was more concerned than usual about their captive. Thorolf thought it would be the worst of luck if the Skraeling were to get away from them, while under his care. Nor did Sigtrygg reproach him for the extra bonds he placed on the man though, before this, they had only seen fit to bind their captive in this manner at night. After awhile, Thorolf went to Sigtrygg and asked him how long he was to continue with these extra precautions and Sigtrygg replied "as long as necessary" though he was unwilling to say anything further about the matter.

One morning, not long afterwards, when all the Greenlanders were still asleep in the main house, as was their custom, with the Skraeling safely secured in their midst, Thorolf found himself awakened by a thin stream of sunlight poking through the timbers of the wall above his head. He was not an early riser and he rolled over to avoid the harsh light on his still sleep-heavy eyelids. Yet, when he turned his face away, his eyes flickered open, momentarily, and then he saw that the Skraeling was not lying bound in his accustomed place. Although he would have preferred to go back to sleep, the absence of his charge now struck Thorolf like an axe blow and he sat up at once and began to look about him for some sign of their captive. He thought it exceedingly strange that the man should have found it possible to escape from the midst of the Greenlanders, bound hand and foot as he was, and he at once went over to Asmund, his fellow Icelander, and told him to get up.

"What is the meaning of this?" asked Asmund, for he was no more anxious to cut his night's sleep short than Thorolf had been.

Thorolf hushed him up at once and told him the situation.

"How do you know the Skraeling's gone?" Asmund demanded, no happier than before, now that he had discovered the cause of his early waking. "Have you looked everywhere for him?"

"Certainly," replied Thorolf, "but the man is not to be found in the house."

"Then we had better have a look outside," said Asmund.

Thorolf said these were his thoughts as well, but that he preferred they keep the matter to themselves, if at all possible, since the task of watching the Skraeling had been his, "and I don't know how Sigtrygg will take this loss."

"He will take it a whole lot better, if we find the man before he has gone too far," Asmund answered. "And the best hope for that now lies in waking the others." So they quickly set about rousing the rest of the crew.

Arnliot was angriest of all, when they had awakened him, not because of the early rising but because he said that everything was happening just as he had feared. He told Thorolf that if the Skraelings now came and drove them out of the country, it would be due to his negligence and that he hoped the Icelander was, at the least, prepared to give a good account of himself in the event these fears should prove true.

"I have never been backward in swordplay, before this," Thorolf replied.

"Then you will certainly have your chance to prove your mettle, if I have my way," Arnliot said, "for, if we do not catch this fellow, I have no doubt his kinsmen will pay us a visit before very long. But whether they come or not, I mean to test you out myself."

The crew all got their weapons down from the walls and armed themselves. Then they rushed out of doors into the early morning sun which was shining brightly over the trees. They stood about in a group, adjusting their eyes to the daylight. When they had got their bearings they began to move as a group toward the settlement's edge, but only then did they notice that Vragi was not with them.

"Where is the old man?" asked Olvir, for he was the first to notice the viking's absence. "It seems that no one has bothered to wake him, though he is certainly the most experienced among us and the man we are most likely to depend on at a time like this."

"Had he been in the house," answered Arnliot, "he would certainly have risen with the rest of us crewmen, for no one can accuse these Icelanders of being overly quiet. In my opinion he must have gone out before us."

"It doesn't pay to wait, in any case," Asmund said to them, "since every moment we spend in talk, now, is wasted where our prisoner is concerned. I don't think any of us is likely to doubt that fellow's speed, once he has got into the forest."

"He is certainly unlikely to be waiting around for you men to decide whether or not you mean to pursue him, in any case" said a voice to their rear.

They turned at once and saw the old viking leaning on his spear, behind them. Swiftly they told him everything that had occurred, although it did not seem that it came as much of a surprise to him.

When they had finished, Vragi came up and stood in their midst. "I don't think there's much chance of our overtaking the Skraeling, however we proceed now," he said at length, "for you men are no more at home in this wilderness, than he would be out on the seas. But some people might think we have had more luck in this matter than we deserve, since you have been so remiss in your duties."

They asked him what he meant and he told them to keep silent and follow close behind him. They now walked in a cluster to the edge of the forest and, when they had come to a small clearing, they saw Sigtrygg sitting quietly in the grass, the Skraeling seated cross-legged before him. Everyone was greatly surprised by this and Thorolf most of all, for he was still worrying about the consequences of his carelessness and was unable to quickly reconcile the sight before him with the memory of waking to find the Skraeling gone. Neither Sigtrygg nor the Skraeling seemed to have anything to say, until Sigtrygg finally looked up at them and asked Vragi what had taken them so long.

The rope was still about the Skraeling's neck, although Sigtrygg was not holding it, and it's end seemed to be lost in the tall grass.

"It doesn't say much for the vigilance of you men," Sigtrygg added, after awhile, "that I and this Skraeling can steal away so lightly in the night from amidst such sound sleepers. Still, I admit, it was hard-going cutting this fellow's bonds under Thorolf's groaning nose."

Arnliot stepped forward and asked Sigtrygg what his purpose was waking them in such an unusual manner.

"Not much," Sigtrygg admitted, "except that you men are now to go back to the camp and gather up whatever you can carry on your backs, for there is a short journey I intend to make."

"What do you have in mind?" asked Vragi.

"It seems to me we have been strangers in this country long enough," Sigtrygg answered him, "and I, for one, am anxious to have a more thorough look around."

Sigtrygg now told the crew they were to secure all those goods in the camp, which were too bulky to be carried, and conceal their ship, as well as they were able, from unwelcome eyes. Then, he said, they were to gather up the rope and all the woolen cloth they had brought out with them from Greenland, and whatever food-stuffs they could carry, and bring these to the forest's edge. "And take along whatever arms are left in the camp, as well," he added, "for I have the feeling they will prove handy."

"I don't see what good it will do for us to go about in this country so heavily laden with goods," Arnliot said, "since it will only prove an added weight, if trouble starts. We'd be better off to leave these things in camp and come back for them when they're needed."

"I'm not sure we'll have the chance," Sigtrygg said.

Vragi now asked if Sigtrygg knew the direction he wanted to travel in.

"That will be up to Bjorn," Sigtrygg answered, "for he is to be responsible for that."

Olvir asked if Sigtrygg didn't think they would be better off to go wherever he had in mind by sea, rather than overland, "for that is the fashion in which our predecessors explored this country, when they came out here; and we are certainly more acquainted with travel by sea than by land."

"In that case," Sigtrygg replied, "our Skraeling would be as useless to us as we would be in the forests, to him, for he is no more familiar with the seaways along this coast than we are with those trails leading inland. Besides, we would certainly need to come ashore at some point, and then others may note our landing, unseen by us."

He now asked the Skraeling if he thought he could lead them in such a way as to avoid meeting other people and W'tnalko replied that he could, if they did as he advised.

"Then that is how it is to be," said Sigtrygg.

Arnliot now said he thought it "rather sudden, to be putting ourselves into the keeping of this little man," but Sigtrygg replied that he did not see any problem with it, despite Arnliot's misgivings, "for we have had this Skraeling in our keeping, all winter long."

They now gathered up all the items which Sigtrygg had directed them to take and, before the morning sun was much above the eastern trees, they walked into the thickly forested country which lay south of Leif's houses. The trees quickly closed about them and it was not long before they came to unfamiliar country. Aside from Sigtrygg and, possibly, Vragi, few among them had any love for the heavily wooded lands which lay all about the settlement and, for this reason, they had always stayed close by the coast, in sight of the sea. Yet it was not long before they saw that they had left the sea far behind them and, in the dark forest, it seemed to them they were completely cut off from the good grey surf of the ocean.

For most of that first day they travelled ever deeper into the woods. The trees seemed to grow larger and much close together, the further they advanced, making the going difficult. Sigtrygg stayed out front with the Skraeling, the man's neck rope held firmly in his fist, and the others followed over the unfamiliar ground as swiftly as they could. But before the first day had ended, Sigtrygg suddenly came to a dead stop and all the men behind him halted, too.

Vragi asked him what he was thinking.

"We are certainly a noisy group of men, when travelling in this country," Sigtrygg said. "Though each man of the crew has surely done his best, walking through this forest is not the same thing as sailing on the open seas, for there's no telling who is nearby when the trees are as close together as they are here. And then others are likely to hear us, long before we become aware of them."

Vragi said this was probably true and now he asked Sigtrygg what he thought they should do about it.

"I think we must divide up into three parties, as we have done before," Sigtrygg replied, "each group to go along its own path, but keeping the others in sight. Then, while we may be more likely to be seen by strangers, since we will be travelling over more ground, at least we will not be taken by surprise, or all at the same time, if others should come across our path."

Vragi said he thought this a good plan, since there was no telling what lay ahead of them, and now he offered to lead one of the groups, "for, though a sea-going man, I have made my way overland through many a hard campaign before this."

Sigtrygg said he would accept this offer and now he told Arnliot to take a second group and that each of them was to follow at a discreet distance, "but keeping the Skraeling and me in sight."

Then they broke up into the three parties which Sigtrygg had decided upon, Vragi taking five of the crew with him off to the west and Arnliot taking his comrades to the east. Sigtrygg remained with the Skraeling, and with Olvir and his Brattahlid men, and these soon took up the march again, heading south and west, in the direction which W'tnalko led them.

The going did not become any easier, the deeper they went into the forest, for the country was broken by many rivers and lakes and they had to cross over or skirt round a great many of these. They soon had to admit they would be hard-pressed to find their way out of these woods again, without the Skraeling's help. Still, Sigtrygg urged them to press on; and so they did.

Each night they made three separate encampments and set a separate watch over each, for Sigtrygg said he didn't see much use in taking unnecessary risks. They also kept their cook fires low and put them out as quickly as they could, nor did they roam about for the purpose of taking game, though the animals in the forest were plentiful. "We have more than enough food along, for this passage," Sigtrygg told them, "so there's no need to go running through the forest, stirring up the beasts."

Some of the men thought it a hardship to subsist on dried meat when there was so much fresh provender about, but Sigtrygg would not yield on this point and no one seemed willing to argue the matter when they were so far from any recognizable landmarks.

When they had been travelling about in that country for more than a fortnight and had, as yet, seen no sign of any other human beings, Sigtrygg took the Skraeling aside and asked him if they were now close to their destination, "for it seems to me, Bjorn, that you foretold a shorter journey than we have now made."

W'tnalko said that Greenlanders did not travel as Skraelings did and that he was not accustomed to such a slow pace but that they were certainly moving in the proper direction. They now pressed on for several more days until, one morning, W'tnalko said they had come into a country where Skraelings were more likely to be found than before.

Sigtrygg said: "Yet, I have seen no signs of anyone else about."

The Skraeling made no answer to this.

Sigtrygg now told his men they were to begin traveling much closer together, since "I want to reduce the risks that any of us will stumble upon the people who live in these parts, before we are ready for them." Accordingly, the three little bands of men now fell in together and they began to advance much more cautiously through the thick trees. After another day's journey, they made their camp in a closed-in defile which was surrounded on all sides by dense woods.

Because spring was now upon them, the foliage had begun to spread over the forest floor and in the trees, and this made it easier to conceal their presence in the camp. But Sigtrygg said he had no desire to take unnecessary risks so he forbade them to light any fires that night and he set men to watch all about the perimeter. But nothing untoward happened and they awoke, on the following day, with no more indication they had come any closer to the Skraelings than before. They silently shouldered their burdens and followed W'tnalko back onto the forest floor and now the unusual quiet of that place seemed to lay especially heavy on their hearts.

Arnliot said: "In my opinion, this captive of ours has been leading us deeper and deeper into these woods without any hope of our finding our way out again. And that's not surprising, since he can have little cause to look out for our welfare."

Many of the crew thought the same way Arnliot did and these began to mutter.

"Better to cut this little troll's throat before he does us any further harm," some of them said.

"If he meant to guide us true, he would not have taken us such a roundabout way," said others, "so that we are now entirely cut off from the sun in the daylight, or the stars at night."

Sigtrygg told them to hold their tongues, though he was, himself, not a little concerned that they had lost their bearings since he still could see no sign of the people which W'tnalko had assured him were to be found there.

Vragi saw Sigtrygg's uncertainty and now he asked him what he wanted to do, whether to press on or try to find their way back?

"I don't see anything to be gained by cutting our travels short, at this point," Sigtrygg replied, "for we have already come a long way from our home base at this Skraeling's word. Returning now cannot be any easier than what lies before us, but it will cost us all the hard work we have put into the journey thus far."

Vragi said: "In that case, my advice is to push forward as quickly as possible, for these men are growing restive and there's no telling where that will lead."

"They are certainly better sailors than walkers," Sigtrygg agreed, "for they were out on unknown seas for a great deal longer than they have now been roaming in these woods."

That day W'tnalko led them through some of the thickest brush they had seen up till then. About midday they heard a change in the forest's sounds and a gurgling noise in the distance. Sigtrygg stopped and asked W'tnalko what he thought this meant.

"It's just as you think," the Skraeling replied, "a river."

"How far?" Sigtrygg asked.

"Not far," W'tnalko said.

They went on until the sounds were clearly discernible to all that company and now they could tell they were not far away from a fairly large body of moving water. "Now we are to be especially careful," Sigtrygg told them, "for the cover of the forest will certainly fall away, the closer we come to this waterway. And then we will be as easily seen as the ducks and geese which are likely to make their home there."

Accordingly, they all got down on their bellies and came up, with great care, to the river's edge. Just as Sigtrygg had guessed, there was little in the way of foliage, the closer they came to the water, though the grass was high enough to conceal them so long as they kept low to the ground. The first thing they saw were the birds, sitting on the narrow river, and most of the crew became very excited about this since they had not caught or eaten any fresh game from the day they had left Leif's houses. They also thought it a great thing to see the sun in the open sky once more, without the dark green shroud of the forest trees to block their view. Nor was the sight of the water, itself, unwelcome to these men who had spent their entire lives within sight of the sea.

Sigtrygg said he thought the river was not much of an ob-stacle, "although it's too deep for an easy crossing."

Now while he was speaking thus, he felt a hand on his shoul-der and he looked around to see Arnliot close beside him. The big Ketilsfjordman was gesturing to a place on the other side of the river where the tall grass had moved slightly.

"What do you see?" Sigtrygg asked him.

"I'm not sure," Arnliot replied, "but there is certainly a patch of brown color moving about in the grass on that side of the river."

Sigtrygg looked in the direction in which Arnliot had pointed and now he thought he could see the same thing.

"What do you think it is?" Arnliot asked.

Sigtrygg did not give a quick answer but lay there on his belly, with the others, making no sound. After awhile, the grass moved again and now they could all see how a large doe was pushing her way uncertainly through the grass to reach the edge of the swiftly flowing river. She put her head down and began to drink lightly from the stream, her ears flicking quickly, back and forth, over her head.

"Here is tonight's dinner," said Arnliot, "though she is on the other side of the river, for I don't see how we can pass by such an opportunity as this is."

Sigtrygg reminded him that they had refrained from chasing the creatures in the forest, until now, to avoid making their pres-ence known to others who might be about, "and since we have now come into Skraeling country, this is a matter of even more urgency than before."

"Even so," said Arnliot, "we crewmen of the Gull have been without fresh meat for far too long, to my way of thinking, and now we have the solution to this problem put into our hands. There's no need to make a big fuss over this either, since the beast is not far off and the area about the river is open enough to see that we are not observed."

"Still," said Sigtrygg, "she is not as close as some would think. If you miss your aim, she will not be easy to bring down, for the river lies between us."

"I'm not likely to miss," replied Arnliot, "or do you think you are the only one who can cast a well-aimed spear?"

Sigtrygg agreed that there were certainly others who might be able to throw as well as he, or as far, but added that they would only get one chance to spear this creature, in any event, so the man who tried had better be sure of his mark. "Still, if you are so intent on this, I won't stand in your way," he said.

Then Arnliot picked out a spear for himself and ran his finger along its edge and carefully felt its weight. When he was satisfied with the quality of the weapon, he slowly stood up in the midst of the high grass and drew the spear back behind his head, sighting the forest creature on the river's farther shore, all the while. The Greenlanders held their breath, for they were already dreaming of the feast the doe would provide them with, after living so long on the dried meats they had carried with them out of Leif's houses.

Now Arnliot held steady but did not cast, since the creature seemed skittish; and Sigtrygg looked up at him, after awhile, asking if he meant to take the animal before it had finished its business at the river, "or do you think she will be an easier mark when she has drunk her fill?"

"Some people would think it better done to wait till the beast is least likely to bolt, than to make a hasty cast and leave our supper to feed other bellies," Arnliot said. Then he again pulled the spear back the full length of his arm and, smiling, added: "Now we shall see whose spear flies truest."

But at that moment the creature seemed to jump in her place and, landing stiffly on her hooves, began to move sideways into the tall grass. Arnliot leaned forward to hastily throw the spear, before the deer was entirely lost to sight, but Sigtrygg leaped up and caught him as he sought to cast the weapon, pulling him down into the shelter of the grass and undergrowth, where the other Greenlanders were lying.

"Do you so fear another's skill," Arnliot said sharply, "that you would deny these men fresh meat for their supper?"

"Keep still," Sigtrygg said, "or that spear of yours had been our bane."

"What do you mean?" asked Arnliot.

They could now see that the deer was leaning sideways into the grass and that a large red spot had formed on her chest, just below the neck. As she toppled backwards, on unsteady legs, the feathered shaft of an arrow stood out from the creature's tawny fur and protruded upwards. Then the deer fell and was lost to their view.

"Who shot that?" Arnliot said.

"I have no better idea than anyone else here," Sigtrygg replied, "but it certainly did not come from our side of the river."

They all looked about them and then at W'tnalko, who was lying silently, watching the opposite bank. Sigtrygg followed W'tnalko's gaze and soon he could see a man coming out of the undergrowth where their captive's eyes had been fixed. The stranger was stooped low and running soundlessly toward the place where the deer had fallen. Sigtrygg could see that he was clad much as their captive was, entirely in the skins of animals, and that he wore various shells about his person. In his hair were birds' feathers.

Arnliot said: "That Skraeling means to have our dinner unless we take it back from him." And now he half rose in the grass, gripping the spear he was carrying tightly with his fist.

"There's no use hoping for that," Sigtrygg said, catching the larger man by the arm, "for you can never get across this river without him seeing you first. And then you may find it hard going, for there will be no advantage of surprise in your favor."

"Still, he is but one man," answered Arnliot, "and I don't think anyone is likely to think me unequal to this task."

"Yet there may be more," Sigtrygg cautioned him, "for they can hide on that side as easily as we conceal ourselves here."

"If so," Arnliot asked, "why have they not shown themselves yet?"

"Perhaps for reasons not dissimilar to our own."

As Sigtrygg said this, two more Skraelings suddenly came out of the undergrowth, as though arising out of the earth itself, and now these two made their way to where the first man stood, bending over the deer. These new men were garbed in the same fashion as the first and all three wore their hair in the most outlandish manner, with parts of their skulls shaved and the hair tied up in knots which fell over their faces or about their necks. The first man bent over the fallen deer and lifted it up by its head while one of the others took out a stone blade and drew it quickly across the animal's throat. Then they began to tie the dead creature's legs together and one of the strangers placed the carcass on his shoulders.

Arnliot said: "I don't think there are any more than these three about, or they had come into the open by now; in which case we are certainly a match for them. Nor does it seem fitting to sit idly by while they make off with our kill."

"They have not yet seen us, or they had not shown themselves so readily," Sigtrygg replied. "But then you cannot call them thieves, since they could not have known that others had a claim on that beast."

"Still," said Arnliot, "it would be dishonorable to let them go without giving them something to remember us by, especially since they have taken the food from our mouths."

"In my opinion, it's better to leave things just as they are," answered Sigtrygg, "since there's no telling how many more are about, beyond this river." He now turned to W'tnalko and asked him if he knew who these men were.

The Skraeling replied that he did not, though by the cut of their garments he thought they came from further down river, where, he said, a great many such Skraelings were to be found.

"In that case," said Sigtrygg, "I don't think it can do us much good to show ourselves to these men."

He told Arnliot and the others they would have to content themselves with eating their dried provisions for just a little while longer and then he turned back to W'tnalko and said: "Now it is plain to me, Bjorn, that you have not been deceiving us, though others in this crew have certainly doubted you before this. Still, I want to know how you think we should proceed from here?"

The Skraeling replied that there was nothing else for them to do but go further up river.

"That seems like very sensible advice, to me," Sigtrygg agreed.

So that was the direction they now decided upon, though they traveled, afterwards, far back from the river bank, keeping well within the line of the trees.

CHAPTER XVI

AN UNSOUGHT MEETING

They walked for three more days, following the course of the river, but staying far back from its bank to avoid being seen by any of the Skraelings who lived in that part of the country. On the morning of the fourth day Arnliot said he thought they would have been better off to have gone down river, instead of the direction they had taken, "for then, at least, we would have had the chance of seeing other people, or did we come this far only to count the trees in this land?"

"There are certainly an overabundance of these," Thorolf agreed, and now the other members of the crew began to grumble at the harshness and seeming pointlessness of their travels.

"Other men who have come out to this country have spent their time gathering a rich cargo to take back with them to the home countries," some of them complained, "rather than chasing through these endless woodlands, as we are now doing." Others added that, while there were riches enough for the taking in this new land, there was little likelihood that they, themselves, would benefit, from these, "for we can't even hope to find our way back to our ship from here."

Sigtrygg, when he heard these mutterings, asked them if they thought they were indeed worse off than the other Norsemen who had come out to Vinland before them, "though these all met with much greater difficulties than we have had so far? Nor did any of them fall in with a Skraeling to take them through the country, as we have now done."

Arnliot replied that "it still remains to be seen what good this Skraeling means to do us since, in my opinion, he is no more to be trusted than those other wretches, who so lately robbed us of our rightful dinner."

After he had listened to such talk for awhile, Vragi said: "I don't think you men can hope to get very far with this kind of thinking. Most people will agree that successful people usually know how to make the best of difficult circumstances and are not daunted by the things they have not foreseen, while you men are always groaning and seeking to run back across the sea, as soon as things become the least bit unpredictable, to sit in comfort on your back-country farms."

Sigtrygg said that these were his thoughts as well and he now asked those of his crew, who seemed the most put out by their travels, if they would prefer to part company with him and find their own way back to the coast, "for I have no intention of holding this matter against any of you; and I think I am likely to be far better off traveling about, with only those who think as I do."

Asmund said: "It's not likely any of us will be able to make our way back to Leif's houses without this Skraeling's help, in any event."

"I would not be overly concerned about that," answered Vragi, "for I think we can point you in the direction of the coast, at the least, for it seems to me this river is no different from others which I have known; in which case it will certainly find its way into the sea, when it has gone its full length. And then it is a small enough matter to follow the way northward to Leif's houses. It's early enough in the season, too, so you need have no fear of losing your way before winter. Only keep a sharp eye out for those Skraelings who live down the river, for it is plain they have a penchant for seashells from the coast."

"There's no use trying to divide us by such words," Arnliot now said, "for we Greenlanders are not so easily frightened as some people might think. Still, in my opinion it had been better to sit in Leif's houses and let these Skraelings come to us."

So now they all agreed to continue on, just as before, with Sigtrygg and the Skraeling leading the way, and it was not long before they were again following that path which the Skraeling showed them, between the thickly growing trees. Now, the longer they walked, the farther away from the river they seemed to wander and Sigtrygg asked W'tnalko if he were as certain of the path as before. W'tnalko replied that he had no doubts in the matter and that they were now not very far off from their destination.

They came to a small clearing, surrounded by dense trees on every side, and here they paused, the men putting down their burdens while W'tnalko wandered over to where the woods seemed to shut them in. Overhead the leafy branches of the trees grew so tightly together that only a little of the sun's light was able to come through to the place where they stood. Sigtrygg said this was certainly a different sort of country than they were accustomed to.

Vragi replied: "The world is a much wider place than most men know and it would not surprise me if this country had a great many more unusual sights in store for us than this."

Now, when he had spoken these words, they heard an odd buzzing sound, which seemed to rush past their ears, and then another and yet a third, and these were followed by several dull thuds and the voice of a man groaning. When they turned they saw that Aki Erlendsson lay on his side upon the ground, a feathered shaft lodged in his throat, his blood already pooling where his face lay, half buried in the dirt. His mouth was open too, making a gurgling sound, for he was still groaning through the blood which rushed out from between his parted lips.

"Put up your shields," said Vragi quickly, "and form a wall against these trees."

The Greenlanders did as they were told and soon the dull thud of more arrows followed, striking their shields and the nearby tree trunks.

"What is the meaning of this, Bjorn?" Sigtrygg asked, and then he urged W'tnalko to take shelter with them inside the shield wall.

"There's no need for that," the Skraeling replied without showing much concern, "for our attackers are not likely to cause harm to me, though it's clear the same cannot be said for you Greenlanders."

Sigtrygg said: "If you do not fear these arrows and will not stop them, you must certainly have had a part in this. In which case you cannot hope to leave here alive, for I still have that rope which binds you in my hand."

W'tnalko replied that he was not responsible for the predicament they now found themselves in, although it had certainly been very foolish of Sigtrygg to have thought he could come upon the Skraelings unawares in their own country. "Still," he added, "it's all the same to me, what happens now. But my death is not likely to do you much good, since you men cannot see your attackers, while they can readily see you. Nor are you likely to find your way out of this country again, before their arrows find your backs."

"It's not so easy to strike a Norseman down as that," said Arnliot in hot anger, "though you forest people hide behind your trees and toss these puny, stone-tipped arrows in our direction. Now we are alerted and will not easily be taken by surprise again."

"I don't see how you will get the chance for that," W'tnalko said and he sat himself down outside the circle of shields, which the Greenlanders had made, and waited for Sigtrygg to tighten the rope and drag him into the circle and kill him. All the while the arrows continued flying in the direction of the Greenlanders and these seemed to be coming from every side so that it was soon apparent the Skraelings were all about them.

"How many of them do you think there are?" Sigtrygg asked Vragi and the old viking replied that it was not so easy to count men you cannot see, "but there are certainly more arrows than I would like flying about our heads."

Sigtrygg again asked W'tnalko if he were willing to come into the shield wall but the Skraeling made no answer, just as before. Now suddenly the arrows stopped and voices were heard in the

Skraeling tongue, just beyond the nearest stand of trees. W'tnalko replied to these, too swiftly for Sigtrygg or any of the other Greenlanders to catch his words, and then the voices behind the trees spoke again.

"What do they want?" Sigtrygg asked W'tnalko.

"They want to know if they are to kill you."

"And what was your reply?"

"That you must be spared, if you will lay down your arms."

"Some people would think that a foolhardy gesture before an enemy who will not show you his face...or his intentions," Sigtrygg replied.

"Still, it is better than dying in these woods," said the Skraeling, "without any hope of finding your way home. For those of you who are not killed today will certainly be hunted down tomorrow, or afterwards, till all you Greenlanders lie spitted in the earth like that man of yours who took the arrow in his throat."

Arnliot said, in a low voice, that his counsel was now to rush the nearest line of trees in one group and, once into the woods, see how many of the Skraelings they could lay hands on. "In that way we will give the best account of ourselves so these forest people will not soon forget what kind of men we Norse folk are."

"We carry our shields with us," said Olvir quickly, "and most people would think that is enough. But these Skraelings have the trees all about them for their shields. I do not think we can make much headway against such men in this place, for the advantages are all with them."

Vragi said he thought this well-said "for shields are likely to be more of a hindrance than a help when fighting in such close quarters. Nor are you men accustomed to the manner of fighting which these Skraelings practice."

"Still we cannot stand here all day till they get the better of us," said Arnliot, "for it is hard enough to see them while the sun is above these trees. How much more difficult, after the sun has set?"

Sigtrygg called out to W'tnalko again and asked him the

Skraelings' terms.

"Your lives," said W'tnalko. "No more."

"We must keep our arms," Sigtrygg said.

"Certainly not," W'tnalko replied.

"Then what guarantee will we have that you will offer us peace?"

"No more than you gave to me," answered the Skraeling, "when you took me and my companion in the forest."

"We are better off to take your head," Arnliot said to him, "and let the consequences fall out as they will."

"That is certainly within your power to decide," W'tnalko agreed.

"How is it you have betrayed us in this fashion, Bjorn," Sigtrygg now asked the Skraeling, "seeing that I have given you my friendship?"

W'tnalko made no reply to that and now Arnliot said: "This only shows the folly of trusting strangers, as I have long warned you. But there's no use making a fuss over what is past. It's time we taught these Skraelings how Norsemen can die."

Sigtrygg now asked Vragi if he agreed that this was the only path open to them.

"Some would think killing as many of these people as we can, an honorable way to leave this world," Vragi replied, "and I have thought as much, in my time. But now it seems to me you have come into this country for a very different purpose than the meaningless death, in these woods, which you are now contemplating. Nor am I entirely sure these other men will think your promise to them well-kept, if you ask them to lay down their lives here, with no deeds yet to their names but death in this unknown place. And none to record it."

"Still," Sigtrygg said in a low tone, "it's not certain they will be better off in the hands of these Skraelings, for we don't know what kind of people these are."

"That is certainly true," said Vragi, "but we have seen somewhat of their nature in this captive of ours, and that has not been without merit. As for you, it seems you are a man who rushes on to embrace his fate, whatever the portents. Still, some would think your tale not yet told out, since your dreams still lack an end. As for these others, who can say?"

Sigtrygg now asked W'tnalko if he and his kinsmen were willing to discuss terms.

"What do you have in mind?" W'tnalko said.

"I want to know what is to become of me and my men, if we give ourselves into your hands."

"That will depend on what others have to say," W'tnalko answered, "but, if you choose instead to make a fight of it, I can certainly predict how things will turn out."

Sigtrygg now took the knife from his belt and tossed it to the Skraeling. "Whatever occurs from here on," he said, "there's no use holding it against you. You only did what you thought right in defense of your kinsmen, though I cannot say how you called to them when we had you under such close guard every moment you were with us."

W'tnalko readily took up the knife and, after handling it a moment, applied it to the rope at his neck and quickly cut the tough hide away. He arose then and, holding the knife high above his head, let out the strangest sound the Greenlanders had ever heard from a man's throat. It began like the barking of a dog but seemed, after a moment, to become a wolf's howl. Answering howls now suddenly arose all around them and it seemed as though the forest was full of these strange noises.

"That was badly done," said Arnliot, after they had heard the answering howls, "to have cut our only hostage loose in this fashion. Still, at the least we now know where these men are to be found."

"It's not likely to do us much good, in any case," Sigtrygg replied, "since we still can't see them among these trees."

There was another thudding sound, this time at their feet, and, when Sigtrygg looked down, he saw that W'tnalko had returned his knife to him, though the Skraeling, himself, was nowhere to be seen.

"There's no use looking for him now," Arnliot said when he saw Sigtrygg looking about for the man, "for he has gone off to join his fellows. And that will certainly be a cause of regret for us since he, alone, had been able to show us the way out of this country."

"I don't think we will be leaving so readily, in any event," Olvir said, "for these forest men, it seems to me, are determined to prevent it."

Now they heard W'tnalko's voice from the woods, where the other Skraelings lay hidden, and he called to them and asked if they were ready to put aside their arms.

Arnliot replied that he was certainly unwilling to go along with such a cowardly policy but Sigtrygg said they would do as W'tnalko demanded, nevertheless, and now he told the Skraelings, in as loud a voice as he could, that his men would lay down their shields if the Skraelings would stop shooting their arrows at them, as well.

They got no reply to this, but the woods seemed to fall silent after a little while and the hail of arrows, which had plagued them, suddenly ceased. Sigtrygg now told his followers that there was no other choice, if they were to save themselves, but to put their lives into the Skraelings' hands.

"This is not the kind of ending you promised us when you begged for our support back in Greenland," Arnliot said. Still, he put his shield down on the ground with the others.

Now there was a rustling among the trees and several Skraelings stepped out into the open, showing themselves for the first time. They were small men, dark complexioned as W'tnalko was, and clad in animal skins like all their kind. They carried their bows, with arrows nocked in the bow strings, and these were pointed at the Greenland men. Several also held small stone-tipped axes and clubs in their hands. W'tnalko now came out of the woods, behind these men, and he told Sigtrygg that the Greenlanders must now set down their swords and other weapons, as had been promised.

Sigtrygg told his followers to do this and he, himself, now

placed his sword on the ground. W'tnalko came forward and took this weapon, as well as the knife from Sigtrygg's belt.

"Some people might think there is little honor in returning a borrowed knife to its owner," Sigtrygg said, "if you only meant to claim it again for your own."

To this W'tnalko offered no reply but continued to walk among the Greenlanders, with several others of his kinsmen, taking their weapons. The other Skraelings were much in awe of these men, for they had never seen people of such great size and with such unusual weapons. They showed a special interest in the iron edges on the Greenlanders' arms. Several of the Skraelings now struggled to pick up the large, two-sided war axe which Arnliot carried, but they were unable to lift it easily. This only made the great size of the Norsemen, and especially of Arnliot, who was surely the largest man they had ever seen, all the more impressive to them.

Sigtrygg and his crew could now see there were about thirty Skraelings in this band and that all were as poorly armed as W'tnalko had been when they had first found him, except that each of these had a drawn bow in his hands, which he did not scruple to aim at the captives. After seeing the quick, hard death of Aki Erlendsson, none of the Greenlanders were eager to test the Skraelings' aim again. Still, they did not find the appearance of these forest people, once they had come out from behind the trees which had shielded them, particularly worrisome. Arnliot said, in a very low voice, that he thought they were now much better positioned to rush their captors than they had been before, "and give a good account of ourselves besides, for I doubt we would find it very difficult overpowering such men as these."

But Sigtrygg told him to hold back since he wanted them to keep the terms of the agreement they had made with the Skraelings, "at least for now."

The Skraelings went about, from man to man, plucking at the Greenlanders' clothing and taking their weapons and other goods from them. They surrounded Arnliot and he looked down upon their dark heads, his angry look gradually fading to the wry smile of former days. None of the Skraelings were willing to come too close to him and he seemed to find this especially humorous.

The Skraelings now took the arms and goods from every man, in his turn, until at length they came to Vragi, who had been carrying nothing more than the long spear which he had cut for himself at Leif's houses, as had been his custom ever since they had begun their travels inland. By signs and words, the forest men told the old viking he was to give up the spear, but Vragi pretended not to hear or understand them. This made the Skraelings who were about him exceedingly ill-tempered and they began to shout and gesture wildly at him. Still, he affected not to notice these signs of their discontent until one of them raised a stone axe as though he meant to bring it down on Vragi's skull. The old man looked calmly, with his single eye, at the angry Skraeling and the Skraeling stepped back and dropped the axe to his waist. Other Skraelings now rushed up and surrounded Vragi, pointing their arrows at him and shouting fiercely.

W'tnalko ran to where the noise was greatest and asked his companions what the cause of all the commotion was. They pointed to Vragi and told him the old man, alone among their captives, was unwilling to give up his weapon.

"Why do you resist us," W'tnalko now asked Vragi in the language of the Greenlanders, "since all of your friends have accepted the terms which have been granted them? I cannot be responsible for your safety if you continue to act in this fashion, though I have promised you your lives if you will put yourselves in our hands."

"It's not resistance," Vragi answered, "for I am an old man who has seen his share of the dead and dying. Nor do I imagine I have the years left to me, which you younger ones can count on, so that death in these woods, or elsewhere, does not seem to be such a dreadful matter to me as it does to some others. Without this stick to lean on, it is unlikely I shall find it an easy task keeping up with the rest of this company and so an axe stroke or an arrow, from you Skraelings, may yet prove the lighter path for me."

W'tnalko turned to his fellows and waved them off, saying

Vragi was to keep the spear, if that was what he wanted, and so they let the matter pass.

Now the Skraelings all pressed in on the other Greenlanders and herded them into a tight group with their stone-tipped arrows and axes. They picked up the Norsemen's weapons but made their captives shoulder their own burdens, as before, and told them they were to follow W'tnalko and several others, single file, through the darkest part of the woods. The Greenlanders did as they were told, looking all about them for their captors, who now seemed to fade once again into the trees and heavy undergrowth of the forest.

When Arnliot saw that most of the Skraelings had again disappeared from view, he began to mumble that they had missed their best chance to overcome these people and would now have to await a better opportunity. But Sigtrygg replied that patience was certainly their best weapon in this case, and a watchful eye, and he urged his crewmen not to do anything out of the ordinary, unless he told them to.

"At the least," replied Olvir, when they had gone a little ways into the forest, "we have done better than those of our countrymen who came out to this land before us, for we, at least, have met these Skraelings on their own ground, whatever else now befalls."

CHAPTER XVII

IN THE SKRAELING CAMP

The Skraelings now led them back toward the river and, when they had reached the river bank, turned them northward again, proceeding up river. They traveled, thus, the better part of the day until they began to hear voices faintly in the distance. Then they saw what appeared to be a number of houses, built entirely of tree bark and animal skins, on the other side of the river and people running out of these down to the water's edge to see them. The people were all one with those who had taken them in the forest, being swarthy in complexion and dressed in hides like those men, except that these were mainly women and children. The children were all nearly naked, but the older women wore skins wrapped tightly about their bodies and held fast to the youngest of the Skraelings, lest they rush impetuously into the river. There was a great deal of shouting and gesticulating, but none of the Greenlanders could understand what was being said for they were too far away.

W'tnalko now came up to Sigtrygg and told him they were to cross the river and go into the Skraeling village. So now the Greenlanders went into the water, which was quite shallow at this place, and began to wade across. At its deepest point, the river rose no higher than their chests and Sigtrygg said to Arnliot: "It seems you are to get your wish, afterall, and cross this river."

"It's all the same to me," Arnliot replied, "so long as we can have our way with these people."

As they came up onto the farther shore, the people all fell

back, for they were quite as surprised at the appearance of these Greenlanders as their men had been in the forest. They made a great deal of fuss as each of the Greenlanders came up out of the river and, when Arnliot himself, climbed onto the shore, their voices seemed to rise in admiration and fear at his size, though, in truth, they thought all the Greenland men quite impressive to look on.

Then their Skraeling captors urged them to move on toward the houses and Sigtrygg led the way, his crewmen following. They came into a small clearing, between several large booth-like structures, and looked all about them. There were carcasses and skins of small animals hung up all around the clearing on long poles which had been tied together to form racks. Near the center of the area there was a small fire burning and a rack of fish hung over it, surrounded by smoke. On the booths, here and there, were feathered implements, as though for decorative purposes, and stone-tipped spears and other weapons lay about on the ground.

The people who edged closest to them had a dirty look, for their hair was dark and generally tightly bound while their faces seemed somewhat blackened from the smoke.

"These are certainly a poor people," Sigtrygg said, "for all the richness of this country."

"And that is just as I told you," answered Arnliot, "though you thought my words of small account before this."

W'tnalko said they were to drop their loads where they were standing but must move on, past the booths, to several larger houses which stood behind these. Sigtrygg replied that they would do this for now, if that was what was required, but that he was eager to meet their chief man, if they had one, and make a present to him of the goods they had brought, "for these are in payment for that man of your kin whom my men slew, that we may get an agreement of peace between us."

"I don't know what good there is in trying to pay for that killing now," Arnliot said, "since they have already slain one of our men, when they took us in the woods, and most people would agree that the one death cancels out the other. Still, the killing of that fellow Aki cannot be accounted such a great loss to us."

W'tnalko said that the death of Aki carried no weight in the matter at all, as they would presently see, but he urged them to speak up when they were brought before the Skraeling chief and make whatever offers of peace they thought right, "for much may depend on it."

Then they followed the Skraelings to the large houses and all the women and children went before them, assembling between these structures and making a great deal of noise. The Skraeling men followed close behind the Greenlanders, shouting as loudly as the women, but keeping their weapons trained on their captives.

Now a bear skin which hung over the entryway to the largest of the houses began to flap and was suddenly thrust aside, revealing two men and a woman who came out of the opening and stood before the Greenlanders with very serious faces. The first man was somewhat squat, with greying hair and a rounded belly which he made no effort to conceal with the animals skin he wore draped over one shoulder. The second man was smaller than the first and very frail looking. He seemed to be exceedingly old and his narrow hands shook with a slight tremor. His face was entirely covered over with brightly colored paint, giving it a rather fearsome aspect, and on his head he wore a most remarkable hat which seemed to consist of the fully feathered carcass of a large black raven, wings outspread, head and beak and sharp bird's eyes still intact.

When Sigtrygg saw this unusual sight he stepped back in some surprise and, for the first time, the men of his crew thought he showed uncertainty. But this passed quickly and he soon turned to W'tnalko, asking him who these men were.

"The man with the round belly is our chieftain," W'tnalko replied, "and he is called Anyok. The other is the oldest of our people, although no man knows how many winters he has seen. He is called Manitikaha and he is our Dream-Speaker, for he can see what will be, in the hours when most others are asleep. The woman is Tanakrit, the wife of Anyok, and she has a great deal to say about everything that happens in this clearing."

Sigtrygg looked at this woman who stood between and a little behind the two men. She was somewhat stout with greying hair, like her husband's, although her face was smooth and broad, and Sigtrygg said later that he thought she must have been a fine looking woman in her younger days.

The man they called the Dream-Speaker now began to sing a song in a low voice to himself and, when he did this, everyone in that clearing grew unusually quiet. Anyok, the chieftain, stepped aside and permitted the singing man to stand alone before the Greenlanders. Now the Dream-Speaker began to rock backwards and forwards on his heels and then he opened his eyes suddenly and fixed them on the Greenlanders and, most especially, on Sigtrygg.

"What does this mean, Bjorn?" Sigtrygg asked W'tnalko.

"That is still to be seen," W'tnalko replied, "although he has certainly taken an interest in you."

Now the Dream-Speaker began to walk about in the clearing, looking at each of the Greenlanders in turn, until he came to Arnliot and then he walked right up to him and stood beneath the large man's gaze. Though Arnliot frowned and made the hardest looking face he could muster, the old Skraeling did not even flinch or make the smallest effort to move back, as the other Skraelings had done when face to face with the big man from Ketilsfjord.

"Here is one who does not take you for the mighty man you'd have the rest of us believe you to be," laughed Sigtrygg.

"I'm not so sure you would find this as amusing, if I were to reach down and snap the fellow's back," Arnliot replied, "for he does not seem to me to be much stronger than some dried out stick."

"That would not be advisable," Sigtrygg cautioned him, "for then you would put us all at risk."

The Skraeling, who was called Dream-Speaker, looked for a long time at Arnliot and then he moved down the line, giving the same treatment to each of the crewmen until he came up to Vragi and then he stopped suddenly and looked into the old viking's single eye. He began to sing his song again, louder than before, and all the Skraelings in the clearing seemed to groan at this. The men who had brought them in raised their weapons and pointed these at the Greenlanders, watching the Dream-Speaker sing his song under Vragi's unmoving features.

"What is the meaning of this?" Sigtrygg now asked W'tnalko.

"That is hard to say," W'tnalko replied, "but it seems you have brought a very unusual person into our midst."

The Dream-Speaker now began to move back and away from Vragi, yet he kept a close watch on the old viking, as though unwilling to take his eyes from Vragi's one good eye. During all of this, Vragi neither spoke nor moved, though he also kept a careful watch on the proceedings.

The Skraeling sooth-sayer gave up examining the rest of the captives after this and now he hastened to the side of the chief of that people, whom W'tnalko had named Anyok. The two men conferred briefly and then the chief stepped forward and demanded to know who the leader of the Greenlanders was and why they had come to the Skraeling's country.

Sigtrygg said that he was the leader and that he had come with goods, by which he hoped to make amends for the wrong his men had done the Skraelings when they had killed that man who had been traveling with W'tnalko. He now tried to explain what had occurred and how the killing of the man, whom W'tnalko had named Aselekah, had come about. The Skraeling chief listened to these words without comment and asked W'tnalko a number of questions so swiftly that Sigtrygg could not catch the meaning. Then he turned to Sigtrygg and asked him where he and his crew had come from.

"From over the sea," Sigtrygg said, "a very great distance from this place; and many days' sailing."

The chieftain asked how many others there were in the country they came from and if all the people there were like them.

"They are not much different," Sigtrygg said. "We live in large houses by the sea and are not afraid to cross the ocean to get to those places we wish to travel to. As for our numbers, there are quite a few of us, though we are spread out over many lands which can only be approached from the sea."

W'tnalko now told the chieftain that Sigtrygg had said his home was in a place where it was always winter and that men did their hunting on great sheets of ice or on the sea itself. All the Skraelings thought this news indeed and they began to murmur loudly among themselves at the strangeness of this.

"I have heard of such a country where it is always winter," Anyok, the chieftain, said. "It is far to the north of here and the people who live there must go about in furs and many skins all year round. Still, I have not heard of any such sea people, as yourselves, though many have wondered who it was built those strange houses on the coast to the north and east of here."

"My grandfather, a great chieftain named Leif Eiriksson, built those houses," Sigtrygg replied, "and now I have come to live there and claim that land which lies about them, which we call Vinland, for my own."

Anyok turned to W'tnalko and asked him what he thought of these people. W'tnalko now recounted the tale of what he and his companion had seen, when they had first espied the Greenlanders, and how they had been surprised and fled before these men and been run down afterwards so that Aselekah, his companion, had been killed and he, himself taken captive. Then he told the chieftain, in great detail, about the nature of each of the Greenlanders as he had come to know them, without omitting anything, however insignificant it might have appeared. He told how it had been Arnliot who had run down and slain Aselekah and who had then seized him as well and how Sigtrygg, the Greenlanders' chief, had spared his life. Then he told about the treatment he had received, at the hands of the Greenlanders, over winter, and how Sigtrygg had conceived of this journey and ordered him to guide him and his crew to the Skraelings' home.

He said all of this so quickly and in such great detail that

Sigtrygg, for all his skill with the Skraeling tongue, could not follow half the words, yet it seemed to him that W'tnalko gave a fair account of how things had been. When W'tnalko was finished there was a long silence in the Skraeling camp, where before there had been loud shouts and howls at every new thing W'tnalko told them. The chief looked over the Greenlanders without saying anything and then he turned to his sooth-sayer and to Tanakrit, his wife, and these three began to speak among themselves.

"What do you think the outcome of this is likely to be?" Sigtrygg asked W'tnalko.

The Skraeling said he did not know, but now he told some of his kinsmen to bring up the goods, which the Greenlanders had carried with them out of Leif's houses, and lay these before the chieftain. This was quickly done and the Greenlanders' packs were cut open on the ground, before Anyok and his wife, and the contents emptied onto the earth. There was plenty of woolen cloth in those packs, which the Skraelings seemed to marvel at, and fine seal skins, as well as iron tools and implements which the crew had brought with them out of the house where their ship had been kept by the Leifssons, over the winter. The Skraelings also spread out the Greenlanders' weapons, though they made certain to place these well out of the reach of Sigtrygg and his men, and Anyok and the others all crowded round to see these unusual items.

Sigtrygg now told the Skraelings that all the goods had been brought as gifts to pay them for the unfortunate killing of their kinsman and as a gesture of peace between their two peoples. Anyok straightened at this and asked W'tnalko if the weapons were also to be included in the gifts that were offered.

"That is not possible," Sigtrygg replied when he heard this question, "since each is the personal property of one of my men and will be needed by us to hunt and sustain ourselves in this country. But the rest we have cheerfully brought to present to you."

Anyok said he thought the weapons were especially interesting and that they would certainly be as useful to the Skraelings for hunting, as to Sigtrygg and his men.

"Still," Sigtrygg said, "no man can readily give up his arms and hold onto his life for long in such a wild country as this is."

Anyok and the Dream-Speaker and Tanakrit, the wife of Anyok, now returned to the doorway of the large skin-covered house, out of which they had come. All three stood about there without speaking, though the chief continued to look at the Greenlanders, his expression fixed and altogether unreadable.

Sigtrygg turned to W'tnalko and asked him if this meant that the Skraeling chief had now accepted his offer of gifts and friendship. But W'tnalko made no reply.

"If he thinks to take our arms, as well," said Arnliot, "it will be a much graver matter; and then I think we cannot stand idly by while these people rob us of what is ours. Nor was it wise to show them such weakness, as we have now done...as though begging their forgiveness for that killing up at Leif's houses will put things right."

"Most people will think we have overpaid for the killing, in any event," said Olvir, "even if they leave us our arms."

The chieftain gestured to the Skraeling men who stood all about the clearing with their stone weapons drawn and told them to close in on the place where the Greenlanders were standing and then he told the Skraeling women to gather up all the goods, including the Greenlanders' arms.

W'tnalko now turned quickly to Sigtrygg and said they were to leave the chief's presence and go to the house that had been prepared for them, where they were to be kept under close guard until the chief had made his decision concerning their fate.

"This is not the sort of hospitality I had expected," Sigtrygg said, "when I thought to make this journey and bring these goods to your kinsmen."

"Still," said W'tnalko, "it is no worse than what you provided me when I fell into your hands."

The Skraeling warriors at once surrounded the Greenlanders and began to gesture with the sharp points of their arrows toward another house, near the center of the village, telling them they were to go there. The Greenlanders moved sullenly off to the place they were shown and each of them stooped low to go in through the small and narrow opening that served for a doorway. Once inside, they could see there was little light and nothing in the way of furnishings. The walls were made entirely of sticks and animal skins and the Greenlanders stood about there until one of the Skraelings in the doorway said they were to sit on the ground. They did as they were directed but with no great willingness.

Vragi was the last to come up to the house that had been assigned to them, leaning on his spear, and when he came to the doorway the Skraeling guards seemed to fall back as though afraid. He stood at the entrance a moment and looked about him and then W'tnalko came over, going much closer than any of the other Skraelings had shown themselves willing to do before this. He put his hand on Vragi's spear and the old viking looked at him, for a moment, with his one good eye. But W'tnalko held the spear firmly in his grasp. Then Vragi let it go and, without a word, stooped low and entered the house with the other men.

Sigtrygg now called from inside the Skraeling house and W'tnalko, who was still standing nearby, with a number of the other Skraeling guards, asked him what he had on his mind.

"I don't see why there is such a need to consider this matter, Bjorn," Sigtrygg said to him with great urgency, "since we have come from so far off and with the best of intentions. Besides, your men have already killed one of mine, for whom I have claimed no payment; though, by rights, his death ought to be paid for as well, or, at the least, offset against the death of your man. Or does this chief of yours think our goods so unworthy he will not even consider making a settlement between our two peoples?"

"It is not the worth of your goods," W'tnalko replied, "but another thing which troubles the heart of the chief. And this bears on the question of the goods, and on your very lives."

"What other matter can have such weight?" asked Sigtrygg.

"Kinship," W'tnalko replied, "for my companion, Aselekah, whom your men slew, was our chief's son."

CHAPTER XVIII

HOSPITALITY

They now sat for the remainder of that day in the Skraeling house, pressed closely together, with little room to move about or light to see by. When they lifted the skin covering which lay over the doorway, they could see a number of Skraeling men ranged about, keeping a careful eye on their doings. These Skraelings made no reply, when spoken to, and seemed rather grim, keeping their hands firmly on their weapons.

"They are certainly not pleased to see us," Arnliot said, when he had looked out at them for the third time.

Asmund said he thought they should wait until it grew dark and then make a run past their captors, into the forest, "for they are not well-armed and we are a great deal larger than they are."

"I don't think that will do us much good, for they will be expecting that," said Sigtrygg, "and will know the grounds here better than we do, ourselves. Besides, I don't think we can hope to get far in these woods, as things now stand."

"Still, it doesn't make sense to sit here and do nothing," Arnliot said, "when bolder men would have put these people in their place, before now."

Sigtrygg turned to Vragi and asked him what he thought they ought to do.

"These Skraelings are unlikely to have any more advantage over us later than they have at this moment," answered Vragi, "so there's no need to rush things, in my opinion. It's best to see where matters are headed before taking further risks."

So now they agreed to spend the night in that Skraeling house in which they found themselves, without attempting to break free, and they settled down as best they could in the close quarters allotted them. When night came on, they could hardly tell that the sun had gone out of the sky save for the loss of some small slivers of light, which had previously poked through the gloom, here and there, along the makeshift walls of their prison. The birds now ceased their calls and the crickets set to, and the Skraelings outside seemed to become a great deal less talkative.

As the Greenlanders had no fire, they huddled against one another for warmth in the cold dirt on which they were bedded down and muttered unhappily at the sorry condition they now found themselves in. Arnliot grumbled the most, saying "we are certainly a great deal worse off here than we were that night we slept in your kinsmen's cowshed."

But Sigtrygg made no response to this, for he was carefully watching the Skraelings, who guarded them, through a gap he had found in one of the walls.

"Are there any fewer now than before?" Arnliot asked him after awhile.

"Not as far as I can see," was Sigtrygg's reply, "for they have just as many men guarding this place, although most of the others in this settlement seem to have gone off to their beds."

Olvir asked if, in that case, this did not change matters enough so that they might now reconsider running off, as Asmund had suggested earlier, but Sigtrygg said that "the situation is no different than before, for they will know how to find us, in these woods, while we will certainly be at a loss, the more so since we will lack the sun to guide our steps." Still, he agreed they should now look to their own safety and he set guards from among the crew to watch over them throughout the night, in case the Skraelings should prove to have some treachery in mind.

They were awakened by loud noises and a great deal of shouting from without. Sigtrygg was the first of the sleepers to lift his

head and he now asked what was causing the commotion. One of
the crew, who had been keeping watch, replied that the Skraelings
had apparently risen with the sun and that now a large group of
them were just outside, engaged in some sort of dispute.

"That does not sound very promising," Vragi said.

Before anyone could reply to this, they heard loud pounding
on the sides of the house. "I think it's time to have a better look,"
Sigtrygg told them and he made his way to the skin-covered doorway and pulled the covering aside. There was a cluster of Skraeling
women standing a few feet off and they had an angry look on their
faces. They were pelting the wall, about the doorway, with bits of
food.

When Sigtrygg pulled his head back inside, the crew asked
him what was going on. "Not much," he replied, "except that I
think these Skraelings have brought us our breakfast."

In a short while the doorway covering was pushed aside again.
This time it was the Skraeling, W'tnalko, standing before them
and he stepped through and sat down in their midst without a
word.

"I would have thought you'd be afraid to come among us again
after all that you've now done for us," Arnliot said but W'tnalko
made no reply to this. Instead he folded his legs under him, as
though he had no reason for concern at all and sat down opposite
Sigtrygg.

"This is certainly a different matter from those times we spoke
together in the forest," Sigtrygg said after awhile, "for then I thought
you meant to keep your word and bring us peacefully into this
country."

W'tnalko replied that the fault had been Sigtrygg's for "a promise freely given is always worth more than that oath which a man
swears to save his life." Still he added that the Greenlanders had
treated him kindly, despite their slaying of his companion, and he
was minded to return the favor, if he could.

"In that case," said Sigtrygg, "you must now speak up for us with
your kinsmen, so they will accept a settlement for this killing."

W'tnalko said the matter was still to be decided but that things did not look as hopeful as he would have liked, "for you Greenlanders have chosen a poor time to pay us a visit."

"How so?" Sigtrygg asked.

W'tnalko now explained to them that all the Skraelings in that part of the country were tributary to a certain Skraeling king, who went by the name of Nahinanto and who made his home in the western part of that land. This king ruled over a people who called themselves the Tulewat and who had come from a place where many waterways converged, far beyond the country in which they now found themselves. It was the custom of this king, said W'tnalko, to travel about the country, once each year, with a number of his followers, and visit those Skraelings who owed him their allegiance. He did this in the spring, when the Skraelings had just left their winter lodgings, for the purpose of collecting what was owed him. "And this is that time of the year," W'tnalko added.

"In my opinion," said Sigtrygg, "your king would certainly do better to wait until the summer is past, for the hunting is likely to be best then, in which case his goods will be the most increased when he claims his due of those who are under his sway."

"It is not our goods alone which he takes," W'tnalko said, "for he has as much, or more, of these as we do ourselves. And many to hunt for him, besides."

"What then?" Sigtrygg asked.

"Our young men and women," W'tnalko replied, "for it is the custom of this man and all his people to strengthen themselves, at the expense of others, by claiming the best for themselves. They take the likeliest of our children, once they are grown, and adopt them into their nation. These become servants to Nahinanto and his people and, if they prove themselves worthy, full-fledged followers of the king; or wives of their great men. In this way Nahinanto and his nation increase their number, while diminishing their enemies."

"Some people would think it an honor to serve such a powerful man," Sigtrygg said.

"Yet, this is not done by choice," W'tnalko replied, "for they take whomever they want, both of our young men and our women."

"Still, I don't see how this concerns us," said Sigtrygg, "since we have nothing to do with this king of yours."

"Some might think otherwise," W'tnalko replied, "for you have come at a time when Nahinanto and his followers are yet to arrive and our chief, Anyok, has much on his mind."

"What does he intend then?" Sigtrygg asked."

"Since you have killed his son," W'tnalko said, "he is unwilling to set you free or accept the payment you have offered him. Still, he thinks you men are too numerous and too large to keep safely in our company, even as captives, for he thinks you will do us some harm if you are allowed to remain here for any length of time. Nor can we feed such men as you, when game grows scarce in the winter, for you will be a drain on our people if you are not free to hunt for yourselves."

"That is certainly sound judgement on his part," Arnliot said.

"Then how is this matter to be resolved?" asked Sigtrygg.

"That is still to be seen," replied the Skraeling, "but for now, you men are not to be denied the hospitality of this camp." When he had finished speaking, he arose and called to several of the women who were gathered outside, telling them to bring what food they could find for the Greenlanders, who were now to be considered their guests.

Sigtrygg followed the Skraeling to the doorway and lifted a corner of the animal skin, looking at the large crowd of women which had formed outside. These had been joined by children and some of the younger men, all of whom were shouting angrily and throwing stones and pieces of deer bones at the Greenlanders. The camp dogs also were now to be seen skulking at the edges of the group and running about, whenever some piece of food was thrown, snapping up what they could. "I'm not sure everyone feels the same way as you do, concerning our welcome," Sigtrygg said.

W'tnalko told them not to pay any attention to this display, "for it is only natural that people will be angry when one of their own has been unjustly killed," and he promised they would be treated well and have nothing to fear, until their fate was decided. A number of the women could now be seen leaving the others and, in a short while, they came toward the Greenlanders, though somewhat uncertainly, bringing provisions. These they carefully laid in front of the doorway, after shooing off the hungry dogs. The women, however, were unwilling to get too close and so they piled the items they were carrying hastily in the dirt and ran quickly back to the safety of their companions.

W'tnalko laughed and said: "They do not know what to make of men such as you, for they have not spent a winter in your company, as I have."

Sigtrygg could now see that many of the women were quite young, no more than girls, and these did not seem so angry or fearful as the older ones, although they were just as unwilling to come near. He now told his men to carry the food they had been given inside, and the Greenlanders came, one by one, to the entrance to gather up the items the women had left for them. These provisions consisted largely of partly chewed over deer bones and strips of dried meat. The Skraelings had also brought them a dish made of animal blood and fat, which had been stored in hollowed out tree limbs, along with river water carried in the dried bladder of a large bear.

When the Greenlanders came out to take these goods, they seemed to look, for the first time, at the people who had brought them this repast. They were especially heartened at the sight of the young girls and they called to them, urging them to come closer.

"That won't do you any good," Arnliot said to the others when he came out into the light to see what all the fuss was about, "for these people are certainly too timid to trust themselves with men like us. And maybe that is not to be wondered at." Still, he said he thought that some of the Skraeling maids seemed fair enough, after such a long journey as they had now made, and would not be unwelcome company.

Sigtrygg replied that they were to keep their minds on the business at hand, "for we are certainly not out of danger here. And it still seems to me these people are not overjoyed to have us in their midst."

"Even so," said Arnliot, "I don't see how it can do us any harm to get to know some of these people a little better than we do now."

"That is certainly a different tune which you are singing," said Sigtrygg. "Still, I don't want any further cause for difficulty between us and these Skraelings, at least until the matter of our guesting has been settled with their chieftain."

But Arnliot said he thought negotiations with the leader of these people should have very little to do with how they conducted themselves with the young women, particularly since the women seemed as curious to get to know the Greenlanders as the crew was to know them. And, in truth, Sigtrygg had to admit that the Skraeling girls did seem fascinated by the Greenland men, for all their apparent timidity. They stood about, behind their elders, careful to hide themselves but unwilling to look away from the big Norsemen.

Foremost among these was one young woman who seemed more intent than any of the others, and somehow more serious, for, when Sigtrygg caught her large black eyes with his, she did not look away, as the others did, but returned him stare for stare. Still it seemed to him there was a sadness in her face, despite the boldness, and something which he thought oddly familiar, so that he now found that he was unable to take his own eyes from the face of this young woman, which seemed in color most like the sleek brown coat of a forest deer.

W'tnalko said: "You men are now to eat as much as you like of the food which has been brought to you, and then we will see how things turn out."

They went back into the house which had been assigned to them at this, carrying their provisions, and W'tnalko left them. But they soon found their accommodations no less unpleasant than before, since they remained confined, despite the offering of food, and dared not venture out of their prison. And, though the people outside seemed to become less interested in their fate, and now went about their work with less regard for them than they had shown at the first, there was a certain grimness in their actions and a mood of sadness which seemed to hang over the entire settlement. Sigtrygg was the first to note this and he said he thought these people had certainly taken the killing of W'tnalko's companion much harder than anyone would have thought, "even if he was the son of their chief."

"It's not altogether clear what is causing this unpleasant demeanor in these people," Vragi agreed, "but it can certainly do us little good, if the matter of our fate were now to be put to a vote."

Sigtrygg placed himself in the doorway of that house in which they found themselves, with the skin flap tucked up behind his back, and took to watching the comings and goings of each of those Skraelings who passed nearby. Some of the other crewmen clustered close about him, eager for the sunlight, which his placement in the doorway allowed, and for the sight of the open air which lay so near. But Vragi and Arnliot and a number of the others showed little interest in any of this and remained well inside.

This state of affairs now went on for most of the morning, until Sigtrygg began to notice that certain of the Skraelings were showing more interest in the Greenland captives than the others. He soon saw that the same young woman he had noticed before seemed especially interested in the Greenland men, for she stood about in the clearing, though at some distance, watching Sigtrygg even as he watched her kinsmen. Sigtrygg found that he could still not take his eyes from her when he had seen her again and he thought this exceedingly strange, for she was certainly no great beauty by Greenland standards. Still, she had a sad and distant look, as though judging some far off thing, and her skin was smooth and brown and shone like a bright, wet pebble, lying in the shallows of the river, reflecting the clear sun of that country. Her hair, like her eyes, was black as a raven's wings, and Sigtrygg could not shake the sense that he had seen this young woman before, though he could not say where.

When he had pondered this for awhile, he became more perplexed than ever, but he did not cease watching the girl until she herself suddenly slipped off, as quietly as when she had first appeared. Then Sigtrygg got up slowly and went inside to where Vragi was sitting alone, leaning up against the farthest wall of their Skraeling prison. The old man sat there quietly, appearing to be asleep, until Sigtrygg sat down softly beside him. Then he opened his one good eye and asked Sigtrygg what he had on his mind.

"I'm not sure we are likely to be better off waiting here for matters to run their course, afterall" Sigtrygg now said, "than if we had tried our luck last night. At the least, we would then be matching ourselves against these people, man for man, instead of just sitting about here now like so many sheep waiting to be sheared."

"Or perhaps we would already be lying dead in the forest like that poor shipmate of ours," Vragi answered him. "Things have certainly not changed all that much since last night to cause you such concern," he added, "so it seems to me that something else must be troubling you."

Sigtrygg said he did not have much to say about that, "except that I have never seen such a heavy-hearted people as these are; and that is not likely to work to our advantage, when matters are put to the test." Still, he agreed there was also another matter which he now thought worth mentioning.

"And what might that be?" Vragi asked.

Sigtrygg told him about the young Skraeling woman and the odd sense he had that he had seen her somewhere before. "She has certainly got a familiar-looking face," he added, "and there is something uncanny about that."

Arnliot laughed when he heard Sigtrygg's words and said it wasn't very likely that any of them had ever laid eyes on these Skraelings before, "unless in our dreams; but most people would agree there are better things, than these people, to dream of."

Vragi said the best thing was to go and have a look. So now they got up and went to the doorway. But, when they pushed their heads out, they could see that a crowd of Skraelings had again begun to gather and these seemed just as unhappy as they had earlier, except that they were now much quieter and seemingly more restrained. The young woman was nowhere to be seen, though Sigtrygg looked carefully over all the Skraeling faces that were before him.

"Where did the woman with the deer eyes go?" he asked one of the crewmen, who had remained sitting in the doorway. But the man replied that he did not recall such a woman, for there had been a great many Skraelings coming and going throughout the morning and all of them, he said, had looked pretty much the same to him.

It was now about midday and the Skraelings seemed to have put aside their other duties to come and gaze at their captives once more, though their purpose remained unclear to the Greenlanders.

"Perhaps they have come to invite us to the noon meal," Arnliot suggested, after a time.

After awhile they saw that W'tnalko was coming toward them again from out of the crowd and that this time he had a very grave look on his face. The Skraelings who were guarding the Greenlanders stepped aside for him at once and, when he came to the doorway of the Greenlanders' house, he motioned them to go back inside. Then he followed close behind them.

When they were again within, Sigtrygg asked how things had gone.

"Not as well as we had hoped," W'tnalko replied, and now he told the Greenlanders that the chieftain of the Skraelings had come to a decision concerning their fate and that it was not likely to be one which Sigtrygg and his men would find entirely to their liking. "Our chieftain meant to put you men to death," W'tnalko said, "for he has taken the loss of his son very hard. But there were some who spoke against this. I, myself, spoke up for you Greenlanders, though my words do not carry much weight in the chief's house. But others thought as I did and so it was agreed your lives are to be spared."

"Then that is good news, and not the sort to cause a man to go about with such a long face as you are now wearing," Sigtrygg said.

"I won't deny that," the Skraeling replied, "but some people might think that life is not always the best prize a man can hope for."

"Whatever the terms, it is certainly better to live a little longer," Sigtrygg replied, "for then there is, at least, the hope we can forge a friendship between us. And now I want to ask you about a certain young woman whom I have seen about this camp, for it seems to me she is not as unfamiliar to my eyes as these others. Yet I know for a fact that I have never been among you Skraelings, or seen any of your kind, besides yourself, before now."

W'tnalko said that Sigtrygg should describe the woman and tell him where he had seen her and this Sigtrygg now did.

"It's not hard to tell who it is you have seen," W'tnalko replied, when he had heard Sigtrygg out, "for her name is Chinokwa and, if she seemed fair to look upon, that should not be surprising either, for she is the daughter of our chieftain, and sister to that man you Greenlanders killed on the day we first met. Nor is it any wonder she seemed familiar to you, for she was born in the same hour as her brother, Aselekah, and her face is all one with his."

"In that case, it's no wonder there is such great sadness in this woman's eyes," Sigtrygg said, "for it can have been no easy matter for her to have lost her kinsman."

"It is not the loss of her brother alone that causes this woman to grieve," W'tnalko said, "though that is a weighty matter."

"What then?" Sigtrygg asked.

"For herself," said the Skraeling, "for she is of an age to please those men who come to us every year, at this time, to take our young people for their own."

"Is she to be taken then?" Sigtrygg inquired.

"It is certainly possible," W'tnalko replied, "if she catches their eye, but that is a matter for our chieftain to set right. And he is certainly not eager to part with his only daughter, after losing his son, as well."

"This is a strange country," said Sigtrygg, "for, where we Greenlanders come from, it is considered an honor to enter the king's household."

"Many enter," said W'tnalko, "but few who do ever return to their kinsmen. And it is a harder matter for young women than for men, since the king and his nation have a custom where such women are concerned. Once, each spring, a maid is selected, from among those adopted into their nation, to be offered as a sacrifice to the morning star. And then they cut the heart out of her breast."

The Greenlanders all said they thought this very unseemly behavior, but W'tnalko replied that it was an old custom which most in their country willingly accepted. "But Anyok loves his daughter, the more so since she is now all that is left to him."

"In that case it's not hard to see why he desires to circumvent the wishes of his king," Sigtrygg said. "But what does all this have to do with us?"

"A great deal," replied the Skraeling, "for you men have come along at just the right time. It was the word of Tanakrit, the chief's wife, which convinced Anyok to hear my pleas and spare your lives. And of Manitakaha, our Dream-Speaker, for he warned that you were not to be harmed. Anyok would have had it otherwise, for he is very grieved over the death of Aselekah. Still, he means to get some benefit from your presence here since Chinokwa is now more dear to him than anything else in the world."

"That is certainly not hard to understand," said Sigtrygg, "since few things are as strong as the love of a father for his children. But matters are much less clear where we Greenlanders are concerned, for it is hard to see how he can save his daughter through us, though we were prepared to pay a very steep price to make amends for the killing of his son. And yet he was reluctant to accept that, though most people would have thought our offer a handsome one."

"There's no use worrying about it now," said W'tnalko, "for the matter is to be settled in another way, since our chief means to ransom his daughter from Nahinanto, if he can. And you men are to be the price."

The Greenlanders now asked W'tnalko what he meant by these words and he replied that it was just as it seemed, for the Skraeling chief had accepted the advice of his wife and the Dream-Speaker and now intended to offer the captive Greenlanders to his king for slaves, in place of the young men and women of the town. This was not as bad as it sounded, W'tnalko hastened to assure them, for it meant they were not to be killed, as Anyok had first intended, but would only be required to serve the Skraeling king, until they proved themselves worthy.

"And then," he added, "you may find a place in Nahinanto's following, for you are big men and likely to be of use to him."

CHAPTER XIX

THE BLOOD PRICE

"I don't think we can afford to offer this Skraeling chieftain self-judgement for very much longer," Arnliot now said, when he had heard W'tnalko's words, "or we will find ourselves on their cook fires, before the matter's done."

Sigtrygg asked W'tnalko if this was indeed to be the outcome of their case, though they had come, of their own accord, to make a settlement with the Skraelings.

"There is nothing more to be done," W'tnalko replied, "for it is not long before Nahinanto will come, and then he will take whomever he will, unless you men are given into his hands. Still life is better than certain death, as you have said yourself. And at the least you will be granted yours."

"Then you will be thinking your debt to us is paid," Sigtrygg said and W'tnalko replied that it most certainly was "since now I have won your lives for you, just as you spared mine."

Arnliot said: "There are those of us who will think they have cause to regret such rashness...and that it is not too late to undo the error."

"It won't make much difference, in any event," W'tnalko answered him, "for then you will follow after me. And it is unlikely your spirits will find much rest in this country for we will hunt you, through these forests, in death, even as in life."

Sigtrygg now asked when this Skraeling king was likely to arrive and what manner of man he was.

"He is much larger and fiercer than any of us Skraelings you have met so far," said W'tnalko, "and he always goes about the country with a large body of equally fearsome supporters. There are not many people willing to stand up to him, so that he always gets his own way in any dispute. As to when he will make his appearance, no man can say. But it's not likely to be a long wait now."

Vragi said he thought this Nahinanto would at least prove to be the sort of king a man like Arnliot would find to his liking, "for you would do well in such a lord's service." But Arnliot replied that he intended to "choose any lord I serve, and not be sold to him like a common slave."

"Still," laughed Vragi, "some people would think it makes the most sense to abide by the customs of the country you find yourself in."

Sigtrygg now asked W'tnalko if he thought this Nahinanto would accept Anyok's offer and take the Greenlanders in place of the people he had come to claim, even though there were no women among them.

"That remains to be seen," W'tnalko replied, "for he will have his pick of the young women from other Skraeling settlements which owe him their allegiance. And you Greenland men are certainly of an unusual type, which he is not likely to have seen before."

"Yet he may take us and your women, too."

W'tnalko admitted that this was certainly possible and that Anyok had thought of it, as well.

"What then will you do, if matters go thus?"

"Not much," admitted the Skraeling, "for Nahinanto is too strong for us."

"And what," asked Sigtrygg, "will you do when he returns next spring, to claim his share of your people again? Who will you trade for their lives then?"

"If Chinokwa is married by then, and with child, they will not touch her," W'tnalko answered.

"But what of the others?" Sigtrygg demanded. "Will you get

all your young women with child, then? And what of your young men, in what fashion will you protect them? And those children in this village who are not yet grown?"

W'tnalko said that no one knew what was likely to happen tomorrow, much less the day after that, so that it made little sense to worry about things which were still far off. "But at the least," he added, "Anyok's daughter will now be saved, and that is a small price to pay for the life which you took."

"Some people would say you have more than a passing interest in the life of this woman," Sigtrygg said, "whatever her brother's worth," but W'tnalko made no reply to this.

Sigtrygg now went on, saying that "such an interest as you are now showing has been known to give rise to serious errors in judgement when great matters are afoot, since things may not be seen as clearly under such circumstances as they ought to be."

"How so?" asked the Skraeling.

"Because you will trade away goods, whose true value you do not know, on the off-chance this one woman will be spared. And you cannot even be certain of that. Or do you think we Greenlanders will prove any less valuable to this king of yours, once he has seen our size and skill in battle, than we now seem to you?"

W'tnalko said: "You men will make strong slaves for the house of Nahinanto and his kin, and they will have reason to thank us when they have brought you into their town. And that is a better fate than you would have met, had they taken you in battle, for then they would have caused your deaths, with great pain and suffering."

"Even so," said Sigtrygg, "they are likely to find even more reason to thank you and your kinsmen if, as you have said, it is their custom to accept strangers into their midst, to strengthen their ranks, for we Greenlanders are not likely to be backward when matters are put to the test."

W'tnalko said he didn't have much to say about that, but it seemed plain to Sigtrygg and the others that he had not considered this before.

"Perhaps it would have been better to have killed you men afterall, as our chieftain had urged," the Skraeling said at last, "for then we would be no worse off than before."

"But no better, either," Sigtrygg said. "In my opinion, you Skraelings have not thought this matter out as well as you might, though you pride yourselves on your cleverness. And now I want you to take me to see this chieftain of yours, for I have a feeling he will see the flaw in your plans, more readily than you have yourself."

"What do you have in mind?" W'tnalko asked him, but Sigtrygg replied that this was for Anyok's ears only and not for his.

"In that case," I shall have to consider the matter further," W'tnalko said, and Sigtrygg replied that he should take as much time as he thought necessary, "although some people would think it wise to settle things, one way or the other, before this Skraeling king of yours arrives."

Some time later, near dusk, W'tnalko returned to them and this time he had with him a number of other, rather dour looking Skraelings. They told Sigtrygg to come outside and follow them, so now he arose and took leave of the crew. These men were not happy to see him go but he told them that things would fall out as they were fated and he urged them to remain quiet until his return. Then he went out among the Skraelings, amidst the lengthening shadows of the forest, to a small booth on the outskirts of the camp. Inside this booth, several people were seated about a fire, wrapped in pieces of the woolen cloth which Sigtrygg had made his men carry overland from Leif's houses. Some of the faces of these people were strange to the Greenlander, but he soon saw that the man who was called Anyok was among this group and that his wife sat behind him. W'tnalko told him to go in and take a seat by the fire with the others, and so he did.

For a long time, no one in that little group spoke, although they passed a wide bowl around, between them, from which each in that company took a taste; then each taster passed the mixture on to another. When the bowl came to Sigtrygg, W'tnalko whispered that he was to do just as the others had done and so he carefully observed their custom, taking neither more nor less than the others had taken. After this, the Skraelings produced a long-stemmed stick which was hollowed out and which had a small, stone bowl set on one of its ends.

One of the men applied fire to this bowl and the bowl's contents began to burn. Then this man began to suck on the hollow end of the stick and draw the smoke from the stone bowl into his mouth. He devoured this smoke seemingly with great satisfaction and, when he had taken his fill, passed the implement on to the next person in that circle. This went on for a long while, each person taking as much of the smoke as he pleased, until the stick was passed to Sigtrygg and then he did as the others had done. After he had applied the hollow end of the stick to his mouth, and taken his share of the smoke, he handed the strange device to W'tnalko, who sat close by his side. The other Skraelings watched all this with great interest, but they seemed to have little to say on the matter.

When they had passed the burning stick around to all those seated at the fire, and each person had taken as much of the smoke as he desired, Anyok spoke. In a very low voice, which Sigtrygg found very difficult to make out, the Skraeling chieftain recounted the words which Sigtrygg had earlier spoken to W'tnalko, concerning the likelihood the Greenlanders would join forces with the Skraeling king and increase his power thereby. He now asked Sigtrygg if he did not agree that the best thing, in light of such a possibility, was for Anyok and his people to put the Greenlanders to death, rather than allow them to be used to strengthen their enemies.

"That is certainly one means of dealing with this problem," Sigtrygg agreed, "but, perhaps, not the best means."

"What is better?" asked the Skraeling chief.

"Some people would say you men are in a difficult situation," Sigtrygg replied, "for you are beholden to a king who is more conqueror than lord; and his interests are not entirely at one with your own. Such a ruler is often more burden than boon to his subjects and we Greenlanders know a thing or two about this, for our own ancestors fled a land where such a king held sway, nor do we call any king our lord to this day."

Anyok said: "Are there no men then, such as Nahinanto, in your country?"

"Only chieftains like yourself," said Sigtrygg, "although many of my people hold the king of Norway in such repute that they will go overseas to serve in his household in order to win wealth and a good name, thereby. And, in truth, this Norwegian king is a kinsman of mine, though I have never made the journey, myself, to his country."

"What manner of man," asked Anyok, "is this Norway king?"

"Very fierce and warlike, or so I am told," Sigtrygg said. "And exceedingly shrewd. But he is a long way off, while this man, Nahinanto, whom your people find so formidable, is certainly a lot closer to home."

Anyok now asked if it was the custom of the king of Norway to claim the children of his servants or to sacrifice their young girls, after the manner of the kings of his country.

"Certainly not," Sigtrygg replied, "for he is a Christian king, nor would our people stand for such behavior as this. But all those who enter the service of the king of Norway do so of their own free will."

"Then he must not be so strong or formidable as Nahinanto is," said Anyok.

"Some would say he is stronger," said Sigtrygg, "for his army fights with iron and steel, and can put great fleets of longships on the seas."

Anyok laughed at this, for he said Sigtrygg had never seen Nahinanto and could not understand the power which this man could command. "And though we know nothing of your longships, Nahinanto can call forth such an army as would blacken the river, from here to the sea, with war boats."

"Yet he, for his part, knows nothing of iron and how it can bite," said Sigtrygg, "unless your man has misled me."

But W'tnalko now leaned forward and said he had only told Sigtrygg the truth concerning the Skraelings in that part of the country and that none of them had ever seen iron before, to the best of his knowledge. Anyok now confirmed this, saying he too thought this reliable information for he had never seen such hard weapons as the Greenlanders carried, until the day W'tnalko had led them into his camp. And now he asked if the Greenlanders could teach his people how to make edges of the sort which their weapons bore, for the Skraelings' tools.

"That is a very great matter," Sigtrygg said, "for we cannot easily make such weapons here, ourselves, although it is not impossible that this could be done in time."

"Yet," said Anyok, "we do not have such time, since the day of Nahinanto's arrival is now due and we must be prepared, if we are to purchase his goodwill. Some people have advised me to do this with you and your men, but now it seems that this is certainly too high a price to pay, for such men as yours would make our enemies even stronger than they now are, if you were to win a place among them."

Sigtrygg said that this was probably true.

"But if we kill you," the Skraeling chieftain continued, "we may keep your iron edged weapons and this will be a great gain for our hunting. Still, it is unlikely to make us strong enough to save my daughter, if they decide to take her, and I don't see how they are likely to overlook such a woman as she is. Perhaps I will send her into the forest, with a few of my young men, and hope the others do not find them. Then we can kill you Greenlanders without further concern."

Sigtrygg replied that it was not unlikely they could solve their problem in this way, "although this seems to me rather shortsighted, since you will leave yourselves at your enemies' mercy forever afterwards though you had the means at hand to rid yourselves of this scourge now. Nor can you be certain to save your daughter by such a stratagem, since this Nahinanto has men who know the woods as well as you do, yourselves."

Anyok said that Sigtrygg should now say clearly what he had on his mind, since he had led them to believe he had a proposition of some import to make, adding that W'tnalko had urged them to give him this hearing.

"It's easy enough to say," Sigtrygg replied, "for we Greenlanders are not men who are accustomed to go quietly to our deaths, despite appearances, thus far. Nor will it be as easy to kill us as some would think. We came into your country for the purpose of making a settlement between our two peoples and for that reason I have held my men back. But others have found us to be most formidable adversaries, before this."

Anyok laughed and said the Skraelings were perfectly willing to try them out, if it came to it.

"As it may," Sigtrygg agreed, "though we have offered you a settlement, which we will not willingly break, if you hold to your part of the bargain. But some people might think you'd do better to fight beside us, than against us, for then we will see what this king of yours, who has your people locked so tightly in his hands, is made of."

"That is foolish talk," Anyok said, "for you do not know the strength of these people or their means of making war. When the Tulewat come against any nation, they come with great swarms of men, decked out like demons. And they fight just like demons, too. Whoever they kill on the battlefield, they cut up into pieces and take away with them. But those they capture they bring back alive to their encampments; and then they cut these people into pieces while they are still alive, and burn the flesh from their bones so that they die a most dreadful death. They torture and devour the women and children of their enemies in this fashion, too, except for those they take as their slaves. But only a portion of their captives are spared for this. There are too many of this nation for men such as we are, or even for those like yourselves, to contend against."

Sigtrygg said: "We Greenlanders are not frightened by such odds or we had never set foot in this country. Nor are we such light fighters that our enemies can hope to get off scott free in any engagement with us, however fierce they think themselves to be. But I had thought you Skraelings were sturdier men than your words now show."

"We live in a hard land," Anyok replied, "but there's no reason to see our race die out for pride's sake and an unwillingness to give way before stronger people."

"Still, you're not likely to save your daughter, by such caution, though you save your kind," Sigtrygg said.

W'tnalko now asked Sigtrygg if he thought his followers, big as they were, could fight against such men as Anyok had now described.

"Ours is a strong race," Sigtrygg said, "and men of our kin have laid much of the world across the sea under scot, so that kings and princes and chieftains tremble at the word that our ships have come to their shores. My own kinsman, King Harald of Norway, fought for many years in far off lands and never lost a battle, before coming home to claim the kingship in his native country. Most people think he is the boldest sea-king who ever raided another man's shore, but I have heard he is but a shadow of the great lords of our race who sailed the seas before him. Your king, Nahinanto, is unlikely to be half the man that Harald is."

Anyok said: "Still, you are not many. While Nahinanto can fill the forests with his men."

"Will he come with such great strength, then?" Sigtrygg asked.

"No," said Anyok, "for he has no reason to expect war from us, or from others of our kind who live in this part of the country."

"Then we will take him by surprise," said Sigtrygg, "and that is all the better."

At this, the men sitting round the fire began to mutter to one another. After some time Anyok asked Sigtrygg if he did not think it would be more sensible for him to take his fellow Greenlanders and flee into the forest, "for then you will have a chance to live, since you may be able to outrun my hunters and the men who come after you from Nahinanto's following when these have come among us?"

"Do you think to distract them, then, from taking your children by sending them after us instead?" Sigtrygg asked.

"At the least we will see what your boasts are worth," replied the Skraeling chief.

"And forego any chance to put an end to this irksome tribute which these people exact from you," Sigtrygg said.

"You are certainly a big talker," said the chieftain, "but you took the life of one of our kin, without a moment's hesitation; and now you want to put all my people at risk."

"You must decide what is best for these people," Sigtrygg agreed. "But I don't think you are likely to spare your daughter captivity among these loathsome men who are your tormentors if you are timid now."

The Skraelings about the fire began to fidget at such harsh words and the chieftain, Anyok, became very quiet. His eyes narrowed and he turned away from Sigtrygg and now he would speak no further.

W'tnalko, when he saw how things were, leaned over and said that Sigtrygg must now take his leave of them, for the Skraelings had begun talking softly among themselves and appeared to take no further notice of him. So Sigtrygg stood up and W'tnalko rose with him.

Anyok looked up suddenly then and said: "You are a brave man, stranger, though you come to us from unknown lands. Still, you go forth as one who does not yet see the nature of the beast he hunts, and so goes out too noisily into the woods."

"Better to go thus and startle the bear, if I can, than to hang back and starve for lack of courage," Sigtrygg replied.

The Skraeling chieftain said there was some truth in these words but added that it was not fitting, in his opinion, "for a stranger, like yourself, to lead us in our own country. Had Aselekah lived, he would certainly have been the man to lead his people one day, though now he has been taken from us because of you foreigners. There is only one way to set things right now," he added, "though you may find it harder than serving Nahinanto."

Sigtrygg said: "There is no honorable task that a bold man will shrink from."

"In that case," said Anyok, "I mean to accept your offer, for it is bravely made, and you are taking no less risk with your men than I with mine. But there is one condition I shall make for a stranger cannot know our ways or be depended upon to look out for our good in times of trouble. If you will do as I ask, I mean to let you and your men go free; and then we shall make our stand together against those who would take from us what is ours. But, if not, I shall settle things as seems best in my own eyes."

Sigtrygg asked what condition the Skraeling chieftain had in mind, but now Anyok only looked away from him once more and began to stare into the fire as he had, at the first, when Sigtrygg had been brought into his presence. Sigtrygg asked again, but still could get no response for the Skraeling chieftain seemed to have entirely lost interest in the proceedings.

It was dark when they left the chief's house and Sigtrygg looked sharply about him, for he had not yet seen the Skraeling camp under the moon's light, having spent the previous evening in that prison to which he had been confined with his men. W'tnalko now took Sigtrygg by the arm and told him to come along to his own sleeping place, "for tonight you are to sleep with us."

"But what is that condition which your chief has placed on our agreement?" Sigtrygg asked. He was unwilling to take his leave until he was certain how his proposal had fared.

"Not much," W'tnalko replied, "except that tomorrow you are to decide if you will accept the gift which Anyok means to give to you. And then we shall see if you will stand with us, as you have promised."

"But what kind of a gift does he have in mind?" Sigtrygg asked him, "since I am far from my own country and cannot readily repay him in kind?"

"More than you had sought," W'tnalko replied, "for Anyok wishes you to understand that there is only one way to make a settlement with him over the killing of his son. And that is not through the payment of goods, as you would have it, for we think this too light a price for the man who has been slain."

"What kind of payment, then, does your chieftain desire?" Sigtrygg asked him.

"Nothing less than your own life," W'tnalko replied, "for he means to test your courage and strength, according to our customs. If you die, then matters will go much as we had planned at the first, and the Tulewat shall have their foreign slaves. But if not, you are to be taken in Aselekah's place as the chief's son."

CHAPTER XX

AT THE RIVER'S EDGE

Just before sunrise, the next morning, they awakened Sigtrygg in the place where he had been sleeping, among a large number of Skraeling men. A group of young women came into the sleephouse and began to silently strip him of his clothing despite his protests. Then they told him he was to get up and follow them outside, which he did, and now they led him down to the river. He was completely surrounded by the silent young men, who had shared their sleeping place with him the night before, and by the women. When they came to the river's edge, the sun's light was already beginning to spread and lighten the eastern sky and Sigtrygg saw that W'tnalko was waiting there for him in the company of Anyok and many of the others and that these all had rather stern looks on their faces. Tanakrit, the Skraeling chief's wife, and the Dream-Speaker were there, too, and this man now came up to Sigtrygg and, uttering many harsh words, began to mark Sigtrygg's naked body with dark colored paint.

Sigtrygg asked W'tnalko the meaning of this but the Skraeling said he was to keep silent and, when the Skraeling sorcerer had finished his work, they left him standing alone at the water's edge. Five young men, whom he had not seen before, suddenly appeared before him. These were attired for war, with fiercely painted faces and great feathered headpieces strapped about their chins. In their hands were short spears with very narrow points made of some kind of animal bone or horn.

All the Skraelings now ranged themselves in a large half-circle about Sigtrygg and the strangely attired men who faced him, and these began to move slowly toward him, singing and howling in a most unsettling manner. Sigtrygg now looked from one to the other of them and then at W'tnalko, but none of the Skraelings spoke or gave him any indication as to what they expected of him. Since he was entirely naked and unarmed, he began to move about cautiously, his back to the river, for he meant to avoid these men who were now stalking him, if he could.

It soon seemed plain to him that he could easily elude these hunters, if he were to suddenly turn from them and plunge into the river, for he was a strong swimmer and escape in this fashion would not have been difficult for him. Yet he thought they would count him a coward, in that case, since he would be saving his own life at the expense of his companions, whom he had brought into that country, leaving them to whatever fate the Skraelings intended for them. Besides, Sigtrygg thought the opportunity to flee by way of the river, too easily gained, so that he doubted its efficacy. Therefore, he thought it best to face the hunters, although he knew he could have little chance against them, so long as they carried those spears while he was yet unarmed.

The men before him now circled about, still singing their strange song and thrusting with their deadly looking weapons. The spear thrusts were made slowly, at first, and rhythmically, in keeping with the sounds of the men's singing, and Sigtrygg soon found he could easily anticipate each thrust the Skraeling warriors made by listening to the rhythm of their voices. Still the singing became quicker and louder, as the strange hunt progressed, and soon Sigtrygg had all he could do to keep ahead of those men as they pressed him back toward the river with their sharp spear points.

Then, without warning, one of these Skraelings suddenly stepped out from the others and, waving his spear before Sigtrygg's face, made a quick lunge at his stomach. Just as swiftly, Sigtrygg grabbed the man's weapon, behind the spearhead and, grappling with his attacker, he drove the spear point harmlessly into the ground before him. Then he caught hold of the Skraeling, who had lunged at him, and seized the man's two arms. He wrenched the weapon from his grasp and, bending his enemy's arms back, at the wrist and elbow joint, Sigtrygg forced him down into the dust at his feet. The other Skraeling hunters seemed so startled by this that they broke off their steady singing and stood watching as Sigtrygg and his adversary grappled there in the dirt. Then Sigtrygg arose, as suddenly as when he had first grasped the out-thrust spear, and stood over the fallen Skraeling, brandishing the stolen weapon in his hands.

The other Skraeling warriors now quickly recovered themselves and charged into Sigtrygg with their weapons pointed at his upper body. There were four of them left, now that the one had been disarmed and wrestled to the ground, and Sigtrygg held the spear he had taken from his defeated foeman and lowered it toward his attackers. A great hooting noise now arose from those other Skraelings who stood all about them, watching these events unfold, and Sigtrygg raised his eyes to see what was afoot. There was a look of great seriousness in the face of the Skraeling chief and on the faces of those who stood about him and Sigtrygg let out a triumphant yell and began to feint and thrust with his own weapon, pushing the four remaining Skraelings backward, up the riverbank toward their chieftain.

With each push of his sharp spear point, the attacking Skraelings gave way and Sigtrygg cut first one and then another of them on their arms and legs, as they fell back before him. So skilled was he with the spear, that he could have buried its point in any one of these men, had he wished to, but he saw that this would only immobilize the weapon he held and leave him unarmed against the others. Thus he feinted, this way and that, with his strange opponents, and yet was unwilling to close with them.

Now the other Skraelings all about him fell strangely silent. Looking about him, Sigtrygg could see that they looked even grimmer than before. The morning sun was becoming visible, too, over the tops of the trees, and the four Skraelings before him had completely stopped their singing, for they now had all they could do to fend off Sigtrygg's hard spear strokes. Sigtrygg came to a stop then, when he saw how things stood, for, as he said later, this had been the hardest of any fight, which he had fought up to that point in his life, and he had lost himself entirely in the blood-lust of the moment. Yet now he saw that things had certainly not gone as the Skraelings had expected and that this was a cause of much consternation to them. Turning about, he could see, too, that the first Skraeling whose spear he had taken, had now fled the half circle in which the battle had been fought and that he was quite alone with the other four men.

Yet, it seemed to Sigtrygg that the Skraelings who ringed him in had an unfriendly look about them and that, while it was clear he had had great success against the five men they had sent against him, it was unlikely he could overcome that entire company, should they take it in mind to cut him down. Still, he was not standing so far away from their chieftain that he could not reach him before they could do him some harm and so he suddenly leaped past the four men who opposed him and was quickly beside the man they called Anyok. Then Sigtrygg seized that man about the shoulders with one arm and, with his other, he placed the point of his spear up under the Skraeling's jaw.

"Now," said he, "you are to turn me and my crewmen loose, if you value this head of yours."

The chieftain made no answer to this but stood still as stone, his eyes half-closed. The other Skraelings were also silent, though they did not seem any more willing to give way than before.

W'tnalko said: "This is no way to repay a great man's gift, though it is not unexpected from men such as you Greenlanders."

"I only want freedom for my crew and for me," Sigtrygg told him. "Those men came here at my bidding, and not by their own choice, so there's no use holding their presence in this country against them. And you Skraelings have certainly done little enough to make them welcome, in any case."

"It is unlikely this can end well...for you or us," W'tnalko now replied, "for whatever happens, our chieftain is prepared to die well, if it is his time. Yet, it will not gain your freedom for you."

Sigtrygg now looked all about him. He could see that the other Skraelings had begun to move closer to him and that they had their weapons raised. "At the least," said he, "I will take this man with me," and now he pressed the spear point harder into the Skraeling chief's throat, but still his captive made no move to pull away from Sigtrygg's strong grasp. Sigtrygg began to walk the man backward, towards the Skraeling town, and all the other Skraelings who had gathered about them now followed close behind.

Anyok uttered no words during all this, but went silently and without resistance in the direction Sigtrygg urged him. Now Sigtrygg spoke to him directly, asking once more if he were willing to free the other Greenlanders.

To this the Skraeling chief made no more reply than before and Sigtrygg could now see there was no hope for it but that he kill this man. But even this seemed unlikely to gain him what he sought, for there were armed Skraelings all about them, and these stood blocking the way back from the river. Sigtrygg looked from each of these men, in turn, and then his eyes came to rest on W'tnalko and now he saw a sadness in this man's face, which he had not seen before.

It now seemed to Sigtrygg that these Skraelings thought matters had taken a more unfortunate turn than they had had cause to expect, so that, marking their looks, he suddenly ceased to press the advantage he had won. Even the loss of their chief would not turn these Skraelings from their purpose, he thought and, seeing this, he lost all desire to bring about their deaths, if it would not gain him his purpose.

"Well, we have come into your country unbidden, Bjorn," he now said to W'tnalko, "and perhaps we have found the welcome we deserved. If you had come among us, I think you would have fared no better." Then he let the spear he had taken fall to the ground and stood back, empty handed, releasing his grip on the Skraeling chieftain.

All the Skraelings now rushed forward and seized hold of him with many angry shouts and they began to pull at his arms and legs, threatening him with their stone weapons. They bore him down, under their weight, and would have killed him at once save that their chieftain now intervened and told them to carry him down to the river again. So they lifted him on their shoulders and bore him down to the water's edge and placed him there, on his feet, with great shouts of triumph, making many fierce gestures and brandishing their axes and spears. All the Skraelings seemed to be about him then and Sigtrygg stood there, entirely unarmed and in their power. Now the one they called Dream-Speaker appeared before him, once more, his great raven hat shaking as he shouted harshly into Sigtrygg's face, and then the Skraelings grabbed his arms again. Those four men who had fought him with their spears were there, too, and they now thrust these weapons at Sigtrygg without further ceremony and at once began to cut his flesh with the bone-tipped points.

Now Sigtrygg fell back from them until he came to the water and felt the cold wetness lapping about his ankles. There he stopped and would go no further as the Skraelings pressed the points of their spears into his bare flesh, as though urging him to flight. They suddenly began to sing again, exactly as before, only this time Sigtrygg made no move to take their weapons from them for, as he said later, every man must face his death some time and no manner of dying, in the end, is any worse than another, if you have lived well.

When they saw that he would not run from them, they began shouting even more loudly than before and to press their weapons more deeply into his flesh, exactly where the Dream-Speaker had made his numerous markings. With each thrust of their long narrow bone points they caused great searing pain to course through his body. Still he would not go into the river, though the blood began to spurt from his wounds and run down his bare sides, reddening the river water in which he was standing.

They gave him numerous wounds in this manner, until all his

flesh was crisscrossed with streaks of freshly flowing blood and still he stood his ground, unwilling to flee from his attackers into the safety of the river. He stood thus, until the morning sun was clearly visible over the tree tops, in the face of the strange singing sounds which all the Skraelings were now making, swaying and bloodied at the river's edge until, at length, he saw the old man, the one they called the Dream-Speaker, come down again to the river and now this man was flanked by a number of young boys bearing lighted brands in their hands.

Then Sigtrygg's attackers fell away from before his eyes and none but old Manitikaha stood before him, the great raven-winged hat bobbing unsteadily under his nose. The old man began to shout at him in the same angry tone as before and then he gestured with his hand and one of the boys brought forth a burning brand and others seized hold of Sigtrygg's bloodied arms and the old man leant toward him with the fiery stick and pressed it into his flesh, where the blood ran.

Then he moved it along Sigtrygg's chest and struck him with it, again and again, until the searing fire filled Sigtrygg's eyes and washed away all images of the Skraelings before him. Attacked thus, again and again, by the hot fire which the Skraeling soothsayer wielded against him, Sigtrygg fell down at last from the weakness brought on by loss of blood and by the stinging brand, until he tumbled, face-forward, into the bloodied water which swirled about his feet.

The sun was at its full height in the sky, when Sigtrygg was again awake, and then he lay on a bear skin, close by the running sounds of the river, staring blankly at the sky. He still heard the sounds of Skraeling singing but it was softer now, and somehow different, and, when he rolled his head about, it seemed to him he could make out the shape of a brown deer, crouched nearby, softly singing the Skraeling words. Overhead the trees moved with the cool wind and Sigtrygg shivered as the wind blew, for he suddenly felt extremely cold. Only then did he realize that he was still unclothed. He recalled the combat on the riverbank and its outcome and how the Skraelings had sought to slay him without any resistance on his part and, for a moment, he was greatly shamed. He tried to rise but he soon found he was too weak for that and his head swam. Then he let it fall heavily back onto the softness of the bear's skin.

The deer that was sitting nearby now arose and seemed to amble over to him. The singing stopped for the moment. He tried to see the deer's face but it was a brown blur before his eyes and it seemed to move about above him. It spoke but he could not make out the meaning of its words. Again he tried to lift his head but he soon found that he could not even remove it from the fur of the bear which lay between him and the earth.

"Do not move for you are too weak," he thought he heard the deer say and he tried to answer, but no words came.

After a time, he opened his eyes again and now every thing seemed much clearer except that he thought the sun was a good deal lower in the sky than before. The brown deer was still nearby and he found that extremely reassuring. He tried to speak to it but it did not appear to understand him. He asked about his men and then about the ship and if all were ready to go back to Leif's houses and put out to sea. The deer, though it became unusually silent, made no attempt to answer him.

"We found grapes and the houses Leif built," he said aloud, "and no one thought we had any chance of that. And we found Skraelings, who were the cause of Thorvald Eiriksson's death and Thorfinn Karlsefni's flight from this country. But they could not drive us away," he said.

Sigtrygg now became aware of something soft touching him, moving gently over his body, and then a voice, very sing-song and melodious, and words which he could not understand. Then he opened his eyes again and saw the brown deer's face hovering over his and large black eyes and, as he watched it, it slowly began to shift until it became the face of a young girl floating cloud-like in the sky above him. The girl had an oddly familiar look and a friendly smile and her skin was smooth and shining. It had a nut-brown color to it. Her hair, bound close about her face, was raven black.

She was speaking strange words in his ears and Sigtrygg had to listen very closely before he could understand. Then he knew they were Skraeling words and this a Skraeling girl and that he was alive, after all, though he had offered himself up for killing by the Skraeling men.

"You must lie very still," the girl's voice said, "for you are very weak from blood loss."

"Where are the men who cut me?" Sigtrygg asked in the Skraeling tongue, but his own voice was low and he could barely make himself heard.

"Gone," said the Skraeling girl, "but I have dressed your wounds and you will soon recover. You are very strong, for you took many wounds and yet live, though few others could have stood as much. But it would have been better to go down quickly and put an end to the hunt."

"Some people would have thought it better if I had cut my way through and taken those men with me," Sigtrygg said.

"Then they would have stabbed you till you died," said the girl, "and that would have been a great loss."

Sigtrygg looked up into the girl's face and saw the sad but pleasing smile which she had on her lips and which seemed to shine down on him like a hearth fire in some distant and unknown farmer's house.

"I am Chinokwa," said the girl, "the daughter of Anyok, our chief. And of Tanakrit."

Sigtrygg said that he knew this already, as he had seen her watching him and his crew the day before, "though your sadness was a matter of great concern to us since we were responsible for it, in that we took your brother's life."

"Do not speak in this fashion," she warned him, "for that is yesterday's matter, whereas today my brother is reborn."

Sigtrygg now said he wanted to get up but the Skraeling girl told him he was to remain where he was until he had got his strength back. Now she brought out water and the food made of blood and animal fat, which the Skraelings had given to the Greenlanders before, and she made Sigtrygg take as much as he was able to, from her hands. When he was finished, she told him he could rise if he wanted, but he was to do so carefully, since his wounds were still fresh.

Sigtrygg very carefully got to his feet and when he stood up he saw that he was still without clothing. Chinokwa gathered up the bear skin and helped him to wrap himself in it. There was no one else to be seen on the riverbank but the young Skraeling woman, and Sigtrygg now placed his arm on her shoulder for support, walking thus, slowly up the bank, to the Skraeling town.

The Greenlanders, in their prison, were surprised by all the commotion outside their house and they came to the doorway to see what the cause was. The Skraelings were gathered all around the clearing and they were heavily armed, after their fashion, with paint all over their bodies, giving them the most hideous appearance. They were singing and shouting at the top of their lungs in a warlike manner and Arnliot, when he saw how things stood, said he thought that matters had now come to a head. "Either we chase after them and crack their heads with our bare hands at once, or else we sit quietly and allow them to butcher us like so many cattle. I certainly did not think, when I came out here, that it was to serve as the main course in some Skraeling feast."

The Skraelings seemed to become more bellicose with each passing moment and most of the Greenlanders now said they agreed with Arnliot, that the time had come for them to take desperate action. Vragi said they should do what they thought best, "for it is certainly the case that things do not look promising here, the more so since our skipper has not been returned to us."

There was now howling and shrieking to be heard from the midst of the Skraelings and many of their younger men kept running out from the place where the others were clustered, striking the blade end of their weapons on one of several poles which stood about in the clearing. These poles were large affairs and were adorned with feathers and bones and animal skins. Each time one of them struck the pole, he let out a hideous sounding shriek, as though he were in great pain, and then all the others began to howl and shriek in answer.

The Greenlanders all gathered near the opening of their prison and they could soon see that the Skraelings had worked themselves up into such a frenzy that they were paying very little attention to their captives. "This is certainly our chance," said Asmund and Olvir agreed that they would never have a better one, but Arnliot now said they were to wait until he gave the word and then they were to run for the nearest of the Skraelings and overpower them.

"Take whatever weapons you can from them and kill as many as you can," he said. "Then make for the woods and run as hard as possible, until the sun has set, and that should not be long now. Afterwards we must go to ground for the night. Then, when the sun comes up, we'll make our way, as best we can, down to the coast."

They all agreed that this was the best plan they could hope for, under the circumstances, and now they got themselves ready, waiting until Arnliot saw their chance to move.

The screaming and wild dancing of the Skraelings seemed to increase with each passing moment and the Greenlanders thought they had never heard such hellish carryings on. Despite their resolve, the Skraeling behavior unnerved them and they did not feel entirely confident in their plan in the face of such strange foes. Still they meant to see it through, for they had concluded they would not have another opportunity, if they failed to take advantage of the one that was now before them.

Suddenly, and much to their surprise, the wild carousing stopped and the Skraelings fell silent. Now things were as quiet in the clearing where the Skraelings had their town, as in the nearby woods, and it was as though none of the strange rantings and howlings which had been going on, but moments before, had ever been heard. The Skraelings turned to the Greenlanders and all eyes in that clearing seemed to bore in upon them.

"We waited too long," Olvir murmured, when he saw how things had gone, and the others said they thought this was certainly true.

"No matter," Arnliot said, "for a brave man will fight, whatever the odds. Whether we have it in our power to take them by surprise or not, we are still the better men. In my opinion, there's no use being backward in this matter."

The large gathering of Skraelings, as silent now as they had been loud and rowdy before, began to separate, leaving a large open space in their midst. In this place a number of their leaders now appeared, clad from head to foot in animal skins and with great feathered headpieces atop their heads. Then there was a rustling at the sides of this gathering and a number of the young Skraeling men stepped out of the shadows, carrying the swords and shields and other weapons of the Greenlanders. They piled these, one atop the other, in the cleared space in their midst and then withdrew, leaving the arms sitting, unclaimed, on the bare earth.

"Here is a turn in our luck, then," Arnliot whispered, "for these could not have been left any closer to us, if they had meant to return them to us themselves."

"Perhaps they do," Olvir said.

The man whom they recognized as the Skraeling chief, Anyok, now strode toward them and told the Greenlanders, in a loud and imperious voice, that they were to come out of their prison. Arnliot said this was just what he had been hoping for and he now walked boldly out, looking neither to his right or left at the strangely appareled forest people who ringed them in. After him, Olvir followed and then Asmund and the others. Vragi came out behind all the rest.

The Skraeling chieftain stretched out his hand toward the arms and, when Arnliot approached the pile, he backed quickly away. Arnliot stooped and found his great war axe, lifting it carefully, as though examining it for harm. Then he took up his sword and shield and the other Greenlanders came about him and began to pick through the pile to find their own arms, as well. The men of Brattahlid seemed especially eager to find their shields and, when every man of them was again armed, they turned to face the Skraelings, who now seemed somewhat chastened at the sight of these big Greenlanders, girded for war and in such close quarters.

"Some people would think you Skraelings have finally come to your senses," Arnliot said, "where we Greenlanders are concerned, though you still seem to lack sufficient fear when facing men like us, despite the fact you have handled us so roughly."

Now several other Skraelings, who seemed to be garbed even more richly than the others, came out and stood beside Anyok. These men were covered in long, brightly decorated robes and each had, on his head, a more elaborate headpiece than the next. Their faces glinted in the waning light of dusk from the brightly colored markings which were painted across and around their features and they did not show any fear at all, despite Arnliot's harsh words. One of them stood out from the others, for he was taller than the rest and he carried a sword and shield, just like the Greenlanders. His face was painted in the most hideous fashion, as though streaked with blood, and his eyes were blackened all about, from the sides of his nose to the outer edges of his face. His chest, which was partially bare, was also brightly painted and streaked with freshly made scars and this made him all the more awful to look at.

Arnliot lifted his axe toward this man as he strode out toward the Greenlanders and then lowered it again.

He said: "I did not think to see you among us again friend Sigtrygg, and especially dressed in this fashion, for you look as much like one of these creatures as they do themselves. Some people would think there is truth in the stories which have been told of your birth, for the clothing which this nation wears surely suits you."

"Put aside your arms, Arnliot," Sigtrygg said to him, "and tell the others to do likewise, for these Skraelings will do them no harm."

"Some might think otherwise," Arnliot replied, "for they have certainly been less than accommodating thus far. Nor do they look overly friendly now."

"Pay it no mind," said Sigtrygg once more, "since it is their custom to celebrate in this fashion, and to make a warlike display when great matters are afoot."

"Whatever their customs," Arnliot replied, "we Greenlanders now intend to leave this place, for we have little interest in the friendship of such a people as this, who would as soon sell us for slaves as feed us our dinner."

"There's no reason to be concerned about that any longer either," Sigtrygg answered him, "for these men have given you back your arms, as I have instructed them to do, so you are well able to defend yourselves should the need arise. Yet, no further harm or discomfort is to befall you here. You are to be treated, henceforth, as honored guests, since they have sworn this to me. And we, for our part, are to make common cause with them and fight in their ranks; for I have sworn this to them."

"I think that is a matter best left for us Greenlanders to decide," Arnliot said, "and not to you and these Skraelings, for few men, in my opinion, will risk their lives to help those who meant to do them harm."

"I'm not sure that harm has been done, in any case," said Sigtrygg, "though we entered their country without their leave and took the life of one of their young men, to boot. But have it your own way, as is only right, for each of you must decide for himself what he means to do to win a name for himself in this land. Now I have bought your freedom for you and you can leave this place if you like. But I, for one, mean to stay on with these people and fight alongside them, as is only right since their chieftain has taken me for his foster son."

Arnliot said he did not know what to say to such news as this but added that he thought it highly irregular, in any case, "since these Skraelings have thus far shown little enough friendship to men of our nation."

"Nevertheless," Sigtrygg told him, "that is how matters now stand, though you are free to make what you will of it."

Now Vragi, when he heard Sigtrygg's words, pushed his way past the others and came up to where Arnliot stood.

"It seems our ship's skipper has won some authority for himself in this strange land," he said, "whatever else has befallen, and there's no use denying that this is good news for the rest of us since it gives each of us crewmen a place beside the chieftains of this country on the field of battle. And a fair claim to whatever is won, besides. There's not much more an old viking like me can ask for than that."

Olvir said he felt much the same way and that he too meant to stand with Sigtrygg. He and the other Brattahlid men now came forward, as well, and ranged themselves beside Vragi. These were quickly followed by the two Icelanders, Thorolf and Asmund.

Several of the other crewmen now said they would also stand by Sigtrygg, if that seemed good enough for their shipmates and when Arnliot saw how things were he began to laugh as loudly as he could and all the Skraelings looked at his great frame with wonder, for his laughter was so loud and forceful that his whole body seemed to shake with it, as did the very tree limbs above their heads.

"It seems you mean to hold to your purpose in this as in everything else," Arnliot now said to Sigtrygg, when he had caught his breath again, "no matter what others of us might think."

Sigtrygg agreed that this certainly seemed to be true.

"In that case," Arnliot replied, "I don't think you will find me the kind of man to split this company up, whatever else occurs, though these Skraelings are certainly not the sorts of fellows I would have chosen for allies if I'd had my way. But the proof of the blade is in the cutting, as the old saying has it. So now let us see what manner of steel you have found for us in this new country."

CHAPTER XXI

OF SHOES AND BEASTS

Although he had come through the ordeal the Skraelings had set for him without serious harm, Sigtrygg had actually been greatly weakened by the loss of blood he had sustained and it was not long before he began to sway on his feet, despite his best efforts to appear completely well, standing there in the center of the clearing among that strange gathering. When the Greenlanders saw this, they became greatly alarmed and wanted to take him back at once to the house the Skraelings had assigned them, but this the Skraelings would not permit. Instead, these people now formed a close ring around Sigtrygg and began to carry him off.

The men of his crew protested but Sigtrygg said they were not to make anything of this "but pass your time as best you can, for these Skraelings have sworn to treat you well."

And so they did, for though they carried Sigtrygg off with alarming speed, the Skraelings who remained now made a great fuss over the rest of the crew, inviting them to join in a feast which they had set for them in the open area of their encampment, about a large fire. There was then much shouting and dancing although the men of Greenland found the manner of these Skraeling festivities somewhat strange. Yet they willingly took part in the celebration, for they saw that it betokened the Skraelings' happiness at the adoption of Sigtrygg by their chief. And this Vragi had told them was the case.

Sigtrygg was now gone from them three days and during this time the Skraelings proved much better hosts than before. They brought the crew all manner of foods, which they had not provided to them earlier, including various fruits and herbs, which had been gathered in the forest, and fresh game and fish. In all, the Greenlanders found little cause to complain, since they shared equally in whatever provisions the Skraelings had for themselves and were given the freedom to come and go just as they pleased. Arnliot and the others now made the most of this and took for themselves that part of the Skraeling settlement which they found themselves in, setting their shields about the perimeter and discarding the Skraelings' goods which they found there. In all, they did whatever they could to make their new home as much like a Norse steading as possible, though they were somewhat limited in this regard by the paucity of things which they had brought with them out of Greenland.

On the morning of the fourth day Sigtrygg suddenly appeared outside their ring of shields and now he strode into their midst and looked all about him. He was dressed, still, in the skin clothes of the Skraelings, but he bore his sword and shield in Norse fashion. He seemed less happy to see them than they were to see him and he now asked them the meaning of the changes they had made in their living conditions.

All the crewmen were lying about, near the house the Skraelings had given them, and they looked quite pleased with themselves. "We thought to make this place more suitable for men such as us," replied Asmund, "since many of us have a longing to see our homes again, after such a lengthy and unprofitable voyage as this has been. And there's no use denying these Skraelings know little of the amenities to be found back in Greenland or Iceland."

"There's little chance of getting back to those countries, in any case," Sigtrygg said somewhat harshly, "if you men persist in such folly as you have now undertaken, for you are strangers here and should conduct yourselves in a manner befitting that status, without striving to bring undue attention on yourselves."

"That's easy enough for you to say," Arnliot replied. He was half lying beneath a tall tree which stood near the house which the

Greenlanders had claimed for their own. "You wear these Skraeling clothes as though you were born to them," he said, "and have made a place for yourself among this unpleasant people, besides. But, as for the rest of us, well, we must find our comfort where we can."

"In my opinion, you won't find that tree so comfortable when things heat up around here," Sigtrygg told him and he now began to walk all around the area which the Greenlanders occupied. Wherever he found a spear or shield stuck into the ground, or propped against a wall, he threw it angrily into their midst. All the Greenlanders thought this highly unusual behavior and they now asked him the cause of it.

"Only this," replied Sigtrygg, "that we are sitting here, awaiting an enemy who, by most accounts, is more numerous and stronger than we are and who we mean to attack as soon as he is encountered. Yet all the advantage is likely to be with him, unless we take him by stealth. Yet you men now want to boldly announce our presence, before the first blow has even been struck."

"At least no one can fault us for killing from the shadows," Arnliot said and the others seemed to agree with this.

"Then do as you see fit," said Sigtrygg, "for you men are free to follow your own counsel...in this as in all things. But my advice in the matter is clear."

They now consulted together and the end of it was that each man took down his shield and other arms, which had been displayed so prominently, and piled these up, out of sight, inside the house. As to the Skraeling goods, they returned these to their places, as well as they were able and Sigtrygg said he was satisfied with that. Not long afterwards he told them about those events which had so lately occurred, explaining how it had come about that the Skraeling chief had taken him for a kinsman.

"These people," he said, "have some very unusual customs, not least of which is their manner of honoring the dead. Whenever any important man dies among them, his kinsmen are free to choose some stranger, if there is one nearby, to adopt in his place. Then it is as though the dead man, himself, has returned to life; and so they believe. So now they have taken me for that Aselekah, whom we killed by Leif's houses, and given me his name."

He now described all that had occurred on the riverbank and told them of that strange battle he had fought with the Skraelings there. The bloodletting, he said, and the singing, which he had found so disturbing at the time, had been meant to lure the ghost of the dead man back to the land of the living, in order to offer it a new body in which to reside. If the spirit returned and found the offered body to his liking, the Skraelings believed he would enter it and take up his residence there.

But if the man being offered was found wanting, either in courage or strength, then the dead man's ghost, they believed, would spurn the body offered to it. And this, they thought, the worst possible turn of events, for then the ghost would be condemned to wander forever, lost between the worlds of the living and the dead, to haunt those people who had summoned it back, while the stranger who had proved so unreliable a vessel was condemned to a quick death.

"I'm not sure I'd have let these wretched forest folk poke such holes in me," Arnliot said, "whatever the bonds of kinship to be gained."

"Then that only shows the difference between you and this man who led us out here," Olvir said, "for he had, uppermost in his mind, the well-being of his fellow crewmen, while you would have looked to your own skin."

"I think we were on the verge of gaining our freedom, in any event," said Arnliot, "though I'd have done it in quite another manner. But now I want to know how this new Skraeling prince of ours proposes to deploy his men against the Skraeling king's host, when they come upon us, for it seems to me that that is a matter more worth prating about."

Sigtrygg said: "We are to take them by surprise and in close quarters, for this will make the most of our good Norse weapons. Only thus can we hope to overcome their greater numbers."

"I'm not sure you will find it as easy as you hope to surprise such men," Arnliot replied, "since they will know this country better than we, and the day of their arrival, besides."

"Then we must begin at once," said Sigtrygg, "and waste no more time in talk."

He now sent for W'tnalko and the other Skraelings and told them he wanted the encampment restored to the condition it had been in before the Greenlanders arrived, "for there are to be no signs that men such as we are have come into your midst."

W'tnalko now asked him what he had in mind and Sigtrygg explained that he wanted to conceal their presence completely from the Skraeling king. That, said W'tnalko, was a very sensible strategy, "but if you really want to hide these men, you will have to do much more than that."

"How so?" Sigtrygg asked him.

W'tnalko now said he thought it would be easy enough to conceal the Greenlanders' goods and even the men themselves, when the Tulewat came, but that their shoes were certainly a different story, since their markings would be readily distinguishable, on the ground, from those which Skraeling shoes left. "And we Skraelings are very keen-eyed, where such things are concerned," he added.

"Then what do you think we should do?"

"You must exchange your Greenland footgear for such shoes as we Skraelings wear," W'tnalko replied, "if you hope to fool the followers of Nahinanto."

Sigtrygg said he was more than willing to do this, so now it was agreed that all the Greenlanders were to give up their shoes and W'tnalko sent them a number of Skraeling women to measure their feet and cut skins to make shoes for them, after the Skraeling fashion. The Greenlanders thought this great sport and the Skraeling women were, themselves, much amazed at the size of the feet which these men showed them, for these women had never seen such big men so close up before. Arnliot said he thought matters had certainly taken their best turn, so far, since they now had the chance to get better acquainted with the women of this tribe, and all the other crewmen readily agreed to this.

Now while they were busying themselves with the Skraeling women in this fashion, a young woman appeared nearby who had not been seen there before. She stepped hesitantly toward the place where Sigtrygg was sitting, a tight wrapping of deer skin in her arms. W'tnalko, when he saw her coming, got up suddenly and went to her, placing his hands on her arms. But the young woman pushed past him and walked into the midst of the Greenlanders.

W'tnalko said: "There's no need for you to come to this place, Chinokwa, for there are plenty of others to do this work." But Chinokwa replied that it was only fitting for her to do her part and make those shoes, herself, which her brother, Aselekah, was to wear.

As soon as he saw her, Sigtrygg rose and made a place for her at his side. She sat down then, without further words, and began to tug at the shoes which Sigtrygg still wore. When these had been removed, the young Skraeling woman began to look more thoughtfully at him and now she asked if he were well, for she said she did not wish to see her brother overtaxing himself, before his wounds had had a proper chance to heal.

"There's no need to worry about that," Sigtrygg replied, "since I have had such care for my injuries as no Greenlander could have dreamed of, before now, in this strange land."

Chinokwa said that that was only to be expected, when people were looking after their relations, and she now unrolled her wrapped skins, pressing these up against the soles of Sigtrygg's feet. She was soon busily at work, cutting and shaping the deer skins with a small stone knife and with her teeth. Then she fitted the parts she had made, about each foot and, when she was satisfied with her work, she began to sew them together with a small needle, made of animal bone, and with thread of deer sinew. During all this time she did not speak and Sigtrygg kept his silence, as well.

When the shoes were made, and this did not take so long as may be imagined, for these Skraelings had great facility in such matters, Sigtrygg stood up and began to walk about in them. The other Greenlanders were up and doing the same, except for Arnliot who alone remained somewhat forlornly on the ground, since it took several women and quite a number of skins to cut and shape the shoes which were destined for his feet. This proved to be the cause of much laughter among the Greenlanders and Arnliot replied that they could amuse themselves at his expense, if they wanted to, but that the size of his feet only showed how much more of him there was, than of other men, and that this would be most readily apparent on the field of battle. "Even these Skraeling women can see what a man of my size can do," he laughed.

Chinokwa now asked Sigtrygg if he were pleased with the shoes she had made for him and he replied that he was, so that she quickly looked down and away, her face seeming to color somewhat in the shadowy light of the forest. Sigtrygg reached out then and took the maid's chin in his own hand, lifting her eyes up to his.

"There's no use hiding it," he now said to his crew, in the Greenland tongue, "for I have never seen a fairer looking maid than this new kinswoman of mine...however darkly complexioned these Skraeling folk are."

"At the least," answered Arnliot, "we have not seen any better, since we came to this country, so we must make do with what is at hand."

Sigtrygg replied that Arnliot was to bear himself in a manly fashion and not press matters overmuch with the Skraeling women, unless they and their kinsmen were willing, for he said these people were, in his opinion, no better or worse than those they had left behind in Greenland, however odd their ways.

But Arnliot replied that "there are some would think manliness a different matter entirely."

"Nevertheless," said Sigtrygg, "I want you to show some forbearance where these Skraelings are concerned."

"That's easy enough for you to say, since you have already taken one of these maids for your own," Arnliot replied. "But others of us, who have not yet been so lucky, will think we are entitled to taste of the same provisions, as we are all crewmen on the same ship."

"Chinokwa is my foster sister," Sigtrygg said, "though our bonds of kinship are but lately formed, and I mean to treat her in just that fashion. You other men would be well advised to do the same with those Skraeling women you fancy, until matters are a lot more settled between us and these people."

Sigtrygg now asked Chinokwa if she were willing to walk with him and she said that she was, so now these two went down toward the riverbank, leaving the crew of the Gull behind. When they came out of the trees and saw the river below them, Sigtrygg stopped suddenly and looked down at the rocks, along the water's edge, which still glistened in places with the bloody markings of three days before. Chinokwa saw him hesitate and asked if he wanted to turn back, but he replied that there was no need for that, "since I have already forgotten what has been left behind on those rocks."

They now found a place for themselves in the tall grass which grew above the river and Sigtrygg asked the Skraeling woman if she were willing to tell him something of the man, Aselekah, whose name he now bore. Chinokwa said she would do so, if he insisted, and Sigtrygg said, in that case, she must hold nothing back.

"My brother," said she, "was a very promising young man who was greatly loved by the chief, my father. But he sent him away with W'tnalko, out of fear of the king, Nahinanto, since the Tulewat always claim the best young men for themselves. My father thought to hide them by sending them off to that place where the ghosts of your kinsmen dwell, for that was considered a journey worthy of any young man. And Aselekah would never have gone willingly, had he thought it a matter of fleeing his enemies or seeking safety for himself. But my father thought the ghosts who lived among those houses, which your kinsmen built, less formidable than the Tulewat, and so he took the loss of his son very hard, when he learned of this, having thought my brother safely hidden there."

"It's not clear to me," said Sigtrygg, "how he could have thought him safer amidst ghosts than among men."

"Manitikaha cast many spells to safeguard them there," said Chinokwa, "and he assured my father that he was stronger than your countrymen's ghosts. Still, it's plain he did not count on living men."

Sigtrygg said he was sorry for the loss of her kinsman, though it had not been done by his will. "Still I am certainly responsible for it," he added.

"We must speak no more about this," Chinokwa replied, "for the way we Skraelings see things, my brother is now returned to us; and you are the means for that."

Now it seemed to Sigtrygg that, even as the young Skraeling woman was speaking, he saw again that same vision, which he had seen before, of a brown deer sitting over him as he lay bleeding on the rocks beside the river, and he thought Chinokwa's dark eyes seemed to grow exceedingly large and to become one with that strange creature's. He reached out, unthinking, and took her by the hand.

"Tell me," said he, after holding her hand for a time in his, "how it is that I thought I saw a she-deer in your place, on that very day you awoke me from death; for, while it was certainly these same black eyes which gazed down upon me, it was not this form, but that of some animal which called me back to life."

Chinokwa said she could not answer for what he had seen but that he must tell her everything, just as he remembered it. So now he carefully recounted his vision to her, in every detail, and, when he had finished, he asked her what she thought it meant.

"Some people would say you are luckier than most," she replied, "for few are able to see as far into things as you have now done."

"How so?" asked Sigtrygg.

Chinokwa now told him that all the Skraelings had a spirit form, as well as a bodily one, and that these spiritual manifestations took the shape of beasts. "What you have seen," said she, "is nothing less than our true natures, and the form we take, after we die. But each of us has his own nature and the animal form which suits him best."

"Do we Greenlanders have such forms, then, too?" Sigtrygg asked her.

"That is unknown to me," replied Chinokwa, "for you men come from a long way off and may not be the same as we are. Still, if you have such forms, they may take the shapes of creatures which we have never seen; but that is a matter for our Dream-Speaker and not for one such as me."

Sigtrygg said he thought it highly unlikely that there was much difference between Greenlanders and Skraelings and that, if the Skraelings had animal forms, "then we Greenlanders must as well. But some people would find it hard to believe, in either case."

"Still," said she, "you have seen it with your own eyes."

"A man may see a great many things, when he is lying close to death," Sigtrygg replied.

"At the least, you have my brother's spirit," insisted the young Skraeling woman, "which has now been joined with your own. And that is not to be denied."

Sigtrygg agreed that he saw no reason to question that, but added that "this only makes me the more eager to hear about that man whose name I have been given, for I would like to know the nature of the creature which your brother's spirit wears as its garment, since I am anxious to learn as much about him as I can."

Chinokwa replied that she could tell him very little concerning that, "for these things are not easily discovered. But some say the spirit form of a man is most likely to make itself known, when the need is greatest."

"Then, that," answered Sigtrygg, "would certainly be a thing worth seeing."

Not long after this, the Skraeling chieftain sent for Sigtrygg and asked him what he planned to do concerning the defense against Nahinanto, "for my young men," he said, "are eager to put themselves at your disposal, and will not shrink from even the hardest fighting."

"I want to remain here, just as before," was Sigtrygg's reply, "without making a great deal of fuss about it, for, in my opinion there's no reason to go chasing about the countryside in search of an enemy who might still be far off and who will surely know the woods as well, or better, than you do yourself."

"Still," said the Skraeling chief, "it is often best to make war when the blood is hot in men's veins. And the sight of your bravery and great strength has already done much to encourage that. Yet such ardor may cool, as quickly as it arises."

Sigtrygg said: "It will burn again when the Tulewat come, and that will be soon enough for my purpose."

The Skraeling chieftain told him to have it his own way and said he was now to have sole responsibility for the defense of their town, "since that is the proper role for a chief's son."

Sigtrygg thanked him and promised to do whatever was needed to protect his new kinsmen and the old chieftain replied that he had no doubts concerning that. "But," he added, "you are to look after my daughter, whatever else befalls, since it is for her sake alone that I have taken you into my house."

CHAPTER XXII

THE CONJURING

Some time later the Skraelings gave out that old Manitikaha, the Dream-Speaker, was to cast his spells in order to determine how near their enemy was to them and the likely outcome of the expected encounter. Anyok told Sigtrygg he was to attend, along with all the most important men of the Skraeling town and Sigtrygg agreed, on condition the other Greenlanders would be welcomed, as well. Anyok said he was to have his own way in this, so Sigtrygg now told the men of his crew to join them at the appointed time.

On the evening when the conjuring was to take place, the Skraeling women made a small fire before the opening of Anyok's house and placed an old wolf's skin on the ground beside it. Then they piled a number of feathers and bones carefully on this skin and hung a sack from three poles which had been placed nearby. The poles formed a tripod, with their ends bound tightly together at the top.

When these preparations had been made, the old soothsayer, Manitikaha, came out of the house and seated himself before the fire. He had little to say at first but, shortly, he began to sing in the Skraeling fashion, and, as he sang, he cast dried leaves from the skin sack which dangled beside him onto the burning sticks at the fire's center. When the fire began to become very smoky from this and the Greenlanders, who were seated nearby, found it hardest to breathe because of the harshness of the smoke, the old man muttered some words and then several young boys ran forward and laid a number of flat rocks across the flames and smoke. The old man then took the animal bones, which were lying on the wolf skin, and placed them on the flat rocks. Then he took hold of the feathers and began to wave them about. All the while he kept muttering to himself and singing in his sing-song fashion.

Now it happened that Vragi observed all this with a much keener interest than any of the other members of Sigtrygg's crew and, after the proceedings had begun, he arose suddenly from his place and walked toward the fire where the Dream-Speaker sat. He had his long spear in his hand and, when the Skraelings saw him going toward old Manitikaha with the spear, they stood up at once and placed themselves in his path. Foremost among these was W'tnalko who, of all the Skraelings, had shown himself the least willing to give way before the old viking. W'tnalko now put up his hand, as though to push Vragi backward, and Sigtrygg half rose from his place beside the Skraeling chief. But the chief's hand restrained him. "Aselekah, of all men present, must keep his place," he said.

Then the Dream-Speaker stopped his chanting abruptly and said that W'tnalko and the other young Skraeling men were to step aside; and now he made a place, beside himself, and gestured for Vragi to take his seat there. This Vragi did so that these two were soon lost, together, in the enveloping smoke. Now the con-juring went on, just as before, and all those who were present as witnesses, both Skraelings and Greenlanders, kept silent. The smoke became so thick that those nearest the fire were soon lost to the view of those sitting furthest away and no man could see clearly the features of his fellow, though he sat no more than an arm's length away.

The Greenlanders found the smoke very tiring, as it seemed to induce in them a state of great sleepiness, while burning their eyes and throats. Yet, it did not affect the Skraelings in this way, at all, for they seemed to be hardly moved by it. After a time, the soft sing-song of the Dream-Speaker faded off and then there was only silence and the drifting smoke which hung about their heads. Then the Skraelings set up a great shout and now they rose to their feet, as one man, and began to disperse the smoke.

The Greenlanders could now see that old Manitikaha was quite worn out, for he sat slumped in his place, as though he was no longer able to speak or even lift himself up. The young Skraeling men quickly gathered the Dream-Speaker into their arms and assisted him out of the circle, while the women came and hurriedly gathered up his things, covering the fire with earth and waving away the last of the smoke.

Then Sigtrygg turned to Anyok and asked him what had been accomplished and what, if anything, the old man had seen.

Anyok said there was not much to tell and now he got slowly to his feet and looked at Sigtrygg for a long while. Then he placed one hand on the Greenlander's shoulder. He said nothing but looked, for a long time, into the younger man's eyes and Sigtrygg said later that he thought the eyes of the Skraeling chief seemed rather distant at that moment, as though he foresaw what was to come, for himself and all those who depended on him. Sigtrygg repeated his question concerning what the soothsayer had seen, but Anyok only shrugged and took his hand slowly back from Sigtrygg's shoulder.

"You will fight well, as befits a chief's son. And that was only to be looked for from you, Aselekah," he said. Then the chieftain went off, without saying anything further, and he seemed to Sigtrygg much older than before. All the other leading men of the town quickly followed after him.

The Greenlanders now came round their skipper and asked him what the outcome of the spells had been, but Sigtrygg replied that he was as much at a loss concerning these events as they were, "though it would seem these Skraelings have learned some news tonight, which it would be good for us to have."

"The only news I think worth having," said Arnliot, "is that this Nahinanto, whom they call their king, is to be soundly trounced beneath our feet; and that mine are to be the feet which do it."

Olvir said he thought this only showed how little was to be gained from such pagan practices as these Skraelings engaged in and that "many will find cause to blame us for our backsliding, when we have got back to Greenland."

Some of the others now said they thought the same and that they would all be better off, the sooner they were away from these devilish Vinlanders.

"I don't know what it was you men hoped to find out here, when you agreed to ship out with me and come to this country," Sigtrygg said to them, after he had heard their complaints, "but it certainly could not have been a land and people like the ones you left behind. Nor do I think it can do us much good to despise those things which seem strange to us, or hard to understand, now that we are here."

Vragi said he thought this well-spoken, "for such carping and complaining as I have heard on this voyage, until now, has never been known in all the days that vikings rode on the open seas since I was a youngster. And that does not speak well for men of our blood."

Arnliot replied that events would soon prove who was fit to call himself a Norseman and who was not, and Vragi replied that this was certainly true. "But until then," he added, "this petty bickering and second guessing is likely to do us more harm than good, for who knows what state our foes are likely to find us in, when we finally cross paths, if we are unable to agree on things now."

Olvir said that fighting was one thing and speaking one's mind quite another and that he thought they must be prepared to do both.

"Still, we have not seen much fighting yet from you Brattahlid men," Arnliot said, "though you have always been willing enough to have your say; and this despite the unimpressive manner in which you came aboard our ship in Eiriksfjord."

"There's no need to keep reminding us about that," Olvir said, "for we four have shared all the hardships equally with you others and have by now earned the same rights as any man of this crew. But some people would say you Ketilsfjordmen are no strangers to empty boasts, yourselves, for you have done no more than any of the rest of us to make a mark in this country, despite your big words."

"Hard sailing will prove the ship, in any event," Arnliot replied.

Sigtrygg said this, at least, was certainly true and that they could all expect the chance to test their rigging before that wind which they now found themselves in had played itself out, "for, in my opinion, rougher seas than we have so far seen are no longer far off. Though only these Skraelings seem to know how low on the horizon the storm clouds are lying."

"Five days," said Vragi.

"What's that?" Sigtrygg asked him.

"What the soothsayer saw," Vragi replied, still leaning on his spear shaft. "In those bones which he threw onto the fire. That old Skraeling sorcerer has certainly got much keener eyes than you Greenlanders give him credit for. The Skraeling king these people fear will be among us in five days, and he looks to be a very formidable opponent, if my judgement is still worth anything in these matters. That is what old Manitikaha saw written in the bones."

"Then we have very little time," said Sigtrygg, "if this is true. But how, then, do you think we ought to proceed?"

"No different from before," Vragi said.

Sigtrygg now turned in earnest to preparing their defenses. He told each of his crewman what they were to do and then he instructed the Skraelings and set W'tnalko over them, to see to their preparations. He told them they were to build no fortifications nor change the appearance of the Skraeling town in any way. "I want everything to look just as it did before," he said and W'tnalko promised that this should be so. But Sigtrygg also told them to cut a number of large tree trunks and bind these with ropes on either end and conceal them about the edges of the town.

He also directed the Skraelings to prepare large snares, such as those used for taking birds, with strips of the wadmal he had brought with him from Leif's houses, and these he had carefully laid in certain of the pathways between the houses.

When all this was done, he told his crewmen they were to conceal themselves in various of the Skraeling houses when the time came and assigned each to his post. Then he took W'tnalko aside and asked him if everything had been accomplished exactly as he had requested.

"Nothing has been done differently," the Skraeling replied, "but it might be wiser to stop these men from coming among us, in the first place, instead of leaving everything open to them in this fashion so that they can walk so easily into our midst."

"I don't think we are likely to have much luck, denying them entry, if they are minded to pay us a visit," Sigtrygg said. "But perhaps things will fall out in such a way that they find it harder to forsake our hospitality, once they have tired of it, than they found in accepting it."

Sigtrygg now told W'tnalko that, if things got rough, he was to see to the removal of the women and children and any others who were not fit for fighting, "for we will find it easier going if we are not impeded by those we most desire to protect. And I especially want you to see to the well-being of Chinokwa, my foster sister."

W'tnalko said he was willing to do this, but that he thought Sigtrygg would have need of every man in the town, should fighting break out.

"One man, more or less, will make little difference," Sigtrygg replied, "but the loss of Chinokwa or any of these others will undo all our efforts. However, when you take the women away, I want you to do so by way of the river. Then, if Nahinanto and his men have come upon us by boats, you are to find and break apart every one of these that you can, leaving nothing which can be used by them to escape on the river."

W'tnalko said he would do whatever Sigtrygg asked of him

and Sigtrygg replied that that was no less than he had expected.

On the eve of the fourth day, the entire Skraeling town was strangely silent and both Greenlanders and Skraelings stood about uneasily. Sigtrygg walked among them to ensure that everything was ready. When he had gone into all the houses and seen to all the preparations, he took Anyok, his foster father, aside and asked him if he were content with how things had been handled.

"Only time will tell about that," the Skraeling chief said, "but you have certainly done your part."

"I don't know how things are likely to turn out, myself," Sigtrygg now told him, "and there's not much more I can do to prepare for this encounter than I have already done. Still, whatever befalls, I want you to know that we Greenlanders will fight as hard as any to protect this town."

The Skraeling chief said he had no doubt of this and that he thought they had already demonstrated their sincerity, "but no man can know how a thing will fall out, before it has occurred."

Sigtrygg now told his men they were to take themselves out of sight and hide in the houses to which they had been assigned, "and sleep as well as you are able, but lightly, for there's no telling when you will be needed."

Anyok, for his part, told the Skraelings they were to go about their business, just as they always did at that time of year, and take no actions which might appear suspicious or lead others to think that all was not as it seemed. The Skraelings did as they were told but, as the fourth day drew to a close, Sigtrygg began to feel a growing uneasiness concerning these preparations, for everything seemed much too quiet to him, and to be moving at a slower pace than seemed natural.

He now went into the chief's house and found Vragi sitting on the ground there, with Olvir and another Greenlander. These were busily engaged in cleaning and sharpening their arms. Nearby Chinokwa sat, with Tanakrit, her mother. W'tnalko sat in the farthest corner of the house and seemed very deep in his own thoughts.

Sigtrygg went to where Vragi and Olvir were and now he seated himself beside them. Vragi asked him what was troubling him.

"Things seem overly quiet, to my way of thinking," Sigtrygg said, "and that is likely to put our quarry on their guard."

"There's not much you can do about that," Vragi told him, "for men are much the same, wherever you find them, and fear, in the face of uncertainty, cannot be entirely hidden in circumstances like these."

"Still," Sigtrygg replied, "this matter is not likely to go as well for us as we had hoped, if others smell a trap. And then we will be hard put to hold our own, from all that I have heard of these Tulewat."

"We may be hard put, in any event," said Olvir, "for there are so few of us."

"Men have been known to make up in spirit, what they lack in numbers, before this," Sigtrygg said, "though you Brattahlid men have yet to put that to the test."

"There's no use worrying about such things," Vragi told him, "for you have done all that you could to prepare these people. So now we must let things run their course, as the old saying has it. But my advice to you is to take what rest you can, for I have the feeling you will need all your strength when morning comes."

Sigtrygg said this was probably so and now he stretched himself out beside his men.

After awhile, W'tnalko arose from his place by the Skraeling women and went over to where the Greenlanders were sitting. He watched them silently for awhile, until Olvir and the man with him had stretched out, as Sigtrygg had done, and only Vragi continued sitting in his place. The old viking was intently inspecting his spear's point, seeing to its seat at the end of the long shaft to which it was affixed, as though to assure himself it was still securely bound in its place. With a flattened stone, he struck the edges several times, causing the metal to ring shrilly. Then he put the blade down, for he seemed quite satisfied with it.

W'tnalko looked intently at this weapon and asked its purpose, in the Skraeling tongue, but Vragi made no reply.

"What use is a weapon like this one?" the Skraeling asked once more, for it seemed to him that there were much better spears to hand and that all the other Greenlanders certainly had better arms than did this old man. Vragi again offered him no response. Then it seemed to W'tnalko that Vragi was like most of the other Greenlanders and had not learned many Skraeling words, for, in truth, he could not remember ever having heard the old man speak in the Skraeling fashion.

So now he spoke more roughly, but in the language of the Greenlanders, and asked if the old man lacked sufficient understanding to answer him in the Skraeling tongue.

Vragi looked up at this and said: "You have certainly learned to talk like a Greenlander, and maybe that is not to be wondered at since you have spent so much time in our company. But then you Skraelings are full of surprises."

W'tnalko replied that he thought the Greenlanders no less strange than they found him to be, "but most people will seem odd to those who do not know them. And you seem the most unusual, of all the Greenlanders, to me."

Vragi said he thought this very funny and that it was no doubt due to the fact that he was no Greenlander at all.

"Then what manner of man are you?" asked the Skraeling. "For you seem to know a great deal more about things than others of your kind, and even our Dream-Speaker is unwilling to cross you."

"I am not much different from these others," Vragi answered him, "though older; and one who has seen a great many things besides. And now I have seen this country too, which is better than most men my age could have hoped for. But the answer to your question is not difficult to provide."

"As to the kind of man you are?"

"As to why I carry such a large and clumsy looking weapon, when others seem to have better."

W'tnalko said he had not thought the old man could understand his question since he had posed it in the Skraeling tongue.

Vragi only laughed and said he could understand a great many more things than most people gave him credit for. "And spear making is not the least of these."

"In that case," said the Skraeling, "I want to know why you do not choose a better weapon for yourself than this one, for there are many spears lying about in this place which will be easier for a man to handle," and now he offered to find Vragi a lighter spear, such as a man might carry into the woods, for casting at fleeing beasts to quickly bring his quarry down. "And then," he added, "you can bind the iron point to it."

Vragi thanked him but said there was no need for that.

"And why not?" the Skraeling asked.

"Because spears like this one are not made for beasts," Vragi answered him, "but for men."

CHAPTER XXIII

A HOST ON THE RIVER

On the following morning, they were awakened by the rustling of feet about their heads. Sigtrygg opened his eyes and saw that it was Anyok squatting nearby, with a number of his men not far behind him, the light from the doorway casting them in shadow. The Greenlanders sat up and Anyok said that Sigtrygg was to come with him at once, "for there are boats on the river."

Sigtrygg told the others to remain in the house and he went out with the Skraeling chieftain, and W'tnalko behind them. They went quietly past the other houses to a place which was well-wooded, overlooking the river. Now they could see how a number of long, narrow boats were coming toward them from up river. Each boat contained a large number of men who sat, one in front of the other in single file, paddling softly downstream. The lead boat was by far the longest and had the most men, all of whom appeared to be decked out in feathers and were quite bare, from head to waist, except for the strange painted markings which covered their bodies right down to where these disappeared below the boat line. Each man wielded a small paddle, with which he pushed the boat he was in along, except for one man who sat foremost and unmoving in the first boat's prow. This man did not paddle like the others but rather sat, quite still, his arms clasped before his chest.

The longer Sigtrygg watched, the more boats he could see coming into view and, as the lead boat drew closer, he saw that the men in it also carried a number of long poles projecting out over the river. Several large, ball-like objects seemed to hang from the poles and Sigtrygg asked his companions what they thought these might be.

"Heads," W'tnalko replied. "Those are the heads of the men they have killed."

Sigtrygg said they must go back, at once, to the town "and everything is to be done just as we planned. I want no one to give an alarm or betray our intentions in any way."

They now hurried silently through the woods to the Skraeling encampment and Sigtrygg told his crew to conceal themselves as they had previously agreed and he, for his part, went into the chief's house once more. Anyok and W'tnalko followed him in and now Sigtrygg took W'tnalko aside and reminded him of their discussion of the day before. "I want you to do what you promised me," Sigtrygg told him, "without any concern for what may occur here; for, in my opinion, that is the hero's part."

W'tnalko said he would do whatever was required of him.

Sigtrygg now asked for help in painting his face, in the Skraeling fashion, and the chief's wife squatted down before him and began to apply the markings.

They could soon hear shouting coming up from the river bank, the voices of a large number of men, but there were no answering shouts from the town. Everything was now quiet among the houses, although the deep, guttural voices of the men at the river appeared to grow much closer. Sigtrygg told Olvir and his companion to place themselves by the doorway and tell him everything they saw.

In a moment Olvir said there would be no need for excessive vigilance in this matter, "for I think they are already among us."

Sigtrygg crawled to the doorway and Vragi came right behind him. Outside they could see a number of very fierce looking fellows, entirely unclothed except for a wrapping of skin about their buttocks and strings of bone and shell which they wore over their chests. Their faces were streaked with paint, in the Skraeling fashion, and there were bold stripes of paint all across their chests and arms. On their heads were bright feathers and they carried stone-tipped spears in their hands, and what appeared to be spiked war clubs. Their eyes glowed like fiery coals in their painted faces and they seemed just like birds of prey to the Greenlanders. Each of them bore a small shield before him, which seemed to have been cut and shaped from tree bark.

As they watched, more and more of these men seemed to come into view. Sigtrygg said they were to count as many as they could see, but without showing themselves. One of the Greenlanders said he thought he could see ten of these men but Olvir said he thought the count closer to twenty, or even thirty. Sigtrygg replied that he thought this last number was probably right and, since they could not see everything from where they sat, he told them they must assume there were even more than that. "In my opinion," he said, "there will be forty or more of these fellows, from the large number of boats I saw coming down the river."

The war-like Tulewat who had come up first from the river now seemed to be somewhat surprised by the silent nature of their reception in the Skraeling town and they began to walk about with great deliberation, touching first one thing and then another with the extended points of their weapons. They did not speak much among themselves and were clearly on their guard. Vragi said he thought these were men who were not unused to war.

Now there was a rustling among the strangers and a man who was considerably larger than the others came into their midst. Although these Skraelings were all somewhat larger than W'tnalko's kinsmen, this new fellow was certainly the largest, by far, for he seemed nearly as big as the Greenlanders, themselves. He wore a long wrapping of fur on his shoulders and, on his head, a more elaborate head-dress than any of the others. Amidst the feathers and shells which adorned this headpiece, two large deer antlers protruded. His face was painted, beneath it, in jagged bolts of lightning and his eyes were circled in pools of red-seeming blood.

Behind and beside this man walked several others and these bore the poles which Sigtrygg had seen before, from which dangled the severed heads of the slain. Several Tulewat held these out before the large man, as he walked about amidst the Skraeling camp, projecting the heads in whatever direction he turned. This man, for his part, carried a spear in one hand and a war club in the other, out of which long shards of bone seemed to protrude. A somewhat smaller man went before him, bearing one of the tree-bark shields.

Anyok, who had been sitting quietly, until now, suddenly rose to his feet without speaking. Tanakrit and Chinokwa hastened to place a furred robe on his shoulders and then stepped back so that the Skraeling chief could walk, unimpeded, to the doorway. Sigtrygg rose at this, too, and took a furred mantle of his own, which Tanakrit offered him. He placed this on his shoulders in the same manner as Anyok had done.

"There are certainly more of them than there are of us," Olvir said softly, "and they seem a good deal bigger than we have had cause to expect, up till now."

"They will not seem so large after you have stuck a few spears in their bellies," Vragi told him.

Anyok, the chieftain, now went to the doorway and the Greenlanders carefully drew back so that he could pass through without hindrance. Sigtrygg went out after him, carrying his shield and sword in his hands.

When the leader of the Tulewat, who had come up from the river, saw Anyok step out into the open, his eyes seemed to glisten. He greeted the chieftain with a sound from deep in his throat and now he asked why things were so much quieter than usual and where all the people of the encampment were. Then he saw Sigtrygg come out behind Anyok; and Sigtrygg was by far the larger of those two and bore his shield out in front of him in a most war-like manner, though pointing his sword to the earth.

The Skraeling leader asked who this stranger might be and Anyok replied that it was none other than Aselekah, his son.

"Had I known your son would become such a man as this," said the Skraeling king, "I would have long ago claimed him for my own. But I think he has changed a great deal since last we passed this way."

Anyok said this might well be, but that it only showed the strength of his spirit, if true.

"Yet, it seems to me," said the leader of the Tulewat, "that this man is attired for war, though there can be little cause for that in this country. Or have events occurred hereabouts of which I am uninformed?"

Anyok said there was little news to tell of, except for the killing of one of his young men by some strangers who had come from over the sea, "though that matter has by now been resolved, according to our customs."

The Tulewat lord now asked if Anyok knew much about the men who had done the killing, but the chieftain replied that he did not, though he thought them unusually large men, and of a sort who would prove hard to deal with.

"In that case," said the Tulewat, "you will not find it difficult to make room for me and my men by your fires, since there are few in this country who would willingly stand up to us," and now he asked Anyok if he were prepared to provide them with the usual hospitality, as was the custom in that country, "for we have come a long way and are in need of refreshments."

Anyok said they were short of provisions for that and that he thought the Tulewat king would find a better welcome further down river, "where the hunting and fishing have been better."

"I don't see much reason to travel any further than here," the king replied, "though you appear eager enough to send us on our way. Besides there are still certain matters to be settled in this place, or have you forgotten your obligations to us already?"

To this Anyok offered no reply.

Seeing that the Skraeling chief seemed at a loss for words, Sigtrygg now stepped forward, his shield before him, and stood side by side with the Skraeling chief.

He said there was no need for the leader of the Tulewat to remind them of their obligations, "though it seems to me you would do better looking elsewhere for the captives you desire, since we are even shorter here of people, for your purposes, than of the means to entertain you."

"This Aselekah, your son, speaks with great bluntness," said the Skraeling king to Anyok, "yet he does not seem to understand our ways as a chieftain's son should. Still he is young and can be taught. I would consider it an honor if you will grant me the service of such a man, along with the others whom you owe me."

Anyok said that this was for Aselekah, himself, to decide.

Then Sigtrygg said: "There's no use hoping for that, king, since you and your followers are not welcome any longer in this place; and now I advise you to go to your boats, while you are still able to do so."

The Skraeling king said he thought this very unseemly talk and his eyes seemed to cloud over with anger. He said that Aselekah should learn to speak more cautiously to his betters, "for I am Nahinanto, the lord of this country, as all men who dwell here know, and it doesn't do for strangers to carry themselves about with too much pride." He pulled himself up to his full height, when he said this, and his eyes flashed hot anger.

Sigtrygg answered that he was no less a lord in his land than Nahinanto was in his, "for I am Vinland's king, by right of inheritance and blood," he said, "and that is no small thing."

The Skraeling replied that he had never heard of such a country as Vinland, or of its king, but that some people would think it wiser to tread carefully when in foreign parts, "for it is plain enough to see you are a stranger here; and one of those, perhaps, who has come to us from over the sea."

Sigtrygg said he wouldn't deny that and now he took another step forward and pointed with his sword at the nearby houses. "Think whatever you like about the matter, king," he said, "but the people who dwell in this place are now under my protection, as before they were under yours, so there's no use trying to throw your weight around here as things now stand. In my opinion, your best hope is to leave here as quickly as you can, since this may not be offered you twice."

Nahinanto gnashed his teeth together when he heard the words which Sigtrygg spoke, and he and all his followers began to shake their weapons in a most war-like way. The Skraeling king said there was room for only one lord in that country and that he did not intend for it to be anyone but himself. He now said that Anyok and Sigtrygg were to throw down their arms and beg for mercy, which he promised to consider, after he had made a proper review of the captives he was due.

"I don't think we are likely to be following such advice as that, any time soon," Sigtrygg replied, "for you men are in a much more difficult situation than you imagine."

When he said these words, he called aloud and now Vragi came out of the chief's house, leaning on his great spear, and Olvir and his companion after him. These now put up their shields on either side of Sigtrygg and Anyok, while Vragi, for his part, placed himself off to one side, his eye on the Skraeling king.

Nahinanto said he did not think such menacing behavior was likely to do them much good, "for there are a great deal more of us than of you; and we are all well-versed in war."

To this Sigtrygg responded by calling aloud once more and now the others of his crew quickly came out of the houses in which they had been hiding, bearing their shields and other weapons before them. The Skraelings of the town also appeared at this time, placing themselves in a large circle around Nahinanto and his followers. Then the men of Sigtrygg's crew began to beat their weapons against their shields and Anyok's Skraelings commenced shouting in their own harsh and warlike manner.

"Now it seems to me," Sigtrygg said, "that matters have gone somewhat differently than you had hoped and it is your place, and not ours, to throw down your arms."

Nahinanto and the men closest to him looked around the little Skraeling town at the strange group of warriors which hemmed them in and their eyes came to rest at once on Arnliot, who tow-

ered like a giant among the other large men. They had never seen
such men as these and this could be plainly discerned in their
eyes, and in the hesitation they showed when confronted in this
unexpected fashion. But their uncertainty did not last long, for
they were men accustomed to war — and to death.

Before the Greenlanders could cease drumming on their war
shields, the Tulewat let up a great and evil sounding shout, which
filled that place like the voice of a single man, and then each of
them leaped upon the fellow nearest him. Now the Greenlanders
were taken aback by the fury of this onslaught, and they fell back
before the harsh Skraeling attack. But Arnliot, thrusting his shield
forward, fended off those Skraelings who rushed at him, as though
flicking flies from a beast's carcass, and then he ran into the midst
of the enemy, urging his fellows to follow close behind him.

Striking to right and left with his sword, the Ketilsfjord man
cut himself a path through the midst of those Tulewat who opposed him. All the other men of the Greenland crew, when they
saw how things had gone with him and how fiercely he broke
through the ranks of the Skraelings, now took heart and plunged
after him into the fray. Sigtrygg, for his part, flanked by the men
about him, charged forward as well, toward the place where the
Skraeling king had stood, though, when Sigtrygg reached that spot,
the man was no longer there. Vragi, wielding his long spear, in a
great sweeping motion, rushed forward, piercing first one of the
Skraeling king's warriors and then another without cease, and the
chieftain, Anyok, followed with great shouts, leaping on those who
stood before him, to club them down with his stone war axe.

The mass of fighting men rolled, first one way and than another, about the clearing and there were horrible, blood searing
screams, as men attacked and fell on both sides. But the end of it
was that the surprise, and greater size of the Norsemen, bore the
fury of the more numerous warriors of the Skraeling king down
before them; these, having been badly bloodied, turned, at last, to
flee to the river. Now Sigtrygg sprang the traps he had set for them
and the snares were let loose, to catch at the fleeing men's legs,

tangling them in their headlong dash to the river bank, while the tree trunks were suddenly swung out across their paths, cutting off their retreat. Then the Skraelings of the town and Sigtrygg's own men overwhelmed those they caught up with, beating and stabbing them to death, and the fleeing warriors lost their lives in great pools of blood, wherever they fell. Although the Skraeling king had come with a large force of men, these did him very little good in the end, for he was caught in a trap which he had been unable to anticipate and he was faced by warriors he had never had occasion to encounter before.

Anyok's people, when they saw how things were going, let out a great victory shout and it was soon clear that more than half the warriors which the Skraeling king had brought with him lay dead before the chief's house. As to the others, they were fighting their way desperately to the river but, when they came there, they saw that all their boats had been broken in and were completely useless to them.

The people of the town, with Arnliot and the Greenlanders at their head, now came running down the embankment and threw themselves against the remaining warriors of the king. Many of these now turned and plunged themselves into the river, rather than face the furious onslaught from above, and Sigtrygg came down behind them, his shield gone but his bloodied sword raised high over his head. In his left hand he waved the headpiece of the Skraeling king, himself. He carried this fiercely before him and cried out that the Greenlanders must find the man who owned it quickly, for he had no desire to see the king escape.

But they could not find that man, though they turned over every body which lay face down in the watery mud and chased hard after those who fled across the river. Sigtrygg angrily urged them on for he said there would be no rest for them until they had taken the head of the man the Skraelings called their king. Still there was no sign of him, among all the dead, and when the Greenlanders returned, splattered all over with blood, they threw themselves down on the river's edge and said they would look no further, for this killing had been harder work than they had been accustomed to, up till then.

Sigtrygg now gave over the chase and stood to count up his men, seeing that none had fallen, though a few had taken serious wounds, and he went about, from one to another, to see to the binding of the hurt men and to stanch the flow of blood. He stopped at Olvir and his companions, those serving men from Brattahlid, and saw that they were bloodier than many of the others, and that their shields bore the nicks and red markings of battle. "This was boldly done, shipmates," he told them, "and no less than I had expected of you."

Then he knelt over Olvir and tied a strip, torn from his own shirt, about the man's bloodied arm.

Vragi, too, made his rounds though, unlike the other men of the crew, he seemed completely unhurt. Only the point of his spear still dripped heavily with men's blood and he put this aside now, as he bent to look at the wounds of the others.

Arnliot had a gash on his forehead, where a well-aimed stone axe had struck him, and his side bled profusely from the spear thrusts which the Skraelings had made against him as he ran them down. He seemed quite exhausted from all his exertions, but there was a rather satisfied smile on his face. Vragi looked over the Ketilsfjord man's wounds and bound those which he thought required it. Then he told him to rest while he could, but not to take too much pleasure in the moment's respite, "for I have the feeling there will be more to do, before we are finished in this country."

They now began to look about them, as well, for the wounded among their Skraeling allies, for Sigtrygg said it was these men, above all others, who had made their victory possible, "since we are not numerous enough, however fierce, to have driven this Skraeling king off by ourselves." These men, because they were less well-armed than the Greenlanders, had taken the brunt of Nahinanto's attack, and so had got the worst of it.

Once he was satisfied concerning the condition of his own men, Sigtrygg went about, seeing to the state of those Skraelings

of the town who had fallen in the pursuit of the Tulewat across the
river. Here and there he came to a man who had fallen and then he
lifted him up and guided or carried the fallen warrior half-way up
the river bank. Then he went back to bring another, and then
another, and soon those other Greenlanders who seemed strong
enough to get about were up and helping him.

Now, when he was coming up from the river's edge for the
third time, as he was about this work, he looked up and saw
W'tnalko standing above him and that Skraeling was altogether
unbloodied, though the sweat glistened hotly on his skin. He had
a dark look in his eyes, too, and his jaw seemed rather grimly set.
When he saw this, Sigtrygg put aside the man he was helping and
went up the embankment to see what had befallen.

W'tnalko said he was to come at once, back to the Skraeling
town, so now these two ran swiftly over the embankment and
away from the river.

A little while afterwards the other Greenlanders followed. They
were greatly elated, though quite spent from the force of their
exertions, and they dragged themselves back to the center of the
town without much talk or banter. Still, they thought they had
done rather well for themselves and, here and there, a man or two
of them broke into song.

When they drew near the chief's house they saw a cluster of
people standing about near the doorway and Sigtrygg and W'tnalko
foremost among these. Vragi at once went there, and Arnliot right
after him. Then the other Greenlanders came up to the chief's
house and pressed closely about the smaller group, straining to see
what all the commotion was about.

Sigtrygg told them to stand back, "and let us have some air
here," so they fell back and away, as they were bidden. But Vragi
pressed through the crowd and the Skraelings who stood there let
him by. The old woman, Tanakrit, was standing beside Sigtrygg
and beneath them W'tnalko could be seen, kneeling now, beside
the Skraeling soothsayer. The raven-winged headpiece was all that

was visible of Manitikaha and the old sorcerer's familiar sing-song voice could be heard droning on in his peculiar fashion.

Sigtrygg turned to Vragi, when he felt him by his side, and gestured at the body of the fallen man which lay before them and which all present seemed to be watching with such intensity. The man on the ground was breathing shallowly, his eyes half-closed, a wide gash opened in his rounded stomach from which dark blood was seeping. Nearby lay a stone-pointed spear, still wet with the same dark blood.

"Things have gone much as I had feared," Sigtrygg now said, looking at the fallen Skraeling, "for, despite all our preparations, we have been unable to overcome this man's bad luck. And I'm not sure anyone can live with a stomach wound like this man has; or if any man will want to."

"That is yet to be seen," Vragi said to him.

He now knelt down beside the others and had a good look at the wound. Then he straightened up again. He said that Sigtrygg's eyes were no worse than they had been on that far off day when they had fled Eiriksfjord, "for you gauged this wound well enough, without taking any closer look. Few people will think there's much to be done for this man now."

"Still," said Sigtrygg, "I want you to do your best in this matter, since he is my fosterfather, and that is a tie which cannot be lightly undone."

Vragi said that things happened much as they were fated and that there were some wounds which even the cleverest physicians were unable to heal, "or men would not die in warfare as readily as they do."

Still he promised to do what he could.

CHAPTER XXIV

THE CHOOSING

When they had got the Skraeling chieftain inside and laid him down, Vragi told them to make a fire outside and heat some water over it. This was quickly accomplished and then Vragi sat down beside the injured man and cut away the garments near the wound so they could see how things stood. And now it was plain to all that the wound was every bit as grave as Vragi had suspected, since the spear had gone in very deep and done a great deal of damage. Vragi said he would remain with the Skraeling chieftain for as long as he was needed but that Sigtrygg had other matters to attend to. Accordingly, Sigtrygg now went out, and W'tnalko followed after him, and now those two went about the town, seeing to the people who had fallen there.

Arnliot and Olvir and some of the other Greenlanders now came up with them and they could see that Sigtrygg had a stricken look on his face so these forbore to speak for some while, until, at last, Sigtrygg himself spoke up. "In my opinion," he said, "things have ended much worse than we had hoped, since that man these Skraelings call king has not been found among the dead, while my own foster father, who is the chief here, lies near to death in his own house."

"That was not to be helped," said Arnliot, "for you were warned that this Nahinanto would be no easy foe to overcome, though you have certainly done better than most people would have expected."

"Still, his flight will be a matter of concern to us if he is now able to return to his own country," said Sigtrygg, "for one thing is certain above all else: that where enemies have arisen before, more will be found."

"Then this, surely, is the beginning of wisdom," Arnliot replied, "or did you fail to consider such a turn of events when you undertook to fight for these people?"

"There's no use worrying about it now," Olvir put in, "for Sigtrygg has already set the course for us. It won't do us much good to run for shore when we are already so far at sea. My own advice is that we now look to the seaworthiness of our craft, so we can ride out this storm."

"What do you suggest?" Sigtrygg asked him.

"I'm not too sure about that," replied the man from Brattahlid, "but I have the feeling this king of theirs will certainly find his way home again, since he has been clever enough to elude us in battle; and then we are not likely to find the sailing as smooth as we have so far had it."

Sigtrygg asked W'tnalko if he thought the same and the Skraeling replied that there would be very little to hinder Nahinanto on his journey home, though it would be somewhat longer by foot than by the river, "since the king has his stronghold up country, in the land where this river arises and in a place where there are many other lakes and waterways, besides."

Sigtrygg asked what manner of stronghold the king maintained but W'tnalko replied that he had not been there, himself, since it was not the sort of place people were eager to visit. "But he keeps many men there," W'tnalko added, "and most folk agree it is a large and well-fortified town, not at all like the one in which we now stand."

"That certainly does not sound promising," said Arnliot, "for we are certainly too few for a head-on assault against such a place as this fellow now describes."

"Still, we cannot sit idly by here while they gather their forces against us," Olvir said. "And I'm not certain it can do us much good to run back to the coast either for, even if we can find our way back to Leif's houses, we will be hard put defending that place against such a host as this Nahinanto might raise against us."

"He has still to find us there," said Arnliot.

"That is unlikely to be as hard a matter for the men of this country as it would be for us," Olvir replied. "And now, I think, we have given them ample reason to seek us out."

Arnliot laughed and said: "In that case, they will still have to overtake us, which will not be so easy for them, once we have got the Gull back on the sea, for I doubt these people have the means to travel about the oceans as we Greenlanders do. In my opinion we can quickly sail away from this country, if we must, and find another place to make our land claim, where these fellows can have no hope of reaching us."

Sigtrygg said: "I don't have any intention of doing that, for Leif's houses are my claim," and now he turned to W'tnalko and asked if the Skraelings who lived further down river were also tributaries of the king, Nahinanto.

W'tnalko said that they were and that there were quite a number of them though they were all as fearful of the Skraeling king as his own people were. Sigtrygg asked him how near were the closest settlements and if these could be reached in a day.

"In one or two, if you travel by river," W'tnalko said. "But they are not likely to provide a warm welcome to strangers."

"Nevertheless, I now want you to send messengers to them and tell what has happened here," Sigtrygg said. "Tell them, as well, that they are to send their chief men to meet with us, since their own safety now depends on it."

"I'm not sure they'll be willing to do that," W'tnalko replied, "for they will have little to gain in helping us and a great deal to lose, if Nahinanto proves the stronger."

"Yet they will get no better chance than they now have of throwing off this tyrant's yoke, for we Greenlanders are the men to beat these Tulewat, as has now been proved. But if they hold back when the opportunity is at hand, they may get no other chance, hereafter."

Arnliot said: "Then you mean to widen this war, when an easier and surer course is at hand?"

"If I must," replied Sigtrygg, "though you and any of the others who choose to are free to go; and take the Gull if you desire, for I am unlikely to have need of a sailing ship in this campaign."

"Then that will leave you without means to flee this country, if the matter goes against you," said Arnliot. "And that is certain to occur if you send us Greenlanders away now, for men such as we are the only advantage you can hope for against a stronger foe."

"I need no support from those who begrudge it," Sigtrygg said, "so those of you who are eager to put out to sea for Greenland or some other landfall are now free to go, with whatever goods you can carry back with you. But I mean to make my stand in this place, beside my foster kinsmen."

Olvir said: "There's no use hoping to send us off that easily, for we all swore to uphold one another, whatever befell; and even we Brattahlid men are party to that oath now. Or do you still think we are worth less to you for the manner of our joining this crew?"

"No less than any other," Sigtrygg said, "for you have proved it in hard fighting and with your blood. But what say you Arnliot?"

"That you would be hard pressed without a few good Greenlanders at your back," Arnliot answered him. "I'll not leave you here to face our enemies alone, any more than this serving man of your uncles would. But I think it a difficult matter you mean to undertake. And that this may be the death of many of us."

"Then each man is to choose for himself," Sigtrygg said, "for I would ask no man to face his death for me."

They now gathered the other crewmen to them and told how things were and Sigtrygg offered the Gull, as before, to any who thought it wiser to depart that country than to remain and fight with him. But none thought it better to sail back to Greenland till they had got some measure of renown in that land they had come to, and won the war which Sigtrygg urged on them. So now they pledged their fellowship anew and swore that Sigtrygg, and no other, was to be their leader and Sigtrygg said he was satisfied with that.

Afterwards they went about the Skraeling town and Sigtrygg asked how things fared with the townspeople, telling his men to do what they could to help repair the damage from the battle. There were a great many dead laying about, but these were mostly the followers of Nahinanto so they did not occasion much concern on either the Greenlanders' part or that of their hosts. In fact, the Skraelings of the town thought they had got themselves a great victory, despite the grievous wound which their chief had taken.

During all this time, Sigtrygg kept a sharp eye out for Chinokwa, but nowhere did he see the young Skraeling woman and because there was so much to be done, he put her from his mind.

Not long afterwards, W'tnalko came to see Sigtrygg with a number of young men and he told him that these were the messengers who had been selected to go down river and speak with those who made their homes there. Sigtrygg saw, at once, that one of these had a familiar look to him and then he recalled that this was the same man whose weapon he had won on the banks of the river, when they had speared him to entice the spirit of Aselekah to return to the land of the living. This man seemed frail and barely more than a boy to Sigtrygg now, without the fearsome garb with which he had adorned himself at the river, and Sigtrygg asked the fellow his name.

"Naruk," replied the young man.

"Naruk," asked Sigtrygg, "are you not too young for such a hazardous mission as this is likely to be; and were it not wiser to remain behind to help us with repair of the town, leaving such hard journeys to others more experienced than yourself?"

"Aselekah," replied the young man, "I have now fought beside you against those who call themselves our rulers and bloodied my axe in the skull of one, and run down another in company with my kinsmen, so that there is no man here to say I have failed to do my part in this affair. Surely I am no less able to do the bidding of the chief's son, when he requires it of me."

"Have it your own way," Sigtrygg said to him and now he had W'tnalko tell each of the messengers what they were to say when they came to the other towns.

"Tell them," said Sigtrygg, "that we have destroyed the following of Nahinanto here and that the king, himself, was forced to flee from us, with barely his life to show for his troubles. Tell them, too, of the strength and warlike manner, which you have seen among us Greenlanders, and that we have come here to break the power of this Skraeling tyrant who has you all so tightly in his grasp. And say, besides, that I, and no other, am the leader of this troop and that I am a man who is descended of kings and a kinsman of kings; and that I am Aselekah, the son of Anyok, your chief, called back from the dead."

W'tnalko carefully instructed each of the messengers in what he was to say, exactly as Sigtrygg had spoken those words, and he rehearsed them carefully so that none would falter or misstate the message. But when he was done he arose and went to Sigtrygg with a troubled look on his face.

"What is the meaning of this?" Sigtrygg asked him, for the Skraeling made no effort to conceal his misgivings.

"You are certainly few enough, for all your big words," W'tnalko replied. "And it is unlikely that others will be willing to throw in with us, whatever we say to them now, so that, in the end, we are likely to stand entirely alone before the might of Nahinanto and his nation. But, where you men can flee across the sea, if things go badly, my people shall have nowhere to hide from the anger of the Tulewat."

"There's no use worrying about that now," Sigtrygg told him, "for the game was set when first we bloodied this king and his men. Had we not done so, your life would certainly have gone on much as before, and then they would have taken your kinsmen as they wished, to serve in their households; and Chinokwa from her father's fire."

W'tnalko said: "It would have been better had we killed them all, when we had them in our hands."

"That is certainly true," Sigtrygg agreed. "It was bad luck the fellow slipped through our fingers as he did, and worse that your chieftain took such a hard wound. But there's no way we can change any of it now, so we must deal with things as they are. When will your men go down the river?"

"At once," W'tnalko said, "though I am not certain of the reception they are likely to receive. It would be better if we sent some token to the chiefs who live there, to strengthen the words the messengers will speak, for then they will see for themselves the kind of people they have to deal with."

"What is the custom in such matters?" Sigtrygg asked him.

"Some sign of bravery and of the things which are to come," W'tnalko replied. "That may impress them, where words alone will fall lightly on unwilling ears."

"In that case," said Sigtrygg, "you are to hold these messengers of yours up, since it seems to me that I know what is best to send to the chiefs down river."

"What's that?" W'tnalko asked him.

But Sigtrygg turned away without giving him an answer. He now went into one of the Skraeling houses and, when he came out again, he held a sword in his hand. It was a rather plain looking weapon, and not overly long, but it had a good edge to it and Sigtrygg passed it, once or twice, quickly before his face. He went over to Olvir and showed him the weapon, asking him if he had any familiarity with such arms.

"Not much," the Leifssons' steward admitted, "for we did not have much occasion for sword play on the farm at Brattahlid."

"Nevertheless, I want you to have this weapon," Sigtrygg told him, "for it was formerly the sword which Aki Erlendsson bore, though I don't think he is likely to have much need of it hereafter. On the other hand, there is no more likely a man, in my opinion, to carry this blade henceforth than you."

Olvir took the weapon and thanked Sigtrygg for it, promising to do his best with it.

"In that case, you will need to practice your strokes," Sigtrygg said to him, "for wielding a sword is not like swinging an axe about, or playing with a spear."

"What do you want me to do?" asked Olvir.

"That's easy," Sigtrygg replied. "You are to go among the corpses of those Skraelings we have killed and choose the ones with the best heads; and then you are to strike these off with your sword and bring them to me."

Olvir said he would do this and, before long, he reappeared, bringing the heads.

Then they wrapped these carefully in skins and gave one to each of the messengers, whom W'tnalko had chosen, and sent these men on their way. When the last of the messengers had pushed off downriver, Sigtrygg turned to W'tnalko and asked him if he now thought better of their embassy, since their messengers had been more appropriately outfitted.

"I'm not sure about that," replied the Skraeling, "but at the least the people who are to be visited will know what kind of men they have to deal with here."

CHAPTER XXV

PURSUIT

Sigtrygg now said he was satisfied, and more than satisfied, with how matters had turned out, despite the difficulties of their condition, for he thought they had made the best of their ill-luck and were now as likely to win their war as not. "But I want to see to my kinsmen," he added, "while we are awaiting the outcome of our mission to the lower river people. And I especially want to look after the health of my foster father, since it seems to me that much depends on it."

He said W'tnalko was now to bring Chinokwa to him at once, since he had not seen her at the side of the fallen chief, though most others who had ties of blood to that man had been present. But W'tnalko replied that he had not, himself, seen the young woman "since the battle was fought."

"Yet this entire town is by now astir with those people whom you hid at my urging," Sigtrygg said to him, "so it is unclear why my foster sister is not among them."

Swiftly they went about the Skraeling settlement, searching for the maid, but it was soon quite clear that none had seen her, or certain others who had been hidden away with her. Sigtrygg said: "Bjorn, you must now tell me how you followed the instructions I gave you; and in what manner you hid those people I placed in your care."

W'tnalko replied that he had done exactly as Sigtrygg had requested and gone to the river bank where the Tulewat had left their boats. There he, and those who were with him, had broken the hull of each of the boats precisely as Sigtrygg had desired. And this had been no hard thing since the Skraelings made their boats of tree bark and skins. Then they had gone further up river and into the woods.

"I found three places of concealment there," W'tnalko said, "and divided those in my charge into three parties and hid one party in each place. But Chinokwa I kept with me the longest, out of regard for her father, and left her safely in the last of the hidden places."

It now became clear to them that Chinokwa, and those who were missing along with her, were all of that group which W'tnalko had left last and Sigtrygg said he thought it strange that these, alone, had not yet made their way back to the encampment. W'tnalko replied that he would go at once in search of them, for he knew the way, but Sigtrygg added that he meant to go too. So now they ran out of the town, with a number of men close behind them, both Skraelings and Greenlanders, and into the forest in the direction which W'tnalko led them.

They ran to where the trees seemed to grow thickest and W'tnalko had the lead, while the others pushed themselves to keep him in sight. When they came up to him, he showed them a certain copse of trees, which was all overgrown with bushes and brambles, and said that this was the first of the places he had found to hide those whom Sigtrygg had placed in his keeping.

Then they ran on to a second spot, and this one was rocky and dropped suddenly into a gully, which was hidden from sight in the woods unless you came right up to it and peered down. W'tnalko showed them where he had hidden the people in this place, too.

"This is all well and good," said Sigtrygg when he had looked in the direction W'tnalko pointed, "but these people have not been lost, since they all seem to have found their way safely back to your town. It is the fate of those you placed in your third hiding place which most concerns us now."

W'tnalko took them deeper into the woods than before and

now the trees seemed to grow so close together that the going was very difficult, since the trees appeared tangled and became intertwined at their very roots. Still, they pushed on until they came to a clearing, and then W'tnalko stopped suddenly, while the others came up beside him. The first thing they saw was a strip of deer skin, such as the Skraelings used for their clothing, hanging like a banner on a thorny bush. W'tnalko reached out and took it from the bush and brought it up to his face. He held it there for a moment and then handed it to Sigtrygg. It was still wet with traces of blood.

They went into the clearing and now they could see the signs of carnage all about them, for there were bodies lying about everywhere, young women and old, and many of the children whom W'tnalko had taken with him out of the town that very morning. They walked among these, carefully examining each, and they could now see that many had been killed by a skull-crushing blow from a club or axe, while others had had their throats slit. They counted up the bodies and Sigtrygg said these were the worst killings he had ever seen since the slaughtering of the seals which the Greenlanders did when laying in provisions after a particularly hard famine. Everyone thought the matter very grave indeed.

The Skraelings went about from one body to another and counted these up and, after a time, W'tnalko ran off into the woods. When he returned he said to Sigtrygg: "All have been accounted for but one and that is our chief's daughter for Chinokwa's body is not to be found in this place."

"What do you think has become of her in that case?" Sigtrygg asked.

"I'm not sure about that," answered the Skraeling, "but there are tracks which lead off from here to the west and they show that seven men have passed this way. And they are Tulewat."

Arnliot asked W'tnalko how he could be so certain of that.

W'tnalko said only that "this is a thing which some people will know better than others."

"Is the woman with them?" Sigtrygg asked.

"There's no sign of her feet on the ground," W'tnalko replied, "but one of the men seems to be carrying a large burden on his back, for his feet cut much deeper into the earth than the others, and his stride is wider."

"Then that will be Chinokwa," said Sigtrygg, "for there is nothing else to be carried away from here than her. And she will still be alive, since otherwise they would have left her here among these others. But do you know any reason why these men would have spared my kinswoman while killing everyone else?"

"They could not take all these others with them, if they are to go quickly," answered W'tnalko, "and yet would not leave them unharmed, since they have suffered so greatly at our hands. And, if Nahinanto is among them, he would know the daughter of Anyok and think his claim on her as good her father's."

"Then there is hope yet," Sigtrygg said, "despite the harsh work which has been done here. How far ahead of us do you think they are?"

"Not as far as they would like," W'tnalko offered.

Sigtrygg now said that those men who were with him must see to the dead which they had found in that clearing and carry the bodies back to their kinsmen. "But Arnliot is to come with me and W'tnalko will lead the way. I don't think we will have much trouble overtaking these fellows, and then we will see what kind of weapons-play seven Skraelings can make with men such as us on their heels."

Olvir now said he wanted to go along, as well, "for you will need the help, if you come up with them."

Sigtrygg said there was no need for that since he thought Arnliot, alone, could cut these men down once they had found them, "and this will be a hard chase, besides, which a man of your background may find somewhat taxing."

"It would not be much repayment for the sword you have given me if I turned tail and ran back to safety the first time you had need of its edge," Olvir answered him. "And for this reason, alone, I am unwilling to remain behind."

Arnliot said: "If this serving man thinks he is man enough to run with us and guard our backs, then let him come along, for every sword edge will be of use to us, however feebly swung."

Sigtrygg told them to have it their own way, and now he told the others to go back to the town, as he had instructed them, and tell Vragi what had occurred. Then he said that W'tnalko was to take up the trail and, very quickly, they were away and into the forest. They now ran hard through the dense brush, W'tnalko ever before them, looking at the ground and at the markings on the forest growth which only he could read. The countryside was harsh there and not easily passable but still they pushed on, striking the forest aside wherever it severed or blocked their path.

They traveled thus the better part of that day, until it became too dark to see what lay ahead of them. Then W'tnalko said they must make their camp and settle in for the night. Sigtrygg replied that he could see little reason to rest from their pursuit now. But W'tnalko said it didn't pay to press their hunt in the dark "since I cannot see enough of their trail to assure that we come any closer to them than we now have. And they will certainly be taking their rest, too."

After some thought Sigtrygg agreed and now they made their camp and slept fitfully. In the morning, before the sky was fully light, Sigtrygg was awake and told the others to get up, as well. W'tnalko found them some roots and native berries which he said were good for a man to eat and they refreshed themselves on this poor fare. Then they were on the trail of the fleeing Tulewat again. But it did not seem as though they were able to come any closer than before. Sigtrygg asked W'tnalko if he thought they had made any gains but the Skraeling replied that he couldn't be sure, "for these Tulewat are good woodsmen."

They came to a river and to a very rocky country and now W'tnalko began to run back and forth along the edge of some large rocks which ran like the spine of a great beast along the middle of that country. Sigtrygg asked him what was the matter and W'tnalko replied that he had lost his way since the Skraelings they were hunting had gone out onto the rocks where a man's feet did not easily leave their imprints.

"Then they know we are following them," Sigtrygg said.

W'tnalko replied that he thought this was true.

"In that case it will certainly be harder to come up with them," Arnliot said and he placed his great axe on the ground before him.

"We are likely to make faster progress if you leave that over-sized weapon of yours behind," Sigtrygg said, "in any case. And then you can reclaim it if we pass this way on our return."

"I think you will be sorrier if I leave it here, than if I carry it with me on our journey, however much longer it may take," Arnliot replied and added that he had no intention of parting with the axe under any circumstances.

W'tnalko now called sharply to them and they looked up. He said he had found the trail again. So off they ran without any further words, and now they ran down off the rocks and into the forest once more and they ran thus for a second day.

When night fell again, Olvir said he thought they had better start looking for better food than roots and berries if they meant to keep up their strength, "for we will need more than that just to keep up this pace, whatever fighting lies ahead of us."

That night W'tnalko snared a small rabbit and a bird and they made a fire and cooked these, eating the bones clean and leaving themselves nothing for the morning meal. Then they slept, just as uneasily as before, and were again up before the first light of the dawn. They came to a river and crossed it and then they came to another and now they followed W'tnalko for a ways along its bank. They stopped to refresh themselves and take some fish from the river, which they ate heartily around midday. Then they pushed onward again, crossing over this river, too, until they came to a mountainous region, broken by many rifts and small valleys. Here they stopped to take their bearings and here, for the second time, W'tnalko seemed to lose his way.

Since it was already sunset they made their camp in a small gully there, with their backs up against the gully wall.

"I don't like stopping now," Sigtrygg said, "since we have lost track of those we are pursuing. It will only make it harder to take up the trail again once the sun has risen. "

"There's no help for it," W'tnalko replied, "for we are unlikely to have any luck finding their trail after it has grown dark."

So they spent the third night in that place, eating as well as they could from what was to be had there. But Sigtrygg was exceedingly discontented.

On the following day, they were unable to find any sign of the fleeing Skraelings though they scoured the countryside all about them. Arnliot said: "This does not seem to be the easy chase you promised us, for this Skraeling king now seems to be just as far ahead of us as before. And perhaps he is doing even better than that, since we cannot locate any sign of him."

It was not until late in that day that W'tnalko came back to them from the woods and now he had a pleased look in his eye.

"This will mean he has found our way again," Sigtrygg said to the others and W'tnalko replied that it was so. They quickly followed him into the woods, in the direction he was pointing, and picked up the trail. But, because so much of the day had been lost, they could not go far and so they settled down for a fourth night in the forest.

The pursuit went on thus for five days and nights and Sigtrygg's mood darkened considerably since he thought they were not making all the progress that they should. He became exceedingly moody and short-tempered so that Arnliot and Olvir took to walking by themselves behind him, unwilling to give him cause for complaint. Olvir noticed how Arnliot was now holding back and how he seemed to prefer the company of a servant from Brattahild to more vigorous men and he remarked that he thought this was certainly a change from how Arnliot had been accustomed to behave before this. "There's no need to give that man any further reason for concern," the big man from Ketilsfjord replied quietly with a gesture toward Sigtrygg, "since he has plainly taken the loss of this woman to heart."

Sigtrygg was sharp, too, with W'tnalko, at this time but the Skraeling pretended not to notice, though once or twice the Skraeling, himself, seemed somewhat out of sorts over the matter.

When they camped for the sixth night Olvir asked W'tnalko why he too seemed so despondent and insisted on keeping to himself as Sigtrygg did.

"Because I am the one who lost this woman," the Skraeling replied, "although it was for her sake that all this has been done."

During the sixth day the Skraeling briefly lost the trail again but this time he was not long in finding it so that they did not lose as much time as before. He now told Sigtrygg and the others that he thought the Tulewat were surely taking a rather round about way to their home country, to throw them off the track, and that, if they were willing, he wanted to try another means to come up with their quarry.

"What do you have in mind?" Sigtrygg asked him.

"These men certainly mean to make their way back to their stronghold, where their kinsmen and others of their kind are to be found," he said. "But, if so, there is no need to follow that path which we have been taking, for I know how to come to their country another way, which is swifter than this one. Still, to do so, we must leave off this chase and strike out in another direction entirely. And then we will lose touch with them and with the young woman whose safe return we most desire."

Sigtrygg said he should do as he thought best, for they were certainly not making any better progress following on the heels of the Tulewat than they had at the first, "in which case these churls are likely to win to the safety of their homeland before we are close enough to do them that harm they have so richly earned."

Arnliot and Olvir said they had no dispute with this strategy either and so it was agreed that they would leave the trail of the fleeing Tulewat; and that's what they did on the sixth day after the battle had been fought in the Skraeling town.

CHAPTER XXVI

IN THE TULEWAT COUNTRY

W'tnalko now led them cross-country toward the west without paying any heed to the trails or signs of passage made by men or beasts in the woods. They traveled steadily, in this fashion, for two days until they came to a very high and rocky country, broken up by many streams and rivers. Then they climbed up to the top of a rock strewn promontory and W'tnalko told them to make their camp there.

"I don't see much need to rest now," Sigtrygg said, "for nightfall is still a long way off, while this climb has barely winded us."

"Even so, we are to rest here," W'tnalko said, "for this place seems to offer us the best vantage over all this country and, if those men we are hunting mean to make their way to their homes, they will have to pass this way. And then we are certain to see them before they have seen us."

They now lay down on that stone perch and spent the rest of the day watching the countryside. From where they were they had a clear view of much of the open land before them, although they could still not see into the wooded areas. But W'tnalko said he thought their quarry would have to cross the open country, if they were headed westward, for that was where the main Tulewat town was said to lie.

"Have you ever been this far to the west?" Sigtrygg asked the Skraeling.

W'tnalko answered that he had, "but no farther than here, although I have heard a great deal about that country which lies beyond this place." He added that he thought this was the most likely route which people on foot would take to reach it and that this gave them their best chance of intercepting those men they were pursuing.

The day now wore on and they continued to search the horizon to the east, hoping to see the appearance of the Tulewat king and his followers. But there was nothing to be seen, however hard they scanned the countryside. Toward evening Sigtrygg asked W'tnalko if he thought they should go down for the night and make their camp at the foot of the promontory, "where we have some chance of finding food."

"Do what you like," the Skraeling replied, "but I will stay here."

Sigtrygg said he would do the same but he now told Arnliot and Olvir to climb down and see what they could find, "but don't make a big show of it, for I don't want to give our position away."

As the shadows lengthened with the setting of the sun, it became harder and harder to tell what lay to their east. Still they watched the distant horizon, and the trails and open places which led out from the woodlands.

It was not Sigtrygg or W'tnalko who first saw something but Olvir, when he was halfway down the face of the mountain. He turned then and scrambled up again, with Arnliot close behind him. When he came out on the flat promontory he went over to Sigtrygg, gesturing hastily to the north.

"What seems to be troubling you, shipmate?" Sigtrygg asked him.

"There are men coming from the north of us and not from the east, as we had expected," he said, "and I think there are at least seven of them. They are dragging a captive behind them, too, bound at the wrists. And they are making a path which crosses behind this rock, into the west."

Sigtrygg and W'tnalko instantly arose and went down the side of the mountain to where Olvir said he thought they would be able to see what he had seen. When they came to the vantage point, they were able to see around the side of the rock in a northward direction, just as Olvir had told them and now they could see, off in the distance, a line of men with a prisoner disappearing into the woodlands again.

"They have outflanked us," Sigtrygg said. "They must have guessed our purpose in leaving off the chase. Still, we are closer to them now, so we must try to overtake them before they are lost to us again among the trees."

They now ran down the side of the mountain until they had gained the forest floor, but by the time they had got down off the rocks, the Tulewat were again out of sight. W'tnalko ran about seeking their trail and, when he thought he had it, he called quietly to the others and they all ran toward the deepest part of the woods. Still, the shadows were so dark from the sun's descent below the horizon at this time that they were unable to follow closely behind those they pursued. W'tnalko again said he thought they must give over the chase for the night, but Sigtrygg replied that he was unwilling to do that, "for we are so close."

Accordingly, they moved awkwardly through the forest, despite the deep gloom of evening which fell over them, and the blackness of night which followed hard behind. They stumbled about for a long while, without any firm sense of where they were, until, at last, even Sigtrygg had to admit that they were thoroughly lost. Then he sat down on the forest floor and would not speak to anyone and the others came and sat nearby but said nothing to him for fear of disturbing his thoughts.

On the morning of the ninth day they were hard put to find their way again, or to pick up the trail of those they were hunting. It seemed that the Tulewat, throwing caution to the winds, either because they sensed how close their pursuers were or because they knew the countryside in which they were traveling so well, had kept going all that night without pause. Now there was very little fresh sign of them to be found. At last W'tnalko called Sigtrygg to him and showed him a single mark in the soft earth beneath them.

It was a half print of a foot, seemingly no larger than that of a small boy's...or of a woman's.

Sigtrygg said: "We have them now," and they started off swiftly in the direction the foot seemed to be pointing.

They went as quickly as they could, without making any more noise than they had to, since they thought they were now quite close. Still, they could not hear any sounds of those they pursued, however close they thought they were drawing, and the signs in the forest were not easily read. After awhile W'tnalko said they had come to a place where many others had passed, and not so long ago that it would be easy to distinguish one set of markings from another.

He told them they were to keep even quieter than before, since there was no use alerting others to their presence, "for this is not friendly country."

Arnliot said: "Matters do not seem to improve much, however hard we press things."

W'tnalko now lost and found the trail several times more and Sigtrygg began to become quite impatient. He said that he thought the longer they spent dawdling in those woods, the farther ahead Nahinanto and his followers would get, "and then all the advantage from that shortcut we took will be lost."

Arnliot replied that there was no use hurrying things if it took them off in the wrong direction, as it had the night before, when Sigtrygg had got them hopelessly lost. "And I would prefer to go more slowly, however long that takes, if it brings us closer to the men we seek."

Sigtrygg made no answer to this but he left off urging haste.

They came to a place where the forest seemed to end and where the country opened into a large ravine, rock strewn and steep on either side, the slopes going up and away from them, both to their left and right. The trees were much sparser here but the large rocks offered plenty of room for concealment and so they went warily, unwilling to show themselves in the open. When they had crossed the ravine they came to another heavily wooded area and now they made their way through this, as well.

Once again they were obliged to spend another night, without pursuing their prey, though, by this time, none of them were eager for the enforced idleness. Still, Sigtrygg had learned his lesson and showed no further inclination to urge them forward in the darkness. So they slept and woke by turns in the night and, as they had done each morning, since their chase began, they were up and moving again before the first rays of the new day's sun could be discerned in the sky.

They now found themselves moving steadily westward until they came, at last, to a place where a number of rivers seemed to run down from higher country. Here they moved up to high ground, for they wanted to get a better view of what lay beyond them.

This time it was Sigtrygg's own keen eyes which first saw their quarry. These were out in open country, moving toward the nearby riverbank, but now there were more than the seven they had been pursuing. There seemed, in fact, to be twice that number, or three times it, but it was certainly the same men in the midst of the others for they had, between them, a woman captive.

"I'm not sure how we are to get at them now," Sigtrygg said, "for it seems they have won to their own country, despite our best efforts."

"It can do us little good, in any event," said Olvir, pointing to a place where two rivers seemed to join, not far below them. This place seemed to lie in precisely the direction the Tulewat were headed and a great walled town could be seen there, surrounded entirely by a stockade of roughly cut timber. Within the stockade there seemed to be a hundred houses, all larger and more impressive than the biggest of those which they had seen in W'tnalko's village; and hundreds of people seemed to be moving about in their midst. There were people, too, on the broad, calm waters beside which the town was built, traveling about on small boats or walking along the shore.

W'tnalko stood quite still when they saw this place and did

not seem to have anything to say.

Sigtrygg asked him if he knew where they were and the Skraeling replied that he thought they had come to the chief town of the Tulewat, the stronghold of Nahinanto, and that much sooner than he had expected.

"Then they have other towns like this one?" Sigtrygg asked.

"Some," replied the Skraeling. "But this is their largest. And all the other chiefs of the Tulewat serve the man who rules in this place."

"Then we have found our way into their country, at any rate," Sigtrygg said. "And this we would have had to do sooner or later, as things now stand."

"I would have preferred to find these people at another time," Arnliot replied, "when we are better manned to storm their defenses."

Olvir said that that would prove a harder matter than they were prepared for, in any case, "since we have no army numerous enough to overcome this host, however much we may deceive ourselves."

"Still," said Sigtrygg, "battles have been won before this, against even greater odds."

W'tnalko suddenly gestured toward that company of men who now seemed to be approaching the open stockade of the town, their captive in tow. People were running out of the gateway to meet them so that these men were soon surrounded by numerous other shouting Skraelings. These new people now seized hold of the bonds which held the captive woman and, dragging her with great commotion from the safety of those men who, until now, had been her only companions, pulled her behind them into the walled town. Then the Tulewat warriors let up a very loud and harsh cry and the whole countryside seemed to ring with similar shouting which echoed from one end of the great valley, in which the town was situated, to the other. And, from within the walls of the town, hundreds of answering shouts rose up as if in reply to these.

"There goes our enemy, into the safety of his walled city," said Arnliot morosely. "And he has got the woman with him."

They hid themselves throughout the day on a ridge overlooking the Tulewat stronghold, sizing up the town, eager to gauge its defenses. Sigtrygg, himself, seemed especially grim and paced about while the others sat together and talked over what lay before them. At last Arnliot came to him and told him he must join them, "for there is a matter we mean to put to you."

Sigtrygg went over, then, and squatted down beside the others.

"This is how it is," said Arnliot after they had squatted silently in that place for a time. "Though we have come a great distance and endured many hardships, neither Olvir nor I think we can have much hope of rescuing this woman now, since they have got her securely in their midst. There are too many of them, even for us, and we certainly cannot find our way into their town by stealth, for we will be recognized at once since we don't look anything like these people. The only thing for it, now, is to get back to our fellow crewmen downriver and talk the matter over with that old viking shipmate of ours. At least he may have some idea of how to proceed in this matter."

"This is timid talk for a man of your size," said Sigtrygg, "though it is, perhaps, not unexpected from this other one who has spent his life as a servant to others."

Olvir replied to this that he was willing to do whatever Sigtrygg decided but that he and Arnliot were just speaking good sense, "for most people will think it unprofitable to throw away their lives on an enterprise which is so clearly beyond them."

Arnliot said they were willing to abide by the judgement of the majority, in any case, if Sigtrygg meant to put it to a vote.

"Is the Skraeling to have a say in this, too?" Sigtrygg asked.

"If that is how you want it," Arnliot replied, "but that may make it harder to reach our decision, should the vote be equally divided."

"There's no need to worry about that," said Sigtrygg, "for I will not gainsay you all; but if even one man votes with me, I mean to stay here and try my luck out with these people, whatever you others decide."

Arnliot and Olvir said this was agreeable to them. So now they called W'tnalko over and put the matter to him as well, urging him to think hard on the heavy odds which were now arrayed against them.

But the Skraeling replied that, like Sigtrygg, he preferred to remain and do what he could, whatever their chances.

"So that is it," said Sigtrygg. "The Skraeling and I are to stay here while you two go back to find our companions."

Arnliot said: "In that case, we are not likely to find you alive on our return. And then our fellow crewmen would certainly hold the matter against us." Olvir added that he thought this was certainly true and that he, himself, had not pressed so hard to come along on this journey only to go back now, "when others are getting ready to test themselves in battle, however uneven the odds."

"Then the matter is decided," Sigtrygg said, "for I do not mean to leave this place, whatever befalls, until we have won Chinokwa's freedom."

"Or those Skraelings have otherwise proved too much for us," Olvir put in.

"That will take some proving, in my opinion," answered Arnliot, "for these people have yet to taste the bite of this old war axe of mine; or to face such men as we are."

It was now agreed that W'tnalko was to go down to the Skraeling town and have a look around, if he could, for they thought he had the best chance of passing undetected in the Tulewat's midst. So he left them in the late afternoon and went toward the town by way of the river. There they saw him stop to mingle with those who were fishing in the water; and then he disappeared from their sight.

They now waited the remainder of the day but saw no sign of

the Skraeling, though they listened and watched closely for his return. The sun moved steadily into the western sky and, when it began to sink down toward the horizon, they still had no better idea of what had become of him than before.

"He may have fallen into their hands," said Arnliot when the lengthening shadows of the trees began to darken the valley below them "for he does not look entirely like these Tulewat, to my way of thinking."

"Then that may be worse for us than had he never gone," said Olvir, "for what is to prevent him from revealing our presence to those others, once they have got their hands on him? In my opinion we must now be especially vigilant and on our guard."

"There's no need to worry about that," Sigtrygg said.

"And why not?" asked Arnliot.

"Because our companion wants this woman back as much as I do, myself" Sigtrygg said.

After the sun had set, it became quite dark, for it was an overcast night, with little glow from the moon to light up the place where they had hid themselves. The three Greenlanders sat uneasily together without fire or food. In the darkness they could not see very far into the valley and so could not tell if anyone was approaching from the Skraeling town. Only the night sounds of the forest seemed to surround them. Toward morning they fell asleep, for they were hungry and exhausted and even the expectation of trouble could not hold them awake any longer.

It was not the grey morning sky which woke them, but footsteps about their heads. Sigtrygg sat up first and then the others, grabbing for their weapons. W'tnalko was standing over them. He was armed with a Tulewat war club and had dressed his head with feathers, after the fashion those people affected. He made a gesture for them to keep silent.

The Greenlanders now got stiffly to their feet and the Skraeling threw a large sack into their midst. Sigtrygg bent and opened it. It contained strips of dried deer flesh and fish. When they saw this, they immediately sat down and began to eat their fill, for it had been a long while since they had had such food. W'tnalko squatted down beside them and took some of the dried meat for himself. "This will give you strength," he said between mouthfuls.

"What did you find?" Sigtrygg asked when he had eaten a portion of the meat, for he was eager to know the fate of that Skraeling woman whom he counted his kinswoman.

"They have her," said W'tnalko, "just as we thought. They are keeping her in a long house, near the town's center. But, there is no hope of coming to her there unobserved."

"How long will they keep her thus?" Sigtrygg asked.

"Not long," answered the Skraeling, "though it would be better if they held her longer in that place."

"And why is that?" asked Sigtrygg.

"Because then we would have the time to find a way to free her," he said. "But as things now stand, the time is too short for that, since they have chosen her for the sacrifice. And they mean to bind her, this very day, to the stake."

CHAPTER XXVII

THE STRONGHOLD

Sigtrygg now asked if there was any chance of reaching the woman before they brought her out but W'tnalko said that was out of the question, "for they will tie her to the stake when the sun has reached its highest point in the sky. And then they will dance about and sing until sundown, filling all the places between the town walls and the place where she is bound. There will be no way to get near her."

"And after the sun has set?" Sigtrygg asked.

"Then only the warriors will remain," replied the Skraeling, "but they will not sleep, nor allow their captive to sleep either, for they will dance about as much as before, so that Chinokwa will have no rest until morning. And then, when the morning star alone is visible in the sky, all the people will come out of their houses and they will kill her."

"How is that to be done?"

"She is to be shot with arrows," replied the Skraeling. "And then they will cut out her heart."

"These are a very harsh people," said Arnliot, "though some of us could think of better uses for such a maid."

"Is there any chance of freeing her in the night?" Sigtrygg asked.

"Not much," replied the Skraeling thoughtfully, "since they will be on their guard; and none of the men will be sleeping."

"In that case, even a direct attack against this stronghold is unlikely to reach the woman before she can be slain," Arnliot said.

"So now it seems to me even more unlikely that we can achieve what you have set for us, shipmate. Still, if you are as determined as before, there is nothing to stop us from firing this town of theirs; and that, at the least, will give these wretches something to shout their war cries over."

"Then there will be no hope at all," said Olvir, "for the woman will surely die in such an attack. And it is not unlikely that we will do the same."

"There is nothing to stop you from running off now and re-joining our companions, if that is your concern," replied Arnliot, "for no one is forcing you to remain with this company. Yet even that will bring some good, it seems to me, since then you at least will live to tell the others how we met our end here; and that we died like Norsemen."

"In my opinion, there is another way," said Sigtrygg, "which, while no less risky, at the least gives some hope of regaining the woman."

"What do you have in mind, shipmate?" Arnliot asked.

Sigtrygg said: "Since we cannot assault these walls or steal the woman, unseen, from under their noses, perhaps we must do both at once, if either effort is to have any chance of succeeding."

He now told them his plan which was to send W'tnalko back into the Tulewat town, while creating a diversion to draw the main body of the enemy away from their captive. "This Skraeling com-panion of ours," he said, "has shown himself capable of moving about quite freely in the enemy's midst, though we would be un-able to do the same. So it is for us to make a frontal assault and draw the Tulewat away from the object of our efforts, that Bjorn may get near enough to cut her free and take her out of the town."

"What kind of diversion do you have in mind?" Olvir asked.

"There isn't anything likely to cause these people more con-sternation," said Sigtrygg, "than if men like us just walked out of the forest and into their midst, through their front gate."

"If so, it's unlikely we shall walk as boldly out again," warned Olvir.

"I'm not sure what is likely to happen, once there," Sigtrygg agreed, "but, at the least, we shall make enough of a commotion to give our Skraeling companion the chance he needs." And now he asked W'tnalko if he would agree to undertake Chinokwa's rescue on these terms.

The Skraeling replied that he was certainly prepared for that, so now it was decided that Sigtrygg's plan was to be the means by which they attempted the rescue. "But this won't do us any good until they have brought the woman out in the open," Sigtrygg added, "for then that entire nation will be in the open, too, and they will have their eyes on us, without any hindrance, when we have come into their midst. Thus our companion can be assured that no one, with any cause to look elsewhere, is lurking about unseen to betray him once he has undertaken the rescue."

Olvir asked if their plan could not be more profitably employed after nightfall, but Sigtrygg said he doubted it would be as effective, "since we are likely to make the biggest splash when we are most easily seen. Besides, the woman will be too tired to flee, the longer we wait, and I have the feeling that just cutting her loose from her bonds and taking her from this town will not be sufficient to bring her to safety."

So now they agreed to wait until midday, as W'tnalko had assured them that all would be quiet until then, and Sigtrygg told the others to sleep again, "for we will need all our strength before long." And so they did.

When the sun was directly above them in the sky, Sigtrygg awoke, suddenly, and now he had a strange look in his eyes. Though he was rather more darkly complexioned than most Greenlanders, he seemed unusually pale to his two Norse companions and his limbs were shaking, too, while sweat stood out on the flattish features of his face. The others were looking at him oddly and Olvir asked what had occurred and if he had slept poorly.

"Not at all," was his reply, but he seemed uncertain to them. "There's no use holding things back," said Arnliot, "if you have had a dream which concerns the rest of us, for we are companions in arms and each of us has the right to know what portents the others have seen if it concerns him."

"It does not, in any case," Sigtrygg answered, "but such uneasiness in sleep, as I have now had, is only to be expected when men bed down in harsh circumstances such as we have here; whereas those dreams which count for something are most often given to those who lie untroubled in their own beds."

Now he got up and took his weapons and went apart from the others and there he sat for a time, keeping his own counsel.

Arnliot, Olvir and the Skraeling said no more about it, though it seemed strange to them, since Sigtrygg was not a man who was accustomed to show uncertainty in times of great stress. Still, they left him alone and now took what food remained to them and divided it into four parts, each man taking a share and the last portion to be given to Sigtrygg. The Skraeling brought this to him and Sigtrygg ate it, though he had no more to say than before.

He did not speak to them again until the shrill war cries from the Skraeling town could be heard coming up to where they sat above the walled Tulewat stronghold. Then Sigtrygg arose and went to the edge of the rock on which they had hidden themselves and, when he saw how things were and that they were too far off to see affairs in the town clearly, he told them they were to creep down closer, to get a better look at the goings-on below. They did this and, when they had come as close as they dared, they paused to take the measure of their enemy. Now they had a better vantage point than they had had before and could readily see that someone was being brought out and bound to the pole which stood alone in the center of the square.

Arnliot asked if anyone could tell if this were the woman they were seeking and Sigtrygg replied that it most certainly was.

Olvir now looked more closely himself, saying that no one could deny that it was a woman, "for it can be readily seen how they have stripped her to the waist. But it is not so certain that it is the same woman who was stolen from our camp."

"It is unlikely to be any other," Sigtrygg answered him. "And my eyes can make out the features well enough from here to assure us of that. Or do you think I have lost that keenness of vision which served us so well when we were sailing out to this country?"

"In that case," said Arnliot, "there is no reason to delay this matter any longer, if we mean to teach these Skraelings how we Norsemen make war," and, so saying, he hung his shield on his back and took hold of his war axe with both hands, half rising from the ground.

Sigtrygg told W'tnalko he was to take his leave of them then and, when the Skraeling was gone, he said that Olvir and Arnliot must stay close behind him, for he wanted to approach as near as he could to the Skraeling town without being seen.

They now went down into the valley, under cover of the forest, until the trees fell away. Then Sigtrygg said they were to throw caution aside and walk forward, three abreast, as boldly as they pleased, up to the town's gate. He told Olvir to put up his shield, too, when they had got within shouting distance of the walls, and to carry his sword in his hand and walk swiftly, looking neither to right nor left, so that the Skraelings could not detect any fear in the manner of their approach.

Then they walked out into the open field, which lay before the Skraeling town, and in through the opening in the roughly made stockade, into the midst of the astonished Tulewat.

A large number of people stood about there looking toward the center of the town. These did not, at first, see the Greenlanders for they were watching the warlike dancing of those who were participating in the festivities within. Nearby and up against one side of the stockade stood a strange-looking pile of dried skins which had been scraped entirely clean of flesh on the one side but which seemed quite bare on the other, without either hair or fur. Sigtrygg said he thought these had the look of human hides to him and now he urged them to walk right past them and make for the center of the town; and so they did.

The people by the stockade walls saw the Greenlanders only as they came past the gate but they did not know what to make of them, for they had never seen such men as these, and especially the yellow-haired giant which Arnliot seemed to be. He, for his part, had his usual grin on his face, which he reserved for those times when he meant to show his prowess to others, but Sigtrygg and Olvir had only the very grimmest of looks and they cast these balefully about at those Skraelings who stood in their way, until these people fell back from them.

It was soon quite plain that those who were standing about at the gate and who gave way so easily and with such astonishment on their faces before the Greenlanders were not the formidable warriors of this race. Rather, they seemed to be those servants and slaves, of whom Anyok had told Sigtrygg earlier. The Tulewat, themselves, all seemed to be engaged in the ceremonies within. So strong did they take themselves to be, that they did not appear to think it necessary to post guards against their enemies, if, indeed, they thought they had any in that country. So now Sigtrygg and his companions went boldly forward until the excited warriors of that nation at last caught sight of them and then these stopped their wild dances and looked at the three and a great silence seemed to descend on the town.

The Tulewat were not warriors who were ordinarily accustomed to show fear, but the shock of seeing these three unusually attired strangers walking so fearlessly and purposefully into their midst seemed to unman them and they fell back before the newcomers. Sigtrygg pressed this advantage at once, for he now strode straight to where he thought Chinokwa was being held, at the town's center.

The painted warriors, for indeed they had garbed themselves for war in anticipation of that rite by which they meant to dispatch their captive, made no move against them. Thus, Sigtrygg and his companions came within sight of the woman they sought and now they could see how the Tulewat had bound her hands above her head, to the tall pole, and that she was held there by a tight rope about her ankles, as well. A bright red line had been painted from the crown of her head down the middle of her torso to her waist and her hair was untied and now hung loosely about her shoulders.

The woman had a calm look about her, for her eyes were tightly closed. But, when she heard the commotion, as the Greenlanders approached the place of her imprisonment, she opened them and then she saw Sigtrygg.

The Greenlanders stopped now, for the Tulewat seemed to recover themselves and were closing ranks in the space between Sigtrygg and the bound woman. Olvir whispered, in the Norse tongue, that they must be careful not to get much closer than this, "or all our plans will be undone."

"Then let them drive us back," said Sigtrygg, "for that will lend credence to this charade."

All around them the Skraelings seemed to have taken up their weapons again with a purpose, and now they hemmed the Greenland men in on every side. There was a sudden hum of voices and then a large man, bigger than any of the others, strode out to meet them, and he glowered at them harshly from the midst of all the other menacing Tulewat faces. He wore a long skin cloak and the features of his face were painted in a familiar manner.

"It is not surprising," he said in the Skraeling tongue, after having placed himself in a position to bar the Greenlanders from advancing further, "that Aselekah has now come among us in search of his sister. Though," he added, "I had thought him lost, more than once, in that chase we led him in the forest."

"It's unlikely we would have found it difficult tracking such clumsy woodsmen as you Tulewat are," was Sigtrygg's swift reply. "Still, you men certainly ran hard enough from us, whenever we came too near. But now I want to offer you your lives, and honor, too, if you will return my sister to me, for it was not her doing that we made you such a warm welcome, when last you paid your respects in our part of the country."

"Perhaps not her doing," replied the Skraeling king with some thought, "but it was certainly for her benefit, or was it not your intention to deny us those captives which are our due?"

"Something like that," Sigtrygg agreed, "but matters have now taken such a turn that I am minded to offer a settlement for that damage which we have done you, however severe it may have seemed in your eyes."

"What do you have in mind?" asked the Skraeling king, more slowly than before.

"If captives are what you seek," said Sigtrygg, "here are three before you, if you let the woman go free. Nor are you likely to find us backward in serving your interests, since we are all accomplished men. And there are more of us, besides, whom I have left behind in that town where we first met, who will gladly enter your service, if I bid them to."

"It seems to me," said the king, "that, as to the three men before me, these are already in my hands and in no position to offer service, since I can take what I want of them; and even their lives if I desire it."

"This may be so," Sigtrygg agreed, "but then you are unlikely to gain their support, and such men as we are will not readily be found in all this country."

The Tulewat chieftain said he was willing to take that risk. And, as to those others, "too much blood has already been shed to make peace between us now, for I mean to hunt them down, when the time is right so that others may see how the Tulewat repay their enemies. But the woman is to remain with us, for the sacrifice is now due and we are short of captives for this purpose. It is only fitting that the sister of that Aselekah, who is responsible for our lack of captured maidens, shall now serve this need in lieu of others."

Sigtrygg replied that he thought this exceedingly unreasonable, "since we Greenlanders are men who can offer a great deal to those willing to accept our friendship."

But Nahinanto said he didn't have much need of that, and now he promised that the newcomers would not find his hospitality any less warm than he had found theirs.

"But you men will be seeking to refresh yourselves after such hard traveling," he added, "so now I will offer you a taste of that sweetest of all dishes, which only our most important men may partake of, and that only once each year; for you are brave fighters, at the least. But you will have to wait until tomorrow for this repast. And then you are each to be given a taste of the maiden's roasted heart, before we send you to your deaths."

Sigtrygg replied that the tales he had heard of the Tulewat's cruelty had certainly not been softened in the telling. But, he added, men who boasted in advance of the event were often the least likely to recount their exploits afterwards. And now he took a step toward the Tulewat chieftain, his sword raised over his head.

At once three Skraelings interposed themselves between Sigtrygg and their king, lifting their own war clubs in reply. But Sigtrygg rushed at them, paying their weapons no mind and sweeping his sword out before him. In one stroke, he severed the head of the nearest Skraeling man and brought his blade down firmly into the neck of the second. The third rushed on him at the same time, but Sigtrygg caught him with his shield and thrust him back. Then he pulled his sword out of the second man's neck, leaving the head half-torn from the shoulders, and drove his weapon deep into the chest of the third man who was still staggering backward from the hard shield blow.

Quickly, four more Tulewat leaped forward to take the place of their fallen comrades and all the other Skraeling warriors closed round the Greenlanders, shouting and lifting their weapons in a threatening manner. Sigtrygg dropped to a crouching position and began to turn about in a tight circle as the four Skraelings moved past and around him, their war clubs dancing about in the air before his face.

Olvir said to Arnliot that they must join the fray at once, "for our skipper is in a bad way," but Arnliot replied that they were to hold back for the moment. "We will know when the time is right to give him assistance," Arnliot said. "But let us see what the man is worth, while we are waiting."

Sigtrygg lifted his sword once more and struck at the nearest of his foes and, in a single blow, he severed the arm of that man so that he dropped his hand, with his war club still firmly grasped in it, and stood standing as though in shock at the bleeding stump which now stood out from his shoulder. Then Sigtrygg struck again, sweeping the man's right leg off at the knee.

"That was well-done," Arnliot said, "and worthy of any Norseman."

The other Skraelings seemed quite stunned for, except for those who had been with the Tulewat king in the first enounter, these people had never seen the work of iron on men's flesh before, and Sigtrygg seized this moment and turned on the others who menaced him as well. Turning round in a tight circle he struck swiftly at the other three who had been blocking his forward movement, striking each, in turn, with a hard blow of his sword. Each man fell as the sword struck home, for they had no protection against the harsh bite of the steel. Now Sigtrygg pressed forward again, in search of the Skraeling king, but this man seemed to recede farther back, the harder Sigtrygg pushed to reach him.

More Skraelings suddenly came forth to bar the Greenlander's way and these proved more cautious than the others, having seen the damage which Sigtrygg's sword could wreak. They did not close with him at once but endeavored to strike at him from a distance, or from behind. To this Sigtrygg replied with his shield, which he used to ward off their sharp blows until he saw an opening. And then he dropped down to the earth and rolled under their legs, striking at will, until the surprised Skraelings fell like so many trees cut down in the forest, their legs shattered and bloodied by his swift sword strokes.

Sigtrygg stood up again, when he was past those who had

sought to bar his way, and now it seemed to him that he was closer to the Tulewat lord than before, though all around him only the faces of the harsh Skraeling warriors were to be seen. He was entirely in their midst and they had an ugly look to them, but Sigtrygg turned round in a great circle again, brandishing his bloodied weapon which dripped, now, with the fat and flesh of slain men. Yet the point of it, when he held it over his head, still glistened cleanly in the bright sun and so he waved this weapon fiercely in the face of those who opposed him and these men seemed to fall back, despite the advantage of numbers which they had over him.

Now the Skraelings advanced on him cautiously, closing in the circle which they made and Sigtrygg swept his fearsome weapon about in their faces, promising each man death or dismemberment if he came too close. But this was not enough to halt them for, however much they feared the keen bite of Sigtrygg's blade, they knew they would overwhelm him and slay him, in the end, by the sheer weight of their numbers. Still, it was as though these men had cornered a maddened beast, for each knew that the ones who came in first were doomed to a terrible death from the creature's claws, so they advanced only slowly and with great care.

Sigtrygg now straightened up in his place and put an especially wicked look upon his face and then he smiled at those who crept in on him and told them, in their own tongue, to come forward if they would and taste death at his hands, "for you men will know who it is you have been fighting before this day is done."

So on they came, for they could do nothing else, and he struck them swiftly, stroke upon stroke, until he thought his arm ached with the hard swinging, but still he kept his sword aloft. And, each time it flew up, another Tulewat fell, bloodied and battered, to the earth. Now a great keening cut the air all about him and this was a harsher and stranger noise than Sigtrygg had ever heard in that country before. It seemed to drown out the Skraeling war cries which, until then, had filled the air amidst all that harsh fighting, and even the Skraelings who beset him seemed to pause in surprise at this new sound.

Then the odd noise became a horrible wailing, and men's death cries and the dull thudding of bodies flying about could be heard as though these were part of the strange new tune. Sigtrygg looked up and now he saw a man's head come flying over the wall of Tulewat warriors which still besieged him and then blood and broken torsos and severed legs and the wall of men fell away before his eyes as a great axe broke through it, splitting a man's spine as it came. Behind the axe Arnliot stood and he was terrible to behold for his face and arms were awash in men's blood and the great axe seemed to rise, in his hands, as though with a will of its own, and descend with great crashing thunder upon those men whose misfortune it was to block his way. His eyes had a frenzied look, too, and he was singing a Norse war song, between each heavy stroke of his axe, and howling like a beast, mad for the taste of men's blood.

Even the Tulewat fell back in haste before this terrible apparition, but this did them little good, for Arnliot struck harder and faster with his great weapon than these men could flee, though the very sight of him, and the bloodthirsty bellowing he made, seemed to strike fear into their own fierce and war-like hearts. Whatever weapons they threw against him seemed to bounce harmlessly from his flesh and, when they saw that their weapons could not bite him, they began to break and flee.

But Arnliot's battle rage was hard upon him and he turned with his axe in a mighty circle, sweeping every man in his path before him, howling his death song at them and cutting heads and arms and waists and whatever else stood in his way. He cleared a great space in this manner and Olvir came rushing in behind him, his own sword raised and reddened with Skraeling blood, and took up his position there beside Sigtrygg, whose arm now drooped with the strain of that hard fighting which he had had.

Arnliot made ever wider and wider circles about his two companions with great sweeps of that war axe of his, and his singing became louder and more garbled so that it was soon difficult for even his fellow Norsemen to comprehend. The Tulewat fought back but they seemed unable to drive away that fierce giant who now, alone, held them at bay. When his axe was utterly covered with the fat and blood of man-flesh and the smell of that place where they now found themselves had begun to reek in their nostrils like a farmer's slaughter house, Arnliot rushed over to where his companions stood and raised his weapon high over their heads, shaking it fiercely at the astonished Tulewat.

"Come forward and feel the weight of good Greenlanders' steel on your scrawny necks," he cried in the Norse tongue, but none of the Tulewat seemed willing to step to the fore, either because they could not comprehend his challenge or because, as is more likely, they had been utterly cowed by his fierce onslaught. Then he placed his feet squarely in the blood-reddened mud and stood beside Sigtrygg and Olvir.

"Bare is that back which has no brother, shipmate," he whispered to Sigtrygg in a very low voice; and his laughter had a strange and blood-curdling quality to it.

"Never have I seen such ferocious fighting, in any case," Sigtrygg said. And: "I did not know you were of the berserker kind."

"Nor did I," answered Arnliot. "Until now."

"Whatever kind," said Olvir, "this has opened the way for us. And saved our lives for the moment; though I'm not sure how much longer these Skraelings are likely to be impressed by this performance of yours."

And now it could be seen that Olvir had judged matters aright, for their enemies had again screwed up their courage and begun to press in on them, placing their confidence, once more, in their greater numbers. Arnliot replied that this only made him the more eager to show them how Norsemen fought when in a tight corner, and he lifted his axe high over his head and began to howl again, in that manner which seemed to have so terrified the Tulewat warriors before. He rolled his eyes about in his head, too, and chewed in a rage on his beard, while white drool ran down the sides of his mouth.

"There may not be as much need for this now, as before,"

Sigtrygg said, "for our purpose is already half-accomplished, if I am any judge."

They looked quickly to where Sigtrygg's eyes were fixed and could see, at once, that the stake where Chinokwa had stood bound, but a brief while ago, was now quite empty.

"In that case," said Olvir, "we must make no less noise than before, if we are to assure the woman time to flee; and this even though we mean to fight our way through these heathen in another direction entirely."

It was now agreed that they would continue fighting, but that they would make for the town's gates, if they could, and fight even harder than they had done thus far, so that the Skraelings would have no time to take notice of the loss of their captive. Accordingly Arnliot and Sigtrygg began to move sideways toward their foes, back against back, while Olvir came up close behind them and then the battle was quickly engaged again.

But, once the Skraelings saw that the Greenlanders were now intent on flight, it was as though a spell had been lifted from their eyes and they no longer seemed to hold these strangers in as much awe as before, when they had thought the Greenlanders fought like demons and not men, for they saw that these strangers, too, were afraid and eager to save their lives.

So now they attacked with even more fury than they had shown at the first and Sigtrygg and his companions had hard fighting every step of the way. Yet the Greenlanders placed themselves in the form of a triangle and each guarded the side he faced as they fought their way slowly through the press of their foes. In this manner, they came to a place where the open square of the town narrowed, between the roughly built Skraeling houses, and here they broke free of their foes and began to run as well as they could, seeking, always, for an opening in the town gate.

When they came out of this narrow space, they found even more Tulewat warriors arrayed against them than before and these quickly pressed them back. Now the madness began to come on Arnliot anew and he stepped into the midst of their foes, sweeping his great, blood-soaked axe before him. They had come to a place where a number of cook fires were burning and Arnliot stepped over these as though they were not there so that it seemed to the Tulewat that even fire could not touch him. At this, they broke again, for he seemed to them just as inhuman as before.

In this manner Sigtrygg and his companions made more progress than they had thought possible. Arnliot ran out into the midst of the enemy, brandishing his great axe and howling like a maddened beast, and the Tulewat scattered again before him. But, while Arnliot was about this, with Sigtrygg close behind, striking both to left and right with his sword, Olvir stopped for a moment and bent over one of the cooking fires which they had passed. Sigtrygg saw him and, turning, urged him to get a move on, "for," he said, "this is no time to be hunting for your dinner."

Olvir made no response to that but remained by the fire as his companions carried their fight to the Skraelings who were opposing them on every side. Then, sheathing his own weapon, Olvir gathered in his hands a number of burning brands and ran to catch up with the others. Once he had reached them, he began to throw the brands in every direction, onto the roofs of the Tulewat houses.

Sigtrygg saw this and slapped the man on the back, saying, "in my opinion you are worth more to us each day than you were the day before," and now he ran to another nearby fire and began to do as Olvir had done.

The Tulewat surged around them in fury, throwing their stone weapons at the Norsemen, but these, at first, only bounced off the shields which Sigtrygg and Olvir held aloft before them. For his part, Arnliot seemed entirely impervious to the missiles the Skraelings threw at them, just as he had at the first, for he did not seem to feel the blows of the stones which struck him.

Amidst the spreading flames the Norsemen pressed their retreat, drawing ever closer to the town's gates, cutting a pathway of blood before them, though after awhile it seemed that some of that blood was their own, for Sigtrygg and Olvir began to take some wounds, as the weapons of the Tulewat came at them in greater numbers than before. But Arnliot still appeared quite unhurt and now he led the way, his companions fighting, step by step, behind him.

They came out, once more, into a large, open area and now they could see the gate of the Skraeling town before them. But all around this place the Tulewat warriors stood shoulder to shoulder, barring their way. At their backs the hot flames, which were now spreading quite rapidly in the enemy town, bit at their heels and seemed to urge them on. So they could not go back, but they could not break down that wall of fierce fighting men which stood before them either.

"It seems to me that here is where we are to make our stand," Sigtrygg said, when he came up, at last, to Arnliot.

The big man from Ketilsfjord was covered, from head to toe, in the grisly gore which his axe had wrought from the midst of his foes and he now put that weapon, head down, in the earth before him, between his widely placed legs. Then he took his stand there, the familiar smile crossing his face once more and giving him a rather troll-like appearance. Olvir came up to them, too, and he still had one blazing brand in his hand. He said: "Now everything is happening just as I predicted, for I foresaw that we would be unable to win to safety, once we had placed ourselves in the hands of these people."

"Even so," said Sigtrygg, "at least we have given a good account of ourselves."

At that very moment a loud cry went up behind them, as though sorrow and fury had been mixed together in equal parts, and Sigtrygg turned back to see what had occurred. There was wailing and shrieking and, then, great angry bellowing from that part of the town where they had lately been and a rush of people back to the place where the great wooden stake stood. The Tulewat behind them seemed to have suddenly lost interest in their pursuit and were now running about, as though searching for some valued piece of property which had been lost. Sigtrygg said: "They have realized the woman is gone and now they will turn back to us, if they cannot recover her. Yet if she is captured, all that we have now done will have gone for nothing."

Swiftly he grabbed the last burning stick from Olvir's hand and threw it over the heads of those men who were still standing between them and the opening in the timber stockade. The brand fell among the dried human skins which were piled high against the wooden wall and these quickly caught fire and began to burn hotly behind the Tulewat warriors opposing their retreat. The Skraelings sought at once to cover the fire and smother it, but the skins had been left too long in the sun and allowed to dry and turn brittle, so that they now proved a fertile field for Sigtrygg's planting. Sigtrygg told his companions they were to charge the Tulewat at once, whatever the consequences, "for we will never get a better chance than this," and so they raised their weapons and ran straight toward the rapidly burning stockade wall.

The Skraelings met them amidst the smoke and heat of the blaze and hurled themselves bodily against the oncoming Greenlanders but these did not slacken their pace, for all the fierce heat of the fire which consumed the wooden wall before them. Now weapons clashed again, as Norse steel shattered the stone arms which the Skraelings bore, and Arnliot cleared that fiery place of foes with great swings of his war axe. The other Skraelings, who had been behind them, but who had become momentarily distracted when the loss of their captive had been discovered, now realized what had occurred and these rushed up in a great mass after the fleeing men into the place where fire and battle were raging together.

Then Arnliot said: "We will never win to freedom if we are to stand and fight each of these men, in turn. You two must go on ahead, while I remain to give them a proper Norse greeting."

"I don't see much hope of that," said Sigtrygg, "for I doubt we could outdistance them, in any event, without your help. So now we are all to remain here, until these Skraelings have borne us down by sheer numbers, or else we must run through this fire together and try to put some distance between ourselves and our pursuers."

The entire stockade now seemed to be aflame and Arnliot said that Sigtrygg and Olvir should suit themselves where these Skraelings were concerned. He now ran along the fiery wall and Sigtrygg and Olvir followed him until they came to the place where the stockade ended and they could see the distant forest before them through the smoke. Arnliot said they were to run through there while he held the Tulewat back with his axe; and now he swung that weapon about him, again, in great circles, causing their pursuers to fall back. Sigtrygg and Olvir did as he bade them and, as they fled, the Tulewat let loose a flight of arrows against them, though they had not used these weapons before because of the close quarters of the town.

Now Arnliot worked his way backward and, when he had come to the place between where the two sides of the town wall broke to form a rough gateway, he suddenly turned his axe against that wooden wall which stood on the farther side of the opening, where the fire had not yet reached. With several quick strokes, he cut down those timbers which supported that side of the wall, bringing them down across the opening through which his companions had fled. Then fire leapt across the fallen timbers and swept angrily onto the farther side of the stockade and Arnliot, howling as though in triumph, leaped over these and ran for the woods after the others.

Sigtrygg and Olvir met him at the place where the trees seemed thickest and clapped him on the back. There were arrows standing out on his shield, which still hung from his shoulders behind him, and in the thick, padded leather of his garments. But he seemed otherwise unhurt though quite spent.

Each of the others was bleeding in numerous places, but Sigtrygg said that none of their wounds were life-threatening. "Still, we cannot afford to rest now, for I doubt these Tulewat mean to let us off so lightly."

They could now see that the Skraelings were spilling out of

their burning gate in large numbers and heading toward them, shooting arrows and crying their war-cries. Sigtrygg asked if Arnliot thought he could go on, "for it often happens that berserkers will be as weak as children, when they have finished with fighting, and, if so, we are quite prepared to make our stand here."

But Arnliot replied that that was not the case with him and so they now began to run as hard as they were able into the woods and away from their Skraeling pursuers.

CHAPTER XXVIII

THE VALLEY OF STONES

They ran hard through the woods following the way they had come into that country and Arnliot, for all his exertions before, was soon setting the pace for them, his great strides devouring the wooded land which lay before them. They paused once to see to their wounds and then Sigtrygg quickly made bandages from their clothing and bound up their cut flesh, wherever he could, but, when they heard the Tulewat coming up rapidly behind them, they ran again toward the east. Twice a number of their pursuers came up with them, and then there was hard fighting, but each time the Greenlanders broke away and managed to leave the Tulewat behind. After the second time they made such gains that Sigtrygg thought they would lose their foes and he told his companions to slow up, "for I don't want them to lose interest in us while Bjorn is still in the woods with the woman."

"There's little hope of that, in any event," said Arnliot, "for we have now done them such harm that I doubt they will pursue any others while we are still at large. Nor do I think we will find it difficult keeping them in sight."

And now they could see the truth of this for, before Arnliot had even ceased to speak, they heard the voices of their foes and these were not far off. Then they ran again, as swiftly as they could, though they had no time to conceal their tracks from those who were behind them, and so had to rely alone on that speed which their legs could muster. The countryside was not overly rugged, where they now found themselves, and they were able to make good progress among the trees. When night fell, they sought what shelter they could and took their rest. But they rose again before the sun was up and took flight once more, with neither time to search for food nor to eat it, but pushing on deeper into the woods, knowing that the others would surely find their tracks and come after them without cease.

After further hard running they came again to that place where the forest fell away and only a great rock-strewn valley seemed to stretch out before them, offering little by way of concealment to mask their passage. Olvir said: "There are no trees now to protect us from those hounds which are baying at our heels and I think crossing this rocky country will be no light task, either."

They could now see that the man who had once served the Leifssons on their Greenland farm was more badly hurt than they had thought, for his bandages had loosened and were wet with fresh blood. His legs were soft under him, too, and he now sat down on the ground.

"I think you men must go on without me," he said after awhile, "for I am unlikely to be strong enough to cross this place which lies before us; and it is certainly too much to hope that I could keep pace with you, in any event."

"There's no reason to expect these Tulewat to be any more gentle if they come up with you now than they have shown themselves to be before," Sigtrygg said, "so I don't intend leaving you behind."

"I don't see that you have much choice, where that is concerned," Olvir replied, "for I cannot run alongside of you two any longer; nor can the two of you fight all of our enemies off by yourselves, if you stay behind, for then we will all meet our ends in this country, instead of me alone."

"It may happen that we will meet our ends here, in any case," Sigtrygg said. "But it did not seem to me, when I made you a member of my crew, though contrary to your will, that I was bringing you out here to die."

"No man knows what fate awaits, wherever his luck may take

him," Olvir said. "And I do not regret how things have turned out, in any case, since this is better than dying of old age among the closed-in houses of Greenland's farms. But now I want you to take back this sword which you gave me, for it has served its purpose well-enough and should not be allowed to fall into our enemies' hands."

"I do not intend to take it," said Sigtrygg, "for no man has a better right to this weapon than you, shipmate. And you may yet have need of it."

Olvir said he should have it his own way then, and now he urged them to run out among the rocks if they would save themselves, "for my ears tell me that our pursuers are not far behind and you will have hard running if you are to cross this country ahead of them."

Arnliot said he agreed with the Brattahlid man in this at least, "for there is a time to stand and fight and another for running, though some people seem to think that any time is good enough for bandying words about."

Now he unslung his shield and tossed it away and then he handed his axe to Sigtrygg. "You are to carry this, shipmate," he said, "although you thought it rather cumbersome and a hindrance when first we came out this way. Still, I would take it amiss if you were to lay it down now."

Sigtrygg said there was no need to worry about that. So now Arnliot went over to their fallen comrade and lifted him onto his shoulders.

"I have run with heavier burdens than this across the ice floes in Ketilsfjord," he said, "and most people thought I got the better of the ice there, despite the unsteady footing underneath. But you must stay still, shipmate," he now told Olvir, "and don't wriggle about overmuch."

Olvir said he would keep as still as he could and they now left the shelter of the trees and began to run out among the rocks. Sigtrygg set the pace and Arnliot kept even with him and it did not seem to either of his companions that Arnliot ran any slower than he had before, despite the extra weight on his back. It was not long before they heard the Tulewat war-cries coming up behind them and, when they turned, they could see these fierce-looking warriors leaving the line of trees and surging down into the rocky valley. There was now no hiding from them and the Greenlanders ran harder than they had before, but the harsh pace had at last begun to take its toll of them. The Skraelings' shouts soon seemed much louder and, when they looked backwards, they could see the faces of their foes closing behind them.

"It's no good trying to outrun them now," Sigtrygg said, "for they will be on us before too much longer, and then we will be hard put fighting them off in the open like this."

"What do you suggest?" Arnliot said.

"Make for that large rock up above us," Sigtrygg shouted, "for there at least we can control the number of our foes who can come against us at any one time. And that will give us our best chance, if we can hold them off till dark."

They turned at once toward a large, flat rock which Sigtrygg had seen and which stood out above the valley, nestled against the sheer side of a low cliff.

"I don't see how we will be able to get away, once we have gained that foothold," Arnliot said, "but it is certainly better than letting them run us down in the open country like this."

The climb to the rock was not overly difficult, until they came to the place just below it and then it became quite steep and the going was very rough. Still, they pushed on though the Tulewat were now right beneath them and grabbing at their feet. Sigtrygg turned back and struck blindly at the Skraelings who were closest to them with Arnliot's axe and these men fell swiftly in bloody pools at each blow of that formidable weapon. Then he turned and fled up the slope again. Arnliot was now above him and he reached his arm down and took the axe. Then he lowered his hand again so that Sigtrygg could get hold of it and, when he had him, he pulled him up behind him. Then Sigtrygg went on ahead and climbed up through a crease in the rock until he had gained the stony lip which stood out above them. Arnliot now handed up the weakened form of Olvir to him and afterwards his axe and then he pulled himself up, just behind his companions, as the Tulewat surged around him striking him from all sides with their weapons.

Even Arnliot was now bleeding profusely when he gained the top of the ledge and the Skraelings, when they perceived that they had, for the moment, lost their prey, began to howl with anger and frustration, and to shoot their arrows up onto the rock ledge. Sigtrygg and Arnliot carried Olvir to the innermost part of the ledge and Sigtrygg placed his shield over him, for he alone, of his companions, still had this. Then they ran to that steep pathway which led up to their haven and began to strike with their swords at those Tulewat who were now striving to make the same climb which they had made to the safety of the ledge.

They took turns hacking at their pursuers for, so narrow was the means of ingress to that place which they had chosen, that it needed but one swordsman at a time to hold their position so long as their assailants did not land some lucky blow against them. Sigtrygg and Arnliot each took his turn at the gateway while the other leaned hard against the cliff side, catching his breath in order to regain his strength for further fighting.

Thus it went for much of that day, while all of the Tulewat at last came up to that place and gathered beneath the rocky ledge, shouting insults and laughing at the predicament which their enemies now found themselves in. Although they were unable to come at the Greenlanders, they saw that matters could not remain as they were forever, since the Greenlanders would soon tire and would be unable to provide themselves either with food or sleep. So the Tulewat began to settle in about them and to make fires on the slope below and soon they brought meat and put it to cook on the fires so that the rich aromas of the roasting flesh floated upward onto the rocky ledge.

"They mean to kill us with our own hunger," Arnliot said.

"No doubt," replied Sigtrygg, "but I think, if we weaken now, it will be our flesh they'll be turning on the spits above their cook fires and not that small game which they have now slain."

"Better to die thus," said Arnliot, "than of starvation up here, especially since there is so much worth fighting for down below."

Olvir now wakened and, when he saw how things were, he said they had better keep their wits about them, "for these Skraelings are not about to leave off the hunt until they have snared their quarry. And now some people might think there was wisdom in my words when I urged you men to leave me behind and save yourselves."

Arnliot asked Sigtrygg if he now had any ideas concerning how they were to make good their escape, since they had attained the safety of that precipice which Sigtrygg had directed them to.

"I am certainly too exhausted to think any further about that," Sigtrygg replied, "let alone for running beyond where we have now come. But if we can hold them off until darkness, perhaps we shall find some way out of here which we have not seen before."

"There's not much promise there," Arnliot said. "Still, I suppose it's better than trying to run past that assemblage while the sun is still aloft."

So now they settled in to await the evening though the Skraelings continued to shoot their arrows up at them, even while they were dancing and laughing about their cook fires.

Toward the end of the day, when the sun could be seen drifting lower in the sky, they heard a voice calling to them and now they crawled out to the edge of the rock on which they were perched and peered down at the faces below them. Nahinanto, the Skraeling king, stood underneath them, midway down the slope into the valley. He was surrounded by a number of his chief men and he was calling the name of Aselekah.

Sigtrygg answered him and asked what he wanted.

"To come up," said the king. "Or for you to come down to us, for it won't do you any good starving like a frightened rabbit in this fashion. A man should die like a wolf or a panther and not like one of the grass-eating beasts."

"What do you mean to do with us if we come down?" asked Sigtrygg.

"No more than you deserve," replied the king, "for we will put you to death. But you shall die like warriors and not like women, for you have earned that, at least."

"I don't suppose there's any reason to think you'd be willing to accept a settlement from us now, since you were so unwilling to do so before, when you had less to hold against us?"

The Skraeling king only laughed at this and then he fell silent.

"In that case," said Sigtrygg, "Aselekah prefers the safety of his rabbit's hole to the wolf's death, for now. Though who can say how matters will fall out in the end."

Nahinanto said he could have it his own way, if those were his final words on the subject, "for we will take your heads, however long we must wait. But if you men fall from weakness and starvation, and not in battle against us, your deaths will certainly be the harder when, at the last, we have laid our hands on you."

Sigtrygg said he was willing to risk that.

Now the Skraelings began to assault the Greenlanders' position once more, with arrows and a quick rush up the steep rocky slope. Sigtrygg and Arnliot hurried to the narrow pathway up which they had come and began to take their turns fighting off their attackers one by one, just as before. But now the Tulewat pressed much harder and nearly drove the Greenlanders from the entryway which guarded their rocky perch, for Arnliot faltered and lost his footing so that his sword fell from his grasp onto the rocky ground below them. Then the Skraelings would have pulled Arnliot down with it for they were all about him and he seemed completely exhausted, except that Sigtrygg crawled out over Arnliot's shoulders and began to strike at the clawing hands which had grabbed the big Ketilsfjord man and were pulling him down. When he had cut their attackers away, he pulled on the larger man and drew him to safety, placing himself between him and them on the steep pathway.

Just then he heard shouting and, looking above him, saw that two Skraelings had managed to gain the lip of their rock from its steeper side and were even now pulling themselves onto the ledge. Arnliot lay limply behind him and seemed unable to rise to defend himself, while, before him, the other Skraelings continued to press their assault up the narrow path. Sigtrygg struck at these warriors as swiftly as he could but could do nothing to stop the others who had now gained the ledge. Still he raised and lowered his sword without cease, unwilling to give way before the men below him.

Now, as he struck repeatedly with his blade, he suddenly felt the clang of steel on steel and, looking down, he saw that one of the Skraelings had got hold of Arnliot's sword and was striking at him with it. Swiftly Sigtrygg whirled his own weapon about his head and brought it down and around the other man's sword arm and this swept the blade from the Skraeling's hand, for these Tulewat, however fierce with their own weapons, were quite unfamiliar with the manner of weapons play which swordsmen practice. Sigtrygg now continued the sweep of his blade so that it lodged in the armpit of the man who had lost the sword, and that was his death blow.

The other Skraelings fell back at this and Sigtrygg turned to face those men who had gained the ledge while he was engaged elsewhere. But now he saw that these two were staggering backward over the fallen body of Arnliot, for Olvir had gotten to his feet and was striking at them mercilessly with his own sword. Sigtrygg rushed to join him but he arrived too late, for Olvir had driven their assailants to the edge of the rock and, with sword and shield before him, he pressed both men until they lost their footing so that each now fell backward to the steep sloping ground below.

Sigtrygg said: "It's a good thing you have got your sea legs again, for it will now fall to the two of us to defend this place since our shipmate seems unable to lend us his support for the moment."

"There's no need to worry about that," Olvir replied, "for I have had my share of rest and am eager to try my blade out against these foreigners. But Arnliot must be pulled to safety."

So now Sigtrygg sheathed his sword and drew the fallen Ketilsfjord man to shelter under the cliff face while the Skraelings renewed their assault against them with arrows and Olvir ran to guard the pathway.

"It will not be long before they overcome us at this rate," Olvir said to Sigtrygg, when he had joined him again at the place where the sloped earth came up to their rocky redoubt, and Sigtrygg said that it certainly looked that way, "though they will not do so without a great deal more of that hard fighting which they have had from us, so far."

Now, as he spoke these words, they heard a loud cracking sound above their heads and this was followed by a second, equally as loud, and then a third, in quick succession. Three large rocks suddenly came crashing down on the place where they were standing and it was soon apparent that these sounds were the noise which the rocks made as they hit the cliff face, above them, in their sharp descent. Sigtrygg looked up and saw that more rocks were coming down at them, in the same manner as the first three, and that arrows, too, were now being directed toward them from the upper reaches of the cliff. These began to fall about their feet and several of the stones struck them on their backs and shoulders.

Olvir said: "They have got above us, as well as below," and Sigtrygg replied that, in that case, they must now retreat to the safety of the cliff wall, "where they will find it hardest to strike at us cleanly."

"Then we will be unable to defend this place," said Olvir, "and they will come up through that narrow passageway, which is the only means of entry onto this rock, and then there will be too many of them to fight off, since we are now in such a weakened condition."

"There's no help for that," said Sigtrygg, "for, if we stay out here in the open, we will be slain just as surely. But if we run to the rock wall and make our stand there, we may yet preserve our lives, if only for a little longer."

So now they turned and ran back to the sheer cliff, which loomed above them, amidst that storm of stones and arrows, and took their places there, backs against the rock, legs braced widely, their swords raised high over their heads. They could see, at once, that the Skraelings began to pour onto the rocky ledge, through the undefended portal, as soon as it was clear to them that Sigtrygg and his companion had forsaken their defense, and Sigtrygg and Olvir now stood shoulder to shoulder over the slumped body of Arnliot.

Sigtrygg said they were to strike at those Skraelings who were first to reach them "with all your strength and take them down, so those who come after will know what awaits them here. But under no circumstances are you to let them take you alive, for they are not likely to deal kindly with us after this day's work."

Olvir said: "Is this the end, then, which you foresaw for us Sigtrygg, when you slept so uneasily yesterday; though you were unwilling to speak of the matter afterwards?"

"It is not so different," Sigtrygg agreed, "but I could not have abandoned our quest, in any event."

"Nor would we have abandoned you, whatever your dream foretold," Olvir said. Arnliot lifted up his head at this and added that his only regret was that he was no longer strong enough to swing his axe, "though that is the great weakness of the berserker's fever, once it has come upon a man."

The first of the Tulewat warriors now reached the Greenlanders with war clubs raised and hideous cries on their lips, their painted faces contorted in fierce anger, and Sigtrygg and Olvir struck at these men, simultaneously, each sweeping a Skraeling head from its body. But behind these were others, who came without let up, and the weight of their bodies seemed to overwhelm the two Norsemen so that there was no longer room for them to swing their swords. Then Sigtrygg drew his knife and began to stab at those men who pressed above him, though he was, himself, bleeding heavily in many places. Still, he struck wildly with his blade at the bare Skraeling flesh of his enemies so that the ledge on which they fought soon ran red with men's blood. His own body was bathed in it, his eyes blinded by the stinging, hot spray which spouted forth from the wounds he inflicted on his Skraeling assailants.

Then there was a loud thud, followed by a second, and the force of the Skraeling attack on them seemed to halt. The weight of the Skraeling bodies which pressed them down eased somewhat and Sigtrygg pushed the wounded and dying men who sprawled atop him aside and struggled to his feet. Above his head he heard another heavy thudding and, looking up, he saw a great shadow falling toward them from the cliff face above. It bounced several times against the steep rock wall and then fell with a wet, cracking sound not far from their feet. Two more such sounds and two more bodies of Tulewat warriors seemed to fall upon them, from out of the sky, in the same fashion as the first one, and Sigtrygg could now see that others were tumbling from the top of the rock wall, as well. They came, one after another, as though cast aside by some angry giant, raining down upon the rocky ledge and the sloping ground below like great stones, except that the places where they struck were soon flooded in bloody pools as the life ebbed from their broken bodies.

Sigtrygg and Olvir pulled themselves out onto the ledge and now they saw a scene they had not dared hope for until then, for the whole countryside below them seemed to be in turmoil. The Tulewat who had besieged them were themselves now under harsh attack and this from a host of other Skraelings who seemed to appear, as though by some strange sorcery, from behind the huge boulders which lay all about the sloping valley in which they found themselves. Waves of fighting men poured down upon the stunned Tulewat host who had been so intent on taking the three Greenlanders, they had neglected to post guards on their flanks.

All that valley now seemed alive with war cries and the Tulewat were hastening to meet the sudden assault against them.

There seemed to be a great maelstrom of seething people beneath the lip of that place where Sigtrygg and his fellows had sought safety and the attack on the Greenlanders' position was now quite obviously forgotten by their foes, since these seemed to have all they could do just to meet the onslaught of those others who had come up on them so suddenly. Above the line of the battle, standing amidst the few trees which ringed the valley's upper edge, Sigtrygg and Olvir could now make out the bright glint of sun on steel and, looking closer, they thought they could see a Norse shield wall forming. Then the wall seemed to become a wedge, as either side of the formation fell back and its middle thrust forward and down along the rocky slope, the men behind the shields breaking into a hard, steady run, their deep voices rising to an ominous boom.

"That will be the kind of help which men like us can depend on," Sigtrygg said, and he got stiffly to his feet, using his sword for support. He now told Olvir to see to their comrade, "and bind those wounds which need it, for I think there is still work to be done, for those of us who can stand, down below." And, so saying, he hobbled down onto the sloping ground which spread out beneath them.

The shield wedge hurtled down the slope like a rock fall, gathering speed as it came, a great spear point at its apex, and it struck the remaining Tulewat in the valley below like the great blow of a hammer on anvil, shattering the Skraelings there as though they were brittle stone. The Norsemen at once fell to and struck at the fleeing enemy with a fury born both of anger and of the heavy weapons they carried, so that the Tulewat fled in all directions without thought of defense. But now those other Skraelings, who had first attacked the Tulewat, rose up against them again and slew them in every direction that they turned, and there was great killing in the valley and the cries of men fighting for their lives and of those who were dying.

Sigtrygg rushed into this battle as swiftly as he was able, though his wounds were great and his legs stiff beneath him. Still, he was not minded to let the others fight it out without him and so he pushed forward until he had come up with Vragi and the crewmen he led, who were laying all about them with their Norse blades. Vragi had his long spear before him and none, it seemed, could stand against it for he twisted it first one way and then another, so that it caught those who opposed him on its point, before they could get near enough to do him harm.

Thorolf and Asmund quickly came up on either side of Sigtrygg and, when they saw him, shouts of joy escaped their lips simultaneously. They raised their swords in salute and rapidly began to strike at those Skraelings who were nearby, so that Sigtrygg and these two now advanced, as one, into the midst of the fray where Vragi had taken his stand.

"It seems we have arrived only just in time," Vragi now shouted, when he saw Sigtrygg coming up with him, and Sigtrygg replied that this was so, "but we had them on the run, in any case, so you would not have found many left to test your weapons on, if you had delayed much longer."

"Still, it was a good thing we came across that Skraeling companion of yours in the woods, or we had not known the direction of your travel," Vragi said. "And then you men would have fought yourselves to exhaustion against these wretches, so that sleep had claimed you before you were done with them."

Sigtrygg said: "Is the woman safe?" And Vragi replied that she was, "though she's quite worn out from the hard running she's had in the forest."

"In that case," said Sigtrygg, "there is much to repay these Tulewat for."

Vragi replied: "There are many in this country who think the same, for the Skraelings who now fight beside us are those who answered that summons which you sent to the people who make their homes on the lower part of the river. And it wasn't hard work convincing them to join us, once they saw the sort of weapons we had with us and the work these had wrought on their enemies."

Sigtrygg now said they were to finish with their foes if they could and Vragi pressed forward, all the Greenlanders clustering close behind him. The fighting was hand to hand and exceedingly bloody, for the Tulewat were not craven fighters, however matters had gone against them, but the Norsemen led the way into their midst and the end of it was that the Tulewat fell before them and their allies.

Now the fighting swirled toward the upper edges of the valley, where the trees grew more thickly, and here they caught up with Nahinanto, himself, considered by the people who lived in that country to be their king. This fierce leader of the Tulewat now took his stand, with the trees at his back, his war club swinging out at those of his enemies who approached him from whatever direction they came and it seemed to all those who saw this that none could come near him and live. Sigtrygg at once ran up to him, but Vragi ran in first and thrust his great spear out at the enemy king, before that man could swing his club at Sigtrygg's head. "That is no light weapon," Vragi warned, "and this man is well-versed in the use of it."

Sigtrygg said he didn't much care about that and added "you are to withdraw your spear at once, for this man is mine."

Vragi said: "You are a bold fellow, yet I think too weak to stand against such a hardy foe as this, for you have bled more than you know."

"Nevertheless, no one is to take his head but me," said Sigtrygg and now he pushed Vragi's spear aside with the flat of his sword.

At once the Skraeling king leaped forward and swung his great club at Sigtrygg's face and the Greenlander barely had time to turn his head so that the spiked end of the club left a deep gash in the side of his jaw. Sigtrygg returned this gesture swiftly with a sweep of his sword, but his arm was much weakened and the sword barely cleared the ground as he raised it from the earth, where he had held it, until then, to support his unsteady legs. Then the

Skraeling king leaped high in the air and let out a fierce war cry, like some great cat intent on his kill, and brought his club down onto Sigtrygg's unguarded head. At the last moment the Greenlander raised his sword and struck the blow aside, grabbing the Skraeling with his free hand and digging his fingers tightly into the man's throat. The Skraeling released his war club, then, and at once began grappling with his foe, the two men falling to the ground and rolling over and over one another, down the steep slope toward the valley below.

They landed with Nahinanto atop the bloodied Greenlander, and striking him repeatedly with a rock he had seized as they fell, Sigtrygg groaning under the repeated blows. Then Sigtrygg got his two hands free and caught the arm of the man who was thus pounding him, and the rock fell from the Skraeling's hand. Sigtrygg now took the flesh of the man's face in his two hands and rolled out from under his foe, even as he tore skin from bone and the man shouted hideously from that bloody attack. Sigtrygg rose first, to a half-sitting position, and immediately fell on his enemy again and now these two began to roll, once more, down the slope and toward the bottom of the valley. The Norsemen ran to follow the two as they tumbled in a seeming death grip.

Sigtrygg was on his knees again when they caught up with him but he was unarmed, for he had lost his sword. Still, he grappled fiercely with the Skraeling king and this man fought back with all the strength of his body, which was not inconsiderable, so that these two seemed, for a time, as though they were one seething mass of bloodied flesh and hatred. Sigtrygg had the man, at last, in a strangle hold, such as wrestlers use, and squeezed hard to choke out the life's breath of him but, in the end, he had no strength for that and he fell back, releasing his grip. Then the Skraeling king arose and struck out at the Greenlander, though he too was overcome by that hard fighting and his blow fell uselessly to the earth where the Greenlander's head lay.

Thorolf and Asmund came up to them first and pulled the Skraeling chieftain from the ground. Thorolf thrust his sword at the man's belly, but Sigtrygg spoke sharply then and told him to let the weapon fall, "for I have already said it, that no one is to take this man's head but me."

"If I slit his gut, the head may still be yours," Thorolf said.

But Sigtrygg said that the head belonged to him who took the life of his enemy, "and I am too weak for that."

"Then what will you have us do with him?" Asmund asked.

Sigtrygg now climbed weakly to his feet and regarded the Skraeling king. "He is a mighty man, whatever his other faults," Sigtrygg said. "And it seems to me that we made the mistake of killing too quickly once before, which caused us no end of difficulties thereafter. I want to offer him peace, if he will take it from us."

"That is not wisely done," said Vragi who had now come up to them, with the others behind him. "This man is your enemy and has shown himself to be the harshest of foes when weapons are drawn. It won't do you much good to leave him alive in this country, for he will know its pathways and secrets better than you."

"Even so," said Sigtrygg. "There are other chieftains among these people, or so I have heard; and these are lords we have not yet met. Perhaps it will serve us better if this man lives to tell these others of the kind of men we are, and the fate he has met at our hands, than if we slay him now and so must prove our mettle to his kinsmen and fellows, without benefit of his testimony thereafter."

He now turned to the Skraeling king and asked, in the man's own tongue, if he would accept his life of them, in exchange for a settlement between the Tulewat and the Skraelings who lived to the east.

Nahinanto replied that he was willing to do that, so now Sigtrygg called those Skraeling allies of his, who were nearby, to witness, and he laid out the terms of the peace. And these were that the Tulewat must agree to leave the Skraelings in the east unmolested and to seek no captives or other tribute from them, hereafter. In exchange, Sigtrygg promised the Tulewat leader, and those who had been taken with him, their lives and peace in their own country. "But if this peace is broken," he said, "then let the peace-breakers be swallowed up by that fire and bloodshed which their own treachery shall have raised in the land."

Everyone agreed that this was a good oath, except Vragi who now said he thought it only showed how headstrong some Greenlanders were, since it proved they were unwilling to listen to those who had greater experience in such matters. Sigtrygg agreed that this was probably so, but said he meant to have his own way, in any event, "since I understand these people better than you others." And now he sat down upon a nearby rock, for he had been greatly weakened by the day's events.

But when he sat thus, he heard a soft voice behind him and, turning, he saw the face of Chinokwa, and she was coming up from the valley bottom with the Skraeling, W'tnalko, beside her. He had a broad grin on his face and his hand tightly on Chinokwa's arm.

Sigtrygg rose, weakly, to greet these two for it now seemed to him that it was for these alone, and no others, that he had hazarded his life and challenged the king of that country, and vanquished him at such great cost. Leaning on his sword he stood there unsteadily and said: "Welcome, Bjorn, for you have done what no other could have and brought back my kinswoman to me, though others misgave your chances for that."

When the Skraeling woman saw how weak Sigtrygg appeared to be she let out a cry and broke free of the other, and now she ran to him and caught him round the waist with her small dark arms. Those two sat down, together, upon the rock and looked hard, each upon the other, and no words passed between them for a time. Then Sigtrygg said: "I did not look to see you again, when the enemy pressed round me. But I would have died in peace, at the least, knowing you'd been brought in safety out of that evil place."

But Chinokwa told him to keep silent, "for you must save your strength." And now she clung to him, as though she would pass her own strength into his, and then she began to tremble and Sigtrygg saw that she was afraid.

"What ails you, kinswoman," he asked her, "were they as close upon your trail as on ours? If so, I shall cancel that peace which I have now made with them, at once, if it seems to me that they have done you any further harm than has already been wrought in their grim town."

But Chinokwa said it was not for that she was trembling, "but to see you thus, for you have taken many wounds and have been much nearer death than I had known. I would not have had you die for the life of one woman only."

Sigtrygg said there was no better cause which he could think of, "but I am alright, in any event, and will surely recover in your good care, though this trembling of yours unsteadies me, somewhat; for I will need a sturdier shoulder to lean against, if I am to leave this rock."

Chinokwa said she would help him with that and now these two arose and clung tightly to each other so that Sigtrygg laughed and said he was not so weak as to require such careful tending as she now gave him. But the Skraeling woman made answer, saying he was to hold his tongue, "for I know what kind of man you are and how strong. Still, you have taken grievous wounds, such as would kill lesser men, and this I have seen for myself, for the saying is true that a man's spirit is best seen when his death is near."

"How so and have you seen that beast which haunts my pathways, then, kinswoman," Sigtrygg asked her, "even as I have looked upon your own?"

"No less," replied the Skraeling woman, "for it seemed to me, when I opened my eyes upon the stake of my enemies, and saw you in their midst with your weapon aloft, that I saw your guardian beast there, too. And he stood above you then and encompassed you; and all the Tulewat seemed to tremble before him and were afraid."

"Then I have much to thank your brother for," said Sigtrygg, "since we had such hard fighting in that town that every ally, even of the ghostly kind, had been gladly received."

"Yet, I'm not sure my brother had much to do with it," Chinokwa replied, "for this spirit-beast was like no creature ever seen in this land. I thought it was a mighty bear, larger than any which dwell hereabouts and, when it rose up, its great paws seemed to sweep the sky."

"Large bears are not so odd," Sigtrygg said, "even in this part of the world."

"But this one surely was," replied the maid, "for it was white as new-fallen snow, and I have never seen its like before."

W'tnalko now came up to them and stood nearby, putting his hand out as though to lead Chinokwa away. But she clung to Sigtrygg and would not part from him. "You must come home now," he said after awhile, "for your father's sake."

"There's no use pressing the matter," Sigtrygg told him, once it was clear Chinokwa preferred to remain by his side. "Still, you have done us a great service, Skraeling. My thanks and good will for that. But I will see her safely home, now the fighting is done."

W'tnalko said he would prefer to look after Chinokwa himself, since there were still many days travel ahead of them, until they came into their own territory again, "and there are plenty of dangers about in this open country."

"They are not likely to be much trouble for men such as these," Sigtrygg replied, "who have overcome the Tulewat host. But take your rest now, Bjorn, for none have earned it more than you."

So now Sigtrygg went down to the place where the main battle had been fought, holding the little Skraeling maid close by his side and leaving W'tnalko standing above them on the high ground. In the blood strewn valley below, the Norsemen were already moving about, counting up their dead. Five of Sigtrygg's crew had fallen in this fight and countless Skraelings, on both sides.

Vragi now sent those who could still stand up the slope to fetch Arnliot and Olvir and those two came down, though slowly and only with their shipmates' help. Olvir seemed in better shape than the Ketilsfjordman for he could walk on his own, but Arnliot had to be lifted by the others and that was no light task. Still, when he saw the dead on the field of battle he cried out in shame and anger that he had been unable to stand beside his comrades when they had driven their enemies off.

But Olvir, for his part, said that that was a small enough matter since enough blood had surely been spilled without their aid. And now he urged the others to bury their fallen shipmates so their bodies would not be torn apart by the wild beasts of that land. But Vragi said there was little time for that and that the ground in that part of the country was too hard for digging graves, in any event, so that he now advised the Norsemen to heap up mounds of large stones over their fallen comrades and this was what they did. When they had finished, Olvir went about and cut sticks of wood for crosses and placed these on each of the grave sites. He said he thought the dead men would rest more quietly in that strange country, if they had proper burial markers.

Afterwards, they gathered up what armor and weapons were left from those men who had fallen and tied these onto their backs for Vragi said there was no use leaving such valuable items behind, although in former days it had been the custom to place a man's arms with him in his grave. "But these are hard to come by, in this part of the world," he now added, "so I don't think our comrades will begrudge us what we can carry away on our backs."

Thereafter, they gathered up their company and went into the woods away from the place where the sun seemed fast to be falling below the line of the trees. But when they had gone a little ways, with Vragi leading them, the old viking suddenly called a halt and all in that fellowship obligingly slowed behind him. Then he turned about and looked at his companions and at the place from which they had come and no one had anything more to say, for it seemed to them that they had done much and seen more. Then Vragi spoke to them in a very low voice and made these verses:

West over water
we sailed into strange lands,
wandering, aimless,
'midst this luckless folk.

Feasting, they fed us
their paltry provisions,
fostered our ship's lord,
proclaimed him their chief.

Then promised us treasure
if we'd hunt the harsh men
who harried their kingdom,
taking their wealth.

So west into woodlands,
all rock strewn and riven
with boat-ways and fish trails,
we plunged, never failing.

Pursuing the long spear
to shatter the shield walls,
our foes raised against us,
lopping off Skraeling heads.

Then up flies the long sword
lightly borne by our battle lord,
seeking repayment
for deeds badly done.

There blood spatters boulders,
where vengeance is suffered,
bold men lay their heads down
to sleep under stones.

And Sigtrygg our swift lord
takes back what was taken,
the maid and the country of
Vinland are won.

After this everyone seemed to grow even quieter than before and no one had anything more to say for a long time. They walked thus into the deepest parts of the forest until they could no longer see behind them to the place where the fighting had been and then they continued on even farther than this so that they nearly lost sight of one another for the heavy growth of the trees there.

And so it came about that the crew of the Gull, which had sailed out of Eiriksfjord in such great haste the summer before, and with fewer men than seemed advisable to many at the time, was diminished even more by that fight which they made against the Skraelings in that place which afterwards they called the valley of the stones. And this valley lay to the west of Leif's houses in the land called Vinland, which was so named by those who had sailed to it before. But the names of the fallen men of Sigtrygg's crew are nowhere recorded and remain unknown to this day, although they won much honor in that place because of the size of the host which the Skraelings sent against them there. And that was the second battle which Sigtrygg fought against the Skraeling king, and in that one, too, he had the victory.

PART 3
BLOOD TIES

CHAPTER XXIX

AN OLD MAN'S WORDS

When they returned to the place by the river, where W'tnalko's kinsmen had their settlement, they found a better welcome awaiting them than at the first for all the Skraelings there thought matters had gone exceedingly well, considering the price which had been paid. These people were unstinting in their praise of the Greenlanders, thinking that nothing which could be done for such men was too much, and now they brought them food and drink and made a great fuss over them. Fires were lit, too, and a celebration prepared throughout the encampment. Sigtrygg spoke for a time with those chieftains who had come up from the lower part of the river to join in the attack on the Tulewat, for these men thought him a great hero and the Greenlanders especially bold men for the fighting skills they had shown and Vragi encouraged this, saying he thought it particularly useful to foster such thinking.

But Sigtrygg did not remain long with these people, going as soon as he was able to the bedside of Anyok, the chieftain of W'tnalko's kin. He found this man lying propped up, on the ground, in the Skraeling fashion, inside a booth in the center of the encampment. He was lying on a bed of skins and covered over by some of that wadmal cloth which Sigtrygg had brought into the country with him. This cloth was stained a dark, wet color, all along the line of the man's legs, and the place where the man lay had a rank odor to it. Tanakrit, the chieftain's wife, and the Skraeling soothsayer were both in attendance there and now Sigtrygg came inside, as well, with the maid Chinokwa and W'tnalko at his side. He knelt down at once beside the injured man and told him the news.

The Skraeling chieftain listened closely to Sigtrygg's words, though he did not take his eyes from his daughter, all the while that Sigtrygg spoke. The young maid, for her part, placed herself close by the stricken chieftain's side and set her hands on his forehead. Sigtrygg now gave a thorough accounting of the battle which had been fought with their enemies in the west, but he said little of what had drawn them there or the role which Chinokwa's captivity had played in the matter. He made no mention of his own efforts on the maid's behalf, at all, although he told the old man everything else which had occurred from the time of the Tulewat's pursuit of them until the final assault, which was made by Vragi and the allied tribes from the lower part of the river.

When he had finished describing these events, the ailing man reached out and took his daughter's hand in his and held her tightly for a time. Then he pushed her from him, saying he was not surprised at how things had turned out, considering the manliness which Sigtrygg had shown earlier. And now he added that he had already heard somewhat of the events which Sigtrygg described to him, from those who had returned beforehand.

The old man's voice was so weakened from his fevered condition that Sigtrygg found it difficult to make out what he was saying, so now he asked W'tnalko to assist in this. Accordingly, that Skraeling came forward and placed his ear by the old man's lips. After a time W'tnalko looked up and said that they should not be surprised if the injured man knew a great deal more about those events which had occurred in the battle, and in the time leading up to it, than they had expected, for others had not been as reticent in describing events as Sigtrygg had been. "And now the chief desires to know what your plans are," W'tnalko added, "since you have served him so bravely."

"I haven't thought much about that, for I have been too busy," said Sigtrygg.

In that case, said W'tnalko, "our chieftain wants to offer you Greenlanders the right to remain in this country, for as long as you choose, and to share in the hospitality which he and his kinsmen can provide. Nor is it likely you will find better accommodations in all this land, or firmer friends," W'tnalko added, "although Anyok is now much grieved that he will be unable to ensure you men are thanked in more proper fashion."

Sigtrygg replied that no man could see all that lay ahead for him and least of all one whose mind was clouded over by the pain and discomfort of a wound which was still in the process of healing. "But some people would think the debt to be paid was mine and not yours, chieftain," he said directly to the injured man, "since we took your son from you."

When W'tnalko told the old man these words, the Skraeling chieftain opened his eyes wider than before. And now he lifted himself halfway off the skins on which he lay, his face stretched tight as a ship's sail when it has been caught in a head wind. "Aselekah," said the chieftain, in a much louder voice than he had used until then, "Aselekah. You have certainly taken great losses from this fighting and your men are now fewer than before; and we, for our part, have suffered no less than you."

Sigtrygg said that no one could deny this.

"In truth, all the people who live along this river have given of their blood," the Skraeling leader continued, "which was only right. But you Greenlanders and we have been hurt the most. Now I want to propose that we join our forces, for this is a harsh land and few will prosper in it if they are not strong."

Sigtrygg asked him what he had in mind and W'tnalko replied for the Skraeling chieftain saying that he thought the time was now not far off when his kinsmen would be seeking a new leader, since Anyok thought it unlikely he would recover from that wound which his enemies had dealt him.

"Now I have no son of my blood to lead this people," W'tnalko said for the chieftain, "but only you, a son by adoption, though you are unaccustomed to our ways. Yet you have shown yourself a mighty man and an honorable one, and are certainly not unfit to lead in my place."

"It is unlikely these people will take me for one of their own," Sigtrygg replied steadily when he had heard this, "for all their willingness to fight beside me."

W'tnalko spoke into the old chieftain's ear, as Sigtrygg bade him, but the Skraeling leader now spoke for himself again, saying that "matters may be as you say, but I don't think they will find a better man than you, however hard they seek him. And they will certainly have need of such a man for there will be many who will desire to take their rights from them and deny them those hunting grounds to which they may lay just claim."

"This country seems large enough, that men need not quarrel over such matters," Sigtrygg replied.

"Yet quarrel they will," the chieftain said, "for that is the way of men. But those people will do best who speak with a strong voice. And I think these here will need one, such as you, to speak for them."

Sigtrygg said his skill with the Skraeling tongue, while better than that of the other Greenlanders, would certainly not be sufficient for the purpose which Anyok now envisioned and he urged the man to choose another, "for," he said, "I am not one of you."

"It is not my choosing," the chieftain replied, "for I did not bring you into this country; or make you what you are. Yet some would think you are more like us than you know. Of all your kind, you are the most suitable for this undertaking."

But Sigtrygg replied that it was not possible that he could do as the Skraeling chieftain urged for he thought his own affairs would draw him away before long. "And I have a land claim on the coast, which must be seen to."

But W'tnalko now told Sigtrygg that the chieftain would not be swayed, "for this has been foreseen by our Dream-Speaker."

Sigtrygg said that he didn't see how this matter could have a good end, if he now followed such advice as was being offered. But W'tnalko leaned closer to the old chieftain's face, listening with even greater care than before to his words. As the old man spoke, W'tnalko's own features seemed to grow more intense and now he narrowed his eyes slightly and tightened his mouth over his teeth. At length, he straightened and turned again to Sigtrygg, saying: "This is what our chieftain would say to you, Greenlander. If Aselekah doubts his skills, or the willingness of those in this place to accept him as one of their own, let this put his mind at ease. Anyok, who rules beside the fast flowing river, now gives his daughter, Chinokwa, to Aselekah to be his wife. And this will ensure that the others accept you and that your words do not fall unheard onto the earth for Chinokwa's blood is no less good than her brother's was, since she too is the child of Anyok; and of Tanakrit, herself a daughter of chiefs."

Sigtrygg now looked to the maid, Chinokwa, and to the other Skraelings in the house but none, it seemed to him, had understood the import of those words which had been spoken since W'tnalko used the Greenlanders' own tongue which he alone, of all the Skraelings, had command of. W'tnalko sat impassively above the stricken chief and said nothing further and Sigtrygg looked again on the face of the young Skraeling woman who sat nearby.

"I don't know how she will take this," Sigtrygg said after a time, "for she has been as a sister to me."

W'tnalko remained silent and Sigtrygg now asked him if these were in truth the words of the old chieftain.

"They are certainly not my own," replied the Skraeling.

"Yet," said Sigtrygg, "the maid may have other wishes for there must be many young men in this place who have taken her fancy or who desire her for a wife. And there is another concern besides, for I am not here alone in this country. It would be unjust if I were now to take a wife, however strongly it were urged on me, while leaving my men unwed. They have been long out of Greenland and no man can stand idly by, while others find happiness of this sort, if he himself is denied the same reward."

W'tnalko said this was true enough but that Sigtrygg must

now decide whether to accept the old chieftain's offer, "for he is too weak to speak longer on this matter."

Sigtrygg replied that he did not find the prospect of Chinokwa as his wife unappealing but that he had to consider the well-being of those men in his following who might see the matter in a some-what different light, for "I would lose their support and goodwill if I were to accept this offer as it now stands. But if wives could be found for each of them, as well, it would be a different matter. And then I would be free to marry Chinokwa...if she were willing."

W'tnalko asked if that were the response he desired to make to the chieftain and Sigtrygg replied that it was. So now the Skraeling leaned over and spoke again in the old man's ear. After a time, he turned to Sigtrygg again. "There aren't enough young women of marriageable age in this place for what you are proposing, our chief says. Yet your followers are certainly fewer than before, so it is not unlikely the chieftains of those people who dwell below us, along the river, will think they have an interest in this matter, too. And then they may be willing to provide brides for those of your men who cannot find them here."

Sigtrygg said he thought this quite sensible, since such an arrangement would have the added benefit of binding the peoples of the river together in a fashion which fighting side by side, in a single battle, could never hope to do. So now he agreed to the chief's plan. W'tnalko leaned closer to the ailing chieftain once more and whispered the outcome of the matter in the wounded man's ear, and the old chieftain nodded to him and then he closed his eyes.

Then W'tnalko arose without saying anything further and went out of that place before any of the others could follow or speak with him, and that was the last they saw of him on that day.

Chinokwa, herself, did not give an immediate response when her father's words were told to her, but she hid herself all that day from those of her kin who sought to speak about the matter with her. Nor would she venture out to speak with anyone in the camp, however hard they entreated her thereafter. Sigtrygg, when he heard how matters stood with the maid, said he thought that things did not have a promising look to them, but he told his men he would abide by the young woman's decision, whatever it might be, for he had no desire to cause her any further unhappiness. The other Skraelings also seemed to view the matter with some concern, for these now separated themselves from the Greenlanders and left off that easy camaraderie which they had had with them, until then, since the battle in the west.

When they saw how matters stood, the Greenlanders went off by themselves to that part of the camp which had been set aside for them, since they had become the Skraelings' guests, and now they remained there alone, while those Skraelings who had formerly shouted exultantly at their return watched them in silence from a distance. Olvir said he thought matters had taken a somewhat unexpected turn "and not one which is likely to end well, for us." But Sigtrygg replied that they must be patient, "for we are certainly free to depart this place, whenever we desire, since no one here has set himself up as our enemy."

And now he sent word for W'tnalko to come and speak with him, since he thought him the Skraeling in whom he could place the most trust.

But W'tnalko did not come and the Greenlanders remained uneasily in the midst of the Skraeling camp, fewer in number than before and still recovering from those wounds they had taken in the hard fighting against the Tulewat. There was now much muttering against Sigtrygg's decision to remain among the Skraelings, but no man of them wanted to speak out openly against him and, in truth, few were in any condition to strike out alone and without the support of the others. Only Vragi seemed unperturbed by the way things had gone and his silence and lack of concern gave the others some reason to hope that matters had not got out of hand. But they were exceedingly depressed by their isolation, nonetheless.

Toward the end of that day Sigtrygg became restless and began to pace about and Vragi asked him what he was thinking.

"That we have gone rather suddenly from being the friends of these people to being their outcasts," Sigtrygg said. "And that I am the cause of it."

"You won't get very far blaming yourself for that," Vragi replied, "for these people are not like those you have known in Greenland and it is not to be expected that they will behave in just the same way. Still, they are flesh and blood, as the war with the Tulewat has now shown. And that will prove the most important factor, by far, in the end."

Sigtrygg said he was prepared to depart on the following day, in any event, if the situation did not improve, "for there's no use remaining in a place where we are not welcome."

"Have it your own way," Vragi said, "but some people would think you young men are too eager and proud to judge clearly what is in your own best interests."

Sigtrygg asked him what he meant by that.

"Not much," replied Vragi, "except that pride often breeds rashness; and rashness is the work of fools."

Sigtrygg said there was no use bandying such words with him for his mind was now made up. "And I do not intend to sit any longer among these heathen, when they have so clearly turned against us," he added.

"I'm not sure that they have turned against us," said Vragi, "or if you have simply lost your faith in them, for the woman's sake. But whatever has caused this change of heart of yours, one thing is certainly true. And that is that this woman has now got a greater hold on you than your enemies in that Tulewat town were ever able to obtain."

Sigtrygg said he thought there was little truth to that since his only concern was for the safety of the crew, now that their position had become so much more precarious than before, but when he said this last, he looked up suddenly. And now he saw before him the dark eyes of Chinokwa, watching him from the edge of that clearing in which the Greenlanders sat. She stood beneath a small tree and her face seemed to shine like burnished bronze in the reddish light of the declining, afternoon sun. Her black hair was wrapped loosely about the smooth, brown orb of her face and she did not avert her eyes from him though he gave her back look for look.

Sigtrygg stopped in his tracks, then, and fell silent and Vragi turned back to the others, saying only that "you must look sharp now Sigtrygg for the enemy is upon you; so put up your shield and gird yourself for the battle, since this is no feeble Tulewat warrior they have sent out to face you."

Sigtrygg moved slowly toward the tree where Chinokwa stood and now it seemed to him that her full lips were creased slightly, in the semblance of a smile.

Afterwards the matter was put to the other Skraeling chieftains, as well. At first, they could get no agreement among themselves for most thought the proposal of Anyok somewhat irregular, since they knew so little of these men who had come to them from over the sea. They thought them strange, both in appearance and manner, although it was generally agreed that they were hardy men and good fighters.

Still, they agreed to Anyok's plan in the end, and so a number of young women were sent for from those settlements which lay further down the river. These were brought up, after several days, and the Greenlanders met them at the water's edge and helped them onto dry land, leading them up the embankment to the Skraeling camp.

There was now much laughter among these girls for they thought the strange looking men from over the sea great sport and the two sides got on well together. Then Sigtrygg told his men they were to choose wives for themselves from among these women and the Greenlanders did not find this as difficult a task as some others which they had been obliged to undertake.

Arnliot, who was still recovering from his wounds and the exhaustion of the battle, which seemed to have taken a greater toll on him than on all the others, said he thought this the best news so far and only proper payment for the service they had performed for these Skraelings, considering the ungrateful manner in which these people had so recently behaved toward them. The other crew members voiced their agreement as well and said that they, too, were more than willing to enter into the marriages which Sigtrygg now proposed for them. Only Vragi objected for he told them that, in his opinion, he was now too old to take on the responsibilities of husbandhood, since he had had more than his share of wives in his youth. He added that his only desire now was for that peace which a solitary life could provide a man.

Arnliot, when he heard this, said that he would willingly perform that service which Vragi now rejected, since, in his opinion, none of the maids ought to be sent away from them disappointed. The old viking said he was not opposed to this. So now it was agreed that Arnliot would take two of the Skraeling women for wives, but the other Greenlanders were to choose one each and then they were to celebrate the nuptials in the Skraeling fashion at a great feast which was to be held that very night.

But Olvir came forward at this and said he thought they were all behaving in a most unseemly fashion, since they were taking no steps to ensure a proper Christian wedding feast. "And," he added, "most people would think that one wife was more than enough for any good Christian man."

Arnliot replied: "There are no priests in this part of the world for us to turn to in our need, shipmate, and we have certainly not had the foresight to bring one along with us. But that lack does not stop these Skraelings from seeking one another out and forming marriage bonds, after their own fashion. Nor do these people find it odd that one man should have two wives, if he is man enough to provide for them."

Sigtrygg now interposed himself between these two and said that since they were in the Skraelings' country there was little blame to be attached if they conducted themselves according to the Skraelings' laws, "but you, Olvir, are free to remain aloof from them, if you so desire, and give your share to another."

But Olvir said he was not willing to do that.

So now no one raised any further objections to the arrangements and things proceeded exactly as Sigtrygg desired. The Skraeling maids came and sat in the company of the Greenlanders and the two groups spoke to one another all that day, until each had made the choice which seemed most suitable to maid and man, and until Arnliot, himself, had singled out the two women he desired for his own. Then the Skraelings built up the cooking fire which burned in the middle of their encampment and roasted meat in the open air and sat round the fire on the earth, after their fashion, holding a loud and raucous celebration at which all the chiefs from the nearby settlements readily joined in.

Then it happened that a number of Skraelings came forth and cleared a place by the fire, after which others came out, bearing a litter between them. In it Anyok lay, wrapped closely in furs and skins. They set him down beside the fire, and everyone moved aside to make a place for the ailing chieftain. He now made a great show of taking food and ate as much as he was able, as a sign that the matter proceeded according to his wishes and that he meant to put his blessing on those marriages which were now to take place. Tanakrit, the chief's wife, came and sat close at his side and ministered to him all that evening while the other Skraelings of that settlement and their guests, made a great fuss over the newlyweds, dancing and singing about them, according to their custom.

Sigtrygg now told those of his crewmen who were to take a wife that they must present a gift in token of this act to the Skraelings, according to the usages of that country. So each now arose, in his turn, and placed some possession which he had carried with him out of Greenland into a large pile beside the fire.

Arnliot was the last to do this, getting to his feet rather stiffly and making his way to the place where the goods were being laid up. There he put down a belt buckle and a small ring, beside the other goods. "These should suffice to pay for the first two, at any rate," he laughed. "And I have more besides, if there are other maids in this country in need of a good husband."

Sigtrygg said he should content himself with what he now had, "for I have no desire to empty this country of marriageable women, even for your sake. But you, Arnliot, would certainly have done better to pay for your wives with something more worthy than those trinkets for it seems to me you are getting much the better part of this bargain."

"What did you have in mind?" Arnliot asked him.

"Nothing you possess has greater value than that axe of yours," Sigtrygg replied, "and it seems to me that that weapon has now served its purpose and should, by rights, be handed off to another. It is certainly worth two maids, at the least, and few people would fault you for parting with it now."

"I am unwilling to do that," Arnliot answered him at once, "for this weapon proved rather a treasure, in my opinion, when we fought together with it against those Tulewat in the west."

"Yet your father told me something of its history," Sigtrygg pressed him, "before we left Greenland. And now that you have borne it in battle and gained a victory from it, it will have other properties which may prove less desirable to him who possesses it."

"Those stories which you are speaking of are not unknown to me," Arnliot replied, "but I am not afraid of them, either. Nor would my father have allowed me to take this weapon, if he had not thought I'd have need of it in this country. In my opinion, there is time enough to part with the axe, for I am still young and have not fought many battles with it, while both my grandfather, and his father before him, carried the weapon a long while before its curse was felt...if, indeed, such a curse exists at all."

"Still, there's no telling when these things will strike," said Sigtrygg, "and this is a different land than men like us have come to before, so there's no way of knowing how things will fall out in such a place."

"I did not take you for a superstitious man," laughed Arnliot at last and now he turned away from Sigtrygg and took up with the two Skraeling women who sat there on either side of him.

"I have seen many strange things since we came to this country," Sigtrygg answered him, "so it does not seem odd to me that a weapon which will inspire berserker fever in a man and enable him to overcome so many, despite the odds, such as that axe of yours, should have other properties, as well. Or that it should prove to be the kind of weapon most people would prefer to avoid."

"I am not like most others," Arnliot replied. "And I am not willing to part with this weapon, either, whatever others may say in the matter."

"To each his own way of gaining fame," Sigtrygg said, and now he too turned away, directing his attention to the maid, Chinokwa, who sat by his side. She had, all this while, sat silently in her place but when Sigtrygg's eyes fell upon her she seemed to flush in the hot light of the fire which blazed up before them and she turned her eyes from him.

"What ails you, sister?" Sigtrygg asked, for he still found it hard to address her in any other manner.

"Not much," replied the maid, "except that I have not yet seen the gift you mean to pay my father for me, though these other men have already paid out the bride price for their wives."

"That is because I have no goods which are equal to your worth, sister," Sigtrygg told her, "and I am ashamed before your kinsmen."

"Still, if you don't pay something," said the young woman, "others will not think much of this marriage, and then they will consider me cheaply bought indeed, which will be a greater shame for me."

"Then you must choose the bride price, yourself," Sigtrygg said to her, "and I will pay it out as readily as I am able."

Chinokwa replied that she was unfamiliar with the kinds of goods which the Greenlanders carried about with them but that, if she could have her way, he would give her father a white bear skin such as the one she had seen in her vision in the Tulewat town, "for that is a prize which is not likely to be found in this part of the world, and most others will envy me for it."

Sigtrygg replied that he could not offer that, "for we are very far from that country where such bears are to be found." But he promised to kill the largest bear he could find in the country they were now in, as soon as he could. And now he reached into his shirt and drew forth two large white ivory tusks, asking her if she had ever seen their like before. Chinokwa admitted that she had not and Sigtrygg grinned and described the beast for her, from which such tusks were taken. She and all the other Skraelings who were near enough to hear his words now listened intently to that tale which he told them concerning the taking of the walrus.

Sigtrygg leant closer into the fire and told them how a man must go out onto the ice, to find such creatures, where only the white bears dared to go besides, and how such a man must lie out there in complete silence, sometimes for days on end, until the walrus came up for air. And then he must spear these creatures and struggle thereafter with them, to pull them to the surface, despite their great strength. "These teeth will testify to their size and power," he added, and all those who heard agreed that it would be no light work to bring such a beast to land.

"Then this is the bride price I mean to offer," Sigtrygg said, "for these teeth have been dearly bought and they are the last goods of this type which I have in my possession."

Sigtrygg now handed these over to the old chieftain and Anyok looked them over for a bit and then said he thought them fair payment. Everyone at that feast now agreed this were a handsome price, indeed, and Chinokwa seemed content.

Now, when all the payments had been attended to, Tanakrit suddenly arose from her place and the Skraelings fell silent at the sight of her standing above them. The old woman took a long breath and began speaking in a very soft voice, so that all those present must strain to hear her words. As she spoke, her voice seemed to grow louder and soon there was nothing to be heard but its hard rasping, like an insistent tree branch in the wind, amidst the night sounds of the nearby forest. She said that all men who were present could now see the manner of that man, Aselekah, who had been taken, first of all, as her son and now as husband to her daughter. He had, she said, shown himself to be a warrior of unequaled strength and courage in the fight against the Tulewat and now, by the bride price he paid, he had proved himself a manly hunter as well. If anyone thought himself his equal, the old woman went on, then that person must now stand up and present himself before the assembled company and declare his challenge.

But no one moved.

In that case, continued the old woman, Aselekah was now to take his place in the house of Anyok as the husband of Chinokwa just as he had been previously acknowledged as the old woman's own son. These, she said, were the words of Anyok, her husband, who could not, now, speak them for himself. If anyone thought otherwise, she added once more, he was now to speak up. But, again, no one arose to deny what the old woman said.

Sigtrygg sat uneasily beneath the woman as she spoke for, though her words were highly formal, after the Skraeling fashion on such occasions, and, thus, rather more difficult for him to follow than usual, he grasped most of what she said. He could see from the faces of the Skraelings that the matter seemed a grave one to them, as well, and he was not certain how matters would fall out.

But the old woman did not falter. She continued to speak and all the Skraelings gave her a respectful hearing for it was plain they held her in high regard.

It was Anyok's wish, she went on, once it was plain that no one intended to challenge her words, that all those who were now present should welcome Aselekah and his following into their fellowship and that they should swear to take Sigtrygg, himself, for their chieftain, when the time should arrive that Anyok could no longer lead them. The Skraelings murmured among themselves at this but still no one raised any objections. So now Tanakrit said that the men of that kin must rise up and greet their new brother and, in a rather formal ceremony, these men slowly did so, coming one by one to the place where Sigtrygg sat. Each now spoke words of welcome to the Greenlander and Sigtrygg looked hard into each man's face, for all were known to him, since they had fought together in two battles.

Last of those to come before him was Manitikaha, the Skraelings' Dream-Speaker, and he spoke certain words which Sigtrygg found hardest of all to understand. But all the other Skraelings seemed to think the old man's mutterings highly satisfactory for, after he had spoken, a great howling went up among that company, such as wolves and other wild beasts are wont to make in the woods, and everyone there seemed rather pleased with themselves. Now when all these had come before him and Sigtrygg had greeted each in his turn, it seemed to him that one man, alone, was yet unaccounted for. He looked hastily about him, among those who sat by the fire and at those standing further back from it and now he thought he could see the face of one who had held back. It was the man W'tnalko.

Sigtrygg now spoke up and asked him whether this unwillingness to join the others reflected his desire to exclude himself from his kinsmen? Everyone now looked to the man who stood at the edge of that company, barely illumined by the fire, since he had placed himself so far away from it. But W'tnalko made no move to step forward or to offer a response of any kind to Sigtrygg's query.

Sigtrygg asked again whether W'tnalko was excepting himself from the wishes of his kinsmen by this refusal to step forward with the others and then in the Norse tongue he added, "or do you mean to forsake that friendship which I have shown you, Bjorn, by setting yourself against me?"

W'tnalko replied in the language of the Greenlanders, as well, saying: "It was not friendship which brought you men here; or which caused the death of my companion, whose name you have now taken and whose sister you have claimed. And I do not think it is for friendship that you sit, now, in the place beside Anyok, our chieftain."

"What then, Bjorn," asked Sigtrygg, "for I did not seek what has now been thrust upon me. Nor would it be a service to your kinsmen, if I turned away from this charge, for they will have need of my leadership now that they have been bloodied by this war of ours with the Tulewat."

"Yet, this was a war of your own urging," replied the Skraeling, "and some people would think you have gained the most by it; while my kinsmen have certainly suffered for their part in the matter."

"It is unseemly for two such as we, who have fought so closely and for the same purpose, to fall out now," Sigtrygg replied, "snarling at one another like two angry beasts over the kill. Better we make amends here. But tell me what will you have of me, Bjorn? Only speak up and I will give it to you, that we may be friends and companions, as before."

"What I want," replied W'tnalko, "you cannot now grant; and I fear you will not bring luck to my people by your presence in our midst. Still, I will not stand in the way of those who see matters differently than I do. But you are not to think, by this, that things between us are as they were before."

And so saying, the Skraeling now stepped forward into the light of the cook fire and came before Sigtrygg and welcomed him, in the Skraeling tongue, as all the others had done before him.

And now a great shout went up and all the Skraelings began to dance about the fire and to sing in their fashion, and many of the Greenlanders got to their feet and began to dance and sing, as well. But W'tnalko stood in silence above the place where Sigtrygg and Chinokwa sat and looked down upon them for a long while as though he would speak, but no words came from his lips. Still, he seemed unwilling to leave them until, at length, Chinokwa turned her face away, and then he took himself into the shadows.

The festivities now proceeded just as before until, one by one, the Greenlanders and their new brides arose to go into those houses which had been assigned to them. Sigtrygg and Chinokwa were last to arise and they now went to the place which Sigtrygg had taken for his own. It was a large, booth-like structure, no more impressive than any of the other enclosures which the Skraelings used for their houses and its floor was of bare earth.

When they saw that they were alone inside it, the Skraeling woman made a bed of skins and furs upon the ground, and placed herself upon it.

Then Sigtrygg went to her and lay down beside her. And now these two thought there was no better place in all the world to be on that night than that small plot of earth on which they now found themselves.

CHAPTER XXX

STRANGERS

The high keening of a woman's voice awoke them on the following day, even before the first warm rays of the sun had begun to penetrate the skin and bark covered house in which they had slept. Sigtrygg and Chinokwa hurriedly pulled the furs in which they had wrapped themselves from their bodies and went outside. Nearby, the great fire which had burned so brightly the night before lay smoldering in the midst of the camp, only blackened ash and charred wood remaining where before hot flames had brightened the night sky. A long bundle of skins was stretched along one side of the place where the fire had burned. Over it a woman seemed to be lying. They went up to this place and others came out now, as well, in response to the same high-pitched wailing, and began to gather nearby.

The woman who was stretched out beside the fire seemed to be moaning and howling in a most uncanny fashion and Chinokwa, when she heard this, rushed to her at once and fell across her there and began to howl in just the same way. Then Sigtrygg knelt down beside them and lifted the woman's face. He saw that it was the old woman Tanakrit. Beneath her stretched the lifeless body of Anyok, still wrapped in the furs in which they had carried him out to the fire the night before. His face was sunken and his mouth opened, as though he had died in the midst of some speech which he had been, even then, in the course of delivering.

Sigtrygg saw at once that the loss of this man must have a great effect on the people who called the man their chieftain so now he stood aside while all the women of that tribe came forth and, on seeing the condition of their fallen leader, commenced to wail and groan in a most unnerving manner. The men showed themselves more steadfast but it was clear from their dour looks that they took the passing of this chieftain no more lightly than their women did.

After a time Tanakrit ceased her wailings and slowly arose from that place where she had spent the night, above the body of her husband. Adopting a rather severe look she seemed suddenly to take control of matters, in a fashion which quite belied her earlier demonstration of grief. She now told those men who were standing about to gather up the body and carry it to the Dream-Speaker's booth, which was built at the farthest edge of the village. They did this at once, just as she commanded, raising the corpse with great ceremony and conveying it to its destination. Then they put it down once more beside the seer's doorway.

They waited there, in what seemed a most respectful silence for a long while, until, at length, the Skraeling soothsayer pulled aside the skin covering which hung over the entryway to his dwelling and stepped outside. The old wizard was dressed in a long bearskin which covered him completely from the soles of his feet to the upper part of his neck and on his head he wore that raven-winged hat in which he was wont to appear when matters of great import were at hand.

It now seemed to the Greenlanders that the Skraeling sorcerer began to sing a long and melancholy song in a language which none of them could understand. This went on for the better part of the day. During all this time, the women stripped down the dead man's body and began to paint it, after the Skraeling fashion, and to adorn it with necklaces and arm bands of strung sea shells. Lastly they brought the fallen man's weapons and placed these on and about the body and in the man's hands, prying the frozen fingers apart to ensure he could grasp those instruments which they placed there. Then the men made a litter for him, of tree branches and leaves, and the women lovingly placed the body and all the goods they had gathered for it onto this.

The men now lifted this burden, with just as much ceremony as before, and raised it high above their heads and then they began to walk off silently with the corpse into the woods. All those who had no part in carrying the litter now began to follow this group, forming a long procession which wound its way out of the Skraeling encampment and Sigtrygg and his Greenlanders now followed along, as well. Only the voice of the old sorcerer could be heard and this seemed to them to be coming from farther and farther away. They followed this sound and the people who went before them into the deepest part of the woods until they came to a place where the ground seemed to rise up beneath them and then they found that they had come to a place on a hilltop where all the Skraelings had stopped and placed themselves silently amidst a number of raised platforms. On each platform the remains of a man seemed to reside and all the Skraelings in that company maintained a respectful distance from these.

Sigtrygg asked if anyone knew what place it was that they had come to and Vragi replied that he thought it was the burial place of the most important people among these Skraelings, "although it is plain they do not follow the custom of placing their dead chieftains into the ground, as is done in most other parts of the world."

"I am not certain what customs are practiced elsewhere," Thorolf now said, "but it is somewhat unnerving to think they leave their dead lying about in the open like this...and so near to that village in which we are now residing."

"I don't think you've much cause to be concerned about that," answered Vragi, "for things are not the same in this country as in other parts. If there were any reason to be afraid, I doubt these people would have built their homes where they did. But see how carefully they walk about among these platforms? They are certainly giving them a healthy respect and you would be well-advised to do the same, for the fact that they have never brought any of us up to this place before shows how highly they regard those who have been placed here. In my opinion they will not come up to this place except when their purpose is as it is now, and then they are not likely to spend more time here than duty demands."

The Skraelings now raised up the litter on which the body of Anyok had been carried and placed it onto one of the platforms which had been newly built for this purpose. Then they all began to moan and howl, once more, and the old soothsayer threw earth and leaves up into the sky above the place where the body of the dead chieftain lay. Afterwards all the Skraelings hurriedly left that place and Sigtrygg and the Greenlanders followed close behind them.

Sigtrygg now found that his new wife was much affected by the death of her father and he remained apart from her for as long as she desired it, because of this.

Accordingly, Chinokwa now went with her mother and the other women into the woods for a number of days, after first going down to the river to cover their faces and bodies in the dark mud which was to be found along its banks. But afterwards, they returned to the village and Chinokwa to Sigtrygg's household.

Sigtrygg asked her, when she had returned in this fashion, if she were willing for things to go on as before or if she now preferred to take up her residence elsewhere, but Chinokwa replied that that would not be right since she belonged to Aselekah and only desired to make him as happy as she could. Sigtrygg said that he thought her presence alone enough to banish all concerns and, after this, these two seemed to get on even better than before.

Matters now proceeded in this fashion for some time, until the summer leaves began to thicken and the people of the village began to speak of laying in winter supplies and of moving their encampment to a more protected location as was their custom when the weather turned colder. The old woman, Tanakrit, now took over direction of these people and everyone came to her whenever any important decision was to be made. She appeared to have a great deal of wisdom in their eyes, which they continuously sought from her, and nothing of any importance could be decided in the village unless she was first consulted.

One day Sigtrygg told Chinokwa that he wanted to see the old woman, himself, to talk things over with her.

"What do you have in mind, husband?" Chinokwa asked him.

"Not much," Sigtrygg replied, "except that I have been too long apart from my own affairs, and there are matters which must be seen to."

"Can no one else do this for you?" she asked.

"That is not likely," he said, "for some things a man must do for himself."

Chinokwa had little to say to this but begged him to put off the matter. And so he did, for a time. But it so happened one day that he raised the matter again with her and this time he was more adamant then before, for he said he could not delay any longer concerning the question of his own affairs.

"Have I been such a poor wife to you then, husband?" the Skraeling woman asked.

"Not at all," he replied, "but I would be the poorer husband if I did not now look after those matters which you, as my wife, are entitled to a share in."

The end of it was that Sigtrygg went to seek out Tanakrit and, when he found the old woman, he told her that he thought the time had now come for him and his men to depart the Skraelings' country and return to their land claim on the coast. The old woman listened gravely to what Sigtrygg had to say and then sat silently in her place for a long while, making no answer. Sigtrygg became uneasy when he could get no reply from her and pressed for some response.

"What do you think is waiting for you there?" the old woman asked him after a time.

"My ship," said Sigtrygg, "and those houses which my grand-father built. And that land which he claimed there for his own."

"You have more here," the old woman replied, "for you are a

chief's son and husband to his daughter. And you have all the honor which goes with that."

Sigtrygg said he would not deny this but that he thought it unjust of them to restrain him from seeing to his own affairs, now that matters were settled in the Skraeling village, "for I have done all that was asked of me. Have I not defeated your enemies and won back your daughter as I swore to? And, indeed, I took her for my wife, besides, though this last was no hard task in itself. So now it seems to me that I should be free to go and attend to my own affairs, just as I have seen to yours."

Tanakrit said that he was certainly free to depart, if that was what he desired, "but what is to become of us if you do? Are you not Chinokwa's husband and the man who has been chosen to lead us, in the event our enemies return?"

Sigtrygg replied that he did not plan to be gone for long, "but only until I have seen to the proper upkeep and preparation of my property for winter, since it will do no good to allow my ship to go to rot. After that I shall return and take up our life here just as before."

"So you mean to return before we move house to our winter camp?" the Skraeling woman asked him.

"I do, indeed," replied Sigtrygg, and he meant this in all sincerity.

"Then whom do you propose to take with you?"

"Not many," Sigtrygg said, "but I will need all those crewmen of mine who came out here with me. And some of your own young men, to guide us, besides, for we are not so keen in the forest as you Skraelings are. And we propose to take our wives along, as well, if you are willing, for it is a long way off and they will ensure we return to you before winter, since they will never find peace with us unless it is among their own kinsmen."

Tanakrit said she thought this was certainly true and that Sigtrygg could have his way in this, so long as he gave his word to return by the time they struck their camp. Sigtrygg replied that he was more than willing to do that. So now he arose and left the old woman, going about to all his crewmen to tell them what he had in mind. It now turned out that these were not so keen, as before, to undertake the arduous trek back to the coast, for most of them had come to enjoy their life among the Skraelings. But Sigtrygg urged them up, promising that they should soon return and, when they learned they were to bring their wives along, the matter did not seem so burdensome as before.

Within days they had formed up their party and bundled what goods they meant to take along, meeting on the outskirts of the Skraeling village by that low river bank across which they had first sighted these people with whom they had now taken up living. The Greenlanders came with their wives in tow and a number of the younger Skraeling men joined them, and now all the other people of that settlement turned out to see them off. Tanakrit, herself, led those people who were to remain behind, standing in silence among them on the highest part of the land, above the river's bank, and she seemed to have a very odd look on her face.

Sigtrygg, when he saw this, asked Chinokwa what she thought this could mean but the younger woman only shrugged for she said there were very few people, of any age, who could fathom her mother's thoughts.

Now, when they were about to go into their boats, for they meant to make the first part of their journey along the river, a sudden commotion and splashing was heard and a young Skraeling man suddenly dashed out from behind some underbrush and into the water ahead of them. He stood still in the river, the current lapping at his waist. He was armed and painted all across his face and body and, all in all, he made a very fierce appearance.

Sigtrygg saw at once that this was W'tnalko, though he had seen very little of the fellow since that night when he and the other Greenlanders had celebrated their weddings. He now asked the man what the meaning of his display was and whether he thought to block their passage by it.

"Not at all," replied the Skraeling man, "but it seems to me you will have need of someone who has gone this way before, both to the coast and back again, and few others of my kind can say as much."

Sigtrygg said that he thought this was certainly true but that he had misgivings about bringing someone along who had shown himself to be no friend of his, before this.

"I will not deny that," W'tnalko replied, "but I am certainly a friend to some in this company, and would not desire to see any harm come to them. If you men lose your way or come upon those who mean to do you some harm, it will serve you better to have those about who are as concerned for the safety of your wives as you are yourselves."

Arnliot said: "I'm not certain his concern for our women will work out to our benefit, for this man led us astray once before; and there was no telling then how things were destined to turn out."

Sigtrygg asked W'tnalko if he didn't think the other Skraeling men who were coming along with them sufficient to help them find their way back to the coast, or to stand beside them in battle, should it come to that. "Or," he added, "do you think we Greenlanders are so unskilled in these matters as to be unable to fend for ourselves?"

"None of these," replied the Skraeling, "but one more pair of hands can do you no harm. Unless you are more afraid of me than of any of those others you may meet along the way."

Sigtrygg replied that there was very little in that country which would cause him concern, for he thought he had met the worst that Vinland had to offer and overcome it. "So have it your own way," he said, "if you must, and throw your lot in with ours. But keep a sharp eye out, and see you don't fall behind us, for it is often hardest to tell a friend from an enemy in the depths of the forest."

They now went into their boats, which were of that small river variety which the Skraelings, in that part of the world, made use of. One man sat at either end, with a paddle in his hand to guide the craft, while the others placed themselves in the middle with all their goods. Arnliot said he thought these rather flimsy vessels for men such as they were, but Sigtrygg replied that it usually made the most sense to travel about in a strange country in the same manner as the people who lived there, "for they will know the best means of arriving at their destination."

So now this company went down river and came, by turns, to each of the settlements where those Skraelings, who had made common cause with them, dwelt and they found a good welcome at every landing place. Those of their wives who had kinsmen in each settlement they came to now rejoiced to see their own kind once more, and these were warmly received in their turn.

The upshot was that the Greenlanders now spent a good deal of time in each of the villages which they came to, receiving many gifts from the residents there. Sigtrygg, for his part, gave gifts to their chief men, in return, and all the Greenlanders now took to adorning themselves in the Skraeling fashion, with feathers and shells. Vragi said he thought this rather senseless vanity but not surprising in such young men, and Arnliot replied that it made little difference what they took for themselves in any case, "for there would not be much among these people worth taking, if it were not for their women. Had I thought otherwise I would have certainly urged another attack on that Tulewat stronghold in the west. But as things now stand, there's no use shedding more blood where so little is to be gained."

Sigtrygg said he had pledged peace to the Tulewat king, in any event, "so it's no good talking about such things. And I have the feeling such an assault would not have been as easy as some would have it, for we had luck and surprise on our side the first time. But that is not likely to serve us again."

After this they left the Skraeling settlements along the river, and those boats by which they had proceeded from town to town, and struck inland into the thickly wooded regions which lay to the east, having visited all those Skraeling settlements with which they had made alliance. They now bundled their goods onto their backs and went on foot into the heavily overgrown forested coun-

try and Arnliot said it seemed rather strange that the tribute they
had gathered among the Skraelings should weigh so much and be
so bulky since it was of such little value, and now he urged them
to discard these goods in the forest.

"I don't see much reason to do that," was Sigtrygg's reply,
"but you, shipmate, are certainly free to lighten your shoulders, if
you find the going so rough. In which case you won't have much
to show for all your efforts when we have got back to Leif's houses."

"I shall have these women," Arnliot replied, "at the least. And
they are twice the goods which any other man of this crew has
carried back with him." But he did not lay his burden down,
despite such talk.

Now there is not much to tell of their journey back, for they
passed through the forest without further incident, though they
went by a different route than they had traveled before. But because of the stopovers along the river, it took them somewhat longer
than they had expected, although this forest trail was more direct
than the earlier one they had followed. But one day they heard the
sounds of the surf beating against the nearby shore. Thereupon
they dropped their bundles and ran, as one man, towards the sound
of the ocean and, when they came out of the trees, they saw that
sight which seemed sweetest to them of all the sights in the world
— the wide grey ocean, white-crested where its waves beat steadily
upon the land.

That night they camped beside the sea and it seemed to the
Greenlanders that they had never found a more beautiful place in
all the world than this one and, for a time, they forgot entirely
about those Skraelings who had accompanied them. They lit fires
and sang songs of home and urged their Vinland wives to lie down
with them upon the sand and, in this manner, they passed their
first night, since they had left Leif's houses, beside the sea.

On the following day they were wakened by the sun which
appeared above the ocean and shone full in their faces and every
man of them was heartened, for no dense growth of trees stood
above them to block the brightly lit sky. Vragi was already up and

about and now he asked the others how they had slept and if they thought they detected anything unusual.

Sigtrygg stood up and looked about him and the others rose as well.

"Not much," Olvir replied after a moment, "except that we seem to be much fewer than before."

The rest of the crew muttered agreement for it seemed that all the Skraeling men had stolen away in the night.

The wives of the Greenlanders now arose and they appeared to be quite as surprised as their husbands. Sigtrygg turned to Chinokwa and asked her what she thought had become of the others but she only shook her head for she said this was certainly an unexpected turn of events. Sigtrygg asked Vragi what he thought they should do.

"Not much," replied the old seaman, "for there's no telling what lies behind this. But I now think we should press on as quickly as possible and find our ship."

Everyone thought this made the most sense so they swiftly gathered up their things and began to walk up the coast, in the direction in which they thought the ship lay. They moved along briskly, for they did not see much sense in prolonging the matter further, until they came to a place where a headland jutted out and a number of small islands could be seen offshore. Then Sigtrygg went out onto the headland, with a number of the others but leaving the main part of the crew to look after the women. Arnliot followed close behind him , saying: "I don't think surprises of this sort are likely to bode well where these Vinlanders are concerned."

But Sigtrygg replied that it never did anyone much good to jump to conclusions before all the facts were known, "though it certainly won't hurt us to be on our guard, and see what lies before us from the vantage which this headland provides."

Not long after he said this, he suddenly came to a halt and those behind him stopped in their places, as well. Seated directly before them, upon a large boulder, a Skraeling man could be seen and he was looking out across the ocean to the north. He turned his head when they came up behind him and now they could see that this was one of those people who had accompanied them out of the forest. The man gestured them to be silent and then he slid down off the rock and came up with them.

"What is the meaning of this?" Sigtrygg asked him and the Skraeling replied that all would soon be made clear.

Rather suddenly a number of their other companions made their reappearance and these came round them in a tight circle. At last W'tnalko stood before them and he seemed to have a very strange look in his eyes. He said: "You Greenlanders have certainly slept better than most, for you have brought your women along to keep you warm in the night, when the winds blow unopposed off the great sea, but we Skraeling men have no such comfort to rely on and so must find our shelter where we can, among the nearby trees."

Sigtrygg said that, even so, this was no cause for them to have crept off so silently and without any word of warning, "as though you meant to abandon us."

But W'tnalko said that that was the very last thing on their minds, "though we made better use of our time than you others, who slept so soundly beside the waves until the red sun woke you, for we went on ahead to that place which you Greenlanders claim as your own."

"To what purpose?" Arnliot demanded.

"To see how matters lie there," W'tnalko said.

"And what did you find?" Vragi asked.

"Something," replied the Skraeling, "but it is better that you have a look for yourselves." He now told Sigtrygg to follow him up onto that large rock which had served as a perch for the first man they had seen.

Thereupon, Arnliot climbed up behind Sigtrygg and then Olvir followed them both. Then these men stood upon the rock and gazed into the distance where the Skraeling pointed. A narrow expanse of sea lay before them and, across it, a low-lying, wooded promontory.

"There," said W'tnalko, "lies that place where you have built your houses, on the other side of those trees, where the land faces the waters on its farther side, at the place where the waters rush outward and just as speedily return again. Only we have approached it from the seaward side now and not from the land."

"Then we shall have to backtrack and turn inland," Arnliot said, "for we will find it hard to come by it from here without seaworthy boats."

W'tnalko said that this was true enough but now he urged them to look more closely and tell him what they saw.

"Not much," said Arnliot, "for we are quite a ways off and will have to get a good deal closer if we are to scout out that country. Is that what you brought us up here for then, to show us how far we have gone astray from our proper road?"

"Not at all," replied the Skraeling, "though it is clear that a man like you will never do well on his own in this country."

Sigtrygg said: "There is certainly something out there worth seeing, for now I think I can make it out, too."

"Where?" asked Olvir, and Sigtrygg made a sweeping gesture with his hand toward the farther shore.

Vragi now came up beside them and asked Sigtrygg what he thought he saw.

"Smoke," he answered at last, "a thin line of smoke arising from the place where Leif's houses are sited."

"That is so," said W'tnalko, "and just what we saw ourselves."

"Then someone has settled there in our place," said Arnliot, "who will certainly need to be shown the door. Or do they think the kind of men who built such houses so easily dealt with that they need only move into our holdings to claim them?"

"First we had better reconnoitre," Olvir warned them, "to learn how many of them there are. And how strong. Then we can see about eviction proceedings."

"There's no use wasting time with that," replied Arnliot, "for there cannot be more of them than of those Tulewat whom we overcame when we walked right into that town of theirs, without any one's leave but our own. And then this axe of mine scattered our foes about our feet like so many felled trees."

"Until forced to flee with their arrows in our rears," Olvir said quickly, "and run for our very lives into the safety of the forest."

"Nor would we have had the luck to overcome them, even then," added Sigtrygg, "if our own companions had not been following close behind us into their country. In my opinion Olvir's words make the most sense, for we must first determine who these men are, and their strength, before hazarding an attack."

"You have certainly grown more timid, the more battles you have won," Arnliot now said.

But W'tnalko said there was no need to ask further about the strength of the strangers, "for while you men were sleeping in the arms of your women, my companions and I went much closer to them than this and counted heads. And now I can tell you that they are certainly more numerous than we are."

"Then this only shows the difference between you Skraelings and men of our kind," answered Arnliot, "for we are not daunted by numbers, even when the odds seem heaviest, as our victory against the Tulewat has now shown."

"Yet, you may find it harder going this time," W'tnalko said to him, "for the men who have occupied your encampment are likely to be much more formidable than those you fought against in the west."

"And why is that?" Arnliot inquired.

"Because, they are men like yourselves," said the Skraeling.

CHAPTER XXXI

A MEETING ON THE COAST

Vragi now said it was news indeed, "if other Norsemen have found their way to this country," and that they must go, at once, and have a closer look.

So now they left the headland and returned, by the route the Skraelings showed them, to the heavily wooded countryside. And then it did not seem very long before the land began to have a more familiar look to it. Sigtrygg said he thought they had now come to a place which was not very distant from Leif's houses and that "even those among us who are more at home on the open sea, or the icy floes of Greenland, should have little trouble finding his way to our land claim from here."

Then they went forward and soon they came to a place where the land seemed to rise up in front of them. Sigtrygg told the others to keep silent but he, himself, crept out over the rise, to a place where the trees fell away. And then he could see Leif's houses in the clearing below him. A great many people seemed to be moving about there too and, beyond, the large black hull of a ship sat beached and secured, not far up the shore. Vragi came up suddenly behind him and asked if he thought there was anything familiar about the sight which was now before them and Sigtrygg replied that there certainly was, "for that is the Norwegian's ship, which we left behind us when we fled from Eiriksfjord."

"You certainly have a good eye for such things," Vragi said, "and the makings of a real seaman, for most landlubbers will find it hard to tell one such vessel from another, however distinctively lined each ship might be."

"It's not hard to tell which ship that one is," said Sigtrygg, "for I had a good look at her when I sailed her deck, up from Herjolfsness to Eiriksfjord. And when we left her beached, thereafter, at Brattahlid."

"Then you will know the crew that has sailed her here, as well," Vragi said, "for the skipper is not readily parted from the ship."

Sigtrygg said: "I have no doubt that these are the same men who guested with my kinsmen in Eiriksfjord the summer we departed, for even then they had designs on this country."

He now went back to the others and told them what he had seen.

Arnliot laughed at the news and said he thought it strange the Norwegians had taken a whole year to find their courage and come out in pursuit of them, but the other members of Sigtrygg's crew seemed to think it a much more serious matter, considering the manner of their departure the summer before. Olvir asked what other men were there with the Norwegians, but Sigtrygg replied that they were too far away to determine that.

"Then we must go down and get a closer look," said Olvir and everyone agreed with him.

"There's no use skulking about here among these trees in any event," Sigtrygg added, "for these men are occupying our houses and acting, in all things, as if this property was theirs. And that is a matter which I am not prepared to tolerate."

"What do you propose to do then?" Vragi asked him.

"To go down and claim what is mine," Sigtrygg replied, "whatever the cost."

Vragi said that this was boldly spoken, "but some people might think it overly rash, since the Norwegians' ship is so much larger than our own and fully crewed, to the bargain, while ours has been somewhat undermanned from the start. Nor was the manner of our leave-taking, when last we parted company with these fellows, such as to inspire confidence in the reception we are likely to receive at their hands now."

"Still, they did not give chase when they had the opportunity to do so," Sigtrygg said.

Vragi agreed that this was true but added that there was no telling what their disposition towards them would now be, "for who can say what has passed among them in the year since our departure?"

Arnliot said that he thought they were wasting their words in such discussions "since it is better for us to discover ourselves to them now, than that they learn, first, of our presence and we lose the benefit of surprise in this affair — for we have seen how useful that can be when dealing with a foe."

"It is not yet clear," Olvir said, "that these men are our enemies, for they have given no sign of it."

"Nor will they," Arnliot said, "until they know that we have returned."

Sigtrygg said: "They are occupying the land claim which we have made here and that is sign enough of enmity to me."

But Olvir answered him, saying that "the houses were certainly empty and unlived in when these Norwegians found them and it's no crime to borrow a man's roof for shelter, if there's no one at home to gainsay it. In my opinion, it's how they behave afterwards which will best tell this tale."

"Then we must not give them the opportunity to behave badly, first," Arnliot said.

Vragi said there was truth to both sides of the argument and now he urged them to proceed as cautiously as possible. So Sigtrygg told the women to hide themselves in the woods "while we men go down and greet these fellows, to see what kind of reception is waiting for us there."

He then told his crew, and the Skraeling men who were with them, to carry what goods they could on their backs. "But," he added, "you are each to keep your arms handy, in case things should prove considerably warmer than Olvir, our shipmate, has now fore-seen."

The Norwegians appeared to be taken completely by surprise when Sigtrygg and his company emerged suddenly from the woods. They ran all about, calling to their fellows, when they saw these strangers walking briskly down the sloping land towards them, and those who were in the houses came out at a rush. There was a great deal of confusion then and men went for their arms.

But the Norwegian skipper quickly appeared in the midst of his crew and, when he saw the nature of their visitors, he told them to lay their weapons aside, and this they now did. Then he went up to where Sigtrygg stood, with his following, and gave him a fair greeting.

"This is more than we looked for from you, Greenlander," he said when they met. And now he looked over Sigtrygg's compan-ions, noting the odd manner in which the crewmen of the Gull were dressed and the Skraelings who were in their company. He grinned and said he thought there were certainly more of them than there had been before, "though there are fewer here of those who sailed out with you last summer from Greenland."

Sigtrygg replied that he should not find this too surprising, "for we have been to the country of these Skraelings and won much renown for ourselves there."

Now all the Norwegians clustered around them and gazed with great curiosity at these men who had come so suddenly upon them from out of the woods. Sigtrygg looked about from man to man and now he thought he saw among them certain familiar faces and Osvif, the skipper of the Norwegian ship, laughed and said it was just as he thought, "for your kinsmen are certainly among our number. Or did you think you were the only man in Brattahlid to know the way to Leif Eiriksson's landfall in the west?"

"I'm not sure about that," Sigtrygg replied, "although I am certain that I'm the only one with a rightful claim to this place. And now I want to know the purpose of your journey here and why you have occupied these houses just as if they were your own though they have been lawfully pledged to me?"

"That's easy to tell," Osvif said, "for they were unoccupied when we arrived here and no one barred our way to them. As for our journey, the reason is clear enough, for this is a rich country and a ship, well-stocked with Vinland goods, will bring a good price in any of the northern lands, as most men know. Besides, some people think it worthwhile sailing to a new land, if only a few have been out there before them, and I am no different from these."

It now fell out that certain men in that crew, who were from Eiriksfjord, came forward and it was quickly seen that Thord Thorkelsson and his brother Thorstein were foremost among them. Beside them were several farmers' sons from that district where Thorkel Leifsson and his brothers held sway and these now ranged themselves protectively around the Thorkelssons. When Arnliot saw this he laughed and said it wasn't surprising that the men of Eiriksfjord went about in such numbers, since they had formerly fared so poorly when they had matched themselves against their betters "out on the fjord beneath Brattahlid."

But Thord replied that there would have been little cause for mirth that day, "if the wind hadn't come up and blown you men out to sea, denying us the chance to close with you and show you how we Eiriksfjorders repay boat-thieves in our district."

"You can't steal what is already yours," Vragi now said to him. And Arnliot added that it made little difference, in any event, since "a man must be strong enough to hold what he claims, and you men of Eiriksfjord have shown yourselves incapable of that."

Thord did not take this well and answered briskly saying "we shall see who is capable of holding what." And now it seemed that the two sides would come to blows. But Sigtrygg placed a restraining hand on Arnliot's arm and urged him to hold his peace for the while. As he did this, two other men pushed through the Norwegian crew. One had a thin face and close-cropped chestnut colored hair, and on his mouth a tight-lipped smile, and he came right up to Sigtrygg and offered his hand to him. Beside him was a larger man, very grim looking, his right arm dangling loosely from his shoulder which was rather stiffly held, and he followed the first man, though it was plain he had little liking for this. Sigtrygg recognized both men at once.

The man with the close-cropped hair gave Sigtrygg a good welcome and Sigtrygg returned this greeting and took his hand warmly and now these two embraced. The man said: "That was good sailing which you showed us up in Eiriksfjord, for a fellow who had spent his days, before that, on the ice floes with the bears," and Sigtrygg replied that he had not thought to get clear of the other's ship "before hard blows were struck, but for the good luck which blew for us that day, down off the ice."

"Good luck and good casting," replied the other man, "or had you never thrown a spear before that?"

"He has certainly thrown his share," replied the larger man who stood beside them, nursing his crippled arm, "and I am the proof of it."

Sigtrygg turned to him and said: "Still, it is better to see you alive than dead, kinsman Lambi, for, in truth, I had thought you lost to us, after I saw you go into the sea. But now I am relieved to know that matters turned out otherwise and that the blood of my relations is no longer on my hands. For that, at the least, I will give you a good welcome, and offer you the hospitality of this country. And so it will be for all of you," he added, turning now to Osvif and the others, "for it is a good day when bloody deeds are undone and those we thought dead walk again on the earth."

The thin faced man, who was none other than Girstein Eiriksson, now said: "That is well-spoken kinsman, for we have sailed a long way to find this place and it would be ill-natured of you to deny us a welcome."

"Ill-natured or no," replied Thord Thorkelsson, who had stood by, all this while, in uneasy silence, "there's no use seeking that which is not within this man's power to give, for the question of the land claim is still unsettled. Or did we all not see, with our own eyes, how this man stole that vessel and goods which our fathers rightfully had claim to?"

"I'm not sure about that," said Girstein, "for it seems to me that oaths were sworn and pledges exchanged concerning this country and the means by which to come to it."

"Yet the ship was not yet given," said Thord, "nor did this man have the means to sail her, in any event, so that the taking of that vessel, despite my father's words, must be accounted theft and the blood spilled in the process man-slaughter. And these things must now be paid for."

Vragi said: "Yet this claim of yours, friend Thord, hinges alone on the lack of means but all men in your father's hall clearly heard that eighteen men at the oars were as good as twenty, in the Leifssons' opinion, and we sailed out of Eiriksfjord with no fewer than that number. In which case, there was no reason to withhold the ship and no theft to be claimed."

"But you came by your number only after the theft was committed and after an unlawful assault upon those persons who rightfully pursued you," said Thord, "and so this is no valid defense against those claims which I have now laid against you."

There was now general agreement among the Norwegians that there were claims outstanding and settlements to be made, for, at the very least, Sigtrygg had brazenly stolen his ship from that place where the Leifssons had placed it, and no man could deny the killings and assaults which had resulted from that. But, as to where blame was to be laid, there was less consensus, for some felt that Sigtrygg's hand had been forced while others that he should have waited to bring the matter to law, either before the Eiriksfjord assembly, as his uncles had urged, or by the promised duel, which he, himself, had desired. And so they went back and forth on this matter until, at length, Vragi stepped forward again and said there was no use debating the finer points of the law where this question was concerned, "for we are a long way from any assembly of men where such matters may be resolved. In which case, my advice is that we lay this issue to rest for the while — or until such time as the legal case on both sides may be presented."

But Thord cried out that there was no use hoping for that "since this question has already been considered, before we set sail, and provisions have been made in the matter."

Sigtrygg asked Girstein what this meant and his kinsman replied that Thord was speaking truthfully, if rather thoughtlessly, considering the situation which they had now found, "for our uncle, Thorkel Leifsson, assigned all matters in this case to those of us who are tied to him by blood, before we sailed across the western ocean, in the event we should find you in this country. And then we were to prosecute our cause as fully as we were able, although, in truth, I did not attach much importance to it at the time, for I thought the sailing directions we had so vague that it were unlikely we would fall in with you here. But our ship's skipper has certainly proved a better navigator than any of us could have hoped since he brought us so unerringly to your own landing place."

Vragi said: "It's not difficult to follow the directions of those who have sailed before you, if they were as able on the high seas as your kinsman, Leif Eiriksson. But I don't see how you mean to pursue this legal case of yours in such a wild country as this is for there is no court in this place to hear your claims."

"We are certainly prepared for that, too," said Thord, "for we kinsmen have assigned jurisdiction in the matter to King Harald of Norway, since we are so far from the laws and courts of Greenland here, and to King Harald's representative in this country, Osvif Thorleiksson, who is fully authorized to review this matter and give judgement concerning it, in the king's name. And as to our claims, know that we have each taken over a portion of the case, as befits a proper proceeding of this type."

Vragi asked him what he had in mind and Thord replied rather pompously that all would presently be made clear "for we have not been idle in this matter as you ship-thieves had hoped. Concerning the theft of the boat, itself, and all the goods which were housed with it and those men who were slain in its pursuit, no less a personage than our kinsman Girstein Eiriksson has taken it on himself, under oath, to prosecute this case. And he has the most reason to pursue the matter since you men fled from him in Eiriksfjord."

Sigtrygg now asked if this were true and Girstein said that it was.

"And as to that blow which was struck, against all ties of kinship and good will, upon our cousin, Lambi Gunnarsson," Thord continued, "there is no one here better suited than Lambi, himself, to press the claim. And Lambi has sworn to do this, for your spear cast, kinsman Sigtrygg, has deprived him of the use of one limb, leaving him no better than half the man he was."

At these words Lambi looked away and would not meet Sigtrygg's eye, though his jaw was firmly set. Sigtrygg turned to Thord and said: "You have certainly thought these matters out with great care, kinsman. But what role do you purpose for yourself in this matter since you are the eldest son of my uncle Thorkel, who is, for his part, that man who claims Leif Eiriksson's chieftaincy for his own — though there are some who would question his rights even to that?"

"There's no need to ask about my role in this matter," Thord replied, "for I have taken the hardest claim of all upon myself. And that is the question of Arnliot Torfisson, who some call Keelfoot, who pillaged the countryside in Ketilsfjord before coming up to join his fellow brigands in our district, where he conspired with you to steal our property from beneath the very noses of those who gave you guesting in Brattahlid."

"What nonsense is this?" Sigtrygg demanded and Arnliot grasped his axe tightly by its neck, where the shaft joined the base of the broad, two-headed blade.

"No less than the truth," replied Thord, "for Grimkel Vesteinsson, who is the chieftain in Ketilsfjord, learned of the predations of this man after he returned to his own part of the country and had him declared an outlaw for his thefts there. And then he turned the case over to me, should I fall in with the fellow, as I now have. And the proof of the matter is that very axe which Keelfoot carries, for he stole that, too, from off the wall of his own father's house before setting out to join his companions in theft. It was with that very weapon that he broke open the larders of half a dozen farmers in the Ketilsfjord district and drove them back again when they sought to reclaim their own."

Sigtrygg turned to Arnliot and asked if there was any truth to these accusations and the big Ketilsfjordman replied that there was indeed, if a man was to be blamed for taking back what was rightfully his, "for that man they call a chieftain in Ketilsfjord wrongfully looted my father of all that he owned and hounded me, thereafter, in my own district, even after a settlement had been brought about between us. I certainly do not count it a crime," he added, "to have recovered my due from those men who supported farmer Grimkel, and who prospered so unjustly from it afterwards. And as for this axe, what matter if I took it with my kinsman's leave or otherwise since that is a matter between us alone?"

Sigtrygg said that this was not what he'd had in mind when he'd urged Arnliot to make his way as quietly as he could up to Eiriksfjord, but that there was no use bewailing what was already done, "for we shall never be able to settle things as they now stand, till we have returned to Greenland and had our say. Nor do I intend to grant judgement in this matter to King Harald's man — or to any other."

But Thord said: "That is not for you to decide, kinsman, since those of us who make this claim have already acknowledged the king's authority in this country. And we are prepared to enforce it."

Vragi said: "These hounds are relentless, though they do not yet know the manner of the beast they have brought to bay here."

"I do not grant King Harald or any other man overlordship in this country," Sigtrygg said when he had heard his kinsman's words "for, if the truth be known, there is a king here already, and he is now standing before you."

"Are you claiming the kingship for yourself, then, Greenlander?"

Osvif the Norwegian asked him.

"By right of inheritance, I am," answered Sigtrygg, "for ownership in this country has been pledged me by my uncles. And paid for, to boot, with my own property back in Greenland. And by right of battle I claim it, as well, for I led these Skraelings whom you see before you, and a host of their kinsmen, in war against that king who, before now, held sway in this land. And then I defeated him and gave him his life, on condition he relinquish all his claims in my favor, which he has now done. As for those Skraelings who followed me into that battle, they are pledged to uphold my rights in this matter as will soon be seen. Moreover, I am here while Harald is elsewhere — over the wide the sea."

"These Skraelings of yours certainly don't look very formidable, whatever else may be said of them," Thord now pronounced and the Norwegians who were standing about all laughed at this for they thought it very funny.

"Yet, there are a great many more of these people than you now see before you," answered Sigtrygg, "all well-schooled in the arts of woodcraft and war, as these things are practiced in this country. And they are not far off."

"There's no telling how close or far such men may be," Osvif now put in, "but one thing is true enough and that is that we Norwegians are the more numerous and better armed of the two sides who have now met in this place. Still, it would be an unhappy matter if we were to come to blows now."

"It would be the least happy for those closest to hand," said Arnliot grimly and he raised his war axe to his shoulder.

Thord told his brother and the other Eiriksfjordmen to close about him and unsheathe their swords at once, for he had his eye on the keen edge of that axe which Arnliot now held aloft, where it stood gleaming brightly above him in the morning sun. Then the two sides began to draw forth their weapons amidst angry words and it seemed that the peace was again to be broken. But Girstein stepped up to the others and said that, in his opinion, it was not for bloodshed that their fathers had sent them out with the Norwegians to Vinland, but to claim a good cargo to carry back with them to Greenland's fjords. And Osvif added that there was certainly enough wealth in that country for all without any one of them striking another in anger.

"Yet the claim to these houses has still to be settled," Thord protested, for he was determined to give the matter no rest. "And who is to have the most say in this place, for against our kinsman's claim of a pledged exchange of lands must be laid these charges of theft, and the killings and injuries which arose from them."

Now another voice could be heard from the rear of the Norwegian party and the men of that crew stood aside at once and made a path in their midst so that this speaker could come forward. Then the voice was heard again, saying that "this only proves the old saying, that men make the poorest peacemakers," and it could then be readily seen that the speaker was a woman, for her long red hair streamed down the sides of her white cheeks as she walked past the Norwegian sailors and right up to the place where Sigtrygg stood. Then her eyes fastened on his and the grim set of her lips relaxed and she smiled in greeting saying, "it is no less than I had expected of you, kinsman, that you would dig your heels in even harder, once you had come to your land claim, than when you were seeking it. Still," she went on, "you would be better served, in my opinion, to make a place for these others now that they have followed you here, since it's unlikely you can hold onto all that you have gained if blows are exchanged now."

Sigtrygg recognized Thjodhild at once and now he looked on her, as though seeing her for the first time. His mouth softened into a smile and he took her hands in his and there was a long silence between them. Behind Thjodhild the little serving maid, Fridgerd, came up and she seemed rather uneasy in the midst of the Norwegian crew, placing herself close under the shadow of Thjodhild, as though seeking safety there. Then the serving girl looked all about her until her eyes alighted on Arnliot who was nearby, his axe still raised in anger above his head, and she laughed at the sight of him, poised in this manner as though he would strike at the very air before him. Then the big man lowered his weapon and smiled back rather sheepishly, for he seemed to think it ludicrous that she should see him standing thus and all that gathering began to laugh at the sight of Arnliot so unmanned and everyone put aside their weapons and now it seemed that matters had taken a different turn.

At length Sigtrygg turned to Osvif and said: "I did not think you would have brought women with you on such a hard journey as this is." But Osvif replied that the matter had not been entirely of his choosing, since it was the Leifssons' decision concerning who, among their kin, was to sail out with him, "and they alone knew the guide posts which must be followed if we would make Leif's landfall."

"You should not be too surprised at this turn of events, in any case, kinsman," Thjodhild now said to Sigtrygg as well, "for each of your uncles had it within his power to choose those whom he would send to look after his interests. And my brother, Lambi, certainly had reason to support my plea, for he finds it harder now to see to his own affairs than before."

"Still," said Sigtrygg, "it is no light thing to make that voyage which you have now made and this is a harsh country for women of our kind. I would certainly have opposed you in this, had I known your mind in the matter."

"Then it's well that you did not," said Thjodhild, "for a man like you is not used to being thwarted, and I would not willingly have been the cause of it. Still, I'd have come, despite all."

Vragi said: "These are certainly not the first women to sail out to this country — nor the first of your kinswomen." But Sigtrygg said that made little difference to him, "for the seas are a hazardous pathway for such as these to travel and this Norwegian has not done well to ferry them here with him."

"I don't think you can fault me for that, friend Sigtrygg," Osvif replied, "for your kinswoman has proved as handy a sailor as any man who ever shipped with me, and that is testimony to the hardiness of your Greenland women, who are as sturdy at the sail as at the butter churn, and fairer to watch than our homegrown ladies, in either place."

Sigtrygg now said that he thought matters had come to such a pass that an arrangement must be made between the two sides, "lest we fall to squabbling again, amongst ourselves, and needless blood is shed."

"I think that is wisely spoke," said Osvif, "but what do you propose?"

"That we share out these houses, for the while," Sigtrygg replied, "until those claims which have been raised here can be laid to rest."

But Thord now spoke up angrily and said he was not willing to do that since they were all sworn to pursue those matters which the Leifssons had raised against Sigtrygg.

"Is that how it is to be then?" Sigtrygg asked and Osvif and Girstein replied that that was, indeed, how things must go, "unless we are all to be parties to a settlement with you. And then even your cousin Thord must willingly join in."

"There's little hope of peace, in that case," Vragi said upon hearing this, "for few men are as single-minded, or as short-sighted, as Thord is. And in that he is not much different from Thorkel, his father."

Thord said: "You men can have it your own way but I mean to keep to that oath which I swore when I undertook the case which Grimkel Vesteinsson assigned to me against his outlaw, Arnliot Torfisson," and now he recited his claims against Arnliot and named witnesses to each of the parts which he asserted and to the passing of the case, from Grimkel Vesteinsson's hands into his own, and he called upon Osvif Thorleiksson, as King Harald's agent, to hear the case and find in his favor, according to the kings's laws.

When he was done there was silence for awhile and then those men who were named as witnesses, both Norwegians and Eiriksfjordmen who had sailed out there with them, stepped up, in the order in which they had been called, and took oaths of their own as to the claims asserted by Thord. Osvif said he thought that matters were proceeding in precisely the wrong fashion, considering the circumstances they now found themselves in but, since he was the king's agent, he could not disregard the suits which were now being raised and so he said that he would hear the case in the king's name.

Then Lambi Gunnarsson stepped forward and named his witnesses as well, and charged Sigtrygg with an unlawful assault upon his person with intent to kill, while in flight from those who were lawfully seeking the return of their stolen property. When he had finished he asked Osvif if he were willing to hear his case, as well, and Osvif replied that he would. "Then," said Lambi, "I think it likely that justice will be done."

Now all men turned to Girstein and he said that matters had certainly gone much farther than wise men could have hoped, "but I am sworn, no less than the others, and I do not intend to be any more remiss in my duties than they have been in theirs." And, so saying, he looked at Sigtrygg and seemed to smile slightly, and then he also recited his charges, to wit that Sigtrygg and his companions had wilfully and in the middle of the night slipped into a boat house which the Leifssons maintained near Brattahlid and stolen that ship with which they had later fled out of Eiriksfjord. And then he named all those who had been present at the theft, among Sigtrygg's crew, and named his witnesses to those claims which he had made.

When Girstein finished, Thord said that things had gone just as he had expected and that the cases were now before the proper authority and that justice therefore would surely be done. He then turned, for the first time, to Olvir and the others who had been serving men at Brattahlid and said they were now free to return to their rightful places among the men of Eiriksfjord "and we will see you safely home, when all these matters have been put to rest, so you can take up your duties there as before."

But Olvir answered that he and his companions preferred to remain where they were for the time being, "since we are members of this crew, no less than these others."

"Have it your own way," said Thord, "but things are not likely to get any better for you, the longer you are with these outlaws."

Osvif now asked Sigtrygg if he, himself, had anything to say in the matter but Sigtrygg offered nothing in his own defense.

Now when she saw how Sigtrygg stood by in silence, Thjodhild herself spoke up, saying that she thought the Norwegian skipper could only judge the matter fairly if he took into consideration the nature of her kinsman's claim, since she thought that Sigtrygg had merely acted to safeguard his interests "for events surely outran even the wisest man's reason, that day out on the fjord."

Osvif replied that he would certainly take her words into account and then he turned to Vragi and asked him if he too had something to offer in Sigtrygg's defense, "for you are also a party to this matter and not entirely guiltless, if there is blame to be laid."

"I have little enough to add to what has already been said," Vragi replied, "except that you are to bear in mind two things. And the first is that this case, which has now been placed before us, stems from the theft of a boat whose ownership, most people would agree, has not been clearly established — although there are those of us who think our claim the better one. As for the second, you have already been warned, and that is that neither you nor your king have authority to give judgements in this country."

Now, when he had said these words there was a stir in that gathering and everyone of the Norwegians seemed to look out beyond the cluster of people around Sigtrygg and toward the line of trees which skirted the clearing in which they were standing. Then Sigtrygg and his crewmen turned about, as well, in the direction in which the Norwegians were looking. And now they could see a number of other people emerging from the woods and coming down towards them. These were the twelve Skraeling women who had been left behind, in the cover of the dense woods. They had become uncertain at the length of time which Sigtrygg and his band had spent with these strangers until, at last, seeing no signs of violence or conflict from their distant vantage point and impatient to rejoin the men, they had prevailed upon Chinokwa to lead them down to the others. This she now did, walking confidently at their head until she came up to where Sigtrygg was standing.

Osvif, when he saw this, said: "It seems you did not mislead us concerning the matter of these others who were close by, Greenlander, though you said nothing to us of women. Or are these the fierce foemen you promised us?"

"As with any people, there are both women and men among these Skraelings," Sigtrygg answered him, "so it did not seem necessary to warn you of the presence of both. But now that you have seen them with your own eyes, you may not find it so hard to believe that there are still others about; and that they call me their king."

Thjodhild said: "If you are their king then who is this?" And she looked hard at Chinokwa who had placed herself behind Sigtrygg and taken hold of that satchel, which he bore across his back, in a manner which suggested that she thought she had a share in those goods he carried.

"She is called Chinokwa," Sigtrygg said in a very low voice. "And she is the high-born daughter of a great chieftain in this country and much revered among her kind. And she is also my wife."

"How long have you been with this woman, then, kinsman?" Thjodhild asked.

"Not long," Sigtrygg replied, but he averted his eyes from hers, when he said this, in a manner which seemed to all those present rather unusual for him. And Thjodhild, too, looked away.

"Well, it seems that it did not take you long to take to these Skraelings and their ways," said Thord grandly, "but that was only to be expected of a man of your uncertain bloodlines. Still, I am a little less sure what excuses these other fellows, who are with you, can make."

"There are no excuses to be made, kinsman Thord," said Sigtrygg, "for we have done in this country what seemed right to us, and that is what was to be expected, since we have possession of

Leif's holdings here and all these lands, as far as the eye can see...and further, still, for this country is mine by right of conquest. And now you men have placed yourselves in my hands, as guests, and I am minded to treat you in that fashion, though you meted out somewhat harsher treatment to me when I spent time among you in Eiriksfjord."

Osvif then asked Sigtrygg how he wanted to arrange things, since matters had taken such a hard turn and a court of judgements was now to be held, "though I will need some time to prepare for it."

"No different than before," was Sigtrygg's reply for he was eager to keep the peace between them if he could. "These matters will be sorted out, one way or the other, however we dispose ourselves now. But your company is more numerous than mine so you are to have half the houses for your own use, if you have need of them, while we will keep the others for ourselves since we were first here and the right of ownership is with me."

CHAPTER XXXII

OF OATHS AND CLAIMS

There was a man in the Norwegian crew at that time named Asgaut Asgautsson who was called Gaut for short, and by some Gaut the Swordsman, for his great skill with that weapon. He was a large, back-country Swede who had been with King Harald east-a-ways in Russia and, still later, with the king when Harald captained the Varangian Guard for the Byzantine Emperor during the long years of his exile. This man Gaut had come west in the king's company when Harald returned to claim a share in the Norwegian crown, which was then held by his nephew King Magnus. Now Magnus did not live long after Harald's return and Harald succeeded him and became sole ruler of Norway. Yet Harald was a hard man and soon proved a harder king and it fell out, not long afterwards, that this Gaut the Swordsman was forced to leave the king's court, because of a killing, despite their years of comradeship in the east. So he sought a berth on Osvif Thorleiksson's ship before it sailed west from Trondheim.

Now this Swede was not much of a talker and did not readily form friendships with others for he counted few men his equal. But he took to Girstein Eiriksson as soon as he met him, thinking him a promising man. Accordingly, these two became fast friends during the long voyage out to Greenland and later during their stay over winter at the Leifssons' holdings in Brattahlid.

The Swede Gaut had a number of fine swords in his possession of which he was inordinately proud, and he spent all his free time while at Brattahlid cleaning and sharpening these and, when he could, practicing his swordstrokes. Girstein admired the man's weapons skills and commended him for this to his kinsmen. And these, for their part, thought Gaut the finest swordsman they had ever seen although, if truth were told, they were none of them well-travelled enough to have seen many swordsman before this. The Swede had unusually long limbs and big hands and he held even the largest of those blades which he owned so lightly in his hands that it seemed to the Leifssons, when they watched him raise one of his swords overhead, that three blades flew about, where one alone ought to have been. He was also the sort of man who could fight equally well with a sword in either hand, or in both at once, favoring neither his right side nor his left.

The Thorkelssons soon saw how this man, Gaut, had become such a close companion of their kinsman Girstein. Accordingly, they did everything they could to ingratiate themselves with him as well. They made certain that he had whatever he could ask for during his stay at Brattahlid and afterwards, when they had all come out together to Vinland, they were even more solicitous of him than before. Thord, especially, made it a point to ensure that Gaut always got first choice in everything and, after Sigtrygg's return, he and his brother kept even closer to Girstein and the Swede, "for," he said, "we kinsmen must stand by one another, whatever anyone else says in this country."

Girstein told him to have it his own way and now it seemed that the Thorkelssons and their following became inseparable from Girstein and Gaut, though the Swede paid very little attention to them, preferring to spend his time seeing to his weapons, as before. But Thord thought Gaut a very formidable man and so he came and sat beside him as he worked on his blades that first day after Sigtrygg had reappeared and tried to speak with him. The Swede usually showed very little interest in what other people had to say and things were no different this time. Still, Thord asked him how he thought matters were now likely to go for them, since their claims were to be placed in the hands of Osvif Thorleiksson.

Gaut replied that he had little to say about that, for matters of law did not much concern him, "though this case could certainly have been handled more speedily, that day out on the fjord or even before, if you kinsmen had had the heart for it."

"But that is precisely the reason I have come to you," said Thord, "for it seems to me that events may not always go as a man predicts, though the law is in his favor, since even the best of courts are made by men, and men may be swayed."

"Do you think our skipper unlikely to render a fair verdict, then?" asked Gaut. "Or that he will make a separate settlement with these people?"

"Not at all," replied Thord, "but, in my opinion, he is not as firm in his conviction as to the rightness of our case as he ought to be. And he may be swayed by false arguments, or by those feelings which will often intrude upon a man's reason, for it seems to me he has some admiration for this outlaw, who is our adversary here."

Gaut said that men will often think highly of those who take big risks and are successful despite the odds, "and this kinsman of yours has certainly shown himself to be that sort."

"Then," said Thord, "you won't think it strange if I ask your opinion of our case."

"I have nothing to say about that," replied Gaut, "for my concern is first of all with this sword which I have in my hands and secondly with coming safely home again to Norway when this voyage is behind us. As for these petty squabbles which beset you kinsmen, there is little enough to trouble those of us who are here and yet have no part in them."

"Still you are in our camp, for the sake of your friendship with our kinsman, Girstein Eiriksson, and that is not to be denied," said Thord. "And he will press his case as strongly as we others."

"That is still to be seen," replied Gaut.

But Thord said: "He will lose as much as the rest of us, both of honor and wealth, should the ruling go against him. Yet, in my opinion, he is a proud man and not one to let such matters lie."

"That may well be," said Gaut, "but what do you want from me?"

"Your support," replied Thord, "should it come to blows, for one way or the other I am determined to have my way in this. And it is not unlikely there will be a share in the winnings for those who cast their lots with us."

"I am not in the habit of selling my sword for gain," said Gaut but Thord replied that he had certainly not held to such scruples when he had served with King Harald in the employ of the Byzantines, "or afterwards, when you used your sword arm to win a pouch of silver, though it cost you the king's favor."

Gaut said there was a great deal of difference between serving kings and "little men who fancy some grievance over a land claim, which none can hope to hold, in any event — for this country is too large, and too far away from all other parts of the world, for that." Still, he promised to consider Thord's words and then he left off speaking and turned his attentions again to that weapon which he held in his hands. After this Thord arose, seeing how things were, and left the man to himself.

Osvif Thorleiksson soon gave out that he would hold the court in three days' time, for he said he needed at least that many days to familiarize himself with the parts of the law which might apply to those cases which were to be presented before him and that it was only right that Greenland law should be used, if this could be managed, since the matter had arisen in that country and chiefly concerned Greenland men. Now in those days the laws of Greenland were not so different from those of Iceland, from which they had derived, save that in Iceland all duelling had, by then, been banned, from the time that Gunnlaug Wormtongue had fought against Skald-Hrafn Onundarsson on an island in the Oxara River for the affections of Helga the Fair. Accordingly, Osvif now shut himself away from others for the three days he required, and invited into his presence only those with some knowledge of Greenlandic or Icelandic law and then he spoke with them at some length.

In the meantime, the Thorkelssons set themselves up in the

midst of the settlement and, together with those they counted their allies, began to behave in a very lordly manner toward Sigtrygg's companions. They blocked their way when any of these people wanted to pass by and were especially harsh toward the Skraelings who were with them. This came to Sigtrygg's ears on the very first night after they had returned and he became angry, for he said that, in his opinion, his kinsmen were showing very little appreciation for the hospitality he had granted them.

Arnliot said he would teach them better manners, "if you desire it, for these people have certainly not learned very much from their experiences with us out on the fjord."

But Sigtrygg replied that they should let it lie for the while, "since matters are to be put to the test, soon enough, and then we shall see which way things are likely to go."

"I'm not certain they will go as well for us as they should," Arnliot now said, "if we are to depend on this Norwegian's interpretation of the law. In my opinion, he has no standing here and it is a mistake to sit quietly in this place as though he did. For, if he finds against us, we will be hard-pressed to dismiss his judgement, since then it will look to others as though we had rejected a lawful decision."

"There's no need to worry about that," said Sigtrygg, "for I have no intention of allowing him to hold an assembly of law here...or in any other part of this country."

But Vragi now intervened, saying "I'm not so certain that that is the wisest course, shipmate."

"And why not," asked Sigtrygg, "since these men are no closer to their homes here than we are to ours, and can have no stronger claim of rule, for that? And it remains to be seen if we are to be overborne by sheer numbers alone, for others have tried this, it seems to me, and with no great success."

"Yet that was a different matter than this now is," said Vragi. "And I'm not certain the legal aspects of our case will work to our disadvantage here."

Olvir asked what he had in mind and Vragi replied: "Only

this, that Girstein Eiriksson, our skipper's kinsman, is no fool and yet I think he presses a case which is fatally flawed. And that, seemingly, with great willingness, in service of the oath he swore before his uncles when he departed Greenland."

"And the claim of this Lambi Gunnarsson can be no stronger," Thorolf the Icelander now added, leaping up, "for, as every man knows, one assault will cancel out another and his was the first spear cast, in any event, as my own scarred leg will show. And besides, our skipper struck him with his own weapon, and that should be evidence enough to any man as to who made the first assault."

But Asmund, his companion, said: "There's no use hoping for such a happy outcome as that, shipmate, for it is the weakest of those defenses which we may now put forth. Or were you not named outlaw, along with the rest of us, for the theft of that ship we sailed out to this country? In my opinion, most people would agree that an outlaw has few rights against those who strike at him in lawful pursuit."

"All true," Vragi now said, "but it is Girstein who is pressing the claim of outlawry for ship-theft, and that is a different matter."

"How so?" asked Sigtrygg.

"Because," said Vragi, "he must name the culprits before witnesses, as he has now done. But it is a flaw in the proceedings to leave out any, if you know them; and even more so for a man, who is equally guilty with those named, to bring charges against the others. For that is how Mord Valgardsson discredited the case against the Njalssons of Bergthorsknoll, when they slew their foster brother, Hoskuld Hvitaness-Priest, back in Iceland, since Mord was party with them to that killing, although secretly. And yet it was he who brought the charges against them."

"And Girstein, my kinsman, helped us with the ship-theft?" Sigtrygg said.

"As did Thjodhild, which Girstein knows well," said Vragi, "though he did not name her. So now it seems to me that, by taking this claim on himself, instead of leaving it to one of your other kinsmen, this man has undercut the very charges against you which your uncles sought to lodge. Yet he is a clever man and must have known we would see through this and raise the matter in any proceeding of law, if it came to that. In which case, he must know the claim will now be undone and that your kinsman Lambi's claim must, therefore, also be discredited. If we were not outlaws, and this can no longer be established, then your throw against him was no crime, since his was the first assault. At the very least, as Thorolf has now said, the two throws will cancel each other out."

Sigtrygg said: "In my opinion, matters have certainly taken a better turn than I had hoped, for if what you say is true there is no reason to think these men will be able to disqualify my claim to this country by these actions which they have now raised."

"Yet there is still one matter which is unresolved," said Vragi, "and I am not entirely sure how to handle it."

"Which one is that?" Sigtrygg asked him.

"Those charges which have been brought against our ship-mate, Arnliot Torfisson, and his companions, for these have now been admitted to, by Arnliot himself, before all men. And we have no counter-claim to throw against that."

"There's no reason to be concerned," said Arnliot quickly, on hearing this, "for it's unlikely they will be able to enforce any rulings against me in this country. And I will deal with these matters, if I must, when we return to Greenland. What is between me and this Grimkel Vesteinsson has long demanded a final settlement, in any event."

"Still, the case belongs to Thord Thorkelsson now," answered Vragi, "and he is unlikely to let the matter lie until you both have found your way back to Greenland."

"Then let him churn the waters to his own undoing here," Arnliot said, "for I have no intention of knuckling under to him; or to any other in that company."

Sigtrygg asked Vragi what he thought they ought to do now and Vragi said: "It is my advice that you seek a settlement with your kinsmen in all three of these matters, for we have the stronger case in two of the suits, while they have the advantage in the third. And a win before the law may not count for much in this distant country, in any case, where they will have grudges to nurse against us...and are more numerous than we are, to boot."

"What manner of settlement do you advise, then?" Sigtrygg asked.

"I'm not sure about that," Vragi admitted, "for it's not entirely clear what they will be seeking. Still, if I am any judge of men, they will want a share in this country, and that will be the hardest thing for you to grant them."

"I certainly have no intention of inviting my kinsmen to share in these houses, or the land claim which attaches to them," Sigtrygg said. "But I will not oppose their settling elsewhere, if they desire it."

"Nor could you," Vragi laughed, "since the country is so large and far-flung. But, in my opinion, they will want a share in the houses which Leif built here...and nothing less."

"That I am not prepared to do," Sigtrygg replied, "for these were pledged to me, in payment for my father's farmstead. And that is a matter of law and sworn oaths."

"Then you will find it hard-going to press this case of yours, no matter the strength of your claims and counter-claims," Vragi now said.

On the following day, Sigtrygg was awakened in the place where he was lying beside the Skraeling woman by loud and angry shouts from without. He and the others inside the house at once arose and Sigtrygg, leaving Chinokwa's side, went hastily down to the beach, with a number of his crewmen, to the place where the noises seemed to be coming from. There they saw that a fight had broken out between the Thorkelssons and some of the Norwegians, on the one hand, and W'tnalko and his Skraeling companions, on the other. These Skraelings, it seemed, had arisen earlier than others in Sigtrygg's camp and, being fascinated by the large

Norwegian ship, had approached it, in the first light of the morning, to get a closer look. Some of them, overwhelmed by curiosity, had then climbed up onto the ship's hull and this had alarmed the Norwegians who, upon waking and seeing what was occurring, had rushed angrily down to the beach, with the intention of chasing them off. Thord and his brother had at once joined the Norwegians and, when they saw how things were, began egging these men on for they said that the Skraelings would surely do some damage to that ship "which is our only means of returning home. And who knows if it is not their intention to do so?"

Sigtrygg and his companions now ran into the midst of this fight, as soon as they reached the place where the ship stood, and at once set about separating the two sides. But hard blows had already been struck between the combatants and the Skraelings had gotten the worst of it, for they had been taken entirely by surprise by the Norwegian assault and were not so big as the Norwegians were. Many of them were now badly hurt and Sigtrygg had all he could do to pull them to safety.

Then Osvif came down, following close behind Sigtrygg, with the remainder of his followers and he was very angry when he saw the fighting which was going on around the ship. He went, at once, to examine the condition of his vessel and, when he had satisfied himself that no serious damage had been done, he turned to Sigtrygg and said that he must now see to it that those people who owed him their allegiance were kept well clear of that place, "for they will not know how such a ship as this is to be treated."

But Sigtrygg replied that some people would think the Norwegians ought to know better how men were to behave while guests in another's house and that it seemed to him there were things to be learned on both sides.

"It remains to be seen, who is the guest and who the host," Thord now said, when he heard Sigtrygg's words, and Sigtrygg replied that this was indeed so, "though you, Thord, are not likely to be the one to benefit by the decision, however matters turn out."

After this the two sides separated and feelings ran very high between them so that each group gave the other wide berth. Chinokwa and the other Skraeling women now saw to the injuries which the Skraeling men had received while Sigtrygg told his crewmen they were to keep well apart from the Norwegians, just as before. "Though," he added, "I don't want you to give way before them, if it should come to blows."

Arnliot said there was no reason for anyone to be concerned about that.

Thus, by the second night of their return a great deal of tension had arisen in the camp and Sigtrygg's companions thought it best to keep a watchful eye on the movements of the Norwegians. It seemed to them that matters had grown rather serious, since the Thorkelssons were exerting such a strong influence upon the men of the other crew and there was much talk among them of taking the fight to the Norwegians before daylight should return and cost them what little advantage they now thought they had.

But Sigtrygg put a stop to this talk when he heard it, for he said he had no intention of being party to such a treacherous attack as was now being proposed, "however many more of them there are than of us."

CHAPTER XXXIII

AN OFFER IS MADE

That night Sigtrygg gave orders that those Skraelings who had been injured in the earlier fighting were to remain indoors and now Chinokwa and the other Skraeling women went about, once more, seeing to the wounds of the men. Though little blood had been shed, many of the Skraelings had been badly hurt and were suffering from numerous bruises and broken bones. W'tnalko had been among the most seriously injured, for his face and upper body were badly swollen and battered, and Chinokwa went first of all to his side to see to his care. But the Skraeling was a proud man and refused all her ministrations until the young woman straightened up at last and went over to Sigtrygg to tell him how things stood. Then Sigtrygg told the injured Skraeling that he wasn't showing much gratitude for all the concern which others so obviously had for him. He added that "you wont find gentler hands than this woman's, Bjorn, or a more healing touch, though, if you like, we Greenlanders can look to your wounds instead. Still, I doubt you will find our care any more pleasing."

W'tnalko said he had no desire for anyone's assistance in the matter and turned away from the others and, after this, he had little to say, though the other Skraeling men readily accepted whatever help was offered.

Shortly afterwards Asmund came in to Sigtrygg, for he had the night watch with several others at that time, and said there were two men outside who wanted to come in. Sigtrygg asked who these might be but, before Asmund could answer him, the two came through the doorway, pushing aside all who stood in their way. The first man, it could now be seen, was Sigtrygg's own kinsman, Girstein Eiriksson, and the second was the man called Gaut. These two looked about them and took in, at once, the sorry condition of the Skraeling men. Then Girstein said: "You have certainly chosen poor allies, kinsman, for these fellows have given a rather poor account of themselves in the fracas with the Norwegians. Though maybe that was to be expected since they are so unimpressive to look at." And now he walked over to the fire pit and squatted down beside it.

The big Swede, Gaut, followed close behind, though he seemed less interested than Girstein in the condition of the Skraelings, or in anything else, for that matter, until his eyes fell upon that big war axe which Arnliot had propped against one of the house walls. Then this Gaut cast a long look up and down the shaft of this weapon, and marked how the color of men's blood had got into the grain of the wood itself, and how the broad, two edged blade at the end of the shaft seemed to glisten in the smoky light of the pit fire. When Arnliot saw this man's keen interest in the weapon he grinned broadly and went over to it and placed his own hand carelessly on the shaft. Thereupon these two men exchanged looks, and now it seemed to those who were nearby that neither was willing to be the first to look away.

Sigtrygg followed Girstein to the fire, and Vragi and Olvir came afterwards, and then these men sat down and Sigtrygg asked his kinsman the purpose of his visit.

"There's not much to tell about that," was Girstein's reply, "for most people would think that matters have now come to such a pass between us that it will be hard for either of our two sides to remain long in this place without further violence and peace-breaking."

"I won't deny it," Sigtrygg said, "for the men in this Norwegian's crew are an overbearing lot, and we are not accustomed to that."

"Still," said Girstein, "I now want to know if you intend to abide by the settlement which our skipper is prepared to make in King Harald's name?"

"Things are no different than before, regarding that," replied Sigtrygg, "for your captain has no authority in this country to speak for anyone but himself, since Harald has no claim here. Therefore this Osvif, however highly he stands at the Norwegian king's court, is unfit to pronounce any form of settlement, whatever his pretensions, unless others are willing parties to it. But if it is a king you seek, no one here is more suited for this than I."

Girstein said that this was exactly what he had expected Sigtrygg to say, "though it is not likely to bring matters any closer to a resolution."

Olvir now spoke up and said that Girstein had certainly not come to visit them to hear the same words repeated which he had heard on the morning of their arrival and so he should now say clearly what was on his mind. Girstein looked across the fire at him and smiled. He said: "Many things are found in places where they are least expected, and not least of these is a serving man who speaks his mind to those he once took for his betters. And now I will tell you what I came here to say, since you have asked it so gently of me." Then he looked about at the others sitting nearby and at the Skraelings who sat or lay in silence along the walls.

Girstein said: "Kinsman, in my opinion, you are in a weaker position than your words now acknowledge for we are more numerous than you. And these Skraelings, upon whom you seem so much to depend, are unlikely to be of much value now that they have shown themselves entirely unable to hold their own against Norsemen like ourselves. Accordingly, it is not clear to me that Osvif Thorleiksson's pronouncements will make much difference in this matter, however the judgement falls out. For there are those among our kinsmen who are unlikely to happily accept any finding which is not wholly favorable to their view of the matter, while you, for your part, have already made clear your own unwillingness to do the same."

Sigtrygg said he thought this a true enough picture of their present state of affairs.

"In that case," said Girstein, "there is not much to be hoped for in the matter among those of us who would see an amicable settlement between the two sides and peace restored among our kinsmen."

"Peace is to be had," said Sigtrygg, "when my kinsmen recall those oaths they have sworn to me and fully acknowledge my rights here."

"That is unlikely to occur when such headstrong men, as are now involved in this question, are concerned," said Girstein.

"Then things will happen as they are fated," answered Sigtrygg, "for there's no use seeking to avert what cannot be changed."

"Yet no man knows what fate has in store for him," said Girstein, "and least of all those of us sitting out here now, so far from our homes, on this distant shore. In my opinion, it is just as likely that peace can be made as otherwise, if men act wisely. And who is to say that we are not fated to do thus?"

"What do you have in mind, kinsman?" Sigtrygg asked him.

"Only this," said Girstein, "that these claims and counter claims which have now been raised are unlikely to lead to a clear-cut resolution of these difficult matters under the law, whatever judgement is now rendered, for there are strong men on both sides, who are likely to seek further redress, before we have left this country. Yet, I do not think it was for this reason that our two ships' crews came out to this land, for there is plenty here for the taking, if only we do not stand in one anothers' way."

"I have no desire to hinder your interests in this country," said Sigtrygg, "or those of my other kinsmen. Let them go off in any direction they choose and take another land claim, for there is enough here to be shared by all. Only leave Leif's claim, and the lands it touches, to me. And, if you choose a site within my domain, then let the Leifssons and their kinsmen take me for king here, as these Skraelings have done."

"This is well-spoken," said Girstein. "But Leif's claim, as is commonly known, has long been held to be in the best part of this country, since it is not overly peopled with these Skraelings whom you have now found and brought into our midst. In truth, others had worse luck than Leif, when they came into this country and tried to settle in other parts than here, for they ran afoul of these forest people and found it hard to establish themselves for that reason. Though hardly formidable, man to man, these Skraelings are too numerous in most parts of this country for our safety."

"That is yet to be seen," said Sigtrygg, "for we have traveled about, somewhat, and found the country safe enough, if a man is willing to fight for what he wants."

"Most men of our kind," Girstein replied, "will find life among these Skraelings as undesirable as continuous warfare with them, for our ways are not theirs, and it is unlikely we can make common cause with them as you have now done. So now the matter is thus, that you must agree to share this place with those others of us who have come out here in your wake, so we may join forces to our common profit, or that you remain obdurate...in which case, both sides will be made to suffer."

"This is a big country," said Sigtrygg, "as has already been seen, and it is not unlikely you men will find another place as free of Skraelings as this place has been. You are certainly free to sail on and explore these coasts, if you desire it."

"There's no use searching for safer havens than this," said Girstein, "and it is out of the question that our kinsmen will agree to do so, since they count their claim here as good as your own. And, in truth, there is something to be said for that since it is not clear that Leif's houses were our fathers' alone to give, for there are others of us who may assert a claim to them."

"I have nothing to say to that," answered Sigtrygg, "since it seems to me that the Leifssons alone rightfully speak for that property their father held before his death."

"Yet such holdings belong in part to all our kin, and this matter was never put before those others of us who ought to have had a say in such things. Still, the law, it seems to me, is with you since it was their error, and not yours, in the manner in which they disposed of this holding. But," Girstein continued, "you cannot retain it, yourself, by force alone if we oppose you. And Thord and the others certainly will do that. So now I want to make an offer of peace between us, for there is still a way that this can be done."

"I don't see how," Sigtrygg replied, "after all that you have now said."

Girstein took a burning brand from the fire and stirred the flames about. He said: "You must bind the others to you in a stronger fashion than that kinship which was between our fathers before us, for that will split those who are opposed to your claim in this land, at the same time it ties them more tightly to you."

"I'm not sure what you mean by this," said Sigtrygg, "but it certainly does not sound promising, for I doubt that the Thorkelssons, or Lambi Gunnarsson, are eager for closer ties with me than they now have."

"That may be," said Girstein, "but there is one other, at least, of our kin, who has a say in this and she is not unwilling to make her peace with you. Or did you think Thjodhild Gunnarsdottir came out to this country for love of seafaring and rough seas only?"

Sigtrygg now grew very quiet and for a long while he said nothing. At last he turned to Girstein and said: "It was ill-done to bring that woman out to this country, kinsman, for there are many dangers here. And many a ship has been lost on these unknown seas, besides."

"I thought you had heard our skipper's words, when he told you how things were," said Girstein, "for it was not within his power, or any man's, to decide whether Thjodhild was to sail with us or not, once she had made up her mind in the matter. Nor is it any more likely we can compel her now, than before, for, if truth be told, it is she who has the most say where she and her brother are concerned. And as to our cousin Thord, he cannot press this claim of his without Lambi's full support."

"Then this is a very different Lambi than the one I knew in Brattahlid," said Sigtrygg; and Girstein said that this was not to be wondered at, "for that man was lost to us, as surely as the whale who sinks beneath the hunter's blows, on that day you speared him on the fjord."

Sigtrygg said: "I did but return him gift for gift...though, perhaps, my aim was sharper."

"I think he'd have preferred the duelling island, in any event," Girstein replied, "for then his chances had been better. But now he will do as Thjodhild says, for she has always been much the cleverer of those two, and he is at a loss without her."

"Still, I don't see how this will change things, where the Thorkelssons are concerned," said Sigtrygg, "and it is Thord Thorkelsson who is certainly the most eager to press his case in this matter."

"It will change everything," answered Girstein, "if you were now to wed Thjodhild, for then what you own would also be partly hers and there would be no reason for any other of our kinsmen to contend against you, since they would have a stake in this country, too, through this union."

Sigtrygg looked for a long while in silence at Girstein and then he said: "They have certainly opposed such a union before this, so why would they give way now?"

"Because," said Girstein, "matters are now much different than before."

"And what does Thjodhild say to this?" Sigtrygg asked.

"In my opinion, she will look favorably upon such an offer, though the matter must be put to Lambi, since he is her elder brother."

Sigtrygg said he had not thought much about the possibility which Girstein was now proposing for, in truth, "I have been much too busy for it. Still, if I were now to do as you suggest I should have as partners those men who wished only ill-luck and failure upon my undertakings before."

"Yet, it may be the only means to preserve what you have won," answered Girstein, "for, in my opinion, no settlement is likely to hold for long in this country unless the ties are now bound so tightly that that man will choke who seeks to undo them."

"You have certainly thought this matter through," said Sigtrygg, and now he stood up and began to pace about. "Yet," he added, "it seems to me that I detect another's hand in this, as well. In which case, I would know what it is that Thjodhild herself wants in this matter, for she will have her own ideas where these things are concerned."

"Only you for a husband, kinsman," Girstein replied, "for this she has confided in me: that she has long set her mind upon it. And that you now make peace with those of our blood, against whom you have been striving, and make a place for them in this country besides. And lastly that you send away those Skraelings whom you have brought here and most of all that woman you call your wife."

Sigtrygg did not speak for a long time after he had heard these words and, in truth, he seemed somewhat distracted to the small group of men who were sitting nearby about the fire. He now ceased walking about and turned back toward Girstein who grew silent in his turn. After awhile Sigtrygg spoke again, saying that he thought these "harsh terms, that a man should give up all that he has won, and those he counts as friends besides, for this union you have now proposed."

But Girstein replied that it was only to be expected since every woman counts herself as worth more, in the balance, than all others "and Thjodhild is no different in this from the rest. Still, she is certainly a better prospect than that Skraeling woman you are keeping in your bed."

"I don't see that there is much to be gained by discussing this further," Sigtrygg now said, "for you are seeking concessions which I am not prepared to give, whatever the consequences," and then he turned abruptly about and walked to the farther end of the hall.

Girstein and Gaut looked at one another in silence and, when it was clear to them that Sigtrygg desired no further conversation on the matter, they arose from their places. Then Girstein looked from Vragi to Olvir and then, one by one, into the faces of each of the other crewmen. He said he thought Sigtrygg ought now to put the matter to a vote, "for this will concern all of you men as much as your skipper, who thinks it so hard a matter to wed the most desirable woman in all Greenland, despite the fact that her love for him is so great she will not share him with others."

But no one had anything more to say about it than Sigtrygg had. Thereupon Girstein, seeing how things were, took up his sword and walked to the doorway and Gaut went along beside him, for it was plain to them that they would make no further headway with the men in that hall. Only then did they see that Arnliot Keelfoot had placed himself squarely in their path and stood, now, with his big war axe in his hands, holding its double bladed head lightly against the earth at his feet.

Girstein said: "That is a large weapon, Ketilsfjorder, and certainly too big to swing about in these close quarters, where it is likely to do more harm than good to those you count your friends. But if you really want to test this axe's balance, and see how she flies about when swords are aloft, then my advice is that you now carry her outside, and then we shall see how she fares under the open sky."

Arnliot said he thought his axe would do equally well, wherever he raised it, but that he had no more objection to swinging it about beneath the stars than in the smoky light of the pit fire and now he moved to let Girstein and his companion pass, for he said he was unwilling to be any less courteous to them than they had been to him. But Sigtrygg came up at once and placed his hand on the large man from Ketilsfjord, saying he was to remain inside with the others, "for these men are my guests and no harm is to come to them since they have been received in peace under this roof."

Arnliot replied that he could have it his own way this time, if that was how he wanted it, but that things might not always be as they now were and then there was no telling which of them would be proved the wiser in the end, "whether it had been better to settle things tonight or await a better time."

Girstein thanked Sigtrygg for his intervention and now he went out through the doorway and Gaut followed after him, showing very little concern for the others in the hall. Still, it seemed to some that the big Swede stopped for a moment in the shadow of the open doorway and looked back at the men inside and that his eyes fell, finally, upon the figure of Arnliot Keelfoot. And then he looked harder at this man than at any of the others.

CHAPTER XXXIV

THE KING'S COURT

Now the time came when Osvif the Norwegian had promised to convene the king's court. Accordingly, he went out with his crew and had stakes driven into the ground, near where his ship sat beached upon the shore, and then he had ropes tied to the stakes so that a broad area was marked off. Into this area he told his men to carry a number of benches and he had them place these on the highest part of the ground that was within the marked off land.

When Sigtrygg learned of these preparations, he told his own crewmen to arm themselves. So now they went for their weapons and each took hold of what he could and formed up outside their houses, both the Greenlanders who had sailed out with Sigtrygg from Eiriksfjord and those Skraelings who were then in their company. But Sigtrygg told Chinokwa and the other Skraeling women to remain inside and that they were not to show themselves, "whatever strange noises you may hear."

This was on the third day after Osvif Thorleiksson had agreed to hear the Leifssons' legal actions, and the weather did not seem especially promising, for there were heavy clouds then forming over the sea's face to the north of them. W'tnalko showed Sigtrygg how the birds were flying, at that time, just above the treetops and added that he thought this a sign the weather would not hold and Vragi said he agreed with this man's judgement, "for these people will know best how to interpret the storm signs in their own country."

"Nevertheless," Sigtrygg replied, "I am not willing to allow these Norwegians to hold their court without my presence, whatever uncertainty the weather offers; besides we are on dry land here, should the sea blow a strong gale against us."

Vragi told him to have it his own way. So now they formed up to go down to the marked off land, where the legal proceedings were to be conducted. But when they counted up their number they saw that Arnliot Keelfoot was not among them and they thought this highly unusual, since he was always the first to show himself when any sort of trouble was afoot. Sigtrygg now asked if anyone had seen the big man from Ketilsfjord but no one had anything to say about this.

"I don't think much good can come of our proceeding without him, under the circumstances," Sigtrygg now said, and so he went into each of the houses which stood nearby in search of this man.

He found the big Ketilsfjorder at last, in one of the smaller booths, standing about with a very perplexed look on his face. Everything inside was overturned, but Arnliot seemed no less satisfied for that, and he had, in his hands, a bundle of animal skins which they had taken with them out of the Skraeling country. He was wearing his sword and carrying a very large shield, but he seemed intent on the bundle in his hands and on nothing else. He tossed this angrily to the ground, just as Sigtrygg walked in, and then he turned about and his face seemed very red. Sigtrygg asked him what was causing such strange behavior and Arnliot replied that it was nothing less than the loss of his axe, which he counted a very serious matter, since it was a family heirloom that had come down to him from his great-grandfather and namesake.

Sigtrygg asked if he had not kept a careful watch on this weapon and Arnliot replied that he most certainly had for he always slept with the handle of the axe close beside him.

"Then I don't see how anyone could have taken it from you," Sigtrygg said, "though some might think you'd have been better off to use it as a pillow under your head for then you would have been less likely to lose track of it."

Arnliot replied that, in his opinion, there was no one brave enough or sufficiently skilled to have taken the weapon from him, even while he was sleeping, yet he was now at a loss to explain what had occurred.

"Perhaps one of your Skraeling women has now played a joke on you, for it is common knowledge that you prefer the company of that war-tool to either of your wives," Sigtrygg laughed.

"I'm not sure about that," answered Arnliot, "but it is certainly the case that whoever is responsible for this theft will now be made to pay for it."

Sigtrygg laughed again when he heard this and said there was not much to be concerned about, if that was all that was bothering him, "for I am the one who has taken that weapon of yours into my keeping, for our friendship's sake, so there's no need to take it out on those women."

Arnliot took one step toward Sigtrygg on hearing this and said: "I don't see how you can call it friendship, if you have taken for yourself what is plainly the property of another."

But Sigtrygg replied: "It was not theft, shipmate, for you freely gave me that weapon, when we fled the Tulewat town, or had you forgotten? And then you thought very little of the matter, since our lives seemed to depend on it."

"I did not give it to you," Arnliot answered him slowly, "but only placed the axe in your hands for safekeeping, since a man cannot do his best when he is carrying more burdens than he should...and I had our shipmate from Brattahlid upon my shoulders. But if you have this weapon, as you now say, I am asking that you return it to me at once, for there is no honor in hanging onto that which belongs to others."

"It's not clear to me who has the rights to this weapon, in any event," said Sigtrygg, "for you willingly placed it into my keeping when you had it in your power to do so. And that, as Torfi Gudvesson has said, is the proper means for ridding oneself of this war-tool. Besides, the weapon has a curse on it; and the way to avoid this curse is to give the axe freely to another, as you have now done with me. And I am certainly prepared to accept it of you, and that for our friendship's sake."

"It is a fine show of friendship," answered Arnliot, "in any case to act thus behind a man's back."

"In truth, I did not think you would willingly give it up," answered Sigtrygg, "once you had it again in your own hands. Yet I took the weapon for your good; and for that of this crew, since I doubt there is much to be gained should that killing fever which possessed you, when you fought with the axe against the Skraeling king, come upon you again. And that, too, was surely the work of this weapon's curse."

"You may yet have cause to regret this choice," said Arnliot, "should matters go against us at the Norwegian's court."

"There are those there I would not see harmed," answered Sigtrygg quietly, "but that will mean little to a man in the throes of berserker's rage. Nor do I think there is much chance of preserving the peace, in any case, once you have that weapon again in your hands; so now leave it in my keeping, shipmate, as I have said, and this will be best for us all, since you have already played the hero's part and won great renown with it."

But Arnliot only ground his teeth together and said: "There's no use hoping for that, since I am not afraid of curses nor am I less able to wield this weapon than those kinsmen of mine who came before me. Still, since you are so fearful of what is to come, I will let matters lie, for the while, and leave the axe where you have placed it. But I do not relinquish my claim to this weapon, by the gesture which I am now making, nor do I acknowledge that any man has a stronger claim upon the axe than me."

Sigtrygg said he thought this very foolish, but that he would accept these terms for now, whereupon these two went outside to join the others. Vragi now asked what had been responsible for their delay, since he thought it very unusual for them to be dawdling about "when such big matters, as we are now involved in, are at hand," but neither had much to say on the subject.

Then Vragi looked at the big Ketilsfjord man and remarked

that he seemed rather lightly armed.

Arnliot replied that there was not much to be worried about, where these Norwegians were concerned, and that a sword and shield would certainly be "more than enough to deal with such men as these are." Then Sigtrygg added that he thought they should not spend any more of their time bandying words about but go down at once and see what "these others have in mind, for they have certainly been making plenty of fuss down by that ship of theirs."

Vragi said that this was true but now he asked them to hold off a bit longer, and then he brought out a large sack in which he was accustomed to store all his goods, while on his travels. He reached into this sack and took out a broad piece of dark blue cloth. It had a rather old look to it but it seemed in good condition, for it had been neatly rolled and its edges were neither torn nor shredded. He now unfolded this cloth and held it up to them and it seemed to the crewmen of the Gull that the cloth glistened as brightly as the sun itself and, when they looked more closely, they could see that this was because it had been worked throughout with numerous strands of fine gold.

Vragi now took hold of this cloth and tore a long strip from it and handed it to Sigtrygg, telling him to tie it about his head, "for it is only fitting that a king should be set apart from other men by the crown of gold he wears. And this is the closest thing we have to that."

Sigtrygg took the cloth and thanked him and now they went down to the beach.

When they came up to the area which the Norwegians had staked out, they were met by a number of men of that crew and these told them they were to set their weapons aside, "for it is against the rule of law for men to come armed into the presence of the king's agent." Sigtrygg replied that there was no such person, to his knowledge, in that country, but Vragi said that it was the custom in most places for men to leave their arms behind, when entering a law court, so now the men of the Gull and the Skraelings who were with them did as the Norwegians asked and piled their weapons to one side, before stepping into the staked-off area. Once within, they could see how the Norwegians had cordoned off two places, one of which now stood quite empty. There was also a third place in which a number of benches had been set. Osvif sat on the highest of these and beside him several of his crewmen, and with them Thjodhild. She was placed off to one side, but on a seat nearly as high as Osvif's own. Behind her stood the serving girl, Fridgerd, and her eyes seemed to widen when she saw Arnliot coming in with the others.

Thjodhild sat very straight and still in her place. She was wearing a brightly colored gown and her red hair had been braided in such fashion that it fell down along either side of her face and lay upon her breast in two rope-like coils, shimmering there in the bright glow of the sun. And now the braids of her hair, and her very eyes, seemed to leap suddenly to life as Sigtrygg entered the cordoned-off area with his followers, and it seemed that a tremulousness took hold of her and the soft hair on her bosom rose and fell with each breath that she took.

Sigtrygg went with his following to the empty place which the Norwegians showed them and now he could see that the other space, which lay opposite to where they were given to stand, was occupied by the Thorkelssons and by Lambi Gunnarsson and their supporters. Girstein Eiriksson was also with them there, along with the big Swede called Gaut.

Thord Thorkelsson was the first to speak when he saw Sigtrygg arriving and he cried out, at once, that they had violated the sanctity of the law ground, "for Sigtrygg has brought these heathen Skraelings into our presence, though it is certain that such men are not fit to stand before the court in proceedings of this type."

Sigtrygg answered that he was not certain who was "more fit to stand on this ground, for these people were born in this country while you, Thord, are barely more than a guest here. And it is not yet clear to me that there is even a court to be convened, since that will depend on whether there is any rightful king nearby."

"There is certainly a king," replied Thord, "for none is stronger in the northern lands than Harald of Norway. And this man, Osvif, is his representative. But if you have any doubt about it, you must know that we have all voted on this question and acknowledged him in the matter, and there are more of us than of you. Or else, why have you come here to answer those charges which we have now brought against you?"

"I would not be so quick to count heads, in your place, cousin," Sigtrygg responded, "for there are many more Skraelings in this land than men like us from over the sea. And if their votes were to be counted, I think they would have something very different to say concerning who is to have the rule here."

"Still," said Thord, "they have no vote in this and are not now present in such great numbers as to change the outcome, in any event. So now I claim that these people must be removed at once, or that you have forfeited your case by violating the sanctity of the law ground."

Sigtrygg said he thought they were getting off to a very bad start, where questions of law were concerned, and that, if they hoped to air the matter at all, they must do so within the hearing of both sides "so that everyone will be party to any settlement which is arrived at here. But, if you insist on evicting any of my followers, we shall all depart, and then you may see what manner of judgement you are able to achieve in our absence."

Thord replied that it made very little difference to him whether Sigtrygg and his companions were present to hear the verdict or not, "for we intend to enforce it, nonetheless. Nor am I certain your attendance here will be of much help to your case in any event."

"You are certainly overconfident, kinsman," Sigtrygg said, "and that is not to be wondered at, for you have always been given to such heedless judgements. Still, there's many a slip between tongue and lip, as the saying has it, and it's not entirely clear to me that you are any more likely to have your way in this now, than when we sailed out of Eiriksfjord."

Osvif now stood up and said there was no use their going on in this way, "for it is my place to deliver the judgement, and now I rule that these Skraelings can stay, if Sigtrygg desires it, for this is a different country than the lands we are used to and different rules will apply here. If this were Norway, then the heathens would certainly be excluded, until they had come over to the true faith, and likewise in Iceland or Greenland. But in Vinland, I hold that these people have as much right to attend this court as we Norsemen do."

Now most of those present thought this a reasonable judgement so Thord fell silent, seeing that he was so clearly overborne.

Sigtrygg thanked Osvif for his decision but added that this in no way changed matters "concerning this proceeding, for I see no more reason now, than before, to accept King Harald's authority in this land. Or you as the man to speak for him."

Osvif said he could have it that way if he insisted but that it would then be even more unlikely for him to achieve a settlement with his kinsmen, "for they will never acknowledge your sole sovereignty in Vinland, however often you claim it."

"It's all the same to me, what my kinsmen say," answered Sigtrygg, "but one thing, at the least, is certain. And that is that we cannot remain in this place together, in peace, so long as they do not hold to those oaths which my uncles swore concerning this land."

"That the oaths were taken is not to be denied," Thord now said, "but their terms are not what our kinsman Sigtrygg has maintained, for they only concerned these few broken down houses and the land on which they were built. For the rest, no man has any greater claim than any other. Still, our kinsman has certainly failed to keep to his side of the bargain, since he stole a ship and other goods from us, as all present here must know, and did great violence in pursuit of these lawless actions, to the bargain."

"I don't see how you can blame a man for taking what is already his," Vragi now put in, when he heard Thord's words, "for everyone is agreed, at the least, that the ship was promised, along with the land claim and the houses."

"A ship, certainly," answered Thord, "but only if she could be fully crewed, and yet she was not."

"And yet we sailed out of Eiriksfjord with eighteen men, which was no fewer than your kinsmen demanded," Vragi replied.

"With men who were taken by violence," said Thord, "in the course of which two others were killed and a third maimed by an unlawful assault upon his person. And that man of the finest blood-lines in all Greenland. You ship-thieves have certainly shown your-selves to be arrogant and overbearing men, since you thought you could do just as you pleased, despite the will of my father and the law. But now these matters are to be put right, for Osvif Thorleiksson has sworn to deliver a fair verdict here, in light of the facts and the requirements of this court. And we have put our trust in him as King Harald's man."

Osvif said: "As to this claim of unlawful seizure of the ship, the matter is not entirely clear to me, for I have as yet heard nothing in those oaths, which were sworn, concerning the size of the crew which was to man her."

"Yet," said Thord, "no one will deny that Sigtrygg took it upon himself to raise the needed crew."

"I did," Sigtrygg agreed.

"Then what did you have in mind, kinsman?" Thord asked. "Did you think any number of men would do, or that you would be allowed to take the ship with two men, or with three? Or did you think we would give her to you for five, or even ten, knowing the value of the vessel and the risks involved? We kinsmen hold that the oath only bound us to make over the ship if Sigtrygg did his part, and that was to raise the crew needed to man her. But our cousin was unable to do that and so he had no right to the vessel, though he took her anyway and shed much blood in the act. So now we call upon this court to hear our oaths concerning the mat-ter and to render a judgement in our favor, both for the unlawful theft of the vessel and for the damage which was done in the taking of her."

Osvif now asked both sides to repeat the oaths, word for word, which had been sworn between Sigtrygg and his uncles and when he had heard these he became very quiet. After awhile he said: "It seems to me that the Leifssons have the right here, for Sigtrygg did agree to raise a crew, though this was only partially done at the time of the theft."

Arnliot leaned forward and whispered in Sigtrygg's ear, saying the Norwegian's words only showed how matters were likely to go, now that they had put themselves in his hands "for this man will never render a fair judgement where your kinsmen are concerned. And now I think you will have cause to regret my leaving that war-axe of mine behind."

Vragi at once pushed himself forward and asked leave to speak and Osvif said that he was free to do so, if that was his desire.

"In that case," said the old man, "I would ask these kinsmen of Leif Eiriksson how it is that they know this theft, which they have accused us of, in fact took place, or that the matter has been properly put before this court?"

Osvif said this was an unusual question, considering the circumstances, but that he was free to raise the matter if he wanted to and Vragi replied that he did. But Thord only laughed at this and said that everyone now present had been a witness to the events out on Eiriksfjord "and as for the bringing of these charges, no less a man than Girstein Eiriksson has placed them in evidence before this court. And he has the case duly assigned to him by oaths which were properly witnessed by men who are standing before you today."

Vragi asked if this were so and Girstein replied that it was and now those men who had witnessed the assignment of the case were brought forward and they gave oaths to this effect, saying that everything was just as Thord had said it was. Then others came forward to testify to the charging of the culprits in public hearing and to their summonsing to stand before the court.

Vragi turned to Osvif and asked if he thought this sufficient to support the claims being made and Osvif said that it certainly was.

"In that case," said Vragi, "I now declare this entire case null and void, for it has been improperly summonsed from the start, in that the man bringing the charges is himself a culprit in this case, for Girstein Eiriksson was with us when we took the ship. And, indeed, we could not have accomplished the matter without his aid since he, alone among us men, knew where the ship was hidden."

Osvif stood up from his seat when he heard this, and the others with him, so that only Thjodhild remained in her place, of those who had before been seated. There was now a great uproar and Thord shouted above the others that this was some foolish trick. Lambi looked over at Girstein but he only stood by in silence, with a slight smile on his lips. Osvif now turned to Girstein and asked if there was any truth to this outlandish assertion and, after a time, Girstein spoke up and said there most certainly was for, he added, he had indeed helped Sigtrygg and the others to take the ship before any violence had been done, since he had been hoping to avert a confrontation between the kinsmen by his actions.

Osvif said that this was all very irregular and a serious matter, "or didn't you know, shipmate, that it is a fatal flaw in a case like this to bring charges against men, if you are equally guilty with them?"

Girstein said that he had had no idea of this, "for I am not skilled in matters of law," adding that he had ceased supporting the thieves as soon as violence had been reported of them, and that he had then done everything in his power to prevent them from fleeing Brattahlid.

"That is of no matter where this case is concerned," said Osvif angrily, "for you are the man who has the claim in his hands, yet you are no less responsible than these others for what occurred. How are we to proceed with such an irregularity in this case now?"

Thord pushed his way up to where Osvif was standing and leant over to him, saying there was no reason to give way before such an obvious ploy to disqualify their case as this was since everyone already knew the truth of the matter "and it is of little concern who brings the case, in any event, whether Girstein or one of us other kinsmen, for the ship was taken despite the terms of the sworn oath and this may not be denied."

"Yet the law is the law," answered Osvif in a very low voice, "and all of us here have sworn to abide by it. You cannot now prosecute a case which has been improperly placed before this court."

"Then how can this thing be righted?" Thord demanded.

"A flaw must be found in the assignment of the case to Girstein Eiriksson," said Osvif. "And then it must be assigned anew to some other. Or Thorkel Leifsson and his brothers must undertake to prosecute the matter themselves. But these men are yet in Greenland, and so it cannot be reassigned or prosecuted by them in this court. Nor do I think we are likely to find a flaw in the assignment which they made of the case to Girstein, your kinsman, for we have all heard the oaths and agreed that these were properly done."

Now there was even more shouting than before and Thord seemed especially put out by this turn of events and he had many harsh words for Girstein, his cousin. But Girstein only shrugged and continued to plead his ignorance of the law.

At last Thord said: "Still, we have these other matters, and these are no small things, for two servants of my father were unlawfully slain in the taking of the ship. And my kinsman Lambi Gunnarsson has a just claim for compensation besides, in that Sigtrygg Thorgilsson willfully made an attack upon his person with intent to slay him. And various other goods were seized by these men at the time when they spirited away the ship from under our very noses...and all of this is yet to be paid for. So now I claim compensation in Lambi Gunnarsson's name, and for my father and his brothers, for their loss in both goods and men."

"What say you to that?" Osvif asked, turning again to Vragi and fixing him with a hard look.

"Not much," answered Vragi, "since all of these charges are asserted in the matter of the ship's theft, yet that cannot now be established under the rules of this court. If men were slain or otherwise injured in the course of these events, such harm must be shown to have been unprovoked. Yet it is certain that we fled before you others, and if we fought back and did some harm to our attackers, it was for no other purpose than to safeguard our own lives."

Thord became even more angry at these words than before and said: "What manner of game is this which you are now playing, old man?"

But Osvif put up one hand to silence him. Then he said: "It is certainly the case that a man may fight to defend his own life, if he is blameless in the matter, but it is not altogether clear that that was so in this case."

"Yet," Vragi replied, "you cannot now show that a theft occurred, while all those who are present here know how it was for us that day, when we fended off numerous boatloads of attackers. And if Lambi Gunnarsson learned to his detriment that his spear throw was less true than that of his kinsman, he has at least to be thankful that he was spared a worse fate when they pulled him out of the icy fjord waters alive. Yet I have known men who took harder blows, in the midst of battle, and never voiced a complaint concerning these."

Osvif said this was certainly true and now he sat back down in his place. The Thorkelssons and their supporters were very annoyed with how matters seemed to be going for them and Thord at once demanded that Osvif declare summary judgement in their favor, since the ship theft and the bloodshed which followed were well-known to those who were present in the court. But the Norwegian now had little to say in the matter and seemed lost in his own thoughts. Then Thord turned to Girstein and asked what he meant to do, "since this case now seems to be going so decisively against us, and you are the cause of it?"

Girstein replied that, in his opinion, "there is little enough we can do, for the law seems to be with them."

Thord said he would never accept such a judgement, and now he denounced the proceedings, as did his brother Thorstein and those other Eiriksfjordmen who were with them. Osvif turned to Lambi and asked him if he saw matters the same way.

"I'm not sure about that," replied Lambi, "but I would certainly prefer to have redress for my wound, than to leave this court with no compensation at all."

"In that case," Osvif said, "I now want to know what offer you, Sigtrygg, are prepared to make to this man, Lambi, in consideration of that wound which you inflicted on him, however justified you took yourself to be at the time?"

"I don't have much to offer concerning that," answered Sigtrygg, "unless my kinsman is also prepared to offer payment to Thorolf the Icelander for that unprovoked wound which he gave him."

"It's not entirely clear that it was unprovoked," said Osvif, "though the Icelander has certainly recovered without any ill effects, while your kinsman has not had the same good luck. So now I want to ask you again what you are prepared to offer to each of your kinsmen to get peace from them?"

Vragi said that Osvif, himself, should make a proposal in the matter, "for it is you who have set yourself up as lawman here."

Osvif laughed and said he had the same proposal to make as before and that was for both sides to divide the houses and the land claim between them, "in which case, I think we should now let matters stand as they are and each side keep what they have taken."

"I am not willing to do that," Sigtrygg said. And the Thorkelssons now said the same.

"Then," said the Norwegian, "I don't see how there can be any hope of peace between the two sides."

It now happened that the sky, which had been steadily growing darker above them, during these proceedings, became completely grey and the sun slipped suddenly from sight. At the same time a sharp, cold wind came up from the sea and began to sweep over them and then the rain began to fall, in heavy hail-like droplets, driven by the seaborne gale, and it quickly swept across the face of the land so that there was no sheltering from it and everyone was overwhelmed by the harsh rush of wind and the sea which the wind seemed to carry with it.

At this Osvif said that he thought the matters now before them would be better dealt with at another, more propitious time and no one disputed this so that the law-gathering at once began to break up. Some of the Norwegians hurriedly sought safety under the hull of their ship, but the ferocious storm seemed to drive everything before it. Thus, many in that company now broke and ran for the cover of those houses which they had left on the higher ground above them. Sigtrygg and his companions did the same and, because the houses which they occupied were nearer to the shore, they reached shelter first. They rushed inside while the Norwegians raced on past them. Arnliot now placed himself in the doorway of one of the houses and stood there laughing at the discomfiture of the Norwegians as they fled to higher ground. "These foreigners are certainly finding this country harder to claim than they had expected," he said, "when even the clouds in the sky cast their votes for us."

Now they could see the others straggling up through the muddy grass to their own shelters, with the wind and harsh rain at their backs and the sky streaked with white, as the thunderous rumblings of the storm rolled in behind the wind. A small group of people hastened up the path nearest to the place where Arnliot stood athwart the doorway he had claimed for his own, and now he urged these people to greater speed for he said laughing that he thought "this storm will sweep you all out to sea and back to Greenland, if you are not more careful than you have now been."

These people now stopped and it could be seen at once that it was Girstein Eiriksson in the lead there and beside him the big

Swede, Gaut, and between these two were Thjodhild and her servant. The women looked utterly spent, for the harshness and speed of the rain seemed to catch all of them unawares and all were now soaked entirely through to the skin. Thjodhild's hair hung tightly around her face and shoulders and her long gown clung to her body as though it were a part of her. Her serving girl hovered behind her, seeking to shield her from the worst of the rain with a long cloak which she held out weakly behind and above her mistress, but this did little good for it flapped wildly in the steady gusting of the storm, and the rain seemed to roar right past it, washing over the taller woman. Thjodhild had her head down and Girstein reached out and took her arm and drew her up toward him and when he did this he turned to Arnliot and asked for shelter, "for we are still a good distance from our own lodgings," he said, "and this storm shows no sign of abating."

"You should have thought of that, before you selected such an inauspicious day for your court actions against us," the big man from Ketilsfjord replied, "for we are not bound to offer you lodgings here since we have given you men too much, in my opinion, already."

"Still," said Girstein, "these women have done you no harm and this wind and rain are harder on them than on us."

Arnliot agreed that this was probably so and looked at the two women for a moment. Then he said: "We have women of our own here, in any case, and I am not certain there is room for these others, as well. But you will know best how to bring these two to shelter, before things get much worse, for I have heard a great deal about your quick thinking and resourcefulness."

"Quick thinking often makes for quicker dying," said the voice of the Swede from behind the others, and when he spoke he shouted so that he could be heard over the pounding of the wind.

"That, at least, remains to be seen," said Arnliot smiling. But he made no move to step aside from the doorway.

At that moment there was a scuffling inside and now another man's head appeared beneath Arnliot's big arms, which were braced against the wind and rain on either side of the narrow opening. When this man saw what was happening, he pushed his way through and stood in the lee of the overhanging roof, and at once extended his hand to the others. "You had better come inside, if that's what you want," he said, "for things are not going to get any better by debating the finer points of the law in this matter as you now seem to be doing." It was Olvir, the Brattahlid man, who said this, and he gestured to Arnliot to let the others pass within.

"There's no need to give hospitality to us," said Girstein when he saw the man's offer, "for I have the feeling that that is likely to end badly, however good the intentions. But in my opinion it would be unseemly to deny entry to these women who are now seeking your protection from the harsh forces assaulting us from the sea."

Olvir said he thought the same and urged the women to come in at once, which they now did, Arnliot making no move to prevent this despite his earlier strong words. Then Girstein and his companion thanked the former serving man from Brattahlid and Olvir said they should come in as well if they wanted to. But Girstein repeated what he had said before and added that, in his opinion, the storm would now be much easier to endure, "since the women are in your hands."

Girstein and Gaut now turned back toward the shore and began to make their way again down to where the Norwegian ship was beached, fighting against the stinging wind and rain which hammered them from the sea. It could now be seen that many of the Norwegian crew were still about their ship, fighting to keep her from being toppled over in the wind and it was obvious that Girstein and his companion meant to help the others in this task if they could. Arnliot stood there a long while watching their progress, until it was plain that they had reached the hull of the big merchant ship, and then he saw how they grabbed hold of the lashings with the other crewmen and began to pull on these and how, when they had added their strength to that of the others, the big ship seemed to move back to its place despite the rough rocking and buffeting of the wind.

Olvir now told Arnliot that, in his opinion, there was no further need to keep guard over their door, since it was Sigtrygg's desire that they offer shelter to anyone in need of it.

"And besides, it looks like the rest of them are too busy to come pounding on our door, in any event," he added, staring down toward the shore in the direction the big Ketilsfjord man had been looking. Olvir had spoken in this fashion just in time to see the great ship righted and swung round to its proper place and they could still hear the groaning of her timbers, even above the harsh howling of the storm winds.

"That is man's work," Olvir said at last, seeing how the Norwegians were striving so forcefully against the storm, and Arnliot said he thought that that was certainly true, "though it is no less than what we, ourselves, have done many times before. Still, I think it a strange matter that those two thought to pass so close by to us, on their way to finding shelter for these women, when others of their company found it so much quicker to go to their own lodgings by other paths."

Olvir said that he too thought it odd, but added that, if so, "it only shows the boldness of these two men, and especially of Girstein Eiriksson who, among all the Leifssons' kin, is considered by many to be the most promising."

"I'm not sure about that," replied Arnliot after a time, "for there are more men than one, of that blood, who can lay claim to great achievements in this country. Still, in my opinion, his companion is certainly the sort who will bear watching."

CHAPTER XXXV

UNLOOKED FOR GUESTS

When Thjodhild and her serving girl were taken inside, they were wet to the very skin and the crewmen of the Gull brought them dry blankets in which to wrap themselves. Then they placed them beside the fire and Sigtrygg told the Skraeling women to put on more wood, which was quickly done, and after this a great blaze arose in the pit so that it soon became extremely warm and close within the hall. Sigtrygg went and sat down beside the two Greenland women, while the fire was being stoked, and asked if there was anything he could bring them, but they said there was nothing they desired at that time more than dry clothes.

"We don't have much provision for that," Sigtrygg said, "for we did not come out to this country with women's gowns in our cargo; and you two should know that better than most, since you were both present at our leave-taking."

Fridgerd said she would make do with whatever could be found and Sigtrygg turned to Chinokwa and told her to bring what she could for their guests. The Skraeling woman now went off and came back again with a wrapping of skins, which she unrolled before them on the ground beside the fire. Sigtrygg then asked Thjodhild if she were willing to do as Fridgerd would, and replace her ruined garments with others of Skraeling manufacture.

"I see no reason to do that," answered Thjodhild, "for the clothing I am wearing is of a better sort, and I have more of whatever I need, among my own goods, in that house where I am lodged with my brother and the Norwegians. But Fridgerd is certainly free to do as she sees fit, if she is so bereft of pride as to put such rough rags upon her own body."

Sigtrygg said: "Your own dry garments are yet far away, lady, while these are close to hand. They will serve to keep you warm, while the wet clothes, which you are now wearing, are set to dry by the fire. But it will do you little good to sit here in this heat if you remain wrapped in these sodden woolens, for many a man, and woman too, has been taken with fever for less cause than this."

"Nevertheless," said Thjodhild, "I have no desire to don such barbarous garments, for whatever reason, though we are certainly grateful for the hospitality you have shown to us in our need. So now we will sit by this fire, until the rains cease, and warm ourselves, as best we can. And then we will take our leave of you, as soon as this weather lifts."

"There's no need for that," Sigtrygg said, "for this house is at your disposal and you are to be treated as honored guests here while you are in our midst."

"Neither my serving girl nor I have any wish for that," Thjodhild replied, "for the matter is quite clear to us, namely that people of my blood are to be regarded as intruders in this country, which you have taken for your own."

Sigtrygg said: "You are no intruder, Thjodhild."

But she replied: "Can I be anything else, seeing as you have declared your enmity with our kin?"

"They have made the matter, thus," he said in answer, "for they have foresworn those oaths which they made with me."

"Yet, you are the cause of the breach which divides the Leifssons, now," Thjodhild answered him. "Or did you not see how the matter went before King Harald's man when he urged a settlement on you?"

"Shall I settle for half of something, when all is mine by rights?" asked Sigtrygg.

"No man may own the whole earth," said Thjodhild, "nor all of Vinland either. Did you come out here first? Yet others have followed after, and they are no less justified in taking a portion of this country for their own since they have won this right by their courage on the open sea. Or do you think to hold all this land with your tiny crew and these Skraeling servants whom you have found in the woodlands? They are certainly no match for men of our race and will do you poor service when the matter is put to the test."

"If I permit my kinsmen and their companions to settle here," answered Sigtrygg, "they will take whatever they please and act, in all ways, as though they have more rights than me. Yet, if they will take me for their king, as these Skraelings have done, then matters, I think, may still be settled without undue strife."

"It will be hard for men of your own blood to acknowledge you their overlord," said Thjodhild. "But why must it be thus, for there are no kings in Greenland, or even Iceland, yet men live in peace together there?"

"Because," said he, "that is how matters are arranged in this land. If I do not rule, then some other must...and I have seen the nature of that king who held sway in this country before me. Nor am I minded to bow my head to any other in this land which is my inheritance."

Thjodhild said she thought it very odd that Sigtrygg thought the rights he held to Leif's houses entitled him to all that country round about as well, but Sigtrygg now replied that, in his opinion, no one could hold Leif's houses if he did not also hold broader power in that land, "for these Skraelings are too numerous for anything less."

"Then," Thjodhild said, "that is reason enough for men of our blood to abandon this country, since we cannot hope to hold sway over such a people, who are so different from our own kind...and so widespread. Or did you think to find contentment among them by taking one of their own to wife?"

Sigtrygg looked away from her when she said this.

"I did not think to see you again, kinswoman," he replied. "And, truthfully, the matter arose as a means to exercise power over them. And to fulfill a promise which I had made to their chieftain, to look after those people who, before this, had depended entirely on him."

"Yet you find the alliance a pleasing one, kinsman?" asked Thjodhild.

"The Skraeling woman makes a good wife," Sigtrygg replied, "and what she lacks in knowledge of our Greenland ways, she compensates for with the gentleness of her heart. Besides, a Skraeling wife is no ill thing in this country."

"A Skraeling wife for a Skraeling king," said Thjodhild, "if that is your desire. But most northern men are unlikely to be satisfied with a woman of lesser race, though it has been said your own father found his solace among such as these."

Sigtrygg said: "Lady, things have certainly taken a different turn than what was dreamed on when we two stood alone in your father's barn, feeding the cattle. Yet, I would not see you harmed in any manner. Ask what you will of me and I will grant it, if I am able, for you had the right to more than I have now given."

"Dry clothes, Sigtrygg," Thjodhild now said. "Only my own dry clothes which I have stored among my goods in the lodging you granted the Norwegians; for, if truth be told, I shall freeze to death, despite this fire you have built here, unless I can remove this gown which I am now wearing."

Sigtrygg could now see that Thjodhild was trembling within her blankets and that Fridgerd was shivering too, for she, like her mistress, had chosen not to remove her wet garments, in deference to Thjodhild's wishes. Sigtrygg now got up and, calling Olvir to follow him, ran outside into the storm which was still raging with no less ferocity than before.

These two now went up to the Norwegians' hall and rushed inside, surprising the few men Osvif had left to guard his goods, and now they began to tear apart whatever they found there until they came upon a trunk with women's clothes inside. Then they took two dresses from within and wrapped them carefully in wadmal cloth and ran outside again, before any of the Norwegians could prevent them, bringing the garments they had found at once to

Thjodhild and her servant. But these two were now so cold that their features had taken on a bluish cast and Sigtrygg at once gave orders to the Skraeling women to strip them of their wet garments and wrap them in the driest skins which they could find and this was now done.

Sigtrygg stood over them all the while, unwilling to leave, watching to see that they were treated with the utmost care, and Chinokwa and the other Skraeling women hurriedly peeled off the ruined garments from the shivering bodies of the two Greenland women. When they had taken the last piece of gown from Thjodhild's flesh, the Skraelings looked down at her and stared without shame for, it seemed to them, that they had never seen such fair white skin on a human being before and they thought this a great marvel.

There was a small building in the shadow of the larger hall which Sigtrygg had taken for his own and he now commanded his followers to build up the fire within it. When this was done, he had the two Greenland women carried inside and placed carefully on the ground on either side of the burning pit. Then he told everyone to leave except for Olvir, whom he set to keep watch over the two women.

All that day thereafter Sigtrygg paced about, finding the close confinement of the hall little to his liking. Yet, since the storm raged on outside, he could do little else but remain within with the others. Several times he sent word to Olvir to ask him how matters stood with his charges but the Brattahlid man responded, each time, that things were no different than before. Then Sigtrygg resumed his uneasy pacing and no one could lighten his burden for he seemed to be consumed by the matter.

After night fell, the storm outside eased somewhat but Olvir did not return to them and, when Sigtrygg sent to ask if the women had recovered, Olvir again replied that there had been no change.

Once the storm had abated, the men of the Norwegian's crew

sought rest in their dwellings, for they had struggled all that day as the storm raged to ensure their ship remained securely lashed on the beach and safe from the winds and storm-driven tides. Yet, they did not come, thereafter, to reclaim Thjodhild and Sigtrygg said he thought this a strange thing, since they left her, by this, in his keeping. He said that, in his opinion, this only showed the small regard in which they held her. Still, he did not offer to send her back to them.

That night, when others had gone off to their beds, Sigtrygg remained seated before the fire. Chinokwa came softly up to him and asked if he intended on going out.

"That may well be," Sigtrygg replied, "for there is little enough here to encourage a man's sleep."

She asked where he meant to go, but he gave her no answer.

"You are certainly more likely to find what you are seeking," she said, after a time, "if you are willing to speak of it to others."

He looked for a long while into the fire and then he turned and fixed his gaze on her. "There's little hope of that," he said at last, "for each of us must follow the path that lies before him. And now I want you to return to your sleeping place and think no more on this matter, for I will let no harm come to you or your kinsmen, whatever else befalls."

Chinokwa said that it was only right that she remain by her husband's side, when he was wrestling with such weighty matters as those which were now before him, but Sigtrygg answered that there was no need for that. "Besides," he added, "you cannot hope to understand questions of Greenland law."

"We Skraelings often see much farther into things than men of your kind will give us credit for," she said.

Sigtrygg said he thought this might be true but that there were some things which neither Greenlanders nor Skraelings could clearly see "and then it is for those who are on the path to find the way themselves." And now he arose and went out of doors and left the Skraeling woman alone before the fire.

Although the harsh storm had ceased, the sky remained over-

cast with no moon above for light and the air had a heavy damp-
ness to it. Sigtrygg went, first of all, down to the place where the
Norwegian ship was beached and then to the sea's edge, and now
he could see how the water had risen and left, in its wake, all
manner of seabed debris. He picked his way among these things
until he came to a place where the line of trees came down to the
water and then he turned back and followed these again to the
higher ground. He returned in this manner to the place where Leif
Eiriksson's houses stood and now he found himself beside that
small structure in which Olvir kept the vigil and, seeing that all
was quiet and no one about, he went inside.

Olvir gave him a fair greeting and said that nothing had
changed, though he thought the women slept more easily, now
that the rains had ceased. Sigtrygg thanked him and told him he
was free to go, "since you have given up a night's rest to look after
these two. But I will keep the watch now, for both of us, until
morning comes."

Olvir said he could have it his own way and got up to leave.
Then Sigtrygg went and sat down beside the sleeping form of
Thjodhild. It seemed to him, then, that the woman stirred and he
reached out one hand to touch her face. He found it cool against
his fingers and he thought this better than the fevered burning he
had expected. Then he brushed the flame-red hair hastily from
either side of her face, and now it seemed to him that there was no
fairer woman to be found, on either side of the western sea, than
this maid of Brattahlid and he let his hand linger there, upon the
soft downy cheeks of the sleeping woman. Something in his touch,
perhaps, or in the low-crackling of the fire which now burned
itself down into the earth, or in the shifting of the air, as Olvir
went out, seemed to reach out beyond his fingers to her then, for
all at once he could see that her eyes were no longer shut and that
she was watching him, in her turn.

Sigtrygg said "are you awake then, kinswoman," and Thjodhild
said that she was.

"Then matters have gone somewhat better with you than we

had cause to hope," he replied, "for many have taken to their beds with fever, for far less cause than you have now had."

"Did you not hear the Norwegian skipper's words, concerning the hardiness of Greenland women?" Thjodhild asked him softly and he replied that he had, "although I thought the words were meant to please you, more than to praise others."

Then he took his hand away from her cheek and asked how she was getting on, "for the rains have now let up, and that is surely no loss to us, so you are free to leave, if you want to."

Thjodhild made no answer but remained silent for awhile.

After a time she reached out and took hold of his hand and placed it again where it had been. She said: "I am not certain about the rains, kinsman, but there are other losses which I have known...and felt more keenly."

Sigtrygg said: "It was unwise of you to come out to this country, lady..."

But Thjodhild put her finger to her lips and silenced him. She said: "There's no use worrying about what cannot be changed. Still I want to know if you are now prepared to change those things which can?"

"To each person, his own fate," Sigtrygg answered, "however hard he may strive against it; and I don't think things are likely to be any different in this case."

Thjodhild said that this was exactly the answer she had hoped to hear from him. "But what of the Skraeling woman?" she asked.

"I will not be the cause of any harm to her," he said.

"But you will send her away?" Thjodhild asked.

"There is no need of that," he replied, "for the customs in this country are not the same as those by which people in Greenland abide."

"But I am of Greenland," answered Thjodhild, "and not this land."

Sigtrygg sought to withdraw his hand from her but Thjodhild held him fast. She said: "Now you must choose one thing or the other kinsman. Either make your peace with those of us who are of your own blood, and I shall be the means for that, or let the matter lie...and then you are to leave me in peace, so I may return to our kinsmen in the Norwegians' camp."

"I am not certain that that is the alternative you will prefer," Sigtrygg replied.

"Nevertheless, that is how it is to be," said she. And now she loosened her grip upon his hand and turned her eyes away.

Sigtrygg left his hand where it lay upon her cheek and then he stroked her gently along the outer edge of her face and down the inside of her neck. "I would not cause you greater grief than I have already done," he said, and, hearing this, she turned her face once more toward his and opened her mouth as though she would speak again.

But now Sigtrygg bent down to her and took the covering, which lay over her, away, so that she lay, glistening and white, in the smoky light of the pit fire, unclothed beneath his eyes. Then he placed his face against hers and told her to keep silent, lest they wake the serving maid, and Thjodhild nodded her assent, and in this fashion he lay down beside her and held her for a long time against his chest. Thereafter he began to kiss her, very slowly at the first, but afterwards with greater urgency, and she did not offer up any resistance to that siege which he now brought against her defenses. And soon no other sounds were to be heard in that place but the soft clashing of their limbs and their whispered words as they clung tightly, each to the other, beside the dying fire.

After a time Thjodhild placed her hands hard against his chest and pushed him upwards so that he seemed to hang there in the air above her. She said: "There is yet one thing more I would have of you kinsman." And Sigtrygg replied: "Speak lady, for there is little I am minded to deny you."

"In that case," said she, "you must now promise to send these Skraelings away...and most of all that one you have taken, in my place, to your bed."

To this Sigtrygg made no answer, but he lowered himself gently onto her again, covering the length of her body with his own.

And then he kissed her for a long time, and she did not refuse this but offered him back kiss for kiss, until the morning light crept through those crevices which the passage of years had left in the walls of that roughhewn house in which they lay.

CHAPTER XXXVI

RECONCILIATION

When Sigtrygg rejoined the others on the following day he had little to say, one way or the other, and kept even more to himself than before. Still, he gave orders that Thjodhild and her serving girl were to be treated with every consideration and he sent them back to the Norwegians with so many gifts that it took nearly half the men of the Gull to carry these for them.

Thord, when he saw how things were, said he thought it a very strange thing that Sigtrygg should treat one of their blood with so much honor, when he had shown only contempt for the rest of them. But Girstein laughed at this and said it was plain his kinsman had little knowledge of human nature, "or of how these two got on in former times, when we all sat safely together on our fathers' Greenland farms."

Afterwards Sigtrygg sent a message that he desired a meeting with them and that this was to be at the place which the Norwegian skipper had claimed for his law court, beside the beached merchant ship. When they came to this place they saw that Sigtrygg and his men had already arrived there before them and that they had claimed the high ground for themselves. Sigtrygg, himself, had taken that seat which Osvif the Norwegian had previously occupied and on either side of him stood Vragi and Arnliot, with the others nearby. They were all fully armed.

Thord said that this was a fine situation, "for our kinsman now shows that he has taken matters into his own hands, and it is quite clear how he means to deal with us." But Girstein replied that they must be patient "and let matters take their course, since it is not as plain to me as to some others that this man means us ill."

Sigtrygg invited them to come into the open area before the high seat and it could now be seen that he wore the cloth of gold thread, tied tightly about his head, as before. He said: "Since you men have sought a judgement, it is only right that I should render it, for there is no other as well-suited in this country for that than I."

"Then you propose to claim King Harald's rights here for yourself?" asked Osvif.

"My kinsman, the king, has no rights in this land unless I grant them, and I have not done that," answered Sigtrygg. "Still, it is in my mind to put the matter to rest, one way or another, since it is clear enough that you men will never find peace in this land until a decision concerning the claims you have raised has been given."

"It is unlikely that you will be the one to deliver a judgment which is suitable for that," said Thord. "So now the best thing is that you remain here while we go for our weapons, and then we shall see which of our two sides is likely to get the better of this matter."

Arnliot lifted up the shield which he held and half-drew his sword from its scabbard. He said: "We are certainly not willing to do that Eiriksfjorder, for you have the advantage on us in numbers. But now we are armed and you men aren't and, in my opinion, that is most likely to even up the odds between us."

Sigtrygg said: "There's no need for weapons play here in any case, since I did not bring you men to this place for fighting but for a settlement. Or is that not what you were seeking?" And now he arose from his place and told them he was prepared to offer peace on terms which he thought they would be willing to accept.

Thereupon Girstein stepped up and said: "Then you must tell us your terms, kinsman."

"Willingly," answered Sigtrygg, and he now asked if Thjodhild were present.

"I most certainly am, kinsman," she said, coming forward, for, until that moment, she had been standing well to the rear of the others.

"In that case, I want to ask Thjodhild to name the terms herself," said Sigtrygg, "for she is a better spokesman concerning these matters than any of you others."

"That I will not," said the woman, "for how shall I know what is in another's mind where such things are concerned? Since you have brought us out here," she added, "it is for you to speak first and offer what you will."

Sigtrygg laughed and said: "It is not surprising that you are unwilling to speak up, lady, since these others in your company have proved such thick heads, before now, concerning this matter. In my opinion, it would be difficult for anyone to persuade them to accept even the fairest of offers. But if you will not deliver a verdict for us, then it falls to me do so. And now I want to know if my kinsman, Lambi Gunnarsson, is also present?"

Lambi said that he was, although he too had remained apart from the others and was now standing outside the roped off ground. Sigtrygg told him to step inside the boundaries, with the others, "for all agreements made on such land will have the strongest hold on those who swear to be bound by them, and I will not have any less for the settlement which I mean to offer you men here."

Lambi agreed to do this and now he entered the area where the others stood. But Thord said: "It's not altogether clear to us, kinsman, that this land has now got that sanctity which you have claimed for it since the storm washed away those first markers which we placed here, under the eyes of King Harald's man. It is not certain that these other markers which you have put down have been properly laid out after them. And besides, you men have brought your weapons onto this ground, which is certainly a violation of all custom and practice concerning such things."

To this Sigtrygg replied that the ground had that sanctity which he, alone, proclaimed for it and Vragi added that "in every land, the king has the power to lay down those usages which make the most sense for those under his rule, and things are no different in this country."

"I'm not sure about that," answered Thord, "but it's certainly clear that my kinsman intends to have his own way, whatever anyone else has to say in the matter. In which case, there is little enough to be done now, though some will think the issue hardly closed whatever now befalls."

Sigtrygg said: "You are a hard man to treat with, kinsman Thord. But, in my opinion, this only makes it the more challenging, to arrive at a settlement which all those who are now present will agree to honor."

"What is your offer, then?" asked Osvif the Norwegian.

"My offer is to Lambi Gunnarsson, first of all," said Sigtrygg and now he asked if Lambi were willing to hear him.

"I am," said Lambi.

"Then, kinsman," said Sigtrygg, "I want to pay you for that wound which I gave you when we met out on the fjord beneath Brattahlid. Though, in my opinion, the blow was not unmerited, yet it did you more harm than I could have wished, once the moment was passed, and it seems to me the honorable thing to pay you now for what you have suffered. But first I want to know if you are willing to take this payment from my hands?"

"And why should I not?" asked Lambi.

"Because you must take it as from the king of this country, and not as though it were a matter which is solely between kinsmen."

Lambi said: "That will depend on the manner of the payment you are offering."

Thord now grew exceedingly angry, on hearing that Lambi was willing to treat with Sigtrygg, and said that it was folly to listen to such idle chatter as this, "for Sigtrygg is no more a king in this land than any of us, and has no more right to make himself out as such than you or I."

But Girstein told him to hold his peace and now Lambi said

he was willing to hear what Sigtrygg offered.

"Then that is well done," Sigtrygg replied. "But first you are to tell me if you are equally prepared to hear a request from me?"

"That will depend," said Lambi. "Yet, since you have asked this in such an honorable fashion, I see no reason to refuse. But what can you want of me?"

Sigtrygg said it was not a difficult matter to discuss "between men like us, for I want only one thing of you that is in your power to give and that is your sister to wife. It is your right to speak for her, for you are her nearest kinsman in this country."

Lambi said this came as a surprise to him, considering all the hard feelings which had been between them until now. And then he added that it was certainly not a matter which he had looked favorably upon in former days, "though you were somewhat less well-off then than now. But what does my sister have to say in this matter?"

Lambi turned then to Thjodhild and she looked boldly back at him. She said she would not oppose Sigtrygg's request though she thought the matter best left in Lambi's hands, "for you are the one to speak for our father now that we find ourselves so far from our home."

"I did not think that I was bringing you out here to preside at your wedding," Lambi said. "Nor do I think our father would consent willingly to this, if he were present."

"Nevertheless," Thjodhild said, "you are here, and not him. So it is your right to speak for me and act in his place."

Then Sigtrygg pressed him, saying: "Are you willing to give your consent in this matter, kinsman, since so much depends on it?"

But Lambi said that this was a very different matter than the question of his claim of unlawful assault, or of the stolen ship, and that it would certainly require more thought than he was now prepared to give it. "In my opinion," he added, "this is not the sort of thing which a man should decide upon without the advice of others."

"Yet all those claiming kinship with you in this country are now in this place," Sigtrygg said, "and you will be hard put to find a better time to consult with them than this. But if you mean to put the matter off till you come again to Greenland, it is unlikely you will get the settlement in these other matters which you have been seeking."

Thord said: "Pay him no mind, kinsman, for there is no reason to offer the hand of Thjodhild for a share in this country. Nor will those we left behind think well of us for it."

"They will not think well of us, in any case," added Girstein Eiriksson, "if we make so little of this expedition that we fall to fighting now among ourselves, and take no profit with us out of this country when we sail back to Greenland. My advice, therefore, is that we leave the matter to Thjodhild herself, for she alone will know how this is to be decided."

Lambi again asked his sister if she were favorably disposed to the offer which Sigtrygg was now making and Thjodhild replied that, as far as she was concerned, the matter was entirely in her kinsman's hands. "But," she added, "some people would think a marriage feast a better way to spend one's time than the hard words which we have been exchanging all this time . . . and the fighting which will certainly follow close behind, if we forego a settlement now."

Sigtrygg said he thought this showed that Thjodhild's wishes were clear in the matter and now he asked Lambi again for his decision.

At length Lambi said he would agree, since Thjodhild was willing, and now they fell to discussing the terms of the marriage. Lambi asked what his sister could expect as her share in the arrangement they were making between them, "for Thjodhild comes of the best family in Greenland," he said, "and is not, herself, without wealth and position."

"She is to have half of all that is mine," answered Sigtrygg, "and that is all this country called Vinland."

"That is fair," Lambi agreed. "Yet I cannot offer you anything in return, for that property which is held by our kinsmen back in Greenland is not now in my keeping. Still, I promise to speak up for you in the matter, when we have made our way home again, and to see that Thjodhild is given her share of the goods which our father owns, either in land or other wealth."

Sigtrygg said that this was acceptable to him.

They were now about to conclude the betrothal on these terms, with each man calling witnesses to what had been said, but, before the proper oaths could be declared, it happened that Thjodhild, herself, suddenly spoke up and asked Sigtrygg and her brother if, indeed, they now thought that they had settled every question to the satisfaction of all present. Sigtrygg replied that he could see no other obstacle before them and Lambi, her brother, said that he too was in agreement, "provided our kinsman proves as honorable in this matter as his words have now made him out to be."

But Thjodhild said that, in her opinion, there was still one other matter which concerned her, "for I cannot wed you, Sigtrygg, so long as the question of my possessions is unresolved and I must go to my marriage bed undowered, like any common serving girl. People," she added, "would think ill of me for it."

Sigtrygg said this was of no great import "for I will certainly accept the word of Lambi Gunnarsson, concerning the disposal of your goods, when he has gone back to Greenland."

But Thjodhild said she did not want others to laugh at her behind her back, which would surely happen if she brought no property of her own to their new household. "I am certainly not the sort to wed a man with nothing to show for it in my own name," she said.

"What do you propose then, lady," Sigtrygg asked, "for it seems to me that this wedding feast was a thing which you were seeking, but a short while ago, no less than I? Yet now some people would think you have joined our kinsman Thord in opposing it."

"Not that," replied Thjodhild, "yet I will not be bought like some common slave, even for all this wide country. But you may still bring a resolution to the matter, if you are willing, in another way."

Sigtrygg said he would do whatever she wanted "if only to put an end to this haggling. So come, lady," he added, "and speak your mind here."

Then Thjodhild asked Sigtrygg what manner of settlement he intended to offer her brother. Sigtrygg replied that he planned to offer him half of all those goods, still remaining in his possession, which he had brought with him out of the Skraeling country. "And I will give him, and those who are with him, the right to remain in Vinland, besides, for as long as they desire it, and allow them to take out with them whatever goods they can secure for themselves, while they are here. Furthermore," he said, "they are to be my guests, whenever they sail out to us, and have the free use of Leif's houses while they are here."

"These are very generous terms," Thjodhild admitted, "and most people will think them acceptable; nor do I think you will find the men who sailed here with Osvif the Norwegian ungrateful for such an offer. But in my opinion you must now promise something more to those of us who are bound to you by blood and to whom you owe a greater debt."

"What then, lady?" Sigtrygg said.

"If you would have my hand, kinsman," said Thjodhild, "it must be as equals, in which case you must now grant land to my brother to hold in our father's name as payment for the harm you have done us . . . for Lambi has lost the use of his arm from that spear you cast against him, and that is no light matter."

Sigtrygg said: "That is a high price for one arm."

"No less than he has placed upon it himself," answered Thjodhild, "in which case you will get no peace for any lesser settlement. But if you fear the outcome of sharing out your birthright in this manner, there is no need, for Lambi will grant me the land which you pay to him, as my share of our father's holdings. And then I shall be dowered, as is my right, while the land which you have given up will be returned into your keeping for as long as we are wed."

Sigtrygg thought about this for a while and, after a time, he nodded his head and said he thought it a good plan. So now he asked Lambi if he were willing to do as Thjodhild had proposed, "for then you and your companions shall be the guests of your kinswoman, no less than of me, whenever you sail out to visit us, and you may find this more to your liking than otherwise."

Lambi said this was acceptable to him but Thord now added that he didn't see how this could settle all the differences which were still between them.

"In my opinion," Girstein said, "this only shows how clever our kinswoman is, for none of us men could formulate a settlement acceptable to all the parties before now. And yet Thjodhild has shown us the way to this. I, for one, will be pleased to accept hospitality in this land, from whichever of my kinsmen will offer it, and I urge you others to do the same."

"I'm not sure about that," said Thord, "for there are yet other questions to be resolved."

Girstein said: "As to the matter of the ship, we have already seen how that case has gone and it was not to our benefit. Nor do I see how we can reopen the question until we have found our way home again to Greenland; and then it is not entirely clear that matters will be resolved in our favor. Still, our kinsman is willing to pay Lambi for that wound he gave him, though his debt remains uncertain until the status of the ship has been determined. And that is nobly done, whatever anyone else says concerning these other matters."

Sigtrygg now thanked Girstein for his words and promised him his full friendship in that country, "both as king and kinsman, for you will always find a welcome here while I have any say in the matter. And now I want to offer you, Thord, settlement as well, for you seem to be the least satisfied concerning the outcome of your case here. But while you have taken on the claims of another, which are more properly to be prosecuted elsewhere, I still want to offer you the right to submit the matter to my judgement, for then you may gain some satisfaction and be content."

"There is no settlement but full restitution of all the goods which have been stolen from chieftain Grimkel's followers," said Thord sharply, "and outlawry, besides, for the men who took them."

"We can't offer you that," answered Sigtrygg, "for the goods are not in our possession to return. And outlawry seems rather harsh and is not something I am willing to impose, in any event. But I will see that payment is made for what was taken." Sigtrygg now turned to Arnliot, who had stood all this while in silence beside him, and asked what he was willing to pay to those bringing the claim of theft against him.

Now Thord began to laugh at this and Sigtrygg turned to him once more and asked the cause of this strange outburst.

"Only this," said Thord, "that we never thought to see you playing at kings, when we were boys together in Eiriksfjord, for then it seemed to us that you were the least likely of any of our kin to make a place for himself in this world; or to strut about so, as you are now doing, with such pretensions of royalty."

Sigtrygg's face darkened on hearing these words, but he did not alter his tone in replying to Thord, but said in a low and steady voice that, "things will often happen in a manner that is least expected, and this should not seem surprising to you, kinsman, for none can know his fate at the start...or how matters will end for him afterwards. And now, it seems to me, that our paths have certainly taken a very different turn, for you are destined to remain a farmer's son, who loves wealth more than honor, and his life more than either of these, whereas I have won a kingdom in this new land."

"Even so," replied Thord, "I am not obliged to honor you for it."

"Yet you will take my judgement," said Sigtrygg, "if you would have satisfaction in this case which you have brought."

"Not even that," answered Thord, "for I would prefer nothing than to accept this false claim of kingship which you have made here."

"Then nothing," Arnliot now interjected, "will it be, for I am certainly not inclined to offer satisfaction to one such as you, in any event."

Sigtrygg said, at once, that these were ill-considered words and now he turned to the Ketilsfjorder and urged him to withdraw them, "for no peace is made which is only partially offered."

But Arnliot replied that he was unwilling to unsay the words he had spoken and now Thord said the same, adding that "I will certainly press my claim against this big man in other quarters, where false kings do not set themselves up to obstruct the course of justice. And, if need be, I shall see a sentence of full outlawry levied against Arnliot Keelfoot at the Greenland Assembly, where I and my kin are not without some influence."

Sigtrygg said this was an unfortunate turn of events and urged Thord, once more, to accept a settlement, "for I will pay it out myself, if my shipmate will not."

But Thord said he was still not willing to do that.

And now he turned and stalked angrily from that place of assembly with his brother, Thorstein, and those other Eiriksfjord men who had sailed out there with them on the Norwegian's ship.

Girstein, when he saw how things had gone, said they should not allow Thord's abrupt departure to upset those other agreements which had now been made, "since his grievance is a small one and cannot be pressed further in this country, so long as we others are of the same mind."

"I, for one, am certainly willing to keep my word in regard to the agreements made here today," Sigtrygg said and now he asked Lambi whether he would still take the land claim which Thjodhild had sought for him.

"I see no reason to do otherwise," Lambi replied.

"Then I can see no reason not to grant it to you," said Sigtrygg and he asked his kinsman where he planned to make his claim.

Lambi said he had not given that much thought but would

settle wherever Sigtrygg advised him.

Then Thjodhild spoke up again, saying that she had already made up her mind concerning the land claim, even if her brother had not, and that the place she desired was not far off.

"Where then, kinswoman?" Sigtrygg asked her.

"Through these nearby woods," said she, "and not far from where we are now standing either, for there are houses there which are not unlike those our ancestor, Leif, built in this place. And it will be easy enough to restore them and build a proper steading where they stand. And a hall for the wedding feast, besides."

CHAPTER XXXVII

THE DOWRY

Sigtrygg listened to her words and grew uncommonly silent. After a time he said: "You must choose another land claim, lady, for that is an ill-omened place and I would not be the cause of harm to you or others by giving it into your hands."

"Are you afraid of ghosts, then, Sigtrygg," Thjodhild laughed, "though you spoke so boldly against these on that night we two stood above the hall at Brattahlid?"

"Not the sort that walk about, which some people fear," answered Sigtrygg with some firmness, "but I have seen enough to know that there are things best left undisturbed. And so it is with that place, where hard deeds and injustices were done by those who counted themselves our kin."

"Nevertheless," said Thjodhild, "that is the land claim which I would make for the houses on it can be readily restored for our purposes, while the land itself is close by the coast, yet well-shielded from any sea-borne gales such as those we have now seen. And the place has a pleasing look to my eyes, besides."

Sigtrygg said: "In my opinion, this is a bad choice, for there are many other places nearby which are just as fair and which carry no burden of past crimes as that place does, Lady."

But Thjodhild said that no other place had houses built upon it, which were ready for occupancy with only a little effort, and that her mind was made up concerning this in any event, "or do you regret, already, the oath of betrothal and the promises you have made to me, kinsman?"

"Certainly not," was Sigtrygg's reply, "but I did not think you had this in mind."

"Then that is a different tune from the one you sang to me the night before," answered Thjodhild, "when you thought there was little in this world you were willing to deny me."

Sigtrygg said: "Have it your own way, kinswoman, for I will not deny you this, either, if you have set your heart upon it. But I want you to promise me at least that you will build another hall, beside the two which are now standing there, and that you will not take up residence in either of these."

Thjodhild said: "It is unseemly, kinsman, for a man like you to show such fear of ghosts as this, for these are well-built structures and it would take us much longer to build anew than to restore what is already standing on that ground."

"Have you not heard," said Sigtrygg sharply, "what manner of crimes were done there? Or that men say the brothers Helgi and Finnbogi lie buried in that ground who, among all others, have special reason to hold a grievance against members of our kin?"

"I see no reason to be concerned about the opinions of dead men," answered Thjodhild sharply, "and you did not, either, when we two were together back in Greenland. Still, I will abide by your wish in this, if that is how you would have it, and build a third hall for the wedding feast. Yet, it seems to me, that you are not so bold a man as the one who sailed out of Eiriksfjord on that day we last parted, when neither ships nor spear points nor the clamor of angry kinsmen could turn you from that path you desired to follow."

After this the two sides parted and now Thjodhild invited Osvif and all his crew to join her at the inland houses, "since we have already imposed too long on the hospitality of this country's king." And then she added that she thought there was too much risk, besides, if the two crews remained longer together, "for fighting over one matter or another is certain to break out."

So now the Norwegians left the houses in Leif's settlement

which Sigtrygg had lent them and went inland with Thjodhild and her kinsmen and set up camp on the ground which had formerly been used by the slain Icelandic brothers. There Thjodhild asked the Greenland men who were with them to lend a hand in cutting trees for the new hall she had promised to build for the wedding feast and Osvif said that he would set his own followers to work beside them, as well, "for it is only right, lady, that we repay you for our upkeep."

But not everyone was in agreement with this plan for it seemed to many a great waste to be building a third hall when two others, which could so easily be restored, were so close by. Thjodhild reminded them of the promise which she had made to Sigtrygg but Thord and the Greenlanders who were with him said this made no difference to them for they had no desire to undertake more work than was needful. Many of the Norwegians said they felt the same way and the end of it was that Osvif persuaded her to allow them to first rebuild the two houses which were already on that ground, "so we may have a dry place to stay, at the least, before winter finds us. Nor are the storms we are likely to encounter in this country any less severe than that one which we have only just been through."

After this they set to work and it was not long before they had cleaned up and re-thatched the houses of the Icelanders. Then they made their home in these, with Thjodhild and her kinsmen and those who were with them taking the one hall and Osvif and his followers the other. There was some grumbling among the Norwegians about this for they thought it rather an unfair division of the property, seeing as they were more numerous than those who were with Thjodhild, though they had to make do in a house of no greater size. But Osvif silenced them, saying they were Thjodhild's guests and that it only made sense that their hosts would have the better share of things.

All this while, Sigtrygg remained with his followers at Leif's houses hard by the coast and now they thought things had gone very well for them, indeed, since all that ground which they had claimed before was now returned into their keeping. Arnliot, especially, went about with those of the crew who had attached themselves to him and took possession of all the houses once more, placing Greenlanders and Skraelings in each of these, "so we do not lose our claim here a second time," he said.

The Skraelings in Sigtrygg's following soon set up their own houses in the midst of those which Leif had built, as well, so that the settlement began to take on the look of a Skraeling village. The men of the Gull found this strangely comforting for it reminded them of the other Skraeling settlements in which they had been and of the glory they had won there. And now, one after another, they moved out of Leif's houses and took up living in the booths which the Skraelings made and Sigtrygg laughed at the sight of this, saying, "now these men are truly a part of this country." And then he added that "it will not be long before we have bred us a host of new Vinlanders to take our place here, and support us against those who would make themselves our enemies."

Still, despite this mixing of Norsemen and Skraelings, Sigtrygg soon found that all was not as quiet as it seemed for W'tnalko now set himself apart from the others and several of the young Skraeling men who had come out there with them joined themselves to him. They now came and went without leave of the others and built shelters for themselves at the edge of the forest, somewhat removed from the place where Leif's settlement was. Sigtrygg went once or twice to speak with W'tnalko there but the Skraeling showed little interest in conversation and, in the end, Sigtrygg gave the matter up. After this he went to Chinokwa and asked her to speak for him to W'tnalko, since he wanted to win the man's allegiance back, but she replied that she did not think there was much she could do in this matter.

"And why not," Sigtrygg asked her, "since you are a woman of his kind and one for whom he has risked much besides?"

"Because," said Chinokwa, "he holds me to be the cause of his pain as much as he does you . . . though I am not certain that I have gained as much from it as was to be hoped."

Sigtrygg said she should now speak up more clearly if some matter was troubling her, but the woman replied that she had little to say concerning this, "for you will not be disposed to heed my words, in any event."

"I would not be so certain of that," was Sigtrygg's reply, "for I, too, faced harsh odds to win back your life for you, and this will have been of little account if I turn my face from you now."

"Yet, that is just what you mean to do, is it not?" asked the woman. "Or what is that oath you have made to take that Greenlander woman to wife?"

Sigtrygg said: "I did not think you Skraelings would have learned of this so swiftly."

"W'tnalko speaks your tongue as well as you speak ours," replied Chinokwa, "so it was only to be expected that some will talk and others hear. And that is surely the cause of his anger with you, inasmuch as I chose you, despite all his hopes, when the matter was mine to decide. "

"Still," said Sigtrygg, "it is not unheard of that a man may have two wives, for this is common enough among you Skraelings. And one of my own men is the proof of it."

"This Greenland woman has spoken otherwise," replied Chinokwa, "or has she not said she will have you for herself . . . or not at all?"

"Words spoken are not things done," said Sigtrygg. "Besides she is new to this country and has little understanding of its ways. In time she will see, as I do, how things must be here. And then she will not find it hard to welcome you, as her sister, into her house."

"As you took your sister to your bed, Aselekah?" asked the Skraeling woman.

"This was at your father's urging," Sigtrygg replied. "I had never claimed you as a husband, otherwise."

"Yet now I would know how you mean to repay him for bringing you, thus, into his household and raising you up as a great man among his kindred?"

"It seems to me," said Sigtrygg, "that I have already done my share, having saved the life of his daughter and defeated those who were his enemies besides. If I took you, afterwards, to wife, it was in fair exchange for that duty to guard your kinsmen, which your father exacted of me. And I am no less prepared to do that now than before."

Chinokwa said: "And yet it is not clear to me how that is to be done, husband, if you make common cause with these others who have come from over the sea after you since they are no friends to us Skraeling folk as has been readily seen."

"They will come in time to think differently, as the men of my own crew have," answered Sigtrygg. "And as Thjodhild, herself, will, for they will see the need for allies and friends on these shores."

"I'm not sure about that, husband," said Chinokwa, "for these are very different people from most others and they do not seem the sort to mix easily with those of us who are not of their kind. But now I want to know what you have in mind for me, since you cannot wed the woman with sun-red hair if I remain nearby."

"You are to return to your kinsmen by the river," Sigtrygg said, "until I come again to claim you, and then I will bring these others and we will establish a large town in that place such that no enemy, in future, will dare to trouble those people who make their home there."

Chinokwa said: "These are fair words, husband, yet it is not in my heart to depart thus, for I think I shall never see you again if I travel this path . . . and that is a thing which I am unwilling to do."

"Still, that is how it must now be, wife," Sigtrygg answered her softly, "for I have given my word to these others and I cannot undo that. But I will ask W'tnalko to render this one last service to us and see you safely conveyed to the dwelling place of your kinsmen, where you are to await my return. And this, I swear, will not be overlong."

Chinokwa said that this was much against her will and that if she could have her way she would remain exactly where she now was, "whatever the Greenland woman says." But Sigtrygg placed his hands on her shoulders and bent down towards her and gave her a single kiss upon her forehead. He said: "This may not be little sister, for I have business to do with these kinsmen of mine, and oaths must be redeemed. But I will come for you, as I have said, and then things will be with us as before."

After that, he sent her to gather her belongings and went, once more, to where W'tnalko had made his camp and this time he would not be turned away but insisted on speaking with the Skraeling warrior. When W'tnalko at last came out of the rude shelter he had made for himself, Sigtrygg gave him a friendly greeting. He said: "You have certainly come a long way Bjorn, from those first days when we found you fleeing amongst the trees, for you have now gained authority with these men so that they take you for their leader. And that is no less than I should have expected, since you acted so boldly when we faced the Tulewat in their stronghold in the west."

W'tnalko made no reply to this but asked Sigtrygg what he now desired of him.

"Only this," answered the Gull's skipper. "My affairs have now taken a somewhat unexpected turn and so it is necessary that we part company for the while. I want you to take Chinokwa, and any others who wish it, back to the village by the river so they will be safe from harm. And I will follow when I am able."

"Then you mean to marry the woman with fire in her hair?" said the Skraeling.

"What is to be, will be," answered Sigtrygg. "But you must see to the safety of Chinokwa, for that is a thing which will matter to us both."

Then it seemed to Sigtrygg that the Skraeling's eyes brightened and the tightness with which his lips were drawn eased, if only for a moment, so that he again had the look of that youth they had stumbled on in the forest nearly a full year before. But this did not last long, for a cloud passed quickly over W'tnalko's features and hid his thoughts once more, as surely as the clouds in the sky obscure the sun when they pass before it, and Sigtrygg was unsure of how to read this man. He said at last: "W'tnalko, I have placed this woman who is both sister and wife to me in your keeping, for I know that you, of all men, will do whatever is necessary to see that no harm befalls her. And now I want you to choose out as many men as you think necessary for this journey, and I will instruct them to do as you desire."

"I will need no more than these few who have joined me here," said the Skraeling in answer, and he pointed to three other warriors who had seated themselves nearby. "They have had enough of you Greenland men, as I have, and will be pleased to leave this place."

"You shall have others if you desire it," Sigtrygg told him, but the Skraeling said there was no necessity for that.

"In that case," said Sigtrygg, "I want to know when you plan to take your leave of us," and W'tnalko replied that they would be gone "before the sun has dropped below the trees," on that very day.

But Sigtrygg said that that was certainly much sooner than he had hoped, and somewhat hastily arranged "for a journey of such importance as this is."

Now it chanced that Thjodhild's serving girl, Fridgerd, came into Sigtrygg's camp not long after this and sat with the crewmen of the Gull and then she had a great deal to say to each of them. They, for their part, thought it great sport, for they found it pleasant to spend time with a woman of their own kind who spoke their language and seemed to think them all great heroes for the tales they had to tell of their adventures among the Skraelings. But Arnliot soon put a claim on this woman and then none of the other crewmen seemed eager to speak with her further for fear of angering the big Ketilsfjordman. Thereafter, he put her on his lap and made much of her, holding her fast even after she indicated a desire to return to her mistress. Though she squirmed about in the big man's grasp she could not free herself until Olvir came up to him and said, in a low voice, that he was now to let the maid go, "for it is plain enough this little bird desires to fly off in search of some other perch than the one she now finds herself on."

Arnliot laughed and asked Olvir if he thought he could provide a stouter landing place, but the Brattahlid man replied that this was for the maid, herself, to decide, "although I am certain I can do no worse than you Ketilsfjord farmers."

Arnliot said: "At the least you are talking bigger than that serving man used to, who joined us after we dumped him and his fellow slaves into the sea. And then you were doing the Leifssons' bidding like any common house dog, lapping up the table droppings which they tossed your way."

"It's no dishonor to keep one's word and serve those who feed and clothe you," answered Olvir. "But some people might think it less than manly to press a young girl to stay when she desires to do otherwise, especially when you are so much larger than she is."

"I am much larger than a great many people," said Arnliot, "as many have found to their sorrow. And I am no less large compared to a man like you."

"Even so," replied Olvir, "you are now to let this woman go her way, for it is unseemly to press her to remain against her will."

Arnliot laughed again and said: "She is just a serving girl and no stranger where I am concerned. But perhaps that is why you are so intent on taking her out of my hands, for like goes to like, as the saying has it."

"Say whatever you will in the matter," answered Olvir, "but you are to release her now, if that is her desire."

Arnliot tightened his grip about the girl's waist and pulled her closer to him and now she ceased to struggle in his hands for it seemed to her that the big man had all the advantage in the matter and that fighting against him would only increase his anger. Thereupon Arnliot kissed her hard on the face and looked up at the other man in triumph for now it was clear to all that the serving girl had given up her struggle to free herself from his grasp.

Olvir said: "Still, you are now to release her shipmate, or things will go hard between us."

"It seems to me," answered Arnliot, "that you have forgotten who it was saved your life when we two fled before the screaming warriors of the Tulewat town, for I broke through their town walls with my hard-swinging axe and afterwards carried you, at great risk, on my own back to safety on that rocky ledge where we made our stand against those people."

"Yet I fought beside you there," said Olvir, "even after you, yourself, had fallen before the Tulewat's fierce blows. And then I stood between you and those who would have taken your head until our shipmates came to aid us. Nor had I sought your aid when my own legs gave way under me, though I had given as much as you, and more, in that town."

Arnliot laughed once more and now he said that all of this was certainly true and that it was a shame to let one little maid come between men like them, when they had fought as brothers, back against back. Then he pushed the serving girl from him and patted her briskly, saying she must now go off, if that was what she wanted, but he promised her a place on the perch she now vacated, "if the little bird should seek to alight there again."

After this, Olvir took Thjodhild's servant by the hand and led her back to the others' camp, saying she must now go about more carefully where men such as these were concerned, "for they have seen and done harsh things and are no fit company for those of us who have lived less adventurous lives."

But Fridgerd said she doubted that Olvir was now any less manly than these others, "though you were certainly rather more timid when you served as farm steward for Thorkel Leifsson."

Olvir now brought her safely back to Thjodhild and the others and when he came there he saw how they had labored over the two houses which the Icelanders had left and how they had rebuilt and enlarged both of these buildings. But nowhere did he see the third hall, which Sigtrygg had charged them to build. Thjodhild came out with her kinsmen to greet them as soon as she saw them coming through the trees. But once she heard how matters had fared, she had only scolding for the serving girl, who now ran hastily into the larger hall. Still, Thjodhild gave Olvir a fair greeting and asked him to stay for awhile and sample their hospitality.

"I haven't much time for that," said Olvir, "for my companions will be seeking me."

"Are you worth so much to them, then, steward?" Thjodhild asked. "But that would not be surprising, for I remember the place you had in my uncle's household. Even he would never have parted willingly with your services."

Thord now came up to them and said that this was certainly true and then he asked if Olvir thought he was as well paid "among these heathen, as when you kept track of things for my father and his brothers on that good farm at Brattahlid?"

"Well enough," replied Olvir, "for I have an equal share in everything with each of my shipmates. And we have won some little renown in this country, and the goodwill of the people who live here, besides."

"Still, there is a great deal of risk to this sort of life," said Thord, "and what is won today may be lost tomorrow. Or do you think our kinsman can hold himself a king in this country forever?"

"I don't know about that," said Olvir, "for no man may live longer than his allotted time, or keep more than his due. But he is no worse a master than some I have served. And better than many."

Girstein was also there with them at this time and he said this was well-spoke and thumped the former serving man hard on the back. This caused Olvir to stumble somewhat and now everyone thought this very funny. Girstein grinned and said he must come into the hall and accept their hospitality at once, but Olvir only thanked them again, saying he preferred to wait until they had built the third hall which Sigtrygg expected of them. "These other two," he said, "are fairly decked out, but there is something about them which makes a man uneasy since such hard deeds were done beneath their walls."

"Are you afraid of ghosts, then?" asked Thorstein Thorkelsson rather too loudly and he made a gesture at the sword which Olvir wore. "Certainly you have come here well prepared to defend yourself, should the need arise, though I'm not sure that a man of your background will know what to do with such a weapon as you are now carrying, once he has it in his hands."

Olvir said that he'd had plenty of opportunity to learn about swordplay, although most people would agree that such arms were of little use where ghosts were concerned. "Still," he added, "I have seen worse things to fear than walking dead men, and these will be living men, against whom a sword stroke may be counted a fair defense."

"Are these Skraelings worth fearing then, serving man?" asked Girstein.

"Some are," said Olvir, "but that will depend on where you meet them. And when."

Thjodhild said there was no use talking about Skraelings unless it was to discuss those which Sigtrygg now had in his company, and then she asked if any of these had been sent away and, if so, which they might happen to be.

"None, lady," answered Olvir, "to my knowledge, though I am told our skipper now means to send off the one he has taken for his wife, just as he promised to do. But you have still to build the hall which you promised, for he will not want to celebrate his wedding night in either of the two houses which are now standing here."

Thord said there was no use talking about that, "for these two buildings are in excellent condition and we've already put a great deal of effort into readying them for use. There's certainly no reason to make such a fuss over this, in any case, unless it is to throw up obstacles to what has already been agreed."

Thjodhild now asked Olvir to speak with Sigtrygg and get him to pay them a visit so that he could see for himself how things were, "and then he will know that these houses will certainly serve as well as any for the purpose which he has in mind for them."

Olvir said he would do what he could and now he took his leave of them.

Sigtrygg was not pleased when he heard what Olvir had to say for he thought that the Icelanders' houses should have been left alone and a new hall built in their stead. Still, Olvir urged him to go and see for himself, "for Thjodhild has asked this of you."

So now he went along with Olvir and some others into the forest until they came to the meadow where the Icelanders' houses stood. There he saw the two halls, newly restored with fresh cut timber. Thjodhild, herself, came out to meet him and brought him to the larger of the halls. Thord Thorkelsson and his brother Thorstein stood within the doorway there but they had little to say when they saw Sigtrygg. Girstein, however, now came over to him and Lambi Gunnarsson was close behind, and they gave him a good welcome to Gunnarsstead, for so they called the land there and the two houses which stood upon it.

"So this is the work which you have done here," Sigtrygg said when he saw them, "though I told you to do otherwise."

"Don't be angry, kinsman," Girstein said, "for the work was hard and Thjodhild eager to see an end to it. And so it seemed better to us to repair these buildings than raise a new one entirely, since that would have taken much longer and been a great deal more work besides. But these two were good buildings, since our predecessors built so strongly when they came out to this country."

Sigtrygg now walked along the length of the larger hall and admired the size of it for, truly, they had made the Icelanders' work better than before. It stood, like an upturned ship, upon the grassy meadow and its timbers were shorn of bark and glowed a clean, bright yellow in the day's sunlight. The man who had named himself King of Vinland now counted off the paces which he must make to mark the length and breadth of this building and he marveled aloud at how much bigger the hall was than before.

"Will you not come within, kinsman?" Thjodhild now asked him, when she saw the surprise and admiration in his face.

Inside the walls arched steeply overhead, to close in a high peaked roof, three-times the height of a tall man, and now well covered with thatch. Light entered from slit windows, at both sides of the hall, while, on the earthen floor, stood two long, newly built tables with a pit for fire between them. At the farther end of the hall, a dais had been raised, as in the finest nobleman's house, and upon this another long table stood. From the rafters hung brightly colored strips of cloth, and wreaths of flowers and green leaves so that the hall smelt of new-cut wood and meadow grass.

"Here lies my dowry before you, kinsman," said Thjodhild softly, "so that all will know I do not come to your bed like some common serving woman but, as befits my station, with property and wealth in my own right. All this I bring to you, kinsman, husband to be, for on the night we drink from the nuptial cup, I shall put this hall and all that it contains into your hands."

"Lady," said Sigtrygg at last, "this is a fair gift and a fairer dowry, as only one who is shortly to be a queen in this country may rightly bestow. Still, I doubt the wisdom of it since there is somewhat of ill-luck attends this place, as you well know. Indeed, it were better to have left this place untouched, to my way of thinking, until some priest or two had sprinkled water round about, than to have taken such liberties with it as you have now done."

"I had thought you'd have accepted this of me in better grace," said Thjodhild with something of a sulk in her voice.

"It is not the offering," said Sigtrygg, "but the history of this place which holds me back. I think you'd have done better to leave this house and the other untouched. But now the matter's sped and I will not disdain what you give, if you would have it so."

"Then this is a better answer than the first," replied Thjodhild and now she told those who were present to clear the tables and lay out food and drink. But Sigtrygg said there was no need for that, "for we will be feasting in this hall soon enough," and he turned to leave, his companions following close behind. Now Thjodhild said: "Kinsman, will you set the date of the marriage feast?" And he replied that it should be of her own choosing, since she had got the hall ready so speedily.

"Then in one week's time," said Thjodhild, "for that will give us sufficient days to lay in the meat to feed our guests and to make a rough sort of wine for the toasting, from the grapes to be found in the countryside roundabout."

"Then that is how it is to be," Sigtrygg agreed and now he went out and back to his own houses, hard by the coast.

CHAPTER XXXVIII

THE FEAST IS HELD

Now it happened that the Skraeling, W'tnalko, prepared to take his leave with those who desired to return to their homes in the country of the Skraelings. But each day Sigtrygg held him back for he said there was no need to act in haste and that such a journey should be well-thought out to avoid the dangers of the countryside. W'tnalko said there was little reason to be concerned about that, for he knew the trails which would bring them safely to the river country, but Sigtrygg urged him to delay, nonetheless.

For her part, the Skraeling woman, Chinokwa, now went apart from the others and made a sleeping place for herself outside the hall which Sigtrygg had taken for his own. These two now had little to say to one another, though Sigtrygg often went to sit above the place where Chinokwa slept out in the open. And then he watched over her, without giving any sign of this, to her or to others, so that she might remain untroubled by both men and beasts in the night. W'tnalko, alone, saw how Sigtrygg kept the watch and sometimes he came and sat beside him for awhile, but neither man spoke to the other during these times.

After three days Thjodhild sent word that she had laid in all the supplies she thought they would have need of and asked Sigtrygg to come and take a count of all that she had prepared. But he replied that there was no need for that, since he was certain she had the matter well in hand, and he urged her to rely on Girstein and on Osvif the Norwegian for her purposes since he was otherwise preoccupied with the affairs of his camp. When her messengers returned to her, Thjodhild asked them what they had seen and if Sigtrygg had now sent his Skraelings away. But they replied that everything was just as before, except that Sigtrygg had turned the Skraeling woman out of his bed.

"Then that is better than nothing," said Thord when he heard this news, "but it is yet a far cry from the promise he gave you, kinswoman, to discard this Skraeling concubine of his, entirely, and send her back to her own kind."

"It is to his credit," replied Thjodhild, "that he finds it so difficult to part with this woman. Still, he must do so if we are to keep to those oaths we have sworn."

She now sent for Olvir and he came at once and these two talked for a very long time together, away from everyone else, and then Olvir returned to Leif's houses on the coast and sought out Sigtrygg. Olvir told Sigtrygg, when he found him, that Thjodhild thought the time had now come for him to keep his word to her, since the wedding feast was nearly upon them, "and you cannot have this Skraeling woman and Thjodhild, too."

"Are you prepared then to give up the Skraeling woman you have to wife, shipmate?" Sigtrygg asked him.

"Not at all," replied the Brattahlid man, "but I most certainly would, if I had such a fine woman as Thjodhild in exchange. And I am not pledged to do so, in any event."

"I am not certain that I am bound to do this either, for she has not kept faith with me in that she has rebuilt those two houses, though I commanded her otherwise."

"It was not Thjodhild, but her kinsmen and the Norwegians who did the building," said Olvir, "and I have her word that this was much against her will. You cannot hold such a matter against her, shipmate, if it was beyond her power to prevent it."

"There is much that is beyond any man's power, I think," said Sigtrygg, "and not least of these is the choice of a straight and storm-free course upon the open seas, if the winds will otherwise. Now I have to hand that woman whom I sought, since we both were young farm folk on our kinsmen's land in Eiriksfjord. And then we thought we had made firm promises, each to the other. Yet I find I am unable to drive out from before me the vision of those dark eyes which I first saw from our place of imprisonment along the banks of the Skraeling river."

"The Skraeling woman can be no fit wife for one such as you, Sigtrygg," said Olvir when he heard this, "for she is not of our blood, or so high-born as Thjodhild is, who claims descent from that great chieftain, Eirik the Red."

"Yet was Chinokwa's father any less a chieftain, in his country, than Eirik in his? Or Leif after him? And am I any less than these men, for my own uncertain parentage, though some have said as much?"

"On the contrary," answered Olvir, "it is well-known how you count your descent from kings, on your father's side, and this is better than any of them. So a man such as you must choose from the best, lest he demean himself."

"How would you choose, then, shipmate?" Sigtrygg asked him.

Olvir said: "That is not hard to tell, for I would choose the one most highly born and to whom I had given oaths."

"Then I will do so, as well," Sigtrygg said.

Not long after this conversation a man came out of the woods, a Skraeling, and he was brought at once into Sigtrygg's presence. Sigtrygg asked his purpose and he said he was a messenger from the people who lived by the river and that Tanakrit had sent him to seek out Aselekah, her foster son.

Sigtrygg told this man to speak up and deliver that message he was charged with carrying, whereupon the Skraeling said that the lady of the river now begged Sigtrygg to remember those words he had spoken at his departure from their country and return at once, "for the lords of the Tulewat have gathered together in council in their chief town in the west, and none know the purpose of this."

"Is it an unheard of thing, that these men will do thus?" Sigtrygg asked him.

"No," replied the Skraeling, "for they will often gather in this fashion when great matters are to be decided. Still, they have summoned their kinsmen from the most distant parts of the country and Nahinanto, their chief man, sits at their head."

On hearing this Vragi stepped forward and said: "Here then is the proof of earlier folly, shipmate, for I warned you before of the perils of leaving such a man alive."

"I'm not sure it would have made a difference, in any event," Sigtrygg answered him, "for the death of one king leads only to the rise of others and we cannot kill them all. Still, it is not certain that such a gathering as this man now describes will be a cause of harm to us, since these people must keep to their own usages and govern according to their customs."

"And that is unlikely to be to our good," said Vragi, "for they will think they have cause to remember how things went between us the last time we met."

About this time Osvif came up with a number of his men, for the Norwegians had heard, too, how another Skraeling had come out of the forest and they wanted to see the man for themselves. After they had heard how matters stood, they asked Sigtrygg what he planned to do and if the Skraelings in the west were truly as formidable as Vragi and some of the others seemed to think.

"They are certainly worth a mention or two," Sigtrygg agreed, "but they are far away from this part of the country and pose little danger to us."

"Still, it would seem these other Skraelings of yours are not taking this news as lightly as you are, yourself, Sigtrygg," said the Norwegian skipper. And, in truth, it could now be seen that a great uneasiness seemed to have come over the other Skraelings who were present, for these people stood about in silence and each of them had a very serious look on his face.

"There's no use worrying about that," Arnliot said, "since we have shown the Tulewat how Norsemen make war and they are not likely to have forgotten such a lesson as the one we gave them, when three of us walked unaided into their town and set it ablaze; or when we met and defeated them in open battle, afterwards."

Sigtrygg said: "Still, there's no use underestimating an enemy, however matters fell out between us before. So now I want to have a strongly built stockade set up all around this settlement, for safety's sake, and I advise you Norwegians to do the same."

Osvif said he would follow this advice, if Sigtrygg urged it, "but," he added, "what do you mean to do concerning this messenger who brought us the news? In my opinion there is not much to be gained by your returning to the country of these Skraelings when such danger is afoot, however much they beg this of you."

"That is still to be seen," answered Sigtrygg. "But, for now, I want to offer this messenger every hospitality. And he is to be treated as our honored guest, for my foster mother's sake."

After this, Sigtrygg went about much more briskly than before and he sent gifts to Thjodhild from among his own goods and told her to use them as she would in her great hall. In particular, he sent many fine fur pelts which he had from the river Skraelings, saying these were to be thrown over the wooden benches to make them softer for Thjodhild's guests. He also sent deer meat and fish and other game for the feast. But he remained silent concerning the Skraeling messenger and the news he had brought.

Thjodhild now sent once more to Olvir and he came to her, as before, and now these two again spoke apart from the hearing of others. Afterwards, Olvir remained with Thjodhild and her kinsmen, helping them to raise the stockade which Sigtrygg had advised them to build. Thord and some of the others complained about this for they thought it somewhat wasteful to spend their time thus, when everybody agreed that the men they feared were far off in the west. But Osvif said they would be better off for the hard work they undertook now and Olvir said the same, and now he told them many stories of his encounters with the Tulewat so that it soon seemed better to them to build the walls than otherwise.

Now the day came before the wedding feast was to be held and there was a great deal of activity in both camps. Thjodhild directed her kinsmen to roast all the meats which they had prepared and to pour out the wine which they had brewed up for the coming festivities and then she sent word to Sigtrygg that all was now ready. Then Sigtrygg sought out the Skraeling, W'tnalko, and told him how things stood. He said: "You are now to take your leave of us, as we have already agreed, and bring Chinokwa to the camp of Tanakrit and see to her well-being there. Tell them, as well, that I will return when I am able."

W'tnalko replied that, "things have certainly taken a different turn, where you are concerned, for there was a time when you would have risked all to fetch this woman from danger. Yet now you send her back to that place where her enemies are to be found. And this, though you swore to guard her and her kinsmen from those same men."

Sigtrygg said this could not be helped and he urged W'tnalko to prepare as carefully as he could, "for it is possible that this will not be as easy a journey as it had first seemed."

The time of the wedding feast now came on and all those in Sigtrygg's camp, both Norsemen and Skraelings, now arose and went to the place where Thjodhild had prepared the feast and they got a good welcome there and found the tables well spread with all manner of choice foods which the country had to offer at that time of the year. There were savory smells from the roasted meats and fine broths which Thjodhild and her serving maid had prepared, and rich red wines for drinking. Girstein and Lambi greeted the newcomers, as hosts should, and Osvif and his fellow Norwegians offered them a share of the wine and meat.

Vragi led his fellow crewmen into the hall and now he looked about him and said it was not surprising that they had done so well for themselves there, "for the Norwegians among you are certainly no pikers when it comes to building with timber, though you men of Iceland and Greenland are somewhat more deficient where these skills are concerned." He added that he thought they had rebuilt "the houses of these Icelanders as finely as any, of similar size, which are to be found back in Norway."

Girstein replied that "it was only to be expected, that our Norwegian comrades should know how to use wood better than those of us who hail from Greenland since there is so little timber in our part of the world. But now it can be seen that we have found a better country for our purposes, and one which is every bit as rich in resources as Norway, or any of the other old lands in the east."

Vragi said: "Still, it remains to be seen if the wealth of this land is now to be ours for the taking."

After this everyone asked where Sigtrygg was, for he had not come in with the others, and Vragi replied that he would follow along shortly, "since he has certain matters which still must be attended to." Thereupon all the guests fell to feasting and boasting, and to the retelling of those stories which were thought to be the most entertaining. Arnliot was the most forward, of the men in Sigtrygg's crew, recounting for all who would listen how they had faced and overcome the Skraeling king in the west and proved themselves the better men. He said that this only showed how easily the country they now found themselves in could be brought under Greenland rule and that they would certainly find much better prospects for themselves in this land than anywhere else.

Everyone thought there was good sense to the big Ketilsfjorder's words, although they listened in utter silence when he came to the battles which had been fought with the Tulewat, for those people seemed to grow larger and more fearsome, the more Arnliot praised his own courage and that of his companions in their confrontations with them.

Osvif also had many tales to tell, since he had travelled widely and seen a great deal of the world. Therefore he stood up, after Arnliot had had his say, and urged those assembled there to consider that other lands besides Vinland had both dangers and treasure to offer, and these were no less to be sought after than "the goods of these wild Skraelings who live in this part of the world."

He told, now, of his own adventures on the Baltic Sea and of the raiding and trading he had had there, for he was a man who was not averse to either hard fighting or hard bargaining, as the case might have it. And he told of his journeys far to the south where he had seen the country of that people who were called Moors. He said there was a great deal of wealth in the Moorish lands, both in gold and fine horses. And then he added that it was "a pity Vinland had no horses of its own, as far as can be seen, for then this country would be as good as any in the world, in my opinion."

Vragi now replied that he thought Vinland must have other virtues which even the Moorish countries lacked.

"That may be," said Osvif, "but there is no matching them for either gold or horses or strength of arms. Still," he added, looking over at Thjodhild, "it may be that the women here are fairer."

Girstein said this was well-spoken and someone else added that there was certainly no finer gold to be found in all the world than that which graced a fair maid's head. And now there were halloos of assent to this throughout the hall.

Then Thjodhild, herself, arose and looked about her and everyone fell silent at this. Turning to Osvif, Thjodhild said: "My lord, merchant, is it not the custom of the heathen Moors, of whom you speak, to keep numerous wives in their households, after the fashion of the Skraelings of this land, although we Norse folk have one wife only for every husband?"

"Assuredly, lady," answered Osvif graciously, "since, save for the Swede country alone, wherein the old gods still have a hold, the north is now entirely a Christian land and abides by the law of one wife to every man, although the heathen Moors are not so constrained. Yet, for all that, it is not the number of wives which they take, but where they seek them, which tells the tale. And among that nation none, I think, are so highly prized as the women of the north."

"In that case," answered Thjodhild, "they are surely wiser than many of our own folk, who hold some Skraelings as good as their own."

Then Thjodhild sat down again and the Norwegians laughed loudly at this but the men of Sigtrygg's crew began to grumble to themselves and everyone began to ask after Sigtrygg once more, for it seemed to them that he was long overdue and the bridal cup yet to be drunk. Thord Thorkelsson was the first to speak up about the matter and, after him, many others followed suit and then there began to be much murmuring in the hall and asking after the man who named himself Vinland's king.

At length Vragi stood up and said that it was his part to seek the king, "for he will be about business which may require my presence," and he went out of the hall and into the nearby woods.

He did not have far to go before he came upon Sigtrygg sitting alone in the darkness, with his back to a large tree, facing the settlement which Thjodhild and her kinsmen had named Gunnarsstead. From where Sigtrygg sat, the lights and voices of the guests in the hall could just be made out, though their words could not be clearly discerned. Sigtrygg had very little to say when Vragi found him and the old viking now asked him whether he planned to keep vigil in this fashion all the night through, "in case our enemies have followed us here to the coast? Or do you mean to join our guests, before the sun has risen, and wed that maid to whom you are pledged?"

Sigtrygg did not offer any response to this, so now the older man sat down beside him and these two kept their silence for awhile. At last Sigtrygg turned and said: "I'm not certain what strength an oath which has been sworn in this country will have for my kinsmen, once they find themselves in Greenland again, despite all the fair words and the feasts which they have made here. Or if a man is obliged to fulfill all that he has pledged, when more than one oath binds him."

To this Vragi replied that "most men will think an oath is not to be broken, whatever the circumstances, although it is certainly a harder case when two have been sworn. Still, an oath to kin is generally held to be the stronger sort."

"In my opinion," said Sigtrygg, "no oath is worth more than

another, but each will have the strength of that foundation on which it has been laid."

Vragi said: "In earlier times what a man swore to the gods was said to have the greater claim for men feared their wrath more than the anger of other men. But now things are otherwise so you must weigh up the gains to be had by the choices you are intent on making here."

Sigtrygg said he thought this was certainly true and asked Vragi if there was much unease in the hall because of his failure to arrive there.

"There's plenty of that," Vragi agreed, "for most of the men who are there think you are bound to drink the bridal cup tonight with your kinswoman. And they are awaiting the toasting and pledges you are to make in her honor."

"And what do you think?" Sigtrygg asked him.

"That you are bound to fulfill those words you have spoken."

When the sky began to lighten and the first red rim of the sun became visible over the horizon in the east, there was a rustling at the edge of the encampment which the Skraelings had made alongside the place where Leif Eiriksson had built his houses. The houses, themselves, now stood quite empty for all their occupants had gone inland to the feasting at Gunnarsstead and only a few Skraeling men were about. These had little to say to one another but were gathering up their things in silence and placing these on their backs. The Skraeling messenger, who had but recently come out of the forest, was with these others and also a single woman who had her goods strapped to her back; and now these people turned to go into the woods in a single line, after their fashion of travel, the woman safely placed between the men.

They proceeded without speech and stepping so lightly that it would hardly have seemed to any who might then have been watching that they were walking at all, for their steps barely disturbed the grass on which they trod, or the hard, rock-strewn ground which they passed over as they entered the place where the trees grew more closely together.

Still, there was a certain somberness to the mood of these people and the young woman in their midst had a distracted look in her eyes. She turned back frequently, to the place from which they had come, until they could no longer see the outline of the clearing in which the Greenland houses had been built. Then she resolutely turned her eyes to the ground before her and did not look up again as they pushed deeper and deeper into the forested country. The man in the lead kept up a rapid pace, but he glanced back often, to look at the woman.

When they had gone a little ways, he came to a halt and then those who were behind him stopped as well, and now they all began to look about and to prick up their ears at the woodland sounds which enveloped them. The lead Skraeling knelt down on the ground and the others now did so, too, taking the packs from their backs and laying these silently on the earth beside them. The woman seemed as alert as the others, though she bore no arms, as the men did.

The men now reached for their stone weapons, and two of the five men in that company brought out their bows and nocked arrows to the bowstrings.

The shadowy figure of a man suddenly stepped out from the trees directly before them, on that path which they had been following away from the coast, and the leader of the Skraelings got slowly to his feet when he saw this. He had a small club with a sharpened stone head in his hand and he gripped this tightly at sight of the newcomer. The man who stood before them carried an unsheathed long sword.

W'tnalko's eyes widened but he did not allow the features of his face to betray his surprise, or his consternation if, indeed, this was what he felt at sight of the other. But now he lowered his stone weapon, whereupon the other put away his sword, as well. The Skraelings with bows in their hands also relaxed their grips on these and the arrows they held slid slowly downwards, to point at the earth.

The Skraeling, W'tnalko, asked the man his purpose in bar-ring their path like this but the man did not answer him for he was looking at the woman who still knelt on the ground in the midst of the others. At last he walked past W'tnalko and stood over the place where the woman was. She looked up at him and he bent down, taking her by the hands and pulling her to her feet.

W'tnalko said: "Why have you pursued us in this fashion, to keep us from our journey, though you are the one who sent us away?"

"Because," answered the man, "I did not think I could bear to part from you . . . or from this woman, my wife."

"These are very different words from those you spoke before," said W'tnalko.

"Yet they are true, nonetheless," Sigtrygg said.

"A man may say many things," replied the Skraeling, "and think each thing he says to be the truth. But what is true will be found, in the end, in his deeds only, and not in the sounds which his mouth makes. Now you have gone to wed the Greenland woman and she will have no part of Skraeling folk like us, so why do you seek us out here?"

Sigtrygg said he had no answer to this except that he thought the departure of W'tnalko and his party a greater loss than the displeasure of his kinsmen.

"Then you mean to return with us, afterall, to the encamp-ment by the river, as our chieftainess has bid you?" asked the Skraeling.

"It is certainly too soon for that," Sigtrygg replied, "for that would leave those others to do as they will with my houses and land-claim; and I would find it a hard matter to endure, if they had their way in this. But I will certainly keep faith with the lady of the river, as I have said, when matters have been set right here."

It's not clear that there will be time enough for that," said W'tnalko, "if the Tulewat are gathering their strength again in the west. Besides, winter is no longer far off, so you are bound to return to our country, in any case."

"The winters here are not so harsh as those I have known else-where," answered Sigtrygg, "in which case our return can easily be delayed for a while longer. And as to these Tulewat, who can say what they mean to do? But my kinsmen's purpose is clear enough and I must deal with that."

The Skraeling said: "You'd do better, then, to bind yourself to your own kind, Sigtrygg, than to follow after us here, for we are not like those others and you are unlikely to find peace in our midst."

"It is not peace that I am seeking," answered Sigtrygg and now he took hold of Chinokwa's goods and lifted them from the place where she had laid them, on the forest floor, placing these upon his own back.

W'tnalko saw this and told Sigtrygg that it was too late to undo what had already been done and then he quickly turned to Chinokwa, saying they must go forward at once, "for there are many days of hard travel still before us."

The young Skraeling woman seemed to hesitate at this, seeing that Sigtrygg had taken her goods from her, although her companions now appeared quite eager to be off. W'tnalko urged the others to shoulder their packs once more and then he took hold of Chinokwa's arm, pulling her down the trail after him.

The woman looked backward only once and saw Sigtrygg still standing there, the burden he had taken up still upon his wide shoulders. She made as if to speak but, in the end, said nothing as W'tnalko hurried her along the trail. Then Sigtrygg said after her that "this matter is now in your hands wife, for I am unable to follow you any deeper into the forest than I have now done." But, even as he spoke, the Skraelings appeared to turn into a place where the trees grew even more thickly together, so that he swiftly lost sight of them and could soon hear nothing of their faint footfalls amidst the underbrush, as they pushed further and further into the woodlands.

The Greenlander stood there for a time, then, as though in deep thought, and only after awhile did he seem to turn reluctantly away from their path. And then it seemed to him that his feet grew larger and clumsier, and that the burden which he had taken on his shoulders was a good deal heavier than before, but he would not let it fall or otherwise put it aside on the forest floor. He went thus for a little ways and then he stopped and looked about him at the trees which grew up on every side, and he listened closely for the sounds of the surf but could hear nothing save the few birds, which flitted about in the tree branches overhead, and the rustling of the wind, where it caught in the leaves and rippled along the tree tops.

It now seemed to Sigtrygg that the forest, though a quieter place than the sea, was yet less steadying, for the wind there danced through a thousand tree branches and beat out as many small cadences, while out on the face of the ocean its loud, raucous whipping against a single ship's sail was more constant and settling to men. From this, he was to say later, it became much clearer to him how a man could love the sea above all else, especially for that wide faring which was possible upon its pathways, so that one could travel to many distant countries and yet never remain for long in any single land.

He was thinking these things when the sounds of the wind in the tree tops seemed to change again, and then he thought he heard the wind slide down to the forest floor and the rustling seize the branches of new growth which hugged the earth there. He turned at this, thinking still of the sea and the tug of its currents, until he heard a sharp flutter in the nearby brush. Then he lowered his burden at last and stood quietly waiting, his hand on the hilt of his sword.

He did not move again until he saw a form emerge from the undergrowth of the forest, and then he went toward it and met the eyes of the Skraeling woman with his own.

Thjodhild sat alone and without speaking upon the high seat, which she had had built in the hall at Gunnarsstead, until the first grey light of the new day began to brighten the window slits above her, stirring her guests to life once more. Most had fallen off to sleep, by this time, from the food and strong drink which had been given them, and only a few still sat about in small groups, talking in low tones, as the first rays of the sun began to fill the hall again.

Vragi came in then and found his place, without fuss, among his shipmates and Girstein Eiriksson at once took himself over to where they sat and asked if matters had gone well.

"Well enough," the old viking answered, "though the final judgement, in this case, may depend on who is asking."

"It's all the same to me, whether things have gone well or ill for you ship-thieves," Thord Thorkelsson now said, joining them, "so long as you can tell us of that man to whom our kinswoman is betrothed, and if he now means to take the bridal cup from her hands as he has promised."

"I'm not sure about that," admitted Vragi, "for he has occupied himself with other matters, while we have sat the night through in this hall, enjoying the hospitality you kinsmen have offered us."

Girstein said: "What other thing could be so urgent as to detain him, when such important issues as we now have before us are to be decided here?"

"A matter of the heart," answered Vragi and he took a piece of cold meat from the table and began to chew on it.

Thord said: "What treachery is this?" And Girstein asked if it were true, then, "that our kinsman no longer means to redeem that pledge which he has made to us in this affair?"

"He will not take back what he has given, in any event," said Vragi, "for these houses, and the land on which they are built, are to remain with you kinsmen. And you are to be free to come and go in this country whenever you like."

"And what of our kinswoman," asked Girstein, "for she will have sustained the greatest loss in this matter?"

"She is to have a share, with you others, in the land holding," answered Vragi.

When Lambi Gunnarsson, who had also come up to them by

this time, heard these words, he grew very red in the face but seemed utterly unable to speak. He just stood above them rubbing his useless arm with his good hand. Many other people had also gathered round the crewmen of the Gull and their Skraeling companions by this time and there was much mumbling among them at Vragi's words. Girstein said they would now need time to think matters through, "for this will certainly warrant very careful consideration, on our part." Vragi replied that that was only fair, adding that, in his opinion, Sigtrygg would be more than willing to offer whatever additional compensation seemed just to them, "so long as it is within reason."

"There's no need for that," a loud voice now said and everyone looked to where Thjodhild sat. They could see how she had the bridal cup in her hands and was bent forward in her place listening to their words, her eyes seemingly on Vragi alone.

"There's no need for that," she repeated after a moment, "since my kinsman has now made his choice clear enough, where we women are concerned. And I don't think there's any payment to be made which can undo this insult which he has now offered those of us who are of his blood."

"It can't hurt to make a fair settlement, however ill matters seem, lady," Vragi replied, "if you kinsmen stand to gain by it."

But Thjodhild replied that she did not see how there was much to be gained, either in honor or wealth, in the matter, "for what does such a man as Sigtrygg have to give to others? His wealth lies entirely in land which he cannot hope to hold, while he has made plain enough, by his actions, that he is without even that honor which a thief has in claiming the goods he has stolen for his own."

"Words spoken in anger are often those which are most quickly regretted," Vragi said to her.

"I don't have much fear of that, either," replied Thjodhild, "for I will have sufficient cause for regret without worry over a few words when this matter's done." And now she turned about in her seat and sought a place to put away the cup which she still held in her hands, trembling slightly so that the wine spilled over the side of the vessel onto her dress and the high seat and the ground beneath her.

At once Osvif the Norwegian sprang up to the high seat and placed his hands on Thjodhild's, to steady the cup she held, so that the Greenland woman slumped against him, giving over the wine into his keeping. Girstein followed close behind Osvif, and after him Lambi and the Thorkelssons so that these men now stood over her and around her, as though to shield her from the eyes of those others in the hall. Vragi now arose and told his shipmates that he thought they had stayed long enough in the company of their hosts and he urged them to take their leave with him. Accordingly, all of the Gull's crew, along with their companions, now arose and went out the door, except for Arnliot Keelfoot only. The big Ketilsfjordman remained behind and helped himself to another haunch of roasted deer meat and then he washed this down with some wine. After this, he too arose and went to the doorway of the hall. Olvir was standing there when Arnliot approached and he urged the Ketilsfjordman to follow him, but the big man said he thought it a shame to take their leave now, "while there is still so much good food left upon the table." Olvir said there would be food enough in their own stores so now Arnliot went after him out of the hall.

Afterwards there was silence, for no one dared to speak until Thjodhild herself did, and, when she turned about, she saw their faces hard upon hers. She was very pale but her eyes were bright and now she asked if the others had gone. Girstein said that they had, since that had seemed to be her desire in the matter, and she made no answer to this. Then she put her hand out for the wine cup and found that Osvif still held it and she sought to take it back from him.

"There's no need for that, lady," the Norwegian said, seeing what she meant to do, "since I will dispose of its contents, if you wish it."

But Thjodhild said she had no desire to empty the cup except by drinking it herself, "for that is what was intended when we filled it at the outset of this feasting."

"Then," Osvif said, "you must not drink it alone, lady, for this is a heavy draft for so fine a woman as you are. But if you are willing, I shall drink it with you."

Thjodhild now looked at the Norwegian, as though for the first time, and he looked back at her, placing the cup in her hands, but between his own.

She said he should do as he pleased, if that was what he wanted, so he put the cup to his lips and drank deeply from it, and afterwards he offered it to her.

CHAPTER XXXIX

HOW MATTERS WERE SORTED OUT

It was Olvir who brought the news to Sigtrygg and the others, that Thjodhild had wed Osvif Thorleiksson, since Olvir alone of Sigtrygg's men continued to find a welcome at Gunnarsstead. "She accepted this man's offer as soon as it was made," he said, "and that was no longer than it took for us to depart from the hall. Everyone there thought it well-made, and her kinsmen supported him in his suit."

Sigtrygg had little to say about this except that he thought the Norwegian "rather too old for a woman like Thjodhild."

But Olvir replied that "it was not to be thought that such a woman would accept rejection, and at her own wedding feast besides, when a match like this one was to be had. And this Osvif is of good family, and a king's man to boot."

"That may be," said Sigtrygg, "but what did they do afterwards?"

"What every newly wedded couple will do," answered Olvir, "as was only to be expected. And now they have given orders to the men in their crew to cut timber from the nearby forest and lay this out for curing in the meadow at Gunnarsstead; and to lay in meat for winter."

"Do they mean to winter here, too?" Sigtrygg asked him.

"It is certainly too late in the season to be thinking about putting out to sea," Olvir replied.

"It is not much later, now, than when we set sail from Eiriksfjord."

"Yet we departed in haste...and for good reason, whereas these folk have no such cause," answered Olvir. "And you, yourself, granted them leave to stay."

"I won't deny that," Sigtrygg said, "but what are they saying to one another concerning these events?"

"Not much," answered Olvir, "except that they think the country is now to be divided between us; and that Osvif Thorleiksson speaks for King Harald in the matter."

"That, too, was to be expected," Sigtrygg said, "in which case they will hardly think they need leave from me to remain longer in this part of the world if they desire it."

Arnliot Keelfoot, who had been standing quietly by all this time now spoke up, saying: "It seems you will find cause to regret your forbearance toward them, whatever else now occurs, for they are likely to prove a thorn in our sides for as long as they remain here."

"Still, there's not much to be done about that," replied Sigtrygg, "for I have given my word in the matter; and besides, they are too numerous for us to contest this question with them."

"It will not be the first time you have said one thing, but done another," Arnliot answered him.

Sigtrygg now turned back to Olvir and asked him what he intended to do "since they seem to find you better company than the rest of our crew."

"They have offered me a place at Gunnarsstead," Olvir replied. "And I am thinking of accepting it."

"You must do as you think best," said Sigtrygg.

But Arnliot said he thought it spoke very little for Olvir's manliness if he were to desert the comrades he had fought beside now, "to go running back to the service of these people from Brattahlid."

"Think what you like," Olvir replied, "but in my opinion each of us must choose his own path. And I don't think there's much to be gained by cutting ourselves off from our fellow countrymen as must now occur if we do not make some sort of settlement with them over these matters."

Sigtrygg asked him what he wanted to do with the Skraeling woman he had taken for his wife "or with these others who followed you onto my ship in Eirikssfjord?"

"The woman is to be returned to her kinsmen," answered Olvir. "But let my fellow serving men each decide what is best for themselves."

Accordingly, Sigtrygg now put it to each of the men from Brattahlid in turn, if they preferred to remain with him or to return with Olvir to the service of his Greenland kinsmen. They replied that they would rather keep things as they were and so they stayed put while Olvir went off to gather up his things. When he had done this he asked leave of Sigtrygg to go, and Sigtrygg replied that he was free to do this, if that was still his wish. The Brattahlid man said that it was, so now they parted and Olvir went off to Gunnarsstead and told them there how things were.

Osvif and Girstein received the serving man from Brattahlid warmly and made a good welcome for him when they had heard him out, promising to treat him with no less honor than had been his when he was among Sigtrygg's crew. Accordingly, they found a place for his belongings among their own and, afterwards, he went to seek out Thjodhild to tell her, too, of the decision he had made. Thjodhild was pleased when she had heard his words and said he should be first among those "who serve King Harald here."

But Olvir replied: "It is you I have come to serve lady, and not some distant king, for this land has one king already; and if I had wanted to serve kings, I could have remained with him."

Thjodhild said he could have it his own way but that she was glad to see him, nonetheless, "for you have always been a good friend to our house." And when she spoke thus she seemed pale to him though her eyes flashed, he thought, with unaccustomed fire.

After this Olvir remained close by Thjodhild's side, helping her to see to the laying in of provisions and to the upkeep of her household. These two now went about together, with Olvir keeping the tally of goods which the Norwegians brought in. The Norwegian skipper, Osvif, soon came to think highly of the Brattahlid man, saying they were certainly blessed to have someone of such accomplishments in their number, "for he will prove a good fellow when we go to sell this cargo which we are gathering here overseas."

Girstein and the Thorkelssons also had many good things to say of the former serving man, as did Lambi Gunnarsson, though he proved to be somewhat less talkative than the others since he thought he had more to brood over than they did.

One day, when they were all outside, Thjodhild asked Olvir what Sigtrygg and his companions meant to do when the weather turned. Lambi, her brother, who was then trimming some newly fallen trees which had been laid out on the meadow grass, let fall the axe he was holding when he heard this. Thjodhild went over at once and took it up for him, placing it back in his good hand.

"I didn't always need a woman's help when cutting trees," he said, taking the axe from her, "though some people have said that half a man is better than none."

"There's no use worrying about things which cannot be changed," replied Thjodhild, "for you have still got the one good arm, which is stronger than two such on many lesser men."

"That may be," replied Lambi, "but you are a fine one to be speaking, since you have not yet forgotten the hurt you have taken from that ill-born kinsman of ours, and that despite the good marriage you have made for yourself in this place."

Olvir now said there was no reason for them to be berating one another in this way, "for you are both more fortunate having come here than otherwise, or you had never won such a good landclaim as this is."

"I'm not sure about that," replied Lambi, "or if even this is repayment enough for loss of limb."

"Some would call it a handsome payment, nevertheless," answered Olvir, "in that the act which nearly took your life cannot now be undone, whatever other payment had been made you.

And this is certainly better land than you could have hoped for, if you'd stayed in Greenland."

But Thord now said: "Land is no payment for ill deeds, though some would have it so. Besides, the full terms of the agreement have never been met, since the oath to wed and share all equally was not fulfilled."

"They have left us in peace here," said Olvir, "and that should be enough for you."

"And they could do little else," answered Thord, "for we are too many for them. As for the matter of the law, we have that on our side, too, for this land is under King Harald's rule now and his man is all one with us."

Lambi stood silently by, listening to this exchange, and he had little reaction to any of it, save that it could be seen how red-faced he had become as Thord spoke his words.

Olvir said that there was little use in belaboring these points "for matters are at a stand-still where these others are concerned and my advice is that we now make the best of things for the time remaining to us in this country."

"Yet you have still not given me my answer," Thjodhild said and Olvir turned to her and asked what it was she was so intent on knowing.

"What our kinsman means to do over winter," Thjodhild repeated, "for it is unlikely we will find this country as hospitable when the weather turns as we have now found it."

"I'm not sure about that," answered Olvir, "for this land is not given to such bitterly cold winters as we are accustomed to. But in my opinion he will winter among the Skraelings."

"In that case, he will need someone to look after his holdings here while he has gone inland," laughed Thord. "But I'm not sure he will find anyone for that, however hard he may be seeking."

Not long afterwards, Thjodhild told Osvif that she thought they would be better served if they had their ship closer to hand, "given the storms which come up in this country, for we are not likely to find sailing back to Greenland an easy matter if that ship of ours were to be swept out to sea." Osvif said he would not deny that and asked her what she had in mind.

"There is an estuary not far up the coast from where your ship is beached," she replied, "and it leads to a small lake which lies near this meadow in which our houses are built. In my opinion, the ship can be brought into the lake through this waterway, when the tide is up, and I think that is what we ought to do."

"You have the makings of a good ship's captain," answered Osvif, "for that is exactly my thinking, as well." So now he gave orders to his crew to go down to where the ship had been hauled up and secured on the beach, saying they were to refloat the vessel and bring her into the lake as Thjodhild had urged. And he told Thjodhild she was to take charge of the matter, if she wanted to.

Accordingly, Thjodhild now went with the Norwegian crew to the coast and gave out the orders concerning this ship and every man of them gave her words careful heed for they were well thought out and showed good judgement. When word was brought to Sigtrygg what they were about, he came out of his dwelling and stood on the land above the beach, watching the work. Olvir was there among the Norwegians and Sigtrygg went down to him for, while the others of his crew showed little desire to approach this man, Sigtrygg had no such qualms. He went right up to him and gave him a good greeting and asked him how the work went.

"As well as can be expected," answered the Brattahlid man, "but you'd be better off asking Thjodhild about this, for she has charge of this affair."

Thjodhild was at this time walking around the other side of the ship, giving commands to the Norwegians who had by now got ropes on the vessel, at both prow and stern. These men were easing the big black hull closer to the place where the tide struck against the shore. Thjodhild now seemed to be everywhere at once and often took hold of a rope from one group of these men or another, showing them where they were to pull so as to keep the hull from tipping over or taking hurt from the sharp rocks which jutted out along the beach. Sigtrygg came up to her then and stood for awhile but he said nothing, and she did not stop her work to give him any kind of greeting. After awhile he broke the silence, asking what they were intending to do with the ship, once they had it back on the sea.

Thjodhild straightened then and gave him a long look, saying, "it's not hard to tell, kinsman, for we won't be burying this ship in the ground, as men did in earlier times when making graves for their dead."

Sigtrygg said he thought that "things have certainly changed a great deal from when we two stood together upon the beach at Brattahlid, for then we worried over another ship. And I was the one concerned to push it into the sea."

"That was not half so fine a vessel as this is," answered Thjodhild, "and we must take more pains now than before."

"This may be," Sigtrygg agreed, "but it is the rare skipper who will relinquish care of his ship to another, and she only a woman who has never sailed such a vessel on her own before; nor ventured out, save once, upon the open seas. This Norwegian must think very highly of you."

Thjodhild said he could draw his own conclusions but that "most husbands will share what they have with their wives, and Osvif is no different in this than other men."

"I'm not sure about that," Sigtrygg replied, "but it certainly seems to me he is taking a big risk leaving his ship in such inexperienced hands, however capable and well-intentioned in other matters. But, if you ask it, I will order my own crew to give your men some help, and then you may get this big boat safely afloat again, to do what you want with it."

"There's no need for that," answered Thjodhild, "for these Norwegians are better hands with a ship than your land-lubbing crew. And their skipper, even if she is now only a woman, is no less capable than the one who commands those others."

Sigtrygg said: "You would not have spoken thus, when we stood beneath the farmhouses of Brattahlid, seeing to my ship."

"That was another matter," Thjodhild admitted. "But this ship is my affair, just as the other was yours, so now the best thing is for each to stick to his own business, neither giving nor accepting help from the other."

"Still, we are a long way from home and kin," Sigtrygg said, "and there is little to be gained by spurning what has been offered."

"Nevertheless," said Thjodhild, "my mind is made up."

"In that case, it is to be hoped that you are better at disposing of this ship, than you were of that other," Sigtrygg said.

Thjodhild replied that this was soon to be put to the test.

Now, even as she spoke, a loud shouting came to their ears. Then they heard this a second time and Sigtrygg broke off his speech with her and went up toward the houses, in the direction of the shouting. When he approached the settlement area he leaped over the timber and earthen embankment, which had been raised there as a barrier to attack, and ran at once into the compound. There he could see that several of the Norwegians had broken off from the rest of their crew and had come inside the rough stockade, while most of their fellows were still at their work, and now these men had surrounded a number of the Skraeling women. They were pressing in on them, pushing them up against one of the house walls. They seemed to be urging the women, by cajolery and rough handling, to go off with them. The Skraeling women were very frightened by all this and they were the ones who had begun the shouting.

A number of the Gull's crewmen had now come outside as well, along with some of the Skraeling men, and these surrounded the Norwegians as soon as they saw what was happening.

Sigtrygg ran at once into their midst and now he saw that one of the women who had been trapped against the house wall was none other than Chinokwa, his wife. The deer skin garment which she was wearing had been torn away from her shoulder while her black hair was tangled and half concealed her face which was streaked black with dirt. Sigtrygg went toward the men who stood nearest to these women and, when he reached them, he took hold of two at once and spun them away from him. Then he grabbed a third man and threw him to the ground, leaping upon him and pounding his face into the earth while sitting atop the man's back. Other crewmen of the Gull quickly took hold of a fourth man, as well as the first two, and began to beat these as well.

Now these Norwegians' comrades came up and poured into the compound and, when they saw how things were, made for Sigtrygg and his shipmates in an effort to free their companions. Soon there was hard fighting inside the stockade walls and this did not become any less when Arnliot Keelfoot, himself, came out into the clearing, for he had slept longer than the others and had only just awakened due to the great commotion which now ensued.

When Arnliot saw the fierce fighting in the compound, he fell on the others at once, and now it seemed that the Norwegians found it harder going than before since he was such a big man and more than a match for any three of them. This would certainly have gone on until real harm had been done had it not been for Thjodhild and Olvir who now came up, as well, and these began to urge that peace be restored. Olvir, himself, went about pulling men back from the fray and Thjodhild shouted for those of the Norwegians who could hear her to withdraw themselves while they could. She took blankets and animal skins and whatever else was to hand and began to throw these over the heads of the men who were fighting the hardest and least willing to listen to her words. In this manner the fighting was eased and, since no weapons had been drawn, not much damage was done except to men's pride — although this was, itself, not inconsiderable, for many afterwards begrudged the bruises and hurts which they had got on that day.

But, after a time, Thjodhild succeeded in separating the two sides and now she urged the Norwegians in her charge out of the compound.

Olvir found Sigtrygg kneeling beside the Skraeling woman, Chinokwa, and, though he was himself bleeding from a head wound he had taken, he was seeing to the needs of the woman. She now reached out her hand and wiped the blood from Sigtrygg's face, where it was streaming down into his eyes, and he took her hand and held it there a moment, as though unwilling to see her take it away again. Olvir came over to them then and sat down beside these two, and he helped the Skraeling woman wipe away the blood, asking if Sigtrygg thought matters were now better than before.

"They are certainly no worse," was the response, "though I'd have preferred to repay these men for their arrogance by more than this little scuffle."

"Many people will think they have cause for a grievance as a result of this day's work," answered Olvir. "And I'm not certain you will have enhanced your prestige, as king in this country, by brawling on the ground like any common man."

"Had swords been to hand, I would have shown them how a king handles such matters," Sigtrygg said.

"Then there would be harder settlements to be made than may now be the case. But how did these women fare?"

Chinokwa now said that she was unharmed and the other women said the same.

"Then there was less cause for fighting than we had thought," said Olvir. But Sigtrygg replied that there was certainly cause, in any event "since these men meant us no good."

"That may be," replied Olvir. "Still, it was not to be expected that all men would show the same forbearance, when some have what others lack; and we alone have women in our company to match the men here."

"I did not bid them come out here as they have," said Sigtrygg.

Olvir said that this was true and now he stood up and Sigtrygg and Chinokwa followed after him. When they were on their feet again they took a look around and could see how many of their company were hurt and limping about and how the area inside the compound was badly torn up. Most of the Norwegians who could walk on their own feet had by now gone out of the stockaded area. Thjodhild stood over by the gate alone, her skirts in her hand, held out from her so as not to trail in the broken and trampled earth beneath her. She was looking their way, at Sigtrygg . . . and then at the Skraeling woman beside him.

Sigtrygg did not see this at first, but Chinokwa looked up and caught the Greenland woman's eye and, when she did, she stepped back a little and pulled herself closer against Sigtrygg's side, but without looking away. Then Sigtrygg saw how Thjodhild's gaze had settled on the woman beside him and he reached out his arm and put it over her, as though to shield her from the other, and now he turned away and took Chinokwa with him into one of the houses.

Thjodhild remained there awhile after they had gone from her sight, saying nothing, but when Olvir came toward her, as though he would speak, she turned on her heels and walked briskly away.

When Thjodhild returned to Gunnarsstead, Osvif asked her how matters had gone and she told him all that had occurred. He asked if many were hurt but she replied that there was very little damage done, "for I put an end to the fighting before things could get out of hand." Osvif said that that was just what he would have expected of her and that he was never surprised to hear of the things she accomplished. "But what of my ship?" he asked finally. "Has it been safely moved, as we agreed, to its winter harborage?"

Thjodhild said he should go down to the lake and have a look, "for that vessel of yours will be hard to miss on any body of water which is less than the wide ocean itself."

After this she had little to say and mostly kept to herself, leaving the affairs of the settlement to her kinsmen, and most especially to Thord Thorkelsson and to Thorstein, his brother. At the same time, Osvif took over the matter of the ship. Osvif, for his part, now thought he had done rather well for himself, all things considered, since Thjodhild seemed to him to be such a capable and level-headed woman, as good at handling a ship as at the more common things which a wife is expected to do. And she was well-connected, besides, to the best family in Greenland.

In the meantime Sigtrygg and those who were with him restored order to their settlement, as best they could. They told Vragi how things had gone, when he returned to them, for this man had taken to wandering off more and more by himself, leaving the Gull's crew to their own devices. When he had heard them out, after his return, he praised Olvir's part in the matter and said the Brattahlid man had certainly shown good judgement in the affair, adding that it was a shame he had now chosen to cast his lot with those others "for even kings gain when a good counselor is in their midst."

To this Arnliot replied that good judgement, in his opinion, was a poor substitute for courage and that their former companion had now shown, once more, that he had lost what little he'd had when they had fought together against their Skraeling foes.

"Courage and judgement are both manly traits," agreed the old viking, "and neither is to be despised. But if I had to choose, I think the second is best, for courage without judgement has led many a man to his downfall."

Not long after this, word came to them that the Skraeling man, who had first come out of the forest as a messenger from the people who lived by the river and from their chieftainess, the mother of Chinokwa, had returned and was again asking for Aselekah. So they brought him once more into Sigtrygg's presence.

Sigtrygg gave him a good greeting, when he saw him, and asked after the others who had gone off with him, following W'tnalko.

The Skraeling replied that he had little news to give of these men and even less of his kinsmen on the river, "for I have not yet found my way back to them."

"And why not," Sigtrygg asked him, "since that was your intention when you set off with those companions of yours?"

"Because," said the Skraeling, "we took another path and I parted from those others because of it."

"Then you must tell us what has become of them," Sigtrygg

replied, "and especially of that man whom I esteem above all others of your kind in this country, the man you call W'tnalko."

"I have no answer to that either," replied the Skraeling, "for it is a long time since I have separated from him."

"And why have you done that," Sigtrygg pressed, "since you were charged to go with him and fight it out beside him if the need arose?"

"Because," answered the Skraeling, "he did not follow the path we had set for ourselves, towards our kinsmen on the river, but turned off from there and made for the west instead."

CHAPTER XL

DEPARTURE

The two camps, Sigtrygg and his companions at Leif's houses and the people at Gunnarsstead, kept well apart now, keeping even more separate than before. There was very little coming and going between them and each party saw to its own affairs. At Gunnarsstead they busied themselves with preparations for the winter, listening closely to the advice which Olvir gave them since he, alone of their number, had some experience in these matters. He told them how much food they would need to lay in, to be well-stocked during the cold months, and how they should prepare their houses against the frost and he personally took charge of provisioning the household which Thjodhild and Osvif now set up. Everyone at Gunnarsstead thought they had found a great treasure in this man and he was well-treated.

At the same time Sigtrygg told his people they were to gather up their goods and prepare to depart for the interior part of the country where Chinokwa's kinsmen lived. They made a great show of securing their houses and valuables and of preparing those goods they could carry, for transfer overland on their backs, but they remained all the same, from one day to the next, without departing from their settlement. Arnliot said Sigtrygg ought to make up his mind, whether to leave or stay, but that it was plain they could not possibly do both, whatever their desires in the matter. "But if we are to leave," he added, "it is uncertain that we will find these houses of ours standing in this place, should we find our way back here again, for I think our enemies will burn them down or else plunder them for their timber and other building materials, so they can enrich themselves in that settlement they have made up by the lake."

Thorolf and Asmund said they thought this was probably true but Asmund added that he thought the houses would be no great loss, "since there is plenty of timber for building them again and just as much land for the taking, should they occupy what we have here. Still, in my opinion, the loss of our ship would be a more serious matter, for that is a thing we cannot easily build for ourselves again since ship building skills are harder to come by in our company."

Thorolf added that he thought they should now take the Gull out of her winter berth and sail her down the coast to find the mouth of that river on which their Skraelings dwelt. "Then we can sail or row her up river, till we have found those people with whom we have made our alliance and take up our abode with them."

Sigtrygg said there were too many rivers in the country for that, "for we can never hope to find the right river mouth unless we have gone up river first and then followed its course back down to the sea. Nor are these rivers likely to be deep enough for this ship of ours to pass unscathed along any of them, for we have all seen how easy it is to ford them when we had the need."

"In that case," said Asmund, "I am unsure how we can pass over to winter among the Skraelings and still be sure of this ship of ours when we return in the spring."

Arnliot said: "We cannot, and that at least is clear, in which case my advice is that we now break though the hull of the ship so she cannot easily be repaired. Then these others will get no good of her, if they try to take her while we are gone, but we shall still be able to make her whole, with less work than building her like from scratch is likely to require. And we are certainly men enough to repair a ship which has been badly damaged, if not to craft such a vessel from freshly cut timber."

"I can show you men how such a ship is to be built," laughed Vragi, "so there's no need to fret about breaking through the keel of this one, so you can repair her when the mood takes you. Or do you think the repair work which you can do, cannot, as easily, be done by those you count your enemies?"

Sigtrygg said: "In that case our departure now will certainly leave this ship of ours in the hands of this Norwegian and my kinsmen, if they choose to avail themselves of it, and there is little enough to be done about it."

Vragi said that this was true and that the choice now before them "is whether to sit here all winter, keeping vigil over our ship and risking a clash with these Norwegians, or to go back to the Skraeling country as you have promised and make common cause with them."

Sigtrygg said he would rather choose the second than the first and Vragi said this only showed good sense, so now they made ready to depart once more.

About this time Olvir came down to them and asked whether they had made up their minds concerning their winter quarters and Sigtrygg told him what had been discussed. The others did not want to give this news to their former companion but Sigtrygg said they were being rather foolish, considering all the good the Brattahlid man had now done for them, and he sat for a long time with Olvir and told him his plans and what had occurred among them during his absence. Olvir promised to look after their ship, if that was what they wanted of him, and Sigtrygg said he did not think the Gull could be placed in better hands although he begged the man from Brattahlid to reconsider his decision to remain with the others "for I would rather have you in our company again, than know the Gull was being so well looked after."

"It's not possible for me to do that," Olvir replied, "for I have given my word to your kinswoman, and she will need warding in this country, no less than that ship."

"I have heard that she is married now and has a husband for that purpose," Sigtrygg said.

"This is certainly true," answered Olvir, "but these others are strangers here, and besides, I have never voluntarily left the service of your kinsmen, among whom Thjodhild must surely still be counted. I would be a poor servant, indeed, if I left her and these others now to fend for themselves."

"Have it your own way," Sigtrygg said, "but I think we shall both find cause to regret this decision of yours to return to my kinsmen."

With that they parted and Olvir went back to Gunnarsstead. There he was met by Lambi Gunnarsson and the Thorkelssons and these asked him where he had been. When he told them, they had little good to say about it and said he must be careful to keep his distance from his former companions, from here on in, since "those ship-thieves do not intend us anything but harm."

"I don't think they mean to do any worse to you than you have intended to do to them," answered Olvir and with that they fell silent.

Afterwards Olvir went about his business, telling anyone who asked how Sigtrygg and his fellows were now planning to go off with the Skraelings to their winter encampment and leave the people of Gunnarsstead entirely in peace. There was some mumbling about this for some of the Norwegians thought it a bad thing and that Sigtrygg would certainly use this chance to build up his strength among the Skraelings against them, "for he has plainly named himself king in this country and it is not to be expected that a king will tolerate, in his midst, those who will not acknowledge him."

These men urged Osvif to act against Sigtrygg and his companions, before they could depart to rebuild their alliance with the Skraelings, reminding him that he spoke for a rival king. But Osvif only shrugged and turned a deaf ear to their pleadings "for," he said, "you men are allowing your anger to affect your judgement of these others. They have yet to do us any harm that we were not, ourselves, partially responsible for; and they have already granted us leave to share this country with them."

"Still, they have not acknowledged King Harald's sovereignty here," they said, "and that must be done, if peace is to be established between us, for Harald will never tolerate another man's claim to kingship over such a good land as this is."

"There's time enough for that," answered Osvif, "although I'm not altogether certain that our king will find this country worth the long sailing he will need to come by it."

After this the others left the matter alone and Osvif went on about his business. But news of Sigtrygg's impending departure now found its way to Thjodhild. While she had kept herself aloof from the others since the fighting in Leif's settlement, she had yet remained alert to whatever goings on were reported to her. And so it happened that the serving girl, Fridgerd, brought her mistress word of the departure which Olvir had brought back with him, and news of what had been said by Thord and the others, and by the ship's crew and by Osvif, Thjodhild's husband, when the matter of Harald's kingship had been raised with him.

Thjodhild said, when she heard this last, that she was not sure how much her husband could be relied upon to protect her own rights if he were so mealy-mouthed where his king's honor was at stake.

Now she told Fridgerd to fetch Thord and Lambi to her and this the girl did at once. When her kinsmen came in, she gave them a good greeting. They returned this and then Thjodhild asked Thord and Lambi if it were true, as she had heard, that Sigtrygg planned to go off to the Skraeling country and win new allies for himself.

"I have certainly heard that," Thord agreed, "though it is not clear that everyone sees the matter in the same way."

"What does my husband say?" Thjodhild asked.

"That our ill-born kinsman means us no harm and can do little in any case," Thord replied. "But some others think it is Osvif's place to assert King Harald's rule in this country, whatever the cost, for he is the king's man and has his commission in this."

Thjodhild said: "It's not clear to me that Osvif Thorleiksson has the will for it, for I think he is more tradesman than fighter, when all is said and done. But you kinsmen of mine have certainly more cause for complaint than most in this matter, and now you have the king's commission besides, since I have an equal share in everything which my husband owns."

Thord said: "Kinswoman, there is no easy way to address the matter, for Osvif has the Norwegians under his command and he will do nothing, despite all provocations against him. And we Eiriksfjordmen, on the other hand, are surely too few in this country to act on our own."

"You are certainly proving less manly than I had hoped," Thjodhild now agreed, "though you were free enough with your words before this. And, while it is not surprising that my brother should prove reticent in this matter, for he is only half as good as most men for the injury our kinsman gave him, I had expected more from you."

Lambi stood up at this and said in anger that Thjodhild should not now be throwing in his face what before she had thought to make so little of, "for I am every bit as capable of swinging axe or sword, with my one good hand, as other men are with two."

"Still, you have yet to prove it," Thjodhild said.

Thord said: "What do you have in mind kinswoman, since these Norwegians are so unwilling to take our part in this?"

"That you now find a way to repay that man who crippled my brother and cast his own kin aside for these dark-skinned wretches who cover themselves with the skins of beasts and carry stones about with them instead of steel."

"This is a different tune than the one I have heard from you before," said Thord, "and I am not sure what is the cause of it. Nevertheless, we are no more able to do what you would have us do now, than before, without the aid of your husband. And he has shown himself unwilling to offer that."

"Then you must find a way yourselves," said she, "for when our kinsman has departed he will be beyond our reach, and who knows what will come of it."

"Not much," said Lambi, "if he means to take up residence with these dusky men, for they can have little to offer folk like us."

"It is not the men he is concerned with, in my opinion," Thord said.

"Then do what you must," said Thjodhild quickly, "for I will not sleep easily knowing he has treated us so arrogantly and that, after his many affronts, he will now walk off to claim a kingship in this land which, by rights, belongs to my husband's overlord. And, though Osvif will not enforce it for himself, yet I am not minded to let this matter go by without some effort to repay him on my part."

After this Thord and Lambi took their leave of Thjodhild and each of them said that they thought she seemed a great deal more spirited than usual, and somewhat more intense. They went apart from everyone else at first and talked a great deal among themselves. Later they brought Thorstein Thorkelsson into the matter and the other men from Eiriksfjord and asked each of them what they had to say concerning this. All agreed that what Thjodhild was urging was no easy task, if they were to act alone, and that it was unlikely Osvif could be persuaded to throw in with them or Thjodhild would have involved him directly in the matter already. At last Thord took it to their kinsman Girstein, and to the big Swede whom Girstein had befriended, and told these two everything that Thjodhild had said, with Lambi confirming it for them.

Girstein said he found it surprising that Thjodhild had now turned against their kinsman like this, despite the matter of the broken troth, for he had not thought she had taken things quite so badly as now seemed to be the case.

"Nevertheless," said Thord, "we want to know what help you are prepared to provide to us in this."

"None whatsoever," replied Girstein, "for I think this is an unworthy enterprise which you men are now proposing, and I don't see any use in helping to push it further along."

"It is what our kinswoman wishes," said Thord, "and that ought to be enough for a man like you."

"I will speak to her myself," said Girstein, "and learn whether she is sincere in this matter, or if she spoke out of a moment's anger only."

"That won't make any difference," replied Thord, "for I have seen the look in her eyes when she spoke of this and that is unlikely to change, whatever words you are now able to draw out of her."

"Still I mean to see for myself," Girstein said.

After this he went in and spoke at length with Thjodhild. But he found her just as adamant as Thord had said and unwilling to soften her words concerning their kinsman. In fact, Thjodhild now urged Girstein to apply to Osvif for assistance in the matter, "for you are his friend," she said, "whereas I am only wife to the man."

Girstein returned to the others and admitted what he had heard and now Thord asked him again if he were willing to throw in with them.

"Not at all," replied Girstein, "for I think this no better an enterprise now than before, and it is my advice that you men abandon it as well, for I have the feeling Thjodhild herself will regret the words she has spoken here before those events, which you are now so intent on setting in motion, will have run their course."

But Thord said he was certainly not willing to do that and now he asked Gaut the Swordsman what help they could expect from him.

"That will depend," replied the Swede.

"On what?" asked Thord.

"On what you kinsmen are prepared to do for yourselves," said Gaut.

"There's no need for that," said Girstein hurriedly, "for we are now well-placed to winter over in this country and gather a rich cargo of timber and other valuable things which are to be found here, after which we can sail back to Greenland, if we like, and make a nice profit on this year's work. And there is nothing to prevent us from coming back here afterwards and gathering more of the same, for our kinsman has given us leave for that. But if you act rashly now, who knows how matters will end?"

"Nor are you men likely to find it an easy matter overcoming this Sigtrygg's good luck, in any case," Gaut now added, "for you have not done particularly well for yourselves when you have crossed swords with him before this."

"A house may be entered by other ways than the main door," Thord replied, "and I think this is as likely to prove true in this case as in others."

"And we will have our honor, at the least," snapped Lambi, and as he spoke he rubbed the crippled arm which hung uselessly from his shoulder where the spear had pierced him that morning out on the fjord.

CHAPTER XLI

BLOOD AND REPAYMENT

Not long afterwards Thjodhild's serving girl came into Sigtrygg's camp and now she spent some time dallying and laughing with some of the men there. After awhile, however, she grew more serious and told those who were with her that it was Arnliot Keelfoot she had come to see and no other. So someone went off to fetch the big Ketilsfjorder in accordance with her wishes. Arnliot came out at once, when he learned who was seeking him, and said he was glad Fridgerd had come at last, since they could not expect to be spending much more time together after this, "now that we are departing for the Skraeling country."

Fridgerd replied that she thought it would be a hard thing for them to be separated in this fashion and begged him to remain behind with her.

"That is not possible," Arnliot said, "since I am a mainstay of this crew and they would be hard-pressed if I were to leave them now."

"It's all the same to me what happens to these others," Fridgerd said, "so long as you are not among them but here, instead, with me."

Arnliot laughed and promised to bring her back many fine gifts from the land of the Skraelings "and not least of these, the heads of those who oppose me," and now he took her by the hands and urged her to follow him away from the encampment, down towards the sea.

"No," said the serving maid, "but I know a better place and it is in the woods, not far from here, and no one is likely to find us there once we have come to it."

Arnliot said she could have it her own way and so he followed this girl inland a ways, until they came to a small clearing which was surrounded on all sides by trees and thick underbrush, just as she had promised. They went into this place and Arnliot took hold of the girl at once and placed her on the ground there and then he laid himself down beside her and began to kiss and caress her.

Fridgerd said he must not be in such a hurry to work his will, "for it will be a long time before we two are together again, if you have your way in this, so there's no need to be hasty now," but the Ketilsfjordman only laughed at her words. He said: "You would do better, for your part, to abandon your mistress and those who surround her and take up, instead, with men like us who have won a place in this land, for then you will find the companionship you are seeking a great deal more readily than is now likely once we have gone to winter with these Skraelings."

"It is more likely," a voice from behind him now said, "that she will find a place in your household as servant to those two Skraeling concubines which you keep."

Arnliot raised his head at this to see Thord Thorkelsson standing there, above him, his sword drawn. Beside Thord were Lambi Gunnarsson and Thorstein Thorkelsson, and both of these men also had swords in their hands. A number of other Eiriksfjorders were also nearby. All were armed.

Arnliot said: "You have certainly come here well prepared for trouble and maybe that is not to be wondered at, for you men have never shown yourselves overly willing to expose yourselves to danger."

Thord said: "I would not be too hasty when judging others, if I were in your place, for some people would think that caution is better than being caught unawares in the woods with your pants down. Besides, there is still the matter of that claim which Grimkel Vesteinsson of Ketilsfjord has made against you and which he as-

signed to me, or did you think I would leave the matter unsettled
because of your arrogance? Grimkel swore to get a judgement
against you for the depredations you made in his district and to
see you outlawed, if he could. But if this were not possible, he told
me to exact payment from you however I am able."

Fridgerd now scrambled to her feet and pulled her garments
close about her. Arnliot asked if she had known of this tryst with
the Eiriksfjordmen, when she had lured him out there.

"I did," she replied, "though they swore that they only desired
to speak with you apart from the others."

"Then you are not to be blamed," said he, "for you relied on
the word of your betters."

He now arose, pulling his trousers awkwardly up around his
legs and reaching, unthinkingly, for his sword. Yet now he found
nothing, although he had carefully placed the blade beside him
on the earth before lying down with Fridgerd. Thord laughed at
this and held up the weapon he was seeking and said: "We feared
you would injure yourself, big man, thrashing about there on the
ground as you were, so we took it to spare you that shame, for you
would have been hard-pressed, indeed, to tell how you got such a
wound in light of your other tales. And now you will be thinking
that the time has come when you will have need of this sword,
although I am not certain how you think you will be able to reclaim it."

"I have never needed weapons before this against such men as
you, Thord," Arnliot replied. "Or against cripples like your kinsman."

Lambi said: "We will see who is the cripple when this day's
work is done. And who will be walking away on his own legs."

"Legs and arms are all one to me," said Arnliot, "for whoever
loses even one of his limbs does not deserve to continue living, in
my opinion, since he will have become nothing but a burden to
himself and to others."

The serving girl now began to wail when she heard this exchange and protested that Thord had not told her of his intention

of harming Arnliot when he had urged her to lure the big Ketilsfjordman out into the woods and she began to beg him to leave them now in peace.

"It's too late for that," answered Thord, "but you have had the reward which I promised you and that was to lie once more with this man before he leaves us. Yet, if you still feel cheated, in that we came to meet you sooner than you'd hoped, I will show you how we men of Leif Eiriksson's kin play with our women once our work here is done."

Fridgerd said her mistress would never allow that, but Thord only laughed again at her words and said he thought Thjodhild now had other matters to concern herself with and that she was unlikely to trouble overmuch about the fate of one foolish serving girl in any event. "But bide your time awhile here girl," he added, "while we cut down this big tree of a man, and then you may find the entertainment worth waiting for."

Arnliot said: "There are some trees which fall harder than others and not every man is a match for them."

"That is still to be seen," said Thord and now he threw aside Arnliot's sword and raised his own, running in towards the Ketilsfjord man. Arnliot turned aside from this first blow and, seizing the dead limb of a nearby tree which was hanging just above the ground, he snapped it from the trunk out of which it grew and brought it up before his face in time to ward a second strike from Thord's blade.

"A man does not need a sword to defend himself against the likes of you," he said when he had struck Thord's blade aside.

Thord brought his weapon down a third time and this time he aimed the blow at the big man's waist. Arnliot was unable to move the tree branch he held in his hands quickly enough and got a slight wound then across his stomach so that the blood began to spread under his shirt.

"There," said Thord, "now I have made the first cut and it will not be long now before this tree is down."

Fridgerd began to moan loudly at this and threw herself onto

Thord's sword arm, even as Lambi and Thorstein and the others plunged into the clearing and set themselves in a circle around the wounded man. Thord at once shook the serving girl from him and advanced again against the Ketilsfjorder. Now Fridgerd roused herself and ran from the clearing, her skirts in her hand, and she was shouting loudly but Thord paid her no mind but struck twice more at Arnliot and each of the others followed suit. Their swords now came down repeatedly against the man who stood in their midst and he, in his turn, struck back wildly with the large tree branch he had taken for his weapon. Soon, despite the heavy odds against him, he had cleared a space for himself, for he dealt them hard blows with the broken tree limb he held.

After a time the fighting between them slowed and then Arnliot stood before them, the great stick aloft in his hands, though he bled from several wounds which he had received. Yet, it seemed that his attackers had not fared a great deal better than he, for two of the Eiriksfjorders who had come out with Thord and his kinsmen had taken sharp blows to the head and chest and sat now slumped over on the ground and were plainly out of the fight. As to the others, they were now finding it hard going to get in close enough to lay in a clean blow against the Ketilsfjordman, for he swung the tree limb about him in a wide circle with great ease despite his wounds, nor did he appear to them to be breathing overly hard.

"This has not turned out as well for you as you had expected," Arnliot now said to Thord, but the other replied that the matter was still to be decided, "and you are not without wounds in this affair."

"Such loss of blood is of little concern to me," said the Ketilsfjorder, "for I have had worse cuts than these, and then I walked away . . . over the bodies of those men who had made themselves my enemies."

"You are unlikely to walk away this time, in any event," Lambi said, "for either we or you will meet our deaths here in this wood."

"In that case you must be prepared to meet yours," Arnliot

replied, "for I do not think I am fated to be killed by men like you. But you, Lambi, must certainly be eager to part with your own life; and that more than these others, since it is such a burden for you to bear when you are unable to raise a sword properly and fight as other men can."

Lambi gave a howl of rage at these words and hurled himself at once against the Ketilsfjordman. Arnliot stepped directly into this attack and caught Lambi across the face with a blow of the tree branch and this knocked him full off his feet and to his knees. Now before the others could rush in to support the fallen man, Arnliot reached down and seized the sword from Lambi's weakened grip and then he brandished it aloft and shouted at the others in triumph. He said: "This will prove the turning point, for I do not think any of you will dare come close to me now that I have your kinsman's blade in my hands."

The others fell back at this and now Thord looked about and saw that only Thorstein, his brother, and two others were left standing with him.

Thorstein saw how Thord now retreated and said: "Kinsman, it will be a black mark on all our names if we do not bring this man down now." But Thord continued to step back uncertainly, for he thought the fighting had proved a good deal harder than he had expected. Now he lowered his sword slightly and said to Arnliot: "Will you take terms from us, Ketilsfjorder, since we outnumber you here and you have been cut so badly?"

Arnliot laughed aloud and said he thought it was his part to offer them terms and not the other way around, "but I am not yet eager to do that."

"You cannot hope to get off so easily now, in any case," said Thorstein and he urged Thord and the others to advance with him against the big man. This they did, somewhat hesitantly, and Arnliot raised his sword and whirled it about above his head. At this the attackers all fell back at once so that Arnliot was now able to run out at them, chasing them from the clearing and into a patch of trees. Now he pursued each one in turn and they fled from him as though each was alone and had none to depend on but himself. He laughed as he ran at each man, causing first one and then another to stumble over the tree roots and underbrush which blocked their flight. After a time he said: "Now it seems to me that I am free to kill or spare you men exactly as I choose, and you are unable to do anything to prevent it."

Thord said: "Things have not fallen out as we had hoped, but you will not be the one to benefit from it, if I have anything to say in this matter."

Arnliot quickly struck his sword across Thord's gut, before that man could move to defend himself, drawing a line of blood in the man's flesh, though it was not a very deep cut. "Now I have at least repaid you for that first blow which you gave to me," he said, "and I don't think anyone would blame me if I gave each of you the same, for then we should see how well you men bear up under the same blood loss which I have had."

"There's no need for that," said another voice behind them and Arnliot turned at this to see a number of men coming briskly toward him, through the trees. At their head was Girstein Eiriksson and he had his sword drawn. Behind Girstein came several of the Norwegians led by Osvif Thorleiksson, and Gaut and Olvir. They had the serving girl, Fridgerd, in their midst.

Osvif took in the whole scene before him at a glance and shook his head. He said: "Enough damage has now been done here, for the serving maid has told us everything, how you, Thord, lured this man out here in order to waylay him, and how these others supported you in this."

"Yet matters have certainly gone somewhat differently than they had intended," Arnliot added, grinning and waving his sword point under Thord's nose. Although he was bleeding in several places Arnliot seemed not to notice the wounds he had taken.

"Whatever has occurred," said Girstein after awhile, "you men must now put up your swords, for the time is past for such games as you have now been playing."

"I'm not sure about that," answered Arnliot, "for it seems to me that nothing is finished until each of these fellows has been blooded as I was."

"What do you have in mind?" asked Girstein.

Arnliot had a strange look in his eyes. He said: "I mean to give each of these men exactly the same wounds which they gave to me, or I shall never count myself repaid for the bad faith that they have shown here."

"It seems to those of us who have only just arrived that you have already done enough harm to these men," answered Girstein evenly, "for they will not find it an easy matter to live down the shame which they have earned this day. So my advice is that you now put your anger aside and let matters lie."

Arnliot spoke very softly, saying that he was unwilling to do that and that it was not to be borne that these men had set on him in this treacherous fashion, intending to kill him as they had said. "I will not be content until they are each repaid in the manner which they have earned," he added.

"I cannot allow you to do that," Osvif now said.

"Still, you cannot prevent it."

Now the big Ketilsfjord man advanced to where Thorstein Thorkelsson sat sprawled upon the ground and he touched his own thigh where a streak of blood dampened his trousers, saying, "this wound I got from a stroke of Thorstein's blade while I was yet unarmed, and I remember it clearly, as I recall each cut which these others made on my flesh. And now I intend to give to each man exactly what he to gave me; and Thorstein is to be next to receive back what he meted out with his sword hand."

"This is unworthy of you," Girstein said, "for these men are unable to defend themselves."

"As I was when they came upon me with my pants down in these woods," said Arnliot, "and took my sword from me."

Girstein now went and stood between his fallen kinsman and the man from Ketilsfjord and put his own sword up. "There's no use coming any closer than you now have," he said, "for it is not written that you are to do any more harm to men of my blood with that sword than you have now done."

Arnliot laughed and said that was still to be seen and now he brought his sword down upon the other man in a mighty blow which seemed to set Girstein's weapon to trembling when it struck against it. But Girstein withstood the shock and turned his sword flat-sided, letting the other blade slide past him to the earth. Arnliot at once pulled his sword hand back and raised his weapon to strike at Girstein again and now Osvif stepped forward as though he would stop the fight between these two. But Gaut put a hand on the Norwegian's shoulder and restrained him, saying, "there's no need for that, for it is not to be expected that all the men of Leif Eiriksson's blood will prove to be as helpless as these fellows lying about here on the ground have now shown themselves to be."

Now Arnliot rained hard blows down on the other man and Girstein seemed as though he would break beneath this attack, but no sword stroke got past his guard and he met each strike which Arnliot made against him with his own firm counter. Things went on like this for awhile, until it could be seen that the larger man was tiring with his great effort and loss of blood, and then Girstein told him to put his sword away.

"It is unlikely I will do that," answered the big man, "until I have done what I set out to do." But he was breathing much harder now than before.

"Then you will find it hard going, indeed," Girstein replied, "for I do not mean to let you do any more to these men than you have now done."

Arnliot laid on again with his sword and sought to get past the other man's guard to strike at Thorstein, where he sat, hunched over on the ground. But Girstein seemed now to be everywhere at once, before the big man's eyes, and his sword leaped in and out of the fray, until it glanced across the Ketilsfjorder's arm and drew blood.

"Now put down your blade," said Girstein again, "for you are not likely to get any good from this encounter, if we continue it."

The big man paid him no heed but pressed his attack again, so fiercely that Girstein must fall back before him. Then Girstein stepped to the right and then to the left and, with each step, he laid a cut across the Ketilsfjorder's shoulders. "These are only scratches," he said, "but I will certainly do worse than this if you do not now own yourself beaten."

Arnliot said he was not accustomed to giving way in a fight and that he did not mean to start now and he turned to follow the sword which Girstein waved before him. Girstein circled cautiously around the larger man and when he saw an opening he struck, first to the other's legs and then above, at his head. Arnliot parried both blows but it was clear the effort drained him and now the Norwegians began to laugh, for they thought him well spent.

Girstein said: "You are a strong man, but there is more to swordsmanship than brute strength and you have now seen this for yourself. Yet no one will deny your courage or prowess in this affair, for you saved your own life against harsh odds and have fought bravely against a better man than yourself. I will not count it in your disfavor if you ask for quarter now."

"I will not ask that of any man," answered Arnliot softly, his breathing heavy and labored. "Nor do I offer it."

So now he laid on again with his blade and, though his blows were less well-placed than before, they seemed to those who were watching to be no less powerful than they had been at the first. Girstein now stepped into these attacks and struck to great purpose, warding first one strike and then another, and another, turning the bigger man in circles as he moved about him.

Then Girstein brought the attack round to the Ketilsfjorder, himself, and he began to lay blow after blow onto him in his turn, driving the bigger man backward and into the nearby trees. The Norwegians began to laugh again at this, and to urge their shipmate on, and now it happened that Arnliot, in his retreat, stumbled past them and seemed to lose his balance under the barrage of relentless blows which Girstein made against him.

Seeing this, Gaut caught him up at once, as he lurched past

him, and pushed the Ketilsfjorder back towards the clearing, saying "it's unseemly for such a large fellow as you are to be running off without taking proper leave of your companions." All the Norwegians laughed when they heard this and took up the chant for Arnliot to stand his ground and fight.

Then Girstein came up to him and, with one sweep of his sword, struck Arnliot's own weapon from his grasp.

He said: "I thought you would never relinquish your hold on that blade, big man, for yours is a mighty hand and one I would not willingly face again."

Olvir now ran in behind the Ketilsfjorder and took hold of him around the arms, pinning them in their place. He said that matters had now gone about as far as they ought and that, in his opinion, all debts had been paid, "for your kinsmen, Girstein, have got what they earned at this man's hands while you have drawn a share of his blood from him, on their behalf." Arnliot did not resist the hold which his former shipmate now had around his arms but slowly slipped to his knees, for he was winded from this fight.

Girstein said he was well-content with the outcome, so long as Arnliot was no longer eager to press the matter and everyone there seemed to think things had turned out rather well. They clapped Girstein hard on his shoulders, for he was entirely unscathed from the affair and, seeing this, they praised his sword work excessively. Afterwards, they went about helping the fallen men to their feet, although they left Arnliot kneeling in the clearing, with none but Olvir to look to his wounds.

The little serving girl alone remained nearby, when the others were gone, and Arnliot looked up at her from his place on the ground, through the blood and sweat which mingled together on his brow, as though to catch her eyes with his. But when she saw him looking at her she could not meet his gaze but turned at once and fled away, after the others, toward Gunnarsstead. Then the Ketilsfjordman reached out to take the hilt of his weapon again into his hand, but his fist closed on nothing but the dry earth which his curling fingers were able to weakly scratch away from the ground lying beneath him there.

Word soon got round of the fighting which had occurred in the woods and of how Arnliot had been brought down, despite his bold defense, by Sigtrygg's kinsman. It did not matter that he had saved his own life in the affair, against those others who had attacked him, for everyone held these men to have been of little account considering how they had given way when they had all the odds in their favor. But it was thought a bold thing that Girstein, alone, had stood up to the Ketilsfjordman and disarmed him without sustaining even a single cut himself in the fight, and this was soon the talk in both camps.

Arnliot, when he had returned with Olvir's help and lay recovering from his wounds, heard what was being said and was more quiet about things than usual. Still, he said that his exploit would certainly have won more notice, "if that other had not happened along and caught me when my guard was down."

Everyone in Sigtrygg's camp laughed at this so that the Ketilsfjorder grew even less talkative about the matter than before. Still, he sent Olvir away as soon as he realized who it was had intervened to end the fighting, "for," he said, "it is not fitting that a man who serves that kin should find comradeship with us."

Sigtrygg said this was unjust, "since some people might think it was this man who saved your life," but Arnliot replied that he had no intention of changing his mind in the matter, "although you are certainly free to make him welcome here, if you choose to."

Olvir said there was no further need for that, "since I am accounted a more valuable man at Gunnarsstead than here," and added that he was perfectly content to take his leave of them now if that was how his shipmates wanted it. But Sigtrygg would not let him depart in this fashion and, after a time, these two sought out Vragi Skeggjasson together, and told him how things now stood. Then the old viking asked where Arnliot Torfisson was to be found and Sigtrygg replied that he was not likely to be in any place other than "that one in which we have just recently left him, for he has not shown any inclination to rise up from the bench on which he has lain since Olvir brought him back to us from the fighting in the woods."

Accordingly, Vragi went in with the others to the house where Arnliot lay and they found him there in the darkest corner of that darkened hall, lying with his face to the wall, hidden by the shadows which lay like gloom above his head. Arnliot did not look up at them when they came in, or make any sound of greeting, and Vragi went and stood above his head, saying nothing. After a time, the big man rolled over and stared at his three visitors; but, when he saw that Olvir was among that company, he turned his face angrily away again and lay back toward the wall. Vragi said: "You will not get very far like that, shipmate, for there is little worth seeing in the direction in which you have now turned your sight. And some will think you are not showing as much gratitude as you ought for the good that has been done you."

"There's not much good to be spoken of, in any event," answered Arnliot, "when a man's own comrade binds his arms while he is yet beset by his enemies so they can work their will on him."

"In my opinion," answered Vragi, "there are more ways than one to aid another; and the best will sometimes seem the least pleasing to the one who thinks he has cause to bear a grudge against others."

"I have cause enough," Arnliot agreed. And then he was silent again.

Vragi said: "It seems, shipmate, that you have hidden yourself in this place for reasons which are not hard to guess, and now I want to know what you intend to do as regards this matter, for this will have a bearing upon these others who count themselves your friends."

Arnliot again made no answer to this but now he drew himself up and sat facing the wall, his eyes well-hidden by the shadows in that darkened place. "I have little to say about that," he said after awhile, "but those who must have some news of my affairs will have it, when the time is right."

"You will not gain much by such thinking," Vragi now said, "for there is little good can come of worrying overmuch about such matters, and in the darkness, too. But leave the thing to these men, for I have the feeling they will not rest till they have set it to rights."

Arnliot said he didn't see what others could hope to do where he, himself, was concerned, "for no one here is any more ready with his weapons than I am; and yet that Eiriksfjorder will now think he has got the better of me. And others will certainly say as much."

"Nevertheless, I now want you to give me your word," said Vragi, "that you will bide here while these wounds of yours are allowed to heal and let your comrades look after things, for you are not likely to do any better in this matter than they can now do, while others will certainly suffer if you act otherwise."

"That is true enough," said Arnliot, "and yet I am unwilling to leave this work to others."

"Still, that is what you must now do," said Vragi, "for I do not think you are fated to gain as much from this as you would hope, while great harm may yet be done."

Arnliot said he would give the matter more thought if that was what Vragi desired and the old viking replied that this was only good sense, and now he urged the big man to rouse himself and come out into the light of day, "for the sun is a great healer and can be relied on to banish even the darkest of moods which may trouble a man." But Arnliot said he was unwilling to do that and that he preferred to remain indoors "since it's more peaceful here."

Thereafter, Arnliot remained off his feet for only two days more and then he was up and moving about and it seemed to those who saw him as though nothing of any consequence had occurred. Still, he was much more unwilling to accept the company of others than before, and he went about the camp with a somewhat quicker step than usual, and had little good to say to any man. Olvir, when he saw how matters stood, told Sigtrygg that, in his opinion, things were likely to be more peaceful if he now took his leave of them, "for our shipmate remains in rather harsh spirits and I think I am the cause of that."

Sigtrygg replied that he thought there were other causes which were no less serious but that Olvir should do as he thought best, so now these men parted and Olvir went back to Gunnarsstead where he got no worse a welcome than he had found before.

Now it fell out, about this time, that the men of Gunnarsstead went down to the lake where their ship was moored to bring it up onto the beach for the winter. Most of the Norwegians were hard about this task, for the lake was very shallow nearest the shore and the ship had become mired in the mud there so that it was rough work bringing it up onto the land. They had ropes on the ship's prow and sides and logs underneath the hull, beneath the surface of the lake and leading right up onto the shore, over which they were trying to coax the large vessel. Girstein alone had charge of this work, for neither his kinsmen nor any others of importance were present.

The work with the ship went on for the better part of the day and everyone was very tired by the end of it, although it seemed to them that they had made very little progress, for all the effort they had expended. Girstein took a look at what had been accomplished and said that, in his opinion, they should now let the ship sit where she was, "for it is unlikely to go very far in this lake before tomorrow, while we will certainly be more rested and better fit to try this again, after a night's sleep."

Then he made them tie down the ropes they were holding to stakes, which they had driven into the ground, after which he sent them back to Gunnarsstead.

Girstein was one of the last to head back toward the settlement, after the ship was secured, but, when he thought all the work which needed doing had now been accomplished he turned, himself, to go up the slope. But when he did this he thought he saw a glint of metal in the trees above him. "Who is that who is waiting for me there?" he asked, and when he got no answer he asked this again. There were a few others of the crew who were still with him then and these men saw that Girstein seemed somewhat unsure of the path ahead of them and so they asked if he wanted them to go on before him.

"That will not be necessary," Girstein replied, and he picked up his sword and scabbard which he had laid aside during the work with the ship.

Thereupon a man stepped out from among the trees and it could be seen, at once, that it was Arnliot Torfisson. He had in his hands that great war axe, "hand-biter", which he had brought with him out of Greenland. He was holding it balanced against one shoulder.

He paused and shifted the axe, saying: "It's just as you thought Eiriksfjorder. There's no other way back to your friends at Gunnarsstead except past me. And now I want to know if you are willing to try your swordsmanship out again, when I am some-what fresher . . . and bearing a weapon of my own choosing?"

"There's no need for that," answered Girstein evenly, "for you are a mighty man and I have owned it. I have no quarrel with you except you make one, so step aside and allow us to pass."

"It's unlikely that I shall do that," Arnliot replied, "for then people would think that you made me give way, as they now sing your praises concerning that duel we fought in the woods."

"That was no duel," said Girstein, "for I had all the advantage, as you have said, while you were winded and cut and had lost much blood. No one can think the worse of you for a loss in such circumstances. But all will think you a better and wiser man if you spare us now."

"There's no use trying to get out of this," Arnliot replied, some-what sharply, "for my mind is made up, and that is that we two must now test it out between us, for people will certainly say that Arnliot Torfisson was outmatched, otherwise."

Girstein said he had no desire to pursue this matter but that he would not flee, if no other choice was given him, and now he asked what Arnliot intended for these other men, "if things go your way?"

"They shall come to no harm, if they do not attack me," Arnliot replied, "for my quarrel is with you."

"In that case, you shall have your way in this," said Girstein and he drew out his sword, after advising the others that they were to hold back, "whatever now occurs."

Then Girstein walked part way up the slope and stopped.

Arnliot looked at him and his old smile stole across his lips, but his eyes were very hard. He raised his great axe and at once ran down the hill at the waiting man and now Girstein swept his sword in an arc before him, seeking the shaft of the axe, where Arnliot gripped it with his two large hands.

The big Ketilsfjord man saw the sword fly up, as he came into it, and he jerked his weapon higher over his head, above the place where the sword sped past him, and then he brought his great blade down in a single powerful stroke against the other. Too late, Girstein realized that he had missed his swing and fell back, pulling his sword closer to him, to ward the great axe blow which now fell upon him. But he could not dodge this stroke and his sword's edge split in two, as the axe struck it, and then the axe head passed on, through bone and tendon, half-severing Girstein's forearm, where his sword had been only moments before, to lodge in his skull, splitting it like an overripe fruit.

The Eiriksfjord man crumpled to the earth under the weight of the great axe and then he lay there on the damp ground and Arnliot stood above him, pulling at his axe to free it. The others were all silent, but no man went for his weapon. Then Arnliot turned to them and said they were to go up to Gunnarsstead and announce the killing, if that was what they wanted, "for there is to be no secret concerning who has done this."

They asked leave to see to the body and Arnliot said he would not prevent that but he made them promise to describe the fight exactly as it occurred, "for here was a brave man who did not shrink from danger, as others would have, and this deserves to be told of."

The Norwegians promised to do as he desired and Arnliot said he was content, adding only that they were to be sure to tell truthfully of his part in the affair, as well, "and see that the tale is widely told, besides, so that everyone hears of it; and not least that serving maid who came out here with the people from Brattahlid . . . or it shall go with you others as it went with this man."

The Norwegians said they would do as he asked.

CHAPTER XLII

A SETTLEMENT IS SOUGHT

Everyone thought it the worst news when they heard of this killing and there was great consternation in both camps. Thjodhild took it hardest, of all those at Gunnarsstead, for she said that, in her opinion, Girstein Eiriksson had been the best of those men then alive who counted their descent from Eirik the Red and from Leif his son. Lambi and the Thorkelssons were very cast down over the whole affair and Thord had less to say than anyone. But Osvif told Thjodhild that he would see that compensation was paid, "for this man's loss is no less severe to me than to you others, in that he was both shipmate and kinsman to me."

Thjodhild thanked him but said that she did not think there was anything in that whole country which could be counted equal in worth to Girstein's life.

"Nevertheless," said Osvif, "it would be dishonorable to let the matter lie."

Thjodhild said that this was certainly true and now she asked Lambi and the Thorkelssons what they were prepared to do. They had no answer to this and Thjodhild said this only showed how badly they had come off in their last encounter "with that big fighting man our kinsman Sigtrygg has in his company, since you have been so thoroughly cowed by that fight which you had with him. But I think there must be someone in our crew who is not afraid to match himself against such a fellow."

Osvif said that, in his opinion, the matter could still be settled in a more peaceful fashion, "if we put our case before your cousin, for he has not shown himself to be an unreasonable man."

Thjodhild said he could have it his own way, "but I do not intend to put a low price on this loss of ours."

Afterwards Osvif asked Olvir to accompany him and Olvir agreed to this so that these two now went, with several others, into Sigtrygg's camp. They found that Sigtrygg was moved quite as much by the death of Girstein as Thjodhild had been, for he gave them a good greeting and made them come into his hall, seating them beside him and asking how matters fared at Gunnarsstead.

"Not as well as before," Osvif answered him truthfully, "since the killing of my kinsman and crewman, Girstein Eiriksson."

"How is Thjodhild taking it?" Sigtrygg asked and Olvir replied that she had not received the news well at all and that she held it very much against Sigtrygg for harboring such a man as Arnliot Keelfoot.

"And what is your opinion, then, friend Olvir," Sigtrygg asked him, "since you fought beside the man as I did? And some might think we had both been dead today, but for him."

"I think a settlement must be made in this matter," answered Olvir, "for our shipmate's sake."

"It is for that reason we have come," Osvif Thorleiksson now put in, "for we think this will take a very high price and we want to know what you are prepared to do in this matter."

"I will not give the man up for killing," Sigtrygg said, "or outlawry, if that is what is being asked, for it was Girstein, himself, who egged the Ketilsfjorder on to this by fighting against him in the woods. The man's temper is well known and he had good cause to take vengeance on those others, in any case, though Girstein prevented that. And afterwards my kinsman could have fled, when Arnliot came out against him, though he chose otherwise."

"It was not your kinsman's way, to turn tail before an enemy and run off," Osvif replied, "as you well know. But you must make an offer in the matter, in any case, or stand aside, that others of us may kill him."

"I have no intention of doing that," Sigtrygg said, "and you, Olvir, will know more than these others how firm I am in this. And that the task which this Norwegian is proposing is no light one."

Olvir said that he did and now he urged the Norwegian to accept a paid settlement, in place of blood revenge.

"That is not entirely up to me," answered Osvif, "but I will convey the offer, if it's a good one. But that will be difficult, for there is not much of value which is left to you in this country to give to others."

Sigtrygg said this was a strange thing to be telling a king in his own house, "for I possess all the land which you see about you and everything which is in it."

Osvif said: "A king owns what he can hold, Greenlander, and you cannot hold any of this, or keep others from coming here and taking what they want of this country, if they desire it. If you offered us all the land itself, it would have no value now since it is already ours for the taking."

"You shall have the ship, then, if you will take nothing else," said another voice and they turned around to see the lean figure of Vragi One-Eye standing in the shadow of the doorway. The old viking now came in, leaning on his spear as was his custom, and made his way to where the others were seated. He said: "The ship is yours, if our king is willing to part with it, and that is not without value since you can use it to transport more goods out of this country than you would have otherwise been able to. For our part, I think it will not be missed, for we will not soon be sailing eastwards from here."

Osvif asked Sigtrygg if he agreed with this offer and Sigtrygg said that he could see no reason to withdraw it, "for this old man rarely speaks up without good cause."

"Then I will present it to your kinsmen," Osvif said, "for they are to have the final word in this. But, for my part, I think the offer well-made, although even this cannot offset the great loss which we have suffered."

"It is no less my loss than yours," Sigtrygg said.

Afterwards Osvif got up with his companions to depart, but Olvir separated himself from these others and now he remained behind with Sigtrygg.

After the others had gone back to Gunnarsstead, Sigtrygg and Olvir spoke together for a long time and each of them thought they had suffered greatly from the killing of Girstein Eiriksson. They conferred about this awhile and then they went, together, to where Arnliot Keelfoot was to be found, for he had placed himself apart from all others and sat now with his back against a large rock in a place overlooking the sea. He had that axe of his lying nearby, ready to hand. When he saw Sigtrygg coming up to him he gave him a good greeting, but his face darkened somewhat as soon as he saw that Olvir was close beside him.

Olvir spoke first, when they came up with the Ketilsfjorder, and asked him how things now were. Arnliot replied that they were no different than before, "for there will certainly be those who think they have cause to seek vengeance for that killing I did up by the lake, and I mean to give them as warm a greeting as their eagerness deserves."

Sigtrygg had little to say when he heard this, but he kept looking at the large war axe. At last he said: "You were not to take that weapon of yours, shipmate, until I gave you leave, since I had it in my keeping for all our sakes."

"There's no use worrying about curses on this war-wand of mine," Arnliot replied, "for it is certainly dangerous enough to those who stand before it without such tales."

"Its curse," said Sigtrygg, "is that it has now been used for a very bad end in that it has deprived me of the best of my kinsmen . . . and he is sorely missed."

"Are you to be the first, then, Sigtrygg, who comes to me in search of repayment?" Arnliot asked, smiling up at him.

"There's no need for that," said Olvir, "for this man has just offered to pay compensation for what you have done and we will soon know if it is to be accepted, in which case you will be free to leave this big rock which you have found here and trust your back to your companions again."

"What price is to be paid?" asked Arnliot.

"Our ship," said Sigtrygg, "and everything which can be carried in it back across the sea."

"That is a heavy price."

"It was no less heavy a deed," Sigtrygg said.

"I will leave this company," Arnliot said, "for there is no reason that you men should have to pay for what I have done. Let these kinsmen of yours seek me out themselves, and keep your ship."

"The offer has been made, in any case," Sigtrygg said, "so now we must wait to hear if it will be accepted. In the meantime, I will have that axe from you, in repayment for the ship."

"I am not prepared to part with it," Arnliot said curtly.

"Then let me keep it until a new ship has been built," said Sigtrygg, "for I don't want you carrying it about in this company, since it may cause further harm to men who are not deserving of it. Besides, you are more than able to defend yourself with a sword, as you have already shown."

"I will not give it to you," Arnliot said, "but you may hold it for me while the new ship is being built, if that is what you want. However, the time to build the ship is not to extend beyond one winter, after which I will have this weapon back whether the ship is ready or not."

Sigtrygg said this was agreeable to him and took up the axe in his own hands. Arnliot did not attempt to hinder him, although he did not take his eyes from the weapon until Sigtrygg had turned and walked off with it. Thereupon Olvir took off that sword which he was carrying at his belt and bent down to the Ketilsfjordman, putting it into hands. "You will need this now, shipmate," he said in a low voice, "at least until a settlement has been made in the matter of this killing. If I were you I would remain here by this rock, where the vantage is good in all directions, until we send you word that the matter has been concluded."

Arnliot said nothing but he took the sword, and now these

two parted.

Thereafter Olvir told Sigtrygg and the others that he planned to return to Gunnarsstead "to urge the settlement," and Sigtrygg said he should do as he thought best. Sigtrygg went part of the way with him, to the other camp, until they came in sight of the clearing and then Sigtrygg fell back and took his leave of the Brattahlid man, wishing him well.

Olvir now went in to the others and at once sought out Osvif and Thjodhild. He found these two together on the high seat and all their kinsmen were close by.

Olvir gave them a good greeting and asked how matters stood. Osvif made no answer to this but looked at Thjodhild, as though waiting for her to speak. But it was Thord who spoke first. "No different than before, serving man," he said rather sharply, "for this killing will not be easily paid for."

"What then of the offer which Sigtrygg made in this matter," asked Olvir, "for not many men's lives will be held equal to the value of a ship?"

"It is not much of a ship," answered Thord. "And besides, there are those of us who already count the vessel as our own, so that we are not likely to be inclined to accept, as payment, what is already ours."

Osvif said: "It is just as I said before, that this man has little of value to offer us in compensation for the wrong we have endured here."

"Only blood can pay for blood, in this case," Thord now added.

"Yet I am not certain that you are the man to exact payment," said Olvir, "if your past encounter with the Ketilsfjorder is any measure."

"It is not a task for one man, at the least," Thord now agreed. "Still we all have an equal share in this matter."

"Your words are bold enough when you are safe among your kinsmen in this hall," Olvir said, "surrounded by the men of this crew. But you were not nearly so enterprising when you joined with certain others, who are here, to kill that man in the woods whom you are now reviling."

Thjodhild now broke in and said that Olvir ought not to speak up so boldly in defense of the Ketilsfjorder, "since you, yourself, helped bring that man down, when he contended against our kinsman, and this saved his life, for otherwise, they say, my cousin Girstein would have slain him then and there . . . and that would have been the end of it."

To this Thord now added that he, too, thought Olvir was partly at fault in this matter, "for you knew the temperament of the Ketilsfjorder better than others and should have foreseen what would come of sparing his life."

"It is not easy to foresee what will befall any of us," answered Olvir, "but this much, at least, is now clear to me, and that is that, if you Eiriksfjorders do not now accept the settlement which has been offered, no better is likely. In which case there will be hard matters and a great deal more bloodshed to come before this thing is done."

Osvif said: "The man speaks wisely, however harsh the pain we are all now suffering, for I have seen the resolve of this Sigtrygg and his fellows with my own eyes and they are not likely to stand aside for us."

"We outnumber them now no less than before," Thord said, "despite our loss of one, so I don't see why you have continued to be so reluctant in this matter."

"Numbers are not everything," answered Osvif, "as your own encounter in the woods has now shown."

Thjodhild said this was true enough and now she asked those around her what they were prepared to do to "repay that man who is responsible for our kinsman's death?"

At this Thord fell silent and Lambi and Thorstein averted their eyes. Thjodhild turned next to Osvif and asked him what help he was willing to offer them.

"I want to wait until things have cooled down a bit," he said, "and then I will be willing to talk further about the matter."

"It's a fine situation, when a woman cannot count on her husband or kin to right the wrongs which have been inflicted on her," Thjodhild now said, "for, in truth, it seems to me that I feel this loss more keenly than any of you."

Thord said: "Kinswoman, we will gather a force..."

But Thjodhild cut him off, saying, "it will take more than that to stiffen your backs in this, cousin, for none of you are men enough to do what now must be done."

After this Olvir returned to Sigtrygg and told him how things had turned out and then Sigtrygg sat for awhile and had very little to say. Olvir asked if he wanted to try another offer but Sigtrygg said he doubted that anything else would succeed, "if our ship is not sufficient for them."

Olvir asked him what he wanted to do, in that case, and Sigtrygg said he was to go and bring Arnliot back at once "for we must depart for the Skraeling country without further delay, whatever becomes of our possessions here. In my opinion we have already remained here too long."

Not long after this Arnliot came into the camp with Olvir and now he went up to Sigtrygg and said that he had heard how the others were unwilling to take the ship. Sigtrygg said this was true enough, "though now they are likely to have it in any event, since we cannot carry it inland with us."

"Then my advice is to sink it," Arnliot said, "so they will not be rewarded for their arrogance in this."

"I have no intention of doing that," answered Sigtrygg, "for they may see the vessel as a fair payment when things are calmer, after we are gone. And then we shall have bought peace from them, despite all."

"There's certainly no need for that," said Arnliot, "for when we have rejoined the Skraelings we will have no reason to pray peace from anyone."

"They are my kinsmen," Sigtrygg said, "and I would have a settlement, if I can."

"Still, it seems to me your kinsmen see this matter differently," Arnliot replied, "as I do, myself, for the fight with Girstein was a fair one. And I had cause, besides, since he drew blood first from me. But now I mean to have that axe of mine returned, since I gave it to you as a pledge for the ship, although the ship was not taken as payment despite the offer you made to them."

"Let the matter lie till winter is done," Sigtrygg said, "for they may accept the ship in any case."

"They have not accepted it now," said Arnliot, "and those were the terms which we set between us. So scuttle the Gull or leave her for them, if you like, but I will have back my axe."

"That cannot be," Sigtrygg said.

"And why not?"

"Because it is gone," said Sigtrygg evenly. "I have now done with it what I should have at the first, when you brought it on board ship with us, for I ought to have foreseen then how difficult it would be for you to part with the weapon. That, too, is a part of its curse."

Arnliot said: "What is the meaning of this? What have you done with that axe, which I had from my father, and from his, before him, since it came into the hands of our ancestor Arnliot the Strong?"

"Your namesake got that weapon badly and that has been the bane of your kin since the weapon came into his possession," answered Sigtrygg, "and this I had from your father's own mouth, when I wintered with him in Ketilsfjord. So now I have done what needed doing, before any further harm could be wrought by that ill-fated war-tool."

Arnliot said: "Yet, I would know what you have done with the axe."

Sigtrygg said: "I don't suppose it will do you any harm to hear it then, shipmate, since there's nothing more to be done concerning it. I have thrown it out into the deepest part of the bay and, in my opinion, it will soon be swept out to sea, when next the tide turns, so there's no hope now of retrieving it."

Arnliot said this was badly done and asked Sigtrygg where he had been when he had sent it into the sea. Sigtrygg told him reluctantly, so he would see the hopelessness of finding the weapon again. "And there's no use trying to get it back, either," Sigtrygg added, "for it is as though we tossed it off the bow of the Gull, when we stood out upon her, on the high seas."

The Ketilsfjorder said that was still to be seen and now he stalked off in a great rage.

At this same time, at Gunnarsstead, Thord Thorkelsson was also feeling rather put upon, for it seemed to him that Thjodhild had shamed him and his kinsmen before the Norwegian and his crew, for their unwillingness to face the big Ketilsfjorder again. And, while the Norwegian had shown no greater courage, it was plainly not his part but the duty of the men of Brattahlid to avenge Girstein Eiriksson's death. Thord brooded about this and went about with his head down, since he was unwilling to look any of his shipmates in the eye after his kinswoman's harsh words. He was walking thus when he came upon Gaut, and then he saw that the Swede was watching him closely and seemed to be looking at him in a very intense way.

Gaut now asked him if he were still distraught over the loss of his kinsman. Thord replied that he was, "although you should certainly be feeling it no less than the rest of us, since you were Girstein's friend; and partly responsible for his death, to boot."

"How so?" asked the Swede.

"Because," said Thord, "you denied us your aid when we asked it of you, which, had you given it, would certainly have been the death of that big man."

"I'm not denying that," answered Gaut, "for my swordsman-ship is well known. But some people would think you Eiriksfjorders ought to have been more than enough, between you, to have brought that fellow down."

"That may be," said Thord, "yet he has now inflicted a great loss on all of us and we are unable to get our rights in this matter, for he is under the protection of that man who calls himself our kinsman. Although he is as much an outlaw as the other."

"This will not be the first time you men from Brattahlid think you have been denied your rights," said Gaut. "Still, I am not averse to helping you, if you have the courage for it, for there is very little in this world which is worth winning without some risk."

CHAPTER XLIII

THE AXE

Arnliot Keelfoot now found three crewmen who said they could show him where Sigtrygg had thrown the axe into the sea and so he told them to take him to that place. There was a small headland, not far up the coast, and they led him to this. At its farthest end was a big rock which jutted out into the sea. Arnliot went out with them onto this promontory and asked them where they thought the weapon had gone when Sigtrygg had hurled it from him. These men now began to argue among themselves concerning the exact place where the weapon had touched the water and Arnliot became impatient at this. He stripped off his garments and dove off the rock and began to swim out to the place where one of the three was gesturing. Then he called back and asked if he was in the right place and the man who was pointing in that direction replied that he was.

At once he plunged below the surface and was gone from their sight for a time. But when he came up afterwards he had nothing in his hand and he seemed angrier than before. Twice more he dove below the surface of the water in that spot but he had no better luck than he had had at the first. So now he swam to the place where the second man was pointing and did exactly as he had done before. The water was very deep in this location and he shouted to them that he was having a great deal of trouble finding bottom. The men on shore now urged him to come in, for they thought it very dangerous to be swimming out so far from the land. Few men in Greenland were strong swimmers, because the waters about that country are so cold for most of the year, and his companions were afraid for him. But Arnliot called back that they were not to be overly concerned, "for I have knocked about in much harsher waters than these."

And now he went below the surface again and was gone from their sight for a long time.

When he came up again he called to the third man and asked him where he thought the axe had landed. This fellow now pointed even further out than the others, so Arnliot turned about and swam toward that place. When he thought he had arrived he called to the men on shore and asked if he was at the right spot. But now he got no answer from the others and could see no one out on the promontory, where these men had been. Arnliot dove down beneath the surface a few times then but, after awhile, he grew somewhat winded and so he began to swim back to the shore. He reached the rock where he had left his companions and pulled himself out of the sea there and began to look about for the others. At first he could see nothing, except that his clothing and sword were gone, but when he was able to wipe the brine from his eyes he saw the forms of two of the three men who had come out there with him, lying in the grass on the headland. He went over to them and knelt down and now he could see that the belly of one and the neck of the other had been cut open with sword strokes. Their own swords were gone, as well, and he got up quickly when he saw this and began to look about him.

A familiar voice behind him now said: "You won't find what you are looking for there, Ketilsfjorder, if it is the third man of your company you are seeking. He went off toward the landward side of this rock, but he is unlikely to get far since he has been handled no better than these other two."

Arnliot turned to see the Thorkelssons and their kinsman, Lambi Gunnarsson, nearby. It was Thord who had spoken, and each of these men had a sword in his hands. Now the other Eiriksfjorders who had come out from Greenland with Thord and his kinsmen showed themselves as well, for they had been hiding among the trees which grew out there on the headland. All were armed and there were seven of them in total. Arnliot looked from one to the other and now he laughed loudly at the sight of them and said he thought it surprising to see them, "so soon after our last encounter, for you men seem ill-prepared to protect your good names, since you are so eager to face me again despite the dishonor you got for yourselves when we last crossed swords."

Thord said: "The only thing surprising, big man, is that we seem unable to find you with your clothes on. But that will do you little good now, unless it enables you to run off more quickly, as your third companion did, or, if you choose, to return to the sea. For otherwise we mean to finish what we began on that day we found you covering that little filly who serves our kinswoman."

"There's no need to concern yourselves about that," answered Arnliot, "for it is unlikely I will ever need to run off from men like you, armed or otherwise," and now he walked directly up to Thord, causing the Eiriksfjordman to back away.

Lambi said: "You'll get no honor that way cousin," and he rushed in and slashed with his sword at the Ketilsfjorder.

Arnliot dodged away but the sword caught him, all the same, opening a gash on his bare shoulder.

"There, I have drawn first blood," Lambi said. "And now it is for you others to show what you are prepared to do to exact revenge for our dead kinsman."

The others now came at Arnliot with their weapons raised and he rushed out to the edge of the promontory to save himself. There they advanced against him and Arnliot could now see that his only hope was to throw himself back into the sea. He moved cautiously along the edge of the rock, seeking a way past them.

Thord said: "Now you must decide if your life is worth more to you than your honor, big man, for all will know that you fled from us if you run to the sea, whereas death at out hands will be thought respectable since you had no choice in the matter."

"I think few people will judge it honorable to have received their death blow from you, Thord," Arnliot replied grimly. "Nor are you likely to gain much by it, in any event, since there are so many of you. And I am unarmed."

"It's all the same to me what people say," answered Thord. "Besides, people can only speak of what they know and we will tell them how you begged for mercy and sobbed like a child at the moment of your death. Who will there be to say otherwise when you are gone?"

Arnliot lunged at Thord when he heard this and Thord struck him across the chest, a glancing blow with his sword. Thorstein and the others rushed in at this, their own swords raised. The big man from Ketilsfjord was soon bleeding in several places, for he was unable to defend himself against their blades, and he ran out again to the edge of the promontory and stood there as before, his eyes alternately on the men who assaulted him and on the sea. The others moved toward him once more, bright blood dripping from their upraised weapons.

"Now we will see if this big fellow from the Ketilsfjord district has any manliness left in him," said Thord, "for the choice is to stand here and die or go into the sea. But I do not think he is likely to get far in that case either, since he has been wounded so grievously."

Arnliot said they must not concern themselves overly much on that account, "for I have been in harder straits," and now he seized a handful of dirt and threw it into the eyes of the man who stood nearest to him. When this man covered his face and began to wipe at his eyes, Arnliot rushed past him and now he made for the mainland with the others at his heels. He had not run far when another man appeared before him. He was large, nearly as big as Arnliot himself, and he had a sword in his hand and another on the ground by his right foot. Arnliot stopped in his tracks when he saw this man for he recognized him at once. It was the man called Gaut, and the sword beside his foot was Arnliot's own, the very weapon which Olvir had lent him when Sigtrygg had taken the axe.

Gaut stood there before him and he had little to say until the others came up behind Arnliot and then the Swede laughed.

"It has all turned out just as I predicted," he said at last, "for even unarmed and unclothed this Ketilsfjorder has proved too much for you. And if I had not stopped him, he would even now be safe beyond your reach in those nearby trees."

Thord replied that they would certainly have run him down before he had gotten as far as the wood but Gaut replied that he thought that highly unlikely and asked Arnliot for his opinion.

"If you had not blocked my way," said the Ketilsfjorder, "these men would not have seen me again until I had armed myself. And then they would have thought it better never to have met me at all."

"That is exactly what I think, too," said the Swede, sheathing his sword. And now he kicked Arnliot's sword to him and told him to take it if he wanted it, "for this fight is likely to prove a great deal more interesting if you are armed than otherwise."

Arnliot grabbed the weapon from the ground and turned about to face the others.

Thord said to Gaut that he thought this badly done "for you have as much stake in this man's death as we do, since he killed your shipmate and friend." But Gaut replied that it was all the same to him, "since this fellow is already dead, as far as I can see."

Arnliot now raised his sword above his head and began to swing it, first at one of his attackers and then at another, causing each to fall back when the blade came his way. Now the Ketilsfjorder ran at these men and there was hard clashing of blades overhead, but Arnliot struck with such fury that the other men could make no progress against him. His blade bit, too, so that the others were soon bleeding as freely as the Ketilsfjorder and Gaut watched all this without comment. Thord now begged the Swede to take a hand in the matter, "or vengeance for our dead kinsman may never be gained," but Gaut continued to stand back as the others fought with Arnliot.

The big Ketilsfjord man was badly wounded but he stood his ground, just as though he felt no pain or weakness, and the seven men who were attacking him were soon hard pressed, in their turn. Arnliot whirled his sword about him with such speed that the others were held at bay and one by one these men seemed to tire and fall back.

Gaut, when he saw this, said: "This has certainly not gone as you thought it would, Thord, for this man, although hurt, is still more than a match for most other people. And now you are likely to find that you are unable to obtain what you were seeking, when you set yourselves against him."

Thord said he thought they would bring Arnliot down if they could get the help they had been promised. But Gaut replied to this that "I have stopped the man's flight, at least, and you ought to be grateful for that."

Now Gaut strode into the midst of the others and asked Arnliot if he thought he had done all that he could against these men who beset him. Arnliot replied that he still had a good deal of strength left in him, despite his loss of blood, and that he was in no wise ready "to give way before these weaklings."

"Good," said Gaut, "since I think you must now match your sword with mine . . . and I don't want it said that I waited until you were too weak to give a good account of yourself."

Gaut told the others to back away and now he drew his sword and advanced toward the Ketilsfjord man. Arnliot turned to face him, his own weapon poised above his head, and then Gaut struck with his blade and the two men's swords rang together as they met in mid-air. Gaut said: "You have a strong stroke Greenlander, as strong as any I have encountered, but it will not help you much in this case."

Now the two men circled warily about, each facing the other, and the Swede struck again with his blade, and once more the two swords rang out as they clashed in flight. Gaut took his sword back more quickly this time and swept in with a third blow, aimed at the Ketilsfjorder's knees, and Arnliot only barely avoided this deadly strike. Yet, as he scrambled to get clear, he lost his footing and stumbled somewhat. Then the Swede brought his blade back, along the same path it had first come, and caught Arnliot in the stomach so that his gut was laid open.

The Ketilsfjordman looked down at his belly then and sank down on one knee holding his own entrails in his left hand, trying to push these in, despite the blood and fat which poured out and around his hand onto the ground beneath him.

"There's no use trying to put them back," Gaut now said, "for I have seen such wounds before, and there is no help for them."

Arnliot said he thought it had grown much cooler than before and that he now regretted the long swim he had taken, "for I am not accustomed to feeling changes in the weather as intensely as this," and he put the point of his sword into the dirt and tried to lift himself from the ground. Gaut raised his own weapon again when he saw this, for he meant to strike at the big Ketilsfjorder's neck. But now the others rushed in before he could do so and Thord and Lambi each stuck the half-kneeling man a hard blow with their swords. This sent Arnliot swaying to the ground again and then Thorstein and the others plunged their swords into his body, as well. Each of them said, afterwards, that he thought he had given the big man his death blow, for the Ketilsfjorder did not stop moving until the last blade was pulled from his flesh.

Gaut and the others went up to Sigtrygg's camp, after this, and when they got there they stood outside the stockaded embankment and asked if Sigtrygg was within. After awhile Sigtrygg came out with some of his companions and asked what they were seeking.

"To report some killings," said Gaut, "for there are a number of dead men not far up the coast and I think you will know them when you see them."

"Who has been killed?" Vragi now asked.

"Crewmen of yours," answered Gaut, "and a great keel has been overturned there."

Sigtrygg asked if Arnliot Keelfoot was meant and Gaut replied that he should go and see for himself, "although some people had thought that man too big for slaying."

Sigtrygg now asked what had occurred and Gaut told the tale in great detail, for he and the others had been witness to all that had happened from the first moment that Arnliot had appeared with his companions out on the promontory. Gaut said he wanted all men to know that the Ketilsfjorder had been well enough for fighting, by his own testimony, when the two of them had crossed swords and that "your shipmate was certainly not thought too highly of, for all these others were unable to bring him down without my aid, even before he had a sword in his hands. Still, he was no match for me."

"There are not many men who can boast of cutting that tree down," said Sigtrygg. "But who gave him his death wound?"

"That will be hard to tell," answered Gaut, "for each of these men you see before you had a hand in that."

"Then payment will be sought from each of you," Sigtrygg said.

"It's unlikely that payment will be offered for this killing, in any case," answered Gaut, "or for those others who now lay dead out there on that headland. But if you think you are owed some recompense, in light of what has now been done, you must seek it from me alone for I am the one who is responsible for what has now occurred."

"Then you are the one I shall take it from," Sigtrygg said and he moved toward the Swede, his hand on the hilt of his sword. But Vragi took hold of his arm and held him back. He said: "This is not the place or time for that, shipmate, for you are angry and he is expecting this and will put up a good defense with these others."

"It's all the same to me," answered Sigtrygg, "what efforts these men make in their own defense, for they have now done what cannot be forgiven."

"Still they have come and told us of the killings, as the law requires," said Vragi, "and in that they are not to be faulted. If they are to be punished for what they have now done, then judgement must be gotten against them. And that may not be done here."

Gaut said: "Well-spoken, old man. But if judgement is sought, I, for one, am prepared to offer satisfaction in the matter. If anyone who is now here thinks he has a grievance against me for these killings, then let him come forth and say as much, when he is ready, for I will not be far away." And now he said they should find him in his accustomed place at Gunnarsstead.

"I will certainly attend you there, in that case," answered Sigtrygg, "and my advice is that you keep that sword of yours close by against my coming."

"Gladly," Gaut said, "for it has been a long while since this blade last tasted royal blood. And I think it is now time that fast were broken . . . however lean the fare which is offered."

CHAPTER XLIV

CHAMPIONS

When Gaut and the others returned to Gunnarsstead and told what had occurred, it was thought news indeed and everyone had something to say in the matter. Many of the crewmen of the Norwegian merchant ship now went to Osvif and asked him to intervene since they thought these killings a bad business and unlikely to lead to anything good if allowed to continue unchecked. Osvif said he agreed with this and added that, in his opinion, the killings of Girstein and Arnliot should cancel each other out, "for these were men of equal worth. But I fear we shall have to pay something, at least, for these other deaths."

Gaut said: "There is no need to pay anything in this matter, for I am the man responsible for all of the killings out on the headland and it has never been my practice to pay for the blood I have spilled. Nor am I prepared to alter that custom now."

"Nevertheless," replied Osvif, "it will be hard to get peace with these men if we do not offer them something by way of compensation for these losses which they have now suffered."

"It will not matter if we have peace with them, in any event," said Gaut, "for they are certainly too few, by now, to do us harm. But if anyone here is concerned in this matter, I will personally assure the peace since I have promised to answer all complaints, which any man may have against me, with my sword. And Sigtrygg Thorgilsson has assured me of his willingness to take the matter up himself. When I have dealt with him, there will be no further cause for dispute between the two camps and you, Osvif, will have the final word as to how things are to be disposed of in this country . . . in King Harald's name."

Osvif asked Thjodhild what she had to say in the matter but she gave him no answer, at first. Everyone else in that company now seemed to be standing about, waiting for her to speak. After a time Osvif pressed the question again, saying "you have heard how things have gone wife, so now you must tell us whether this is according to your wishes, since it is unlikely the course of this river can be changed, once it has gone round this next bend which crewman Gaut has made for it."

Thjodhild turned her face away, so that neither Osvif nor the others could see her as she spoke, and her voice seemed to them to be rather heavy and slow. She said: "Things must happen as they are fated and I don't think it is my part to seek to alter one man's destiny."

Olvir now spoke up, on hearing this, and begged Thjodhild to reconsider her words, "for this man Sigtrygg is your kinsman and you have thought highly of him, before this."

But Thjodhild replied: "Girstein Eiriksson was also a kinsman of mine, and most people thought him the better man. And as for Sigtrygg, it seems to me that Girstein served him more nobly than he was served, in his turn, by that man who now calls himself Vinland's king."

Olvir said these were rather hard words, in light of all that had gone before, and that he thought Thjodhild would find cause to regret them before the matter was done. "Dead men," he added, "are not soon brought back to life...," to which Thjodhild responded that it was all the same to her, "for I must be guided by my husband's will in this, and by that which best serves his interests."

Afterwards Olvir left the camp at Gunnarsstead and went over to Leif's houses and now he told Sigtrygg and the others all that had been said. Sigtrygg made little comment, when he heard this, but went off by himself, as soon as he could, keeping well apart from his companions thereafter. Olvir now asked Vragi what he thought they could do in light of these events but the old man only shook his head for he said that things had now gone much farther than they could have hoped and that the loss of Arnliot Keelfoot was greatly felt by all of them, "but by our skipper most of all, for he put great stock in that man, both for his prowess and for that hospitality which Torfi the Ketilsfjorder provided him two winters back."

Olvir said: "It's not hard to understand such feelings for I too fought beside Arnliot Torfisson, and then that big man saved my life when those wounds I got from our Skraeling foes overwhelmed me in our flight. But I don't see how this man's loss can be undone with bloodshed now, for this will not bring the Ketilsfjordman back to us, although it may cost the life of one who is an even better man."

"There's no dissuading a man like Sigtrygg from vengeance, once he is bent on it," Vragi said, "for it is not in his nature to sit idly by when he has been wronged. The only question is how the matter is to be accomplished. But things are not favorable for us in this either, since the Norwegians outnumber us so heavily."

About this time word was brought that another Skraeling had found his way into the camp and Vragi said they must bring the man to him at once. When he saw him Vragi recognized him as the Skraeling who called himself Naruk and now he asked him his purpose.

The Skraeling replied that he had been sent by Tanakrit to again remind Aselekah of his pledge to return to them by winter, "although it is now too late for that, since the Tulewat have gathered a great host and are attacking all the people who live along the upper part of the river. Everyone has fled away to the south and we have done so, as well, in fear of our enemies. Now it is too late for Aselekah to return and lead us against these westerners for all are gone from the river country and he would be unable to find enough of our relations there to serve his purpose. But Tanakrit sent me to warn you of what has befallen, in any case, and to urge you to flee at once from this place, for the Tulewat will now range over the whole country and it is uncertain in which direction their pursuit will take them."

Vragi said: "How long ago did you depart from the river camp and did you see any signs of these others?"

"No," replied the Skraeling, "for I left before they had advanced as far as our dwellings, although many others, who make their homes above us on the river, had already felt their anger. But I came here as swiftly as I could and saw no sign of them the entire way."

Vragi said this was a good thing and now he took the Skraeling to see Sigtrygg and urged the man to tell his tale again. Sigtrygg listened closely to the man's words, although he seemed more distracted than was his wont. When he had heard the Skraeling out, Sigtrygg said that matters had certainly taken a rather grim turn and that he now intended to find Tanakrit and the others and offer them his protection if he could.

Naruk said: "That would be unwise, Aselekah, for our chieftainess says there are too many Tulewat to do battle against, however strong you strangers are, and she has taken our people away to find a safer place for them, beyond the reach of our foes. And you, she urged, must do the same, if you would save your lives."

All the Skraelings who were then with Sigtrygg began to raise a great hue and cry for they well-remembered the nature of their western enemy and they were greatly concerned. Chinokwa now came to Sigtrygg's side and took hold of his arm and began to speak low in his ear with great urgency. After a time Sigtrygg looked up and then he asked Naruk how far off he thought King Nahinanto and his warriors were.

"I travelled with great speed," replied the Skraeling, "and saw no sign of them behind me, nor had they even arrived at the place of our encampment on the day that I left. In my opinion they will seek out those along the river who were formerly their servants first, for they will think they have much to repay them for. Nor is it entirely clear that they will find cause to follow the trails here to the coast until they have subdued that country which was formerly under their sway."

Sigtrygg said he thought this good news and now he told his followers to go down to where the Gull was kept and "prepare her for the sea, for I think we will find it safer out on the waves, for the while, than in these houses which my grandfather built."

When the crewmen prepared to do as Sigtrygg urged, he told those Skraeling men who were then in their company to join them, as well, "for bringing a ship down to the sea and making her seaworthy is no light task and you Skraelings are to remain with us, in any case, whatever events fate may now have in store for us."

But Sigtrygg, himself, remained behind when the others had gone down to where the Gull was laid up and now Vragi asked him what he intended to do, "since there is such work before us as will tax the strength of even a full ship's company, though we were never able to lay claim to such a sizeable crew as that."

"I have another matter which still needs tending to," answered Sigtrygg, in a low voice, "and besides, someone must warn those others at Gunnarsstead of the danger which now overhangs this country."

"Let that be, for the while," said Vragi, "for your first duty is now to your crew and these people who are depending on you. Whatever time is now given us, it may not be enough if we are unable to get this ship of ours ready for sailing before our enemies have come. And that will be no light task since the Gull has been laid up, untended, since first we beached her here a year past."

"That is work that you are more fit to see to than I," answered Sigtrygg, "for you have said, yourself, how unlikely a sailing man I made. But there is other work to be done, for which I am fitter than you."

"I don't know about that," said Vragi, "but it is plain enough, at least, that this preparation of the Gull must now be seen to before all else. And every man is likely to be needed for that work. Your errand to your kinsmen will await the morrow, in my opinion, but the Gull cannot wait if you mean to put to sea with her before our enemies have come."

Sigtrygg said he was not happy to accept the delay but he agreed to do so in the end, since Vragi felt so strongly about it, "although I mean to pay my kinsmen a visit as soon as the matter of the ship has been settled."

Vragi replied that this was only fair and they now went down with the others to where the ship was kept. There they joined in with the others and labored throughout the remainder of the day to make the repairs which Vragi thought were needed to ensure the Gull's seaworthiness. The Skraelings worked alongside the men from Greenland and everyone did whatever work Vragi urged on them, which was not inconsiderable. Vragi proved very demanding in all things concerning the ship and he made a great to do over the work, continually finding small gaps and rot which he said must be patched. Thus, all the men, both Skraelings and Greenlanders, were very tired by the time the sun went down from the demands which he had made on them. Accordingly they slept heavily that night, from the hard labor they had lavished on the ship, and the settlement seemed much quieter than usual, even for that time of the evening.

Some time toward the second half of the night, when all else seemed quiet and all the settlement seemed to be sleeping, Vragi arose and went outside, leaning on his spear. He walked slowly round the enclosure which had been built along the perimeter of the encampment, stopping here and there, as though inspecting the defenses, and then moving on again. He kept this up for awhile, until he came to the gate of the enclosure. Then he went outside and walked a little ways, until he came to a place near the edge of that clearing in which the settlement stood, and then he went up to a tree at a point where its shadow seemed to fall across the grassy ground, cast by the moonlight behind it, and there it seemed that the shadow was darker than it should have been and he stopped at this place and waited. After a moment, a man appeared from beneath the tree and came out to face him.

Vragi greeted this man and the other stood silently for a moment, as though seeing no one before him, and then he returned the greeting.

Vragi said: "Have you dreamed again, shipmate, since you are now so restless and unable to sleep, despite all that hard work which you shared with the rest of us when we labored together over that vessel of ours? Or is it that kings need that much less sleep than common folk, even when they have set great tasks for themselves?"

Sigtrygg turned away at this and looked into the woods toward Gunnarsstead. He said it was true enough that he had had another dream, although it was not on that night "but on the day I stood before the Tulewat town with my companions, Arnliot Keelfoot and Olvir the serving man from Brattahlid; and then I thought I stood alone upon an empty field, and all about me were the bodies of those who had come out with us from Greenland."

"That is a hard dream," Vragi agreed, "and some folk would think it is not the sort to be lightly dismissed."

"Nor do I," answered Sigtrygg, "for I saw your own corpse foremost among all the others."

"Even the old gods could not forestall their end when it was upon them," said Vragi, "and things are not likely to be any different in this case. But could you tell if all the crew were there?"

"I cannot be certain of that," Sigtrygg replied, "but Arnliot Keelfoot was in that company without question and most, I think, of the others, too, although all the faces were not perfectly clear to me. And yet, despite this portent, we went into the Tulewat town and got the victory in the end. Few of the men whose deaths I had foreseen lost their lives there in the west and so I thought the matter of little account . . . until now, and this killing."

"At the least it seems that you are to outlive the rest of us," said Vragi after a time, "for you saw our deaths, but not your own."

"That will certainly be tested tomorrow," Sigtrygg said.

"Then you are still determined to face the Swede?"

"There is no help for it," Sigtrygg replied, "for the man has done me great harm in that he took the lives of our crewmen and offered no repayment for it. It is the king's part to see that justice is done in this matter."

"It is unwise, nevertheless," said Vragi, "for this Gaut is a battle-hardened fighter who has fought in many campaigns with King Harald in the east. There he served under Harald, when that chieftain captained the Varangians for the Greek Emperor, and he fought beside him, afterwards, in Russia as well."

"I have fought against my enemies, too," said Sigtrygg, "as you well know, and am not, myself, unbloodied in matters of war."

"That fighting which you have had, however hard, was in no wise the same as those battles which this Swede has fought," answered Vragi. "Besides, the man has something of a reputation as a dueler. According to some, this man has fought more than thirty opponents in single combat with never a loss to any of them. And now people will add our shipmate Arnliot Keelfoot to that list."

Sigtrygg said: "That was an unfair contest for Keelfoot was winded from his swim and set upon by others first, while he was yet unprepared for battle. Had he that axe, which I, in my folly, denied him, the Swede had never overcome him."

"I would not be so certain of that," Vragi replied, "for this Gaut is not cut from the same cloth as your kinsman Girstein who, while skilled enough with the sword, was yet unequal to the bigger man's axe. Gaut has fought many times, against many foes and weapons, and it is said that no man has ever lived who was his equal with a blade."

"Do you think that is the case, then?" asked Sigtrygg.

"Every man has his better," Vragi replied. "But you are not the one where this Swede is concerned."

"Nevertheless, it is my task to exact the blood price in this matter," said Sigtrygg, "whatever now befalls, for I owe that much, at the least, to the dead man and his companions. And to his father who guested me when others would not."

"Your first task is to see to the well-being of those who are now dependent on you," Vragi said. "And this cannot be done if you leave your head on that man's sword tomorrow."

"We will see whose head is left where," answered Sigtrygg, "for I am rather too attached to mine to part with it lightly, whatever the demands which others make on me."

Vragi again said that he thought Sigtrygg's plan unwise, "for you are no match for this man. But if you insist on fighting him, I will now give you that same advice which I have often urged on you before; and you will do no worse to heed it now than you did then."

Sigtrygg told him to speak up.

"It is that you now seek your bed, shipmate," said Vragi, "and sleep as soundly as you are able, for you are unlikely to be at your best if your head is unclear when you go out to meet this man. And in my opinion you will need all your wits about you if you are to make the most of things in this encounter."

Sigtrygg said he thought this as good advice now as it had been before and he thanked the old man for his words. He said that he thought their talk had helped settle his mind somewhat and that he now believed he would have little trouble sleeping. With that they parted and Sigtrygg returned to the house where Chinokwa lay asleep and now he went inside and took his place on the ground beside her as quietly as he could. After he had lain there awhile, listening to the soft, steady sound of her breathing and feeling the warmth of her flesh against his own, a certain heaviness seemed to steal over him and he fell into a deep sleep.

It was still dark, although a few stray bands of grey light had begun to poke their way through the cracks in the walls, when a gentle thump was heard near the wall where Sigtrygg lay sleeping beside Chinokwa. There was another small muffled sound and the Skraeling woman beside Sigtrygg opened her eyes and half raised her head from the earth although Sigtrygg continued to breathe heavily beside her. The woman looked through the darkness of the hall and now she saw the figure of a man, outlined in the dim grey light, reaching up to the wall where Sigtrygg's sword and shield were hung. The man had the shield in his hand first, and then he took down the sword, and after this he turned to the half-sleeping woman. She saw that it was Vragi and that he now stood silently by the wall, his finger across his lips, gesturing toward the sleeping form beside her. It now seemed to the woman that he was telling her to sleep again and so she closed her eyes once more and put her head down against Sigtrygg's shoulder, saying nothing.

Vragi then went silently out with the sword and shield in his hands and, when he had gone a short distance from the house, he paused and strapped the sword, in its scabbard, to his waist. Then he continued on through the woods and did not stop again until he saw, before him, the darkly illumined outline of the settlement at Gunnarsstead. The sky was now brightened by the rising sun and the old viking went purposefully into the stockaded area surrounding the two houses and made his way to the larger of these. There were a few men about of the Norwegian crew and these stopped in their tracks when they saw who was approaching them.

"What do you want here old-timer?" one of the Norwegians now said and the others laughed, for they could see that he had come entirely alone, though he was armed.

"I have come to pay my respects to that Swedish swordsman you count among your companions," said Vragi quietly, "and now you must tell him to come out and receive my greetings, for that is what courteous men will do when summoned by their betters. But you are to tell him, as well, to bring out whatever sword and shield he thinks most highly of, for he will soon have the chance to put these to good use."

"I don't think you will get very far with words like these where this man Gaut is concerned," said the Norwegian who had first spoken, "for he is a hard man and not an easy one to vex. The best thing for you now, old man, is to go back as quietly as you came and we will not say anything of this matter to him, so that this whole affair may be forgotten."

But Vragi said: "I did not rise so early in the morning to be turned away with such poor hospitality as you are now offering me. Nor do I have any intention of leaving here before I have seen this man Gaut."

The Norwegians conferred among themselves and, after a moment, one of them replied that they would fetch Gaut out, if this was what Vragi really desired, "but things are not likely to turn out well for you, in that case, since you have come here armed and the Swede will take this badly."

"It's all the same to me," answered Vragi, "whatever he thinks of the matter, so long as he brings his weapons out with him."

So now one of the Norwegians went inside while the others remained behind, watching the old man. After awhile the door opened again and now the same man, along with a number of others, came out and these ranged themselves around Vragi. In their company were several of the Eiriksfjorders and, after awhile, Thord and Lambi came out and joined them, too. They all had very grim looks on their faces and each of the Eiriksfjorders was armed.

Vragi asked where Gaut was and if his failure to appear now meant that he intended to hide behind his fellow conspirators by staying inside while these others did his work for him.

"I wouldn't count on that," answered Thord, "but you are certainly a rather different visitor than the one we had expected. In which case it would seem that our cousin Sigtrygg has now found a champion for his cause, and that without any risk to his own life."

Vragi said that events would soon tell the tale and again asked for Gaut the Swordsman.

"He is not far away," a voice now answered, and then the Swede came out of the doorway, his eyes still blinking back sleep, for they had only just awakened him with the news of his visitor. Gaut had two swords in his hands, one longer than the other, and he stood a moment and watched the old man, shifting the weapons lightly about as though carefully weighing each. He said: "I could not decide which sword I preferred in this matter, the longer or the shorter, so I took them both. Have you ever seen a man fight with two swords at once old-timer?"

Vragi said he had seen a great many things but few men who were foolish enough to carry two swords into battle when they had the chance to bear a shield on their arm instead, "and this chance I have now given to you."

"I have never needed a shield before," answered the Swede, "and I am unlikely to need one now. But you will certainly have need of one, if I have my say in this, for you are one-eyed and that will prove a great disadvantage to you, unless I miss my guess. So now I will give you the chance which others have not had, when they stood against me, and that is to depart from here unharmed, for there is little honor to be gained in killing an old man . . . and one who is half-blind in the bargain."

"I did not rise so early from my bed, to leave you standing and whole, once I have left this place," answered Vragi in a rather low voice. And as he spoke he lifted his blade and swept the air before him.

"Then you will soon find out what it is like to live without sight entirely, old man," said the Swede, "for I think I will take your other eye before I take your life . . . though you need not fear a long life now, in any case, for I will not leave you blinded long." He now added that he was willing to allow Vragi to arrange for a second to accompany him and, if he desired it, that the duelling ground be staked out according to the old laws surrounding such matters, "for I am certainly willing to give you your way in this, since you are being so insistent."

"There's no need for these formalities where such men as we are concerned," Vragi now replied, "for each of us knows what the outcome of this encounter must be, and neither witnesses nor the niceties of law will alter this."

Thereupon Gaut said he did not see any sense in prolonging the matter further and he raised the longer sword, which he bore in his right hand, and advanced toward the old viking, all the while holding the shorter blade pointing downward to the earth in his other hand. Vragi raised his shield arm to meet the other and caught the first blow of the Swede's long sword on his shield's rim so that the clash of these shattered the early morning peace. Vragi stepped backward under the force of the blow which Gaut had dealt him and now the Swede swept his short sword at the old man's legs, as he gave way before him. Vragi caught that stroke with the edge of his own blade and, at the same moment, the Swede struck at him again from above with the longer sword.

It seemed to those who stood at the edge of the circle, where these two men now met, that Gaut's weapons moved so freely and swiftly in his hands that they were a part of him, extensions of his very arms, and, when he moved about the old viking, he seemed as swift as an eagle seeking an opening for his kill. Vragi stepped back and back again, each time warding himself from the fierce on-slaught of the other's two blades, with shield or sword or both. But the Swede moved without let up about the older man, his arms flying and the sword strokes which he made a blur in the eyes of those who watched these two. Gaut pressed the matter, first on the old man's blind side, but, when he saw the skill with which Vragi carried his shield and how hard it was to find an opening there, he gave this up and then began to attack from every direction without showing any preference.

Vragi met each attack with a sword blow of his own although his strokes were not so swift as Gaut's, since he wielded the one blade only. Still, it soon became clear to all who were watching that the old viking was no more unskilled in the use of the sword, than he was with the shield, since the Swede was unable to swiftly find that opening which he was accustomed to, and the fight went back and forth now in the clearing before the entrance to the large hall. Gaut smiled grimly and said that Vragi was showing more fight than he had expected and that his death would not be the small thing which his age had seemed to promise.

"You will not think your efforts well-spent, in any case," said the old man, "when this day is done."

The Swede laughed at this and now he leaped past Vragi, on

his blind side, and turned, striking hard at him with both swords from behind. Vragi turned, too, and caught the first sword stroke with his shield but the second swept close by his face, slicing a thin piece of flesh from his cheek, beneath his good eye. When the sword sped past, a wake of blood followed it, and this now fell down the old man's jaw, reddening his beard.

Then the Swede stood back and said: "There skinned I the king's cat." And he seemed to take great pleasure in this.

After this he pressed the attack again, both swords flying above him like darting birds of prey.

Vragi raised his shield to withstand these blows and now he fell backward under the relentless onslaught of the other's weapons. First one sword struck at him, and then the other, and this seemed to continue without end so that the old viking could do nothing but move his shield about to ward the keen strokes. Gaut seemed to push forward with every sword blow and circle the old viking tightly, as though to come at the man from his blind side, if he could. But Vragi withstood this attack too and now, when the big Swede paused as though to catch his breath, the old man suddenly pushed into him, in his turn, pressing his shield hard against the other so that the sword which that man carried in his right hand was crowded against his chest and he could not free it. Then the old man struck with his own sword and the Swede caught this with the blade which he bore in his left hand, as though to deflect it. At once, Vragi seemed to wrap his own blade about the extended sword of the Swede and now the two weapons went round about in the air three times, and then the Swede's sword flew from his hand and landed in the earth some distance away.

Vragi now stepped back and looked at Gaut. He said: "There clipped I the other's claw."

It was plain to those who were watching that Gaut thought the weapon was now out of his reach, for he made no effort to go and retrieve it, but stood warily instead before the one-eyed man, his long sword poised high above his head. He waited as Vragi edged toward him and then he brought his weapon down slowly to guard the space before him. Then Vragi halted and readjusted his shield on his arm.

"Now a younger man than I would throw his shield aside and meet you on your own terms," said Vragi after a moment, "for he would think that the fairer test of skill between men like us. But, in my opinion, such a man would be a fool, for it has never been my custom to discard an advantage once gained in battle. And this time is likely to be no different from the others."

Thereupon Vragi advanced against the larger man, putting his shield up before him. The Swede stepped back and then he brought his blade out over his head and down quickly past the other's shield rim. At this Vragi turned slightly and caught the edge of Gaut's sword a glancing blow, to turn it, with his shield. At the same moment the old viking struck with his own blade and now he caught the bigger man on the side of his leg, cutting the flesh so that the blood cascaded down the length of the leg and pooled about the big Swede's foot. Gaut limped backward and Vragi asked if he wanted to call a halt long enough "to bind that leg of yours so it will not slow your steps," but the Swede said there was no need for that. He ground his teeth tightly together and now he rushed at Vragi as though no wound impeded him, at all, and whirled his sword high overhead, so that it seemed to those who were watching that he bore two swords again. He struck fiercely at the old viking from every direction and Vragi raised his shield again, each time the other's sword fell, to save himself from the harsh blows.

So swiftly did the swords of both men seem to fly about now that no one who was watching that day could tell whose sword had the advantage, if either, and the steel blades rang shrilly against one another in the midst of that struggle. But when the two men parted it was plain that Vragi had gotten the better of it for the Swede was bleeding in several places although the old viking remained untouched. Then Vragi pressed the matter further and pushed hard with his shield into the other man, who seemed greatly weakened and was breathing rather quickly now.

When they saw this, the Thorkelssons grew alarmed and they

rushed about, urging their companions to come to the Swede's aid. But no one made any move to do so until suddenly Lambi Gunnarsson ran forward and struck with his own sword against Vragi's exposed sword hand. The old man turned, when he saw this, and struck back swiftly, gutting the other as he lunged, so that Lambi Gunnarsson fell there, cut down by the first blow, and died at the old viking's feet.

Then Thord and Thorstein seemed to find their courage at last and now these two ran as one at the old man and struck at him with their swords above the body of their fallen kinsman. But Vragi was ready for these men, too, and he cut each of them down as they came with a deadly stroke so that the two kinsmen fell there, the one from a belly wound and the other from a sharp slash across the rib cage. Vragi now withdrew his blade and advanced against the other Eiriksfjorders, who had been party to the killing of Arnliot Keelfoot, and each of these men fell back, although their swords were drawn, for they had been prepared to enter the fight before this at Thord's urging.

Vragi said they must each now pay back what was due on that debt they had incurred by sticking their blades into the body of the fallen Ketilsfjordman, and these men, four in all, looked about them for support from their Norwegian crew mates. But the Norwegians made no move to assist them and so they met Vragi's attack together, hoping to overpower him by their combined strength.

But the old man seemed hardly winded by the fighting he had had and he pressed his attack so hard against them that the first of these men fell at once, while two others took bloody wounds in the first exchange of blows. Then those three who were yet alive threw down their weapons and ran from the field, to the jeers and shouts of the Norwegians. Vragi turned then to face the Swede again.

This man was now advancing against him once more, although he was already badly cut in several places. The Swede had a hard look in his eyes, for he had seen how it went with those others who had sought to aid him, and now he took hold of his long sword, both hands wrapped tightly about its hilt, and ran forward to meet his foeman.

He brought his weapon high above his head, then, and struck at Vragi with such fierceness that the blow staggered the viking, though he caught it full upon his shield arm. Then the Swede struck three times more, in quick succession, so that Vragi was driven back under the hard sword strokes, each time raising his shield to slow the onslaught of blows which the Swede threw against him. Now it seemed that the wound which the Swede had got on his leg was as nothing to him, for it did not hinder his attacks in any way, and he whirled the great sword he bore round about over his head so swiftly that it cut the air with a harsh whistling sound. Each time he struck, the old viking must catch the blow with his shield, for it did not seem as though he could meet such strokes otherwise, so heavy were each of these blows when the Swede delivered them.

The sixth blow which the Swede struck finally cracked the old man's shield and, at the seventh, the target split and now a great piece was hewed from it and fell to the ground. Gaut said nothing at this but struck twice more, his jaw tightly set, spinning about with the force of each sword stroke he made. Then Vragi threw what was left of his shield from his arm, aiming this at the big Swede's legs, and took hold of his own weapon with both his hands at the same moment.

This made the Swede stumble, as the broken shield struck against his lower legs, and Vragi lowered a great two handed stroke at the other man's head so that he had been cleft in two had he lingered a moment longer, awaiting the blow. But the Swede saw this in time and turned about and now he brought his own blade in a great circle into Vragi's neck with such speed that this blow, it seemed, could not be stopped by any single man alone. Vragi saw how this sword stroke came at him and he dropped at once to his knee as it flew on, at the same time shifting the hilt of the blade in his hand and driving the point upwards into the empty air above him. And then the big Swede was there, where the sword point found him, so that he was pinioned by the other's blade, as his own sword sped on above the old man's head like the last breath of some ghostly gale on the sea's face.

The Swede stood there a moment, as the blood burst from his chest like a hot-spring geyser of dark red mud, and then he fell forward into the sword which held him and slipped to the ground. Vragi took his sword from the man's chest then and looked about him. Aside from the cut on his cheek, the old man had no wound.

As soon as things grew quiet, the Norwegians rushed forward to examine the fallen men and it was soon plain to them that the Eiriksfjorders were all dead and that the Swede could not hope to survive since his wound was so deep where Vragi's sword had pierced his lungs. They asked Vragi what he wanted to do and the old man said he would report the killings himself. So now they moved out of his way and he went alone into the hall.

He found Thjodhild and Osvif hurriedly dressing, for news of the fighting had been brought to them when the sword play had begun. Vragi stopped in the middle of the hall and looked from Osvif to Thjodhild and back again and now he told them what had occurred, saying that they would have some heavy work before them, "for you will want to bury these men."

Thjodhild was silent at this and Osvif asked if it were indeed true that Vragi had killed all these men alone, "and that Swede who served King Harald, besides?"

Vragi told him to go outside and see for himself if he doubted it, but that "you will not learn more from what you find there than I have now told you."

Thjodhild asked if any of her kinsmen had been spared and Vragi replied "only one lady . . . but he is not in this camp."

Thereupon the woman ran and grabbed a spear which was lying nearby and raised her arm as if to throw it. But Osvif caught her hand and took the spear from her. Vragi said: "That will do you little good lady, in any case, for your brother, with his one good arm, was able to strike a stronger blow against me than you can now hope to do from that distance. And yet it served him ill, in his turn, when he tried it."

Thjodhild said: "If I were a man I would certainly avenge these killings before you have left our hall, viking. Yet, these Norwegians, on whom it seems I must now depend, show little enough eagerness for such work."

Vragi said that he did not doubt Thjodhild's words, but added that she should not place too much blame on the Norwegians "for men will do what they are best suited for, and not every man is a killer. But I have come here on another errand, as well, for Sigtrygg would have me tell you there is danger now in this country and that you must prepare to sail from here at once."

"What manner of danger?" Osvif asked.

"From those Skraelings whom we overcame in the west before this," answered Vragi, "for word has been brought to us that these people have again risen up, under their king, and are on the march against us."

"I don't see any reason to believe such words now," said Thjodhild, "for you have not shown yourselves to be our friends, before this. And it is well-known that my kinsman wants this land for his own."

"What manner of messenger brought this news?" asked Osvif.

"The best kind," said Vragi, "for he is one of those Skraelings who fought beside us before; and he fled through the countryside in advance of our foes to bring us word of them."

"What do you men intend to do then?" Osvif now pressed.

"To sail, the same as you," answered Vragi, "as soon as we are able."

Thjodhild said that, in her opinion, the words of Sigtrygg and his companions were not to be believed "where this land is concerned," but Osvif replied that he could see little reason to doubt this news, "since they can have no need to scare us off to make their claim now, seeing as those who opposed them are all dead. But," and he turned again to Vragi, "I now want to know what manner of payment you are prepared to offer for these killings, in that three of the dead men were my wife's kinsmen. The obligation to claim compensation for them must now fall to me, seeing as there are none with closer blood ties in this country. And all were crewmen on my ship, besides."

"I shall give you the same answer that Gaut the Swordsman gave to us," said Vragi, "when we asked for payment for his deeds, and that is that I am not accustomed to paying for the blood I have spilled, nor do I mean to change that practice now."

"Yet," said Osvif, "you cannot deny that you have done us great harm in this matter, or that we are justified in seeking retribution from you."

"Seek what you will," answered Vragi, "but I do not intend to pay for the lives of such men, who brought their own deaths on themselves by ill-doing. Besides, it seems to me the harm has now been evened out, somewhat, since these men twice ambushed one of ours and killed him at the second engagement, with the aid of that killer whom people used to call Gaut the Swordsman . . . though now I think he will be better known as Gaut Sword-Pierced."

Osvif said: "Still, I cannot let you leave us without some payment, old man, for your killings are the more serious in that you enticed the Thorkelssons and Lambi, Thjodhild's brother, to fight against you, though you are a seasoned veteran and knew full well they stood no chance once weapons were drawn."

"It was their choice and not mine," answered Vragi, "and I am not responsible for it."

"And yet, I think you could have spared them," said Osvif, "if you had desired it."

"There is no way to tell how matters would have fared, had things been done differently," Vragi agreed, "for no man can see where every choice would have taken him, had he made it instead of another. But, as for me, I think I did what these men urged, since they were eager enough for battle when their blades were drawn."

And now the old viking turned about to leave them. "But, you

CHAPTER XLV

TWO LANDS

Osvif Thorleiksson had the body of Vragi Skeggjasson cleaned and the wound closed and then he sent it back to Sigtrygg, together with the man's sword and broken shield. Along with the body he sent the following message, that this man's death "must now bring an end to the strife between our two parties, since he has slain all those against whom you had a grievance, whereas I have now killed him. And, with this death, ends all quarrels which our folk may have had with any in your company, for no one else is responsible for the harm which he has caused us, unless you make it otherwise. But there is no cause for that. Therefore, I now request that we join our crews together to launch our two ships, since you will not have enough men to man your vessel, while I am in need of another ship to carry away the wealth I have gathered in this land."

The Norwegian told his men to wait for Sigtrygg's answer, after they had delivered the body of the dead man, but Sigtrygg took the news of the old viking's death much harder than they had expected and he proved unable to speak when he saw what had been done and how Vragi had been slain by a spear wound in the back. So now he sent the Norwegians away, without giving them any answer to Osvif's plea, and he told his followers to place the body of the dead man in the hall he had claimed for his own. This they did and, when it was done, he sent them all away as well, and went in alone to keep vigil over the corpse. There he sat for the better part of the day and none of his companions were bold enough to go in to him, or otherwise disturb him, for they could see how badly he took the death of this man.

Olvir waited outside the hall until the sun was well past its mid-point and then he sent in one of the Skraelings to see how matters fared. After a time this man came out again and said that Sigtrygg was sitting in darkness beside the body, but was unwilling to speak. Thereupon Olvir, himself, arose to enter the hall. But at the same moment Sigtrygg emerged and stood alone in the entrance way, blinking rapidly from the brightness of the sun which still stood high in the sky overhead. Sigtrygg now told them they were to take the body of the dead man out for burial, so Olvir went in with the others. There they found that Vragi's corpse had been wrapped tightly in what remained of that blue cloth, woven with strands of gold, which the old viking had carried with him out from Greenland.

The men of the Gull now took the corpse up to a high place overlooking the sea and there Sigtrygg told them to dig a grave for it, with the head pointing to the north. This they did and then they lowered the body into the ground. Sigtrygg looked on in silence, all this while, and, when the body was placed securely in the earth, he brought up the long spear which the old man had fashioned for himself and laid it in the earth alongside the body. Thereafter, they covered the body and the spear with dirt and stood for a long time afterwards in that place, with Sigtrygg staring out across the sea.

It was not until the sun stood low on the horizon that they left that place and returned to Leif's houses, with no man of them willing to speak even a few words, for the matter of this man's death seemed to weigh equally heavily upon each of them. But, when they came in sight of the settlement, they saw that a great deal of activity was taking place there and it could be seen that the Norwegians were all about on the beach and that they had taken the Gull and placed her into the sea. Sigtrygg now hurried down to where these men were and asked what they were about and they replied that they were taking the ship to the lakeside by

Gunnarsstead at Thjodhild's urging, "for she has commanded us to load it with all the goods that we can, since we are now to depart this country."

Sigtrygg told them that he had not agreed to this but they replied that Thjodhild thought otherwise, "since you have pledged us this ship in payment for that killing which was done by your man. And besides, there are now too few of you to sail this vessel yourselves, though we are to tell you that you may sail out with us, if you desire it."

Sigtrygg said he did not think the payment which they were now claiming to be a debt worth honoring any longer, "for others have been killed, since then, which have tipped the scales somewhat," and he told them to bring the ship in again.

But the Norwegians now drew their weapons and ranged themselves along the beach and would not consent to this. Sigtrygg told them that he thought this the worst kind of theft, but they replied that men who got their ships by stealing should not be surprised if others did the same to them.

With that they put out the oars and rowed the Gull up the coast to where the estuary was to be found by which they could enter the lake. Asmund and Thorolf said that Sigtrygg should now pursue these thieves and waylay them, if he could, when they tried to sail up river and into the lake but Sigtrygg said he did not think that would do them much good now, "for they are too numerous and will be expecting us, besides." So they returned to the place where the houses stood and Sigtrygg went inside his hall and sat there in silence for a long while, afterwards, and no one came in to disturb him.

Towards evening he arose and went out to where the Skraelings kept their camp and then he sought out the man called Naruk and these two spoke together for a long time. The Skraelings now showed Sigtrygg a number of small boats which they had built for themselves during the time they had sat in the encampment, in his company, and he looked over their handiwork saying he thought these vessels, at least, were unlikely to draw thieves as the Gull had. But he added that they would certainly prove inadequate to carry all their company to safety before their enemies came.

On the following day, while the sun was just breaking above the horizon, Sigtrygg again went down to the place where the Skraelings had laid up their boats and now he commanded that these be placed on the water. The Skraelings and the crewmen of the Gull did as Sigtrygg asked and the Skraeling women followed after them, carrying down a variety of goods and placing these in the bottoms of each of the vessels. Sigtrygg touched the hand of Chinokwa gently as she put her own burden into the boat and then he sent her back onto the shore.

Thereafter Sigtrygg and the other men got into the boats and began to paddle toward the estuary. The tide was then quite low so it would have been difficult for any but such shallow draft vessels as these to pass over and into that small river which emptied there into the sea. But this proved no obstacle for them now and so they paddled in silence up stream a ways, through the tall reed grass which grew wildly there and which stood much higher during low tide than otherwise, until they came within sight of the two ships.

There the great black hull of the Norwegian vessel sat on the lake, not far from the shore, and, alongside her, the smaller ship, riding rather low in the water. It was plain from this that the Gull had been loaded with the produce of the country as the Norwegians had said she would. Both ships' awnings were also up so Sigtrygg and the others could see that these vessels were already crewed. Olvir now paddled up to where Sigtrygg sat kneeling on the floor of his small Skraeling boat, concealed among the reeds in the early morning mist, and asked what he thought they ought to do now.

Sigtrygg made no answer to this, but took a small Skraeling bow from amidst the goods at the bottom of his vessel and all the Skraelings, seeing this, did as he did. Each of them now also took out an arrow, which had been fitted with a stone point and wrapped about, at the arrow head, with a thin strip of dried skin. Each man dipped the head of his arrow into a small container of pitch which they had brought along with them. When they had done this, they fitted these arrows to their bows and then the Skraeling Naruk paddled about from boat to boat with a small fire which he had been carrying and lit the arrow in each man's bowstring. Sigtrygg now said they were to shoot at the larger boat, "and, when we have set it ablaze, we will row up to the smaller and board her and take her back. If any man contests this, he is to be killed, but, in my opinion, they will have all they can do to save their own vessel and will be too consumed with that to make much of a fight of it. If all goes well," he now added, "the tide will soon be flowing back, as well, so we shall be able get her past the tidal flats without much trouble."

Olvir said he thought the Gull was riding too low in the water for that and that it would be a long while before the tide would be high enough for them to clear the sand banks which lay in the estuary in that case.

"Then," Sigtrygg said, "you are to throw all her cargo over the side, since it is more important to us to have the ship than the goods."

Now Sigtrygg turned his attention once more to the two ships and took careful aim at the Norwegian vessel. Then he let his arrow fly and all the Skraelings did likewise so that a rain of fire now fell about the big black ship. Several of the arrows struck in the deck and awning of the merchant vessel and now these leaped into flame. The men on board her were suddenly to be seen, running about, trying to douse the flames. Sigtrygg told his companions to shoot another volley and this was now done so that a second hail of fiery arrows soon followed the first. The Norwegians on board the merchant ship began to gesture in the direction of the reeds where Sigtrygg and his men were hidden, but they could see little there for the morning mist still lay heavily over the water. But they had all they could do to fight the flames for the big ship was soon burning at both ends. Men leaped off the deck of the Gull to board the other ship and join their companions in quelling the fire and, as soon as he saw this, Sigtrygg told his men to paddle in close under the hull of the smaller ship.

This was now done and Sigtrygg and his companions, both Skraelings and Norsemen, clambered aboard the Gull on her seaward side. Those few Norwegians who were still aboard her ran, at once, to drive them off but Sigtrygg was first up the ship's side and on her deck and he now drew his sword and began to attack them. All the while, the others came up after him and soon these men were swarming over the smaller ship's deck and fighting with the Norwegians who had remained and it was not long before they had these on the run. Now the men on board the big merchant vessel soon saw that it would not be easy to douse her flames, for they had put a great quantity of dry timber and vines on board and these caught fire even more quickly than the ship itself. Accordingly, these men began to throw themselves overboard and some swam for shore while others made for the Gull and got aboard her. Now the fighting became even fiercer than before on board the Gull, with the arrival of these others, while those men who made it to shore began to set up a great shout and run up to the houses at Gunnarsstead to get help.

Sigtrygg said they were to get under way, if they could, and his men began to put out the oars although the Norwegians fought hard against this and made the work more difficult than it ought to have been. Sigtrygg told his followers to kill any of those who now resisted them or to drive them overboard, if they must, but that they were to act quickly if they wanted to win this ship again. So now the fighting between the two crews became much fiercer than before and many were killed, on both sides, but the end of it was that the Norwegians still in the lake or nearby on shore now threw themselves bodily onto the oars so that Sigtrygg's crew could not maneuver the ship into deeper water. Sigtrygg went about with his sword, hacking at those who opposed him, both on board the vessel and in the lake and he was still at this when Osvif, himself, leaped onto the ship, his sword drawn and raised high above his head.

Then Sigtrygg gave him a greeting and said: "Now it seems I will have the chance to repay you for that unmanly blow you dealt my shipmate though his back was turned to you."

And Osvif replied: "Have it your own way, Greenlander, but I think others will see it differently for that old man took those killings on himself and afterwards turned his back to me, knowing I sought revenge, that there might be an end to this feuding. But you must let his death end it for that, and I don't think you are willing to do this."

Sigtrygg struck now with his sword and said that Osvif only spoke the truth where Vragi Skeggjasson's death was concerned, "for he was closer to me than my own kinsmen and the point of your spear blow stuck harder in my back than it did in his." Now Sigtrygg advanced against the Norwegian skipper and his sword seemed to fly about in the air so that the other man must fall back and back from the onslaught. Sigtrygg struck first against the man from the right side and then from the left and then from the right again and Osvif stumbled on the Gull's deck which was now slick with blood beneath his feet. He fell to his knees, raising his sword against Sigtrygg's hard blows and then he said: "I'm not sure you needed that old man to fight against the Swede for you, since you are fighting now like a troll or one possessed."

Sigtrygg replied that each man saw what he saw, "and you are free to spin such tales if you desire it, but only a man is standing now against you, though one you have caused great harm to, when you aligned yourself with his enemies."

Osvif scrambled out from under the harsh sword strokes which Sigtrygg now laid over him and, seizing hold of an awning cable, he pulled himself to his feet. Then he struck back as mightily as he could and this caused Sigtrygg to give way, in his turn. "Now we are more equally matched, I think," said the Norwegian, "and I'm not sure you will find that a better turn of events." Thereafter, Osvif took the battle to Sigtrygg and now all those on both sides fell back, when they saw these two contending, for it seemed to everyone on board that ship that these men needed no less than the entire length of the Gull for this affair.

Osvif now proved to be no mean swordsman, though he had had the worst of it at the start, and he struck heavy blows against the Greenlander so that Sigtrygg must now, in his turn, fall back under the hard onslaught. Then these two ran back and forth at each other across the length of the ship, while the others looked on. First it seemed that the Norwegian would have his way and then that Sigtrygg would prove the stronger. Both were bloodied from the fighting but neither seriously and so they fought on, raining hard sword blows, each upon the other. Then Sigtrygg took hold of that same cable awning which Osvif had grasped to his gain before and now he spun himself around it and came at the other man nearly from behind. The Norwegian turned round to meet this attack and caught the Greenlander's sword just as it landed against him and turned it aside. Then he lunged toward Sigtrygg with the point of his own weapon thrust toward the other's throat and Sigtrygg leaped aside so that the sword cut through the cable and brought the awning down between them.

Hereupon, Sigtrygg turned the point of his own sword toward the Norwegian and pushed it through the falling canvas until he felt the resistance of man-flesh behind it and then he drove it home. Now the Norwegian sat down heavily and he had a stomach wound where Sigtrygg's sword had been and he was breathing hard. He said that things had now fallen out in such a manner that it would be the Greenlander's task to finish him and not the other way around and he threw down his sword and let his head slump forward onto his chest. From the nearby shore a shout was now heard and Sigtrygg looked up to see that Thjodhild stood there, her eyes wide, as he stood above the Norwegian with his own bloody sword still in his hand. He now looked at the wounded man and told him to take up his weapon again, if he could.

"That is now quite beyond me," said Osvif slowly, "and I am not certain if I am likely to live much longer, in any case. But there is no one here who will stop you from doing what you have set your heart on and taking revenge for that death which seems to weigh heavier on you than any other."

Sigtrygg looked again at the face of Thjodhild and then at the seated man and now he turned away from the man. He said: "I have had all the blood which that old man's death required. So bind up your stomach, if you are able, and see to your own ship, which will now burn down to the water line if your men allow it. Only leave my ship with me."

Osvif said he could have it that way if he wanted "but I'm not sure it will do you as much good as you now hope," and he lifted his hand and pointed inland. Sigtrygg followed the direction of the man's hand with his eyes and now he could see a blot of grey smoke rising high above the trees, in the distance. Olvir came up beside him and said: "That is coming from the coast, where Leif's houses stand."

Everyone now agreed that the smoke was coming from that direction and that it must be a very great fire to have caused such smoke. Sigtrygg said "that is where our women are," and now he asked Olvir what he thought it could mean.

"I'm not certain about that," replied the other, "but I think we will learn the cause soon enough for I see men running down the hill to us from Gunnarsstead."

They now looked where Olvir directed and they could see several Norwegians coming toward them at a dead run. Behind them, other men came and they were not Norsemen. Sigtrygg said he thought these had a familiar look to them and Olvir replied that he recognized them as well, "and now wisdom bids us cast off the anchor on this ship and put as much distance between us and the shore as we are able."

The Norwegians still on shore now cast themselves into the lake and made for the Gull and Sigtrygg jumped overboard and waded toward them. He took hold of Thjodhild, who had lunged into the lake with the others, and lifted her in his arms, toward the ship, and Olvir reached down and took hold of her wrists, helping her to get aboard. As they did this, arrows began to fall about them and Sigtrygg pushed Thjodhild's legs up over the side of the ship's rail. Thjodhild said: "Kinsman, you must get aboard now, too, if you would save yourself," but Sigtrygg went back toward the shore where the serving girl Fridgerd now stood, shrieking frightfully. Sigtrygg urged her to come into the water, "and I will help you reach the ship," he said, but the girl only stood there as though frozen in that spot. Then Sigtrygg went up to her and grasped her arms to pull her toward him but, as he did this, the girl slumped forward and fell face down into the water. An arrow stood out on the back of her neck.

Then the Tulewat warriors were upon him and Sigtrygg drew his sword and began to hack at these men, cutting the first down his middle and slicing at the neck of the second. At once Asmund and Thorolf leaped overboard, their swords aloft and then Olvir followed, and now other men came to his aid as well, both Norwegians and those of his own crew. Together these men struck at the attacking Skraelings and drove them back. Then Thjodhild's voice could be heard and she was urging them to return to the ship "for more of these awful men are coming down from the hill upon you," she said. But Sigtrygg now broke off from the others and ran up towards the trees, in the direction in which the smoke from Leif's houses could still be seen.

Thjodhild called on him to return to the safety of the ship, but Sigtrygg plunged into the wood as though he could not hear and after him, Asmund and Thorolf and Olvir followed. Soon these men had disappeared among the trees and the attacking Tulewat were all along the shore and plunging into the water so that the Norwegians now threw everything they could overboard and pushed the Gull out to the deepest part of the lake.

Sigtrygg and the men who were with him now ran willy-nilly through the forest, towards the coast, and, when any Tulewat warriors caught up with them, the Norsemen attacked them with such ferocity that these men fell back in disarray. They ran thus through the woodlands until they came to a place where the land opened up and now they could see Leif's houses, how these were all afire and great billows of smoke went up from them and darkened the sky. Tulewat warriors ran all about with their weapons aloft and howling horribly, as though they were maddened dogs or the spirits of the dead. Sigtrygg stopped now and the others came up with him and now Olvir said how things had at last caught up with them and that it was now quite clear that they could do nothing more to reclaim their goods. "And it is just as well," he added, "that that ship of ours has been taken up river for we could never have saved her if she had been left on the beach."

Asmund and Thorolf asked Sigtrygg what he wanted to do, "since events have now gone against us," but Sigtrygg made no answer. He was looking off into the distance where a cluster of Tulewat warriors seemed to be gathered about in a tight circle. Now he advanced down toward the clearing and the other men came close behind, until they could see how the Skraeling women they had left behind, when they went out to reclaim their ship, were now the captives of these fierce warriors. The women stood in a tightly packed group, herded together like so many sheep, while all about them the Tulewat men howled and snarled like wolves.

Sigtrygg broke into a run when he saw this and hurled himself down against the wall of Skraeling warriors while the others followed close at his heels. They struck against the outer wall of these men with such force that the Tulewat gave way and Sigtrygg broke furiously into their midst. Then he began to lay about him in all directions with his sword and Thorolf and Asmund took up the attack on either side of him, while Olvir guarded his back. The Skraelings leaped in against these men and Asmund was now the first to fall for they overwhelmed him and bore him down until they ground his bloodied face into the dust. Thorolf took up the attack to save his comrade but he was felled by an arrow which caught him square in the chest.

Then Olvir and Sigtrygg stood back to back and Olvir said, "this is much like that earlier day when we stood together with Arnliot Keelfoot and braved the very stronghold of these people," and Sigtrygg replied that he thought this was true. Together these two now advanced, one stepping forward as the other edged carefully backward, closer to where the women were being held. Then Chinokwa cried out and Sigtrygg caught sight of her and now a fierce looking Tulewat warrior ran out from the place where the others stood and ran at Sigtrygg. This man was covered in a cloak of feathers and his face was painted black, although his eyes were rimmed a bright blood-red, and, all in all, he had the look of a great and monstrous bird. He leaped high into the air at Sigtrygg and gave a great and hideous cry. He was waving a fierce looking war-club in his two hands.

Thereupon, Chinokwa broke free of her captors and ran out before the others and thrust herself between this man and Sigtrygg. The man came down onto the ground abruptly then and pulled back his war-club barely in time, or he would have crushed the Skraeling woman's skull. But Sigtrygg, seeing this, now leaped past the woman, and without pause sank the blade of his sword deep into the Skraeling warrior's chest so that the man fell at once to his knees. Looking up, this man let out a great cry, which seemed to be one of both anger and pain, yet well-mixed with grief, or so Olvir said afterwards. And then the wounded Skraeling slumped forward and died there at Sigtrygg's feet, his own blood rushing about him in rivulets in the soft earth onto which he had fallen. Sigtrygg now bent to the man and turned up his face with his sword and then he said he thought he knew the fallen man beneath the markings he bore on his face. "It seems," he said to the dead man, after he had looked at him for awhile, "that I was fated to take your life in the any event, however much I strove against it."

And now Olvir could see, too, that the dead man was none other than the Skraeling Bjorn, who called himself in his own tongue W'tnalko, dressed as a Tulewat warrior.

Chinokwa grabbed Sigtrygg's arm and he pulled her to him, lifting up his sword in challenge to the other Skraelings now ranged about them, but no other man came forward to give battle.

Then the field seemed to fall silent and a path cleared before them. A man stepped out of the midst of the others and Olvir and Sigtrygg knew him at once for the Skraeling king, the lord of the Tulewat. King Nahinanto was painted as hideously as all his followers and he had a war club of unusual proportion in his two hands. His chest and arms were covered with blood so that Sigtrygg could now see that he must have only just come from the fighting with the Norwegians at Gunnarsstead, for those who had burned Leif's houses had found no enemies of their own in that place against whom to vent their wrath.

Nahinanto now came forward and looked at the two Norsemen who were standing before him and at the fallen Skraeling at Sigtrygg's feet. Then he looked at the woman clutching Sigtrygg's arm. There was a rather uneasy quiet then until at last this man spoke, saying that he thought it surprising that he had been able to take Aselekah and his countrymen so easily when they had proved so formidable before this. Sigtrygg replied that every man had his time and that this was no less true for them than for others.

Nahinanto nodded at this and now he asked Sigtrygg where that "great yellow-haired man was, who caused us so much harm amidst our dwellings," and Sigtrygg answered that he was dead.

"Then where is the man who killed him?" asked the Skraeling king, "for this was no feat done by any man of mine."

"That one is dead too," was Sigtrygg's reply.

"Then you have suffered a great loss," said the king.

Sigtrygg said that he thought this was true and now he let his sword arm drop for he was exhausted from the hard fighting.

"What do you mean to do now?" Nahinanto asked him, after awhile, and Sigtrygg replied that "that will depend on what others do."

Shouting could now be heard from the sea and Sigtrygg and Olvir looked out toward where the voices seemed to be coming from. They could make out the Gull and the men on board her, who were putting up the sail. The ship was far enough out so that the Skraeling arrows could not reach her but near enough so that some of what the men on board her were shouting could still be heard by those on the shore. They seemed to be calling to Sigtrygg to break free and make for the ship. A woman's voice carried more clearly above all the others.

"It is Thjodhild," said Olvir, when he had listened for awhile, "and she is urging us to get to the ship. They mean to sail out of this bay and back to Greenland if they can."

"It is rather late in the season for that," said Sigtrygg slowly.

"Still they don't seem to have much choice," Olvir replied, "for this country has not been good to them."

"I'm not sure about that either," answered Sigtrygg, "for some people will think they'd have done better here had they been different men."

"They are the men that they are," said Olvir to this, "as we are. But what do you think we should do now?"

It could now be seen that the Tulewat warriors were falling away from them and that they had opened a path, between them, down to the sea. Sigtrygg looked at the Skraeling king and Nahinanto turned his face outward, toward where the Gull now sat upon the bay. He said: "As you once gave my life to me, Aselekah, so will I do no less for you. You have fought mightily in this country and shown yourself a man, yet you have been my enemy and caused us great loss. I grant you your life then, if you are willing to take it, but you are forbidden to return to us with any of your kind, for I mean to kill all such men as these if they come into this country again."

Sigtrygg nodded and said this was acceptable to him and now he took Chinokwa by the arm and turned to go down with her to the sea. Yet he felt the woman pull back from him when he did this. He looked at her and saw that she was afraid, more afraid to go, it seemed to him, than to remain there among those fierce warriors. So now he bent to her and asked if she were willing to sail away with him. The Skraeling woman only shook her head at this.

"There is safety awaiting us out on the open sea, wife," he said urgently, "but who knows what will befall us here if we remain among these men," and he tugged at her arm again, but gently, as though begging her to go with him down to the shore.

But Chinokwa only pulled back the harder saying, "I am not likely to find a better welcome there than here, husband, but you are certainly free to depart, if that is your wish."

Sigtrygg replied that he did not intend to leave her among men who had nearly caused her death before if he could help it, but Chinokwa only laughed at this and said: "It is not likely they will do me harm now, husband. They have not touched any of us women as you can readily see, for we are not as you Greenlanders, whom they have cause to hate. And besides, I am no longer fit for sacrificing since I am with child."

Sigtrygg said: "How is it that you did not speak of this before, wife?"

"You had other matters to see to, husband," said she, "and but little time for such news as we women bring. Still, I don't think there is much to fear from these men now, for they are not as those others, who have come with you from over the sea."

Then Sigtrygg turned to Olvir and said that he was to go down to the beach without him, "for I will not leave this woman behind, but prefer to take my chances by her side."

"This is unwise shipmate," Olvir replied, "for none can tell how these men will behave toward you after we are gone; and it is unlikely we shall be able to return, once the Gull's sail has caught the wind."

But Sigtrygg said he was to go nonetheless.

Olvir again begged Sigtrygg to reconsider, but he replied that he was unwilling to do that and that his mind was entirely made up. So now Olvir took his leave of his companion and went down alone toward the sea, and all the Skraelings who were between him and the shore gave way before him. When he came to that place where the surf struck the land, he turned and looked again at his shipmate, and now he could see that Sigtrygg stood there amidst the foreign men, entirely surrounded by them, yet he could no longer see the small woman who had been standing there by Sigtrygg's side, for the Skraelings all about them were too numerous for that. Still Sigtrygg, himself, stood out plainly above these others and was easily seen, and now he cast Olvir a look over their heads and nodded to him, as though in understanding of what was to be done.

It seemed to Olvir, then, that the other man's eyes narrowed as he watched him stepping into the sea and he thought that he smiled, however slightly, as though he would say some word. But he did not speak again, despite this, and, after a time, he turned his back to him. And then the Skraelings closed so tightly about Sigtrygg that he, too, was lost to view. Then Olvir turned and waded out into the sea until he felt the ground dropping away beneath his feet so that he must swim for it, if he could. But the sword in his hand proved too much of a hindrance for that so he hastily cast it from him, watching where it struck the surface of the water, until it had sunk into the waves. Then he swam as hard as he could, toward the ship, and all the men on board her shouted encouragement to him, urging him on and pulling him up out of the sea, when he came within their reach.

They offered him dry blankets to wrap himself in, but Olvir only pushed these away and went at once to the ship's stern to look back at where he had been. Yet, try as he might, he could not see clearly how matters fared with those he had left back on the land.

Thjodhild came up to him then and stood nearby, looking where he looked, and asked if he thought Sigtrygg meant to follow him to the ship. But the Brattahlid man only shook his head at this. "I don't think there's much hope of that," he replied, "for there's little good waiting for him back in Greenland . . . while he has found kinsmen here."

"What kind of kin is this," asked Thjodhild, when she had gazed for a time at those still milling about on the shore, "who paint their faces in such monstrous fashion and make war just like the wild beasts?"

"The best kind," answered Olvir, "for they have spilled their blood with his on the same ground."

EPILOGUE

They sailed out of the bay then and turned the ship's prow to the east and north, toward the open sea. But they soon found the going much rougher than they had expected and were caught up in a harsh sea and driven further eastwards than they desired. Osvif, the Norwegian, died from the wound which Sigtrygg had given him shortly after they were at sea, and then they were at a loss concerning which way to turn the ship. Accordingly, they set their course as best they could, steering first for Greenland and then, when they thought they had overshot that country, they made for the coast of Iceland. But they were driven about by the gales which arose on the sea during that time of the year and were finally forced onto some rocks which lay off the western coast of Ireland instead. There most of the remaining crewmen lost their lives, but Olvir brought Thjodhild safely to the shore; and, because he had some skill in the Irish tongue, he made his way north and inland with her, until he found a ship to give them passage to the Orkneys. There they wintered at Straumsey, in the earl's hall, but they said little concerning where they had been.

In early summer Thjodhild gave birth to a boy and then Olvir booked passage for them to Norway and they came to Viken where King Harald was then in residence. They sent word to the king through a local man that they desired an audience with him and Olvir told the messenger to stress that they were kin, of a sort, to the king. This the man did and it soon came about that King Harald consented to see them.

So they were brought into his presence and the king asked who they were and how they thought they might be related to him. Then Olvir told somewhat of this tale and Thjodhild the rest and she finished by asking for her share in the estate of Osvif Thorleiksson, her husband, who had been the king's retainer.

When he heard this part of the tale, the king took it rather hard, for he had thought highly of Osvif Thorleiksson, although he said it was much less of a loss that Gaut the Swordsman had met his match out there in the west, "and that at the hands of a man most people had thought long dead." But he promised to support Thjodhild with her husband's kinsmen none the less, and, afterwards, he sent her to them with messages from himself, asking that a share of what had belonged to Osvif be made over to Thjodhild and her son. As to Olvir, the king told him he was free to remain in Norway for as long as he wanted and offered to make him one of his retainers. But Olvir said he preferred to go along with Thjodhild, if she were willing, as her servant. Thjodhild said this was acceptable to her so that was how they left it.

Now, for as long as they were in his company, King Harald made them a fine welcome as his guests, and he sent word over all Norway that they were to be treated with the greatest of honor while they were in the country, and this is what happened. As for Vinland, the king showed a great deal of interest in that land and never tired of hearing their tales of what they had seen there, while they were his guests and afterwards, and he said that his kinsman, Sigtrygg Thorgilsson, held the land in fee from him, if he still lived. He added that he intended to go there himself, in the end, to see if all the tales which he had heard about that country were true. But this did not come to pass for the king soon became embroiled in a war with Swein Ulfsson, the Danish king, and this dragged on for many years, though neither man proved able to overcome the other.

As for Thjodhild and Olvir, they went to live for a time with Osvif Thorleiksson's kinsmen, who treated them well and gave them everything that they could desire in that country, just as the king had commanded. Yet Thjodhild was restless and, when her son was four years old, she sold off her portion of Osvif's holdings and put the boy out for fosterage. She did not have much trouble finding the boy a home, for he was well-provided for and had the king's backing besides, though most folk thought he had a rather odd look to him in that he was somewhat flat of feature and of rather a swarthy complexion. Still, he came of good family so folk would not turn him away.

After she had found the boy fosterage, Thjodhild and Olvir booked passage to Iceland where they came in the summer and settled near a church in the eastern part of the country. There Thjodhild took up the habit and became a nun and, after this, she went into seclusion and did not speak willingly again of her life before her time in Iceland. Olvir remained close by her side until she died, which was not very long after this, for she was always very melancholy about things and did not appear to prosper in her new life.

After her death, Olvir went out on his own and little more is heard of him for some time. Still, this is known, that it was Olvir who told this tale to any who would listen, after Thjodhild died, though most people thought it rather far-fetched and difficult to believe. But Olvir always swore to the truth of it and urged those who doubted him to seek out King Harald of Norway, "for he will confirm much of what I have said."

But Harald, himself, had other things on his mind in those days and did not prove eager for such tales in the end. Nor did he live long after Thjodhild's death in any event, since he went out to England some time thereafter and was killed in that country by his namesake, King Harold of the English, at Stamford Bridge. Afterwards there was no one left alive who could verify any parts of the tale, as Olvir told it.

It is said that the best men of Leif Eiriksson's kin were lost there, out in Vinland, as a result of those events which have here been related and that the men of that bloodline never again attained the primacy in Greenland which they had held before. Nor is it told anywhere else that others of that kin ever went again into the west, seeking the lands which Leif Eiriksson had found. And after a time men even forgot how to come to that country.

As for Olvir, he lived out his life more quietly than most in Iceland and few folk there thought he was the type to have taken part in such adventures as he used to tell of. Still, he would gladly recount, to anyone who would listen, all that he had seen and heard in the land of the Skraelings, and he did this right up until the day of his death after which nothing more is heard of this tale.